Sally Bianco

Mystery Series

by

Rohn Federbush

Gotham Books

30 N Gould St.
Ste. 20820, Sheridan, WY 82801
https://gothambooksinc.com/

Phone: 1 (307) 464-7800

© 2024 *Rohn Federbush*. All rights reserved.

No part of this book may be reproduced, stored in a retrieval system, or transmitted by any means without the written permission of the author.

Published by Gotham Books (March 14, 2024)

ISBN: 979-8-88775-773-5 (H)
ISBN: 979-8-88775-771-1 (P)
ISBN: 979-8-88775-772-8 (E)

Because of the dynamic nature of the Internet, any web addresses or links contained in this book may have changed since publication and may no longer be valid.

The views expressed in this work are solely those of the author and do not necessarily reflect the views of the publisher, and the publisher hereby disclaims any responsibility for them.

CONTENTS

PART I The Legitimate Way
Section A

Chapter One 1

Chapter Two 16

Chapter Three 39

Chapter Four 50

Chapter Five...67

Chapter Six 84

Chapter Seven..94

Chapter Eight..112

Chapter Nine 127

Chapter Ten 142

Chapter Eleven...161

Section B

Chapter Twelve..175

Chapter Thirteen 191

Chapter Fourteen 229

Chapter Fifteen 263

Chapter Sixteen..283

Chapter Seventeen 305

PART II The Appropriate Way

Chapter One 315

Chapter Two 333

Chapter Three 355

Chapter Four 391

Chapter Five 409

Chapter Six 424

Chapter Seven 454

Chapter Eight 495

Chapter Nine 514

Chapter Ten 525

PART III The Recorder's Way

Prologue 529

Chapter One 547

Chapter Two 567

Chapter Three 582

Chapter Four 602

Chapter Five 612

Chapter Six 631

Chapter Seven 644

Chapter Eight 663

Chapter Nine 683

Chapter Ten 697

Chapter Eleven 729

PART I

The Legitimate Way

Section A

Chapter One

Ann Arbor, Michigan
September, Monday

In the middle of a fine afternoon, heading east on State Street, Sally Bianco stopped at the three-way stop in front of the Michigan Union before she noticed the police car parked among the taxi cabs. She kept her foot on the brake waiting impatiently for two students blown with a gust of maple leaves to cross the intersection, only to be further stalled by a straggling professor attached to his cell phone. Finally, Sally eased her old Mustang through the intersection. However, as soon as she passed the cruiser, its flashing lights rotated. Without a siren, it made a quick U-turn and followed her through the next traffic light. The signal was green at Liberty Street, so Sally made a left-hand turn, planning to park in front of the Michigan Theatre to receive whatever ticket the good 'occifer' wanted to award her.

Across the street two bicycle cops, Sylvester and Sam Tedler, escorted Robert Koelz out the door of his second-floor, used bookshop. The cruiser's multi-colored lights created a confusing strobe effect as the Tedler brothers marched Robert across to the cop car.

Sally jumped out of her car and reached for Robert's arm. "Now, what have you done?"

His hands were cuffed behind him, or his fingers would have tugged at his kinky grey curls, as they always did when Robert needed to explain a questionable deed. "Call Sites." He frowned to keep his frustrated tears at bay. "They think I murdered Mary Jo."

"Nonsense." Sally scowled at the brothers for making her old friend weep at such a ridiculous charge. "Sam, you and Sylvester have known Mr. Koelz all your lives."

Sylvester responded by lowering his voice to an officious tone, "There's a warrant for his arrest. He'll need to answer the charges."

"Call his lawyer, Mrs. Bianco," Sam said as he extracted Sally's claws from Robert's sweater. "I'm sure he'll be out before dinner."

A bookish crowd of Border's customers and between-class students crossed Liberty Street and gathered around them. From the back seat of the cop car, Robert called out something to Sam. Sam bent down to fish in Robert's suit coat pocket. When he straightened up, Sam handed Sally the bookshop keys. "Mr. Koelz says to lock up and feed Miss Poi."

Before climbing into the seat next to Robert, Sam turned to his brother. "Sylvester, take care of my bike."

The other infant officer behind the wheel turned off the cruiser's lights and proceeded down Liberty Street toward the county jail. Officer Sylvester Tedler touched Sally's shoulder. "Better move your car, Mrs. Bianco."

"My car?" Sally asked. "What's wrong with it?"

"Illegally parked." Sylvester couldn't meet her glare.

"Well, give it a ticket, Sylvester." Sally's angry tone let him know he was lucky she didn't wrestle his nightstick away from him and beat him to death. "I have a few things to take care of, thanks to your diligence." Instead of rescuing her car, Sally pushed Sylvester's six-foot-two bulk out of her path to cross the street back to the Bibliopole's entrance.

The rare bookshop stairs seemed steeper than usual. Sally was puffing by the time she reached the landing. Leaning against the railing to catch her breath, she checked on Sylvester's activities through the upper hall's Liberty Street window. He had graciously decided not to ticket her vintage red Mustang.

She asked for the Lord's help as she fumbled with the shop keys. Her eyes were smarting with frustration by the time she realized the upper door was unlocked before she inserted Robert's keys. She sighed at her own idiocy, then unlocked the door to gain admission to the shop. Miss Poi, Robert's cat, rubbed against her jeans in greeting. "Just a minute, sweetie." Sally sat down in the nearest chair. Letting her hand keep Miss Poi's fur and ego occupied, Sally tried to get her mind around Robert's present plight.

Seven years earlier, when Sally first met the zealous bookman, she judged him to be an invincible guru. After tracking his goofy endeavors, she eventually understood the motivations behind Robert's discontent with society. However, the energy level at his advanced age of 79 to pursue convoluted schemes against every form of governmental injustice continued to amaze her. Anarchists should retire at fifty, as far as Sally could surmise. "Mellow out," Sally advised the empty air.

The comforting smells of old leather, a heady scent of binding glue, and the odors of accumulated cardboard boxes overflowing with reclaimed books intermingled with the tannic-acid tang on the autumn breeze rustling papers on Robert's metal desk.

Since her husband's death six years earlier, this room qualified as Sally's refuge, the place closest to her heart. The yellowed high ceiling, the carved woodwork, the patina on the oak floors, the jumble of brimming bookcases, and the mismatched chairs assembled exactly the way a mysterious bookshop would. There was room to walk around a set of bookcases in the side room. In the central area, enough chairs welcomed conversation. The freedom-loving customers supported Robert's myriad causes. Sally considered the shop a perfect sanctum for the illusion of peace in a violent society.

Miss Poi mewed.

Andrew Sites. She needed to find the lawyer's phone number. Ignoring the cat, she brushed a stray tear off her nose and searched through piles of correspondence on Robert's desk. A metal pop-up address book provided the number. What should she do first, save Robert or feed Miss Poi?

She had never ventured into the storage room before, but the can opener and stack of cat food tins were in plain sight on the windowsill overlooking the State Street University 'diag.' As she opened one can, Miss Poi leaned into her ankles. Through the dirty window, Sally could see Sylvester Tedler back on his beat, accosting two homeless women asking for funds from passersby at the corner.

With a satisfied Miss Poi curled on her lap, Sally dialed the ancient rotary phone for Andrew Sites' office. His secretary sounded young and efficient. Understandably, Andrew's voice could not have echoed more of a shocked response. "Sally, who made the accusation?"

"Oh, Andrew." Sally used her 'pity-an-old-woman' moan. "I have no idea. Are you able to get him out of jail?"

"Absolutely," Andrew said. "Will you stay at the shop until I bring him back?"

"I need to move my car." Sally knew Andrew wouldn't be interested but couldn't stop chatting, "I abandoned it when I saw Sam and Sylvester arrest Robert."

The lawyer hung up.

After Sally moved her car to the high-rise lot next door, she returned to the rare bookshop and started a fresh pot of coffee. Robert's metal address book flipped open on its own accord, or Sally might have touched its button as she stared at the State Street Theatre marqueè. The large black letters made no sense. She couldn't remember what was playing at the Michigan Theatre just a few steps down Liberty Street. Her mind drifted in a state of transitory shock, or some child in charge of changing the titles of movies was on a lark. The State Theatre sign spelled. "N A M E N O O N E M A N."

Mary Jo Cardoni, the young woman Robert was supposed to have murdered, was skinny and scared with dark, flyaway shoulder-length hair. Big brown eyes flitted behind pink-tinted glasses. Sally had only met her the previous week. Mary Jo had rubbed her nude ring finger as if removing the 'promise of forever' damaged tendons. The young woman had listed her reasons for leaving her marriage, biting her lips repeatedly as if to apologize for the unsavory truths. The only time Mary Jo calmed down and stopped chain smoking was when Robert handed her a book to peruse. She purchased every tome he suggested as if Robert were prescribing exact narcotics for each of the poor girl's anxieties.

Someone murdered Mary Jo?

Sally could believe several people might desire intimacy with Mary Jo. In her vulnerable state, Mary Jo might have encouraged such momentary felicitations. But murder? Surely the police questioned Mary Jo's abusive husband.

Sally pushed the button on the address book again. Would Robert want his friends to know? Without dwelling further on the proper etiquette, Sally started telephoning. Penny Savage, his youngest conquest, answered her cell phone. Sally struggled with a few words. "Robert's in trouble."

"What now?" Penny sounded exasperated. "Who is he picketing now?"

"Worse." Sally managed.

"Really?" Sally heard Penny's intake of breath as if expecting the very worst.

"He's okay." Then Sally asked hurriedly, "Will you come by the shop tonight?"

"Are you crying, Mrs. Bianco?"

"No." Sally lied. "I have to make some more phone calls. See you tonight." Sally replaced the headset in its cradle.

Sally reached for a blank index card. She needed to perfect her presentation. What could she say without telling his friends she didn't know enough even to bother them? Poor Penny. There were other female customers, like Sally, Penny, and Mary Jo, hanging on Robert's every word. They praised his readings of his favorite poetry, prose, and the lyrics of his esteemed Gilbert and Sullivan operettas. Robert Koelz proposed no agenda for his patrons. They were accepted, foibles, wrinkles, stiff joints and all. However, he did not allow pomposity or any cruelty to linger long in the shop. Robert, of course, did not mind if they kept him in business by buying his unlimited supply of rare books.

Sally wrote down her spiel on a salmon-colored index card before ringing up Henry Schaeffer, Robert's buddy since grade school. "Robert needs you to come by the shop this evening." She read from the card.

"His cleaning isn't finished yet," Henry said.

"Robert's embroiled in an arrest." Sally ventured nearer the truth in the next line of her text.

Henry's immediate loyalty spoke volumes. "You know he's innocent."

Sally reassured him, but added from her script, "I'm not aware of any of the details. Andrew Sites is with him, hopefully, as we speak. Can Robert count on your being here tonight?"

"Absolutely." He paused longer than was necessary. "Sally?" His tone highlighted the coming equivocation. "If an arrest hits the papers, my wife will get involved."

"Robert will understand." Sally gently disconnected. Henry's wife, no doubt, would forbid Henry from seeing his closest friend until Robert's name was cleared. The bookshop crew never blamed Henry for his lack of courage at home. Now there was a woman more deserving of Robert's wrath than Mary Jo. The nameless wife, Henry's former model, trapped him by claiming pregnancy and continued to torture poor Henry for their entire forty-eight years of marriage.

At least the index card's prompts were helping Sally Bianco prepare Robert's directory of friends for this fresh disaster. Edward Thatch said his wife, Smilka, needed to stay home with the babies, but he would be on hand. Sally liked the attractive young man. Ed's father had been Robert's high-school teacher fifty years earlier.

Sally failed to venture her voice out into the electronic ether to announce Robert's arrest to anymore of his friends. Robert's eclectic array of friends was a tribute to his expansive intellect and emotional resilience. His stated philosophy was, "Laughter is better than tears, gentleness sought, bitterness naught." But, how would Robert reconcile himself to being accused of murder?

Robert might need her more now. Penny was too immature and busy getting her law degree in Lansing. Sally's resources as a widow with a comfortable legacy might be the only charm Robert recognized if the truth needed to be faced at some future juncture. For the present, imagined her intellect and love of fun entertained the bookman. The flattery of Robert's attention was palatable, addictive even. She found life as a widow becoming somewhat giddy. Nevertheless, Sally would assure anyone on a stack of King James Bibles that the man who ran the Bibliopole could no sooner see to the demise of another human being than the Pope could smoke grass.

Sally felt a grin ease the tension from her face as she imagined Robert's response when or if she recounted the picture of his archenemy, the Pope, toking marijuana. Sally's moment of cheerfulness was interrupted by customers, who had mounted the staircase without her knowledge. Sally fiddled with her hearing aid, turning up its volume, wondering how long it had been since she had changed the battery. 'We're closed." Sally decided on the slim evidence that Robert had directed her to lock up the shop.

The older gentleman shook his head. "The sign says, 'Open.' And my wife needed an outing."

Sally started to explain that she had forgotten to turn the sign to 'Closed,' but the wife was already seated in the chair next to Robert's desk.

"Robert knows Hilda from his old neighborhood." The older man took off his hat.

Hilda handed Sally a stack of photographs. "You must tell Robert I brought him the spirits."

"Spirits?" Sally questioned her husband with a look.

"In the trees." Hilda pointed. "See there's a face, the eyes, the mouth. And here are two in an embrace, and one here." Hilda continued to chatter, while Sally acknowledged she understood the lay of the land to her husband. When Hilda seemed to run completely out of words, she stared at Sally. "When will Robert return?"

"Tomorrow." Sally rose from Robert's chair and gently guided the woman to the shop's door. "I'll explain to Robert about the spirits. Did you want to leave the photographs?"

"Oh, no." Hilda carefully placed the pictures in her handbag. "We'll come again." Her husband bowed goodbye and politely preceded his wife's exit down the shop's stairs as if to buffer any stumble by the fragile woman.

Sally thanked God. Her own husband, Danny Bianco, had retained his mental facilities until the end. Losing a mate to a fog of confusion must be heartbreaking. Sally asked God's compassion for the gentle lovers leaving the shop.

Three hours later, near eight o'clock in the evening, Sally was exhausted but not ready to go home. The shop was crammed with Robert's hoard of friends.

Henry Schaeffer folded his raincoat inside out before placing it over the wooden chair, which faced the drop-leaf writing desk between the Liberty Street windows. He removed a checkbook from his inside left pocket and a small strap-bound notebook from his right-hand suit pocket. Finally situated behind Robert's desk, Henry consulted his notebook. He added up a sum of figures from its pages, while taking care to watch the street below for Robert's return. He wrote a check and placed it under a brass paperweight in the shape of a reclining nude woman engaged in self-gratification, a disgusting piece. Robert said the sculpture belonged to his mother, but Sally didn't believe it. Although he was the same age as Robert, Henry appeared much younger. His blond hair was a bit sparse, his chin line fallen somewhat. His blue eyes dull from living in an unhappy marriage.

According to Robert, the University of Chicago supplied the art degree and the deferment from the World War II draft. Henry's father-in-law owned the dry cleaning establishment that Henry managed. Henry's art was relegated to a weekend hobby. One of his oil paintings of Lake Superior's shoreline, strewn with stones instead of sand, hung in the upstairs hall of Sally's condominium. "No one yet." Henry answered Sally's unasked question about his latest survey of the street.

Penny Savage draped one leg of her torn jeans over the arm of the chair next to Robert's desk. Sally could reluctantly accept the fact that young people purchased attire without knees and frayed cuffs. However, Penny carried the style of scuffed elegance to the extreme. Sally allowed herself an inner censoring, 'tsk.'

Ed Thatch arrived with the evening's libations. He carried bottles of Taylor's Cream Sherry in each of his hands. Ed lifted the bounty over his head. "The liquor store manager says these are on the house to celebrate Robert's release from jail. Where is he?" Ed approached Henry, shook his hand sadly, and positioned himself to appreciate Penny's display of tattered glory. "Not returned?" Ed asked Penny.

Penny straightened her posture as if in deference to the missing Robert Koelz. "Mary Jo is off somewhere flat on her back enjoying…," she turned her attention to Sally and added demurely, "some view."

"Right," Sally said. Sally reminded herself youth held sway in life. Sally's weight and stamina might want to match theirs, but Sally's teeth were not as brilliant, her hair was white and thin, and her step not as sure. Even though her heart was steady, Sally knew her time was waning like a withering moon. Sally allowed herself few regrets. Everything she wanted in life she gained for sometimes shorter periods of time than she would have preferred.

Was Robert Koelz's fondness unbounded? Sally could accept the gradients of favorites easier than she wanted to consider a bottom to Robert's well of acceptance, attention, and, yes, affection. Perhaps Penny and Mary Jo were jealous of each other. As their audience, Sally found no rancor within herself. Mary Jo was too busy pursuing avenues of escape from the demons within her, while Penny somehow claimed Robert's primary devotion.

Eighteen-year-old Penny's interest in seventy-nine-year-old Robert Koelz was recognized and accepted by the bookstore gang as a replacement for her own father's affection. Her father committed suicide by jumping off the Williams Street high-rise apartment two years earlier. Penny told and retold scenes that explained her father of seven's sad need for a final solution. The telephone was regularly missing from the entrance hall table. By following the landline's cord, Penny opened the closet door under the staircase to find her crouched father in tears, talking to his married lover, a mother of eight. The booklovers and customers of the Bibliopole held their sympathy for Penny in common.

A momentary break in the group's conversation, detected Harvey Clemmons on the stairs to the shop. Ed disengaged a plastic chair from a stack in the back corner for Harvey's use. "I tried to explain to my slow-as-molasses waitress." Harvey's melodious low tones rolled over the group, "I mustn't keep the peasants waiting."

Sally recognized Harvey's voice the first time she met him from a radio show based in Minneapolis, which reached her Illinois home. Sure enough, Harvey and his very, very fat wife lived there for a short time. Harvey's dulcet, seductive tones never failed to illicit a negative response in Sally.

Harvey Clemmons phony affectedness was borne by Robert's friends because of his worries at home. The couple adopted a baby boy, who ended up being a charming master of deceit and periodically incarcerated. Supposedly unknown to Harvey until too late, his wife physically abused the child, beating him senseless with a length of rubber hose. She was not arrested and thrown into jail; hence the boy's continued failure to believe in virtue or justice.

Harvey placed his hand on Sally's pant leg. "Sally, when can we expect our Koelz to be delivered from the jaws of the county's tin whale?"

Brushing Harvey's hand aside, Sally offered her solution.

"Mary Jo calls Robert every morning. When she telephones tomorrow morning, this silliness will be cleared up."

Not agreeing with her assessment, Edward Thatch pulled at the tip of his dark beard. "If Mary Jo has come to harm, her husband is the best candidate for a murder suspect."

"He never actually struck her." Sally remembered.

"You can scare people to death," Penny said.

Harvey disagreed. "Fear doesn't usually stop the heart, but it can shorten a life."

"See!" Penny flung her arms wide as if to prove her point.

Ed refilled all the glasses with cream sherry. Sally made another pot of coffee. Finally, they heard the footfall they were attuned to, coming up the wooden steps to the shop. Penny beat Sally to the banister rail. They watched Ed run down to hug Robert. Once Robert was in the shop, Harvey clapped his shoulders and then patted the back of Robert's head. Penny enjoyed a full-frontal embrace. "Look at this motley crew, Andrew." Robert hung his suit coat on a hanger inside the storage room door.

"Fairly respectable." Andrew Sites surveyed the room. "Character witnesses, if we can keep them sober for a day."

"I don't drink." Sally took Robert's hand and kissed his cheek.

Robert hugged her close and then pushed past her to his desk. "Did you call everyone, Henry?"

Henry answered as he rose to relinquish the desk chair, "Mrs. Bianco handled the matter."

"Good job, Sally," Robert said.

Henry made a grand gesture towards Robert's chair, bowing as if offering the king a permit to his throne. A trick of light perhaps, revealed glistening around Henry's eyes. When Robert touched Henry's arm in appreciation for the magnanimous display of solicitude, Henry coughed to cover a sob. Robert and Henry stood cheek-to-jowl. Sally overheard Henry's reply. "Just until it's over." Robert patted Henry's back in response. Henry hastily gathered his overcoat, nodding his goodbyes.

"Defense strategies need to stay within the confines of this room." Andrew Sites, who they had ignored in their greeting of Robert, had accompanied Robert into the shop.

Robert placed his hand on his belt buckle as if to remind himself to pull in his flat stomach. He adjusted the blue silk cravat, which nicely matched his shirt and eyes before he announced. "Andrew promises me this matter will not see the inside of a courtroom."

Chapter Two

Miss Poi arrived from the back room to greet her master. Robert reclined in his creaky desk chair, and Miss Poi caressed his pant leg. "Well fed, I see," Robert winked at Sally.

Andrew continued his legal dictates. "If Mary Jo telephones at her regular hour tomorrow morning, all will be well."

"She did not this morning," Robert answered as the immediate question hung in the air.

"Where was she when she called last?" Harvey asked, his voice drowning out several attempts at the same question.

"I did not inquire," Robert said and added, "Our conversation was on a personal matter…of hygiene, if you must know."

"Herpes?" Penny was indelicate enough to ask.

"No," Robert said.

Sally watched Andrew casually take out a notebook similar to the one Henry kept his close accounts.

"It might be relevant," Ed said.

"I refuse to divulge the nature of her illness," Robert said. "However, she did reveal the transitory nature of an attempt at reconciliation with her husband may have left her open to infestation. Mostly she talked about her rabbits."

"Rabbits?" Andrew kept his pen poised for germane

information. "Her husband is the man who is giving evidence against you as her possible assailant."

"Do they have a body?" Harvey asked.

"If they did," Ed said, "Robert would not be sitting here."

"Your law studies do provide you some solace," Robert said, implying Ed was not helping matters.

"What evidence could her husband have?" Sally asked.

"That will be revealed in the indictment," Andrew said quietly.

"So, Robert was released because right now the case is only a missing person's report." Ed's brain summarized for them.

"Correct," Andrew said, putting away his notebook.

"How can we help?" Sally asked.

"Well," Andrew drawled. "My resources are somewhat limited."

Robert raised his right-hand high. It held Henry's check firmly clutched between his thumb and forefinger. "Ten thousand," Robert crowed. "Do I hear a higher offer?"

Harvey took out his checkbook, "Five grand more enough to start an investigation?"

"Thank you, that will get things started," Andrew said. "But what we really need are feet, cars, airplane tickets, and phone calls."

Penny jumped up. "I'll search the newspaper for reported deaths in Michigan."

"Mary Jo originally fled from St. Charles, Illinois," Sally said. "I went to high school there. What should I ask?"

"Try to find an address and phone number once you get there,"

Andrew directed. "Her place of work, neighbors, family. Anything might help. Do you know if her family was originally from Illinois?"

"I think Independence, Missouri, or was that her husband's?" Robert was pulling on his curls.

Miss Poi left the scene of the crime debate.

"I can take that," Harvey said. "Kansas City has an invitation to join a symposium on my desk. What was his name?"

"Ricco Cardoni," Andrew and Robert supplied in unison.

"Is he in Ann Arbor now?" Sally asked.

"Yes," Andrew said. "The police say he's ready to stay in town until the case is closed. He swears Robert is the last one to see his wife alive."

"Well, that's obviously a lie," Harvey intoned.

"Robert doesn't know the location of the supposed reconciliation," Andrew said, "and Mr. Cardoni is denying anything close to that took place."

"Are they fighting over custody of the rabbits?" Harvey tried to make them laugh. No one did.

"How long has she been missing?" Ed asked.

"A week, according to the husband," Andrew answered.

"But I talked to her yesterday." Robert lifted an empty glass which Ed rapidly filled with sherry.

Penny curled up in Robert's lap. "That's why she was so cagey about where she was. She didn't want her husband to find her."

"I think she had the bunnies with her," Robert said.

"Yes?" Andrew made a note. "Penny, check the pet stores. See if anyone knows if she purchased supplies recently, exact amounts."

Ed put on his coat. "I'm sorry, Robert, I need to get home. Andrew, let me know if my computers at school can track anything down."

"Wait," Andrew said. "Robert, did Mary Jo use a credit card when she bought any books from you?"

"Yes," Robert said, rummaging through his desk's bottom drawer. Penny necessarily dismounted from his lap. She seemed lost, grief-stricken, cast away. Sally moved her arm as if to invite an embrace from the child, then thought better of it. "Here," Robert said.

Andrew handed the receipt to Ed. "If you can find a program to monitor her latest purchases, we can track her whereabouts."

"I know an Asperger nerd who will be glad do it," Ed said to Andrew. "I'll let you know if we find anything. Robert, I'll call in the morning."

Harvey said his goodbye, too. Ten o'clock. Sally needed to get home and pack for Illinois, but she was loathe to leave Robert alone. Andrew took his leave, cautioning Robert not to drink and not to worry. "Penny, make sure he goes to bed early so that he can record Mary Jo's phone call."

"I will," Penny said, shutting off the shop lights.

Sally hugged Robert goodbye at the street door, and he clung to her for a moment, sweeping her cheek with a slight kiss. "I need you," he whispered close to her ear.

"My heart's always with you," Sally said. "I'll call you from

Illinois. Good luck."

* * *

September, Tuesday

Sally Bianco gassed up the Mustang before taking an indirect route to St. Charles from Ann Arbor. She hated Chicago road construction traffic. She claimed to anyone foolish enough to listen to an old woman the cancer rate increased in direct proportion to the amount of new construction on the nation's roads. All the stalled traffic with engines issuing noxious fumes to trapped motorists had to be a contributing factor. So she sped up route 69 to Ludington, caught the four-hour ride on the Badger Ferry to Milwaukee, and drove the short distance to St. Charles, Illinois.

In the late evening, the day after Robert Koelz's lawyer sent her to collect data, Sally Bianco checked into Hotel Baker. She unpacked, trying to ignore the view of the Fox River Dam, which gleamed with the multi-colored lights from the 1920 bus terminal on the far side of the river. She was here on business, and meant to tend to it as soon as she had a warm shower and ordered flowers for the room.

Sally called Art Woods, an old high school sweetheart, to see if he could help. Art decided to become a city cop when his television repair business went under. His father's hardware shop was still in town. She called the police department to reach Art.

"I can put you through to his cruiser," the dispatcher said.

"Good enough," Sally said, wondering if his wife allowed him to lunch with old schoolmates, really *old* schoolmates, widowed schoolmates, ex-girl friends, really old ex-girl friends. Well, sixty-five wasn't time for assisted living, but Sally needed all the help she could get. She laughed aloud at the thought, scaring the delivery boy, who nearly dropped her dozen yellow roses.

"Hello," Art's voice sounded old, too.

"Art, this is Sally Stiles, Bianco, your old girlfriend from high school."

"I wasn't in high school at the time, and neither were you," Art contradicted.

"Nevertheless," Sally insisted. Big deal. she had only been nineteen. Art had told her never to call him unless she was ready to give it up. After another year of celibacy, still a virgin, she called him. She remembered loving his hair, the line of his jaw, those blue, blue eyes, and tight jeans. However, fate or a very personal God had delivered her. Her period arrived, and she didn't know how to break the date nor how to explain her continued un-acceptance of his advances. This was her first contact after nearly fifty years. "Please help me find a home address for someone I'm trying to get in touch with," Sally asked calmly, professionally.

"Another man?" Art asked, up to his old tricks.

"Nope. Mary Jo Cardoni," Sally said. "She's a missing person, according to a very abusive husband."

"What's your phone number," Art asked, apparently ready to help.

"I'm staying at the Hotel Baker. Any chance we can lunch

together tomorrow?" Sally tried to keep her voice upbeat, confident. "I could fill you in on why I need help."

"Let's wait until I can offer something," Art said with what Sally was sure was an Elvis mimic of a sneer.

"When will that be?" Sally asked.

"Let's say dinner tomorrow."

"Won't Gabby object?" Sally asked, innocently, sort of.

"I'll bring her along if that's okay?" Art said.

"Fine with me," Sally lied. Heck, where was the romance in that? At least he was willing to help an old friend. Sally counted her blessings.

***

Hotel Baker, St. Charles, Illinois

Sally rang Robert Koelz at ten o'clock in the evening to let him know she was on the job in Illinois and to see if Mary Jo had called. She would not mind if her trip was not necessary to clear Robert's name.

"Sally." he answered her hello, "It's not Mary Jo," Robert called out, probably to Penny or Andrew.

"Well, you answered my question. Maybe I should get off the line so that Mary Jo can reach you."

"Are you okay?" Robert asked.

"Absolutely," Sally said. "A friend of mine in the police department is running down Mary Jo's address for me. I cannot remember what sort of car she drove."

"Penny?" Robert asked, back in Ann Arbor. "What kind of car did Mary Jo drive?"

"A van," Sally heard Penny's answer.

"Right," Sally remembered. "Blue it was and a VW. I'll call you tomorrow. Good luck, Robert."

"Yes, of course," Robert said. "Be careful."

Sally meant to be. If Ricco Cardoni could falsely accuse harmless Robert with the murder of his wife, maybe Ricco was capable of worst villainy—like making sure the truth wasn't pursued in Illinois.

* * *

September, Wednesday

The next day, Sally Bianco ordered creamed tomato soup for lunch in the empty but snazzy Hotel Baker dining room. The linen-covered tables were set among art-deco pillars. Moorish sculptured windows faced the muddy Fox River dam. She hoped Gabby and Art Woods would choose the hotel for the evening meal because she planned to eat in the round, ballroom dining room, where tables surrounded the balcony. Perfect, if one had an eye for prying into the business of St. Charles' residents.

Sally's glorious retirement plans had boiled down to snooping out criminals and saving the day for friends. She hoped her wardrobe was more up-to-date than Miss Marple's. Sally wore sensible, elegant shoes, flat but expensive. Today her blue leather vest softened with a matching silk scarf, chosen to hide a few neck wrinkles. Her cashmere slacks were blue, too. Who was she kidding? She doubted she would be of help to anyone. She was at the age when the public took no further notice of her. She might easily walk away from robbing a bank or offing an espionage victim with no one stretching out an accusing hand in her direction. Invisibility should have some benefits. Sally dropped her soupspoon on the marble tiled floor.

The courteous, older waiter jumped at the noise but regained his dignity, gliding to Sally's side with a fresh utensil. "Please." Sally gestured for him to take her unfinished bowl away. "If you're not busy, could I ask you a few questions?"

"Sure, Sally," the waiter said. "You don't recognize me, do you?"

"Noo...," she hesitated. He was around the same age as herself. "High school?"

"Exactly," the man said. "John, John Nelson."

"But you and your twin brother," Sally stalled, 'are rich' were the next words on her tongue, but she had enough sense not to utter them. "...are still in town?"

"We own the hotel," John sat down at her, no his, table. The handsome identical twins were the football hero and class president of her graduating class. Not that she could ever tell which was which, unless they stayed in her vicinity shortly after identifying themselves.

"James is at the bank. He'll be glad to see you." John started to rise, "More coffee?"

"Yes," Sally said, worrying no amount of hot could warm up her cold cup.

"I'll get you a fresh cup, too," John said.

This was good. These two would know the town gossip. So Sally asked him when he returned, "Mary Jo and Ricco Cardoni, did, do you know them?"

"Last name sounds familiar." He rubbed his bald head, where luxurious black hair once existed. "James will know. His memory was always better than mine."

"Were you the football player?" Sally asked, thinking he'd probably knocked his brains around too much.

"I am," he blushed from what he thought was flattery, "I mean was. You remembered?" Sally couldn't lie, but she did nod with her shoulder dipping to show it was no big deal. It seemed high school acquaintances revert a person's psyche immediately back to the imbecilic days of high hormones and no sense. "James," John called out at some noise in the hall Sally's hearing aid had not detected. "Look who's here."

James had no clue which of the old dame's names he was called upon to remember. "Sally," John provided. "Sally Stiles."

"Bianco," Sally added, then just to keep the record straight, "widowed for six years."

"Sorry," James said, actually bowing at the waist. "You were a librarian helper for a while for Flash Jordan."

"Yes," she said, surprised James did recognize her or at least remembered her mousey role at school. Miss Jordan, the white-headed, four-foot-eleven librarian, was remarkably quick on her feet and a strict disciplinarian of absolute quiet in the school library. Flash Gordan was the white-tights-wearing space cadet on a popular, science-fiction, black-and-white television program many years ago.

Sally had wanted to fit in at high school. But, the lunchroom gauntlet past the popular kids' table and not knowing how to react to all those lovely boys caused her to dive into books, not rearing her head until after high school and one last romance of Jane Austin's, when she decided to get some romance for herself. The next man Sally looked at, a taxi driver, asked her out. Sally smashed his head, hard, against the taxi's window when he tried to kiss her after a revelation he was married. But life worked itself out. Danny Bianco had been the grand passion in Sally's life.

"We're glad you decided to stay with us," James said, sincerely but professionally.

"Sally wants to know about—who was it?" John directed James to a seat at her table, their table.

"Mary Jo and Ricco Cardoni?" Sally repeated.

"Only from the newspaper," James said. "Wife abuse, I think."

"I could find the article at the library," Sally said, uncomfortable for some reason, probably just teenage nerves from her past. Then she zeroed in on the source of her unease. James wore a wig, not an expensive one, either. Why did he bother? Everyone would know he was as bald as his twin. Probably a wife's vanity required the unflattering rug. "Are you both happily married?" Sally batted eyelashes she no longer owned.

"James is," John said. "I never married." He continued, with an unflattering chortle, "Once you left town, all was lost."

"Right," Sally said, getting her dander up.

"Ricco Cardoni probably has an arrest record," James quelled Sally's nervous reaction to John's taunt. "My wife, Cindy, runs the women's shelter here and filled in some details the newspaper failed to report."

"Like what?" Sally asked, regaining her role as a detective on a murder case. She produced a notebook identical to Henry Schaefer and Andrew Site's. "Do you know where they lived?" Sally realized she had almost blown her cover of innocent inquiry by asking the question as if they were no longer residents of St. Charles.

"Mary Jo worked for Dukane at the time," James said.

"Oh, I remember now," John said. "Hostage scene, guns and all."

"Why didn't they keep him in jail?" Sally asked.

"No one was actually shot," James said. "Mary Jo left the state, and the prosecutor dropped the case, according to Cindy. She, Cindy, was angrier than I think I have ever seen her."

Sally got the impression Cindy's temper knew few bounds. "Was Mary Jo that afraid of her husband?"

"Must have been," John said. "I could drive you out to their house."

"Really?" Sally said, floored by his immediate interest.

"Sure," John said. "I'm their realtor."

"Would you know how to get in touch with Mary Jo?" Sally

asked as cold chills ran up the back of her neck. John left the restaurant part of the hotel to find Mary Jo's number. Sally excused herself to James. "I need to run up to my room for a minute. Tell John I'll be right down."

James caught her hand. "You've become a lovely lady," he said.

"I wish I was young enough to faint without breaking my hip," Sally laughed, but she appreciated every syllable of the flattery. "I'll be right back."

This was fun. She should have come up with this volunteer work years ago. Digging into other people's private business, righting wrongs, playing with old schoolmates—not bad work. They could keep those cards and letters coming. Then her stomach hurt. Mary Jo's life did not sound like a bed of roses. Sally sent her good thoughts to the missing woman and called Robert Koelz. "Is Andrew with you?" Sally asked Robert.

When Andrew took the receiver, Sally told him to contact the St. Charles police department, ask for Art Woods, and have Ricco Cardoni's arrest record faxed to the Ann Arbor police station.

"No word yet," Andrew answered Sally's unasked question about Mary Jo's call.

"I don't understand why she told Robert they tried to reconcile. Mary Jo fled a case here in St. Charles over a month ago. I think Ricco might have harmed her and planned to shift the blame on Robert."

"Me too," Andrew said. "Keep digging for us."

"I don't intend to find a body, Andrew."

"You know what I mean." Andrew Sites never appreciated a sense of humor, but Sally could imagine the grin under Robert's grey mustache as he recognized her probable reply.

* * *

John Nelson opened the front door of Mary Jo and Ricco Cardoni's split-level home. Apple-and-cinnamon room deodorizer scent wafted outdoors as they entered. "You might want to open some windows while we're here to let in some fresh air," Sally suggested.

"Good idea," he said. "Take a look around."

"Did you sign the deal with Mary Jo or Ricco?"

"The sales agreement carries both their signatures," John said defensively.

"Mary Jo signed in front of you?"

"No," John rubbed that glistening head of his. "Ricco said she had to be out of town, so she signed the agreement before she left."

"You know her handwriting?"

"Actually, no. I was hoping to see her at the closing when the house sells. So far, people haven't taken to the house."

Sally could understand why, but she didn't want to discourage John. Scars and telltale signs of a violent environment were everywhere. A missing piece in the frame of a starving-artist oil over the fireplace was complemented by a pair of antique lanterns with the glass missing in one. She caught up to John in the main bedroom. "Do most of your clients know the history of the couple selling?"

"I'm not sure. They don't bring it up, but I notice them pointing out the obvious." He shut the bedroom door to show Sally a fist size hole bashed into the back of it. "Must have broken his fist on that one."

"How long has the house been on the market?"

"A little less than a month," John said. "I don't hear from Ricco very often, but Mary Jo called once to check on the possibility of a sale and if her belongings were still in the attic."

"Does Ricco ask about the storage items?" Sally hoped she was on to something.

"He's never mentioned them."

Sally came clean. "John, a friend of mine in Ann Arbor, is accused by Ricco Cardoni of murdering his wife. He claims my friend, Robert Koelz, was the last to see Mary Jo alive. I came to town to try to clear his name. Could I go through Mary Jo's personal effects?" Sally purposefully selected those evocative terms to imply Mary Jo might be dead. Although she hoped with all her heart, Mary Jo was very much alive, even on her back in some lover's arms, just not dead, not a cause for Robert to be jailed for the rest of his life.

"I'll help you," John said eagerly, the dear.

Access was gained to the attic by a pull-down ladder in a guest bedroom's closet. The attic sported dormer windows, which they quickly opened for fresh air. A trunk, four huge, cheap pieces of luggage, and about twenty cardboard boxes were in the farthest reaches from the attic's entrance. Sally's first thought was that Ricco might not even know the attic storage area items existed. Her hands and hairline started to sweat, and she felt the unusual, at her age, yet familiar heat-flash symptoms start to overwhelm her. "John," she whined. "Is there anything cold to drink in the refrigerator?"

"I keep diet pop in there. I'll be right back."

Even if Ricco had peeked into the opening, his first sight would have been of baby furniture, which might have deterred any further search. A folded-up playpen of white netting, a bath and linen stand, a baby scale, a bassinette with the pink gingham-and-lace trim still decorating the sides, and a few boxes labeled 'baby clothes' and 'baby blankets' shielded the bulk of Mary Jo's belongs.

Sally ignored the luggage, which was probably carefully packed each time Mary Jo had decided to leave her monster husband, and went straight to the traveling trunk. Sure enough, the metal trunk held documents. Personal, dated journals, legal-looking folders, family albums, jewelry, and an address book filled the, chest.

John arrived with the cold drink before Sally decided which items to take with her. The latest, dated journal and the address book seemed the most pertinent. "John, I need to borrow these two items. If you let me copy them tonight, you can replace them tomorrow, no foul, no injury."

"I wish James had come with us."

"I know you defer to your brother, and we can certainly let him know what we've done as soon as we get back to the hotel." Bless his heart. John took the bait.

"No," John said, buffing the outside of his brains with both hands. "One night won't hurt, and I gave you my word I would help."

"Come to dinner with Art and Gabby Woods tonight. Art is gathering more evidence for me."

His grin said she'd hit the mark. "I will," he said. "I like Art, but Gabby...."

"Never shuts up," Sally laughed.

"Yeah," John said and chuckled, too.

* * *

John seemed disappointed when Gabby and Art agreed the Hotel Baker's ballroom dining room was the best place to have dinner. "There isn't much privacy," he said.

"What about the side rooms off the balcony?" she asked. "I remember a birthday party that Bob Burger held in there when we were dating."

"You dated Bob Burger of Burger Drugs?" John looked Sally up and down with what she thought was some gall.

For an old dame, Sally thought she shone fairly well for an evening meal. She had chosen a long black skirt and a cobalt blue wrap-around blouse, with a matching modern, glass bead necklace for wrinkle duty. At least she was not fifty pounds overweight like Gabby. Gabby should have talked even more to keep her tongue busy with hot air instead of more food. Not a Christian thought. If John hadn't seemed so shocked about Bob Burger asking her out long ago for a date, Sally probably would have been less critical of another member of her side of the human race. "Well, yes, John,"

Sally said, clearly miffed he thought such a thing improbable. "Bob Burger and I dated a few times."

Gabby took over, explaining Sally's personal business for Art and John's edification. "The Burgers and Stiles were both Roman Catholics, and their parents probably thought they would become a fruitful couple."

"At least my mother did," Sally disclosed. She needed these people to clear Robert's name. And, she needed to keep her thin balloon of ego in check.

"Sure," John said, hanging his head. "I hadn't remembered that."

"What about the side dining room?" Sally brought John back to the immediate subject, touching his arm and letting her hand linger. All this reminiscing threw her momentarily off track.

"The staff needs to set it up for us," John said. "We could have a drink at the bar until they're done."

"Sure," Sally said. That's about all she needed! Her nerves were shot, and one thing she did *not* need was a drink. Admitting her alcoholism, again, to herself, Sally ordered coffee and dug her fingernails into the bar. She was not, was not going to drink just because that stupid Mary Jo had decided to lead a trail of breadcrumbs to Robert Koelz's bookshop for her dumb husband to hassle.

"How have you been keeping yourself busy since Danny died," Gabby asked.

"Selling used cars to tire salesmen," Sally said out of the blue.

"I'm sorry, Gabby." Sally apologized and took her arm. "A friend of mine has been accused of murdering Mary Jo Cardoni. I'm in St. Charles to find out how to clear his name."

"Wow," Gabby said, struck speechless for the first time in her entire life.

Art smiled at Sally for accomplishing a miracle he, no doubt, had actively pursued for many years.

John cocked his jealous head as if in disbelief in Sally's mission or fresh distaste in front of an officer of the law. "I should ask for Mary Jo's journal and address book back."

"Yes, John," Sally said. "I'll go up and get them." The hotel staff had already provided her with copies of the journal and the address book. John and James Nelson were known for their ability to motivate the cream of any pick of schoolmates, employees, or charity donors.

Art Woods held out his hand for the books when Sally returned to the bar. "Sure," John said. "I guess the police should have them."

They were informed the private dining room was set up and adjourned for a peaceful meal. Gabby was amazing, talking continually about most of the residents in St. Charles while devouring the food on her plate without ever, even once talking with food in her mouth. Gabby inhaled the food once it was atomized by her windy sentences. Art failed even to try to guide the conversation. He mutely handed Sally a stack of index cards from his inside suit coat pocket. His eyes were as blue as they were when he was only twenty, and the line of his chin was unchanged with age.

Gabby watched the transaction without losing a syllable of her discourse. "So now, the assessor's wife only roams her extensive gardens at Fourth Avenue and Main. Her hats change with the seasons. She is completely bald, they say. But few people stop to chat because of the loud, black hound she allows to dog her every step."

Sally impolitely moved her plate of gleaned duck bones to the side of the table and laid out the multi-colored cards filled with relevant case notes about Ricco and Mary Jo Cardoni. She shuffled them back together and placed them in her purse. She would stay up late to glean through all the clues in order to report to Andrew.

Gabby's explanation of the town's villains and heroes continued. The Viet Nam vet's return, the beauty queen's father, the growing numbers of residents in the housing projects littering the cornfields, the addition of traffic lights on Randall Road. The stories droned on and on. John's eyes seemed to glaze over. Art's studied Sally.

The memories flooded back to Sally. The assessor's wife, that was Judy. Judy and her lover, what was his name, double-dated with Art and Sally. Sally remembered the corn husks stuck in the back of Judy's hair after they left the car so Art could make out with Sally. Judy didn't marry her lover. She married the tax assessor. And Sally knew why. The lover had no fortune, no future, according to Judy. Judy and she had once attended a party after a football game. A very rare appearance for Sally. Nevertheless, courage in hand (a glass of wine), Sally approached two young men and even spoke to them. Judy took her arm and pulled her away, whispering, "You're wasting your time. They don't even own a car."

Sally shivered, and John woke up. "It is chilly in here," John said as he rose. "Should I get a sweater from your room?"

Sally stood, too. "No. thank you. I am tired. It's been a long day." She stepped to Gabby's side of the table and watched Art's face as she said, "I'm so glad Art found you. He loves St. Charles and his life here."

Art laughed too loudly for good manners. "Judy's lover killed himself," he said as if he followed her walk among their memories.

Sally sat back down. Art and Glenn, Glenn was his name, were the best of friends. "You were inseparable," she added sympathetically.

"They were," Gabby was off again, recounting more stories. She didn't notice Art's face or the tears sliding down his cheek, unchecked.

Sally interrupted, "I remember a record you two bought that promised to arouse your dates. What was its name?"

Art wiped his face. "Frank Sinatra," he said and lifted his glass in a sort of goodbye wave.

Sally got up and fled to her room. She looked at the pile of papers, which contained Mary Jo's latest journal and address book. She placed the index cards Art had given her on top of them, but couldn't think about Mary Jo. She was overwhelmed by the past and how lucky she had been to escape the disaster of St. Charles when she did. She remembered meeting Danny, an ex-con serving bar at the Elks Club in Elgin. How she missed Danny's olive-toned skin, his thick hair, turned white since he was in his twenties from the antibiotics they gave him in Viet Nam for syphilis he was too much of a scared virgin to contract, about the nude she had sketched of him on her bedroom wall after he died. How she missed him, how much he had convinced her she was loved.

A bitter sweetness enveloped her. Robert Koelz would understand the ebb and flow of her emotions. Robert. Sally dressed for bed in pink silk pajamas and cradled Mary Jo's paper trail to her chest as she climbed up into the canopied bed. Time to study how to clear Robert.

The July 20th entry in Mary Jo's journal seemed close enough to the present mayhem to start. It was written in Greg's shorthand. Sally's could only translate the most carefully written words. 'Husband' was always capitalized. Some details were lost, but the word 'pain' was underlined as were the words 'bruises' and 'escape.'

Sally skipped to August 1st. In Mary Jo's relaxed script, she read, "Ricco will be served divorce papers at Dukane this morning. My face is too swollen to go to work. I'm all packed. My lawyer, Sue Pike's kid brother, promises I will be safe. I'm not sure. I buried my ring in the backyard next to the rose bush he gave me the first time he broke my ring finger. The funny thing is, I'm sad. I guess for all the broken promises of happiness, of the forever of marriage. But it is more important to live, to feel safe, to at least have a second chance. Mother said it was important to be happy. Life is so short."

Mother. Where did Mary Jo's mother live? Sally reached for the address book. Robert had remembered St. Louis for Mary Jo's husband. Harvey was supposed to check it out. What was Mary Jo's maiden name? Sally started in the 'A' section. Not until the 'S' section did Sally notice the number of similar last names and addresses in Florida. Orlando, Vero Beach, Tampa all had the name 'Staples' listed.

"Family," Sally said. They must be family. Eleven o'clock, too late to be making social calls. Sally closed the address book and slipped into dreamland. Danny was taking her picture in her exercise tights.

"Let your hair fall a little on your face," Danny directed.

In the dream her hair was still dark, natural curly, unruly. But Danny loved her and she him, to the bottom of his perfect feet, and the way he placed one hand on his belt, jutting his hip toward the world. My, he was fine.

Chapter Three

Bibliopole
September, Thursday

Andrew Sites received the stack of cards with a quizzical expression. Sally explained for the lawyer as well as Robert. "Ricco and Mary Jo Cardoni's information while they were in St. Charles."

"Ricco's arrest record," Andrew said, handing a blue card to Robert.

"No wonder he left Illinois," Robert said after reading the information.

Penny whisked the card from Robert's hand. "Do the Ann Arbor police know Robert's accuser was incarcerated this many times?"

"They knew he had a record," Andrew said, holding out his hand for the return of the card. "That's why Robert's bail was waived."

"You could skip the country," Penny told Robert. "We could move to Canada."

"That would hardly clear his name," Sally said, somewhat alarmed by the prospect of losing Robert Koelz to Canada's wasteland.

"I have already given the license plate number of Mary Jo's

van to the police," Andrew said. "You did a great job. I hope Harvey has friends in the police department in Kansas City."

"Harvey has friends on the entire planet," Robert said, already in the sauce.

Sally checked her watch to confirm the inappropriateness of his intoxication. Two o'clock in the afternoon. "Did you wait until after lunch, at least?" Sally asked him.

"We haven't had lunch," Penny said.

Andrew shook his head. "Robert, you need to keep a steady head for a couple weeks."

"Nothing wrong with my head," Robert said. "My ticker's been racing. A sip of sherry slows it down, a bit."

"When was the last time you had a physical?" Sally asked, still irked because he was drinking. She realized part of the problem was she wanted to finish more than one bottle of cream sherry and now wouldn't be soon enough to start. At least her friends respected her history and didn't offer her favorite poison. Sally reminded herself, Robert wasn't an alcoholic until he acknowledged it; or rather, not accepting his addiction to alcohol guaranteed the continued consumption of Robert by the booze.

"Doctors are idiots," Robert said. "But I could eat."

"I need to talk to you, Robert," Andrew said, checking his watch.

"I'll go down to the Red Fox and bring you back soup and bread," Sally offered.

"I'll go with you," Penny suggested.

She was a sweet child. Sally did like her and wouldn't mind the company while she waited, or the extra arms to carry back the food. The wait for the order seemed exceedingly long. "I'm still tired from the trip," Sally conceded.

"You look great," Penny said. "I hope I can keep myself up, when I'm your age."

"Oh, thanks," Sally said. "I'm not nearly as decrepit as all that."

"No, no," Penny blushed. "Didn't I say it right? You look great."

Sally nodded and tried to smile away the sag of her chin and the mean lines around her mouth. "You'll always be a beauty, Penny."

"I hope I don't get fat," she said. "I really love to eat."

"You have so much energy. I'm sure you won't stomach becoming a lazy person."

"I'm still a virgin," Penny said.

"Out of the blue." Sally didn't want to talk about the subject.

"I wanted you to know."

"No," Sally said. "You wanted me to explain why Robert hasn't made a move on you."

"Right," Penny admitted.

"He's a eunuch." Sally hoped she would not need to give further details.

"From the war." Penny's blue eyes widened in appreciation, or alarm.

"No, his wife was a virgin when she divorced him," Sally further enlightened her.

"She's pregnant now," Penny said.

"Is she?" Robert had not told Sally this new evidence of his failure. "When did he find out?"

"While you were in Illinois." Penny traced the outline of a glass' bottom, which remained eternalized on the surface of the wooden restaurant table. "Nancy stopped by. She's six months pregnant."

"A pretty picture to set before the king," Sally said, wondering if she had gotten high from the fumes of stale alcohol in the Bibliopole.

"He wasn't happy," Penny said. "I can tell you that."

"He surely didn't say anything out of the way to her, for heaven's sake?"

"No, no, Robert congratulated her, asked the due date. Hoped to see the child when he popped out."

"Popped out?" Sally asked.

"That's how Robert put it." Penny hung her head. "His ex-wife laughed."

"You don't want to have children, do you?" Sally asked with sincere curiosity.

"Yes," Penny was pouting now. "Why not? I'm healthy. I want Robert's child."

"Well, that will be a problem." Sally's stomach was churning. She waved the waitress over to rescue her. But she added for

Penny's mollification, "I'm sure Robert was flattered."

"He said he was." Penny continued to study the wood grain of the table. "But he didn't do anything about it."

"I hope I've explained why he can't," Sally said.

The waitress arrived, somewhat slowly Sally noted, and took their order. "Three chicken sandwiches, one creamed tomato soup to-go, two glasses of milk, and a pot of tea. Is there anything else you would like, Penny?"

"I'm not hungry."

"She is," Sally explained to the waitress. "French fries, sour cream, a veggie burger, and a cup of coffee."

"Beer," Penny said.

"Orange Juice," Sally instructed the waitress, "And coffee."

"Why can't he?" Penny wouldn't let go of the bone.

"I don't know," Sally tried.

"Yes, you do," Penny insisted.

"What makes you think, I know?" Sally asked.

"Because Robert says you've known him longer than Henry Schaeffer."

"Well, that's just not true," Sally said, somewhat shocked at Robert's lie. "I met Robert a year before my husband died. He was in a coma. My husband, not Robert. That was seven years ago."

"Why did he lie to me?" Sally could see Penny's ire was rising. The food hadn't arrived to calm the surge in negative energy.

"Maybe he was confused," Sally said. Then she decided to change the subject, sort of. "Have you ever read Hemmingway's

'For Whom the Bell Tolls'?"

"No," Penny said, sipping the tardy but arrived orange juice.

As the food was served, Sally spilled some of Robert's beans. "The story Robert tells about being a spy behind enemy lines in the Second World War is word-for-word in the book. Remember how the hero falls over a brick wall to pick an early spring blossom and lands on the fat, dead enemy soldier? How he went through his pockets and found a picture of a fat wife and baby?" Sally breathed a sip of hot tea for fortification, "that's all in Hemmingway's tale."

"You're kidding," Penny said, finally interested in something besides her own hide.

Sally shook her head, happily immersed in her chicken sandwich. Thank God Penny had forgotten to inquire about the nature of Robert's inability to perform. There was a medical term for having only one testicle because the other remains internal, but Sally couldn't recall the word and certainly didn't want to impart the exact information. Robert had told her the story of being so immature looking at the age of thirty that the mailman commanded him to stop playing hooky and get back to school.

Penny and Sally marched back to the shop equipped with Robert's food and their satiated stomachs. Mrs. Clankton, Robert's landlady, was talking to Andrew. Robert was pouring himself another drink, not into the glass, down his throat from a water glass.

Penny set the luncheon items before him, removing the glass in his hand and replacing it with a spoon for the soup.

"Thanks," Robert said sheepishly, but enough of an imp to

wink at Sally.

Robert was a handsome man. His attempt to mimic Mark Twain's looks might have been more authentic if his hair hadn't been so curly and contained more grey than white. His mustache wasn't white either, but Sally always imagined a white silk suit would help the likeness.

During her first contact with Robert's embrace, way before Penny's arrival on the bookshop scene, Sally had noticed the smell of apples in his hair. The aroma did not come from cologne. Rather, given the daily evidence, from the cream sherry traces left on Robert's fingers from pouring glass after glass for his customers and himself. Sally tuned into Andrew's interrogation of Mrs. Clankton.

"She was nude in my bathroom on Sunday morning," Mrs. Clankton was saying, "She could have at least locked the door."

"Mary Jo?" Penny asked.

"Yes," Mrs. Clankton said, reclasping her purse with a bang.

"My apologies for her," Robert called, waving his soupspoon.

Mrs. Clankton grinned. Another smitten female. Mrs. Clankton was over eighty. The range of Robert's conquests was phenomenal. The poor ladies all needed a male ear more than any other item of Robert's physique.

Penny was glaring.

Robert offered her his emptied Styrofoam cup of soup for disposal. She threw it away for him and returned to his outstretched arms, cuddling in his lap as he rocked his desk chair.

No harm there.

"Call a cab for Mrs. Clankton," Andrew directed Sally as he left. "I'll be back this evening. Harvey might be in town with more information. You did a great job in Illinois, Sally."

When the cab finally arrived, Sally shielded Mrs. Clankton from the wind. She offered her arm, and Mrs. Clankton clung to it. Such a frail body, Sally worried the wind might pick the woman up and sail her home. She owned the house on Ann Street Robert lived in. Sally was sure Mrs. Clankton's family didn't know the opera and concert companion they had agreed to house entertained livelier company.

Good heavens. Robert could have at least lent a robe to his latest guest. Sunday morning. Three days before, Robert was arrested. How far could a fugitive travel from the hands of an abusive husband in three days? Mary Jo Cardoni could be in Florida. Sally wondered if Mary Jo owned a passport. Andrew would know that. At least the police were looking for her van with her license number.

Sally hoped Mary Jo was safe. Then Robert would be free to find his salvation. Sally thought she should suggest Penny follow Alanon's directions to muddle through the next few months of court dates without permanent damage. Poor kid, in a way two fathers were letting her down, one to suicide and one to a slower self-destructive act of alcoholism.

After a long afternoon nap in her condominium, Sally cooked a substantial supper for herself of baked sweet potatoes, a pork chop, and corn. A shower and change of attire and lots more make-up allowed Sally to return to the Bibliopole around eight o'clock at night, the usual time for her appearance. Andrew, Harvey, and Miss Poi attended the bookman. Penny was nowhere in sight. Sally failed to inquire about her.

"Ricco Cardoni killed his second wife in Missouri," Robert said, quite cheerfully, by way of greeting.

If Sally could have believed Robert was sober, she would have. But Sally knew his habits too well. She turned to Harvey for confirmation.

"Only a remote possibility," Harvey said.

"We would have to pay to have the body exhumed," Andrew explained.

"He drove nails through the heads of puppies while his children watched." Robert was sober for a moment.

"Children?" Sally asked.

"With the second wife apparently," Harvey said. "At least his first wife is still alive. She's taking care of the four children."

"Will she testify against him?" Andrew asked.

"She said to send her a train ticket, and she would be here," Harvey said. "Her sister was Ricco's second wife. All his children: two boys and two girls, are named Ricco."

A chill went up Sally's spine in spite of her cashmere sweater. "A monster is on the loose."

"With apparently no way to rein him in," Harvey intoned. He raised his head from petting Miss Poi. "We should put a bounty on his head."

"No," Andrew said. "The police are keeping an eye on him."

"Well, that's good news," Sally said. "That will do a lot of good if he decides to harm any of us." Sally looked around again. "Where is Penny?"

Robert sat straight up. "He wouldn't."

Andrew straightened in his chair. "Do you know where Penny is, Robert?"

"Yes," he said, pulling on his curls. It was a wonder he wasn't bald. "She called from her folk's home in Toledo. Needed time to think."

If her blood could have pumped hard enough for her to blush, Sally would have. She realized their luncheon conversation had surely sent Penny off to Toledo. "When is she coming home?" Sally asked, cagey with her polite inquiry.

"She'll be here before her morning class," Robert answered, head held a little higher with rightful pride.

"A pretty child," Harvey mentioned. "Gorgeous."

The men refused to comment on the inappropriateness of the liaison, and Sally certainly did not want to be banned from the brotherhood or sisterhood of Robert's admirers. Penny would have to fend for herself.

Here they were. Educated, with resources available for ample entertainment, all bound by this Prospero as easily as Airele or Caliban were tied to Shakespeare's character in the Tempest. Sally was held by her lack of companionship at home, Harvey was vacating his own unhappy scenario, and Andrew was of immediate service. Those present in spirit, if not in body, were also tethered securely to Robert. Ed was tied by his father's memory, Henry by real affection. More a grandfather than father, Robert was a role model who didn't expect anything and left all the doors open to careers and future desires. Possibilities were as open as Robert's need for a family, too.

Robert's only brother, Ted, had committed suicide at eighteen during the Great Depression when college funds were lost in the disaster. His mother and father had both been felled by strokes while Robert was married to his first wife, who had thus paid her dues—twice in Robert's life. Sally was happy to hear she was pregnant, just a little put out Robert had not shared the news.

"Andrew, is there anything else we can do to help Robert out of this mess?" Sally asked, happy to be of service, sad to be so outnumbered by his friends, vying for his affection with supposedly both Mary Jo and Penny at the same time.

"Does Mary Jo know you well enough to visit her in Florida?" Andrew asked.

"Sure," Sally said.

"Well," Andrew told the group, "With the addresses you found for her, your trip would save the expense of hiring a detective to roust Mary Jo out. Besides, a stranger might spook her into running again, if Mary Jo thinks her husband is having her followed."

"Would you?" Robert held out his hand for Sally to take.

If Robert had had a ring, Sally would have kissed the blessed metal before leaving for the further quest of Mary Jo's whereabouts.

Chapter Four

Thankfully for Sally, her relatives with the wherewithal to do so migrated south from Illinois to Florida as soon as they hit retirement age. Her widowed eldest sister, Madelyn, who Sally judged to look ten years younger than her age, possessed plenty of official contacts in Vero Beach. Sally was sure one of Madelyn's friends could be of assistance in her search for Mary Jo.

September was a bit early for her yearly visit, but she invited herself down anyway.

"Tuesday, I'm busy with 'Nu-2-U,'" Madelyn said.

The assisted-living complex, with apartments for the more robust members of the married couples, sold used furniture, clothing, books, and other belongings of the deceased when their families were too disinterested in the worldly remains to haul them away—the paraphernalia, not the dead bodies. So, Nu-2-U flourished.

"I'll drop by Loretta's and see you on Wednesday," Sally said. "Madelyn, could you invite someone for me to meet from the police department or a detective agency? My friend, Robert Koelz, has gotten himself into a jam. I need to find a missing person in Florida to clear him."

"Why do you do this?" Madelyn asked in an accusatory tone. "I thought your analyst told you to give up disasters. I'll be glad to see you, but do we need to tell all my friends that you're involved in clearing a friend of questionable character?"

Family can bring up the past, right when a person only needs their support. Sally's husband Danny didn't hide his Viet Nam history and his confinement in Michigan's State Prison for the mentally ill. No matter how many years of service Danny gave the community after he'd served his time, Danny would always be an outlaw in her family's eyes. Danny hadn't harmed anyone. Maybe he did shorten a few lives of those who witnessed the terror of watching a grown man scream himself into unconsciousness. The siege of suddenly recovered memories of the war caused his breakdown. Sally knew she had aged five years in two hours.

"You're right," Sally said. "If you'll give me a few names, I'll contact them without referring to my connection to you." Sally hated sucking up to people, especially family. "Would that be better?"

"Much," Madelyn said. Then she sighed, adding reluctantly, "I'll pull together a list of names that might help. What's he accused of?"

"Murder," Sally admitted. Why lie?

"Sally," Madelyn took a deep breath in preparation for a long lecture.

"Sorry," Sally did lie. "My cell is breaking up. I'll put in a new battery and call you back."

Loretta, the sister closest to Sally's age, was always easier to approach.

"Oh, good," Loretta said, all enthused when Sally called her,

"Karl and I are planning to visit Illinois at Christmas. I was afraid I would miss your trip."

"Madelyn's busy until Wednesday," Sally said. "Could I come down Saturday night and stay until Wednesday morning?"

"Absolutely," Loretta said. "I have a daybed in my office. Will that do?"

"The Holiday Inn Danny and I stayed in will be fine," Sally said. "But I will need most of your time and Karl's. I'm searching for a lost woman," she said. "I need to find her before her abusive husband can."

Murder accusations were not necessarily the right avenue to take with these two. Karl was a state arson detective with enough contacts throughout Florida to find Mary Jo in the shortest possible time.

"Give me her name, Sally," Loretta said. "I'll get Karl started on tracking her down. Maybe we'll have something for you by the time you arrive."

"Thanks, Loretta," Sally said. "The sooner I find her, the better. I have the license number for her blue VW van, too."

Packing for the trip was a bit confusing. Sally had just overhauled her closets for winter. She pulled out the summer clothes from the trunks she used for storage, searching for the right look. She wanted to appear professional as if she were a detective, but Sally didn't want her sisters to disown her, which they would if she'd worn black slacks and business vests. Sally threw a bright raspberry-colored short vest and all her tan slacks into her valise. A compromise was always the best way to handle any situation—according to her late husband.

Danny did love Florida. Sally thought the state flat, ugly and unpleasant, to say the best of what she thought of the terrain. The people were all insane, waiting for someone close to them to die or not die, counting inheritances and spending them twice before realizing a penny. The whole place was crazy, thinking they knew how to rule the rest of the nation. Their brains were smitten with strokes. The sun addled any other wits they might have originally possessed. The young people only had drug-induced elders to look up to. Peaches rot faster in the sun. Sally tried to keep hers in the refrigerated up north, where all the oldest living people resided. God help them all. Maybe global warming should be prayed for every day. Ten feet of higher ocean surf would rid the nation of its cankerous foot. The world probably wouldn't even notice the limp.

After adding two cans of bug spray, Sally snapped the suitcases shut and called a cab for the airport. If Mary Jo wasn't dead, Sally might off her just for all the trouble she was causing Robert.

* * *

Lakeland, Florida
September, Second Saturday

Lakeland, Florida, the home of the Detroit Tiger's baseball training camp, was a typical town in Florida, as far as Sally was concerned. She struggled to remember where the motel was as she drove down the main drag. Strung out flat along the interstate, the town had no character, no charm. Neon signs greeted Sally on either side of the road. Late Saturday night Sally hung up her clothes in the biggest bedroom suite the motel sported before calling her sister.

"Let me go to church with you in the morning," Sally asked halfheartedly.

"Fine," Loretta said. "I'll pick you up at 7:30."

"I didn't bring a hat," Sally said, hoping for a reprieve.

"No one wears hats," Loretta snickered. "Karl has a whole stack of reports for you to look through. He thinks he's found your girl."

"Have you contacted her?" Sally asked, somewhat alarmed.

"No," Loretta said. "Karl thinks Mary Jo would skedaddle if anyone but a friend asked her questions."

"Good," Sally said. "I think he's right."

The church service wasn't bad, except for a few minutes of arm-raising. Sally's prayers were sincere, but her habits were just not as robust as the rest of the congregation. Nevertheless, Loretta was pleased. Loretta introduced Sally to twenty people Sally would never lay eyes on again. Well, maybe at Loretta's funeral, God forbid.

The last time Sally had visited her sister's retirement digs, a construction trailer with a yellowed and torn linoleum floor and scuffed-up toilet facilities constituted the living arrangements. The lot was huge, fenced with a gate, and lined with untrimmed trees and their neighbor's junk.

Sally was impressed with the newly expanded air-conditioned

cabana. Six-foot porches under one main roof surrounded the mobile home. Five sets of double French doors allowed entry to the mammoth, enclosed veranda from the rear bedroom, the laundry room, the kitchen, the living room, and a back-side door. Loretta proudly displayed her handy work, consisting of red painted cobblestones on the plywood porch. The windows sported sturdy hurricane shutters and screening, rolled down to brass rods, leaving about a half inch to welcome the mosquitoes.

The dining room table overflowed with legal-sized file folders. Karl helped Sally sort out the most pertinent information. They adjourned to the two-person, covered swing on the porch, which served as the couch.

Mary Jo was living an hour away in Orlando, working at a Wal-Mart, and was seen alive Friday morning.

Sally immediately opened her cell and called Robert with the news. She reached the Bibliopole on her third try.

Harvey answered, "Robert's napping. Should I wake him?"

"Andrew isn't there, is he? Where's Penny?" Sally asked.

"No," Harvey said as if looking around the bookstore to find Andrew. "Do you have a number where he can reach you? We don't know why Penny failed to show up."

Dear Lord, Sally prayed, not another missing woman of Robert's. "Tell Andrew Mary Jo was seen alive on Friday." Sally hadn't realized how excited she was. Her heart was palpitating, and her mouth went immediately dry. She motioned for Karl to get her something to drink, raising an imaginary glass to her mouth. He just sat there in a deep, sandbag chair. However, Loretta had seen their father make the same gesture in his lifetime, and she quickly filled a glass with cold water. Sally's eyes watered in gratitude, and her throat unclenched with the water. "Thank you," Sally managed.

"For what?" Harvey asked. "I never liked Mary Jo or Penny."

"Sure you do," Sally argued with the idiot. "You want them alive and well so Robert won't end up behind bars."

Karl and Loretta let out gasps. Sally just wasn't any good at this cloak-and-dagger role. Karl collected the file folders, including the one in Sally's lap, and put them in a briefcase with a padlock on it, for heaven's sake. Luckily, Sally had written down all the information she needed in her small travel notebook.

"I can't be involved in releasing information in a trial without proper authorization," Karl said.

"Sally," Loretta said. "You weren't honest with us."

Sally shut off her cell and spread her hands palm up on her knees. "I knew you would have a problem helping me investigate a murder case, but a missing person would elicit the right response. Obviously, Mary Jo isn't dead. We knew Robert couldn't hurt a fly and her sadistic husband, who wants her found so he can beat her to death, is Robert's accuser."

Karl backtracked pretty quickly. He struggled to his feet. "I know Orlando. Loretta and I will drive you to her address right now."

Sally rose from the swing and hugged her brother-in-law. She didn't do that sort of thing often.

* * *

Orlando, Florida

The number at the address in Orlando was hung a little lopsided to fit into the space available next to the door of the condominium. The complex was back-to-back with the Wal-Mart parking lot. Karl and Loretta stayed in their yellow pickup as Sally approached the door. Sally rang the bell, but no one was home. Back in the truck, Sally sniffled at the profound disappointment.

"Probably at work," Karl said.

"You two stay here," Sally said, "And I'll just walk over to Wal-Mart and try to find her there."

"I wouldn't ask for her," Karl said, "Might spook her."

"Yeah," Sally said. "I'll try to find her by walking the halls." If no luck counted, it was all the luck Sally had walking the aisles of the gigantic store. She tried to stay in the center aisle, spying down each lane on either side of her. All she accomplished was drawing the attention of half-a-dozen workers intent on helping her find whatever she was looking for. Sally ended up being guided to a checkout lane with her basket filled with useless junk. Karl and Loretta both had a great laugh as they piled the bags into the back of the pickup.

"I wish I had a police radio to find out where her van is right now," Karl said.

"Could we stop at the Orlando police station," Sally asked, clutching at anything remotely helpful.

"Not without an official inquiry," Karl said.

"Write her a note," Loretta said. "Slip it under the door with our phone number on it."

Sally tore one of the small pages out of her notebook and wrote, "Mary Jo, Please call Robert Koelz. He's been accused of your murder by your husband. The police will give you protection, but Robert's name needs to be cleared as soon as possible. His lawyer sent me down to find you. She signed the note, "Sally Bianco," and added a postscript, "Call me at my sister's home."

Sally added all the phone numbers she could think of and slipped the paper under Mary Jo's front door. She insisted Karl and Loretta wait an entire half-hour, hoping Mary Jo would return. They finally even inquired at the Wal-Mart, but no one had heard of her, or maybe Mary Jo had asked them not to tell anyone she worked there if there were inquiries.

* * *

"I might have messed up," Sally confessed to Andrew, safely back in her motel room where she could do less harm.

"No," Andrew said. "At least I can give the police something concrete about her whereabouts on Friday. But we'll need more than hearsay to have the charges dropped. Mary Jo still hasn't contacted Robert. He's getting pretty concerned about Penny, too."

"Should I talk to him?" Sally didn't want to hear Robert's disappointment. She didn't want to hear about Penny not attending him, either.

"I'll handle it," Andrew said. "Are you inquiring in Vero

Beach, too?"

"Should I?" Sally thought visiting Madelyn would be a purely social visit now that she'd found an address for Mary Jo.

"Go ahead," Andrew explained. "Maybe she's moved on."

Sally sighed. "I can do more harm."

"Don't think of it that way," Andrew said. "Ricco is still being followed up here. Hopefully, he doesn't have any contacts in Florida."

Robert took the phone, "Sally, keep us informed. You're doing me a great service. I'm sure Penny is just sulking. I called Penny's brother, Mark. He says she might stay in Toledo until she has to take her finals. I think he said that just to mollify me."

That's all Sally needed, a lonesome, troubled Robert to worry about. She assured him of her affection and loyalty, his worth to his friends, and the likelihood that Mary Jo would call him very soon. She re-packed for Vero Beach, frustrated because she had to wait until Wednesday to contact Madelyn. After a sleepless night, Sally decided to go directly to the police station in Vero Beach. What could she lose?

* * *

Vero Beach, Florida

In a country that should be aware of the problem women face with abuse issues, the Vero Beach police department acted like a throwback to the good-ole-boys days. "No, I'm not a relative," Sally said for the eighth time to the fourth Caucasian face in a blue uniform.

"Sorry, I am not allowed to divulge information on law-abiding citizens." The blond, clef-chinned idiot smiled.

"And I'm not a dolt," Sally said to make him pay attention.

"Now, we don't need any trouble from you," an older, pot-bellied woman officer said behind the chest-high entry desk.

"I am the court advocate for the woman," Sally was surprised to hear herself say.

The young guy looked at the older woman. "Court advocate?"

"No such a thing," she said. Her mouth closed into a tight fist of an expression.

"Oh yeah," Sally argued, anger rising, brain non-functioning, "Call Judge Joe Wilcox in Ann Arbor, Michigan; the prosecutor Jimmy Walker, or the defendant's attorney, Andrew Sites." Silence. "If you don't have their phone number, call information." At this point in the discussion, Sally slammed her new, Wal-Mart legal pad in its fake leather binder on the high desk with a resounding slap.

"Steve," the older cop said. "Let's just have some peace and quiet. Look up the address, phone number, and track the license plate for a Mary Jo Cardoni."

"Might take a half-hour." the tall kid grinned again.

Sally was sure his mother taught her southern-bred boy to shine those pearly whites whenever he needed divine help. "I will return," Sally said at first forgetting her legal pad, not meeting their eyes as she grabbed it and nearly ran out the door.

Half an hour. Plenty of time to find a restaurant for lunch and call Robert again. She headed for the beach, where she could see an oil tanker close to the horizon. The wind was high enough to make her thankful she'd remembered to put on sunscreen. The hat she had lied to Loretta about not packing sailed away with the first gust of ocean breeze.

As Sally approached the blue horizon, strange characters milled about the sand. One male's naked torso boasted a tattoo of an alligator, face front, tail wrapped around his skinny back. A long pier with a covered end for fishing caused Sally to forget all about lunch. As she leaned against the railing, out of the way of the men casting their lines, Sally spied two dolphins sporting near the pilings. Cheered by the site, Sally called Robert on her cell. "No news here, there?"

"None," he said, sounding down. "Penny called to say she would return next month. Seems her mother's having back surgery."

"That's a shame," Sally said.

"That woman will do anything to keep Penny away from me, even faking enough pain so that a surgeon is convinced he has to operate."

"Oh, Robert," Sally said. "You don't believe that. You're just lonesome. Have Harvey drive you down to Toledo. Mrs. Savage will love you as much as Penny does."

"I thought of that," Robert said, his voice still in the cellar. "Andrew says I cannot leave the state."

"Should I come home and pay for a detective to run around down here?" Sally offered.

Playing the detective wasn't much fun. Maybe if she had found Mary Jo wandering around Wal-Mart, Sally could have been more enthusiastic about her part of the quest for clearing Robert's name. Money could solve this one. Sally could be with Robert and pay for someone else, someone not interested, maybe not motivated enough. Sally did not mention the quandary she faced.

Andrew took the phone from Robert. "Sally, I understand you want to be here with Robert, but check-out Vero Beach before you return."

They said goodbyes. Sally grabbed an ice cream cone from a vendor and headed back to the police department.

"No address," Steve, the blond desk sergeant, said.

"We found her car in Arizona," the fat lady offered.

"No address," Sally repeated. Arizona was a fairly sizable state.

"Phoenix," Steve said. "Her car is at the Coldwater Courtyard Motel."

"Thank you," Sally said. She didn't care if they saw how disappointed she was.

Sally slumped out of the cold, tiled, low-slung building. She hated Florida, but before she called down floods and tsunamis, Sally thought she should swing by her sister's and head for a plane out of West Palm Beach.

Now Madelyn was miffed that Sally wasn't staying. "I made the bed for you."

"Sorry," Sally said. "I can't find out where Mary Jo is if I stay down here. The police told me she's already in Arizona."

"When did you see the police?" Madelyn asked.

"This morning," Sally said. "I didn't want to involve your name in this mess."

"How do you find people who get accused of murder to fill your life?" she asked.

"Luck," Sally said. "I'm so lucky. Felons fall from fifty trees at the same time."

"Stop joking," Madelyn said. "How did you meet Mr. Koelz? I remember how you met Danny Bianco."

"Before Danny died, I collected what I thought were rare books, and I wrote Robert to ask what the price was for a book describing old bicycles."

"He's an antique dealer?"

"No," Sally said. She didn't want Madelyn believe Robert had money or might need money. That would lengthen the lecture. "Mostly, he collects used books, but sometimes he gets lucky."

"Is he married?"

"He's a eunuch," Sally informed her eldest sister, waiting for the fun to begin.

"How did you find that out?"

"He told me that's why his first wife divorced him," Sally lied.

Actually, his wife divorced Robert for non-support. He never possessed more than a penny or two at any given time. Judge Joe Wilcox owned the building Robert's shop was in. All the books were on consignment. Ed Thatch and Harvey kept Robert apprised of estate sales and divorce liquidations to keep the Bibliopole fully stocked with first editions and rare books, all on consignment to their owners. Henry Schaefer took care of Robert's clothes, and Mrs. Clankton kept Robert housed and fed. The rest of Robert's customers tried to keep the man entertained and solvent.

"He's a remarkable man," Sally added. "Self-educated, opinionated, a card-carrying communist at one point. He claims to have fought in the Abraham Lincoln Brigade in the Spanish Civil War, right before the Second World War."

"You don't believe him," Madelyn said. Madelyn could always read Sally from when she lied as a child about dusting the rungs of the dining room chairs. Madelyn was psychic at the time, but maybe the clinging dust was evidence enough.

"I've read too much Hemmingway not to find too close of a connection to Robert's stories," Sally sighed.

"So why do you like him?" Madelyn asked.

"I think I miss the daily contact with Danny."

"He's been gone six years. Can't you find something constructive to do with your time? Visit hospitals, volunteer at a library?"

Sally looked at her sister. Madelyn didn't have a clue about her life. She didn't remember hearing how Sally had finished writing fourteen novels since Danny died and had the pleasure of receiving more than one rejection for each and every one of them. A few short stories were published, and friends said they loved her poetry, but recognition for publications seemed a long way off. Perhaps 'never' in her lifetime was more realistic. "I keep time free to write," Sally attempted to defend herself.

"You always say that, but look at the time you're wasting now," Madelyn said, setting off on her familiar high horse. "You could be helping people."

"J. C. says we'll always have the poor with us."

"Who's J.C.," Madelyn asked as Sally edged toward the door.

"Jesus Christ," she said reverently.

"Stay for lunch, at least." Madelyn half-heartedly motioned down the long empty hall leading to the facility's dining room.

"Not this time," Sally said. Lunch at the assisted living facility was deadlier than chili in a diner. The food seemed all right but Sally was afraid the decrepitude of the other diners would seep into her bones. They, her bones, had problems of their own. They didn't need sympathy from other grave-totting skeletons.

* * *

On the plane ride back to Metro airport in Detroit, Sally dispassionately considered her options for getting Robert help in Arizona. She could, first, find a detective agency in Ann Arbor and second, interview the staff to see who she could confidently motivate to go down to Phoenix and extract Mary Jo. Thanks to her dead husband's diligence money wasn't the problem. Sally's ability to find the right man or woman for the job might be. She wished John Nelson could help her interview the agents. Maybe she would call him and ask him to phone interview the detectives.

Good idea.

Sally wondered how much time they had before the police set the trial date for Robert. What if they never found Mary Jo? Could Robert be railroaded to jail? It would kill him. All his friends knew that. Robert was a tender soul, besides not being able to harm another human being, any being - animal or plant. Robert's life required freedom. Locked doors, locked minds, anything that reeked of confinement would destroy his spirit.

Chapter Five

Ann Arbor, Michigan

The taxi ride back to Ann Arbor from Detroit's Metro airport cheered Sally. Ann Arbor did not sport Florida's ocean beaches or Arizona's mountain ranges. But Ann Arbor's streets were lined with trees, glorious in spring, luxuriant in summer, resplendent in fall, and stately in winter. Trees, beautiful trees, Ann's arbor.

Sally threw her bags into the condo hallway and walked out the back door to her garage and faithful red mustang to head straight for the Bibliopole.

"Robert," Sally yelled, running up the bookstore steps. "You need a ride in Waterloo."

He was standing next to his desk. Robert's face was a little pale. Sally's shouting might have frightened him.

"Grab a bottle." Penny had returned early. "This will be fun."

Sally acknowledged her joy diminished a lot, but she kept up her end of the invitation. Soon Penny was settled in the backseat with her bottle of cream sherry; Robert was in the passenger seat, paper cup filled to the brim. Sally planned to hit every bump in the road.

Waterloo didn't let them down. At the end of Pierce Road, where the dirt road to the Geology Center started, they craned their necks, hoping to find deer in the fields on the right side of the road while checking the trees crowding the left side of the road. The creek bed was dry at the second corner, and Sally gunned the engine to keep from being pulled into the washboard section. The trees along the sheltered roads of Waterloo retained most of their leaves, and the colors were stupendous.

Robert talked nonstop while Penny broke into lyrics from Iolanthe. Sally was glad any bitterness resulting from Penny's honing in on her planned excursion with Robert faded away with the sounds of the woods feeding her hearing aid through the half-opened window. At the Mud Lake turn around, Sally stopped the car.

"Did I tell you I was a Big Sister to a nine-year-old in Jackson once?" Sally didn't care if they were interested or not. "I brought her here to show her the sandhill crane nest. I told her this place was probably *unchanged* from when Indians roamed the land. I was all excited and asked her what she thought of the place. 'Boring,' the child said."

"I hope you boxed her ears," Robert said.

"No." Sally could still taste her keen disappointment as if the scene had just occurred. "I immediately took her home."

"How long did you stay in the Big Sister program?" Penny asked, in what Sally thought was an almost gracious tone.

"Well, her brothers kept telling her to ask for my camera and to go shopping with her. At the time, I wasn't sure if I could afford all the medical help Danny needed. I didn't think I could or should spend money on her."

"You're not supposed to, are you?" Robert asked.

"No," Sally said, "But I thought about it."

"Did you just leave her hanging?" Penny asked.

Sally looked at Penny as she poured Robert another unneeded portion of cream sherry. She was awfully cute, and even David in the Bible was allowed to keep young virgins in his bed to warm his bones. "I went to the agency and told them my problem. They said they would find someone else for her."

"What about the detectives you're going to hire for Arizona?" Penny asked. Was she trying to be purposefully irritable?

"I'm going to let a high-school friend of mine from Illinois interview people before I send anyone down there," Sally said. She prayed John Nelson would help. He seemed to like her. Hopefully, she was not imposing on his good nature.

"I could talk to them," Penny said.

"Let Sally handle this," Robert said as he climbed back into the car. "Let's visit my parents' grave on the hill and then drive around the pond in Waterloo."

"Do we have time to go out to the bird sanctuary?" Sally asked.

"Better not," Robert said. "Andrew said he would come by the shop at 6:30. Do you want to join us for Chinese?"

"I'd like that," Sally said. "Andrew can probably point me in the right direction for a detective agency."

* * *

The Peking duck was delicious, and the other dishes of spiced Chinese food kept coming until Sally thought she would burst with one more bite. Harvey, Ed, and Sally accompanied Andrew, Robert, and Penny to the second-floor restaurant. Sally hoped Harvey would pick up the bill but knew she would if he were too much in his cups to attend to such mundane amenities.

Andrew had been busy watching traffic cameras from I94 down route 23 for signs of Mary Jo. Since the crime had not crossed state borders, his office was not allowed to pursue the matter farther than the state line. "She picked up a kid at one point."

"A hitchhiker?" Penny asked.

"Could have been a convict," Robert said.

"Looked innocent enough," Andrew said. "About fifteen."

"Mary Jo did have a soft heart," Robert said, then corrected himself, "does have a warm heart."

"The cops caught him with a suitcase that was Mary Jo's," Andrew said.

They all stopped eating. "Did the hitchhiker harm her?" Ed Thatch asked.

"Says he had lunch with her at Cabella's. She didn't notice when he disappeared for a trip to the bathroom. He poked the lock out of her van and snatched her suitcase." Andrew poured himself more tea.

"Slimy creep," Robert said. "What could he do with her personal belongings?"

"Maybe he was a cross-dresser," Harvey supplied.

"She had jewelry in the case," Andrew said. "But there were no police reports of a robbery in the state from her."

"Maybe Mary Jo didn't realize the suitcase was missing until she stopped for the night," Sally said.

"She was probably too afraid of her husband tracking her to let the police know where she was," Ed worried his beard.

"I agree." Sally smiled at her young table partner, Ed. She always sat as close to him as possible. She even dreamt about him. Anyway, Sally was glad Ed was at the restaurant. She found herself smiling and did not think it was just to hide her wrinkles. The boy's good looks cheered her up.

Ed coughed, "Are you missing the fact Mary Jo was alive, so Robert cannot be accused of killing her?"

Harvey finished another martini. "Still missing. Isn't she?"

Andrew explained, "The highway pictures were dated three days before Ricco made his accusations. The case has not been dropped."

"We need Arizona," Robert said, offering Sally a bowl of rice from across the table.

***

John sounded sleepy when Sally called him. "John, I'm sorry. This is Sally. It's one o'clock in St. Charles. I just left Robert and the gang. Are you very busy this week at the hotel? Could you take a vacation with me to Arizona?"

John's voice changed to wide awake. "Sally! Absolutely. I mean, I'll drive out tomorrow morning. Main Street in Ann Arbor, right? Why Arizona?"

"Mary Jo's van was spotted near Phoenix. You really want to come?"

"I can't think of a better place to be than around you."

Sally heard that. "John. I mean, I don't want to encourage you romantically. I don't want to discourage you, but your good company on the trip might not end the way you want it to."

"Sally, I can't think of anywhere I'd rather be than with you. I missed my chance in high school. I'm glad you called. You're not going to revoke the offer, are you?"

"No. I could use your help." But Sally did worry. "I don't want to hurt your feelings."

"Just let the Lord and me worry about my feelings, okay?"

"Okay." Sally laughed. "It's in His hands." After she hung up the bedside phone, Sally couldn't sleep. Maybe she should start her own detective agency. She was enjoying herself. Terrible because Robert's mess might turn out well for her, provide a new career, besides following the exploits of her favorite bookman. Danny would have wanted her to do something constructive with her life. No one could ever replace Danny.

* * *

Third Tuesday in September

All thoughts in the Bibliopole were with Mary Jo. Why hadn't she at least called Robert? Sally found Robert alone Tuesday evening, staring at his silent phone. "Is Penny upset about Mrs.

Clankton's report?" She hoped to keep his mind occupied.

He pulled his attention away from the unresponsive contraption he wanted to ring before facing eternity. "If Mary Jo kept her clothes on, it might have helped."

"Why did she disrobe, Robert?" Sally relaxed in the comfortable chair across the room from his corner desk.

"She wanted to get comfortable under the blankets with me." Robert fixed Sally with his honest stare. "Mrs. Clankton kicked me to the curb."

"Where are you living now? Mary Jo should have kept some article of clothing on."

"She wanted to get lucky." Robert slid his hand over the phone's receiver. "Penny's brother brought over a mattress for the store room. Miss Poi duly anointed the thing."

Sally tried not to think about Robert's housing downgrade. "You should have told Mary Jo before she undressed." The stinking mattress threatened to intrude on her thoughts.

"Well, I didn't." Robert softened his tone. "You were an exception."

"I am," Sally said, letting her ego puff.

Robert shot her down. "And you are a blabbermouth."

"Penny wanted to know."

"And you wanted to tell her."

"Now, Robert." Sally was saved by Harvey Clemmons bellowing in the hall.

"Thank God," Robert said as if Sally's presence was becoming a trial. Miss Poi streaked from under the safety of Robert's desk into the store room.

Sally felt like bolting, too. "I'll just go along." At least Robert would not be alone. Conversation with his friends slowed Robert from exercising his elbow—drink to mouth.

Robert hefted a large dictionary in Sally's direction. "You move, and I'll throw this at you."

Sally laughed. "I'll stay."

"And she's welcome." Harvey rubbed Sally's head with one hand and handed a bottle of sherry to Robert with the other. "At least Sally doesn't drink up the supplies."

"True, true." Robert actually cooed.

"Big bag of wind." Sally straightened her short hair.

Harvey's torso did resemble an opera singer's girth. He paced between Robert's desk and the hall as if awaiting someone. His head was regal, a Roman sculpture. His white beard and shaggy mustache were clipped in a classical poet's style. But mostly, Harvey was wind. His vocal cords produced loud, well-modulated words in resonating deep bass tones, which bounced off the shiny plaster bookshop walls. Sally remembered Voltaire's work, or Shaw's, in which the hero's pride was injured when the heroine told him she didn't agree or disagree with his rants. She just enjoyed hearing his voice. The low tones of males helped seduce their intendeds. Men complained about the lack of sex. Women rightly criticized the lack of prolonged conversation—verbal foreplay.

"Is Andrew expected?" Harvey stepped back to wave Sam

Tedler into their presence.

Sam, the young man who helped arrest Robert, stood in the hall. He wore jeans and a white long-sleeved shirt instead of the city's uniform. He waited for an invitation to enter. Sally could understand his reluctance. "I might be able to help, Sally," Sam said. "The police found Mary Jo's blood in Robert's room at Mrs. Clankton's, too."

"What service do you offer?" Robert asked in a defensive tone.

Sam ducked his head as he spoke. "I put in for my vacation. I could search for Mary Jo with my detective license."

Harvey pounded Sam's back. "The Tedler Brothers moonlight as certified PI's."

"We can't afford much." Sally needed to make the compensation problem clear. Why was there blood in Mary Jo and Robert's rooms? She kept her questions to herself.

Sam brightened. "Harvey thought I should volunteer."

"Mary Jo is traveling in Arizona," Robert said. "How do we know Ricco isn't paying you to find her?"

"Me?" Sam walked over to Robert's desk. "I didn't want to arrest you, remember?"

"Come on, Robert," Harvey said. "Would I bring a traitor into your inner sanctum?"

Sally interrupted. "I hope it's okay, Robert. I gave John Nelson directions to your shop. I wanted you and Andrew to meet him before we leave for Arizona tonight."

"Unusual occurrence," Harvey reached for his lowest

disapproving tone. "Sam arrived just in time."

Robert finished the sherry in his glass. "What makes you think Sam will have the motivation to save my hide?"

"And what is this John Nelson's driving force?" Harvey asked.

"You know, Harvey, not everyone has your sordid inclinations." Sally wanted to strike him up the side of his beautiful head. "A person is allowed to go out of his way to help an old friend."

Undaunted, Harvey hooted. "You're not that old."

Sally opened and closed her purse as if digging for a new subject. "Robert, doesn't Hilda live next to Mrs. Clankton? Surely you could stay with them until you find another place."

"Difficult to broach the subject with the Grangers." Robert eyed the phone.

"I'll take care of it. Write down their number." Sally stepped out into the hall with her cell phone and the slip of paper Robert handed her. "Hilda, this is Robert's friend Sally. Could I speak to your husband about the spirit pictures?"

"Sweetie," Hilda called.

Her husband answered gruffly, "Granger residence."

"Yes," Sally said, introductory words failing her. "Robert Koelz needs a place to crash for a few days. Would you be inconvenienced?"

"Absolutely not."

Sally tried to think of convincing arguments.

"Tell Robert there will be a key under the mat. First room on

The Legitimate Way

the left at the top of the stairs is his. I'll put extra towels in the bath. Will that do?"

"Thank you. I'll tell him." Sally was flabbergasted. She knew most reasonable people held Robert in some esteem, and the Grangers' immediate welcome confirmed her feelings. She returned to the shop. "You're all set, Robert. Key's under the mat." Robert gave her a thumbs up before downing another glass of sherry. "Do we know where Ricco is staying?" She asked Sam.

"I don't think we want to know," Harvey said. "Too much temptation to send people with instructions to pound on him without restraint."

"We'll have none of that." Andrew Sites arrived on the scene, dressed in his court attire, black suit, and blue tie. Sally smiled with pleasure when she saw Ed Thatch accompanied the lawyer.

Ed delivered Robert his news. "My young friend in computer systems agrees with the information Sally found. Mary Jo is moving from motel to motel in Arizona, probably trying to avoid her husband's detectives."

"I thought it was a state offense to abuse your wife." Harvey cuffed Sam's shoulder.

"Oh, it is," Andrew sat ramrod straight in the chair next to Robert's desk. "However, the state needs proof of the crime, just as they need a body to prove Robert harmed Mary Jo."

"What about this new blood evidence?" Sally asked Andrew.

"We will need to clear the case in court, Robert." Andrew leaned toward Robert in apology. "The police are being very thorough."

"Don't they know she's moving around Arizona?" Harvey asked.

"Her van is moving." Andrew shook his head. "I wish Jimmy Walker was not running for Congress. But the prosecutor is determined to make a name for himself."

Sally motioned toward Sam. "Robert's not sure he wants Sam, my friend from St. Charles, and me to search Arizona."

"Robert, you've known this lad since he was born. What could be better in court than a law enforcement officer on our side?"

They continued useless comments about the probabilities in the case. Mostly about the possibilities of Ricco finding Mary Jo before they did. She needed to show up in Ann Arbor before the arraignment. One thing was not mentioned. How would Robert be able to survive jail if he was convicted?

Madelyn's words haunted Sally. Madelyn wanted to know what Sally was doing connected to these people. Danny's death marked the end of Sally's normal life. She joined Ann Arbor's City Club, painted watercolors, oils, attended their writing group, wasted time in long lunches, and was thankful for people to see on the holidays. After a time, perhaps a delayed stage of grief, she stopped being very sociable. She blamed lack of time on her writing schedule. But to tell the truth, she was too depressed to greet her friends.

If the worst happened to Robert and Sally lost him too, she would return to the club, get involved in learning another language, travel, and engage in something to prove she was alive and happy. But Robert, how would Robert be able to live cooped up in prison? Tears rolled down her cheeks for Danny, Robert, and herself. She covered the faux pax for a while, blowing her nose and fumbling with her pocketbook.

Harvey noticed. "Oh, don't." He broke out in loud sobs with his huge chest heaving.

Andrew offered Robert his handkerchief.

Robert said between gulps, "A friend and I were arrested once, out in California, for organizing orange pickers. He started crying about his dad, who died a week earlier. Then they started crying for ourselves and the suffering workers around the world, and finally, even the jailers were weeping for the plight of humanity."

Ed shook his head at the group, probably trying to rehearse how to describe the strange happenings to his unemotional wife.

"Get a grip," Andrew finally said. "I can't be drinking with people slobbering up the place."

Miss Poi chose the sad moment to claim her master's lap, mewing until he calmed down enough to pet her. She crawled up his chest and bumped his chin with her furry head.

"It's not as if Mary Jo died," Ed said.

"If I ever get my hands on her," Sam Tedler said. "I might strangle her myself."

Sally's schoolmate chose the exact moment to appear at the door of the Bibliopole. John Nelson did not hide his shocked expression. "Hello?"

"John." Sally greeted him, wiping the tears off her face. She noticed she needed to pull him across the bookshop's threshold. "Come and meet the extraordinary Robert Koelz."

"Friend to all." Harvey stepped backward unto Ed's foot, who surprisingly swore.

"We are normally a quiet crowd." Robert extended his hand up to John. Miss Poi stayed put on Robert's lap. Ed smiled engagingly at John, who stood a head taller than anyone in the room, and then Ed offered him a full glass of cream sherry.

"I'm driving." John declined the glass graciously. "Very nice to meet you all. Sally told me she made friends with a book dealer." He stopped in his phatic sentences to survey the small shop. "I imagined a larger establishment." Noticing the error in his choice of words, he added, "To have room for all of Robert's friends."

Everyone nodded to each other, pleased with themselves and Sally's newest inclusion to the group.

* * *

Later Tuesday night, scrunched between Sam and John in the taxi's back seat on the way to Metro airport, Sally noticed most of her explanations about the Bibliopole's crew were acknowledged by John's monosyllable grunts.

Sam picked up the same vibes. "Second thoughts about Robert's innocence?"

"Not in the least." John stole a glimpse at Sally. "I'm worried we don't know how to find Mary Jo once we're in Arizona." John bothered his baldhead with one hand. "When does the trial begin? I couldn't tell James how long he would need to take care of my dog, Ginger."

Sally's stomach dropped. She dialed the shop on her cell. "Robert? Is Andrew still with you?"

"She found Mary Jo," Robert called to the group.

"Nonsense," Sally said.

Andrew could be heard wrestling the phone from Robert. "I thought as much. Is there any way to slow the intake of alcohol with these guys?"

Sally sighed. "When is the trial date, Andrew?"

"Don't give it a second thought," Andrew said. "Judge Wilcox will issue for the arraignment continuances until I'm ready to proceed."

"Really?" Sally said.

"That's what friends are for." Sally heard Robert crow in the background.

She shut the cell phone, hoping John failed to hear the replies she was privy to. "The judge is interested in receiving all the information we can come up with. My trip to Florida wasn't wasted on him."

John nudged her side. "That's why I'm here. Once you told me Mary Jo rented a condo and was working at Wal-Mart in Orlando, I wanted to find her myself. For one thing, I do not appreciate Ricco perpetrating a fraud by signing her name to a sales agreement. I had showed the house to six St. Charles families. I took the Cardoni house off the market."

"I'm not sure that was a good idea. Did you inform Ricco?"

"Of course not."

This schoolmate was easily offended, Sally noted for future reference. "Sorry. I am concerned Mary Jo will be found by Ricco's henchmen before we do."

* * *

After enduring the indignities of airport security, Sally was seated in a row with Sam on her left and John on her right, next to the window. "I'm glad I won't need to lie to the police to ask for information."

"What lie?" John asked.

"I told the police in Vero Beach I was the court-appointed advocate for Mary Jo." Sally slipped off her shoes and snuggled her purse under the seat in front of her with her toes.

"Do you flash a detective card?" John asked Sam.

"Try not to." Sam ducked to avoid a bulging backpack of a boarding passenger. "This is the first case for Sylvester and me. Sylvester still needs to pass the test."

"We're apprentices." Sally leaned on John's arm.

"How long before we need to take a test?" John asked.

Sally wondered if John was as interested as he sounded. She hoped he joined the hunt mostly to keep her company, maybe even start a courtship. "Are you sure you want to become a detective?"

"I liked being with you in Illinois." John held her hand. "After forty years, hotel work is getting boring. Realtors are a dime a dozen. I wouldn't mind using my brain to sort out facts, maybe serve justice." He laughed. "Is there some reason for all of Robert's friends to wear blue?"

"Blue?" Sam asked. "Do my jeans count?"

Sally tried to recall how the book crew dressed. Robert always wore blue. She remembered Andrew's blue tie. Her own blue sweater almost matched Ed's. Harvey's blue jeans vest strategically hid half his girth. Maybe each and every one of them tried to let Robert know they were on his side by mimicking his favorite color choice. John wore his yellow rain vest.

"Why didn't you wear blue?" Sally asked John.

"I didn't know blue was required for book lovers."

The man possessed a sense of humor. At least he was observant, a necessity for detective work. What would working alongside him bring about? She felt more alive, ready for adventure than she had experienced in years. She touched her throat with her fingers. "I think I'm having palpitations." John reached for the overhead call button. Sally pulled his arm down and looked into his eyes. "I'm enjoying myself."

He relaxed but wouldn't let go of her hand. "Good." He smiled. "Me, too."

Chapter Six

Mary Jo in Orlando, Florida
Second Monday in September

Mary Jo Cardoni did have the two rabbits with her, but she was not in Illinois or Michigan. She had driven her minivan all night, straight to Orlando to escape crazy Ricco.

Late Sunday night, when she had stopped to check on the rabbits, calling Robert Koelz kept her sane. His wit, warmth, and acceptance provided a tangible lifeline to her warring selves. She lacked the courage to face her husband in an Illinois court of law. All those proven, unsafe hours outside the courtroom kept her unsure of what step to take next. Running provided the room to think. She was careful not to reveal her whereabouts to Robert because crazy Ricco would wheedle the information out of the poor old man with one device or another. Robert did not mention Ricco was harassing him, which relieved Mary Jo's fears somewhat. Perhaps Ricco would eventually give up trying to make her return.

Mary Jo pulled down the orange turtleneck sweater she was wearing and craned to see if the bruises were still visible on both sides of her neck where Ricco had tried to choke her after he was served divorce papers at work a month earlier in Illinois. The rearview mirror revealed the bruises were yellowed but still visible.

The last week in Ann Arbor, her landlady thought she was reuniting an estranged couple when she allowed Ricco admittance to Mary Jo's room.

Mary Jo did not scream during the rape. The old lady was barely able to walk much less provide intervention. No sense for two women to be harmed. Mary Jo was accustomed to Ricco's brutality, enough to know when not to resist. Afterwards, Mary Jo laid a hand on his neck, which he liked after sex, with her standing between his knees. Quite proud of his reconciliation, Ricco rubbed his fingers inside her mouth and then French kissed her. As soon as he finished, Ricco demanded she pack. Which she did, while Ricco watched each move. Sure of her submission, he gave her directions to meet him in three hours at Robert's bookshop. Mary Jo nodded, and Ricco slapped her face hard, just to keep his dictates fresh in her mind.

Mary Jo hardly remembered loading the van, not answering the landlady's questions, but agreeing Ricco was a loving husband to collect her so soon after their separation. Mary Jo did not have the heart to upset the poor dear. Ricco also told Mary Jo to get rid of the rabbits.

She first realized she was not following orders when she placed their cage between two of her suitcases and made sure the bunnies had water. She closed the back door of the van, smiled at the landlady, and slipped into the front seat. When she turned on the ignition, without Ricco in sight, Mary Jo knew where she was headed, and it was not downtown to be humiliated in front of Robert Koelz.

Mary Jo had driven carefully down Stadium to Washtenaw Avenue out to Route 23, thinking at any minute Ricco would ram her van and force her off the road. She planned to keep going anyway and hoped a police car would stop, at least Ricco. On the ramp, headed south, she sang, "So long. It's been good to know you. So long. It's been good to know you." But it was not good to have known Ricco. She would miss Robert, but Mary Jo was gone, out of Ricco's immediate realm of terror.

* * *

Mary Jo discovered the hitchhiker's theft when she opened the van Monday night in Orlando. She accepted a portion of the blame. She should never have been so open with the kid. After he told her about his parents' cruelty, throwing him out of the house for changing the television channel, Mary Jo revealed she was running away from home, too. Of course, he assumed she packed her most precious possessions. She would miss her mother's opal ring more than the necklace and earrings purchased to complement them. Luckily, the hitchhiker passed over the shoulder satchel behind the passenger's seat. Plastic bags of trail mix were stuffed on top of her wallet, which was jammed with high-limit credit cards. She applied for the cards in her maiden name without Ricco's knowledge.

She had married right out of high school, fresh from the protection of her parents. She trusted Ricco had wanted as large a family as she did. After a series of severe beatings and a visit to Cindy Nelson's safe house in St. Charles, Mary Jo's plans to escape included practical schemes.

Her mother's death six months earlier precipitated her final decision. Ricco had refused to accompany her to the funeral. Her mother wisely set up a bank account in Orlando for her legacy to be automatically deposited with Mary Jo's social security number. Ricco never suspected her mother squirreled away a sizable fortune, because she lived amidst the trappings of poverty—a small house-trailer, no car, no show of money, even her mother's food consisted mostly of leftovers. Mary Jo omitted her husband's cruelty when speaking to her mother.

After her mother passed over to the all-knowing side of the universe, Mary Jo was sure her mother understood everything. She would finally be aware of the reasons why her only daughter did not visit as often as she wanted to. Mary Jo did not attend her aunts' funerals in Vero Beach and Tampa. Too many bruises and the resulting sense of shame for marrying Ricco without full knowledge of his background created her rationale for avoiding Florida visits. Now she knew a man's past was relevant.

Nevertheless, with flush accounts in Orlando and Phoenix in banks near the airports and a complete deck of credit cards, a new confidence and an albeit-shifting sense of security possessed Mary Jo. Her mother's foresight supported her continued flight. Relying on her own resources for the first time caused most of her anxiety. Happiness was not guaranteed in married life. Her future lay unknown before her. She was determined to come to her own aid and be responsible for her emotional landscape.

*** * * ***

Orlando to Arizona

Second Saturday in September

After paying cash for rent on a condo and working for a week in Orlando's Wal-Mart, Mary Jo spotted Sally Bianco entering Wal-Mart. Mary Jo slipped out the rear entrance jumped in her van and headed straight for Phoenix without bothering to pack up the condominium. She had kept the bunnies in the van to could feed them during her lunch hour. Her mother's money was a blessing, but Mary Jo planned to work and pay her way in the world. She hoped she was doing the right thing by running away again. She was shaken. Had Ricco convinced a friend of Robert's to hunt her down? She did not blame Sally. Her husband's craftiness was boundless. Any lie would do.

Before she fled St. Charles, Illinois, the man who sold Mary Jo the pistol and license without waiting for clearance appreciated the significance of the ugly marks on her neck. He owned a Polaroid and asked if she needed pictures for evidence. Three colored prints rested in the glove compartment of the van under the cold gun. Even without the violence, Mary Jo recognized she should have left her husband even earlier. Ricco avoided seeing her nude before intercourse. He claimed the dark helped him get excited. If he needed help, Mary Jo thought he should forego the effort.

With a full tank of gas and the wheels of the van humming along, the engine nearly sang as it cleaned out carbon deposits on the cylinders. Moving down the road made it easier for Mary Jo to examine the man she married. Ricco's male friends were too devoted to him. At first, she misjudged their need to hunt, fish, and attend baseball, football, basketball, and wrestling matches each and every weekend as normal male bonding behavior.

One frail chap came to their first apartment, standing as close to Ricco as possible without actually embracing him, staring up into Ricco's face. The conversation was normal: work, sports, their next hunting trip. However, the next day, the boy hung himself in the cellar of his apartment. When they heard about the suicide, Ricco was not upset. He refused to talk about the tragedy.

Within a month of moving into a St. Charles housing development, when Sally was beginning to know their neighbors, one man visited the Cardoni household to say goodbye to Ricco. The handsome neighbor ignored Sally entirely. He made a determined effort not to look at her. She was sitting in the dining room in full view of the entrance door.

The neighbor's wife remained behind to sell their home. She informed Mary Jo that Ricco was the closest friend her husband ever made and was the reason they were leaving. When Mary Jo mentioned the hint of a homosexual relationship to her husband, she received her first beating and a passionless display of manhood in bed.

On the road, with Phoenix as an ultimate destination, Mary Jo's acquaintances in Ann Arbor came to mind. The men and women in Robert's bookshop never lacked for subjects of discussion. She remembered thanking Robert after several visits for his long conversations with her. "You've spoken more to me these last few days than my husband did the entire time I lived with him."

Robert stroked his mustache, pleased. "Conversation is, after all, intercourse."

His kindly voice and an invitation to his room encouraged her attempt at seduction. He said he decided not to take advantage of her vulnerability. She admitted her heightened sexual drive developed after she left Ricco, probably to prove she was attractive to heterosexuals. Mrs. Clankton's 3:00 a.m. visit mortified her. The immediate need for using the facilities caused Mary Jo to at least shut the bathroom door, but she failed to turn the lock, as any decent person should in a stranger's house.

The roads of Florida, Alabama, and Mississippi melted away the worst of Mary Jo's fears. She drove the breadth of Texas the second September Saturday night.

* * *

Coldwater, Arizona
Second Sunday in September

Sunday morning in Arizona, Mary Jo hoped the Courtyard Motel in Coldwater might be a pleasant place to hang out. She did not mention the bunnies to the hotel clerk. No one helped with her luggage. Crouched in the van, she efficiently switched the bunnies from their cage to a pet-carrying case. After depositing them in the bathtub with an emptied box of salad greens, she folded up their cage, emptied the litter box in the hotel's dumpster, and re-provisioned their cage next to her bed. Mary Jo hoped the maid would think she received clearance for her pets.

The smallest, and happiest, bunny scurried past Mary Jo's feet as she tried to fetch the rabbits from the bathroom. An entire hour of flipping towels in the little devil's general direction finally wore the rabbit out. Or, the rabbit pitied her owner enough to stay perfectly still under the towel until Mary Jo could climb over the bed to reach her. The brown, calmer rabbit was transported from the bathroom to the metal cage, once Mary Jo refilled the carrying case with timothy hay and kale.

Two swimming pools promised she could escape any crowd or family group. The marks on her neck were pretty well hidden under pancake makeup. She needed to exercise her travel-weary muscles without encouraging any acquaintances.

* * *

Coldwater to Jerome, Arizona
Third Monday in September

One day of peace was gained before Mary Jo noticed the same smiling faces were showing up too often near her table in the restaurant, hanging around the pool, or stationed in the lobby. If they were not interested in her personally, which she did not need at the moment, they could have been private detectives waiting for Ricco to arrive.

One of the older men summoned up his courage with what looked like a glass of white wine but smelled like gin. He approached her with a straight-forward line. "Are you someone I can ask out?"

Mary Jo lowered her eyes. "Waiting for my husband to join me."

So Monday night she packed up the bunnies and the few items purchased at Orlando's Wal-Mart. She headed for Jerome, Arizona, a touristy, abandoned mining town in the mountains to the north of Coldwater. One night's stay in the upstairs guest bedroom of a mystic, crystal healer of questionable, friendly motives provoked her continued flight.

* * *

Reservation, Arizona,
Third Tuesday in September

A rental log cabin on the reservation north of Lake Chekobee seemed remote enough for Mary Jo on Tuesday night. George Dade, the landlord, asked if she needed food stamps before she handed him the first month's rent in cash. "No." Mary Jo could feel her blush of embarrassment. "I have a bit of money. I need to be alone."

"A writer, then?" George sized her up.

"Just a dreamer."

"Good place for dreams. I could build you a sweat lodge."

"In time." Mary Jo bowed her head, not wanting him to see her eyes. She knew he thought she was on some sort of mystical or spiritual quest. Well maybe she was. Mary Jo lifted her head and looked straight into his deep black eyes. "I need to rest."

"Supplies are a mile away." George pointed to the north. "Give them my name as a reference." Mary Jo extended her hand for him to shake. Instead, George gave her a bear hug, lifting her from the floor. "You are welcome here. My wife will be over shortly with a loaf of bread and a bottle of wine."

"Thank you." Mary Jo felt somehow steadied by the friendly attack and the knowledge the giant's wife knew where he was. As she turned away from her new cabin's door, her eyes tried to focus through her tear-filled eyes on the unlit logs in the fireplace. After transporting the rabbits' cage inside and tending to their needs, she set about lighting the fire. It was not at all cold. She knew she would nap and let the fire go out, but she needed to make the place hers for however short a time she was allowed to stay put.

Chapter Seven

Arizona

Third Wednesday in September

    The only restaurant on the Lake Chekobee reservation sat a half mile from the interstate as if to testify to its historic precedence. The blue-painted flat-roof building in front of the eating establishment reached a block in each direction from the entrance. Native-made tourist articles ranging from oil portraits to life-size stone and woodcarvings of the region's animals as well as every conceivable object remotely tainted with Native American history, stocked the shelves. Three cash registers kept busy with lines of people from the tourist buses. Signs pointing to the back of the building hung low enough for John and Sam to duck. Sally led the way to the A-framed building attached behind the store. The restaurant boasted a three-star classification.

    Thanks to Sam's detective license, after a considerable amount of money and time spent at competing detective agencies in Phoenix, and a future phone bill Sally tried not to think about, a George Dade had agreed to meet them for lunch to tell them what he knew about Mary Jo.

    "Sammy," John directed the officer-detective, posing as their son, to a chair facing the window. Sally thought John might have understood from his hotel restaurant experience older women try to sit with their backs to the source of any harsh light. So, she agreed to sit with her back to the view and placed the red-and-white checkered napkin in her lap. The menu listed no prices. The message conveyed, "If you can't afford it, leave."

John unfolded a piece of paper before handing it to Sally. "While you and Sam were busy on the computers, I interviewed each detective in the agencies. These are the books they recommended to study for the investigator's license."

Sally scanned a list of twenty books ranging from treatises on bones, forensic methods, wire-tap procedures, as well as lists of library resources and web search engines. "No more television for the two of us."

"Sylvester failed the test twice already." Sam surveyed the team of uninterested waitresses. "I could eat," he raised his voice, "a *big* horse."

Sally checked her watch. Since they were seated, no server arrived for half an hour. Sally explained they were in an "Alternate time culture."

"The people behind Sam already ate and received their checks." John clinked his glass with his fork.

A group of French tourists at a table farthest from the entrance was intent on causing a scene. "No wine?" one of the louder members shouted.

"No one can enjoy a civilized meal," his skinny female

companion said, "without a glass of wine."

"Savages can't drink." A spirited waitress with hips enough to challenge the idiots stomped to their table. "You are on a *dry* reservation."

"All the more reason to drink," the third Frenchman said. The waitress pointed to the restaurant's door, so the three unfed tourists left.

"Perhaps our tribal leader gave instructions to wait for him to arrive," Sam said as John waved uselessly in the direction of the serving staff.

"I'd fire the bunch." John hissed. "For ignoring customers!"

Sally said to Sam, "John owns a hotel in St. Charles, where I went to high school."

Sam nodded. "With the loss of liberty, posing as a child eating with his parents, I refuse to comment."

When a man the size of Montana finally arrived, the wait staff snapped to attention. He wore black jeans and a black leather vest. Sally expected to see a bike helmet in his hand, but he carried a lone eagle feather. His shoulder-length black hair shone blue from the restaurant's wall of windows. Sam and John rose to greet him.

"Are you Mary Jo's mother?" the man asked Sally, handing her the eagle feather.

"No." Sally quickly added to keep the giant's attention, "But I want to protect her."

"Good," George Dade said. Four waitresses arrived to fill the four glasses with water. George waved them away. "Do you need to eat?"

"No." Sally stood to join the three men.

George led them through the front part of the building to the parking lot outside. He climbed on his bike, saying only, "Follow me."

They scrambled into the rental car, peeled onto the interstate, and raced after the trail of dust and smoke. When they arrived at the mountain's tree line near Flagstaff, George turned off the road and crossed a narrow bridge. A gravel drive led to an adobe building overlooking the gorgeous mountain stream. Sally struggled to get out of the back seat as fast as she could. "The view is breathtaking."

"My home." George opened the front door, but a small woman with arms crossed stepped out onto the stone threshold.

"Who are these?" the old woman asked.

"Friends looking for Mary Jo, Gran." George bowed, helmet in hand.

"Off with you." His grandmother waved at them energetically as if to disperse their evil spirits.

"Is Mary Jo safe?" Sally's determination was unbroken by the older woman's aggression.

"Never heard of her," Gran said.

"Now, Gran." George pointed to Sally's face, where angry tears were beginning to slide.

John put his arm around Sally. "Madam, just tell us if Mary Jo is with you, and we'll leave."

"Mother Dade." Another woman with grey hair down to her

shoulders pulled the older woman inside. "You know George wouldn't bring trouble to his own door."

George, looking somewhat relieved, ushered Robert's friends into his home. "That was my wife, Constance."

Mother Dade was sequestered into a back bedroom, where they heard the television being turned up unusually loud. Constance returned with a tray of lemonade. "Please excuse an old lady who is not accustomed to receiving strangers."

"Sorry." Sally declined her glass. "I'm allergic to lemon."

"George," Constance said, "bring in a glass of ice water." He also brought in a tray filled with plates, paper napkins, and a chocolate-layer cake.

"We have known Mary Jo for less than a week," Constance said. "Why are you seeking her?"

John and Sam filled their mouths with cake, so Sally explained as quickly as she could. "Our friend in Ann Arbor, Robert Koelz, who is also a friend of Mary Jo's, is being questioned about her disappearance by the police. Her abusive husband claims Robert is involved."

Constance sat quietly on the long, red couch, judging Sally's words. Her dark eyes appeared to look into the depths of her soul, searching for a clue for the correct action. Sally was humbled by the woman's spiritual strength. Constance finally looked up at George, who stood near the fireplace. He gave no indication of any decision on his part. "I'll speak to her." Constance rose. "Now if you'll excuse us, I'm sure George knows how to reach you."

John and Sam voiced their opposition to this plan, but Sally hushed them. "We'll wait at the motel."

Constance turned from her exit to the kitchen, formed a slow but genuine smile, and said, "Mary Jo will appreciate your patience."

* * *

Feeling somewhat defeated, John, Sam, and Sally returned to the rental car. John drove to the first motel outside the Lake Chekobee reservation. It was dark by the time they checked in.

"Does this place have food?" Sam asked. "I'm about starved to death."

John guided Sally away from her motel door toward the restaurant. "Let's discuss our failure over supper."

"We didn't really fail," Sally said. "Should we call Andrew?"

"Eat first." Sam held the Big Boy's restaurant door open. "Everything will make more sense."

Sally took refuge in the politeness of the moment. Andrew could wait for their bad news. Robert was probably already inebriated. They could wait. Besides "no news" was not good news in this instance. Perhaps Mary Jo would be too afraid to return to Michigan from her safe refuge. Sally admitted an army of men would have trouble harming Ricco's wife. As things stood, they would have to go through crazy Mother Dade, mammoth George, and Constance's formidable gauntlet to get to her.

"Nothing makes sense." John slid into the booth indicated by a surly waitress. "That scene was crazy. We should have demanded to see Mary Jo!"

"What, and drag her back to Ann Arbor?" Sally asked.

Sam used his brains. "Why don't we rent a video camera? If they let us back on the reservation and if Mary Jo can't face Ricco's violence. After all, there is no way we can protect her. At least, we'll have a record of her, alive, to show the prosecutor."

* * *

Arizona,
Third Saturday in September

After two days of waiting for word from Constance Dade or Mary Jo, Sally packed to return to Ann Arbor. Trying to relax in the pool with John's trim body hovering around, as he asked for news every ten minutes, was driving Sally crazy. She needed to find an AA meeting, too. The facts were evident. She wanted to control the outcome of their visit to Arizona. She was tired of repeating the Serenity Prayer and digging her nails into the plastic lounge chair. She didn't want to drink, but her state of nerves gave her enough warning to seek out fellow recovering alcoholics. Closing the suitcase, she realized one thing was certain. For some reason Mary Jo did not trust them. Sally urged John and Sam to pack up, too. "She must have seen me in Orlando."

Sam shared the motel room with John. "Mary Jo couldn't think her husband sent you?"

"Let's wait one more day," John said. "You need proof she's alive."

As the word "alive" resonated, George Dade knocked once on

the frame of the open motel door and stepped inside. "Constance says you may return. She has more questions for you." Without another word, he sailed off on his motorcycle. John, Sam, and Sally dropped everything and piled into the rental car to give chase.

"Don't lose him." Sally handed the video camera into the back seat. "Sam, you'll be better able to figure this thing out. It's a miniature computer."

"I hope I don't lose sight of the bike," John said. "Do you remember which road George turned off on last time?"

After they got lost completely, ending up in Flagstaff and backtracking for fifteen more minutes, Sally finally recognized the bridge they initially crossed to get to the Dade residence. "Here, here!" she shouted, grabbing the steering wheel.

John fishtailed the car as he slammed on the brakes. "You're going to get us killed."

Sally readjusted her seat belt, thankful the airbag did not inflate. "I was afraid you would miss the turn."

John backed the car up along the median of the main road before he could turn down the dirt lane.

"You don't suppose Gran could be occupied?" Sam asked.

"What happened?" George stood in the yard, waiting for them.

Sally wondered if this giant was too afraid of his grandmother to knock on the door. She stated the obvious. "Lost."

"We went all the way to Flagstaff." Sam repositioned the shoulder strap of the camera bag onto his left shoulder in order to pump George's hand. George shook his head and indicated John should knock on the door.

"Don't you live here?" John asked, unable to understand the man's shyness.

"When they allow me in."

"Strong women-folk," Sam said in an admiring tone.

Mother Dade did answer John's timid knock with a frown, but Constance was expecting them and encouraged their entry. "Come in, come in." Escorting the old woman from the room, Constance told her, "Mother Dade, Doctor Phil already started interviewing the prostitute."

"Reality's drama plays second fiddle to fakers," George said.

When Sally noticed they were not offered the usual welcoming amenities of cold drinks and cake, she steeled herself for the worst. Constance invited them to sit down at the bare, round dining-room table, not to eat but to better monitor their reactions to her questions—Sally surmised.

"Mary Jo wants to know what Ricco told you." Constance smoothed her numerous strands of turquoise beads against her ample chest.

Sally included John and Sam. "We've not met the man."

"No, Mrs. Bianco," Sam said. "I did see Ricco at the Ann Arbor police station. I heard what Ricco told Robert Koelz and his lawyer." Sam turned to Constance. "Andrew Sites is Robert's attorney. I listened to Ricco's false murder accusations against Robert." Constance extended a hand in Sam's direction to elicit more details. "Ricco claimed Robert was the last one to see Mary Jo alive.

He contends they planned to meet at Robert's bookshop, at Mary Jo's insistence. However, Mary Jo never showed up."

"What day?" Constance asked.

"A Monday, three weeks ago," Sally supplied. Was Robert questioned so long ago?

"The Sunday before, around six in the evening." Sam paged through his pocket notebook. "Was when Ricco said his wife didn't show up."

Mary Jo Cardoni appeared at the Dade's kitchen doorway with a rabbit under each arm, one white, the other fatter and brown. "So, Ricco waited a day before going to the police."

John and Sam stood as Mary Jo entered the dining room. Sam was not shy about placing the video camera on the table, but he made no motion to turn it on or aim it at Mary Jo.

"Join us." Constance indicated a chair for Mary Jo.

"You're safe," Sally said before breaking down from all the tension.

John offered his handkerchief. "Sally's been under a lot of strain."

"I recognize you, who are you?" Mary Jo asked.

"A high-school friend of Sally's, from St. Charles," John said. "You spoke to me about the storage items in your house."

"Ricco's realtor," Mary Jo said to Constance.

"I took the house off the market." John held his hands up as an act of innocence to George, who took a threatening step in his direction, placing a hand on Sam's camera. "Sally wasn't sure the signature on the sales agreement was yours."

"It was mine." Mary Jo gave the brown rabbit to Constance, who let it hop down to the floor. Mary Jo touched the back of her head. "I lost a handful of hair for not signing the papers as soon as he put them in front of me."

"Why did you flee Illinois?" Sally stifled a final sob. "Ricco would have been put in jail by now."

"Would have been?" Mary Jo stroked her throat as if speaking was difficult. "Where do you think Ricco was in Illinois when he wasn't in jail? He was trying to choke me to death. When he found me again in Ann Arbor, he raped me!"

Constance stood and motioned for George to help defend Mary Jo. "That's all we need to ask you. You can leave now."

But Mary Jo didn't rise from her chair. She took a minute to compose herself, stroking the white rabbit before setting it on the floor, too. "Let them understand…everything."

"I'll explain to them on their way out." George indicated the three of them should leave by pointing to the entrance door.

"But Robert." Sally resisted the expulsion and remained seated at the Dade's dining room table, hugging the camera to her chest. "Robert needs proof you're alive."

John and Sam were already escorted outside.

George returned and tugged at Sally's chair.

"Wait," Mary Jo said. "Is there some way we can disguise where we are? Then Mrs. Bianco could take a picture and leave."

Sally fumbled with the camera. "Sam knows how to work this

thing." George closed his big paw over the camera, flipped open the screen, and started filming. He put one finger over his lips, but pointed to Mary Jo, making a flapping gesture with his fingers indicating she should start speaking.

"I'm Mary Jo Staples. My husband, Ricco Cardoni needs to be behind bars before I feel safe to travel to Michigan. Obviously, I'm alive. I cannot reveal where I am because of my husband's violence. Sally Bianco will bring Polaroids of the bruises on my neck which Ricco inflicted when I tried to have him jailed in Illinois."

Sally said, "Shut it off." George complied. "I went to Florida after I found several surnames 'Staples' in your address book. The phones were disconnected, but we gave your license number to the police in Ann Arbor and Orlando." Sally wondered how much time remained before she was thrown out of the Dade house. "Robert's lawyer said hearsay evidence from his friends, testifying about your being alive would not be enough for court. We need to prove you are alive today."

Constance left for the front room and came back with a newspaper. "Mary Jo, hold this up close to your chest. Okay, George, roll'em."

After the filming, Sally let the Dades know Mary Jo's fear of Ricco was well grounded. "Mary Jo, did Harvey Clemmons visit the bookshop when you were there?"

"The museum director?" she asked. "Drinks about as much as Robert?"

"Robert's lawyer thought it was a good idea for Harvey to

speak at a conference in Kansas City to look up Ricco's relatives. Robert remembered your saying he was from Missouri."

Mary Jo listened intently. "I never met his family."

"Just as well." Sally included Constance and George in the conversation. "Harvey found two ex-wives, sisters. The second wife is dead. The first wife is caring for their four children." Mary Jo seemed impressed. "Two boys and two girls. I don't know their ages, but they are all named Ricco."

"Bit much," George said.

"The first wife thinks Ricco might have killed her sister. She's willing to testify against Ricco. However, Andrew, Robert's lawyer, thinks we would need a good reason to exhume the body."

Constance rejoined the two women at the table. She seemed to count her turquoise beads while she considered the new facts. "I suppose the first wife won't be called upon unless an appeal is necessary; that is if your friend is brought to trial and convicted, which can't happen with Mary Jo alive and well."

"Harvey uncovered a worse story." Sally felt reluctant to add to the horror.

George asked, "What could be worse than murder?"

"Should I contact Ricco's wife to help support the children?" Mary Jo asked.

"Once Ricco is incarcerated," Constance said, "when you're safe."

"What's worse than murder?" George slapped the table to get their attention.

"Ricco pounded nails in the heads of the children's puppies." Sally held her throat as she added the rest of the story. "While they watched."

"He doesn't deserve to breathe," George said. The three women agreed even death seemed mild compared to the harm inflicted on innocent minds.

"He is a fiend," Mary Jo said. "Sometimes I thought I was the only one he hated."

"I don't know how you survived this long," Sally said, "under such a vile influence."

In leaving a few moments later, Sally hugged Mary Jo promising to phone Constance as soon as Ricco was incarcerated, at least for causing a false arrest and assaulting his wife. She cautioned Mary Jo, "Robert's lawyer let Ed Thatch track your credit card. I suspect Ricco could hire someone to do the same thing."

"I didn't use my married name on the cards. And I don't live here," Mary Jo said, "with the Dades."

"We collect her mail," Constance said. "Of course, Ricco would know your maiden name, too."

After they were outside, where Mary Jo could not hear him, George told the three detectives, "None of you can protect her."

"Mary Jo won't come to Ann Arbor to clear Robert's name?" John asked.

"Three witnesses swearing Mary Jo is alive and safe should be enough," George said.

"But we're all Robert's friends," Sam said.

"The better reason to believe you and the video." George ducked his head as he eased himself back into his home, closing the door on them quickly in order to keep the rabbits in.

* * *

Even over her cell phone, Sally knew Andrew Sites was not happy with the results of the Arizona quest. "You're kidding? How am I going to explain to Robert or Judge Wilcox?"

"She is safe." Sally was tired, and her cell phone needed batteries or the cliffs along the road were intercepting the signals. "Explain to Robert. Let me talk to him."

"You're welcome to." Andrew sounded thoroughly frustrated with the case.

"What's wrong?" Robert asked in a surprisingly sober tone.

Sally checked her watch: two o'clock in the afternoon. "Everything is fine, Robert." She put a smile in her tone. "We saw Mary Jo. She's in a safe place. We met her through her landlady."

"But what?" Robert asked.

"The problem is she wants to stay down here, out of harm's way. Ricco raped her while she was in Ann Arbor."

Sally could tell that Robert turned to Andrew in the bookshop office. "At least she's under someone's protection. How can that be a problem, Andrew?"

"The prosecutor won't let the judge rely on the testimony of three of your friends."

"Did you take pictures?" Robert asked.

"We prevailed upon the couple she trusts. At least we have

visual proof. We rented a video camera. Also, Mary Jo gave us Polaroids of her neck. She carries a gun."

"I saw the bruises," Robert said.

"I bet you did." Sally remembered Mary Jo's nude romp at Mrs. Clankton's. Robert didn't reply. Sally was sorry to be so light about his troubles. "Has Penny returned?"

"Not yet. Why didn't Mary Jo shoot the bastard when he raped her?"

Sally could hear how his tongue was beginning to be greased with the thick cream sherry. "Don't drink about it, Robert. Alcohol only makes everything worse."

"Slows down my arrhythmia," he said.

"You saw a doctor?" Sally felt a moment of relief.

"Andrew's made an appointment for me." Robert sighed. "Penny's in Texas."

"Texas?"

"She wants you to pick her up on your way back." Robert sounded a little cheered by the outlandish request. "Penny says she has a surprise for me."

"She's joking? We would have to change our tickets. Why can't Penny fly back on her own?"

"She won't come home until you approve her surprise. Please, Sally. I miss her."

"Where exactly is she?" Sally wanted to scream.

"In Houston. She said to fly in tonight and have her paged at the airport. Penny promises to arrange for your ticket to Metro."

"And what about John and Sam? What am I supposed to do with them?"

"That's the trouble." Robert started to slur his words. "You're surrounded by too many admirers."

Sally slammed the cell phone shut. She wished she owned the patience of Constance and the strength of George to shake some sense into Robert. "You're not going to believe it. As soon as we pack up, I have to change our tickets. Robert wants me to pick up Penny in Houston. She won't come back to Ann Arbor unless I see some present she intends to give Robert."

John started to object. Sam beat him to it. "I'll keep my ticket. I am out of vacation time."

Before they saw Sam off at the airport's security lane, Sally hugged the lad. "I appreciate your coming down with us. Make sure you hand the tape of Mary Jo directly to Andrew. He'll make sure the evidence is secured for the arraignment. We never could have found Mary Jo without your help with the Phoenix detectives. I promise to roast a chicken for you when I get back to Ann Arbor."

"Can Sylvester come, too?" Sam asked. "He's been feeling low since you yelled at him about taking Robert in for questioning."

Sally was glad Sylvester felt horrible. "Of course. I remember when you were little, and I offered you a cookie, you always asked for two--one for you and one for your older brother."

"He's not a bad guy, just kind of gung-ho since he got out of the Navy."

"I understand," John said without being asked.

The Legitimate Way

Sally berated herself for not being able to understand Sam's older brother as much as she would like to. The boy was always on a different playing field. Sally never knew what the rules were, but they surely didn't fit in with her ideas of equity and fair play.

* * *

After Sam left for Detroit, Sally entertained mixed feelings about John's loyalty. What were the consequences of encouraging him to stick around? Would he demand a romantic attachment because of all the time and detective work they were doing together? What did that say about the future? Was he going to stay in Ann Arbor at her beck and call, or did he expect her nostalgic attachment to St. Charles would influence her to return to Illinois with him? So she asked him, sort of. "I do not know a more generous friend than you, John."

"Don't you worry about me. I'm having a ball."

"But what's going to happen after we get Robert cleared?"

"We." John rolled the word around in his mouth, too long as far as Sally was concerned.

"Now, John."

"Kidding. One day at a time, right?"

"How did you know?" John knew she was an alcoholic.

"You're sensible, emotional, but not afraid to react." John's eyes glowed with admiration. "You are the most honest person I know. I'm safe with you. I just want to see where all this detective experience leads me, us."

"Well, all right, I can live with that."

Chapter Eight

~×~

Houston, Texas
Third Sunday in September

Paging Penny Savage at the Houston airport at eleven o'clock at night, of course, brought no results. John arranged for connecting rooms in the airport's hotel. Sally was too angry to be of any assistance. Nonetheless, the phone in Sally's hotel room rang too early the next morning. Confused by her new surroundings, she didn't pick up the phone until the sixth ring.

"Boy, I thought you already checked out." Penny's anguished voice alerted Sally to the ridiculous situation.

"Penny." Sally wanted to harangue the imbecile, but she wasn't awake enough to say more than her name. She hoped she telegraphed her disgust at the young girl's antics, but some bell in her head warned, just in time, not to imitate her sister Madelyn's tones of indignation.

"I'm so excited. I'm down in the lobby. How long will it take to get yourself together, or should we come up?"

"We?" Sally wasn't sure she heard correctly. "Do you have a mouse in your pocket, or are you using the royal 'we'?"

"Sorry. I'll wait in the restaurant. How soon will you be down?"

"About an hour," Sally grumbled. "No, I can make it sooner, but then I'll have to pack after breakfast. When do our tickets say we leave for Detroit?"

"Oh, I haven't made the reservations yet. I'm not going if you don't like my news for Robert."

"Your news? I thought you wanted me to approve a present."

"Oh, it is!" Penny laughed, pleased with herself. "Hurry down."

The brat hung up the phone before Sally could find out more.

In retaliation, Sally planned to take her own sweet time dressing. No tickets for home? She merely glanced at her open bags on the second queen bed in the room decorated in uninspired trappings. What was she going to wear? She stepped out of her nightgown and fiddled with the shower mechanisms.

Why couldn't the fixtures in hotel rooms be standardized so weary travelers could figure out how not to be scalded in the middle of a shower? She washed her hair using all the shampoo and conditioner available from the hotel's Lilliputian bottles. Not until the water ran cold with the faucet all the way to hot did she decide to re-enter the confusing world of reality. Usually, her best plans were hatched under running water, but with all the cards for her future in Penny's hands, Sally's mind refused to offer the least hope of a pleasant outcome for their Texas adventure.

Gypsies, she thought, watching herself blow dry her hair in the misty mirror. John and she were becoming roaming vagabonds—moneyed but homeless. Since the first week in September, Sally traveled to Illinois, Florida, back to Michigan, then to Arizona. Now she was stuck in Texas for the Lord only knew how long. 'Please, Lord,' she earnestly prayed, 'give me enough patience for today.'

She was standing in front of the open bar refrigerator. Tempted and with her mouth-watering, she refused to read the liquor bottle labels, knowing they would prolong her agony. Instead, she selected an unwholesome-looking glass bottle of orange juice. "God, grant me the serenity to accept the things I cannot change, the courage to change the things I can, and the wisdom to know the difference." Lacking wisdom seemed to be the rub. Maybe a sponsor could sort out what to change in her life. As soon as she returned to Ann Arbor, she promised to attend meetings until she found a sponsor.

Choosing a tan pair of slacks, matching top, and her wrinkle-proof raspberry vest, Sally applied all the makeup necessary, almost war paint, to face the unknown prospects of the day. Finished, Sally knocked on the adjoining door to John's room. She must have awakened him, because it took forever for him to answer her increasingly loud pounding. "Penny called." Sally apologized to the sleep-rumpled man. "She's waiting downstairs for us. Take your time."

"Five minutes. You look like you've been up for hours. Wait for me."

No problem. Madelyn was right about her. How had she let herself get talked into this fiasco? Robert's feelings were important, and he was vulnerable with the case hanging over his head, but she should have told him to forget this added trip to Texas. Texas did not relate to the case. Penny was Robert's main concern when he should be concentrating on his legal problems. Penny was a problem.

And what did John think of her now? Of course, he might as well know how important Robert was in her life since Danny died. The situation of chasing Penny all over Texas surely seemed ridiculous. Not exactly the way to inspire confidence in a new friend or courtship. Was she allowing John to court her? She should be tending to business, not monkey business. In a way, she was as horrible as Penny—well, maybe not that bad.

Punctual as a clock, John knocked on their shared door in five minutes. Sally opened the door to find him smartly dressed and shaved. "You do look great this early in the morning." He tried to slip his arm around her waist. "We better get started. I have to pack before we leave the hotel for our flight."

"Me, too." John laughed. "I was so mad last night, I threw my things all over the room."

"Penny's lucky I don't add her name to the list of young women Robert could be accused of murdering. She hasn't made plane reservations for us, either."

While they stood in the line waiting to be seated in the airport's crowded hotel restaurant, Penny accosted them. She pulled them past the young hostess, who smiled fixedly at the people they were cutting in front of. "I'm getting married." Penny turned and announced to the waiting crowd.

"Is he the groom's father?" John asked as they approached a table where a man much older than Penny waited.

"Simon, I'd like you to meet Sally Bianco." Penny slipped into the booth next to the straggly-haired older guy.

"Simon Goldberg." The man offered his hand to Sally.

Sally looked at John, who shook the man's outstretched hand. "John Nelson." He pushed Sally down in the seat across from Penny and Simon.

"Simon's a lawyer." Penny chatted away to cover the silence issuing from Sally's side of the table. "He worked at Ford for years, and they paid for his education. Isn't that great?"

"Fine," John said. "Are you the father of the groom?"

"I am the groom," Simon said.

"You are Robert's present?" Sally asked.

"Isn't he great?" Penny did not meet Sally's gaze. "And he's fully functional!"

Sally understood exactly.

"As a defense attorney?" John tried to catch up. Simon smiled at Penny as she laughed, and laughed. The dawn rose in John's red face. "I see," he said, without understanding the previous problem Penny experienced with Robert.

"How is Robert going to be pleased with this present?" Sally asked.

"Oh, that's why I waited for you to approve," Penny said, eyes wide, all innocence personified.

"The marriage?" John asked.

"No," Penny said. "I was worried Robert might not want to see me again...after I marry Simon."

Sally finally met Simon's eyes. She spoke slowly because no one could be this stupid and not need help with language. "A problem worth considering."

Simon wasn't shy about ignoring her implication and instead told them boldly, "Penny thought you two might stand up for us."

"Penny." Sally touched her arm to get her attention. "Should we talk, privately?" Obviously, Simon did not have enough sense for her to bother with.

"No." Penny started to pout like the two-year-old infant she was. She wound her arm around Simon's as if determined to drown with the idiot.

"Mr. Goldberg ..." Sally tried again to bring reason into the situation.

"Simon."

"Simon." Sally sighed deeply. "Did Penny tell you about her father's suicide?"

"I understand your concern. But I think you should know we have her mother's approval. The family has known me for years."

"Yes, I can see you are well acquainted."

"We have to hurry," Penny said. "The preacher is meeting us at Simon's ranch."

Sally checked her watch. She was not hungry. "John, why don't we pack?" She took the menu out of John's hand before standing and pushing herself out of the booth. "We turned in the rental car last night." She tried to keep all her mental ducks in a row. Sometimes life came at her so fast, she wasn't always able to breathe properly, much less think logically. Nevertheless, escape seemed a good plan.

"I'll drive you." Simon offered. "Why don't I order breakfast rolls and coffee to go, and we'll meet you out front in, say…twenty minutes?"

* * *

In the elevator John shook his head.

"Exactly," Sally said. "Should we just pack and board a plane to Detroit?"

"Her family approves. Maybe we should help them out. Do you know how Robert will take this?"

"No." Sally dialed the Bibliopole's number as soon as they returned to her room. "How am I going to tell him?"

"I wouldn't." John rubbed his hands against the side of his slacks. "Let *Penny Goldberg* break the news. Remember, people often hate the bearer of bad tidings."

Sally hung up the phone before Robert could answer. "I'm such a coward," she said, thinking again about needing a sponsor. John sat down next to her on the bed and put his arm around her shoulder. Sally looked up at him. He placed a hand under her chin, but Sally pulled away. "Too much is happening." She apologized for the rebuff and patted John's knee. "I'm so glad you're here with me."

"That's enough for now. Let's get gussied up for a wedding."

"I guess we could leave our bags with the hotel. Should we make plane reservations now?"

"Better wait until we find out the rest of their plans. I don't think we should leave our bags. We don't even know how far away his ranch is."

"Probably Austin," Sally said, entirely out of her depth.

* * *

John Nelson sat in the front seat of the Cadillac with Simon Goldberg, who drove as if Penny might change her mind about marrying a man the same age as her father. He barreled down the interstate out of Houston. John coughed, turning to get Sally's attention. "What is the speed limit in Texas?"

Penny was all cheerfulness and laughter. "Simon's a lawyer. He can talk his way out of a drunk-driving ticket."

"You do need your wedding witnesses to be alive." Sally clutched her purse to her chest.

"I'm pregnant," Penny said as if to cheer her up, and loud enough for John to hear.

"My first child." Simon turned proudly to inform John. The car reacted to the news, too. The right front wheel hit the gravel, and they all bounced in their seats as Simon jerked the car back onto the road.

"Listen," John shouted. "Slow this thing down, or I'll beat you to a pulp as soon as you stop."

Simon slowed down. "Is sixty-five acceptable?"

"Quite," John said, not apologizing for his good sense.

Sally felt a welcome surge of pride. She even smiled at Penny.

At the ranch, with no horses or other domestic animals in

sight, Penny and Simon linked arms as soon as the car doors were shut. "We made it home before the preacher arrived," Simon strolled toward the house. "Time to have a celebration toast."

Penny smiled joyfully and encouraged Sally and John to follow them through the oak double doors of the ranch house. The cool slate floor was relieved at odd intervals with red shag carpeting. The only furniture to be seen were twelve red bar stools in front of a black-and-chrome bar. Floor-to-roof windows opened on both sides of the room.

A mirrored wall behind the bar faced the entrance and reflected Sally's unhappy expression. Sally smiled at herself.

John abandoned her and accepted an empty champagne glass from Simon.

A circular steel staircase next to the bar headed to a balcony, where a rumbled red counterpane lay half on the bed, half on the floor. Another door to the right of the front door led to other areas of the dwelling. Coming from the direction of those unseen areas, Sally could smell meat cooking in something highly aromatic, onions and spices.

"Make yourself comfortable," Simon called to her from across the empty room.

Sally continued to stand in the middle of the living room. "How long have you lived here, Mr. Goldberg?"

"Simon," he said. "Fifteen years, last March."

"Were you waiting for a wife to pick out your furniture?" Sally was honestly curious.

Simon smiled as he popped a champagne cork. "I believe in functional furniture. I drink in here, eat in the dining room, my cook cooks in the kitchen, and I sleep...well, I've changed my habits in the loft."

"A baby will need...." Actually, Sally didn't own a clue about what a baby would need.

"Simon will take care of everything." Penny beamed.

"Well," John said. "For one thing, Penny, I know a pregnant woman shouldn't be drinking."

"I bought non-alcoholic, too. Maybe we'll have twins." Simon slipped his arm around Penny's slim waist.

Sally edged toward the bar, still hoping something or somebody would intervene before the wedding. "Should we wait until after the wedding to celebrate?"

"Too late." Simon finished his glass in one gulp.

John asked about the size of the ranch, the lack of livestock, and Simon's plans for the future Mrs. Goldberg while Sally surveyed her own dire thoughts. If they married, they were doomed. Simon would be off to the city doing his lawyerly duties. Penny would be stuck out in this barren place biting her nails until the birth of...what? Twins? Even Martians if Penny had not stopped drinking soon enough. Either way, they would have no chance to survive in the modern, outside world.

A squat woman, barely five feet tall, approached the group still huddled around the sterile bar. "Now, Simon, bring your guests into the dining room. Sonja, my daughter, is ready to serve the barbecue."

"Yes, Monica." The prospective groom's manner changed abruptly from the stance of a braggart to a gracious host. "Please, please, you're surely hungry. We rushed you over your breakfast." Simon ushered them past the housekeeper, who was dressed in what must have been Mexican garb or the latest retro-ranch fashion. Bare shoulders shone over a red, gathered blouse, hordes of bright colors swirled in her floor-length skirt.

Sally thought the woman was barefoot, too. Her daughter, Sonja, was close to Penny's age, perhaps even five years younger. The girl eyed Simon with what Sally thought was outright aggression. She was a fully-grown beauty, red lips, great dark eyes with lush lashes, and about the same vertical size as her mother but one-fourth the girth. Her attire was the exact match of her mother's. Although similarly barefoot, Sonja walked on her tiptoes as if she just shed high heels, which kept her back straight, her hips swaying.

Penny ignored both serving women and chatted happily with John, who seemed unable to smile for some reason.

Sally tried to ease any tension John might be experiencing by clearing up matters at hand. "Penny, you know how Robert will feel about your marriage."

"He'll be heartbroken," Simon said.

Penny went into her pout mode. "Robert thought Nancy was great for getting pregnant."

Sonja dropped a plate of meat covered in barbecue sauce in front of Penny, splattering brown spots all over Penny's white lace-trimmed T-shirt.

"Careful!" Simon jumped up.

Sonja glared at him.

Penny seemed to notice for the first time. "You love my husband!"

"He's not your husband!" Sonja flounced out of the room.

Simon tried to explain the young girl's infatuation. "Her family has been my family's servants for five generations."

"Until now," John said. "Your wife needs a supportive environment for the baby."

Monica served the rest of the meal in silence without her daughter's angry presence.

*　*　*

After the preacher arrived and awarded the couple the appropriate wedding vows, John asked the cleric for a ride to the airport. The groom was too many miles away from being a sober driver.

"You will need to call Robert," Sally said.

Standing behind Penny, Simon encircled her waist with his hairy arms. He seemed unable to keep his hands off the child. "I'll take care of it."

"You haven't asked about Robert's case." John held Penny at arm's length as she tried to hug him goodbye.

"You found Mary Jo, right?" Penny asked.

"Yes." Sally wondered how a father's suicide could impair or otherwise affect a daughter's brain. "She might refuse to come to Ann Arbor. Robert will need to clear his name."

"We'll be there." Simon's arms re-tightened around Penny.

The Goldberg servants were out of sight, but not out of Sally's mind as they drove away from the ranch with the preacher.

"Known those folks long?" John asked the preacher.

"Monica's a member of my congregation," he said. "She asked me to do her a favor. Seems her daughter is hung up on the employer."

"So you performed the marriage to save her daughter?" Sally asked.

"You could say that." The preacher jerked his stiff collar. "Hope God doesn't mind."

* * *

John brought up another practical concern on the airplane back to Metro. "I would like to be a witness, if Robert faces an arraignment hearing, about the state of Mary Jo's health. Is there a residence-hotel in Ann Arbor where I could stay?"

Sally couldn't help feeling complimented. "I'm sure we can find accommodations for you. I live in a one-bedroom condominium on the west side of town. I didn't see your home in St. Charles."

"I live out west, on 64. James is taking care of my dog, Ginger."

"I remember 64's route all the way to 47. Where do you live?"

"Not far from Randall Road. Do you remember where the road curves enough for a guardrail? There's a small dammed-up pond on the left side of the road. My place is on the right, behind a stand of weeping willows."

"I know the place. I mean, I've seen your house from the road. One story white ranch with lots of flowers along the creek in the summer."

"Do I remember your father was a house painter or a farmer?"

"Both. He wasn't a very good farm manager. They say I inherited his terrible temper. He started painting houses so he could work for himself and not worry about getting fired."

"You do not have a temper. Or, you would have horsewhipped Penny."

"Robert was looking forward to his present. How am I going to explain?"

"Tell him the truth. You didn't approve of the present."

"Do you think Simon will keep his word and show up to help Robert?"

"If he doesn't, I'll go down and haul him up here."

"You love me, don't you?"

"Yep," John said, going all John-Wayne for the moment. "Have since high school."

"You did not." Sally swatted his shoulder.

"I was being honest when I told you why I never married." He held her gaze with his very large brown eyes.

Sally earnestly prayed for help. Here was a man with integrity for the asking. "Please stay." Then she allowed him to kiss her for the first time. Her heart played a warning flip of palpitations, but she didn't mind. She held onto John's earlobe after the kiss and then whispered into it, "I wish I was younger for you."

"Now is all we have, Sally." John slipped his arm around hers. "Is it too early to buy you a ring?"

"Way, too early." She hung onto his huge hand. She was sure he would wait until she was ready for something more. "First, we clear Robert."

"I'm accustomed to life's trials."

Sally thanked God she was too, especially with John at her side. Life could have a go at her. She was ready. "Do you want to hear my favorite poem?" Without waiting for John's permission, she recited. "The Sentence" by Anna Akhmatova:

'And the stone word fell on my still-living breast.

Never mind, I was ready. I will manage somehow.

Today I have a lot to do. I must kill memory, once and for all.

I must turn my soul to stone. I must learn to live again.

Unless – Summer's ardent rustling is like a festival outside my window.

For a long time I've foreseen this brilliant day, deserted house.'

"Not with me around," John said. "I know a good thing when I see her."

Chapter Nine

Ann Arbor, Michigan
Last Monday in September

The Bibliopole's stock of folding chairs was completely utilized the evening John and Sally arrived back in Ann Arbor. Andrew Sites brought along Judge Joe Wilcox and Jimmy Walker, the state's attorney, to view the video of Mary Jo. The usual suspects included Henry Schaeffer, the Tedler brothers in their police uniforms, as well as Robert's co-conspirators, Harvey and Ed. Andrew's laptop computer, which sat on the dropleaf of the secretary between the Liberty-Street windows, displayed a photo of Mary Jo holding up the previous Saturday's newspaper.

Penny and Simon Goldberg were the last bookshop patrons to arrive before Andrew started the video. John straightened his chair from its leaning position with a loud thud.

Sally wished she'd kept her promise and secured a sponsor as soon as she arrived back in Ann Arbor. Robert's dilemma and a dozen other ready excuses, like keeping John entertained with Ann Arbor's resources, let her put off going to a meeting. The increasing tension in the room amplified her thirst. Alcohol was a cunning foe. If she wanted to stay sober, she needed a meeting where other alcoholics would help her remain sane and sober. Everyone of the booklovers assembled held a glass of cream sherry, even John. Sally zipped open her purse and took a sip from her water bottle.

"Look who's here." Robert waved his glass of sherry in Penny's direction, as she entered. "Care to join us, stranger?" Robert aimed his remark at the man accompanying her.

"This is Simon Goldberg," Penny held her chin higher than was necessary for the news. "I can't drink anymore."

"How do you do, Simon Goldberg. Do you read?"

"Lawyer, Penny's husband, and sire of her expected child," Simon said.

"Doesn't read." Robert winked at John.

"Now, Robert," Penny whined.

"Don't now Robert me!" Robert concentrated his anger on his empty glass. "Is this the present you made Sally fly to Texas to approve?"

"Why?" Penny turned her pout toward Sally. "What has Sally told you?"

"Sally didn't tell me you were fool enough to get pregnant with an old duffer and expect me to be happy about it, if that's what you mean." Robert poured himself a drink, drank it as if he had just returned from days abandoned in a sandy desert, and then refilled his glass. His telephone rang. The silence was palpable as they all strained to hear. "Mary Jo." Robert sat his glass down and put his hand over his heart. "Good to hear from you!" He listened, shaking his head affirmatively to the rest of us. "Good," he repeated several times, and finally, "Thanks. See you soon." He looked straight at

Penny when he added, "All my love."

"When?" Andrew asked. "When will she arrive?"

"Didn't say," Robert slurred. "More importantly, she's coming. When Sally told her about Ricco's four children, Mary Jo contacted their aunt. She's interested in supporting the children. I never knew Mary Jo could afford to be so generous."

"Her wealth could be a further motive for Ricco to search for her," Harvey said.

"She's bringing Ricco's first wife with her." Robert opened another bottle of cream sherry, offered it to the group, but poured himself another glass before relinquishing the bottle to Harvey who emptied it by refreshing the glasses of the remaining crew of eight drinkers.

"Are we going to pay for digging up his second wife?" Harvey asked Andrew.

"I'm leaving," Penny said, taking Simon's hand, which held onto his second serving of sherry.

Sally wondered if anyone else in the room knew precisely how much each of them imbibed.

"Nothing to bother ourselves about." Simon brushed his new wife's hand aside, rescuing the liquor. "Your bookman is quite correct. We were foolish, but here we are." He strolled over to where Sally was enthroned in the cushioned chair. "You never drink do you?"

"Not anymore," Sally said.

"Had your fill?" Simon bowed solicitously from his waist.

"I've about had my fill of you, mister." John collared the old man and moved him to the doorway.

"Wait," Sally said. "He did keep his promise to come to Ann Arbor."

"Right," Robert said. "He's just what the doctor ordered."

Penny began to weep and her husband wrapped her in his arms. "Actually, we've decided to relocate to Michigan."

"Remember Sonja?" Penny knelt down next to Sally's chair. "Well, she burnt down the ranch house!"

"Anyone injured?" John asked.

"No," Simon said, "but Monica's out of a job, too."

Penny rallied. "Simon passed the Michigan bar when he worked at Ford. Maybe he can help Andrew."

"Little late for that," Andrew said.

"A little late!" Harvey bellowed. "You've about killed our friend here, worrying about you and Mary Jo. Do you have no feelings for the man?"

"I did the best I could." Penny hung her sorry head.

"Not good enough," Robert whispered, slouching in his chair.

Sally's heart went out to him. But she didn't feel like embracing him, not with John in the room. Maybe, not ever again. "Robert, she is only a child, after all."

"A bad seed," Robert grumbled into his glass.

Ed Thatch stepped between Robert and Penny. "You're talking through your alcohol now. Penny, don't pay him any mind. Congratulations to both of you. We're glad you're here."

* * *

Sally and John were the only two out of the baker's dozen who did not crowd around the laptop presentation of Mary Jo. Afterwards, Judge Wilcox drew Jimmy Walker toward the hall. "Seen enough to dismiss these farcical charges?"

"Absolutely. In fact, I might prosecute her husband for making false accusations."

Ricco Cardoni appeared at the door. Six-feet-four his bulky shoulders testified to football contests or weight lifting. He wore a blue jeans jacket, a string tie, black leather pants and black cowboy boots. High fashion for ugly bullies. Ricco sported great white-hunter crevices down his yellowish face. His lips were full and his mouth filled with protruding teeth. How did Mary Jo ever find him attractive enough to marry? Angry or drunk, Sally could tell he would be dangerous if riled. "Mary Jo told me Robert Koelz threatened her." Ricco glared at Robert, as if he were telling the truth. "If she didn't leave me."

"I did," Sally heard Robert whisper to Andrew. "I said I'd kill her, or he would."

"Oh for Pete's sake," Andrew said.

"Order," Judge Joe Wilcox said.

"You idiot," Andrew yelled at Robert.

"Order!" Judge Wilcox raised his voice over the rising din.

Ricco walked straight over to Robert, reached across the desk, and punched Robert in the face.

Pandemonium erupted, folding chairs collapsed. The Tedler

brothers wrestled Ricco to the ground and handcuffed him. Ed tried to help Robert, whose nose was broken and bleeding. Judge Wilcox stood in the middle of the room, jumping up and down like a four-year-old having a tantrum. The two other lawyers finally calmed him down.

Sally wondered where Miss Poi was hiding and somewhere in the middle of all the commotion, she began to giggle. John, Harvey, and serious-minded Ed broke out in laughter, too.

In the hall outside the bookshop, Sally heard Jimmy Walker say to Andrew, "That's the most fun I've had in fifteen years."

"Well," Andrew puffed out his chest. "We aim to please." He patted the other lawyer's arm as he descended the stairs, still chuckling to himself.

Robert sported blue bags under his eyes and the whites were lined with red. "I need a drink." He forced a grin. "The perfect remedy for what ails me."

Sally's three years of sobriety would not receive any special awards at an AA meeting, but she would feel welcomed. After her first year in AA, she read her confessional Fourth Step to a member. The older woman called her a 'dry drunk.' She was instructed to attend more than one meeting a week, to work on the steps with a sponsor, and daily to strengthen her relationship with God.

As the Tedler brothers led Ricco away, he cried. "She drove me crazy."

"Have you ever heard of anger management therapy," Sylvester asked, somewhat sympathetically.

Anger management. Sally needed some. She wanted to grab a chair and hit Ricco over the head. His weeping softened the men, who probably remembered their need to strike out at someone, maybe even a loved one. The women in the bookshop went all soft, going around a pathetic bend for the poor guy. He wasn't worth a moment of their empathy. As far as Sally was concerned, Ricco was a common kitchen bully, no doubt learned from an anger-ridden father.

In her younger days, when remedy loomed for every evil, Sally had volunteered at a women's shelter in Jackson. She attended classes describing how to relate to the spineless victims. She was taught not to rail against their abusers, but to allow the souls of the women time to recognize better alternatives. Sally told one young woman with two children who were removed from their home by police when she complained of her evil husband's violence. Instead of taking the criminal to jail, the police made the victim and her children homeless! Sally told her to go home, wait until the fool was asleep, borrow the frying pan from the kitchen, and beat him. The president of the shelter's advisory board removed Sally from the safe-house list and asked her to resign from the program.

Now she was experiencing the same frustration because the bookshop crew was so easily swayed by Ricco's theatrics. Penny tried to hug Robert after Ed provided him another glass of sherry. Sally did not see a smile of appreciation under Robert's moustache and his eyes did not brighten. However after Penny helped Robert to his feet, they walked arm-in-arm past everyone toward the washrooms in the hall.

Sally turned to Andrew for his appraisal of the situation. "Ricco will be behind bars for a while." He said to Harvey.

The group stood in silence, until they heard Penny's cries for help. "He doesn't know me!" Penny rushed toward them.

"Call 9ll," Sally said to Ed, who dialed Robert's ancient phone.

They all hurried down the hall. Robert lay on the floor of the latrine. "Get me out of here," he whispered. "Sally, I don't want to die in a toilet."

"John, Harvey!" Sally yelled.

John carried his feet and with Harvey on his left and Andrew on his right, they managed to lift Robert and move him to a wide wooden bench in the hall. Judge Wilcox opened the storeroom door to the hall and insisted they move Robert again, onto the bare mattress.

"I'm having a stroke." Robert smiled lopsidedly at Sally.

"Why didn't you send Penny out to us sooner," Sally asked.

"I knew what was happening," Robert said. "Miss Poi died last night. She had a stroke, too." He looked at Penny. "She's in the big box your boots came in."

"I'll take care of her," Penny said.

"Where's the ambulance?" Sally frantically asked Ed.

"Coming," Ed said.

"Last night," Robert said. "I thought I might not be able to walk over to the bookshop from the Grangers."

Andrew said, "I had no idea you were this ill."

"Doesn't believe in doctors," Harvey said and left the room. Sally could hear him coughing, and then weeping loudly in the hall.

"Hey," Robert called weakly, "I'm not dead yet." Then another spasm passed over him. The line of his mouth slackened and Sally wiped a bit of drool away. The twenty-third Psalm whispered through her thoughts. "Better open the windows." Robert tried to grin.

His bowels let go completely as the ambulance attendants lifted him to the stretcher. "Never mind, mate," One of them said. "We're used to this."

"I can still see you," Robert said to Penny. "I love you all." He raised his left arm. "Tell Mary Jo both my parents died from strokes."

* * *

University Hospital,
October Tuesday Morning

The sorry bookshop crew adjourned to the hospital's emergency waiting room for further news. After three hours, Andrew left with a shaken Judge Wilcox. Harvey and Henry stayed. The group continued to bond with each other over their concern for Robert. Ed finally excused himself to attend to his family.

Henry Schaeffer openly wept. "Are they operating on him?"

"I don't believe so," Sally said.

"Robert's found a way out of this mess," Harvey said.

"Harvey," Henry cried. "He can recover."

"He won't want to be an invalid," Harvey said.

Sally agreed, realizing the implication. "He won't." John nodded and stroked her arm.

A resident walked toward the group, his surgical mask in hand. "He's refused to allow us to relieve the pressure. The stroke is well advanced. He's blind and his right side is paralyzed. The seizures are increasing."

"Can we see him?" Henry was on his feet.

"He won't know you. He has slipped into a coma. He only has a few more hours, at the most."

Penny walked toward them with her new husband and brother, Mark, nearly carrying her. "Robert's gone." She collapsed into a chair. Her young face was ashen.

They all sat in a stunned silence. Sally's first thought was odd. Her sister, Madelyn, would be pleased. There was no reason for being involved with these people assembled in the waiting room. She checked her watch. Three o'clock in the morning was when most births occur, maybe deaths too. Without the bookman, would the people in the room continue to associate with each other?

Henry stood. "I'll attend to everything." Harvey accompanied him out of the waiting room.

"Take Penny home," Sally told Simon and Mark.

John drove Sally to her condominium. "He wasn't a perfect man," she kept saying, feeling disloyal but needing to speak the truth. "He wasn't a saint."

"Robert was your friend," John said. "And you were his friend when he needed you most."

Deep within her bones, Sally knew Robert would always, into eternity, be counted as a friend. But he wasn't perfect. Neither was she, but she was still sober. She thanked God and struggled with her anger against Robert's way of living, trying to let her resentments fade. "I really need a meeting."

"At four o'clock in the morning?"

Sally almost laughed. "You're right."

At her address, John opened the Honda's passenger door. Sally didn't let go of his hand. They walked to her front doorway arm-in-arm. "I'll see you tomorrow morning." Then he kissed her soundly with a comforting embrace before letting her go.

* * *

Waterloo Cemetery
First Friday in October

The funeral service at the Waterloo gravesite was short. Tall evergreens swayed on the cemetery's hill under a harsh October sky. The frost-yellowed grass crunched under their footfalls. Hands were stuffed into pockets or busy turning up collars against the wind.

"We loved him," Judge Wilcox said. "We eulogized him, now we're burying him; but Robert Koelz will continue to live among us as long as we live. Let's adjourn to the shop for a farewell drink."

Sally did not need the drink, or rather, she needed the drink, but a drunken life was not an option for her, not anymore. Without Robert, the entire center of her social activities, after Danny died and apart from AA, was destroyed. Henry was nice enough, but Sally didn't respect his unhappy life with his moneyed wife. Harvey was incorrigible, not anyone she would want to invite for dinner. Ed's wife wouldn't let Sally adopt her husband. Penny's life, even Mary Jo's was of no interest to her. Robert was gone.

John drove her from the cemetery to the bookshop. Was she regressing into the scenes of her high-school days? His bald profile seemed alien, but friendly. Would they develop a friendship? "I'll be right in," she said. "I need to make an AA call."

Sitting in the car, she called three phone numbers of AA women. Each sympathized; reminding her the death of a close friend was not a reason to drink. There were no acceptable reasons for an alcoholic to take the next, first drink. She decided the youngest sounding woman, Grace, would be the best one to sponsor her; the other two were not heterosexual.

When Sally explained a high-school friend was with her, the young woman reminded her, "God, too, is standing firm beside you. How far along are you in the Steps?"

"I've gone through all twelve."

"Read me Step One and when you call tomorrow we'll talk about your thoughts about the step."

"I don't carry my book with me."

"I think you should memorize them for the future. 'We admitted we were powerless over alcohol--that our lives had become unmanageable.' Call me tomorrow morning."

* * *

After Sally dragged her reluctant body up the bookshop's two flights of stairs, she could see the grieving crew was well into their sauce. Sally thanked God she processed enough sense to talk to an AA person before attempting to commune with the drinking bookshop customers. Henry Schaefer was sitting in Robert's chair. Penny, accompanied by her husband and brother leaned against the back bookcase. The Tedler brothers were replaying Ricco's capture. Andrew sat in the place of honor, as Sally always deemed Robert's side chair. He relinquished the chair to Sally and then stood with Harvey and Henry near the Liberty Street windows where Judge Wilcox was enthroned at the drop-leaf secretary. John unfolded a chair and placed it next to Sally.

Faces were marked with their loss. Were they weighing the possibilities of their friendships lasting past the death of Robert Koelz? Then Mary Jo arrived, alive as you please. "I'm so sorry," She repeated the same words for nearly a half hour until the cream sherry began to work on her nerves, too. "I tried to find a babysitter for Ricco's children, but they wouldn't leave their Aunt Harriett so she could come with me."

"Ricco's been arrested for assaulting Robert. He's off the streets, so you are safe." Sylvester Tedler was drawn to Mary Jo's side.

Andrew pushed Judge Wilcox out of his chair in order to offer it to Mary Jo. "There's a body in Missouri I need to dig up to get a conviction of murder." Henry handed Judge Wilcox the phone. After he hung up, the judge told Andrew, "The exhumation papers will be ready in the morning."

"I'll press charges for abuse," Mary Jo said, "if you promise to keep him locked up."

"A bit late," Sally said, more sober than the judge.

Penny pointed to Sally. "Your mouth, the lip line, is the same as Mary Jo's and mine."

Harvey stood clasping his vest labels, elbows extended as if he were mimicking a rooster about to crow. "Robert loved his women."

"And men," Henry said quietly.

"Thank God, Robert taught us to recognize men as human beings," Sally said. Mary Jo and Penny nodded their agreements.

As evening descended on the bookshop, Andrew followed John and Sally down the steps to the street. "I arranged with Sylvester Tedler to keep Mary Jo under protective custody."

Sally agreed, "Even after he's incarcerated, Ricco could hire people to harm her."

"Are the results of his second wife's autopsy going to be faxed to you?" John asked.

"They are, but I was hoping I could send Sam Tedler with you two to Kansas City." Andrew straightened his vest. "I know it's an imposition, but Mary Jo's suspicions would be further corroborated if Ricco's first wife could describe her sister's injuries prior to her death at Ricco's hand."

John answered for them. "We're starting to like our detective work, aren't we?"

Sally slipped her arm around John's waist. "You want us to

convince his first wife to come to Ann Arbor? When should we leave?"

"As soon as possible," Judge Wilcox said, "the necessary paperwork should arrive in Kansas City in the morning. If you could bring the children, who I understand all have the name Ricco and witnessed his violence against their pets and their mother, I think the jury would be willing to give Ricco a life sentence for murder. As soon as I receive the autopsy report, I can bring charges against him and keep him in jail."

Sally hugged the lawyer. "Robert trusted your judgment."

"High praise." Andrew turned away and briskly walked to his car.

"Too bad, men aren't allowed to show their emotions." John shielded Sally from the stiff night breeze. "For instance, I want to be engaged to you. Could I please, please buy you a ring?"

Sally leaned back against his shoulder as he kissed her. "I think that's appropriate." Sally told him after a second kiss. "Separate rooms on the road, until we're married."

* * *

As Sally snuggled under the covers, she repeated the four words of her daily, AA Tenth Step, wondering if indeed she acted out of any fear, self-pity, anger, or resentment. Before her mind let her rest in sleep, she asked God's forgiveness for the resentment she still felt against Robert for ending his life too early by not admitting his addiction to alcohol and for her anger toward men like Mary Jo's crazy husband.

Chapter Ten

∞

Ann Arbor
October, Last Saturday

Sally's grief siphoned energy faster than she could replace her sagging spirits with prayer and sleep. She called her sponsor at eight in the morning. "I didn't drink at my friend's wake."

"Good morning to you, too, Sally. Sounds like everyone else was drinking. I need to tell you this, but you're going to lose a lot of your old drinking friends. But, taking their inventory as we call judging in AA lingo is not going to add to your spirituality."

"I wanted you *not* to worry about the company I'm keeping, to be 'rigorously honest.' Do you think we could move on to the Second Step?"

"Your book is next to you, right? You chopped off the last word of that sentence, 'rigorously honest and tolerant.'"

Sally laughed. She liked the cheerful child. "You know I'm sixty-five."

"Let's see, I'm supposed to say you don't look it, but we haven't met. Step Two: 'Came to believe that a Power greater than ourselves could restore us to sanity.'"

"I am a believer. I accepted Jesus as my Savior when I was twenty."

"When you were drinking, did you consider yourself insane?"

"When I was driving home drunk after being awakened twice by drivers blowing their horns because I was on the wrong side of the road, I realized not stopping the car was insane."

"You're lucky you didn't kill anyone."

"I think my mother's prayers saved me. Now I'm glad I'm an alcoholic. My drinking brought me back to the Lord."

"I use the AA group as my higher power." The young girl coughed. "But I'm keeping an open mind about the possibility of something else out there in the universe to guide me."

"Seek and you will find," Sally said. She was surprised her sponsor's spiritual life was based entirely on AA. "How often do you attend meetings? I only go once a week to King of Kings, if I'm in town."

"Think about adding one more meeting a week. Call me tomorrow and we'll tackle Step Three, again."

The doorbell rang. A thankful bit of brightness appeared on Sally's doorstep. John arrived with his arms filled with flowers. "The neighbors are going to think I died." Sally smiled his gift of a dozen white roses.

"Naw." John shut the door behind him before wrapping his arms around Sally and the flowers. "They'll just notice some fool is courting you."

"You're not a fool." Sally kissed him as proof.

John followed her into the kitchen side of the front entrance, as she secured the last empty vase in the house, ran the water, clipped the end of each of the long stems and arranged the delicate white buds to their best advantage.

Sally shook her head. "The table is already too full of flower vases from Robert's funeral."

"How about upstairs?"

Sally laughed. "You take them up, while I start a pot of coffee. Put them on the drafting table in the study."

"Are you packed?" John called from the stairs. When he returned to the first floor, he sat down at the dining room table to await his coffee. His face showed he was rehearsing his next sentence, or move.

"Never mind." Sally stopped him. "We are not going to venture into the bedroom together until we're married. My sponsor says we should wait. And I agree."

"Am I going to meet this human obstacle?"

"My sponsor?" Sally went over to the sad guy and sat on his lap, as if she were a manipulating girl of sixteen. "I hope you'll be satisfied just being around me for a while." Sally watched his nostrils expand as he inhaled her old-fashioned Arpege perfume. The sweet man was besotted with her. She placed his hand under her brassiere. "When are you going to give me the ring you promised? I'd like to get Ricco dispatched into whatever hole they can dig for him before I concentrate on making happier arrangements."

"Deal." John brightened. "You'll help me pick out a ring? Can I tell James yet? Where should we get married, in Illinois or Michigan?"

"Whoa." Sally laughed. "Ring first; tell James, the rest is up in the air, okay?"

John held her fast. "One more kiss."

She complied with warmth and enthusiasm. She reluctantly left his lap. Standing, she pressed his dear, baldhead to her bosom. Knowing their trance would be broken, she said, "I've invited Sam Tedler and his brother to dinner tonight. Were you there when I promised Sam?"

"Can't remember. My head is swimming with ideas for our future. I know you've been to Europe." He brushed his hands over his slick head as if to clear away traces of her fingertips in order to think clearly. "Florence is so peaceful. Ireland doesn't require any language skills and the people talk to you like southern Illinois farmers. Say hello and they tell you their entire life stories, non-stop. Have you been to Rome?"

"No. Do you want to honeymoon there?"

"That's a great idea," John said, as if Sally thought up the trip's destination.

After spending all day helping her shop for dinner, vacuuming, and setting the table for a salad and a chicken potpie, John asked if he could turn on the evening news. Sally liked a man in the house. She felt more focused, less inclined to worry over the future or the past, less likely to weep about Robert's recent death, or Danny's. After Sally popped the promised chicken potpie in the oven, she joined John on the couch, draping her arm over his knee to make sure he knew. "I'm glad you're here."

"You just want an errand boy." John smiled and lifted her hand to his lips. He ran his finger down the inside of Sally's arm all the way to her elbow, as he watched her tension increase by the widening of her eyes. "I think you're a very alive woman."

The doorbell rang or they might have proceeded faster down the warm path than Sally intended. Sam Tedler walked in first.

His brother, Sylvester, lagged behind. "So sorry for you loss," Sylvester said. "You live in a cartoon," Sylvester said, looking at the walls. "I mean the colors …."

Sally was pleased. "I'm glad you like them. The barn red in the kitchen reminds me to stop and not go in there. I don't like to cook, normally. When the painter opened the can he said, 'Well, this has got to be wrong.'" Sally laughed. "I like yellow in the dining room. I think food should be eaten in a cheery mood, don't you? You cannot paint walls white in Michigan, because the cloudy days turn everything grey, so all the ceilings and the front room walls are sky blue."

"The upstairs is all pink," John said, without thinking; then he added, "I took flowers upstairs for Sally's study."

"It looks like a florist shop went out of business." Sam stepped into the dining room.

Sally batted Sam's shoulder. "Actually, the paint upstairs is called Coral Rose. Come and sit in the front room. The oven needs ten more minutes."

Sam chose one of the red recliners. "Have you two set a date?"

"No," Sally said, as John came to stand next to her slipping his arm around her waist. "We have to wait to put Ricco in his place."

"Good idea," Sylvester said, sitting in the matching recliner. "I mean congratulations, Mr. Nelson."

"Are all the paintings yours?" Sam asked.

"No," Sally said. "Mine are the glorified cartoons. I like Gauguin and see most things I love in basic colors. The texture of oil paint lets me feel I'm sculpting on the canvass. After Danny died, painting cheered me up."

"With Robert gone, will you get back to painting?" Sylvester asked. "I like the blue vases in that painting."

"As soon as you marry, I'll give it to you as a present."

"What if he doesn't marry?" John asked.

"Then, he'll have to visit us to enjoy my paintings."

Over dinner, Sally reminisced about earlier years when she spent time with the boys and their single mother. "Remember when I insisted you both learn how to swim at the Y?"

"Mother was afraid of the water." Sylvester turned to John.

Sam helped himself to another portion of the chicken pot pie. "You made the Y give us scholarships?"

"They wanted to help kids learn how to swim. Your mother worked hard. Wasn't she going to school, too?"

"She wanted us to see how hard she worked getting a college degree as an adult," Sylvester said. Sally refilled Sylvester's plate. John shook his head no, but Sally knew he was waiting for chocolate cake. "Mother's happily married." Sylvester's table manners were more refined than Sam's.

"I'm glad." Sally couldn't remember how many months passed since she heard from their mother. "Does she still live in Seattle?"

"Bellevue," Sam said. "She's married to a retired math professor."

"Do you call her often? You'll have to give me her new address."

"She's pretty busy," Sylvester said.

Sam looked askance at his brother. "I call her, at least once a week."

"She always wants to know who we're dating." Sylvester shrugged his shoulders.

"Sylvester thinks she's still keeping tabs on us. I think she just wants to share our lives."

"Sylvester, you're as judgmental as you think your mother is." Sally brought out plates of cakes and ice cream to make the medicine of her own hypercritical words go down easier.

"Do you think she is an alcoholic?" Sylvester asked.

"It's not for me to say. I've told you two before you should both go to Alanon meetings. You'll be welcome there, because one friend admits she is an alcoholic. Me."

"Maybe when we get back from Missouri," Sam said.

"I won't be able to go," Sylvester said. "I'm on assignment to keep Mary Jo safe. And when I'm off duty, I'm busy with night school. I want to become a forensic pathologist."

"That will take forever," John said.

"Don't discourage the man. I'm proud of you, Sylvester. You

hang in there."

The boy actually smiled. "Thanks."

"How long will we be in Missouri?" Sam patted his big brother on the back.

"I have no idea. Do you know, John?"

"Not me. I'm just going along for the ride."

"You were pretty tough in Arizona. "Remember threatening Simon Goldberg in Texas?" Sally laughed.

"That old fool tried to drive us into the ground." John turned to Sylvester, growling in remembrance of the harrowing car ride.

"Penny invited us for Sunday dinner." Sylvester patted his satiated stomach.

"We're going, too," Sally said. "Monday, Sam, we plan to leave for Missouri."

"At least I'll be well fed. I almost died from starvation in Arizona. My stomach thought my head was cut off."

"Remember Mother Dade frightening the chief of the tribe?" John started collecting the plates from the table.

"She buffaloed me too." Sam said.

"At least we ate well in Texas." John herded them into the front room. "I never would have guessed Sonja was an arsonist."

"Just a fool in love." Sally smiled at John.

* * *

Ann Arbor, St. Andrews Episcopal Church
Last Sunday in October

Sally picked John up for eight o'clock services at the church. "I was raised Catholic, too," he said. "During the sixties, I realized women should be able to serve as priests. I miss the traditions."

In church Sally spoke softly. "I missed the liturgy. An emptiness filled the place where all the poetry resided. This church was built right after the Civil War. I imagine women in hoopskirts waltzing down the aisles. The wires in the skirts were collapsible, like telescopes."

After communion, Sally knelt to ask the Lord to keep her safely beside Him, in His community, next to His heart. She also prayed for Robert's soul to find the Lord's light and eternal peace. The service helped her deal with Robert's absence on her side of the shadow of death.

* * *

When John and Sally arrived for dinner in the evening at the Goldberg's second floor apartment, Sally was surprised at the sophisticated style of the furnishings. "Penny, this looks like a picture right out of 'Architectural Digest.'"

"Penny added all the trees," Simon said. "It's a good thing we left Texas. She never would have been happy in a flat wasteland."

The corners of the living room sported fig trees and other tall plants. Every table held ferns, cactus, flowering annuals. The furniture was a little less sparse than Simon's ranch house, but mostly visitors were greeted with greens. Sally suspected Penny's mother divested her summer porches of wicker furniture. The couch and chairs' cushions were covered in light blue velour. Accents around the room, flower pots, pillows, even the matting around the framed photographs of Penny's extensive Catholic family were a bright basic yellow.

"Up here among the tree tops we don't need drapes." Penny spun around in the middle of the wood floor. "The plants love all this light from the windows."

Sally noticed the inside greens made a stunning contrast against the colorful backdrop of autumn leaves remaining on the trees outside the windows. The plants would also soften the snow-covered branches of the coming winter. "You've made a lovely home." Sally sat on the couch next to John. "When is the baby due?"

"Not until June. Sam and Sylvester are coming to dinner this evening, too."

"Yes, they told us," John said. "We entertained them with stories about our stressful ride out to your ranch house."

"I was so nervous, I was driving like a madman, afraid Penny would back out of the marriage at the last minute."

Those had been Sally's exact thoughts, but the couple seemed happy. At least in Michigan, Penny's family would be close at hand to welcome the new baby. "Babies can be a lot of work."

"Simon's going to hire a nurse to help me. I need to finish my degree."

"I'm opening a law office here in Ann Arbor, specializing in real-estate law."

When Sam and Sylvester Tedler arrived, Sally was surprised to see they brought Mary Jo along. "She needs to get away from her hotel room," Sylvester said. "I'm sure we can keep her safe enough to eat dinner." Sylvester was wearing his police uniform, but Sam was dressed casually. Sally could tell Mary Jo's sweater and slacks were worn more than once between cleanings. She would explain the necessities of life to Sylvester when they were alone. Protective custody should allow some basic amenities.

"I'm glad you came," Penny said graciously. "We're eating buffet style this evening, anyway."

"I made the chili," Simon said. "Penny says she married me because I love to cook."

"Fatherhood was probably more of the reason." Penny laughed in her old childish, unthinking way.

After hugging the expectant mother, Mary Jo sat on the couch next to Sally. "I miss Robert so much."

"Yes." Sally was surprised at a sudden rush of anger. She did not blame Mary Jo's marital problems for Robert's death. "If he could have stopped drinking." Sally reasoned with herself. "I believe he would have lived ten more years."

"I'm mad at him for not lasting long enough to see my baby." Penny turned to her husband. "I suppose I'm awful." Then she served the women bowls of chili, placing garlic bread on the low wicker table in front of them.

Simon marshaled the men into the kitchen to fill their own plates. Sam sat down in a chair across from Mary Jo and Sally. He kept his eyes on his full plate of chili. "I think we all feel angry at Robert for dying too soon."

Mary Jo kept her spoon in her chili. "I'm thankful you don't hold me responsible. If my stupid husband knew how to control his temper …."

"Do you think he killed his second wife?" John asked.

"Her sister, Harriet, certainly does." Mary Jo took a bite of the chili. "The children are beautiful. Their aunt renamed them. Susan is eight. She has dark thick hair. Her sister, Sarah, is six and a redhead. The boys are younger; Melvin is four and Martin just two."

"What does she tell them about their father?" Sam asked.

"Harriet told them he's dead, a soldier fallen in Iraq. They visit their mother's grave each Sunday."

"How did she die?" Sally asked.

"Supposedly a heart attack, at twenty-eight. The doctor told Harriett giving birth to four children in eight years might have been a factor."

"We'll find out the truth when we're down there," Sally said. "Robert mentioned you were helping them out financially."

"My mother left me a considerable amount of money. I guess they accept me as a kind of aunt."

Sylvester stood next to Mary Jo's chair. "Mr. Sites says your inheritance is probably a factor in your husband's hunt for you."

Mary Jo looked up at Sylvester. Sally watched Sylvester's heart melt under Mary Jo's unhappy gaze. Mary Jo's money was only one of the reasons Ricco would hate losing his attractive wife.

Sam noticed, too. "Sylvester, how long should we keep Mary Jo out?"

"I...I guess we should leave," Sylvester said.

Sam picked up their empty bowls and deposited them in the kitchen, before he went along with Mary Jo and Sylvester.

Simon said as part of his good-bye speech, "Maybe you should keep tabs on each other around such a lovely hostage."

Sally wondered if Penny noticed how much her new husband's discourse resembled Harvey Clemmons' mode of salacious speech. Robert's friends, Robert's words were constantly in the forefront of Sally's brain. She refrained from referencing them. Penny's hospitality and present happiness need not be disturbed.

* * *

Independence, Missouri
First Monday in October

October weather in Missouri did not resemble Michigan's. Instead of crisp air, colorful scenery, and sweeps of cold rain, Missouri's world was green, the grass, the leaves, even the breezes retained the warmth of summer. They found Harriett Cardoni's rural home outside of Independence, Missouri, with help from the rental car's GPS system. Weeping willows surrounded the small home's extensive lawns. In the front yard, four children of wicked Ricco played near a swinging bench, which Harriett nearly filled with her mammoth body.

"Don't get up." John called to the hefty woman, even though it was obviously not her intention.

"Mary Jo said we should introduce ourselves as her friends.

I'm Sally Bianco. This is my fiancée, John Nelson, and this is Officer Sam Tedler."

"I've taken copies of these papers to the county coroner." Sam handed Harriett a sheaf of legal documents.

Harriett re-positioned herself to the edge of the swing and holding onto the wooden braces, she hefted herself to a standing position. "Come into the house." She clutched the documents to her chest. "Susan, watch the children don't go near the road."

John and Sam followed Sally to the front door of the house. A thin stone acted as the front step of the entrance. Sam and John ducked their heads to cross the threshold. Sally was sure they could feel the ceiling brush the top of their heads.

"Come into the kitchen. I have coffee and biscuits. Do you boys want a slice of ham with your eggs?" Neither man turned down the Southern breakfast. Harriett's size didn't prevent her from eating right along with them.

"This strawberry jam must be homemade."

"It is, it is." Harriett beamed. "It's better than any store-bought I can find."

Sam was all smiles. "Usually when I accompany Sally and John on their detective missions, I only have time to chew on toothpicks. You're a great cook!"

"I try." Harriett was pleased; but she suddenly noticed something amiss on the front room carpet. She scurried faster than her bulk would predict to the side door and yelled, "Susan, who's been tracking mud into my front room?"

Susan arrived and pointed to her aunt's own shoes. "You usually take your shoes off."

Harriett laughed and kicked off her muddy shoes. Susan picked one slipper up and hit her aunt on the head with it. Harriett only laughed at the child's antics. So Sally, John and Sam joined in. After they calmed down and the triumphant Susan returned to the front yard, Harriett asked, "Is Mary Jo safe? She's not answering her cell phone."

Sam put his hand in front of his mouth, which was jammed with food. "My older brother is helping to protect her."

"Ricco was arrested for making false accusations and assaulting a friend of mine." Sally didn't expand on the statement. "But Judge Wilcox says we need more evidence to bring murder charges against him."

John took over. "Ricco is incarcerated now, but we want him out of the way permanently. We're also afraid he might send others to harm Mary Jo, which is why Sylvester and the local police are guarding her location. They're probably monitoring her cell phone calls."

"Will the children need to testify?" Harriett asked.

"No," John answered spontaneously, then he asked Sam. "Would they ask the children to face their father?"

"We'll do everything we can to prevent involving the children." Sally waved her hand to not accept any more servings of breakfast. "Mary Jo says the children think their father died in Iraq."

"I don't think they need to know what kind of male specimen

fathered them. With Mary Jo's help, we hope to see these babies educated and living normal, peaceful lives," Harriett said.

"With God's help," Sally said. She decided to stay with Harriett and the children, when Sam and John left for the judicial offices in Kansas City. She needed to take a break from her detective obligations and the company of Mary Jo's stepchildren promised to keep her pleasantly occupied.

Eight-year-old Susan's motherly duties for her sister and younger brothers were demanding precious hours of her childhood, as far as Sally was concerned. "How about we go shopping for school clothes?" She asked Susan and Aunt Harriett.

"Could we?" Susan asked, and then added, "Sarah needs some, too."

"We'll take Sarah tomorrow. You can help me find a shopping mall, if your aunt lets me drive her pick-up."

Susan looked at her aunt. "Would it be all right?"

Harriett embraced the youngster. "Of course, baby. You go ahead with Mrs. Bianco." She smiled at Sally. "She's going to need a new raincoat, with a hood, too."

* * *

When Sally and her young charge returned to Harriett's home, the back of the pick-up was filled with boxes. Sally saw no reason for Mary Jo to have all the fun providing what these young orphans obviously needed. John and Sam returned from the city empty-handed, just in time to haul in the booty. The noise level inside the house rose to near pandemonium as the children opened the packages of clothing and boxes of toys and candy. Sam was leaning against the front door or they might never have heard the knock. Mary Jo and Sylvester entered the melee.

Susan said it all. "Look, Aunt Mary Jo, it's Christmas in October!"

Mary Jo hugged the girl. "Mrs. Bianco has been shopping, I see."

"And a new TV!" Young Martin jumped up and down in front of his newly arrived aunt. Then he stopped and doubled up his little fists. "Where have you been?"

Sarah and Melvin came over to where Mary Jo stood, too. "Yeah?" they chorused.

"We've just come to see you for a little while." Mary Jo lifted chunky Martin into her arms. "Susan, Sarah, Martin, Melvin, say hello to this nice police officer?"

"I don't know." Melvin eyed Sylvester. "What's he doing here?"

"He's keeping your aunt very safe," Sam said, then he addressed his brother. "Any trouble in Michigan?"

"Judge Wilcox visited us last night." Sylvester explained. "Mary Jo started talking about how great you kids are and he sent her down to see you, until we need her in Michigan again."

Harriett took Sylvester's hat, shook his hand. "You didn't bring any trouble trailing you down here, did you?"

"No, ma'am. We flew to Canada, before we rented a car to drive down here."

"I bet you're hungry," Harriett said. "Kids let Mary Jo come eat a bite, then you can tell her your news."

All four children dropped whatever toy or article of new clothing they were holding and marched into the kitchen, testimony to their Aunt Harriett's cooking. Sally made their excuses and John and Sam left with her for their hotel room in Kansas City. Sally hugged Mary Jo at the door. "I'll be back out in the morning, if that's okay."

"I can tell you think these kids are great."

"I do. John and Sam can visit the coroner's office, while I'm out in the sunshine with these sparks of life."

"Robert taught us well, didn't he?"

"I guess he did." Sally agreed. Anything life-affirming would be worth Robert Koelz' attention. The cunning trap of alcohol didn't allow him adequate time on earth. Sally sent a plea to her Higher Power for those still suffering under its influence. "I'll miss the sound of his voice for the rest of my life."

"I still hear his words." Mary Jo pointed to her forehead. "In here."

"And here." Sally touched her heart. She prayed the Lord would receive the old reprobate with loving kindness. "He wasn't your most perfect saint." Sally prayed silently. "But we loved your handiwork. Robert will never be replaced, Lord. Keep him close to your heart until we join You." Sally remembered she needed to call her sponsor as soon as she got back to their hotel.

* * *

Hyatt, Kansas City
Sally's Room

"Missouri?" Grace asked. "Are you vacationing?"

"I'm helping a detective unearth evidence."

"Did you take your AA books with you?"

"I'll read you Step Three." Sally appreciated Grace's time, which felt as if her mother's attention was focused on her. "How old are you?"

"Twenty-nine. Why?"

"I was just thinking, I feel like I'm reporting to a parent."

"Is there a problem?"

"No! I'm thankful for your time. 'Step Three: Made a decision to turn our will and our lives over to the care of God as we understood Him.' I noticed on page 34, it says 'We can have faith, yet keep God out of our lives.' I think it's true."

"Have you found a meeting in Kansas City?"

"I've been watching four children, taking them shopping."

"Use the telephone book in your hotel. They'll pick you up for a meeting."

"I don't want to tell you I'll do something and not do it."

"Good. Do it."

"I'll call you in the morning."

"If you can't get a hold of me, keep dialing until you talk to someone. Traveling is very tricky for alcoholics."

Chapter Eleven

∽✠∾

Kansas City, Hyatt
First Wednesday in October

Two days later, Sally's only contact with an AA member was a conversation with a con-man who insisted on visiting her. Well conversant with AA traditions, Sally never gave him her location and repeatedly asked for the telephone number of a woman. Whoever was running the city's hotline needed to police the people answering their phones. When she failed to reach Grace Wednesday morning, she asked the concierge if he knew where an AA meeting was held. After her third call to three different people in the lobby, the manager showed up at her door. "Is there a problem?"

Sally wanted to explain how the room's refrigerator full of tempting liquor should be cleaned out, but her pride refused. "No, no trouble. Thank you."

Thursday her watch informed her five o'clock in the morning was time to rely on her own resources. She repeated the Serenity Prayer and picked up her AA book to remember how to best approach another Fourth Step confession. In Step Three she re-read, "No adult man or woman…should be in too much emotional dependence upon a parent."   or friend or mate. Sally knew her grief which included Robert and Danny could cause her to stop loving, or to stop living fully. Renewed with God's grace, she closed her book and faced the day.

* * *

Napping in her hotel room after another long drive from Harriett's home, Sally felt completely exhausted by the four youngsters' antics. She loved being with the children but her sixty-five years announced themselves in every aching joint and tired muscle in her body. She thought she might have gained ten pounds from Harriett's cooking, too.

John called her hotel room. "We have the evidence. You sounded sleepy when you answered. Do you want to come down to the lobby? Sam's here, too."

"I'll be right down." Sally forgot to hang up the phone. She threw the handset on the bed as she strolled toward the door.

Rat poison was still traceable in the corpse of Ricco Cardoniè's second wife, Anna. John explained, "The coroner's report says the symptoms mimicked a heart attack. Ricco didn't ask for an autopsy, so his young wife was buried quickly without a fuss."

"Thankfully, he didn't think about cremation." Sam re-gathered the documents.

Sally felt relieved, energetic even. "Did they wire the results to Judge Wilcox?"

"We did and I called Andrew. Judge Wilcox recused himself from the case. Judge Kevin Lovejoy will be the presiding judge. I think Sam and I should fly back tonight. Would you mind going back with Mary Jo and Sylvester?"

"No, no. We need to proceed as quickly as we can. Mary Jo deserves her freedom from her creepy husband's threat."

* * *

Independence, Missouri

Sally thought Harriett would welcome the news, but, of course, the wound was re-opened.

"He did it," was all Sally needed to say.

"Take the children outside." Harriett turned her face to the wall in the kitchen.

"Come along." Mary Jo directed the children. "We need to try out these kites while the sun is going down."

Sylvester tried unsuccessfully to herd the children into the living room. "The winds always pick up as they chase the sun."

"The winds chase the sun down?" Martin's bright eyes of wonder kept him nailed to the floor in the kitchen.

Susan hefted him onto her young hip, "Would Aunt Mary Jo's friend lie to you?"

Melvin held the outside door of the living room open for Sarah's exit to the front lawn. "He's telling a story, Martin. Stories don't need to be true."

When all was quiet in the house, Sally touched Harriett's shoulder. "Sit a moment, Harriett."

"I knew he killed her." Harriett slumped into the nearest kitchen chair. "Anna was my maid-of-honor. Ricco always made eyes at her. When I divorced him for terrorizing me, she wouldn't believe how evil he was. He never hit me, just yelled at me when I didn't jump fast enough, or forgot to ask how high."

"I'm sure Anna learned her mistake quickly enough." Sally said, but needed to ask. "Why did she keep having his children?"

"I suspect some of them were the product of rapes." Harriett's face was wet with tears. "Hand me a dish towel."

Sally complied. "Did you try to talk to Anna after Ricco attacked her?"

"Yeah, but he could act like a repentant angel, whenever he had a mind to."

"She thought he loved her?"

"Worse," Harriett re-wiped tears away. "I'm sure she loved Ricco."

"How did you get custody of the children?" Sally asked.

"Ricco brought them over one day after the funeral with hardly any clothes, no toys." Harriett stood and went to the stove to stir a pot of savory soup. "I never saw him again. I don't remember him saying more than three words to me, not even, 'Take care of them.'"

"Did the state help?"

"No, but my church helps out when I ask."

"We need to put the children in your hands."

"No. Mary Jo has asked to adopt them. I know she loves them and she says I will always be at their side. They need a younger mother."

* * *

Airplane to Detroit
Second Friday in October

John and Sam had returned to Ann Arbor earlier than Sally. On their plane to Detroit, Sylvester sat between Sally and Mary Jo. Sally asked for the aisle seat for the same reason most elderly people do. Bladders do not appreciate pressure changes. Mary Jo snuggled into the window seat. Once they were airborne, canceling out the possibility Mary Jo might jump ship, Sylvester kissed her hand. "Will you marry me? I would love to have a ready-made family to work for."

Mary Jo looked across Sylvester's big chest to Sally. Sally shrugged her shoulders. Sylvester was a nice young man, but Mary Jo might want to sample single life.

Mary Jo whispered, "Sylvester, do you think you love me?"

"I know I do. And Mrs. Bianco will testify I would never lay a hand in anger on you, or the children."

Sally nodded. Her ready tongue could think of nothing to say. Where was wisdom when she needed her?

"I know you're a decent man. But, my divorce isn't final. You're willing to adopt Ricco's children?"

"You are a woman with foresight. You've gone through hell through no fault of your own. I see how those kids love you. I want to be around you the rest of my life." Sylvester's voice was rising with the panic of perceived rejection. "I'm surprised how I feel around those kids. I think I could make a difference in their lives. Love them; teach them how to live right." Sylvester took a breath.

"I accept," Mary Jo said. Sylvester broke down and cried, right there on the plane. Sally didn't think the boy possessed such a soft or generous heart. She patted Sylvester's big shoulder, as she watched the stewardess approach. Mary Jo was stroking Sylvester's hand, repeating in a soothing voice, "It's okay to cry. I love you. It's okay to cry."

The stewardess stopped at their row of seats. "Anything the matter here?"

Sylvester straightened up his emotions. "Sorry, no thank you. This lady just agreed to marry me."

"Oh." The flight attendant left them in peace. "Tears of joy."

"Call your mother," Sally said. "She'll want to know."

"I don't want you to think the story I'm going to tell you influenced me, Mary Jo; but I can't very well share it with Mother." Sylvester breathed deeply, as if he were submerging into a deep, black sea. "My sergeant told me a story which happened back in the seventies. This woman they rescued from her husband refused to prosecute. She was all beat up, bloodied from head to foot. Of course, back then the district attorney didn't proceed, because wife-abuse wasn't considered a crime against the state. Anyway, the woman, I think her name was Rose, insisted on going back to her horse farm. Apparently, the property was willed to her by her father. The very next night, she called 911."

Sally leaned over to see how Mary Jo was taking the news. Mary Jo was shaking her head in the negative mode, expecting the worse.

The Legitimate Way

Sylvester corrected the misinterpretation. "Rose didn't have a mark on her, but we called the ambulance to save her husband." Sally hooted. Sylvester shook his head at her. "Rose tied the guy to the bed by sewing the sheets to the mattress after he went to sleep…drunk and repentant, according to her. Then she got a baseball bat and beat the poor sucker."

"Did he die?" Mary Jo asked.

"No. She didn't hit him in the head. She didn't want to kill him. She wanted to make him suffer. But he went into shock. He was barely breathing. She broke both his legs, his arms, and three ribs."

"Mercy," Mary Jo said.

"Violence begets violence," Sylvester said.

"Amen." Sally remembered being kicked off the women's shelter volunteer list for advocating such behavior.

"She plea-bargained for imprisonment for the mentally ill."

Sally matched Sylvester's story. "When I worked for the shelter in Jackson, before they asked me to leave, they invited the district attorney to explain the movie about the woman in Marshall. Remember 'The Burning Bed,' the movie with Farrah Fawcett? The attorney mentioned a case which preceded the Marshall one and involved a husband in Jackson. Seems this degenerate guy found a crowbar to smash an eighty-year-old neighbor lady's legs for chatting with his wife. Then he went after his wife. Both women survived as paraplegics. The dumb judge sentenced the guy man with the words, "I hope the time in jail doesn't ruin your life."

"At least the state changed the law," Mary Jo said.

"Now if we could just change the men." Sylvester squirmed in his seat.

Sally thought, for the first time, Mary Jo made the right decision in accepting Sylvester's proposal. The children would benefit from gentle fathering and faithful mothering. Hopefully, any remembrance of their biological father's actions against their mother and their pets would be left to the realm of dwindling nightmares.

Her AA sponsor's third-step words from the morning's successful telephone call haunted Sally. Was she "a far cry from permanent sobriety and a contented, useful life?"

Were her plans of starting a detective agency with John and Sam part of the Lord's will for her? In a world of real inequalities, could she help balance the scales? Would John want to stick around Ann Arbor long enough to establish the business? Maybe they would eventually drive back to Illinois for his dog Ginger and an engagement bash. The next few days would be filled with Ricco's trial for murdering Anna. Time enough to delve into John's idea of their future together.

John might not be surprised. He knew she enjoyed searching for the truth. What sorts of cases should they work on? Most people were not as lucky as Robert Koelz in attracting a host of dedicated friends. Helping Robert clear his name would have felt more satisfying if Robert was alive to enjoy it. John's cool logic and her intuitional bent could add significantly to the Tedler Brothers agency.

She would give all the love she was capable of to John, who

saw her through the difficult time of losing her best friend. Great men seldom pass by in life and she knew Robert would approve of John.

* * *

Washtenaw County Court House, Ann Arbor,
Fourth Monday in October

Jimmy Walker, the district attorney, asked the Tedler Brother's agency to investigate the backgrounds of the list of potential jurors. Sally was thankful she could follow the proceedings closely. Sam, John and she sat at the prosecutor's table with Jimmy. The thirty file folders stacked alphabetically on the table were the result of two weeks' worth of background checks. Andrew Sites and Judge Wilcox were also advisors to the DA.

The courtroom assigned for the trial was a small, rectangular paneled room. The prospective jurors were seated in the audience section. Judge Lovejoy's high bench with the witness docket attached was on the right side of the room. Windows behind the judge faced the empty tiered jury box. In the arrangement the judge did not face the lawyers' tables. The intimidating set up re-emphasized the power positions of the judge and the jury over the rights of the accused.

Ricco and his young attorney occupied the chairs behind the defense table.

As the prospective jurors' names were called, they proceeded one by one to the jury box where the lawyers took a crack at their eligibility as one of twelve citizens capable of fair and impartial discernment of Ricco's innocence or guilt.

The first, an older man dressed for a day at the office, but with an orange sweater instead of a suit coat, answered the prosecutor's question clearly enough. "No one in my family has had cause to be arrested." He hesitated and then added, "My brother's wife is a lawyer in Milwaukee."

Jimmy nodded his head. "Acceptable." The defense attorney agreed.

Judge Lovejoy excused an overweight, possibly pregnant young woman because she admitted, "My brother-in-law is serving time in Milan."

Thoughts of the imperfect genetic structure of a child with criminals in its lineage who was about to grace the world with its tainted soul worried Sally for a few moments. She prayed the mother's love would cancel out any other negative input. Then, the secretary of the city clerk's office was excused because most of the lawyers and judges recognized her.

Two widows were accepted, one a teacher, the other a nurse. They seemed kindly enough, but one never knew. Ricco smiled at both, which Sally hoped wouldn't hurt the case.

A skinny young man with spiked hair was required to stay, even after he said he was too busy to spend time sitting around. Judge Lovejoy seemed irked when the youngster couldn't come up with an employer's name. "I'm in a band." The child started to pick his nose, but rubbed his eyes instead.

"Not for now," Judge Lovejoy said. "And don't think about not showing up. The law allows me to summon you legally, with penalties of jail time."

"Yes, sir," the chagrined lad replied.

Sally nudged Andrew and raised her eyebrows. She thought Jimmy should ask him to be removed, but Andrew shook his head no. Some sort of lawyer-politeness code demanded the judges' decision not be debated in jury selection.

The remaining eight jurors, five men and three women, were seated after the time-consuming process, which included citizens disclosing their names, addresses, work places and other private information in front of a bevy of strangers and the accused. Sally worried about all the times when convicted felons were in the courtroom for re-offenses with their beefy friends taking down all the pertinent information for future retaliation. What about them? But, Sally could not come up with a better way to select jurors.

* * *

Washtenaw County Court House, Ann Arbor
First Monday in November

Robert's friends attended Ricco's trial to show their solidarity with Mary Jo's future. Harvey, Ed, and even Henry Schaefer made short appearances in the visitors' section. A nearly cheerful Penny and Simon Goldberg stayed for the entire trial. After Mary Jo's and Harriett's testimonies of Ricco's violence against them, Jimmy Walker presented Anna's poisoning evidence from the exhumation autopsy to the jury.

Ricco leaned close to his attorney to whisper instructions. The defense attorney asked if he could approach the bench.

After a short recess, the jury was dismissed and a plea bargain agreed to. Ricco would be imprisoned for life without parole. Sally was pleased because his children would never need to know their father was not killed defending his country in far off Iraq.

In the courthouse washroom, Sally found herself alone with Mary Jo. "Are we going to be invited to the wedding?"

"I think you're going to beat me to the altar." Mary Jo laughed. "I have to give up smoking."

"There is one thing I thing I figured out, but I'm not sure."

"What's that?"

"How the police found your blood in Robert's room."

"Easy answer." Mary Jo smiled. "I wasn't prepared for my time of month. All the tension involved in running away from Ricco caused my period to start a week early."

"Would we have been able to prove the difference between menstrual blood and blood from an injury?"

"See why you're born to be a detective?"

Maybe she was. The Lord surely would help. Before leaving the courthouse, Sally congratulated Jimmy Walker and restated her good-byes to Robert's friends.

John drove her home. "You're awfully quiet."

"One time, Danny and I traveled with a tour group to China. Whenever we assembled in a bus to move to the next airport or boat,

The Legitimate Way

I counted each of the fifteen members. We all did. Then we would tell the guide who was missing, who we needed to wait for. Usually the same people delayed us. Then once we arrived home in Detroit, Danny and I jumped on a bus to take us to the parking lot. I started looking for the other travelers to China in the crowds pushing to get on the bus. I realized, with a shock, I would probably never see them again. I feel the same way now, as if I will never lay eyes on Robert's friends again."

"Since we plan to work with the Tedler brothers, I don't think you need worry."

"Do you think Sylvester and Mary Jo can make a go of marriage with four orphans?"

"I'm more interested in our future. When should we pick out your engagement ring? Should I reserve a quiet corner in the Earl, find an empty ring box, and make you promise to marry me?"

"I don't like basement restaurants." Sally considered his profile. Her second husband? Danny's head of white hair faded in her memory. John's shiny pate would suit her just fine. "Why not today?"

At the intersection of Stadium and Pauline Avenues, John stopped at the red light. "Shall I turn right here?"

"Yes." Sally laughed. "Let's do it." John's smile lasted all the way to the jewelry store. Even after she picked out an emerald surrounded with diamonds, he was still smiling. So she tested the waters. "Are you sure we should pursue this detective business? What if the Tedlers don't attract any cases we're interested in?"

"Then we will rest on our laurels and explore married life together. Did you agree to a honeymoon in Rome?"

"We haven't even agreed on a church, have we?"

"What's wrong with St. Andrew's? We'll have a reason to invite all of Robert's friends to a shindig."

"Sold," she said content with their future together in Ann Arbor.

Section B

Chapter Twelve

Ann Arbor, Late November

Sally overestimated the general public's need for detective services. After Robert Koelz's defense, no new clients appeared waiting in the wings. When no one called the Tedler Brothers' office for more than spousal investigations, John suggested they should retire. Nevertheless after returning from a wonderful week's honeymoon in Florence, Sally asked young Sam Tedler to recommend courses to help them pass the tests for detective licenses.

She had deemed her marriage a success one Saturday morning when John wrapped his arms around her in bed and asked, "Who cares about the rain on such a sunny day."

John spent the first weekend after the honeymoon in Illinois packing up his clothes and reclaiming his dog, Ginger. After his return to Ann Arbor, he busied himself with a renovation project for the Huron River Yacht Club.

Sally rejoined the City Club to pursue her watercolors until someone needed a private detective. She met Donna Leonard, one of many artists at the City Club. Donna was the real thing, not a hobbyist. Donna's husband, David, was a typical scientist with his head continually in the clouds. His smile was genuine, but Sally was convinced if called upon to come up with her name, she might as well ask the Leonard dog to introduce her if they owned one.

David's boss in the Chemistry Department, Professor Paul St. Claire, was engaged to another City Club member, Zelda Cameron, who owned an art gallery in New York City. As Sally's friendship with the Leonards' grew, the idea of representing Donna's art as her agent was discussed. Donna needed to devote her time to painting as far as Zelda and Sally were concerned. So Sally arranged for local groups of artists to include Donna's work in shows, while Zelda tried to convince Donna to present her art in New York.

* * *

Third Thursday in November
Evening

Donna called Sally immediately, hoping she didn't sound too frantic. "The police called. David was involved in a fatal accident at the university." Donna couldn't control her hysteria enough for Sally to ask more questions. "Please come."

When John and Sally arrived, Donna opened the front door unable to stop talking. "Just this morning, I told myself it wasn't as if I cared about David." John guided her to the front room couch. "I found traces of his warmth as I straightened out our wedding circle quilt." Donna took Sally's hand and drew her down next to her on the couch. "I told myself he could pack up his stuff and move out anytime he felt like it."

Sally patted her hand. "You seem devoted to each other, as much as any artist and chemist can be, living in different worlds with dissimilar ways of communicating, logic versus a stream of consciousness."

Donna inhaled the steam from the hot cup of coffee John had provided, then whispered into the warm cup, "I thought he wouldn't leave."

Donna's mother told her as a little girl everyone with gray eyes appears sad to the rest of the world, even to themselves, so Donna accepted her tendency to melancholy. Sally brushed Donna's long hair away from her face and the wide green barrette came loose from its fastening. She normally wore her hair drawn back behind her ears. The unbecoming style was a practical way for an oil painter to keep her hair out of trouble.

"Was David being purposefully hateful?" John asked Donna.

"He treated me as if I were a piece of furniture, a thing not required to share his life." Donna gave a short angry sob. "Now, now, he's gone?"

John sat on the couch opposite the one Donna and Sally shared. He spread out his hands palms up, indicating he possessed no answers. He was not a close friend to David, but Donna knew he cared for her. Sally drew John's attention to the dining room table which was set for the Leonards' evening meal.

When a policewoman and Officer Sam Tedler knocked on Donna's front door at seven p.m., Sally opened the door. When she saw the police under their black umbrellas, she turned around to tell Donna without actually opening the storm door. "Mrs. Leonard, there was an accident," the lady cop called. "May we come in?"

Donna nodded, but could not summon the strength to get up from the couch. Sally waved for the cops to come in. Sam opened the door. The policewoman folded her umbrella. She leaned the wet thing outside against the narrow side window before coming in. Sally followed them into the front room, where Sam and his cohort took seats on each side of Donna.

"We're sorry to bring you sad news." Sam coughed to keep his voice from cracking. "Your husband sustained fatal injuries."

Donna kept her head lowered. "How?" She didn't really want to know, but hoped Sally did.

"I'm Sergeant Cramer," the lady-cop said. "Professor Leonard fell down a flight of stairs in the Chemistry building."

"David always holds onto the railings." Donna raised her head to look steadily at John as if he would agree. She kept her eyes open wide; if she blinked, the tears threatened to spill down her face.

"Is there anyone we can call for you?" Sergeant Cramer asked.

Donna noticed Sally seemed surprised to hear her reply. "Our funerals are arranged." Her voice sounded odd, detached even to herself. "Let me get my purse." She swayed as if she were dizzy when she stood up. Nevertheless, she asked Sergeant Cramer, "Where is he?"

"We'll take you unless your friends want to." Sergeant Cramer pointed to Sam, who was blocking Donna's exit to the upstairs.

"Officer Sam Tedler will drive you to the hospital."

"No. Not necessary," Donna said. "I have to call his sons. What room is my husband in?"

Sergeant Cramer said matter-of-factly. "Ask for the morgue at the emergency room desk."

Donna's legs dissolved. She slumped to the floor. "His sons' numbers are in the book by the phone." She straightened her skirt over her awkwardly placed knees. "Joseph and Norman Leonard."

John tried to assist her to her feet. "Let me help you to the couch."

However, tall Sam Tedler simply picked Donna up as if she were a rag doll and deposited her back down on the front room couch. "Would you like a glass of water?" Sam asked, apologizing for his physical familiarity.

"Diet Coke, please," Donna answered on automatic. "In the refrigerator."

"Your brother?" Sally suggested. "Do you need to call your brother, too?"

"Will he get here before your son?" Sam sounded hopeful.

Donna was sorry to disappoint him. "No, Norman's my husband's youngest son. My brother lives in Milwaukee, Appleton really. He's a trust lawyer and will know what to do."

Sally called Norman to come over to the house. The officers on duty were babysitting Donna as a widow until the family could take over. Sergeant Cramer displayed a fine case of dandruff on the shoulders of her blue uniform, while Officer Sam Tedler, Sally's friend, seemed too big for the room and definitely too handsome for widow duty.

Donna played with her wedding ring, wondering if she would be expected to take it off. How long should widows wear the symbol of the spoiled promise of forever? "You all can go along now. Norman will be here soon." She tried to smile, but her lips did not pass her teeth. "Surely, more pressing matters should be occupying your time, officers." Her voice raised an octave, almost into a fishwife's whine. "Don't you have drug addicts to chase around?"

No one moved. They all watched Donna sip the Diet Coke provided by Sam, of blue eyes and blond hair like David's.

The Coke's wetness released Donna's tongue from the roof of her mouth, but she could not taste the liquid. She realized her brain was shutting down to absorb the shock. The skin on her arms and back hurt too, as if the spirit within her desired flight.

She looked around the room, searching for something less painful to concentrate on. She evaluated the decorating scheme from these strangers' viewpoints. Primary colors dominated. The half-wall between the dining room and the sunken front room was a dark but bright green. The front room and ceilings throughout the condo were painted a pale blue, much like Sally's. The carpeting downstairs was a deep red. She designed the central rug in the front room to match two couches of red, green, blue and yellow. Usually, the colors cheered her, but not today. Donna patted Sergeant Cramer's lower arm. "You know, I'll need to get acquainted with being alone, eventually."

Sam jumped up immediately, but Sergeant Cramer frowned, and he sat back down next to John.

"There will be an inquest," Sergeant Cramer informed them.

"Why is that?" Sally asked.

A fresh terror began to seep into Donna's brain. She could trace its cold path by the throbbing pain in her temples. She closed her eyes.

"A friend was with him," Sam said.

"Male?" Donna blushed, embarrassed for asking. She tightened the grip on her closed eyelids.

"A fellow professor," Sergeant Cramer added quickly. "Harry Terkle."

Donna opened her eyes and shook her head. "Professor Terkle is a small guy, not big enough to catch David." But she didn't want to think about David's accident. "One time," she said, "David caught a professor who fell down the steps in the Physics building." Everyone was staring at her, so she added, "In West Hall. Back then the building was called West Engineering."

"There's a water tank to test out submarines in the basement." Sam added to the non-sequitur.

"Really?" John said.

Donna could tell they thought she was babbling. "The other professor was old, rather frail really. David is a big man. Harry could not have helped."

"He broke several bones," Sergeant Cramer said.

"Which bones did Harry break?" Donna asked, completely

confused by the ambiguous pronoun.

"Not Harry," Sam said. "Your husband."

"Professor Terkle did break four fingers of his right hand." Sergeant Cramer added.

"He may have struck her husband." Sam stood, sounding appropriately outraged.

"He claims," Sergeant Cramer corrected, "his hand was holding onto your husband's belt."

Whirling contradictory pictures swirled in Donna's brain. "Tell me again, did my husband sustain broken bones?"

"Yes," Sergeant Cramer said. "His right femur and ankle were both shattered."

"And his neck," Sam added, stopping any further details at the sound of Donna's sharp intake of breath.

The doorbell rang and Sally commented, "Saved by the bell."

Sergeant Cramer stood up and tugged at Sam's sleeve. Donna thought a dressing down was going to occur shortly, as soon as this woman superior officer could get Sam out of earshot. She imagined some guidebook covered visiting wives with gifts of widowhood.

Norman, David's youngest son, came in and sat down next to Donna. "I called Joseph. We need to tell him when to fly in for the memorial services."

She looked diligently at David's. Not many, if any, of his features resembled David's. Joseph possessed David's light coloring, but he was a head shorter, as was Norman. Donna excused herself and called her brother, Steve. "David's fallen," she said. "I'm afraid it was fatal. I'll call the undertaker. We decided to be cremated. Am I forgetting anything?" The phone dropped out of her hand. She looked at the useless thing lying on the carpet as if it were a bug too big to step on. Sally picked up the phone and further explained the situation to Steve.

* * *

"Tell Donna, I'll come down tomorrow morning and help with the arrangements," Steve said. "I'm so sorry. He was the love of her life." Steve kept talking, but Sally did not pay attention. Her thoughts went off track. The love of Donna's life. But was Donna the love of David's life.

Norman took the phone from Sally's hand. "Yes," Norman said. "Everyone is pretty upset." Norman turned toward Donna for a moment. "Do you need a doctor?"

Donna shook her head. "I've never taken drugs and I'm not going to start now. Tell him there's going to be an inquest." She looked like she felt a strong urge to vomit and rushed to the guest bathroom at the front entrance.

After a decent interval, Norman knocked on the door. "Steve wants to know why there will be an inquest."

"How the hell should I know?" Donna answered between heaving up breakfast and lunch.

After Norman and the police exited, Sally fixated on the dining room table again, which was set for dinner.

Donna followed Sally's gaze to the table. "This morning David prepared breakfast, as he has every morning for the last sixteen years. I heard him opening the refrigerator door to bring the milk and juice to the table. Sometimes his compulsive behavior drives me crazy; but when things get tough, like this morning, I appreciate his slightly nutty traits."

Sally thought it best to let Donna rant on about the last time she saw her husband alive, before asking pertinent questions about the accident. Sally vividly remembered being catatonic, unable to move away from the window above her kitchen sink. Locked in unmoving time, she imagined her late husband, Danny, was taking the garbage out and would return in a minute. But he was gone, seven years ago.

John reclaimed Donna's coffee cup.

Donna looked up at him. "I have been racking my brain to see if I said anything particularly mean last night. I turned away from him, when I told him to stop dating other women when I was busy."

"David would never …" John began, but Sally gave him a look to keep silent.

"The crazy woman next door waylays David every time he leaves the house. She usually claims her cat is lost, but I know she's referring to a more delicate need. I wish I'd been able to summon the courage necessary, at the time, to judge David's facial response. Instead, I escaped to my safe-haven in the studio."

Sally almost asked to see if a new painting resulted from the turmoil, but she restrained her curiosity.

Donna droned on. "The morning light caught the edge of my breakfast spoon as I lifted it half mast, expecting his routine question. He always asks me what I dreamt. But David didn't look at me, just started filling his dish with bran and milk. I waited for him to lift his head, before I told him I dreamt I was screaming again, locked in cement. He called it a nightmare, but without a sympathizing tone. So, I asked him what he would like for dinner to placate his side of the table. He asked me if I needed anything to make a chicken pot pie."

She turned to Sally. "I hate to cook." Then she returned to her soliloquy, "I told him I'd cut up the roast chicken from Busch's." She looked at her twisted hands as if the effort to concentrate on David, alive, required shutting out the reality of Sally and John's troubling presence. "I wondered if he would miss me if he deserted the marriage for another woman. Of course, his behavior this morning denied any intention of packing up before he left for the office." Donna rushed on, as if afraid to face the present reality. "David asked me which book we should read as he opened his Old Testament." She took Sally's hand to explain. "David is teaching himself Yiddish. I compete by attempting to learn at least one word of Italian each day from my Italian Bible."

Sally asked, "Which verses did you read?"

"The twenty-third Psalm. I hoped he would understand the implication of my mood, at the time. Instead, we read Ecclesiastes. You know, dust in the wind?"

Sally realized nothing traumatic happened between the couple, other than a jealous accusation.

Donna sighed. "I wish he shared my quick temper, then he

might realize the remorse I felt. I always make up first. He is beautiful."

Sally admitted the dead man's vanishing hairline emphasized the noble slope of his forehead and nose. No wonder women threw themselves at him like daft hens in need of a rooster.

Donna lifted her chin.

Sally hoped Donna's innate stubbornness would help her adjust to her loss.

Donna droned on, "David took my hand and held it to his chest when he asked me, 'Where would I go? I love you.' I felt the deep bass of his words resonate through his chest to my hands. I do love him."

Sally knew the truth when she heard it. Donna loved David too much, beyond her own good sense.

Donna stood and invited them. "Come up and see the painting my anger produced this afternoon."

John followed Sally and Donna up the stairs. The fresh painting was still on the easel in the studio. With a background of fiery orange, graduating shades of red, purple and blue storm clouds burst upward across the surface of the canvas as if fisted clouds were unleashing their impotent energy. The black silhouette of a boat with a broken mast secured a small central place amidst storm-tossed waves. The sea spray atop the waves resembled sprinkles of blood.

"Geez," John muttered. "Wait till Zelda gets a load of this 'effort.' She'll think you're as crazy as Van Gogh."

John was right. The carnage depicted didn't compare with the normal style of Donna's still life studies, animal portraits or farm landscapes. "You've crossed some kind of artistic barrier." Sally patted the widow's back. "This is certainly not as tame as the rest of your work." As if to hide the evidence of her anger, Donna covered the canvas with a bath towel. "Are you ready to answer a few questions now, Donna?" Sally asked as gently as she could.

"Yes," Donna said. "Let's go down and drink some more of John's coffee."

They sat down at the festive supper table, which David had not been able to enjoy. John picked up the unused crockery and silverware, retiring them to the kitchen. He returned with three mugs of coffee. "Did David say anything unusual before he left this morning?"

Donna seemed about to doze off. She stood as if to keep herself awake.

Sally noticed the time, one o'clock in the morning.

"Come into the den." Donna got up from the table. "I'll try to remember."

"Maybe you should try to get some sleep," Sally said. "I could stay with you tonight."

"I won't be able to sleep," Donna said, nearly sleepwalking across the front room to David's den. "He didn't have much time this morning."

Sally told John to go home, "I'll stay the night. Okay?"

John hugged her good night. "I'll be back at eight. Ginger will need walking."

Sally kissed him longer than she usually did. Another good man suddenly gone, made John more precious to her.

Donna sat behind her husband's desk. She ran her fingernails over the glass top. "David said he wished there was a God on speaking terms with him."

"Why was that?"

"I don't know. I worried more about the oil from David's hand, which I would eventually need to clean off the glass top of the desk. I probably should just let him add to the grime on the antique desk and remove the glass protector. This morning he continued to stroke the glass. I noticed his face appeared melancholy. Maybe because his head was bowed. I asked him if he thought there was a genie in his desk."

"Can you remember what he said?"

Donna shook her head. "We started playing with St. Francis' prayer." Donna rubbed her eyes, like a child with both fists balled up. "David said, 'Confusion seeks truth.' I corrected him. The word was 'error' in St. Francis' prayer. 'Where there is error let me bring truth.'" According to Donna, David said, "Errors seek forgiveness."

"Wrong seeks the spirit of forgiveness. I did forgive David." Donna sat very still at her husband's desk. "But I did not want to forget. I felt something change deep inside me. The seed of hope for first place in David's affection was trampled into dust."

Sally knew David would not have noticed the change in Donna's mood. The truth was he did not pay close attention to his wife's emotional life. Few men did. Like the rest of womankind,

Donna needed to recognize her sole responsibility for her emotional landscape.

"If I asked him, for instance, what the priorities were in his life." Donna's sighing was becoming habitual. "David would surely answer research into the mysteries of chemistry came first. I know I was silly to be unhappy about the implied second place position in his affections." Donna gave a short embarrassed laugh. "I lugged my cup of coffee up and down the stairs this morning. I removed every picture of the two of us from the walls of the living room, bedroom, hallways, and my painting studio. I stacked them all on top of the photograph albums in David's closet. I didn't want to face any evidence of our affection. When David is physically at home, his mind seems in the possession of some other thought, some other direction, maybe not some other person."

David would not have missed the photographs, if he had been able to come home. Sally tried to explain to the widow. "David's constant claim of pharmaceutical research demanding all of his attention was probably truthful. His disconnect from his surroundings surely felt as if he purposefully wiped awareness of you from his inner road map. But David was just being himself, a scientist without many clues to emotions."

"At the time ...," Donna used the last tissue in the box on David's desk. "The rejection smelled of fear, fed my anger, and drained affection away from him. Now he will never return. I will miss him."

Sally ushered Donna upstairs to the bedroom, hoping for her to collapse at some point into the peaceful realm of sleep. However, Donna seemed to be just getting started on venting the problems she perceived with her late husband.

Prone on top of her wedding circle bedspread, Donna said, "If I used the brains God provided, I would have stopped insisting on the use of condoms. I wanted children. But I felt the victims of David's lack of attention would then include children in need of a father. Only my promise to myself, about never being the one to leave, kept me tethered and childless. Research did claim more than David's attention."

Sally tried to comfort her. "Vows do matter or else life is meaningless."

Chapter Thirteen

Third Friday in November

    Sally noticed Donna was still sleeping at ten o'clock the next morning. After consulting with John, Sally called Zelda Cameron and made a date for lunch at the City Club. John agreed Sally should encourage Donna to get out of the house. Did Zelda know all was not well at the Leonard household? Donna gave every indication she didn't consider her painting efforts worthy of as much attention as Sally and Zelda. Zelda and Sally agreed on little else. According to Donna, painting provided the therapy she needed to maintain her marital status. Focusing on the process of creating a tangible idea, with the additional concentration needed for clarity in rendering significant details, as well as the flow of hours, afforded Donna a sabbatical from negative fixations, the black holes in her life.

    Sally wasn't fond of Zelda, who usually attended the Chemistry Department's functions and gravitated toward the friendly clutch of Donna and Sally. Zelda was the significant other of Paul St. Claire, the research supervisor for David and his best friend, Harry Terkle. Sally was as sure of one thing as Donna was. Harry held no animosity against David. David was a living god as far as Harry was concerned.

    Sally once heard Harry comment to one of David's students.

"He's just an amazing teacher. Gifted."

* * *

Lunch time, City Club

Zelda knocked on Donna's door wearing the outfit she donned for every outing. Zelda did not lack funds for a varied wardrobe. A silver fox graced the collar of her favorite three-quarter length coat. An admirer's latest gift of an etched glass broach on her most dependable black sweater topped a long skirt ending with comfortable but expensive flat shoes. The only variation Zelda provided for the austere get-up was her extensive collection of Coach purses. To date, Sally counted 42. One of Zelda's better grooming traits, as far as Sally was concerned, was that she shunned the use of perfume.

Once they had assembled at the City Club, Sally chose a table facing the doorway. With her back to the wall, she hoped her interrogation of Zelda and Donna would entice fewer listeners.

Zelda placed purse, number 43, on the chair next to Donna. "I heard about David."

Donna bent her head and blushed. "Sally insisted I get away from the house."

"I thought the show Sally arranged for you at the hospital started today." Zelda flourished her coat onto the purse.

"It did!" Donna smacked her forehead. "Oh, well. Let's eat."

"I'll order for you." Zelda patted Donna's hand. "Sally, do you need to leave?"

"The show will manage without us." Sally wondered why Zelda was bent on getting rid of her. "The whole town knows about David's accident by now."

"Maybe the committee chose my work in the first place because of David's position at the university."

"Nonsense," Sally said immediately. She was surprised that Zelda did not follow her lead.

"So tell me," Zelda asked pointedly, changing the subject away from the safe area of art. "Why was Harry so angry with David?"

"Harry will be as upset about David's accident as I am."

"Why did you even ask?" Sally wanted to know. Everyone knew David was Harry's best friend. They worked on the same chemistry project and were always seen together.

"You haven't heard?" Zelda purposefully seemed to take a long time stirring cream into her tea. "The police arrested Harry for pushing David down the stairs."

"Nonsense." Sally wondered if she was repeating herself.

"I feel as if I've fallen down a rabbit hole." Donna loosened her barrette, draping her hair over her shoulder. She twisted the split-ends in a distracted manner. "I didn't know anything was wrong between them. David was increasingly distracted." Donna stifled a self-pitying sob. "He acted as if he learned a script for a play about marriage with no heart in the words."

"Mercy," Zelda said.

"When's the last time he went to the doctor?" Sally asked.

"Everything's fine there. I receive his medical reports. I even called Doctor Lorell to make sure he is okay."

Sally's heart went out to Donna. She was having trouble using the past tense in reference to David.

"He did seem pre-occupied, lately." Zelda added.

"Maybe they were both worried about the research results? I realize I seem to be more interested in my husband's reactions to me than to any of his other concerns."

"What about his sons?" Zelda probed.

"Could be. I try not to keep up on their latest disasters." Donna unfolded her napkin. "The one in Arizona, Joseph, is diabetic and Norman, the one living here, is immoral."

"A cause for David's pre-occupation?" Sally sought to defend the dead man.

Donna pushed the lettuce around her plate. "David gave his grandfather insulin shots when he was about nine."

"Did you ask him about his sons?" Zelda always said the obvious things most people try to avoid out of politeness.

"I should have. It was cowardly of me not to bring them up."

"Well, Norman is a problem for your relationship." Zelda offered.

"Only for me." Suddenly Donna blushed guiltily. "David thought everything was fine. I treat Norman okay, don't I?"

"Probably." Zelda laughed. "You don't have the balls to mistreat anyone."

Donna tried to avoid a smile. Sally knew Donna would not

want to jeopardize her marriage by laying down laws for her youngest stepson, who was seven years older than Donna. Sally did have a few opinions of her own on the subject- like not continuing a love affair with a married woman. Norman was 42 and entirely screwed up, living with his mother with no life of his own, no job, no retirement plan, no medical benefits, except his father's wallet. David avoided even speaking Norman's name, but Sally knew the couple went to movies with David's pudgy son twice a week. Being around the sulking young man was surely irritating.

"Norman's latest mantra is that nothing matters anyway." Donna then tried to switch Zelda's attention to a less painful subject. "I need a black dress for the funeral. Could we go shopping?"

"You have not finished your salad." Zelda scolded. "You're wasting good money."

"Spending David's money always cheers me up." Donna paid her bill with a fifty, telling the waiter to keep the change.

"Resentment's roll of money." Zelda picked up her 43rd purse.

"I brought my credit card wallet with all the department store cards." Donna said as they walked to Zelda's white Lincoln.

"Don't you always carry them?" Zelda patted her Coach bag.

"I keep them in a separate wallet in my desk. I only use them for mad-hatter trips. I keep buying until I'm through being angry with David. Normally I only carry one big-limit card."

"This could take several days." Zelda laughed. "I buy a new Coach purse every time I make love."

"To celebrate?" Sally asked. "Or, because you're angry?"

"I always thought I spent money to congratulate myself." Zelda looked down at her latest purse. "But, I guess you could be right. I could be getting even."

"With whom?" Sally kidded, not expecting an answer.

"I guess I'm sticking it to myself." Zelda sighed. "I'm the one laying down the hundred dollar bills."

After trying on a host of outfits at Macy's, Donna's mood lightened. Sally knocked and opened Zelda's changing room door to find out if she could retrace the close-packed aisles of clothing. "When did you plan to leave?"

Zelda hastily pulled the collar of a new sweater around her throat. "Oh, another half-hour." Her nervous laughter added a bit of tension.

Sally saw the bruise. "Are you hiding a hickey?" Sally's laughter nearly matched Zelda's.

"It's nothing." Zelda was actually blushing.

"Well, I'm off for another gathering run," Donna said. "Should I look for anything for you two?"

"A blue scarf," Sally said, "if you pass one."

'Misery does love company,' came to Sally's mind as she loaded down her arms with a plethora of silk blouses in rainbows of color. Overspending was cut from the same cloth as other symptoms of moral decay, like drunkenness. She asked her Higher Power for help in removing this obvious defect of character. Wantonness with money was surely as immoral as other crimes against natural instincts. Watching Donna pay for her purchases with a credit card,

Sally recalled the scripture verse, "Vengeance is mine, saith the Lord." Her daily prayers asked to be delivered from evil. Perhaps the only evil was retribution.

* * *

Stucchi's Ice Cream Parlor

The three women decided ice cream at Stucchi's was required before they could think about going home. Even though Zelda made sure she spent not one slim dime on the trip, the trunk of her Lincoln was filled to capacity. Most of the bags, four in fact, were Donna's purchases.

"Last week, when I took Donna home after shopping," Zelda said. "I wondered if she considered leaving her shopping bags in my trunk."

"In for a penny, in for a pound." Donna said bravely.

"That's exactly what you said. Once inside, I insisted David approve each of your purchases. I didn't intend to leave you in any jeopardy from the spending spree I was a party to."

"David is not capable of even thinking about scolding me. I named people I intended to give most of the articles. One birthday and Christmas is just around the calendar's corner."

Zelda said. "I'll remember the ploy for future dealings with St. Claire. Boring old David displayed no adverse reactions to the loss of his money. I even asked him, 'Do you always let your wife get away with murdering your budget?' But David was not in the least distressed."

Donna mimicked John Wayne's spaced mode of comment. "Well you did try to change harmony into discord." Sally laughed at Donna's antics and Donna smiled. "We have a spending agreement similar to Clinton's policy about gays in the military. David put his arm around me, lifted my hair, and kissed the back of my neck."

"What's the policy?" Sally asked.

"Don't ask, don't tell."

Zelda chuckled and looked away, playing with finding her key in her Coach bag. She bought herself a new purse every time St. Claire touched her in anger. The only other time she felt his hands on her was when she was nude on her back in her own bed.

"But you didn't find a thing to buy." Donna noted.

"That's okay," Zelda said. "I do all my shopping in New York City. You should come with me next time. Scope out my gallery for your paintings."

"New York is so jammed with people." Donna complained. "I feel as if they're using up all the good oxygen."

"Ridiculous!" Zelda raised her voice. After taking Sally and Donna back to Sally's Mustang, Zelda pointed her Lincoln toward the condominium she called home. No good there she remembered, touching the bruise Sally spied as well as the one on the other side of her neck. St. Claire insisted physically she wasn't trying hard enough to become a confidant of Donna's.

"Use some of your New York chutzpa." St. Claire clamped his cold hands on her throat as he pushed her back through the connecting door of their apartments. "Find out about David's plans, now!"

Zelda could report nothing to St. Claire except David became more distracted before he died. He'd removed himself from Donna's world. St. Claire's demands were becoming increasingly difficult to meet. His dominance invaded more and more of her life. When she first met Paul St. Claire in Maui, she chased him with all the womanly and financial ploys at her disposal. His intelligence and academic charm hid his insecurities and anger at the world. Ten years later, and a half-a-million spent out of her daddy's Pan Am trust fund, Zelda felt as far away from claiming his affection as the first day she paid for his Kailua and Cream.

Why she continued to shop and prepare gourmet meals, clean his apartment, wash his clothes, pick up his cleaning, and shine his shoes was the real question. St. Claire promised to become a millionaire on his own without referring to the amounts she invested in their relationship. Any questioning on financial subjects was met with open hostility if not outright violence. It didn't matter, or it did, especially with her recent financial-market losses affecting her future security. She knew where she stood. She was St. Claire's punching bag for all the irritations he encountered in the world.

Time to call Dr. Quincy again. Her therapist would prescribe mood elevators to see her through this latest spell of St. Claire's exasperation with her. With no family to report to, Dr. Quincy was her only friend, rented at $200 an hour. So far, Dr. Quincy seemed interested in really helping her. He insisted she memorize the phone number of the Safe House for abused women. He salved her feelings by explaining the guilt of spending her father's unearned inheritance fed her low self-image. He promised to alleviate those guilt feelings.

However, Zelda didn't really feel any guilt, only confusion. St. Claire's claim on her seemed the only real element in her crazy life. The pills helped. They stayed the nagging voices about her ridiculous premise; she loved Professor Paul St. Claire. Surely, the man would return her love -- someday.

***

Third Saturday in November

Donna could not believe how much time passed when she focused on the studio's wall clock. 2:00 o'clock in the morning! She stretched her arms before realizing one hand still held a paint-laden brush. A glob of blue fell on a white farmhouse on the canvas. She dipped a ragged cloth into turpentine and lifted out the blue mistake. As if awakening from a long sleep, she regarded her finished work. Not a glamorous piece, but neatly done and pleasant enough. She wiped her brush of most of the paint and then immersed it into the crowded mason jar filled with brushes soaking in soap. She re-promised herself to clean the brushes.

When she turned off the four tall lamps facing her canvas, she saw sharp splinters of lightning outside. The thunder was low, continuous. David wouldn't be there when she slipped into bed. Donna ran her hand over his side of the bed. She asked him the night before, "Why are you not sleeping? Are you upset about something?"

"I'm not unhappy because you were painting," David said. "My research may not be going anywhere. I may have wasted ten years."

"That can't be." Donna said softly, close to his ear. "Didn't you tell me, negative results are worth the effort because other experimentalists can skip the false paths in their search for solutions?" She wound her leg across David's. "Have you wasted the fourteen years you spent with me?"

"You're a good wife, Donna. Very mature for a girl of nineteen, from the first day we married." David kissed her. "Roll over and let me rub your shoulders. I'm sure they're knotted up after working so late."

Even without her husband's massage, Donna drifted off into a perfect dream landscape of her canvas farmland. She smelled the golden straw, watched the wind move the heavy heads of oats into patterns not unlike the surf breaking onto a peaceful beach. She reached out her hand to feel the heat of the dream's summer day only to find David's side of the bed empty and cold. Donna tried to avoid thinking of the misery living without David would entail. He was her foundation, the steady plank in reason's sway. What happened?

A steady rain blew at the window.

Sleeping was not David's strong point. He rose at 5:00 o'clock every morning as if released from a Jack-in-the-Box. Sensing the house was too quiet, Donna rolled out of bed and flung her bathrobe over her shoulder as she ran down the stairs.

She was alone.

Sally stayed with Donna the entire first night of widowhood, but Friday night Donna refused. Her bedside digital read, "2:30 am." Sleep appeared part of Donna's lost world with David, a thing remembered but unknown now. She placed a call to Sally at 5:30 on Saturday morning. "When will they let Harry go home?"

"I'm sure he's at home," Sally said. "I left him a message, but it was too late for him to call back."

"I should let you go."

"It's all right. The police won't harm Harry."

"My brother, Steve, and his wife, will arrive this morning." Donna felt as if she were talking to her friend from a far off distance. "I feel as if I'm drugged."

"Well, you're not." Sally comforted her. "Sleeplessness must be your way of grieving. No one knows how they will deal with grief until it happens to them."

"But, I want to think. My mind keeps mulling over the last time David was here. When another person is in the house, I feel more sane. I'll make you a cup of coffee, if you and John will come over."

"We'll be right over. Your body hasn't absorbed the facts yet."

Donna cringed at her own unjust marital complaints aired with Zelda. Even David heard her censure before he died. Oblivion seemed a preferred option. "I wish we'd died together."

"No you don't. It's a healthy sign you don't want to feel the pain of grieving."

* * *

John and Sally were on their second cup of coffee before Donna made a supreme effort to form a normal question. "Have you been in the studio?"

Sally smiled as if she appreciated the exertion required to carry on a normal conversation. "Did you paint instead of sleeping last night?"

"You're going to get curiouser and curiouser, if you don't run up and look." Donna produced a weak smile.

Sally returned from the studio after only a moment's lapse. She clapped her hands in excitement. "Marvelous work, yards above the caliber of your regular paintings." Sally accepted a sweet roll from John. "Emotions do rule expression."

Donna tried to explain. "I dreamt I was in the peaceful painting. I wondered how it would feel to live on a farm. I was guilty about shopping with Zelda. In the past, I threw money around until I wasn't angry, which is not a very constructive option for grief. The terror of living alone without David surfaced somewhere between owning up to my spending addiction and planning my next shopping trip. Then I became paranoid. Do you think Zelda encouraged me to shop in order to share in my budget debauchery?" Donna placed her hand over her mouth.

She felt released from whatever spell kept her catatonic at the table. Perhaps the need to appear rational in front of Sally and John, while facing the gross reality of her husband's death kept her tethered. She stood and pushed her chair under the table. "I need to paint."

She couldn't vomit anymore, couldn't sleep and needed some activity to relieve the longing for David's return. She walked Sally and John to the door.

Upstairs, a fresh canvas stared back at her.

She spread black into all four corners, letting the forms create billowing folds of purple darkness. Halfway down Donna spread a yellow sea crashing into a granite-strewn coast. The heavens she painted white with one, then two trailing clouds of blue rain. In the foreground, she positioned one red and bleeding heart, folded over the edge of a rock like Dali's pocket watch. She added finishing blue tints to a black crow's feathers, who busied itself with the meat of the painting's heart.

* * *

Donna's phone rang.

"Has your brother arrived?" Sally asked. "It's past noon."

"No." Donna took the brush from her hand. "Not yet. I finished another painting."

"I'll be right over. John's busy at the yacht club hotel."

When Sally arrived and absorbed the new painting's message, she sat down on the floor of the studio, bowed her head and wept.

Donna squatted next to her and stroked the older woman's white hair. "Don't cry for me. I'll be all right." She helped a calmer Sally to her feet. "Time for lunch. Come and keep me company." She followed Sally down to the dining room. She felt as if a zombie claimed her soul during the long morning.

Zelda and Professor Paul St. Claire, David's advisor, were talking quietly at the dining room table when Sally and Donna entered. "Professor, is Harry home yet?"

"I'm not sure." Professor St. Clair rose and embraced her, kissing the air on both sides of her head. "I'm so sorry to hear about David's fall."

"Yes, but not from grace."

"What?" St. Claire asked.

"I apologize. I haven't slept much since the police told me what happened."

Sally prepared eggs and bacon for the group. Zelda helped by making a ton of toasted English muffins. "Zelda," Sally said. "Ask Donna if you can go up and see her latest paintings."

"No." Donna said before Zelda could think about it. "I better rest after lunch. Sorry, I'll show you the paintings very soon, but not now." Donna wasn't sure what she thought about her new paintings. She definitely did not want to deal with others knowing the state of her soul. If they compared the angry painting from the previous night with the peaceful farm and the grief-driven one, they might misjudge her. She was sure of one thing; she would never be fully restored after losing David.

At least Donna noticed her taste buds resurrected their heads long enough for her to enjoy the salty bacon. She spread a coating of honey on half of a muffin.

"Not too good for you." Professor St. Claire commented.

"Neither is losing a mate." Donna then apologized for the

second time. "Sorry. Not thinking clearly this morning."

"Understandable." Professor St. Claire said. Zelda and St. Claire exchanged a glance and then said their good-byes.

"How close is Zelda to Professor St. Claire?" Sally asked after they left.

Donna wondered if her suddenly single status helped her realize the nature of the couple's relationship. "Zelda watches every move St. Claire makes. I do know their condominiums are next door to each other."

"I'd want a connecting door." Sally almost giggled. Donna laughed, then covered her mouth, embarrassed by their levity. "Donna?" Sally scolded. "Give me a break here."

"Neither of them would have to haul their asses out into the rain to go home."

"See." Sally smiled. "Doesn't that feel better?"

"Humor is a savior of mankind."

"One of them." Sally agreed.

Then they heard the front doorbell. "That must be Steve." Instead, Donna escorted John into the dining room. "Have you had lunch? We might be out of eggs."

"Plenty of eggs." Sally got busy with the frying pan. "I do need to review the case with John."

"The case?" Donna asked.

"You don't think Harry could harm David, do you?" Sally only knew the short professor by sight. "I've not said more than two words to the man, but he doesn't seem to own a mean bone in his body."

"I know he didn't harm David," Donna said. "I wish I could talk to him to hear how the accident happened."

John rubbed his baldness as if friction on the outside would make his brain come up with something significant. "Maybe Professor Terkle did try to stop the fall."

"I wonder if we could talk to him." Sally asked.

"You might need somebody's permission," John said. "Does Harry live alone?"

Donna sat down to watch John eat. "Won't the university investigate the accident thoroughly? I can't imagine they'll be happy about a professor accused of murdering a colleague."

* * *

Last Saturday in November

Norman Leonard, David's son, resented his older brother for lording it over him.

"We're responsible for her now." Joseph telephoned the night after the accident from Arizona. "Proper." his brother called the necessity to visit Donna every day until the memorial service.

Norman wanted no part of polite, duty calls; but he agreed to stop by his father's house once a day until Joseph managed to arrive. Legally all his father's property was one-third his including, he supposed, the house Donna was presently living in. It would be pleasant to live somewhere away from his own mother's new husband, Chester Pierce. Even Chester surprised him by sending along solicitous messages for the young widow. If his mother owned the stamina not to break down in front of them, Norman felt inclined to shoulder the unpleasant task of visiting his stepmother.

Norman arrived after lunch, just in time to meet Donna's older brother, Steve Morgan, and sister-in-law, Kate. The house was filled with people. Donna didn't need watching over.

"We're staying at the Campus Inn," Kate informed Sally.

Sally took Norman aside. "Did you know Professor Terkle?"

"Yes," Norman said, "He was always irritatingly kind."

Professor Terkle's maid, Henrietta, was Norman's lover. Norman's mother originally hired Henrietta when they were still able to afford a professorial standard of living. However, once Norman finished his Masters in Creative Writing and his father, David, stopped supporting them because of his young wife, Norman's mother let Henrietta go. Inconvenient it was now, with Henrietta being married and all, to find a time and place for a romantic rendezvous. Henrietta no longer expected Norman to rescue her from a life of drudgery. Admittedly, he never intended anything past his immediate needs. Professor Terkle knew the lay of the land, but he was too gentle to confront Norman about his affair. Now Terkle was under some suspicion about his father's accident, actually sitting in jail, a ridiculous situation. "I know Terkle too well to imagine a sliver of hostility anywhere in the man, especially against his professional partner in research."

"For as long as you need us." Steve finally let go of Donna's shoulders. "You look awful."

"Oh, thanks." Donna laughed at her brother.

Norman knew his frown showed his disapproval. Sally offered him an excuse for his stepmother. "She hasn't slept much."

"Hormone swings mimic grief." Steve directly addressed Norman.

However, Norman could feel his frown did not disappear. Embarrassed at his inability to control his face, he thought it best to leave. "Donna, call me if you need anything." He bolted for the door.

* * *

"Were they close?" Kate asked.

Donna rolled her eyes. "I'm sure Norman will miss David. He'll manage to enjoy his third of the inheritance. The boy has not experienced an eight-hour day of work in his life. Nor will he, now."

"How many years older than you, is Norman?" Kate asked.

"Seven." Donna said and added because she knew Kate really could care less. "I was nineteen and David was forty-seven. He would have been sixty-one this March."

"You're thirty-five?" Kate asked. "You look like you're in your twenties.

Steve ignored his wife's bad manners. "Even with an inquest pending, you will need a copy of the death certificate to start the inheritance process."

Donna watched Sally serve up eggs and bacon to her guests. Steve could easily arrange all the legal matters. Money would not be a problem in her future with a third of David's inheritance, an MIT annuity, as well as her mother's generous bequest. "Steve, the police are pretty mixed up about David's death. In fact, they're holding dear Harry in connection with the case."

Sally joined them at the table. Kate, was on the ball, taking over the kitchen's serving duties while Steve questioned Donna. "I met Harry," Steve turned to Sally, "at Donna's wedding."

"Do you know the charges against him?" Sally asked.

"They still have him in custody." John said.

Steve stood up. "Donna, wait here with Kate. I'll take Sally and John down and try to arrange bail."

Donna did not want to wait, but her body seemed logged down with the lack of sleep and heavy realities. She hugged Sally good-bye. "Steve will clear everything up for us." Somewhat amazed at the efficiencies of others in dealing with funeral matters, Donna appreciated everyone's help. When she hung up the phone from Norman's call, she watched the steady soft rain slide down the windows. Emotions drained her energies. David's body remained in the morgue. The autopsy was not completed, and his body was not released for cremation. She tried to examine the need to free David's remains. Partly, she felt violated. Constantly thinking about strangers gawking at the body of the man she knew intimately was driving her crazy. The scene grew into a horrendous obscenity in her mind. She tried to block out the thoughts but the reality needed to be accepted. The only man she allowed to touch her would no longer be able to caress her. She was alone, would be alone. Donna knew she would hate the future days, months, years, the entire rest of her life devoid of her sweet, absent-minded David.

***

Fourth Monday in November

    The third day after David's death, Joseph arrived and arranged the details for a memorial service on the main floor of the university's art museum. Everyone knew David loved to attend string quartets in the marble concert hall. The open space was encircled with a balcony crowded with sculptures of ages past. Without a casket as a focus point, Joseph convinced their mother a round table should be centered in the room to display family pictures, travel mementoes, and research accolades.

    Joseph contacted David's colleagues, family and friends from California, Florida, New York, Minneapolis, Syracuse, Boston and Newark. Norman assumed the responsibility for booking the hotel rooms, rental cars and restaurants in Ann Arbor for the assembling friends. He received a call from Zelda Cameron, who told him his father's research supervisor, Professor St. Claire, would be willing to write the obituary. Thankfully, Donna waived approval and only asked for flowers to be sent to the house.

    "I love flowers," she said, as if the information was confidential. "I'm hoping their beauty will help me accept the fact, David is gone."

    Norman ground his teeth when he hung up the phone. "A lot of good that will do," he said into the mirror above his mother's entrance table.

    His father was off the mortal coil, gone. His brother would

leave within the week for Boston and his mother didn't need him. Norman stared at his double chin. Henrietta's appeal was declining, too. Donna Leonard, the 'widow' still owned her fantastic looks. Norman's prospects were not good for living the rest of his life, happily. He remembered Zelda's offer of help.

"Anything, anytime, Norman." Zelda's voice retained her New York accent. No warmth accompanied the words.

Norman knew he could call as soon as he figured out what to ask for.

* * *

Zelda returned to Donna's condominium on Saturday afternoon around four o'clock. She puttered about the house, straightening pillows, vacuuming David's den, changing beds, even doing the laundry. St. Claire made her mission quite clear with severe tugs of hair at the back of her neck. Any information or materials remotely tied to the pharmaceutical research were his. She was required to bring them to a storage garage off Liberty Avenue, as soon as humanly possible.

"Understand?" St. Claire asked, as he ground the rental key into her palm.

She understood. If she didn't produce something, their relationship would be over, or worse.

At Donna's, flowers in boxes, vases, baskets and wreaths were delivered every fifteen minutes; even though, the obituary request wouldn't hit the papers until the next morning edition. Rainbows of flower arrangements lined the entranceway, covered the dining room table, littered the coffee tables, even the steps upstairs.

"Where are they all coming from?" Donna asked. Bewildered, she instructed Zelda to help her take some of them upstairs to the master bedroom. "The smell of all these flowers is making me dizzy. But, they might help me sleep." Zelda wondered why Donna didn't just tell her to get out of her house. Instead, Donna pleaded. "Zelda, my sleep patterns are messed up. I do need a nap. Could I ask you to leave for a while?"

"Well," Zelda huffed, assuming an injured stance. "I was only trying to help a friend." She quickly recovered her decorum. "I'll bring you supper. Would Boston Market chicken be acceptable?"

"Terrific." Donna hugged Zelda good-bye at the front door. "I apologize for being short with you. I'm dead on my feet."

Zelda did mind how Donna quickly shut the door. Nevertheless, St. Claire would be happy. While dusting every corner, Zelda borrowed an extra house key, neatly labeled, from David's desk.

* * *

When Donna mouthed 'dead,' the word hit too close to home. She slid down the street door, cradling her knees while not bothering to stop the tears. David was as dead as he was going to be, even if his body was still being defiled. After the emotional storm passed, she wandered into David's den. She wished Zelda had not trespassed into his sanctum. Surely, David's spirit would come here to comfort her. The desk's middle drawer was pushed in crookedly. David treasured the old desk she found in a Chelsea antique shop. He carefully aligned the silly drawer each time to close it correctly.

The late November afternoon allowed darkness to fill the room. Donna turned on the desk lamp and sat down in David's high-backed chair and then remembered she needed to wipe away his fingerprints from the glass.

What was it David said? "Confusion seeks truth."

Was he thinking about his research then? Clearly, he was determined to find the truth. She bent down to survey the fingerprints on the desk. Smaller handprints mixed in with David's larger smudges. Zelda must have touched the desk when she pulled out the chair to vacuum. Nevertheless, she did not appreciate Zelda's helpful prints ruining the last traces of David's hand.

Norman appeared at the door.

Donna's concentration did not alert her to his entrance into the house. "Sorry. I didn't hear you knock."

"The door was not locked. I thought you might be sleeping and planned to write you a note."

"I think my sleeping ability died with your father." Donna cradled her head in her hands.

"Did you go through his desk yet?"

"What for?"

Norman laughed nervously. "To see if he kept any love letters from my mother he forgot to share with you."

Donna slumped in his father's chair. "Norman, go home. Why are you discrediting your father to me?"

"He didn't love you." Norman turned to leave. "He never

stopped loving my mother."

"Just a minute, young man." Donna's anger shook her voice. "Do not return to this house." Norman started to speak, but Donna held up her hand. "Do not speak to me and never cross this threshold. I know I will see you at the service. As hateful as you are, I appreciate the help you gave your brother in arranging the funeral. Nevertheless, do not come up to me in the art museum or I will strike you in public."

"Fine," Norman said as he stepped outside.

After Norman left, Donna called Sally. "Dear, do you know if Harry is home?"

"I'm sorry, I don't know. But what's happened? I can hear something in your voice."

"Norman told me David never loved me. He even hinted about a continuing affair with his mother." Donna tried to laugh. Instead, a strangled sob escaped.

"I'll be right over."

While Donna waited, she tried to regain a semblance of emotional calm. That stinker, Norman, never liked her from the first time he laid eyes on her. Norman was so jealous of his father it was a wonder his skin didn't turn green to show his true nature. The only reason she was friendly to the animal was because David loved his sons. Beyond reason, beyond good sense, David's fatherly love for both his sons was instinctual, as natural as his proclivity for research.

* * *

"Of course, you're angry." Sally commiserated with Donna over an aromatic, fresh cup of coffee, bagels and cream cheese.

Donna rousted herself to slice a white onion and a large tomato to accompany the evening's snack. "Distrust is such a seductive evil. I always told myself, I would ask David to leave if I didn't trust him."

"Rightly so." Sally broke the halved bagel into four equal pieces, but did not lift any to her mouth.

"Steve brought David's personal effects back from the morgue. He drove Kate home to Appleton, but they'll be here tomorrow for the memorial service."

Sally broke the bagel sections into smaller bites but seemed to forget why the pieces were in her hand.

Donna tried to focus. "Steve told me the judge refused to accept any bail."

"Unfortunately, Harry admitted he planned to attend the German conference next week. He made his reservation last month."

"They didn't believe he would return for the inquest?"

"As you say, distrust is a powerful agent."

"I can't conceive of a reason for the craziness happening around us."

Sally patted Donna's hand. "Your plate is full. You shouldn't have to worry about Professor Terkle's problems."

Donna swept her long hair off her shoulder and held the mass of sleek hair on top of her head for a moment. "Sally, will you answer a personal question?"

"Of course." Sally straightened the placemat in front of her. Donna noticed Sally was unable to eat, whereas Donna felt incredibly hungry as if she would never be satiated again. "What is it, Donna?" Sally asked, as if aware of the attention Donna was paying to the untouched food in the plate in front of her. "Would you like half of my bagel?"

"I don't feel like a widow."

"I don't think you know how widows feel. Everyone grieves differently. You are an especially unique person."

"I don't want to be without a man."

"Of course." Sally nodded knowingly. "You won't be."

"I mean." A sob interrupted Donna's speech. "I want David – but David's not coming home. Ever."

"It is too soon to worry about your physical future," Sally said as if some sort of commandment was left out of the ten. Donna broke down, heartbroken for herself, for her lost marital world with David. Sally at least understood. "You are a beautiful, loving person, Donna. You don't want to replace David with the first person to show up at your door."

"No," Donna said, not too convinced at the moment. "David could never be replaced."

"Certainly not," Sally said as if she'd heard the end of the matter.

Of course the void left by David loomed as large as before, unchanged even though Donna at least found a voice for one of her concerns. Her mind sought a diversion. "I need to go through

David's office at the university. Will you drive? I am not sure I'm a safe driver tonight. My mind veers off into hopeless directions. I have not slept. Zelda wouldn't leave."

"I'll drive. We could check Harry's email messages for him and cancel his talk at the conference." They unplugged the coffee pot but left the dishes and food on the table.

* * *

Donna was grateful not many people roamed the chemistry building halls Saturday evenings. She wanted to put off the onerous task of accepting condolences. One passing secretary, who Donna vaguely recognized, nodded when Donna unlocked David's door.

Sally closed the door. "Should I lock it?"

"Don't." Donna giggled from nervousness. "I've never been in here alone. Someone may need to talk to us. Here's David's key to Professor Terkle's office. Do you want to look around his office?"

"Thanks," Sally said and left.

Donna breathed deeply. David's masculine scent hung in the room. One of his old, ugly sweaters hung on a metal clothes tree. She lifted the gray scratchy thing from a hook and pressed her nose into its bulk. David's essence would soon dissipate. Could she remember everything about him forever? She placed the sweater on his desk and pulled the pins out of the pictures David kept on the bulletin board above his computer. She stacked the chemistry books outside his door and tacked a note above them saying, "Free for the taking."

David refused to believe he could not teach himself Chinese

long before she met him. So he had. Donna piled the numerous Chinese, Latin, Hebrew and Yiddish orphaned texts into separate corners of the office. Perhaps a library might adopt them. She filled a trash basket with exams from the year before, and then used the box they were stored in to pack David's sweater and pictures. Donna went next door to visit Sally in Harry's office. "Sally, may I borrow a wastebasket to throw David's articles away?"

"Oh bring them in here. Harry will know what to do with them." Sally was sitting at Harry's computer terminal. "I went downstairs to get the systems guy to open Harry's email. Should I call him for David's computer? He can probably help you send a closing message to David's correspondents."

After they finished the final task, Donna's wristwatch claimed two hours had passed. Was she ready to close David's door?

Sally carried one of the boxes filled with David's personal belongings.

A cop with a roll of yellow tape around his elbow strolled towards them. "Officer Sam Tedler," Donna introduced, "This is my art agent, Sally Bianco."

"We already know each other," Sam said. "Sally and John were at your house when Sergeant Cramer and I came over. But you'll have to excuse me. I'll need to look in those boxes before you remove any evidence."

"Nonsense." Donna said not breaking stride toward the exit.

"Ma'am?" Sam called.

Sally stopped and set her box on the floor. "Could you go

through them now? We need to get home for a late dinner."

While concentrating on the role of yellow 'caution' tape on his arm, Sam seemed to consider his options within the realm of police discretion. "Okay."

Donna felt like kicking the boxes or the handsome cop, but she restrained herself. All of this would be over, end soon. And then what? Life stretched out before her with unrelieved loneliness.

Sally chatted with the young officer. "Is your brother happy with Mary Jo in Missouri?"

Sam grinned as he continued unpacking each of the boxes. "She mothers him as much as the children. I think they were meant for each other." He leaned over to help Donna repack a box and they bumped heads as she stood up.

Donna laughed. "Police brutality," she cried, holding her hand over one eye.

Sam apologized and drew her hand away from her face. He gulped as he looked down into Donna's gray eyes. "Are you hurt?"

"No." Donna brushed him away from her. "Are we released from your custody?"

"Absolutely." Sam held both his hands in the air. "You're free to go." Donna laughed, giving Sam a teasing grin. They watched as Sam proceeded to tape an 'x' across both David and Harry's office doors.

Sally shook her head at the madness. "Let's get you home."

When Sally got behind the steering wheel of Donna's car, Donna said. "Your police friend is kind of cute."

"Nice unmarried man," Sally said, as if to set the record straight.

***

Saturday, very late Donna's house smelt of baked bread and chicken soup. Zelda was busying herself in the kitchen. "Who let you in?" Donna asked.

"You forgot to lock the door. Come and eat you two."

The soup was good, but Donna whispered to Sally, "I distinctly remember locking the door."

"When you mentioned Norman," Sally whispered back, "I watched you try the locked door."

"Zelda," Donna called sweetly, "bring a bowl for yourself."

Zelda overheard the comment about the lock. "I confess. I took David's key from his desk. I was so worried about you."

Donna held out her hand, palm up.

Zelda covered any embarrassment with chatter, as she turned over the key. "I evaluated your paintings after I started the soup. The farmland is charming, but the red shipwreck and the broken heart are saleable. After the memorial service, I want to take you to New York. Get your work set up in my gallery. Sally, give your protégé some good advice."

"Please don't go," Sally said, "until we get Harry Terkle cleared."

* * *

Third Sunday in November

In the early hours of Sunday, Donna faced another blank canvass. Sleep beckoned but she refused to enter the master bedroom. In the painting studio, her hands could not recall where she stored her favorite brush. She ventured into the hall; but avoided facing the beauty of all the flowers waiting for her in the bedroom. She stalled outside the open bedroom doorway. The white eyelet skirt of their bed picked up lighting from the hall. Donna took a step backward and returned to the studio, but the paint tubes remained unopened. Throughout the long morning, nothing, no fleeting idea, no hint of creativity called to her from the universal void. Her future stretched out before her as blank as the untouched canvas.

* * *

Sunday Memorial Service

Donna could not remember who drove her to the art museum. Sally and John were sitting on either side of her. She wondered if her own face was as immobile as Sally's stony expression. She touched Sally's hand and watched her try to smile.

Sally whispered. "Hang on, dear. This will be over soon."

Joseph and Norman escorted their mother and an older man to the seating area on the opposite side of the central table.

Donna avoided looking at the scattered photographs. Each one refreshed her memory. David's unsmiling face now lay where the hands and eyes of strangers could dissect his features, view his nakedness in the county morgue. She counted the release of her breath slowly, one, two, remember to inhale, slowly, unchanged, three, exhale, four. Soon, soon the world would end this meaningless charade of insincere attention.

Joseph made his way among the fairly cheerful mourners to Donna's side of the room. John gave Joseph his chair so he could sit down next to the widow. Joseph said, "I want to clear up a horrible impression Norman may have left with you."

Donna stared at him. He was not an evil person and David loved him, so she agreed to listen with a short nod.

"My mother told Norman he was wrong to bring her up during his visit. I think he's evil and mean. Dad never contacted my mother after she deserted him for Chester."

Donna understood Joseph wanted her to know David loved her, but she could not speak.

Sally leaned over Donna's lap and shook Joseph's hand. "Tell Norman Donna sends her condolences to your family." She looked at Donna before adding, "But Norman needn't come to the house to check on how she is handling her grief."

"I understand," Joseph said and withdrew.

Usually, Donna made an attempt to memorize the names of David's colleagues and their spouses. There wasn't much point now. She nodded to the sea of faces, responding as closely to the questions as possible.

One of the mourners asked if food was being served in another room. "I'm sorry. I don't believe David's sons arranged for food to be served. Thank you for coming."

Donna recognized a tall, zaftig dame from the synagogue, where she attended with David on high holy days. Her litany continued. "David spoke of you often," was repeated to more than one graduate student.

To all the faculty wives with husbands to go home to, she said, "Yes, we should spend more time together." Donna knew the invitations would not be forthcoming. She did not blame anyone. Who wanted to share precious time with an available, maybe even attractive female?

"David hadn't told me the story," Donna said to an ancient teacher of David's as well as "Thank you," to more than fifty unfamiliar persons. Also insincere thank you's to the gorgeous women whom David would be proud to see at any gathering on his behalf. Why was she thanking them, for acknowledging David disappeared from their world, from her bed? His cold body was broken, stretched out on an exposed table. Or worse, David's body might have been slid onto a metal slab and then pushed into a dark drawer.

Donna spread her hands on the lap of her black skirt. She was through with shaking the hands of people assembled because David was beyond her reach. Her wedding ring sparkled from the overhead lighting. "Sally," she whispered. "Should I not be wearing my wedding ring?"

"You wear David's ring until you decide the time has come to take it off." Sally covered Donna's ring hand with her own.

***

Third Sunday in November

Zelda Cameron was very busy Sunday morning before the memorial service. The rental truck was positioned in the alley behind Donna's condo. A row of picturesque trees hid the van from early morning occupants of the row of condominiums, who might have looked out their back windows. The temporary haulers sat quietly in the truck sipping coffee. Between the three of them, they finished the dozen donuts Zelda provided with an added explanation for the delay. "We need to wait until my friend leaves. The university doesn't want to disturb her."

But once the deed was done, the file cabinets and computer safely removed and the rental key for the storage unit handed over along with an extra fifty-dollar bill to the driver, Zelda decided to add a few touches to the staged robbery. She enjoyed throwing the books and papers around David's study. Inspired with energizing feelings of revenge, she removed several pieces of cloisonné along with a heavy brass horse. Zelda knew where to market the items in New York. Part of her investment in St. Claire was finally paying off.

***

Sunday Memorial Service

Arriving late to the service, Zelda thrust her mitt at Donna. "I'm late. Sorry."

Donna didn't shake Zelda's hand, didn't want to acknowledge

the woman she had taken into her confidence. Why did she decide to complain about David the day after he died? For fourteen years, not one negative word passed her lips about her husband's business or their lives. Not even to Sally, whom she trusted with her creative output. Donna looked directly into Zelda's eyes, wondering if the woman invited her to criticize David. She remembered Zelda's comments about overspending. Zelda nearly asked David to get angry about the stupid money she spent.

Sally shook Zelda's outstretched hand.

Without speaking, Donna focused on her wedding ring. Her hands seemed helpless, even useless. Then an expensive pair of black shoes in front of Donna's field of vision did not move on, so that the next person could greet her.

"I'm Sam Tedler," he repeated, when she looked up at him. "Remember me?"

"Tedler?" Donna asked the well-fitting suit.

"My name," Sam insisted. "I'm the police officer, you know." Donna cocked her head. From her seated position, the man, about her own age, appeared unusually tall. The gentleman formally bent at his waist, took her hand right out of her lap. "Sam," he insisted.

Donna suppressed a giggle. "Sam?"

Sally shoved her. "Do you remember Officer Tedler?"

"You were not at our wedding." Donna said, trying to remember. The expression on the man's face was all wrong. Too happy to be a mourner for David's soul. And way too much blond hair.

"I am an officer," Sam insisted.

"Are not." Donna was sure she would have remembered this man. Where was his uniform?

"I am." Sam didn't let go of her hand.

Donna noticed his tie was a subdued blue, reflecting in the blue of his eyes, nicely.

"Samuel," Sally intervened, "Could you continue this argument at the house? Donna needs to greet all the mourners. I'm sure you're welcome to come to the house."

"Count on it." Sam kissed the palm of Donna's hand.

When Donna finally moved her concentration away from the warmth in her hand, the new face of a secretary loomed before her. "Thank you for coming," she remembered to say. "Where did he go?" She whispered to Sally.

"You'll see him at the house. Get a grip. People will think you've lost your senses." Sally waved for Donna's brother, Steve. "Help. Could Donna leave now?"

Steve apologized. "I think there are a string of speakers."

"I think everything is catching up to me," Donna said. "I don't appear to be in the proper mood."

"There is no proper mood for these affairs." Sally defended her, waving the line of greeters away. "Donna's not feeling well."

Sam Tedler appeared next to Steve. "We should take her home," Sam said. "She looks ready to cave in."

Donna liked him. He was awfully sympathetic. She really was exhausted. She tried to stand to tell him how glad she was he attended David's service; but the room spun out of control. The canvas blurred and someone caught her in his strong arms.

"I'll go with them." Donna heard Sally say from very far away.

Chapter Fourteen

Third Sunday in November

Sam leaned against the doorframe of Donna's bedroom. The lovely widow awoke when Dr. Linda Lorell, stuck a needle in her arm.

"I can smell them." Donna meant the funeral flowers surrounding her.

The scents were overpowering, almost adding warmth to the air. Carnations, roses and lilies combined to perfume the room. The flowers covered every available surface. The wall spaces between the dressers and the bed were lined with more of the floral homage. Sam could only imagine the range of colors in the dimmed light. Donna's long hair darkened the pillow next to her, probably her husband's pillow. Sam felt an eerie sensation climb his spine when he imagined shadows intermingling with her black hair. They created a force threatening to pull Donna to David's side of the cosmos.

Sam asked the doctor, "Should we take these tributes away?"

"No." Sally Nelson was sitting on the bed holding Donna's hand. "Donna wants them all in here. Could you wait downstairs?"

"Don't," Donna called out, trying to rise, "don't let him leave me."

"Donna!" Sally shared the surprise Sam felt.

"I need to wait downstairs for the robbery squad, anyway." Sam let Sally Bianco bully him into the hall. He ignored his detective partner's unusual display of unfriendliness. Donna wanted him to stay. A tornado would find it difficult to move him from the house. He glanced back into the bedroom where a sweet-scented and temporary oblivion descended on Donna. Sam offered up his gratitude to the Lord for Donna friendship.

Donna's house needed to be secured to investigate the crime scene they witnessed when they brought her home. David's papers were strewn throughout the house, pillows were slashed, file cabinets silhouettes in the rug, and missing computer and media equipment told the old story. The memorial's announcement alerted robbers to clean out the place. Sam was surprised at the trashing of the house, usually thieves made better use of their time.

"Try not to disturb her," Dr. Lorell said. The doctor's professionalism negated her good looks. "I'm hoping the sedatives will let her sleep.

* * *

The room was dark when Donna stirred again. She wondered if days had passed. "How long have I been sleeping?"

"Only three hours," Sally answered. "Try to rest."

"Oh, I cannot lay here any longer with only gloomy thoughts to keep me company."

"If you're up to it, Sam Tedler is still here. He called for backup when we found the front door was standing open."

"Was anything taken?" Donna sat up carefully. She felt strong. "My paintings?"

"They are all safe. After you wash your face, we can go down and talk to Sam."

Before Donna closed the bathroom door she asked, "So, Sam is still here."

Sally sounded exasperated. "He won't leave."

Good, Donna thought. When she looked at herself in the mirror, she did not look guilty. She should be, according to Sally's tonal censure. But the truth was she was glad someone interested in her waited downstairs. True blood, she thought. "I've slipped over the line of sanity," she whispered to herself in the mirror.

Please, Lord, what was wrong with her? Widows did not plan to replace husbands two days after the death of their life-long mate. She wondered how long she should wait. Her father repeated a saying when her mother attacked a widower who re-married, too soon. He said a quick second marriage was almost a monument to the success of the first marriage. Donna was heartened by the adage, but still ashamed of her fixation on Sam. Remarriage was not the issue, if she wanted to be entirely honest. She named the fear of never sharing her sexual being with another man. She didn't want to resemble black swans who died twenty-four hours after their mate. She hoped Sally would forget about her momentary lapse of decorum. Grief demanded release in all sorts of directions.

Downstairs, Sam and John were sharing some joke. They stopped their laughter mid-syllable when they noticed Donna coming down the stairs. "Do I look that awful?" Donna ran her hand through her waist long hair.

"We're surprised to see you up." John took her arm, leading her into the front room as if she were a queen.

"Why are you still here?" she asked Sam.

* * *

Sam felt like a mute giant sent to protect a frail, porcelain princess. The scent of flowers lingered on Donna's breath, or the sedative sweetened her tongue. Her gray eyes enlarged as she tipped her head up to get a better picture of him.

"I requested he stay," John said. "Sam and I solved a murder case with Sally recently. John looked from Sam to Donna before adding, "We're part of his detective agency's team."

"Dead husband," Donna said, as if that needed clearing up.

Sam smiled at her. He could see why David was enthralled with her beauty. He already knew he cared for her, anyone would. What he could *not* understand was how to interpret the facts. Was David's fatal fall strange enough to arrest the man's best friend? Was this robbery way too specific, too much of a coincidence? He briefly examined his prejudices. The world of academe was not above serious intrigues, enough to make this attractive woman a widow. "Could you possibly tell me what is missing in this room?" Sam's pen stood at the ready over his notepad.

"David's cloisonné pieces on the bookshelves." Donna pointed to an empty pedestal near the patio doors. "And the bronze horse."

"David's den was ransacked," Sally told Donna.

Donna rose. Holding onto the back of the couch, she steadied herself then made her way into David's office, where books were strewn on top of papers practically covering the floor. "His computer," she stated the obvious, and then pointed to the indentations on the floor, "and two of his file cabinets. One held his computer discs."

Sally reached for John's arm. "Why did they want his research? I thought St. Claire told him the results were useless?"

"Paul St. Claire told you David's research failed?" Donna asked.

"No, Harry was there when St. Claire told David." Sally pushed Sam to the side so she could stand next to Donna.

"Sit down," Sam suggested. "See if anything is missing from his desk."

"I wouldn't know," Donna sat in David's desk chair. "I've never opened his desk."

John reached over her shoulder to pull out a drawer.

"Don't." Sam raised his voice. "We need to dust for fingerprints."

Donna looked at her hands. Sam noticed her wedding ring was still in place. "I did realign the drawer yesterday."

"Zelda," Sally said.

"Who?" Sam asked.

"Zelda Cameron was cleaning in here yesterday. Seems so long ago. I guess it was two days ago." Donna rubbed her forehead.

"Saturday, yesterday." Sally said. "She told us she took a key out of David's desk."

"She's been over-helping me cope," Donna explained to Sam.

"I met her," Sam said. "We were both late for the memorial service."

"Who would want to rob us?" Donna asked Sam.

"The obituary notice notifies thieves everyone will be out of the house. Of course, because of the upcoming inquest, the police department will look for evidence of more than a simple robbery."

Donna turned to Sally. "It seems to me Harry should be released. He certainly wasn't involved with this."

"Maybe your brother Steve could try again, for bail," Sally said.

"He should be here shortly," Donna said. "Sam, could you go with Steve. The police, you, arrested Harry because he was with David when he fell. You're holding him for no good reason."

"He hasn't been cleared." Sam wished he could return her husband's friend to her side.

* * *

Sally watched Donna focus on Sam as the four of them returned to the front room. He was taller than John, and his proportions were pleasing for a young man. Donna licked her lips. Sally sighed. This child bride certainly had not died with her husband. Sally chastised herself for judging Donna. Perhaps she viewed Sam as an object to paint. Sally finished pouring Sam a cup of coffee. He sat down next to Donna.

Donna asked him, "You know I'm an artist?"

"Yes," Sam shook his head to Sally's offer of a cookie. "We itemized your paintings after I arrived."

"I'm not upset about the thievery." Donna smiled at him. "I've already lost everything important to me."

Sally noticed John was frowning. Sam coughed, breaking away from the intimate exchange, as if embarrassed. "None. No paintings were stolen."

Sally wondered if she needed to speak to Sam about how vulnerable a widow might be. She felt somewhat divided on the issue. She wanted to comfort Donna, too; besides, Sam would be of help on the case. The three of them were a successful team previously.

When the phone rang, John answered. "Leonard residence." He motioned for Sam to take the phone. "Sergeant Cramer is on the line."

John returned to the couch moving close to Sally. He laid his arm in her lap. She held onto John's hand, but she couldn't control her tears. She wanted to apologize to Donna, but her emotions wouldn't let her speak. She felt so guilty to own so much love from a living husband, while wanting to deny Donna any contact with Sam.

Sam returned to Donna's side. "My boss wants me to file a report. They're too busy to send over a crime team."

* * *

Third Monday in November

Donna dipped her favorite brush into the mixture of blue-grey paint. If dreams were seeded by reality, she needed to re-examine her life as a married woman. In her nightmare Sunday night, an earthquake was survived by a brother and sister in their early teens.

In the midnight dream the boy, Sepal, two years older, was the same height as his twelve-year-old sister, Naia. Sepal let Naia's knees embrace him as he sat a step lower on the broken stairs outside their father's place of refuge with their uncles.

Seven men waved them away when the children tried to enter the heated, lit room. The glass windows of a bamboo porch were not broken, even though the house behind was now a heap of gray rubble. Dust covered the windows making the crowded scene appear in a removed, misty world. Brass cups steamed with freshly brewed tea and the circles of hookah smoke rose above the gathered hoary heads. Soft cold rain dripped down Naia's hair unto the boot tops of Sepal. He shivered closer to his sister's offered warmth.

Tang, just sixteen, agreed to marry Naia. Tang dug a cellar under the heated remnant of the porch. Naia's father agreed to the marriage of words, not ceremony. Naia was thankful to lie on the flat, dry blanket next to a travel poster of their country. In the torn advertisement, the mountains were pictured green with flowers dominating half the view, delicate in their soft pink hues. Outside the wind howled and a landslide frightened Tang at the moment of his ejaculation. His cry woke her brother.

Naia did not agree when Tang pulled her hand along the rocky paths to the refugee camps. She did not count the dollar bills Tang pocketed and closed her mind after he ripped the buttons off her blouse to show her budding chest to the giant strangers.

Tang bought a bed and three soft chairs and there was a table, tea and food. Naia awoke from her months of catatonic horror to hold out her hand for some of the money Tang was handing Sepal. "I want a pencil sharpener," Naia said. The boys laughed at her childishness.

* * *

Donna studied the empty paintbrush in her hand. Gold flecks added illumination to the canvas scene of a precariously positioned porch on the cliff of mountainous rubble. The amber was also reflected in the brass object in a young girl's palm outstretched in the foreground as well as the subtle tones of a cloud-dimmed sun, high above the shattered hills.

What price did she pay? Donna wondered. Did she sell any part of herself to David by accepting his marital fortune? Did she freely give her love to him? Or did she reluctantly share his bed; too lazy to demand a life afforded by her own hands? Guilt for the days of luxury with David, for not appreciating his generosity, his love, hung in the air.

Donna dropped the offending brush into the soap-filled jar of paintbrushes. "One problem at a time," Donna whispered to herself as she rolled back into bed, exhausted. The painting of her night's offering glistened in the north light of a fresh dawn.

She awoke late on Monday to the sound of pounding on her

front door. She looked down at the front step only to see her distraught friends, Sally and John Nelson, pacing up and down the sidewalk. Without donning a robe or brushing her hair and still in pajamas, Donna nearly ran down the stairwell to open the door. "What is it? Come in, come in."

"I'm all right." Sally withdrew from Donna's hug. "I'm not all right."

John added to the conversation. "The university sent Harry a telegram. They are rescinding his tenure."

"Can they do that? Steve was no help?"

"He recommended a good lawyer." Sally patted her white hair as if primping would save the day.

"Come up while I get dressed. You can critique last night's painting. I'll go to the police station with you."

"John, could you make us coffee?" Sally followed Donna back upstairs. "Please do not go to the police station. Did you know Sam is sitting in his car in front of your house?"

"He is not." Donna could not see his car from her bedroom window.

"He's parked in front of the garages."

Suddenly Donna could not decide what to put on. Sam was here? Again? "What does he want?" Donna stood in her underwear surveying the racks of clothes in her walk-in closet. Black, think black, she told herself. Instead, she chose a pink sweater over black jeans. Half in mourning.

"What inspired your depressing painting?" Sally watched

Donna brush out her long black hair.

"A nightmare. I can't even figure out what triggered the thing, unless it is guilt about not supporting myself while David was alive."

"What is in the little girl's hand?"

"A pencil sharpener." Donna laughed. "Isn't that a hoot? No one will be able to figure out the symbolism."

"What does it stand for?"

"Hope." Donna went down the stairs with Sally following. "Make us breakfast and I'll go out and drag Sam in here. Maybe he can give us ideas on how to get Harry out of jail."

"He's not a lawyer," John said.

Donna could not remember Sam saying anything about his work as a police officer. Did he talk to her when she was passed out? Donna intended to make Sam answer lots of questions. Outside, her first demand was, "What are you doing out here?"

* * *

Sam smiled and cocked his head as if he were going deaf. He stalled getting out of the car or rolling down the window, taking his time to appreciate the real beauty before him.

Donna pounded on his Cadillac's window. "Get out of there."

"Hi." He pushed the button for the automatic window to open, slowly.

"What are you doing here?"

"I'm keeping watch by night." As she stepped back from the car, he opened the door slowly.

"You idiot," Donna said as soon as he got free of the car. "Get in the house." She shoved the side of his arm. "Sally is making breakfast. You have a lot of answering to do. Are you sitting out here as part of your detective duties?"

She liked him, Sam could tell by the smile teasing the corners of her sedate, but sweet mouth. He didn't care if he played the clown for her; he wanted to cheer her, somehow.

At the table in front of eggs, waffles and fragrant, honey-cured bacon, Donna asked him again. "Who told you to camp outside?"

"Just myself." Sam played with a bite of waffle on his plate, hoping the questions would give him time to eat. "The police can't afford to stake out your house, even though they consider your husband's death suspicious after the house was robbed." He took a bite and rolled his eyes as a compliment to the chef. Sally poured second cups of coffee for all four of them. Sam stopped eating long enough to continue. "The police think the thieves didn't find what they were looking for."

* * *

Donna liked Sam's eyes. He seemed to appreciate her. "That's why they took both file cabinets."

"And I like you," Sam added.

"Well that's inappropriate!" John huffed.

"Why?" Sam asked.

"I don't know." Sally took Sam's plate away. "You don't go around telling widows you like them."

"She's beautiful." Sam defended himself. Donna patted Sam's hand and he quickly turned over his palm, grasping her smaller hand.

Sally stared at their entwined fingers.

"Well," John said, mildly outraged.

Donna withdrew her hand, but stared at it in her lap. How could a friendly touch set off so many nerve endings? "You'll have to go." Donna told Sam. Thinking about a future mate was all well and good, but getting this close to another man nearly sickened her. David had only been gone out of her life since Thursday!

"No, I don't." Sam walked into the front room and made himself comfortable on one of the couches. "I told the department I am on vacation."

"Not in my house," Donna said. John patted her back as they joined Sam in the front room.

Sam smiled at Sally and Donna. "Why don't you let me take you out to lunch before we visit Harry?"

"We do not have permission to see Harry." Sally sat on the couch facing Sam and Donna.

Sam changed the subject. "I saw the lights on in your studio all night.'

"I painted for a little while."

"Go ahead." Sally waved away Donna's implied question about the appropriateness of showing Sam one of her paintings. Sam followed Donna upstairs to her studio. All of Donna's latest paintings were in full view. The Red Sea and the Bleeding Heart were propped on the seat of a rescued church pew under the huge north window. The peaceful farmhouse scene stood against the south wall and her latest earthquake rendition sat uncovered on the easel.

"Moody aren't you?" Sam stretched out his hand as she passed him.

Donna could feel her hair sweep his fingertips. "That's a terrible thing to say to an artist."

"Sorry. You really show your emotions in your art." He took her hand. "I like your moodiness."

Donna tried to tug her hand away, but not too forcefully. "I guess widows are allowed some range of emotions."

"Certainly hope so. Is Zelda going to exhibit these in New York?"

Donna turned to the farmhouse scene. "She doesn't like this one."

"May I buy it?"

"You can't afford to buy the silly thing."

"I can buy every last one of your paintings, if you'd let me."

Donna laughed and listened for Sally's censure from way down in the front room. "Zelda seems to think those two could keep me in kippers for a year or two."

"I like kippers, toasted or grilled?"

"Fried." He liked kippers. Not many people even knew what they were.

"I'm partners with my brother in our detective agency." Sam continued to stare at the farmhouse painting. "We Tedlers keep every dime we make. Sally and John helped put a wife-murderer in prison last month. With our contacts in the police force, you'd think we could get Harry released."

"Why did you never marry, are you gay? Sorry. What a horrible thing to blurt out."

Sam patted her shoulder. "Never mind. I won't tell Sally on you." Donna laughed again waiting for an answer. Sam held her gaze. "I never found anyone I wanted to spend more than three hours with."

"Or make breakfast for?"

"Well, maybe a few times." It was Sam's turn to laugh and a right manly laugh it was.

Donna touched her face. "I'm a widow and my face hurts from smiling."

"We probably should get back to the front room or Sally and John will have more to worry about." He didn't need to explain.

The sexual arousal between them was palatable, if not pitiful. "I'm so sorry," Donna said, as if she made a pass at him.

"Nothing happened." Sam smiled at her as they returned downstairs.

At the bottom of the stairs, Sally stood with her arms akimbo. "Then why are you both blushing?"

"Me? From compliments about my work."

"I have Rosacea." Sam claimed.

"Likely story." John grumbled.

"He wants you two to stay on the case." Donna avoided looking at Sam and toughed out the rest of her speech. "He wants to help prove David died after an accidental fall."

Sally cocked her head in Sam's direction. "Sam seems pretty

surprised to hear about the direction for our investigation."

Sam cleared his throat. "If they won't let us visit Harry, let's find Harry's lawyer."

"Okay," Sally said. "But don't take advantage of Donna's grief."

Donna and Sam looked at each other. "I would never," Sam began.

And Donna interrupted with, "Not ever. He's an okay guy, Sally."

"Sorry," Sally said, clearing the last of the dishes off the dining-room table. "We would be glad for the company. Harry's lawyer looks about fifteen."

"Why hasn't the university provided a good lawyer?" Donna asked.

"They're not sure they want to defend him." John sounded resigned. "Alex Cornville is so scrawny his neck doesn't fill his collar."

"We'll take him out to a buffet," Sam said.

"Great idea." Donna touched Sally's cheek.

* * *

The lawyer met with them at 1:30 at Weber's. After introductions, they walked around the buffet tables where mountains of food tempted them. Alex was the least able to resist. However, Sam managed to devour a large amount of food, considering they just finished breakfast. Then Donna remembered Sally snatched Sam's plate away. The poor guy was as hungry as the underfed lawyer.

By a series of hurried swallows and faster shoveling of food into his face, Alex managed to answer all their questions about Harry's need for defense. "He will be indicted Tuesday morning."

Sally sighed and pushed a piece of a pecan waffle through the rivers of maple syrup on her plate. "Why would they even think Harry had anything to do with David's death?"

"He was the last person to see the victim alive." Alex explained.

"David," Sam and Donna said in unison.

"My husband's name was David." Donna did not feel unduly upset. She smiled at Sam, who had felt the same inclination to clarify the situation to Alex. She did not relish hearing David described as a victim. "Is there any way for you to obtain release of my husband's body from the morgue?" She noticed the nice thing about focusing on David was her guilt about wanting to know Sam completely disappeared. Sam let go of his fork and studied her. At least, Donna knew from the flood of feelings swimming through her veins, she was still alive for whatever the future brought.

* * *

Donna checked her watch when she got home. Where did she hear four o'clock on Sunday afternoons was when more people committed suicide or murder than at any other specific day or hour? But this was four o'clock on Monday. She was surrounded with friends. Sally, John and Sam seemed convinced someone was out to do harm, specifically to mess with David's home and perhaps his widow. None of her escorts were prepared to leave her to her own devices. She shut the door to David's study and started picking up the scattered books and papers. She could hear Sam, Sally and John walking around in the house. They tried not to intrude on her privacy. The three of them hung around all day, bringing in groceries, taking out the garbage, watering the funeral arrays in her bedroom. She heard them go upstairs. The heating vents groaned with their weight. She could not avoid listening each time someone turned on the water. She wasn't ready to relate to anyone, not even Sally and certainly not Sam. She tried to numb all her nerve endings, but the constant attendance of her friends and the handsome, out-of-uniform policeman denied relief.

Her wounds felt raw. Where was the point of entry and when would the pain end? A dryness filled her mouth as if the injury occurred from speaking. Her brain ached and her body screamed abhorrence to the enforced state of grief. The shock of David's death was wearing off and the pain of missing him for the long haul was settling in. David's chair behind his desk offered her some comfort. This was where he sat. His hands were on this glass, his thoughts in this room, once. Only days ago. Would she sleep when the house was devoid of sounds?

Painting, the working therapy, which saved her marriage while her husband was alive, might fail to relieve her grief. Would she ever lose herself in the creative act again? The white canvas and closed tubes of oil paint only stared at her. She needed a reprieve from her emotions. She opened David's door, smiled and nodded at her three attendants. "I need to clean my brushes."

John moved out of the way. Sam said he'd help. He followed her to her studio and then down into the basement where she methodically cleaned every one of the brushes stuffed in the jar of laundry soap. Apparently, Sam owned enough brains not to engage her in conversation. He sat on a folding chair next to the laundry table, silent but companionable.

Returning to the dining room, Donna asked for a cup of peach tea and cream. After the warm liquid hit her empty stomach, her favorite beverage seemed to sour her digestive track. She vomited as soon as she reached the guest bathroom.

In spite of Donna's indisposition, Sally insisted they attend an evening service at St. Andrew's. Sally must have invited Sam, because he joined them in the pew. David rarely attended with Donna. Christmas and Easter, if she asked, would find her Jewish husband by her side, reluctant as an unbeliever in a supreme being, but loyal to his Christian wife. She convinced him the congregation needed to know she was a married woman. Where was he now, when she really needed him? Donna sat down in the middle of the Gospel reading, distraught with grief. The group of friends took her home before communion.

"Sorry." Donna managed, as she shook Sam's hand good-bye. "I didn't sleep."

"I'll bring you Kentucky Fried for supper." Sam seemed concerned, but happy.

Sally intervened. "Sam, obviously Donna is not feeling well

enough to receive visitors."

"I need to protect her," Sam said, in an indignant manner.

Sally looked at Donna who felt at a loss to explain why Sam could not bring her supper. "Oh all right." Sally was exasperated beyond the scope of her usually impeccable manners.

Surprisingly, Donna felt a certain pleasure as Sally and John drove her home. Sam was coming. She should not be looking forward to seeing Sam. Stick to the truth she told herself, else how will you know how to protect yourself.

"Do you need to go home, Sally?" Donna asked.

"No problem. I can stay. If the police only knew how close David was with Harry they would not consider him capable of doing David any harm."

"They were closer than most men. David's mood altered when Harry was scheduled to spend an evening with us."

"I think they both were so tuned into their research the rest of the world seemed an intrusion," Sally said.

Donna remembered how the two of them, David and Harry, locked eyes from the moment they were together. They would stand in the entranceway not talking necessarily just looking at each other until usually David broke the spell. She wondered if it took that long for them to recognize each other, being the absent-minded professors they were; or, were they telepathic and sending research ideas back and forth. A real force of nature was present. Of course, she believed all humans were bi-sexual. A conscious decision was required for the choice in identity, even her own.

The funny thing was, as soon as Donna was in the house, she wanted to paint. Nine o'clock in the evening but her studio called out to her. "I'll just go upstairs, until Sam arrives with the chicken. Will that be okay?"

"Of course, Donna," John said, turning Sally toward him. Donna couldn't see Sally's reaction to being pushed around.

Sally called after Donna as she rushed upstairs, "Fine, dear. We'll wait."

The windowsill in the studio was a still life. And all those clean brushes were lined up ready for use. By the time Zelda interrupted her by pounding on the front door and laying on the doorbell, Donna sketched out the placement of a large blue vase and matching platter. Two small opaque green vases of dissimilar shapes and one crystal vase with three red roses were placed advantageously to permit the light to create a colorful interplay of their shadows on the white sill.

Sally and John stood at the foot of the stairs with Zelda. "Don't let me stop you," Zelda said, as she noted Donna's painting apron. "I'll come up and keep you company."

Without a word, Donna returned to her canvas. Speaking and painting seemed to use alternate parts of the brain. She heard Zelda's babble as white noise, and confessed she was not really listening to the endless chatter about New York's finer points of interest. She stayed in her private world of turpentine smells, shades of color and the shaping of the pleasing forms with the touch of her brush.

When she heard Sam's arrival at precisely ten o'clock, she

realized how exhausted she felt. Her arms were suddenly leaden and she relinquished her paintbrushes, one from her teeth, two from her left hand and one from her right. "What do I look like?" She asked Zelda, meaning was she presentable enough for a male visitor.

"Like a painter." Zelda laughed.

Sam bounded up the stairs. They heard him thud down the hall to her bedroom. Then there he was large, filling the doorway of her studio with his frame. "I thought you were sick." Sam gave the two of them the benefit of his gorgeous smile.

Donna sat down on her painting stool. "I'm just tired." She could feel her face smiling. "I've been painting since nine o'clock."

"She usually paints at night." Zelda explained to Sam. "I always wondered why you left David's bed to paint." They both turned to Zelda, as if she would explain her rude remark. Zelda hung her head. "Completely inappropriate."

"I brought enough chicken." Sam changed the subject and they followed him downstairs like shamed and sheared sheep.

"We have a few more questions." John said, before the last of the chicken was emptied from the bucket. He turned to Zelda. "Sam told me you were late for the funeral on Sunday."

"I was. I don't attend many memorial services and I couldn't find my black purse in time."

"Was anyone with you?" Sally asked. "When you were searching for the purse?"

"No," Zelda said. "Of course, not. Why?"

"Just checking on loose ends." John asked. "You are a friend of Professor Paul St. Claire?"

"Yes, why?" Zelda got up and started to clear the table.

"Zelda," Donna said. "You're worse than David. Sit down. People are still eating, if not devouring the chicken, at least talking."

"Sorry. I brought apple strudel. I thought I would add ice cream and caramel sauce to it, if anyone is interested."

Sally asked John, "Did any of the neighbors see a moving van on the day of the service?"

Sam joined in. "How did they get the filing cabinets out of here?"

"I did check with the neighbors." John covered his mouth, which still contained chicken.

"However," he swallowed, "the alley behind the house is good cover for a small van."

"I drive a van." Zelda placed a perfectly delicious looking dessert in front of Donna.

"She's an art dealer." Donna said in a tone meant to defend the innocent. John nodded his head. Donna was amazed at her own appetite. Sam and Zelda were great to provide all the food. She smiled at Sam and then at Zelda, whose eyes were tearing. "John, look, you've upset my guest. Can we talk about what evidence the police obtained against Harry? David was closer to Harry than his own children." When Sam turned to look at Donna, his knee touched hers. Donna jumped as if shot. To cover her embarrassment, she offered, "I forgot to plug in the coffee." She pushed back her chair to attend to it.

"I already did." Sally pointed to the carafe on the table.

"I guess we should make this a short night. I have painted for hours."

After John and Zelda left, Sally approached Sam with his coat. He sat across from Donna in the front room. He took his coat but remained seated. "Does Zelda have any reason to be nervous?"

"I think she's just embarrassed about taking David's key the first day." Sally dismissed the idea.

"She did go through David's desk," Donna offered.

"How do you know that?" Sam asked.

"Her fingerprints smudged David's. I noticed them. I meant to clean off the glass before he died." Donna noticed her hands needed grasping. She was starting to feel the loss again. This time her hands felt cold and shaky. These fingers will never touch David again, she thought and her tears released. "Sorry." Donna used the handkerchief Sam offered to stop the endless flow.

"I'll bring you a glass of water," Sally said, as if to replenish the loss of liquids.

"I don't like Zelda," Sam said.

"You're just being sympathetic to a silly widow. There's nothing wrong with Zelda."

"She is pushy," Sally said.

Sam stood up and moved around the room. "She's doing something she doesn't like. Her body is jerky, unnatural. I'm sure she's fond of you, but there's something about her I can't put my finger on."

"You met her before the funeral?" Sally asked.

"Memorial service," Donna corrected. "David's body is still at the morgue."

"Those who rise up against me," Sally mumbled.

"What?" Donna asked.

"I don't know," Sally watched Sam roam around the room. "The Bible verse just came to me."

* * *

Before Sam went outside to take up guard duty in his car on Monday night, Sally fell asleep in the front room watching an old <u>Law and Order</u> show. Donna knew Sally saw the episode before, but appreciated her friend's determination to chaperone. However when Sally began snoring, Sam motioned for Donna to follow him out to the kitchen. She trailed along because he was sensibly putting on his coat, as if to leave. "I appreciate your …" Donna stopped unable to identify their relationship.

"Attendance?" Sam smiled. A dimple on the left side of his face presented itself.

"Yes," Donna said, sticking out her hand for a friendly shake.

Instead, Sam hugged her chastely to his chest with one arm, just for a moment.

Donna missed the scent of leather that David's clothing emitted.

Then the very alive Sam Tedler grasped her hand between his huge warm paws while he leaned over to look directly into her eyes. "Please don't tell me to leave your life."

"I wouldn't," Donna said, convinced of at least that.

"Good," Sam said, content for the time being.

After Sam left the house, Donna nursed her own sense of peacefulness as she watched Sally nap on the couch opposite her. Afraid she might join her mothering friend in sleeping on the couch all night, she woke Sally by shutting off the television. After saying good-bye to her detective friend, Donna shuffled upstairs. "Attended," she whispered as she drifted off. The word made her feel less alone somehow. Donna slept well. She dreamt of empty brushes erasing sunsets with each wide swipe.

* * *

Third Tuesday in November

Tuesday morning Zelda rousted Donna out of bed at eight o'clock. She brought pecan rolls and clotted cream, so Donna intended to forgive the uninvited visit. Sally and John's agenda also included an early morning visit. "Harry will be in court this morning." Sally stood and picked at the roll on her plate.

"Not until nine, Sally." Donna hoped she kept any whine out of her voice. Her own appetite surprised her. "I slept like a log last night."

"What time did Sam leave?" John asked.

"I thought you were supposed to chaperone." Zelda scolded.

"Sally was still watching television when Sam left." Donna nursed her coffee and helped herself to more of the thick cream for her third roll.

"I must have dozed off." Sally finally sat to devour the still warm pastry properly. "John, they're good. Have at least one." He did, twice.

Zelda honed in on the reason for her visit. "My gallery in New York is empty until a Thanksgiving show. Sally, please give Donna the break she needs in her career. Let me take her paintings if you will not allow her to attend the show. Donna, I predict I can find lucrative sales for all your work." Sally stopped eating in mid-swallow.

Donna thought to broker a compromise. "Could we wait on a decision until we find out when Harry is coming home?"

"Today." Sally prayed.

"Fine. I'll leave my van here and we can load up the paintings when we get back with Harry." Zelda bulldozed herself through most sticky situations. Sally rolled her eyes in exasperation.

Donna refused to consider a New York show on this particular day, or tomorrow. Too many decisions needed to be made before she would even consider sending off her work to New York. She knew she was not being honest with Zelda. Perhaps the ploy of breakfast sweets should be thoroughly absorbed before she gave Zelda a negative answer. No sense ruining everyone's digestion.

"We'll save you the last roll, Donna." Zelda set the sweet on Donna's plate and then retracted the dish to her own side of the table. "If you run up and get dressed for court."

"Are you coming, too?" Sally asked.

"I hope that's okay?" Zelda asked them.

Donna could not discern any reason for Zelda to come or to stay. She left the question for Sally and John to deal with and hurried upstairs to dress somberly for the court. Sam would surely be there.

* * *

Zelda left her silver-colored van parked on the street in front of the condominium. She drove them to the courthouse in Donna's car. "Should we pick David's car up from the parking structure on the way home?"

"His car," Donna said. "I forgot all about it. I guess we should get his Lexus out of the university's parking lot."

When they arrived, Sam Tedler's blond curls could be seen above the throng in the narrow hallway outside the various courtrooms. Donna ignored Sally's frown and waved to him. Sam made his way through the crowd and stood next to Donna. She moved closer to him in the crush, felt his comforting hands on her shoulders as he helped her off with her coat.

The group of friends sat together directly behind the defendant's table. Donna wondered what the spectators thought of their motley group. Sally could be the mother, John the father, Zelda an aunt. Donna supposed she fit the description of a gangster's moll. Sam Tedler ruined the picture. His polished good looks and his blond innocence warmed the room with a sweet aura of brotherly love.

John shook Harry's hand and Sally embraced him when they let him into the courtroom. When Sally let go, Donna and Sam shook his hand. Harry looked as if someone had dashed his soul into a million pieces. Donna thought his eyes were searching the crowded room for David's form.

"This will all be over soon," Donna promised.

Harry's voice broke, "I can't believe he's gone."

"All rise." the clerk intoned the ancient ritual of justice.

* * *

Nevertheless, justice did not prevail, because Harry said he could not explain how David fell down the steps. "I can't say." He pleaded, weeping as calmly as he could. The judge assumed the worst and would not accept bail, which John offered to pay. After the judge left the chamber, Zelda attempted to guide them toward the exit; but Donna pushed her aside. "We are not going home without Harry." Donna followed Harry through the door to the jail.

Sam stopped her further advance. "That's as far as you can go, Donna."

"No it's not, Sam." Donna pushed directly against his chest "Go get the District Attorney. I'm not leaving until Harry walks out of here with me."

Sam, Zelda, Sally and John, Donna, and Harry's young lawyer, Alex Cornville were ushered into a waiting room, which looked like a typical jury room. Comfortable chairs surrounded the long table. A cooler stood in the corner offering clean water for the dingy world's relief. Donna expected to smell smoke but a hint of bleach was the only odor in the room. She wondered why public buildings chose a palate of greens to dab on the walls and the ceilings. Blue or yellow would be happier colors. Of course, red would be inappropriate with all the blood-related goings on. She pressed her hands to her temples; maybe she was headed over the hill of insanity. She hoped not. Sam and Harry both deserved a sane friend.

Sergeant Cramer finally and a bit reluctantly entered the room. "The DA's office asked me to handle the situation."

"Wire me," Donna said emphatically to Sam. "I'll clear Harry."

"We would have to obtain Mr. Cornville's approval to have you talk to his client with an unrevealed recording device." Sergeant Cramer softened the legalese with a sympathetic tone.

All six of them focused their attention on the youthful lawyer. Alex coughed and clutched his briefcase to his chest. "I cannot recommend that." He cringed as if he expected the group of friends and two cops to pounce on him.

Sam intervened. "Sally, what do you think would be in his best interest?"

Donna smoothed out a silk, spotless handkerchief on the wooden table. She eyed the cowering lawyer and the competent police officers. "Nothing is as bad as having Harry in jail."

Zelda could not stay any longer. Claiming urgent business, she directed Sam to drive the women home in David's car. Donna gave Sam David's keys. Sally and John seemed to approve of the transmittal of the keys to Sam. Zelda left before Sergeant Cramer returned with the written agreement. Alex's client would need to know he was being recorded. Donna was required to get his signature on the waiver.

"No problem," Sam said with an assurance Donna did not feel. Would Harry trust her enough to give up his rights against self-incrimination? She wondered if she would allow such a thing if their positions were reversed.

However, Sally calmed any doubts Donna might otherwise have entertained, "Harry will want to confide in you."

* * *

Three hours later, Donna was allowed to talk to Harry without any lawyers present. As Sam promised, Harry soberly greeted Donna in a windowless room without a two-way mirror. Donna did not con herself into believing the room was free of other bugging devices, besides the one under her jacket; but at least she could not see a camera. Initially, she did not intend to tell Harry about the recording, but the lawyers all insisted on a signed document. "Do you want to go home today?" Donna asked, getting to the meat of the problem.

"Yes, of course." Harry ran his hands through his thinning hair.

"We're being recorded," Donna explained quickly, "and you need to sign this waiver for the District Attorney to remain within the law.

"Okay. I couldn't tell a room full of people, in front of you, what happened."

He started to weep, but Donna stopped him. "We don't have time for grief now, Harry."

Straightening his posture, he signed the waiver without reading the printed matter. "Ask me anything. But David didn't want me to tell you, Donna."

"I need to know. These ludicrous people do not understand you would not hurt David in a million years. Tell me what happened. If your lawyer wants me to testify for you, I will gladly take the stand. David's death was a tragedy, which doesn't need to be intensified by your mistreatment." Harry bowed his head. Donna came around to his side of the table and put her arms around his neck. Their chairs touched each other. "Every detail." Harry sobbed, but Donna did not let go. "Tell me."

"We were laughing," Harry cleared his throat and continued. "I forget the joke. I was behind him. I told the police all this."

"I know you did, Harry; but I want to hear your version." Donna swept her hair behind her ears and replaced her right arm around his shoulders.

"David stumbled on the first step, as if he thought it was lower than it actually was. I replayed his first step a thousand times in my head, but I cannot figure out how he fell. His hand was on the banister. I remember looking to see if he would catch himself." Harry lowered his head nearly to his chest. Donna leaned closer without releasing her arm from his shoulder. Harry turned toward her looking directly into her eyes. "He fell all the way to the first landing." Harry moved slightly away. "His thigh bone stuck out of his slashed pants. He let out one scream."

She dropped her arm from his shoulder and asked. "How did he get to the second landing?"

"I rushed down, tried to hold his head. He was in agony."

Harry showed Donna his own tortured face. "David pushed me away. Somehow, he moved to the second tier of steps. He did not scream again. It was an awful sound, Donna. I dream of the horror every night."

Donna patted his hand sympathetically. "Go on."

"He hung onto the banister," Harry asked for water, drank it and continued. "David pushed his broken, bleeding limb down the stair. I think the pain made him crazy. That is all, Donna. That's all."

"That wasn't all."

"No." Harry was silent. "I can't tell you the rest."

"Yes, Harry, you saw him die. I can at least hear how it happened."

"I was kneeling in the blood holding onto his belt. He was a big man." Harry focused on the floor in front of him as if reliving the scene. "David looked me right in the eye. He was holding onto the banister with two hands, one on each side of the stairway. Then he said, 'I can't live as a cripple, Harry. Don't tell Donna.' And then David let go with both his hands and fell the rest of the way down." Harry looked at the splint on his right hand, broken as David wrenched free from his grip. "I rushed down but they were right, Donna. His neck broke. I closed David's eyes."

The coldness in the ensuing silence crept up from the floor, as if death itself reached out to them. Donna first noticed her knees were shivering. Knocking, she thought, this is what it means. The awareness of death climbed up to her belly, her chest shuddered, and her throat ached from the chill. She stroked her throat, but the cries came out anyway. Hoarse sobs, despairing cries, senseless grief unleashed. Harry scrambled up to get help. Donna heard the door open.

Sam, Sally and John, Harry, and Sergeant Cramer tried to comfort her; but when the paramedics arrived, Donna noticed her throat felt raw from her continuing keening. When the shot started to take effect on the stretcher, she thanked the attendants for her own silence. "Tell Harry," Donna whispered to Sam, "I'm so sorry I could not control myself."

Harry was at her elbow. "I have to stay here, Donna. Do not worry about me. Try to keep calm."

A peace like death descended. "I hope I'm dying." She told the aide in the ambulance.

"No," he said, somberly. "You'll be okay. Never mind."

But of course, Donna did mind. David's suicide made life meaningless. Anger welled up in her, first at the police, then at David.

Chapter Fifteen

Last Tuesday in November

When Donna woke in the hospital, Sam was sitting by her bedside. His face was ashen, his blond hair rumpled. His gorgeous blue eyes were rimmed in red. "David killed himself," Donna said simply.

"We need to know why."

"We may never know." Donna patted his arm, entwined her fingers in his. "Suicide is always a matter of choice. What was he dealing with?" Donna was certain that Sam would be at her side until he found the answers.

"He was not a coward," Sam added.

Donna agreed. "The decision to summon death took a courage I do not possess or understand." Sam did not respond. "I only know I was not convinced he loved me the way other husbands seemed to love their wives. I told myself I could not really judge the private relationships around me. I accepted our routine. I painted canvases with raw colors when life failed to fill all the recesses of my soul. Perhaps David felt the same lack."

"Commonly felt angst at such a low level would hardly force him to stop his life." Sam's hands were in his hair.

"Perhaps …" Donna started and thought better of revealing her fears.

"Perhaps?" Sam asked.

"I wondered about the closeness of his relationship with Harry."

"Did you check out your suspicions?"

"I would not know how to begin. We are all bi-sexual beings." Donna noticed her voice was almost a whisper.

"No," Sam said. "We are not."

"There is his unproductive research."

"Would an academic failure provide enough suffering to end his life?" Sam's steady glance seared Donna's soul.

"Research was David's life." Donna realized the truth.

"Yes. I believe you, but something's not right. The robbery of his work…."

"Failed work. Why would anyone want irrelevant research results?"

"We will find out, I promise."

An RN stopped by to check Donna's vitals and when given the okay to get out of bed, Donna first noticed her hair in the bathroom's mirror. She opened the door to show Sam. "My hair!"

"Looks very distinguished." He lifted the ends of her black hair off her shoulders, holding the long sleek hair in both his hands.

Donna pointed to her temple. "White."

"From your emotions."

The nurse bustled back into the room. "Just dye the roots. Not a problem."

"Not a problem!" Donna said astonished. "My hair is turning white."

"The grief." Sam seemed to need to remind her.

"But my hair?" Donna resigned herself to the added shock. Life would never return to normalcy. Her first call from the hospital bed's phone was to Sergeant Cramer's cell. "You may as well release Harry, David killed himself."

"A release order has not been issued for Professor Terkle."

"I guess I'll call the District Attorney."

Sergeant Cramer coughed. "Call Harry's lawyer, he might be more effective."

"Thanks, Sergeant, I will." Donna returned to the bed.

"Donna," Sam straightened the sheet across her chest. "Try to stay calm, but I have more bad news."

Donna pushed his hands away. "What now?"

The petite nurse popped back into the room. "Problem?"

"Sally and John need to ask you more questions," Sam said. He opened the room's door and let the detective couple in.

Donna noticed the nurses' nametag. Angela placed the call button in Donna's hand. "If these brutes upset you, push the button and I'll clear them out."

"David's car was vandalized," Sally said.

"I called Sam when I tried to take Sally home in David's car," John stood at the foot of the bed.

Sally took her hand. "Someone is getting angry about not finding what they're looking for in your husband's belongings."

"All the windows were broken," John said.

"Harry knows every step of David's research," Donna said. "Why haven't they searched his home?"

Sally coughed. "Harry's house was thoroughly vandalized before we arrived with a search warrant."

"Oh no," Donna said quietly so as not to summon the protective nurse.

"However," John said, "they only stole Professor Terkle's computer. The office computers are being deciphered by Professor St. Claire." Donna noticed how exhausted John looked. His dark eyes slightly bulged the way Sal Mineo's did in one of the black-and-white Turner Classics.

"Who would want failed research?" Sam asked.

Donna compared the two men. "You three act like detectives. Sorry, my drugs must have freed a curb on my tongue." Sam smiled his dimple-inspiring smile reminding her too much of David's lost grin. "Professor St. Claire knows the research is failed."

"He doesn't seem phased about the negative repercussions on his career," Sally said.

"He was happy to assist us." John put on his hat, then blushed and took it off again.

"Too happy?" Sally asked.

"I'll call in some experts from the FBI," Sam said. "They will know who to ask about the research. What chemicals were they testing?"

"Pharmaceuticals," Donna said, "for Parkinson's."

"Crimes are usually solved close to home, aren't they?" John asked Sam. "With so much happening, I delayed in asking Donna about her husband's enemies."

"Zelda Cameron," Donna was surprised to hear herself say, and then negate. "No. I do not know why I said Zelda's name. She wants my paintings for her studio in New York. She tried to put me in a bad light once. She showed David everything I bought on a shopping trip we made together."

"To give him cause to be angry?" Sally asked. "Zelda never sticks around. She's with us until we leave the house then she finds a reason to quit the group."

Donna played with her hair, then remembered the new white highlights. "See what terror has wrought!"

"Terrors by day," John said sympathetically. "Anyone else?"

"His youngest son hates me."

Sam stood up. "That little creep, Norman?"

"What happened?" John was adding items to his notebook.

"He told me David and his mother were still having an affair, but his oldest son, Joseph, apologized at the memorial service. Their mother said there was not a grain of truth in Norman's hatefulness."

"You're going through a rough time." John patted her ankle through the hospital sheet. "I will check out Norman's whereabouts." Sam gently removed John's hand from the sheet. Donna watched Sam glare and John's unspoken apology to him. John made another note, before he expressed his concerns for Donna's safety, then Sally and he left.

"You didn't need to shame the man," Donna said.

"He needs to keep his hands to himself," Sam said too calmly.

* * *

Third Tuesday in November

A week after his father died, Norman decided his stepmother needed to be taught a lesson. Zelda furnished him with the latest news. Harry claimed his father committed suicide. The false statement was dragged out of the vile man accused of murdering his father by Donna, the meddling widow. Now everyone would think his father was a weakling, someone not able to accept a few broken bones. Nevertheless, Norman kept his cool.

He asked Zelda, who he knew wanted to take Donna's paintings to New York, if Professor St. Claire needed any papers from his father's office, mainly to see if Zelda would acknowledge her illicit liaison with his father's supervisor. Norman needed an excuse to go back to his father's house, after Donna commanded he never cross the threshold again. One-third, he repeated to himself, one third of the house was his.

"I'm sure David's supervisor would appreciate any work-related materials delivered to the department." Zelda carefully covered any ulterior motives. "You know, everything Paul thought was pertinent to David's research has been robbed from the Leonard home?"

"I heard. I thought I should make sure anything remaining, of importance, of interest to the department, should be returned -- at least searched for. I doubt my stepmother would recognize a formula, or unpublished paper, if they fell on her head."

Zelda laughed. "Artists aren't often attuned to the ways of science." She encouraged Norman to root about. "I am sure Paul would appreciate your help."

Zelda handed Norman the key to his father's house, one she claimed Professor St. Claire lent her. She had made a copy of the one handed back to Donna.

With Donna in the hospital in some state of hysteria, Norman made use of the opportunity. When he closed the front door of his father's house, the keys in his hand rang against each other. He stuffed them into his pocket, then balled up his shaking hand. He knew fear did not grip his soul. Instead, free-floating rage turned Donna's clown-colored furnishings into a whirling mass of targets.

He needed a knife. Donna's neat kitchen irked him on. He pulled out a stack of dinner plates and calmly walked into the dining room almost as if he were going to set the table. He threw each dish as hard as he could against walls, the china cabinet, pictures, and the light fixtures. He loved the music, the crashing racket of shattering glass.

When he had thrown the last bowl out of the cupboard, he put his favorite oldie into the disc player and turned the volume as high as it would go. Pink Floyd accompanied the bass thuds of books being tossed around until the bookshelves were empty. Fatigue made him remember he was supposed to be looking for something, something important.

He took a steak knife from the kitchen drawer, emptying the rest of the silverware onto the floor. Lovely noise. The knife helped him open up the upholstery on those stupid, yellow, blue and green couches. Norman used the base of the fig tree to smash the glass on his father's desk. He laughed. This was better than a food fight. Then he remembered Donna.

Since his father's death, Norman was not able to make love to Henrietta. They made use of Harry Terkle's place while Harry was in jail. Then his stepmother ruined everything. Harry would be coming home because of Donna's interference. However, while Harry was absent, probably because Donna was so evil at the funeral, Norman was not able to --- to perform with Henrietta, Harry's housekeeper. Oh, Henrietta was okay about his distress. She described their previous more successful encounters. She even got him laughing about the time he hid in Harry's basement. Harry returned home for a forgotten briefcase. Henrietta thought it was a riot. She threw Norman's shoes and pants into the dishwasher, just as Harry opened the front door.

So Norman knew he was justified when he charged upstairs and ripped Donna's bedding to pieces all the way down to the mattress his father slept on with her. But Donna wouldn't know he was the one wreaking havoc on her safe world.

Zelda reminded him the paintings were under her protection. Probably knew some way to profit from them, or he would have made short work of them. He avoided even going into the studio, too much of a temptation to strike at the heart of his enemy. "Plenty left where that came from," he said to the empty house as he left.

* * *

On Tuesday afternoon, Sally drove Donna home from the hospital. On the way, Sally told Donna, "They released Harry and the charges are dropped."

"I guess I can finally liberate David's body from the morgue." Donna brushed her forehead with the back of her hand. "Harry's house was robbed, too?"

"If you didn't insist on speaking directly to Harry, he would still be sitting in the county jail."

Donna remembered what good times they shared, David, Harry, Sally and John. The dinners at Zingerman's, dancing at Weber's. All of the life she shared with her husband was gone. Now she needed to call the crematorium. Where would she find the strength to bury her husband? She thought after talking to Harry, he would understand everything, but she knew no more about David's inner life than she did when he was roaming the rooms in their condominium.

"I wish I'd known David better," Sally said.

"Me too," Donna said, "My idea of who he was doesn't fit with any of the facts."

"He loved you."

"Did he? He never convinced me in the fourteen years I loved him. I wonder why?" Donna almost asked Sally if she ever wondered about the nature of the emotional attachment between David and Harry. She could not broach the subject. A wave of self-pity washed over her.

When they reached the condominium, they could see the front door was wide open. An empty police car was parked out front. "Look." Sally reached across Donna to point.

"I see it, but I don't believe it."

Another police car stopped behind them. Sam stepped out and ran to the passenger side of her car. "Donna, are you hurt?" Donna started to cry because she was so glad to see him. Now she would not be left alone. Sam wrapped his arms around her through the car's open window.

"Sally, was there a robbery?"

"We don't know yet," Sally said.

"Stay in the car, Donna," Sam said. "Let me make sure the scene is cleared."

Donna only nodded her head. One horror followed another these days. John walked out of Donna's door, down the sidewalk toward them. "A neighbor called," he said when he reached them. "They noticed the front door was ajar. Sergeant Creamer picked me up."

A slight breeze blew through the open window of the car. The fall chill made Donna pull her coat collar closer to her throat. Most of the leaves were fallen from the trees, but the condominium's staff failed to collect them. The trees appeared naked with their colorful skirts draped around their ankles. Donna's hands itched to paint the scene.

"You are safe to enter now," John continued, "but I want to

warn you. There has been another robbery. The place is a mess."

"Oh Lord," Sally prayed. "We need your protection."

Donna jumped out of the car, then leaned back through the passenger window. "Sally, go home with John. Sam can handle this."

"Call me when you find out what happened." Sally waved for John to join her.

"No," John said, as he got in the car. "Call us as soon as Sam is through."

"I will," Donna promised, thinking she might wait until Sam left, if she ever let Sam Tedler leave again. Sam's hand was on her shoulder.

A mess hardly explained the disaster Donna encountered in her own home. Every book was emptied from the shelves. The paint on the walls was marred and the framed pictures smashed. Her couches were ripped and the stuffings strewn as far as the culprit could toss them. The kitchen was the worst hit. Every dish broken, every pot out of the cupboards and all of the silverware strewn on the floor.

"Someone is still looking for whatever they didn't find on Professor Leonard's computer." Sargeant Cramer shook her head.

"Did they destroy my studio?" Donna couldn't summon the courage to walk up the stairs.

Sam went up to inspect any damage. When he returned, he said. "Nothing was touched in the painting room but the master bedroom is destroyed."

Donna ran to the first floor, guest bathroom. Was she vomiting in relief? Did her paintings mean that much to her?

Sam came in and held a cold hand on her forehead as she emptied her stomach. "Do you need water?" He provided a chilled glass "Just sip it, or you'll start dry vomiting."

Donna sat on the floor as far away from the toilet as she could without leaving the room. "I think you better call Dr. Lorell for me, Sam." She pulled her knees up to her stomach. "Her number is next to the kitchen phone. I hope."

Sergeant Cramer peeked her head around the frame of the door. "Mrs. Leonard I have to get back. If you find anything is missing, let me know. I am going to file this as another act of vandalism until I hear from you. Take your time."

Sam shed his coat and draped it around Donna. "Just stay there until you feel like getting up."

"We have to stop meeting like this." Donna wanted to laugh, to giggle until she was silly, but she could not.

"I'll make you some tea."

Shortly after maneuvering herself into David's office, Donna sat in his desk chair and completed drinking Sam's effort at making tea, the phone rang.

"Dr. Lorell." Sam brought her the cordless phone.

"Vomiting is not uncommon." Dr. Lorell said.

"For grieving widows?" Donna asked. "I didn't know."

"For pregnant widows." Dr. Lorell said. "The hospital took a routine blood test after your visit to the courthouse prison."

"I'm pregnant?" Donna asked aloud, then remembered Sam

was in the room.

"Make an appointment next week for an exam," Dr. Lorell said cheerfully. "You are two months along, I think. See you then." The doctor hung up.

"But what about?" Donna said into the dead phone. What about raising a baby without a father, what about living a life without a husband, what about ... There were no answers for her in the present and the future was hanging fire.

"David's baby." Sam knelt beside her. "Aren't you pleased?"

"I am," Donna said and then bawled like a baby. She forgot the destruction of her home as soon as Dr. Lorell told her she was carrying David's child.

When the wet storm of tears passed, Sam asked what he could do. "I could move your paintings into storage and find a room for you."

"I'm too exhausted to think about moving. I don't want to call Sally. Do you think you can find Zelda's number?"

"You want Zelda here?" The hurt in Sam's voice was obvious.

"No, but she owns a van and lots of energy."

"How did Sally and you become friends with Zelda?"

"Zelda lives next to Paul St. Claire." Donna wondered if any of her clothes were ruined in the onslaught of somebody's personal vendetta against the Leonard household. "I'll need new clothes," Donna said to herself, thinking of the baby.

"I don't think the vandals ruined yours."

Donna stopped speaking. Her mind was a confusion of

conflicting plans. A baby? Her paintings? Sam was kneeling next to David's chair, waiting for her to continue. She stuck her finger in the pile of dirt from the fig tree still splayed out on the David's desk. "I wasn't crying because the doctor gave me any bad news."

"You've experienced enough traumas in the last week to declare war on the rest of humanity."

"Do you know how handsome you are?" Donna reached for his blond curls.

"Sympathetic friends look good to you, do we?" Sam put his arms around her shoulders.

Donna leaned her head on his arm. "I want to tell everyone."

"How far along are you?" Sam asked.

"I'm two months pregnant." Donna gently kissed Sam.

Sam slid his hand under her hair and held her head, as he returned the friendly kiss.

"David's child." Donna pulled away.

* * *

Sam let go of her. "Babies need fathers." Donna's gray eyes widened. Sam's heart gave a jump. What had he offered? "I mean it," Sam assured himself. "I've been in love with you from the first moment I saw you."

"When you told me there was an accident?"

Sam embraced Donna again, whispered in her ear, "Do I have a chance?"

"I think so." Donna kissed him more than a second time.

They stayed in the embrace as long as they could, both their young bodies cried for warmth, understanding, and physical release from the tensions caused by the continuing traumas surrounding David's accident.

* * *

Thanksgiving Day
Fourth Thursday in November

On the tree-lined north shore of the Huron River, a half-mile west of Ann Arbor but still within the city limits, Sally and John paced off closet areas on the third floor of their planned new home.

"You'll need more room than I will." John stood behind Sally with his arms around her waist.

"I am a clothes horse." Sally let the back of her head rest on John's chest. "But whenever I shop, I fill the emptied department store bags with clothes to give away."

"How is that working out?"

"I'm not giving away as much as I should. I get emotionally attached to the strangest items. I have a sheepskin vest I bought from a Waterloo garage sale for seventy-five cents that I can't seem to part with. The Lord has showered me with possessions."

"My brother and I know our good fortune comes from years of our mother's faithful prayers. But even he says I keep out-of-date duds."

On the way back to the car, Sally thought better of mentioning the hairpiece John's twin brother insisted on wearing. "Don't you love the smell of fresh cut wood?"

"Too bad we have to cover the two-by-fours with wallboard."

Sally noticed a familiar car driving away from the new housing development. Her attention shifted to the Leonard case. "I wonder who is involved in the robberies."

"You're thinking there's a cover-up? By whom?"

"The university?" Sally mulled over the possibility.

"The vandalism seems more personal. I wonder why the paintings weren't hit."

"Wouldn't they be an obvious target? Unless ..."

"What?"

"Hazy thoughts. Let's visit Donna. It is Thanksgiving Day. Where are we going to find a restaurant open?"

"We'll find one. I'm thankful I found you; but we better get out of this cold wind."

* * *

At the Leonard house, Sally wondered why none of the home's windows were broken in the latest bout of vandalism. The paintings and the windows. Something was yelling at her but she couldn't hear the answers or even form the questions. John rang the bell for the third time and then pounded on the door.

"Donna," Sally yelled, in growing concern. Sam Tedler opened the door. "Oh, no!" Sally swayed against John. "Has someone injured Donna?"

"No," Sam said matter-of-factly. "I've been here all night."

"Well, that's not right," John said.

"Come in, come in. Donna's dressing. I mean, she's busy.

She'll be down in a minute."

"What are you up to?" Sally asked.

Sam led them into the cleaned up kitchen. "Paper plates will have to do. Pancakes okay for you two?"

"I thought you were a standup guy, Sam." John sat at the dining room table which commanded a clear view of the kitchen.

"Now, John." Sally remembered AA cautioned about taking anyone else's moral inventory.

"Are you taking advantage of a widow's grief?" John asked anyway.

"She's two months pregnant." Sam answered

"Oh, dear Lord." Sally joined John at the table. "I'm sure she's thrilled and appreciates your support, Sam."

Sam gave Sally a gorgeous smile, she thought, until she heard Donna behind her. Donna hugged Sally's shoulders and kissed the side of her face. "I knew you would understand. I have so much to be thankful for."

"But, someone you know vandalized your house, Donna," Sally said. "Someone who didn't break any windows maybe so the neighbors wouldn't notice the ruckus.

"Someone who hates me, you mean." Donna accepted a paper plate with a pancake on it from Sam. "I don't entertain many people in the house."

They all turned toward the hall, where someone was knocking as if to dispute Donna's statement. John went to open the door. They heard his cheerful greeting, "How are you feeling, Harry?"

Harry made for one of the dining room chairs. "Surprisingly weak in the knees."

"Didn't they feed you properly?" Sally asked.

"I think the shock of losing David, and being accused of actually injuring my best friend." He handed Donna a pie box. "I hope you like pumpkin…for Thanksgiving…I could use a cup of coffee."

Sam delivered the coffee and a stack of pancakes and bacon. Breakfast odors seemed to restore everyone's good nature. Donna embraced Harry and sat next to him holding both his hands. "Thanks for coming over so soon."

"Let the man eat his breakfast," Sally said.

"I needed to warn you." Harry looked around the destroyed rooms, and seemed to size up the situation. "I came too late. I never thought he would do anything so evil. Well, I guess I did. Your stepson …" The distraught man couldn't continue. He pushed his unfinished plate of pancakes away.

Sally asked him. "Do you think Norman has enough hate in him?"

"Yes." Donna answered without hesitation. "He can't stand me. I'm probably lucky to be alive. I hope he doesn't know I'm pregnant."

"Which would cut down on his share of inheritance," Sally added.

Harry calmed down enough to say, first to Donna. "David's child. You are blessed." Then he added for the rest of them, "I fired my housekeeper. She's married and involved in an affair with Norman. I never told David."

"I can have Norman pulled into the police station and questioned," Sam said. "We can let him know he's being watched."

"Wait," Sally said. "Let's think this through. Why would Norman steal David's research? And why didn't he slash Donna's paintings? Whoever vandalized the house went into every room upstairs."

"Someone close to Donna, who loves her paintings, who knows Norman hates his stepmother, who doesn't want the house destroyed, and who has connections to David's research?" John reviewed the clues.

"Zelda!" Sam, Donna and Sally said in unison.

"She wasn't interested in freeing Harry." John agreed.

"We need to trap her into confessing," Sally said. "Don't tell Zelda about the baby, Donna. She might let Norman know and he doesn't need any more incentives to injury you."

"Why would anyone want to steal David's research?" Harry said almost to himself. They turned their attention to him. "St. Claire told us the Parkinson test in China failed. David believed him." Harry hung his head as if determined not to reveal anything more.

"Is that why David was so ready to die?" Donna asked him bluntly.

Harry nodded his head and used his handkerchief unashamedly to dry his face.

Sally understood. "So there wasn't really any reason to steal

David's notes -- unless."

"The pills did work," Sam said.

"St. Claire hinted David was withholding information. A firm in China was demanding better results." Harry looked at each person assembled at the table.

Sally asked, "They weren't using prisoners to experiment on, were they?"

Chapter Sixteen

Thanksgiving Day

As if on cue, Zelda Cameron knocked on Donna's front door. Sam let her in. "So, sorry to hear about the vandalism." Zelda looked around the living room at the obvious displays of wanton destruction. No one seemed ready to converse with her. "Who would want to do something like this? Were your paintings ruined?"

"No." Donna knew the subject of David's failed research needed to be shelved until Zelda was no longer within ear shot.

Zelda seemed honestly shocked. Harry pushed back his thinning hair and accepted another cup of coffee from Sam. Zelda sat down on the arm of one of the ruined couches. She faced the crowded dining room table. "When I first heard about the crime, I thought Halloween pranksters might be blamed." No one commented. She continued to the tough crowd, "Maybe you should get away, Donna. Come to New York with your work. We've missed the parade crowds. What if this onslaught continues? At least your paintings would be safe in New York."

"The trouble might follow you to New York," Harry said, handing Donna a piece of pumpkin pie.

"I think you should go," Sally said. "If you take Sam with you."

Sam and Donna shared a long obvious moment. Zelda chose to dismiss the mute love scene. Harry was too involved in passing around slices of pie to notice. John shrugged his shoulders. However, Sally seemed to agree no harm would come to Donna as long as Sam was at her side. "Make sure no one informs Norman," Sally said to Zelda.

"Why is that?" Zelda asked, sounding too innocent.

"Think about it," Sally said, clearly angry at her for pretending to be ignorant about Norman hatred for Donna.

* * *

Last Monday in November
Zelda's New York Apartment

Zelda's part-interest in the New York gallery included the fixed-rent apartment on the building's top floor. After spending their entire afternoon explaining Donna's paintings to Zelda's patrons, Sam, Donna and Zelda retired to the elevator for access to the living quarters. Floor-to-ceiling windows provided a sweeping northern view of Central Park. A vase of out-of-season peonies filled the open room with their heavy scent. "Isn't this lovely?" Zelda asked the couple.

Donna nodded. Sam slid around the wood floor in his stocking feet, as if his childhood had suddenly returned. "You can hear the traffic." Sam knocked into the leather couch and somersaulted onto the pillows. "Not very homey, though."

"Maybe if you stopped thinking of the place as your personal gym." Zelda tried to hide her outrage.

"I wouldn't want to raise children here," Donna said.

"Raise children?" Zelda's out of control tone continued to rise in pitch and volume. "What about painting here? This is prime north light." Zelda waved her arms around, encompassing the vast expanse of rooms. "You couldn't find a better studio."

"I'm pregnant," Donna said simply.

"Move rather fast, don't you?" Zelda turned on Sam.

"Not mine." Sam held his hands up to the studio's black ceiling as if Zelda's irate tongue was a lethal weapon.

"David's?" Zelda asked but meant the word as a statement. She sat down on the black leather love seat and punched one of the yellow throw pillows.

"Ann Arbor is a more family-friendly place to live," Donna said. "You could still show my paintings."

"New York thrives on personalities. People will tell their friends they met you, a famous artist with her paintings in a prestigious gallery. They'll want to brag about their ability to introduce people to you. No one can relate to you if you are way back in Ann Arbor." The phone rang and Zelda jumped as if her world suddenly ended. "Excuse me," she said, taking the wireless phone into a bedroom and closing the door.

Donna and Sam made use of the time to kiss and hold onto each other, as if their known worlds ended, too. "I'm glad you don't want to live here," Sam said, not letting go of their embrace.

"Break it up." Zelda shouted when she returned. "Sorry. I

received bad news and I need to leave."

"What is it, Zelda?" Donna tried to caress the older woman.

"Nothing, nothing." Zelda broke down. "No matter what I do. It's never good enough."

Donna held her as Zelda cried broken-heartedly. Donna tried to comfort her, "I love the way you hung the paintings, Zelda. Your customers seemed impressed. Sam and I were intimidated by them. They oozed money and culture. Why are you so upset?"

"Who is judging your actions?" Sam quietly asked, "St. Claire?"

Zelda nodded, then denied her action. "No, no." She brushed Donna away from her. "I'll be all right." Zelda stood up and marched around the couch. "So much has been happening. My life is out of control."

"Mrs. Nelson says that all the time." Sam said.

"Sally Nelson?" Zelda stopped with her back to the wall of windows. The couple's obvious affection for each other filled the room with slivers of cutting reality. St. Clair never held her the way these two clung to each other.

"Yes," Sam said. "I'm sure Sally wouldn't mind my telling you. She's an alcoholic."

"You're not supposed to tell people, Sam," Donna said. "That's why it's called Alcoholics Anonymous."

"Mrs. Nelson tells everyone." Sam defended himself.

"Yes, but she can," Donna said. "You're not supposed to."

"I'll explain to her," Sam said. "Zelda, most of us feel as if we don't have control of everything in our lives."

"How about nothing in your life." Zelda leaned against an exposed black beam. She began to weep quietly.

Donna brought her a glass of water from the refrigerator door. "Tell us what's happening. Come and sit down. Maybe we can help."

"No," Zelda sobbed. She let Donna guide her to the leather love seat. "No one can help me." She seemed convinced.

Sam sat next to Zelda. "Do you want us to pray for you?"

"Oh, sure," Zelda laughed, nearly hysterically. "That will work."

* * *

Second Saturday in December

Back in Ann Arbor, Donna continued her life, painting, exhibiting, selling enough pieces to warrant buying more oils and canvas. The City Club provided an outlet when her house, in the midst of massive renovations, seemed to swallow up awareness of who she was. Isolation did not add to her strength of character. Instead, self-pity crept into the hours spent alone.

At first, her women friends were adamant she continue her life, calling regularly for dinner invitations. Unescorted at dinner, or with Sam, Donna tried to stay in the conversation, meaning she spoke more than was necessary. She knew no one expected her to fill in for David, but she tried to provide information about the art world. Eventually the invitations from women friends were changed to luncheons, when Sam was working. Then mostly men began to call, asking how she was 'doing' with David gone from her life.

When the husbands of friends called, Donna would ask about their wives. She implied she would be sure to thank her friend for having her husband call to console her, which stopped most of the nonsense. The real surprise came from the number of single professors from the university who called to invite her out. She knew them all too well to be interested in being seen with them. Marrying a clone of David's was not appealing. Sam Tedler, however, was the perfect houseguest. He cooked, served her coffee in the morning, in bed, and never failed to satisfy her every wish. She knew she should make an honest man of him and marry him, but her responsibility to David's child kept her decision at bay until it was almost too late.

Sam and Donna were wallpapering the baby's room. Sam was on the stepladder and Donna directed traffic. "Is that straight at the top?"

"You to tell me," Sam said.

"You don't have to bark at me."

Sam slid the soft trowel against the glued paper, smoothing out bubbles as he climbed down the ladder and wiped away a last bit of wetness near the floorboard. "Bark at you?" He wrapped his arms around Donna's thickening figure. "I love you. Is everything all right?"

Donna kissed him before struggling to get free. "Hormones, I guess."

"Why don't you go up and paint. I can finish this."

"Without me?"

"With you in a happier state." Sam laughed. "In your studio creating another masterpiece for Zelda."

"You don't like her, do you?"

"We are not having a fight." Sam returned to wetting down another roll of wallpaper, where flop-eared bunnies romped.

"Love you," Donna said sheepishly. She entered the studio without a plan. A white canvas waited patiently. Then an idea hit. She pulled out her 'Family of Man' collection of black-and-white photographs. One of them showed a young Pakistani lad in a tee shirt large enough for a short dress. He was positioned on one knee, looking at a coin he found on a stone patio, his left hand extended behind for balance. His natural grace resembled a ballet pose. Donna sketched the boy quickly and began to paint his limbs and the cobblestones with the same hues of red, pink, and flesh tones. She made the coin a piece of gold and labeled the painting, in her head, 'The Lost Soul.' But the painting wasn't perfect. The tones blended into each other. Even though she tried to lighten the boy's extended arm, the limb seemed to disappear in the matching tones of the stones beneath him. Donna promised to fix the painting and went off to see how Sam was progressing.

The baby's room was finished and Sam was nowhere in sight.

Then she smelled the garlic and onions frying in the kitchen. Supper would be another feast. "Sam," Donna cooed as she slid her arms around his waist in the kitchen. "Do you get enough attention from me?"

Sam put a lid on the frying pan in front of him. "Why? Are you feeling ignored?"

"I asked you first. I get so involved in painting; I hope you don't feel shut out -- like I did when David's research was filling his mind."

"You are first in my thoughts."

Donna smiled. "I'll set the table."

"You are an absent-minded professor." Sam laughed. "Didn't you notice the table? It's already set up with your new dishes."

Donna kissed the side of Sam's face and returned to the living room. Mentioning David made her remember his words, "Confusion seeks Truth." Did David want to summon up a personal God, one who was on speaking terms with him? Donna turned on the stereo hoping to add classical music to the banquet. Instead, the loud, jarring sounds of Pink Floyd blared out of David's disc player.

"Whoa." Sam dashed into the living room to turn down the noise. "Is that your husband's favorite music?"

"No," Donna shuddered, "It's Norman's."

The doorbell rang. Without thinking, Donna opened the door. Norman was standing on her threshold. "I wanted to see if it was true," Norman said.

Donna stepped back, one hand on her offending stomach. Sam arrived big and imposing as he moved between Donna and Norman. "I don't believe you are welcome here."

"I know," Norman said. "I've seen all I need to see." He gave Donna an evil look and walked down the sidewalk.

Sam shut the door and reached for Donna, who was sliding to the floor. "We'll take out a protective order. He won't be allowed within two miles of you."

"Better call the ambulance, Sam." Donna felt unusually calm as the pain tore at something insider her. "I think I'm miscarrying."

* * *

University Hospital

Sally and John joined Sam in the waiting room. "We just finished the nursery." Sam wrung his hands looking from John to Sally, who still held hands. They were together. He would always live alone. His future with Donna was doomed.

Sally pushed him down into a hard chair. "Was Donna overdoing anything?"

"I don't think so," Sam ran his hands through his blond hair. He hadn't protected the woman he loved. She would never trust him now. "Norman came over."

"You didn't let him in, did you?" John asked.

"No." Sam tried to regain some composure. Think like a police detective. "We need to pick Norman up for questioning. He left a disc of Pink Floyd in David's stereo, probably when he vandalized Donna's house."

"Sally, stay here with Sam," John said. "I'll make the report."

Sally took Sam's hand. "I'm glad you wanted to father Donna's baby."

"I asked her to marry me. Do you think I went against the

Lord's will, staying by her side? I thought I was protecting her. Is that why she lost the baby?"

A young female doctor walked toward them. "You're able to visit your wife now."

Sam did not correct her. "Fine. May I bring my aunt in, also?"

"Of course," the young doctor said, pointing to the room she had just exited. "We'll keep her for a few days for observation."

"Aunt?" Sally asked, as she pulled Sam down the hall.

Sam surprised himself by grinning. "Well, friend of my mother's seemed a bit complicated."

Once inside the room, Sam couldn't move. Donna stretched out her hand in his direction. Her beautiful eyes welcomed him. She didn't hate him. Sally took a towel from the room's bathroom and wrapped up Donna's wet hair. "My goddess returned to me." Sam kissed Donna's forehead. "I'm so sorry."

Donna sighed. "What would I have done if you hadn't been with me? The doctor said I'm able to have more children."

"I'm glad," Sally said. "Sam tells me Norman came over. John is taking measures right now to make sure he is jailed or at least legally constrained from coming within ten miles of you again."

Donna shook her head. "Stealing David's research is not Norman's doing."

"But the vandalism is surely his." Sam took Donna's hand. "Donna Leonard, I hope you don't mind repetition. Will you marry me?"

Donna turned to Sally. "He doesn't want his work on the

nursery to go to waste, right?"

"Donna," Sally said. "Answer the man."

"Yes," Donna drew Sam down for a kiss. "Yes, a thousand times and forever, yes."

* * *

Second Tuesday in December

With all the best intentions, John's request for the Ann Arbor Police Department to arrest Norman for vandalism accomplished nothing. The police referred John to the state's district attorney. John was able to demand an appointment and actually see Jimmy Walker in person, telling him the long tale of David's accident, the various robberies and acts of vicious vandalism, and a warrant for Norman's arrest had been duly issued.

The thing Norman liked most about the Saturday he surprised Donna with a visit, was Donna's hair had turned white at the temples. Donna's life was being successfully terrorized. Now he knew Donna was pregnant and his share of his father's estate would be stretched even further to include another heir. Burning down the house of the woman he hated seemed even in good taste. After Donna's house was a pile of ashes, Norman looked at the cans of gasoline still in his car. He'd followed Sally and John earlier in the day to their expensive house being built on the Huron River. All that fresh timber soaked in gasoline made a great blaze. Too bad he couldn't stick around to toast some marshmallows. Driving past the arriving fire engines, he called Zelda. "We have a lot to talk about."

St. Claire handed the phone to Zelda. "Who is this?" Zelda asked.

"Norman, remember when you told me you would be glad to help in any way?"

"Yes?" Zelda said.

St. Claire had pushed the speaker button before he handed her the phone.

"I'd like to leave town," Norman said. "I burned down David's house and Sally's Bianco's future abode. Could I stay at your place in New York?"

St. Claire shook his head. "I'm sorry, Norman," Zelda tried to come up with a convincing lie. St. Claire wrote down a note and shoved it at her. "I sold my interest in the gallery." Zelda read from the note.

"Is there someone with you?" Norman asked.

"Of course not. Why don't you come over and we'll talk about why you want to leave Ann Arbor."

"I will." Norman hung up the phone.

St. Claire advanced on Zelda. "We might as well make this a sympathetic visit." Then for no apparent reason than his own evilness, he rained more than one blow onto Zelda's face.

Finally, Zelda heard a wisp of a voice within herself sing quietly. "I'm all out of love," She knew the truth. She no longer loved this evil man intent on ruining her looks.

The maniac was turned on by the bloody wreck he made of her nose and the slash his ring cut across her eyebrow. St. Claire carried her into the bedroom, stripped her and draped her face with her bloodied clothing, then coldly mounted her. When he finished, he turned his back saying, "You better make an appointment with your beauty parlor." He laughed at his malicious joke. "You're a mess."

Zelda knew she would never let him touch her again. She'd rather die. How had she deluded herself into believing St. Claire was of any worth? His large brain served no earthly good.

* * *

Norman smiled when he started to knock on Zelda's front door. She left the door of her condominium slightly ajar for him. His packed suitcase for a trip to New York was in the trunk of his car. The sooner he was out of the state, the better off he would be. He wondered what the sentence was for arson. Zelda's obvious welcome was a relief. Norman relaxed and took his time appraising her belongings. White deep carpeting, mahogany furnishings and crystal light fixtures signified there was plenty of money here. Zelda wasn't hard on the eyes, really and better looking than Harry Terkle's housekeeper. Norman was sure he could do this, charm the old dame right out of her last sock.

A chilling bucket filled with ice and expensive Champagne as well as a single, slender flute of a wineglass, promised Zelda was ready. He downed two glassfuls for himself. If he'd been as slim as he wanted to be, he would have left his shirt in the living room, but with his physique less than perfect, he settled for unbuttoning his fly. The bedroom door was open. He could see Zelda's form in the wide bed, covered by a blue silk sheet, waiting for him. Her retro haircut hid her face with her black bangs and blunt-cut hair. All the better, as far as he was concerned. "Ready for me?" He tried to make the tone of his voice into a leer. Zelda didn't move, so he kicked off his shoes and shucked his pants. "Plenty more where this comes from," he said, as he turned back the covers. But Zelda turned her face toward him and he lost all interest. "What happened?"

"St. Claire wanted you to make a sympathetic house call," Zelda said through a split and bruised lip. They heard sirens arriving outside. Norman grabbed his pants and fled into the bathroom, locking the door.

* * *

The policewoman took one look at Zelda. "Where is he?" Sergeant Cramer asked. "Your neighbor reported the attack."

Zelda started to laugh but her mouth hurt too much. Instead of indicating the connecting door in the bedroom to St. Claire's condo, she pointed at the bathroom door. "Norman's in there," she said, and then had the good sense to add. "He's been bragging about burning down Donna Leonard's house as well as Sally Bianco's construction site."

Norman was led away in a state of shock.

Zelda refused to go to the hospital for medical care. "I'll see my plastic surgeon." She didn't intend to face a mirror before all the corrective work was completed and healed. It was time for someone to start taking care of her, if it had to be Zelda Cameron herself.

* * *

Second Wednesday in December

Sally and John visited the county's prosecutor, Jimmy Walker, at his request. His office was devoid of glamour. A metal desk, his executive chair behind it and two plastic upholstered metal chairs, passed for furniture. The decorations were books. Where a wall space remained, Jimmy Walker's diplomas and awards were displayed. Sally imagined Walker didn't plan to stay a prosecutor for long. One case worthy of national coverage and he would be launched on a political career.

"I'll bring in Mrs. Leonard after she's sufficiently recovered." Walker pointed to the chairs in front of his desk. "Sam says she's agreed to marry him."

Sally nodded. At least some good news was in the offing. "Has the arson investigator found anything from our house or Donna's?"

Walker placed a blackened key on a white piece of typing paper. "A safe-deposit key was found in the pile of ash from Professor Leonard's desk. Both homes were purposefully destroyed. The igniting sites were doused in gasoline."

"Has Norman confessed to starting the fires?" Sally asked.

"Not yet," Walker said. "But Zelda Cameron told us he bragged about burning down both the houses."

John characteristically rubbed his baldhead with both of his huge hands. Sally found the familiar gesture endearing. His hands were gentle when they touched her. "Did Norman steal his father's filing cabinets," John asked, "during the memorial service for his father?"

"He lives with his mother," Sally said.

"We have searched his home. He thinks Mrs. Leonard is still pregnant. He admits to hating her."

"Why would he burn down what must be part of his inheritance and why attack our home?" John asked.

"Senseless rage. I guess a fourth of something wasn't quite enough for Norman, and you were friends with his stepmother."

"The initial robbery." Sally looked at John for confirmation. "Never made sense."

"If Harry Terkle is right and the research was worthless, you are correct."

"So." John worked it out. "The research was valid; but David kept part of it, a formula, a secret from Harry and his supervisor."

"We're looking into St. Claire's finances. He owns a New Jersey based drug firm on paper; but there is no building at the address site. Very suspicious."

"Harry mentioned Parkinson test results from China being a problem," Sally said, then asked, "Is there a way to find out who St. Claire is dealing with in China?"

"We are going over his phone calls, too. So far, it looks like he set up Norman for a rape charge."

"Zelda didn't charge Norman with rape, did she?" John asked.

"No, she didn't. We have a warrant out to bring her in for questioning. She lives right next to St. Claire."

"They are lovers," Sally stated.

"Norman swears he never laid a hand on her; but Sergeant

Cramer said Zelda's face was smashed to smithereens." Walker moved the safe-deposit key closer to his side of the desk.

"Are you tracking St. Claire's whereabouts?" John asked.

"Yes, we are. We've impounded all the computers used on the research. David and Harry's home computers are missing; but the university gave us access to the rest. We even confiscated St. Claire's home computer. The FBI agreed to provide us with any relevant information from China."

"How are you going to find the safety-deposit box?" John asked.

"I could use some help. You both own detective licenses, right?"

John shook his head no; but Sally produced both of their valid cards. "I just wanted to keep in the game," Sally told John.

"Good deal," Walker said. "I have a search warrant you can produce for the bank managers. Take this key and find us some concrete information." Sally and John got up to leave. "One more thing. Harry says he'll wear a wire and try to trap St. Claire into disclosing the truth about David's research."

Sally shook her head no. "Harry shouldn't be put through more traumas."

"He won't be able to lie," John said.

Walker agreed. "We'll just take our time and crucify the guy with facts."

"Could you charge St. Claire, somehow, for contributing to David's suicide," Sally asked.

"That would be a stretch, but we're certainly going to use every angle to prejudice the jury, if the judge allows it."

"Who's the judge," Sally asked.

"Joe Wilcox."

"He'll allow more than that!" Sally laughed. St. Claire was going to get his comeuppance sooner rather than later.

* * *

Second Wednesday in December

Zelda went to the one place she was sure St. Claire would not look for her. Harry Terkle opened the door and just stood there when he got a good look at Zelda. She pushed past him and shut the door behind her. "St. Claire did it. This isn't the first time."

"Shouldn't I drive you to the hospital?" Harry took Zelda's hand and led her to the couch. "I don't own any pain killers. Would a glass of brandy help?"

"Only if you serve it with a straw." Zelda wanted to laugh, but her face hurt way too much. "I have an appointment with my plastic surgeon on Monday. He phoned in a pain prescription at the Village Apothecary. Could you pick it up for me? Is there any way I could stay here? St. Claire won't think of you as someone I would run to."

"Absolutely. How could he have hurt you?"

"Oh, he's got enough meanness in him. Plenty to go around." But Zelda felt really good, face torn to pieces and all. She felt freed. "You live quite comfortably here, don't you?" Zelda surveyed the walls lined with bookcases.

"I need a housekeeper." Harry blushed. "Norman Leonard was dallying with my last helper."

"Did you know he's in prison? St. Claire set him up for rape charges."

Harry sat down in a padded rocking chair. "Did Norman rape you?"

"No," Zelda waved her hand at the ridiculous premise. "St. Claire wanted him to be blamed for everything. He did burn down Donna and Sally Bianco's houses."

"St. Claire!" Harry was clearly shocked.

"No. Norman did it, because he thinks Donna is pregnant with David's child."

"Well she is," Harry said.

Zelda wondered if this arrangement with Harry, which he wasn't yet aware of, was going to be a match made in heaven or a life-long teaching job. "Donna lost the baby."

"Oh, dear Lord," Harry slid to his knees, hands clasped in prayer. "When will the evil subside?"

Zelda thought that was a good question for the universe to answer. Maybe Harry wasn't as unschooled as he seemed.

* * *

Paul St. Claire was one-step ahead of Zelda. He inquired at the Village Apothecary if Zelda's pain prescription was ready. The pharmacist knew the professor by name and face. St. Claire signed for drugs for his next-door neighbor, with her permission, more than once.

"They've been picked up already." The druggist told St. Claire, after he checked his records.

"That's right. Zelda told me she'd be visiting a friend; but I've forgotten the name." St. Claire was proud of his ability to think on his feet. "Who signed for the pills?"

Without hesitation, the pharmacist relayed the innocent information, "Harry Terkle. He works for you too, doesn't he?"

"Certainly has for ten years." St. Claire smiled a good-bye.

* * *

Harry Terkle rushed back to his house to give Zelda her prescription. After she was asleep, he drove back to the hospital to give his condolences to Donna. The poor kid, after losing her husband to a freakish accident and the resulting suicide, her house was robbed and then vandalized. Now, her hopes of having David's baby were dashed by a miscarriage. On top of all that, her house was burnt to the ground. Harry felt Donna needed support more than Zelda, who surprised him with her levity about her injuries. Zelda didn't seem quite sane.

* * *

Zelda was shaken awake by St. Claire. She didn't ask him how he got into Harry's house, or how he found her. Nothing surprised her as far as St. Claire's intellectual capabilities were concerned. What shocked her was he was carrying a gun, pointing it at her. "Why didn't you just shoot me in my sleep?" Her despair of being free of this fiend arrived with complete calm. She breathed in his familiar cologne. She picked out the blue silk tie he was wearing. She realized he would have a problem finding a maid as devoted as she. The reason for her initial attraction was lost somewhere in her memory. Maui. That was it. The weather on the island was seductive all by itself. She wondered for a moment why fate led her to this bank account of evil.

"I did not want to miss all your sweet pleadings?" St. Claire ran his finger across her broken nose.

Even with the painkillers, Zelda winced. "Well, I'm awake now." She felt happy again. This was going to end, badly for her; but the stretch of harsh days into the future was gone. "Let me see the means of my destruction." Zelda was surprised to hear herself actually coo. St. Claire held the gun in the palm of his hand for her to see. Zelda bent over it, stroking it with her perfectly manicured nail. "Is it heavy?" Somewhere in Zelda's brain a bright light was growing in size. At first, she thought the light was the portal dead people are supposed to look at to find the way to heaven, which didn't make sense with her list of sins. Then, Zelda slowly realized the brightness of the idea forming in her head. St. Claire looked into her eyes, gauging her. She wondered if he could read her thoughts. "Do you want to have a final go at me?"

"That would be too sad to contemplate," St. Claire said, but his voice was husky with thoughts of lust.

"Oh, come on, Paul." Zelda lifted her nightgown. "Give it a go."

The savage instinct in St. Claire ruled and he laid the grey gun on Harry Terkle's blue bedspread to unbuckle his belt. That was all Zelda needed. He was dead before he hit the ground with a bullet hole right above his prominent nose, right between the eyes.

Chapter Seventeen

Third Friday in December

The Nelson table was set for six. Sam was picking Sylvester up at the airport to serve as his best man on Saturday. Donna was sleeping soundly in the guest bedroom, where her bridal gown hung within easy reach of her fingertips. John was experimenting with pecan waffles in the kitchen, sending delicious odors throughout the condo.

Sally was on the telephone with her AA sponsor. "The Fourth Step has been rolling around in my head, but this case was a priority."

"Your program is more important than work," Grace said. "You've done one before, so it shouldn't be complicated for you. What addiction are you working on?"

"Spending. The framework of the house we were planning was torched."

"Are you using the arson as an excuse to overspend?"

"We were thinking of selling my condo and moving to Illinois. John's home is empty."

"You plan to live in Ann Arbor eventually?"

Sally smoothed the pages of her empty journal. "Yes. But, I'm thinking of how best to help with the wedding expenses of a friend."

"Another excuse for your addiction with money? Why don't you list all of them. There are more."

Sally smiled to herself. "Smart cookie aren't you."

"The program is the program. Let's start by you writing down a 'Lady Bountiful' list."

"The needs of the stepchildren of..."

"Make sure your husband sees the list before you call me." Grace laughed. "I expect a few items about redecorating his home in Illinois will be added."

"How is this going to help?" Sally closed her empty journal.

"Your life is going to become manageable with the help of your Higher Power."

"But the fourth step is supposed to list my faults."

"By the time you address all your excuses to outspend any amount of income, we will find out why *you* find it necessary to let a natural generosity turn into a destructive obsession. Next to each item, I expect you to write down how this will improve your conscious contact with God."

"You think I give money to buy affection?"

"This is your inventory, not mine." Grace coughed. "Sorry, I need to run. Are you on course?"

"I am," Sally said. "Thank you." Somewhat humbled by the discussion, Sally stared at the closed journal. She was going to need a great deal of honesty to thoroughly look at her motivations for largesse."

John called for her to join him in the kitchen. "This is the best waffle machine. It beeps when they're done!"

"Shouldn't we wait until we see the whites of their eyes, before you make anymore?"

"Take a bite." John pulled her close to his side as he offered her a fork full.

Leaning into his warmth, Sally opened her mouth like an obedient child. "Oh, they're great."

John squared his shoulders. "Told you."

"Turn the oven on warm and we'll keep these hot. I think you should stop for a while."

"I'll finish this batch and make more when the boys arrive." John hugged her shoulder and looked into her eyes. "Usually your sponsor cheers you."

"She's given me a horrendous task."

"Is she supposed to do that?"

Sally laughed. "Oh yes. Sponsors lead us where God's will points."

"Well all right then." John turned her around and wacked her bottom. "Get to it, before the boys arrive."

"Not that simple." Sally stood in the kitchen's doorway to the entrance hall. Thankfully, the doorbell rang. "They're here."

Instead, Harry Terkle arrived. Sally nearly pulled him to the table. "Sit, sit. I'll hang up your coat. John, here's one customer." After John delivered the waffles and Harry raised his fork, Sally waved at John. "I'll just run upstairs and check on Donna."

John frowned as he sat down at the table. "Stay down here and let her sleep. Harry, tell us what Jimmy Walker needs from us."

Harry swallowed half a glass of milk. "These are superb. You should start a restaurant. Thank you for finding David's notes. Jimmy said he doesn't need any more from us until the trial of poor Norman. Unfortunately, my colleagues don't believe David came up with the answer for Parkinson's. Sometimes a drug can be applied to other uses."

"Like glaucoma medicine or Sjogren's?"

"I'm not familiar with Sjogren's disease."

"Rheumatoid Arthritis." Sally pointed to her eyes. "Dry eyes, no saliva, and joint pain."

"You met Sam and Sylvester Tedler," John said.

"In the hoosegow." Harry smiled first at Sally and then at John. "I need to thank all of you."

* * *

When Sam and Sylvester arrived, Donna was still sleeping. "You both remember Harry Terkle? I'm thinking of a thousand questions about Mary Jo and the children. How do they like Kansas City?"

"They're coming tomorrow, with Harriett," Sylvester dug into a stack of waffles, before patting some added weight around his middle. "See what being married does for a guy?"

"You're beautiful." Sam looked toward the stairway. "She's not awake?"

"Plenty of time," Sally said.

Sylvester encouraged John to refill his plate. "Kansas City is a lot bigger than Ann Arbor. I expect to be promoted by this time next year."

Sam nodded. Sally knew Sylvester pushed himself. His career ascension in law enforcement seemed to be his top goal in life. Sam, on the other hand, let things happen. He was more interested in trying to make a life for Donna, worthy of the girl.

"More criminals per capita down there?" Sally asked just to be polite.

"I don't know what you're asking." Sylvester said, as he sized up Sam. "But there are plenty of cases to go around." Sam ate in silence. Sally could tell being a younger brother to a competitive older brother could be a pain. "John said your bachelor party is being held in the police department basement." Sylvester's tone implied a stodgy gathering.

"Cake and coffee. Is that all right with you?" Sam asked.

"Sure, sure. I came a day early because I thought you might want to go out on the town."

"Had enough of that business to last a lifetime," Sam said.

"I guess." Sylvester was clearly disappointed.

"How's that big family of yours?" John asked.

After devouring more than his share of the waffles, Sylvester said, "Don't tell Mary Jo, but I never thought I would want children."

"Why not?" Sam asked.

"I didn't think Mother did a very good job teaching us how to parent kids. Especially with Dad gone since I was seven."

"I think your mother did you both a favor," Sally said. She knew their cold father only from stories their mother shared.

"At least," Sam said, "we didn't live with bickering parents."

"I don't think I would have minded. I missed Dad."

"When I visit him out in Wyoming, I don't feel he's a warm and fuzzy kind of guy." Sam attention waivered to the empty staircase. "Of course, Mother wasn't perfect."

"You don't know the half of it."

"Ancient history." Sally wished for a moment that Sylvester was too busy on some fantastic murder case to come to Sam's wedding.

"How do you get along with the kids?" Harry asked.

"They're so timid. I guess their father, Ricco, scarred them for life."

"How is Mary Jo with them?" Sally wondered how people changed the perceptions of young children who knew so much personal violence.

"She's great. I wish, sometimes, she spent more time with me. But you can't find fault with the woman for her treatment of those kids."

"What are their ages again?" John asked.

"I've got a picture with me." Sylvester made no attempt to retrieve a photo.

Sam got up from the table without finishing his plate. He strolled over to the stairs as if to listen for Donna's movements. "We're staying at Weber's. You are, too. We'll look for a place after the honeymoon."

"Ann Arbor really experienced a crime wave this year." Sylvester said.

"At least an arson wave." Sally admitted. "We're only providing state housing for one criminal."

"Why's that?"

"The real villain was shot and killed by his mistress," Harry said. "Then she turned around and overdosed on painkillers."

John ushered the group into the front room. "For some reason Zelda, the mistress, took shelter with Harry. Your house was really messed up with a bleeding corpse in the bedroom and a stiff, suicide in his front room."

"Donna's kind of adopted me." Harry smiled as Donna joined them.

"Bring her plate in here." Sally directed John as she watched Donna sit next to a cheered up Sam.

Sam slid his arm around Donna waist. "Sally and John are moving back to Illinois, where John has a house. The dead guy burnt down their dream house, the same week Donna's stepson torched hers."

Harry seemed to take comfort by telling, "The prosecutor assures me Norman will be in jail for thirty years."

"Mary Jo's really looking forward to her trip out here with the kids," Sylvester said.

Donna swept her long hair away from Sam's embrace. "I'm excited to meet them. Is there any chance you would move back to

Ann Arbor?"

"I like Kansas City," Sylvester said.

Sally could tell Sam was judging Sylvester to be more like their dad, not one of those warm and fuzzy kind of guys.

PART II

The Appropriate Way

Chapter One

Wednesday, January 2nd
Route 64, West of St. Charles, Illinois

Heading east on their drive to Wayne, John and Sally Nelson nodded to each other in a state of awe at the winter's pink dawn shimmering on each iced twig, tree limb and snow bank along the road. The sky was sea of soft clouds floating in the rosy glow of sunrise. Sally trusted her new husband to maneuver their Honda over the freshly salted roads. She pointed to the dazzling sight. "How can anyone hate winter?"

"No one who retires to Florida will witness this." John let up on the gas as they approached a banked curve in the road. "Sure a minority lives on the ocean or the Gulf, but they can't possibly conceive of this sustained miracle of beauty."

"Iced in pink grandeur." Sally snuggled into her neck scarf, breathing in a comforting whiff of Arpege perfume. "Let's promise never to retire down south. Anyone with a brain knows how to bundle up against the cold. In hot weather, even nude, you can drip with sweat."

"I've always wondered if brains swell in the summer." John kept both hands on the steering wheel. "Maybe that's why people get to a flash point and end-up lashing out."

"Crime rates sky-rocket in heat waves." Sally stretched out her gloved hands to the dash-board heater. "Although, the cases we investigated didn't involve climate."

"People in the northern hemisphere produced the world's industrial and technological revolutions. In the tropics and deserts, heated brain cells generate fiendish hatreds." John was on a roll. "And, the Holidays need snow."

"Have you read '*The Golden Bough*'?" Sally asked. "I have a copy back home. It's a pagan history describing hunters scurrying around to bring the remaining green trees into their caves to rescue them from the frost."

"I bet they worshipped their fires when the sun diminished." John gestured in the direction of the houses in town adorned with Christmas lights. "Decorations appreciate a background of ice-encrusted snow." He took his eyes off the road for a second to look her way. "We need to make a trip back to Ann Arbor to pack up the rest of your belongings."

Sally laughed. "We better install a few bookshelves in your house first." She loved her new husband's voice, maybe not the decorating scheme of his house. Too starkly modern for her taste. Nothing mattered as long as she could be within John's reach. The Lord could allow criminals to cross her path a hundred times, burn down her house, bury her friends, disperse her family, and move her hither and yon, if He would keep this one man near her. She'd been alone long enough. At 67 finding John, who said he'd resolved in high-school never to marry anyone but her, kept the world fresh and marvelous.

At their New Year's Day wedding reception the day before, John had accepted an invitation to visit Dunham Castle in Wayne. The hazardous and slowed eight-mile drive allowed them to reach the Armstrongs' castle in a little over an hour.

Back in the roaring Twenties, the yellow limestone castle was disassembled in Ireland and then rebuilt on the corner of Dunham and Territory Roads. Sally admitted when she attended St. Charles high school she too had dreamt of someday being a guest of the castle. Bret Armstrong revealed to John that he'd invested most of his father-in-law's funds to change the apartment house, which the castle had degenerated into, back to its original grandeur.

When they walked up to the front entrance and knocked, a butler in a regulation dark suit opened the giant door. "Whom shall I say is calling?"

John banged Sally's back, whispering, "Isn't that cool?"

Sally answered for her husband, "The Nelsons, John and Sally."

With the slightest hint of a frown, the butler ushered them into a small sitting room. The drapes were thick and dark, the tables of antique marble, and the chandelier perhaps a Tiffany reproduction. A hint of pine furniture polish testified to the room's cleanliness.

"Should we to sit or stand?" John asked after the butler closed the door on them.

"Sit." Sally decided, pocketing her leather gloves. "I suspect you should remove your hat."

"Oh," John complained, as he obliged. "I wanted Bret to admire my fur hat. The butler must be our age. Is there a school for butlers?"

Sally smiled not able to hide her enjoyment in her husband of three days. Over six feet, his height belied his youthful heart shining forth in delight with simple things. She'd given him the hat for Christmas and here he was trying to show off in front of a new acquaintance. The Lord was abundant in His gifts. Their shared age hadn't diminished the pleasure of their love or their curiosity for the world around them.

Bret and Matilda Armstrong gathered them from the sitting room. "I've prepared brunch for us," Matilda said, taking John's arm to lead him across the mammoth entrance hall.

The dining room held a requisite long table where four places were set at the far end. Bret and Matilda sat across from John and Sally. A center piece of evergreens and candles ran down the table, which could easily seat twenty. Bret invited them to fill their plates from a sideboard set with a scrumptious brunch of waffles with strawberry and whipped cream toppings, ham, heavenly-smelling sausages, poached eggs, English muffins and cherry or cheese Danish. The Christmas dinnerware added to the festive meal's enjoyment. Orange juice with Champaign was available, but John followed Sally's example and only drank the fragrant black coffee.

"Do hurry along," Bret insisted after brunch. He was set on giving John and Sally the promised tour of the castle's twenty rooms.

Each hall, each bedroom and sitting room, even the bathrooms were decorated with Christmas trees, wreathes, tiny villages, animated toys, and all good and cheery paraphernalia. The castle's abundance of stained-glass windows and dark carved woodwork alone were worth the Holiday tour.

"Matilda enrolled us in the Christmas tour list with the Chamber of Commerce." Bret Armstrong's chest swelled under his red velvet vest. "She loves showing the place off. Now she's reluctant to pack all this magnificence away until next year."

"I believe in year-round Christmas." John laughed. "I hardly leave the hotel during the season." He nudged Sally, "Except for this year."

Sally made a mental note. John could enjoy Christmas every day. She hoped she could find presents he didn't already own. The unwritten thank-you cards for their New Year's Eve wedding gifts still loomed on Sally's mental to-do list.

Back on the ground floor, they found Matilda waiting in the foyer. She'd finished a comment to the butler.

And, Sally recognized Peter Masters, Matilda's father, who she'd met at her surprise wedding reception. He leaned against the outer wall near the door, as if exhausted from an early morning run. But who would run in these wintry conditions? Father and daughter were the same height, taller than either John or Bret.

Matilda's gracious mood had altered. "Excuse us, for a moment." She directed Bret to follow her father into a room opposite the parlor Sally and John were first shown.

Bret turned to John. "Please, come with us."

Sally followed on John's heels into a breath-taking library. Her attention couldn't concentrate on the array of leather bindings on the floor-to-ceiling shelves, for long.

"It's your mother." Peter touched Matilda's arm. "When I got home ..." His voice broke and he straightened his tie for their benefit. "...from the airport this morning." He dropped down into a plush red chair, as if he'd thoroughly explained his distress.

Sally and John exchanged glances. The butler brought in a tray of orange juice, coffee and water, placing it on the coffee table. When Matilda failed to respond to her father or act as a hostess, Sally poured and offered Peter a glass of water.

Without explaining the cause of his dismay, Peter finished off the water. "I'll get a room at the Pheasant Run. Don't go out there."

"To the house?" Bret sat down opposite his father-in-law.

"It's gone." Peter leaned over to replace his empty glass on the tray. He cradled his head in his hands, reminding Sally of John's habit of rubbing his bald head to think. Peter's shoulders shook with sobs. "...in the fire."

Matilda nearly collapsed, sitting instead on the arm of her father's chair, as if trying to digest the awful news. "When did it happen?"

Then Peter straightened, shaking his head in despair. "The firemen are still out there. I had rushed in before they could stop me. They were covering her body in front of the fireplace. She was still holding her pewter candlestick."

"Mother never used those candlesticks." Matilda stood up and then sat down next to Bret. "...her Colonial ancestors..."

The family was going to need professional help to process the trauma and its cause. Matilda already seemed in denial. Sally stepped to the door and motioned for the butler, showing him her detective badge. "Call the police department. Ask for Sheriff Art Woods. Tell him to come out here, right now. Tell him Sally Bianco said, 'Now!'"

John overheard her directions. "Sally Nelson," he whispered.

Sally patted John's bald head before kissing his cheek. "My license is under Sally Bianco's name."

All three of them Art Woods, John and Sally attended the same high school in St. Charles fifty years earlier. Art had already accepted John and Sally's detective licenses on an earlier missing person case. And, with the recent addition of arson expertise due to their latest case when the criminal had set fire to their dream home's construction, Sally was sure Art would want them involved.

***

In a New York minute, before the Armstrongs could thoroughly calm Peter Masters, Sheriff Art Woods, with only a sweater on against the cold, knocked on the castle door. "Where is your coat?" Sally admonished.

"You said now." Sheriff Woods entered the deadly quiet of the library.

After Sally explained all she knew, Sheriff Woods escorted Sally, Matilda, and Peter to his police car. John and Bret followed the cruiser to the Masters' country place less than a half-mile away. Parked cars clogged both sides of West Territorial Road until they reached the Masters' farm lane. Was Art made uncomfortable by his friend's old neighborhood? Tony Montgomery committed suicide when they were all teenagers together.

"Who are all these people?" Peter asked them.

Two television trucks vied for parking spots on the road. A police barricade blocked the lane to the house. After his superior explained who the occupants of the car behind them were, the young officer, Sally recognized as Tim Hanson, prepared to let both cars pass.

Before Tim moved away from the back window of the police car, Matilda touched his arm. "Where are the horses?"

"Your neighbor, the Montgomerys, took them over to their place as soon as Carolyn Montgomery called us. The house was completely in flames."

Matilda had nodded.

The sheriff tugged at his hat as if to remind himself he was no longer the grieving young teenager, she'd known so long ago. Tony's suicide had ended more than their friendship. She and Art Woods, the sheriff, had dated in those baffling, poignant years.

She'd met Gabby, Art's wife, during her last visit to her hometown, when John Nelson helped her find a missing woman. John had followed her to Ann Arbor to assist in the investigation. Sally was glad he was near, when her bookstore friend, Robert Koelz, died of a stroke. They'd solved the crime, finding the husband had killed a former wife. John proved his worth as a stalwart friend throughout their next painful case when a crazy arsonist burnt their dream home to the ground. Their marriage seemed a logical and emotionally solid decision and they'd moved back to John's house in St. Charles.

Sheriff Woods drove slowly toward the pandemonium of fire trucks and police cars. Only blackened walls remained of the Masters' home. A fireplace loomed inside, like an ebony tombstone.

"Everything's gone. Everything's gone," Peter kept repeating as he got out of the front seat.

Sally followed Matilda toward the ambulance, where a body was being loaded. The smell of smoke and burnt flesh lingered. Matilda stood quietly, but her hands reached for Bret, as she scrutinized the form on the stretcher. Suddenly, Matilda caught the arm of one of the attendants.

Sally rushed over to release her grip. "It's all right, dear."

"No." Matilda would not let go of the stretcher. "It's too short for Mother!"

Sally motioned for Sheriff Woods and John to come to her aid. "Calm down, Matilda."

"Sally." John let her know he stood behind her.

Matilda reached for the blanket covering the corpse, but the attendant gently shouldered her aside. "Dad," Matilda yelled, as the door closed on the ambulance. Peter hurried over to Matilda.

Sheriff Woods and Tim now held Matilda by the shoulders, one cop on each side. Sally pulled at the back of Sheriff Woods' uniform. "Ma'am, don't do that again." Sheriff Woods' tone was calm, but threatening.

Sally took a step back. Her old friend, Art, didn't know she had pulled on his sweater. Instead, John's arm wrapped around her.

"Mother is six feet tall." Matilda turned to Tim. Then to Sheriff Woods, she shouted, "That's not her."

"Sheriff?" Tim seemed at a loss.

Sally disengaged herself from John's embrace and walked around in front of Matilda. She nodded to Matilda's stunned father. Another, older cop appeared with a fur-lined overcoat. He helped Sheriff Woods into its sleeves. Sally's brain cells locked on the stray thought that they had all climbed out from under Gogol's overcoat. Harold Bloom's name came next to mind, but not any sober wisdom with the random name. Things were happening too fast to get a firm grip on any theory about the cause of the fire. Secrets and conflicts among long-standing friendships and feuds filled the cold air with conflicting sentiments and unanswered questions.

"Stop the ambulance." Matilda struggled against Tim, her handler. Sheriff Woods held up his hand and the ambulance rolled to a stop. Matilda was freed to stand alone. "Check to see if she has an emerald and diamond wedding ring."

Peter slipped his arm around his daughter's waist, bending his head into her shoulder. Matilda stroked her father's hair. "They'll find her ring in the fireplace." Peter choked on his sobbing words. "She threw it there before I left for Dallas."

Sally signaled for the cops to close in again. Sheriff Woods strolled over. "What's the trouble now, Sally?"

"You'll want to question these people at the station." John motioned to the mourners. "Something's not right."

Sally let out her breath. Father and daughter were conducted without handcuffs into the back seat of the police car. Sally's heart was sending out familiar flipping signals to let her know she needed to relax, immediately.

John handed his card to Tim, who already wore his examination gloves.

Those wedding-gift thank you cards could wait. Sally needed to find out what was going on.

"Our phone numbers are on the card." John seemed inordinately calm. "If any charges are filed, I expect Bret Armstrong will send the Masters' family lawyer over to the station."

Bret took a step toward the moving police vehicle, but John caught his shoulder. "Let's go in our car."

In their Honda, Sally, John, and Bret Armstrong followed the police car back down the lane. Media people and assorted neighbors stuck their IPhones and camcorders up to the windows of both cars. "Don't think the worst," Sally said. "It will all be cleared up, shortly."

"You should stay with Sally and me." John looked at Sally in the rear-view mirror. "Until everything is straightened out."

Bret groaned. "What am I going to do without Matilda? Her life is entwined in my shoelaces. Now some horrible mistake. On television, innocent people get swept up by the hysterical justice system in mysterious deaths. My Matilda!" Bret let his head lean against the back of the front seat. Caught sobs suffocated his breath.

Sally patted his shoulder. "Hang on, Bret. John and I can help figure this out for you. Sheriff Woods only wants to question Matilda and her father."

Sally's mind was bombarded with questions. Why was Matilda initially not upset about her father's news? Was it because she knew her mother was safe? They needed to find Mrs. Masters. And who was the dead woman in the house, holding a candlestick no less? 'Hang on' sounded like a good suggestion, but to whom. Sally straightened up in the car. "Do you pray very much?"

Bret coughed with emotion. "I did when I was younger.

John said, "If I didn't say the Our Father every day, I think I'd lose my place." He smiled at Sally in the rear mirror. "I don't mean my job as a detective or my home. I mean where I am, where my soul resides, hopefully in harmony with my intentions."

"Those policemen," Sally said, "are doing the best they know how. The prayer I say is, 'God, I offer myself to you to build and do with me what Thou will. Grant me victory over my present difficulties so that I can bear witness to those I'm trying to help of your power, your love, and your way of life. Help me to do Thy will always.'"

John interrupted. "We need to wait for things to work out sometimes."

Sally felt like a two year old, wanting everything to be righted immediately. Then her detective instincts slipped back into gear.

When did the fire start? "Let's go by the police station, John instead of taking Bret home."

"Right," John said. "Matilda and her father will need a ride home."

Sally wasn't as interested in being of service as she was in learning the answers to a growing list of questions. "Why was Tim Hanson at the fire?"

"He is a police officer," Bret said.

John picked up the clue. "How did he get there before the sheriff?"

In the rear-view mirror Sally caught John's attention and motioned with her finger over her lips not to say anymore in front of Bret. She needed to bounce ideas off John when they were alone. "Do you want to pick up your car and follow us?"

"Yes." Bret said, rather unconvinced of the suggestion. "I'll do that."

Shoveling the snow and melting ice away from Bret's garage door took more time than Sally planned, but when they were finally alone in the Honda with Bret trailing them in his yellow Cadillac, John asked, "Did Peter say something about when he got home from the airport?"

"But he was with us last night at the reception. We didn't meet his wife." Sally's mind ticked of the unanswered questions. "When did he go to Dallas? When did his wife take off her wedding ring?"

"Maybe Sheriff Woods will have some answers?" John didn't sound hopeful.

"That's the trouble with questioning people," Sally said. "You need to know what to ask."

* * *

Kane County Courthouse, Geneva, Illinois
County Sheriff's Office

Sheriff Art Woods waited for Sally and John to arrive before he interrogated Matilda Armstrong or Peter Masters, who were apparently not speaking to each other. They fidgeted and glared at each other on the other side of the mirrored window. As he waited for the Nelsons, Art propped his cold feet up on his desk. Carolyn Montgomery had called in the fire report. Thoughts of Sally as a teenager swept the scene of the dead woman's fiery demise out of immediate focus. And then, the sad memories of his friend, Tony Montgomery, swept away the present.

It was May in 1957. Six more weeks of the high-school year remained after Art first ran into Sally. He spotted Tony in the school's parking lot. Tony was surrounded by a group of jocks hanging on his every word. Art sauntered over trying not to show his own eagerness. Tony stepped away from the group and clapped Art on the shoulder. "How's the last male virgin in the senior class?" Pretending not to hear the shaming tease, the other untested boys headed for their cars. "Hey," Art said loud enough for the departing gang to hear, "I'm closing in on your girl-friend's buddy."

"Who's that?" Art had hoped Tony hadn't noticed.

Tony climbed into the passenger side of Art's mother's old

Chevy. "The librarian with glasses. Made for each other." Tony grinned without malice. "Virgin on virgin."

"You're really hung up on that virgin label." Art grumbled as he began the long drive out west to Tony's parents' farm. A dreadful guilt rose in Art's stomach. He glanced at Tony, his idol. A god to him really. Tony was smooth, unruffled by the great mystery of women.

Dates were torture to Art, wondering when to put his arm around a girl, bumping heads trying to play kissy-face, and groping more out of curiosity than passion. He hated fending off the aggressive ones, hoping the girls wouldn't blab how he did *not* allow them to play with him. He would someday, but he wanted the act to mean something. Okay, maybe he wouldn't marry the first girl; but he needed at least to like her. And now he had offered up Sally to Tony's dirty gristmill, like a virgin to a pagan god.

"Drive down Dean Street to Randall," Tony said. "You'll get a glimpse of your honey."

Art obeyed and sure enough, Sally with her arms full of books was walking briskly past a small park on Dean Street.

"Want to pick her up?"

"Naw." Art bluffed away his fears. "I gave her enough excitement for one day."

Tony eyed him. "Did you land one on her?"

"Not yet. I'm warming her up first." '*Amazing,*' Art thought, glimpsing Sally's form in the rearview mirror. She meant nothing to him other than a way to get out of paying a late library book fee; but with Tony's prodding, she almost seemed desirable. "Where does she live?" He asked, as they neared railroad tracks.

"Last house on the right."

A small, concrete-block house backed up to the tracks. Behind the house on the far side of the tracks, two iron-stamping plants fronted with brick offices tarnished the landscape.

"Her daddy built the house," Tony said, "with a loan from the Norris family."

"How do you know that?"

"He's painting our barns, in between jawing us to death." Tony laughed. "Name's Denny. The cranky old man threw an open can of paint at our gander when she nipped him. Great sight though, red paint on a mad white goose. Denny said he managed farms before he started painting but his temper kept getting him fired."

"His daughter seems docile enough."

"Probably beats her."

Art laughed. Had she'd ever been struck? She did seem skittish, but for a blushing librarian, she carried herself well, head high, a natural grace. Art knew no one else had staked her out. He punched at Tony's shoulder. "Maybe I should give the kid a thrill."

At the farm, Tony got out of the car, rubbing his shoulder. He came over to Art's open window. A warm breeze from the barns blew acid, fecal smells into the car. Tony leaned over, grinning. "Give her something to think about before we're off to college."

As he drove away, Art stared at Tony in his rear-view mirror. He stood in the lane with his hand on his crotch, thrusting his hips.

Once out of sight of the farm, Art stopped the car. A group of curious steers walked up to the fencerow. Reaching behind the seat, he rolled down the back windows to get rid of the manure smells. As he righted himself, his elbow hit the wheel. The steers bolted at the short blast. He waited until they regained their dignity and amble away. One steer mounted another. Maybe being in the vicinity of all these rutting animals intensified Tony's libido.

Sheriff Art Woods remembered deciding, at the time, he might need to rethink Tony's influence in his life. He wished he'd heeded his own cautions. The Sheriff let his feet fall to the floor in his private office at the Geneva police station.

A much older and wiser Sally Bianco stood in his doorway. "Is Tim here?" She asked.

"No." He said, slowly, knowing Sally would have a reason for asking. She was always sharp and he'd recently worked with her to find a missing abused wife. "He's still at the scene. I asked him to check the fireplace for Mrs. Masters' wedding ring."

"Would Matilda be more comfortable answering your questions with me along?"

"Sure, sure. You go ahead. The two-way glass will let me witness the answers."

"Bret will be here in a minute." John stuck his head in the door.

Sheriff Woods spoke to the desk sergeant. "Direct Mr. Armstrong to my office. We'll be along shortly."

"What about her father, Peter Masters," Sally asked. "Is it a good idea to keep him waiting in a different room?"

"Yes," Sheriff Woods smiled at Sally. "Another good idea."

Chapter Two

After her father left the witness room, Sally observed Matilda rubbed her forehead. "I don't understand, I don't understand."

Yes, St. Frances' prayer about the need to understand others, a daughter should be able to figure out her own father. Across the table from her, Sally put her hand on Matilda's arm. "Your mother is alive, somewhere."

Matilda took Sally's hand, leaning over to search Sally's eyes. "Are you sure?"

Sally's heart re-opened. For the first time, she believed she could provide something of value to this distraught young woman. To be of service seemed as honorable as any other road to follow God's will. She patted Matilda's hand. "We'll get you through this." Wishing she could produce a copy of Daniel Defoe's book, she quoted a passage, "So little do we see before us in the world.... (God) does not leave his creatures so absolutely destitute. In the worst circumstances they have always something to be thankful for."

Matilda's calm seemed restored. "Was that a Bible passage?"

"Defoe's '*Robinson Crusoe,*'" Sally admitted. "How long have you known Tim Hanson?"

"Tim." Matilda said without elaborating. A faint blush crept up Matilda's throat. Matilda must have sensed the heated blood rising to her cheeks. She plucked a hair out of her eyebrow. Sally winced for her, but didn't want to let go of the prickly question. She waited, counting off the seconds. Matilda bent down, as if studying her folded hands. Her blonde straight hair nearly covered her face. Sally could almost hear the gears in her brain racing around. She might be praying. Finally, Matilda raised her head. "I love Bret."

"More than Tim?" The question popped out before Sally recognized there was a reason to ask it.

"No. Yes." Matilda tugged at another bothersome hair in her left eyebrow. "I no longer know." She straightened her posture and met Sally's gaze. "How does knowing Tim relate to the fire?"

"Tim was out there." Sally relaxed as her brain focused on Matilda's responses.

"No he wasn't. The fire department probably called Tim." Matilda shook her head as if trying to produce more excuses. "Don't the police always go to fires?"

"Were you in school with Tim?" Sally shifted her gaze to give the young woman a break.

Matilda worried her pearl necklace. "Not since eighth grade at St. Patrick's."

"When did you get back together?" The answer would implicate Tim, the young man Sally had babysat while she was in high school.

"Before I married Bret." Matilda seemed to relax, perhaps planning how to cover up something. "My father drinks. When he drinks, people get in his way."

"Like your mother?"

"Tim was called to the house. Sheriff Woods, too. More than once. Mother loves Bret. I mean she likes him as a husband for me. A stockbroker and all." Matilda opened her eyes wider to appear more honest. "Tim's future didn't seem promising."

"But you kept Tim on the side."

"Well, yes." Matilda stuck her chin out and then thought better of it. "He wouldn't hurt a flea. Certainly not Mother."

"Your mother hasn't been injured."

"Bret and I were married five years ago." Matilda put her purse on the table, opened it as if searching for her keys.

Sally recognized the defensive, stall tactic. Tim said he'd been a policeman for two years. If Matilda knew Tim before her marriage, five years ago, why did Tim join the police force two years ago?

"I don't know where my mother is." Matilda even batted her eyelashes to enhance the plea for sympathy.

"Don't you?" Sally toned down her harsh questions. "Doesn't she own a safe place your father isn't privy to?"

"She wouldn't be there." Matilda did seem confused. "Because Dad said he returned from Dallas."

"Who is in Dallas?"

"My grandmother."

"Is your cell phone in your purse?" Sally asked.

"Will it work in here?" Matilda retrieved her phone and punched in the numbers for her grandmother.

Sally cocked her head. "Hit the speaker button."

"Rinehardt residence." Was heard on Matilda's cell phone.

"Grandma, I …" Matilda's throat allowed no further sound.

"No," the voice said, "Matilda?" Not only did Matilda's voice fail her, now her brain seemed to shut down. "Who's calling?" The voice sounded off-putting as if expecting to hang up on an inexperienced phone solicitor.

"It's me, Mother," Matilda finally was able to say.

"What's wrong?" Mrs. Masters asked, and then added. "I told you Tim was a problem."

"No! He's fine now!" Matilda sobbed into the phone.

"Was there another accident?"

Matilda stopped crying. "Not one hair on Bret's head is harmed." They heard Mrs. Masters sigh in relief.

Sally reached for the phone and Matilda handed it over. "Mrs. Masters, this is detective Sally Bianco. Your husband has not been injured either, but your house has been burnt to the ground.'

"What, who was hurt?" Mrs. Masters yelled. "Tell me!"

Sally tried in a calming voice, "A female body was recovered near the fireplace. Could you please arrange to fly home? We need your input in the investigation."

"I'll be on the next flight out of Dallas. Tell Matilda we'll talk then." She hung up.

"Excuse me just for a minute, Matilda." Sally started to leave the witness room.

"Before you go." Matilda stood. "Bret doesn't need to know about Tim, does he?"

"That's for you to determine with the help of your Maker."

In the station's recording facility, Sally hugged John just to remind Sheriff Woods where her loyalties stood. Over John's shoulder, she noticed Peter Masters in the window on the opposite side of the viewing room. Peter was answering his cell phone.

Sheriff Woods witnessed the same action; but Sally was surprised because he chose to tease her. "Never got over your religious training, I see."

John's back went up. He must have perceived more in the remark than even Sheriff Woods intended. "Her religion get in your way, did it?"

"Once." Sheriff Woods admitted.

Sally changed the subject. "We might as well send Matilda home with her husband, but Peter still needs to be questioned.

John said, "I didn't hear Mrs. Masters ask about her husband."

Sheriff Woods scratched his full head of gray hair. "Seems I need a word with Tim, too."

"Remember when Tim introduced himself to you?" John asked Sally. John turned then to Sheriff Woods to explain, "We both thought Tim knew something he wanted to tell us at our wedding reception, when we said we were detectives."

"Maybe you should talk to him." Sheriff Woods grumbled. "He seems to think a lot of Sally."

"She used to babysit for him, right, Sally?" John touched Sally's shoulder to get her attention.

"Sorry, thinking. Yes, I did babysit for the family. Tim's not back, right? John, why don't you ask Peter Masters what happened? I need to make some notes."

"I've known Peter long enough," Sheriff Woods said. He plugged in an earpiece. "I'll do it. Use this mike to cue me."

Sally's head was spinning. "I could use a pot of coffee."

"Coming up." They could hear Sheriff Woods direct the desk sergeant to take care of the coffee.

Sipping on the fresh coffee, Sally and John observed the interview room where Peter held his head in his propped up arms. He didn't move when Sheriff Woods entered the room.

"Peter," Sheriff Woods asked, "Tell me who the dead woman was."

Peter carefully placed his hands in his lap. "Should I ask for a lawyer?"

"You certainly should, if you think you're going to be arrested."

"I didn't do anything wrong."

"Did you know the woman?"

Peter nodded. "A trouble maker." Sheriff Woods waited patiently for Peter to explain. Instead, Peter said, "I need to talk to my wife's lawyer."

* * *

Standing in the viewing room, John's index finger tapped the two-way mirror. "He thinks his wife killed the dead woman."

"And his wife thinks Tim Hanson is the dangerous one." Sally looked at her watch. Three o'clock in the afternoon. Her second day in her hometown was wearing her out. "Peter's not going to say anymore today." Sally said into the microphone to the speaker in Sheriff Woods' ear, "I need to go home and get my beauty nap."

Sheriff Woods nodded.

* * *

John and Sally Nelson's Home

Back at their home just off Route 64, Sally approached John on the subject of naps. He hung up their coats, before answering, "I've only known you since you became a detective. You seemed to own the energy of a forty-year-old woman."

"Well, sixty-seven is not forty. Do you nap, usually?"

"I did before I met you. I was trying to explain in my clumsy way."

"Not clumsy, at all," Sally yawned. "The couch or the bedroom?"

"Bedroom. I'll start the gas fireplace in there."

As soon as Sally put her head on the pillow, the world realigned itself. After he laid down next to her, Sally pulled John's hand up to her face, singing softly, "I'm not sick, I'm just in love."

John pulled a red wool blanket from the foot of the bed over both of them. Strange that the gas fire gave off a pine-smelling aroma. In her mid-day dream, Sally recalled the details of first meeting Art Woods as a teenager.

* * *

Rohn Federbush

May, 1957

Just seventeen, Sally struggled to keep the nearly filled cart of returned books from knocking into students in the high-school library. She jumped a foot when Art tapped her shoulder. A senior, Art Woods, blessed her with his full smile. His winter tan broadcast he spent considerable time in an exotic spot for spring vacation. Of course, the book was overdue. Art did not want to pay the fine. During the school break, he said he couldn't return the book. Sally's face glowed as red as the embroidered cherries on her stupid sweater. "There is a book drop." She glanced up to meet his beautiful brown eyes.

Art touched her hand where it rested on the cold cart. "I needed something to read while I was in Jamaica with my folks."

His low voice or the warmth of his hand, seduced Sally into the opposite of her intention. "It's okay," she said, knowing she wouldn't be the last woman to forgive Art's continuing infractions.

"Yes!" He whispered, pounding the cart in triumph.

Sally couldn't draw her attention away from him as he left. Dressed in dark browns, his body seemed to lag behind his busy mind. She imagined a panther's limbs following its hunting gaze. At the door, Art turned and gave her a little wave of thanks. Boy! Her heart was racing, her breasts tingled under the sweater, and her face wasn't the only part of her body capable of a hot blush and sweat. She would pay the book fine herself. She picked up a copy of 'Wuthering Heights' from the stack of books on the cart and tried to concentrate as she randomly flipped through the pages. Forcing herself to relax, she melded into the words of another century. "(When) Heathcliff appeared on the door stones,...(she felt) as scared as if (she) had raised a goblin,...(she resolved) further on mounting vigilant guard, and doing (her) utmost to check the spread of such bad influence ..." Closing the book, Sally placed it on the correct shelf next to '*Jane Eyre.*'

No wonder her classmates laughed at her inane, archaic remarks. Whenever she raised her head from the fictive dreams in books, the unpredictable people surrounding her in reality jarred her sensibilities. She read too many books. Everyone in town thought so, except her mother.

Volunteering as an assistant librarian allowed Sally to hide out in the bright, book-lined room close to the endless possibilities of the written word and away from troublesome people. However, not one syllable prepared her for Art Woods. He probably wouldn't approach her again. He dated every pretty senior girl and most of those in her own junior class, except for Jill Wisnewski; because Art's closest friend, Tony Montgomery, went steady with Jill.

When the library cart was empty, Sally chose three more books to read at home; one on mythology, one named '*Lilith,*' and one on how to construct a log cabin. Reading felt like an addiction at times. She needed to know each word hidden between the covers of any book. How much could she remember from all these books? Maybe words filtered out after stimulating the brain. The brain fluid contained the same chemical make-up as tears. Perhaps the words were wept away. She'd suffered enough to cry for the rest of her life.

Ugliest daughters needed to weep, frequently. She gathered her schoolbooks from her main-floor locker for the last time in the school year.

As Sally was leaving the school building, Jill hailed her, reminding her to call. And report what? Nothing ever happened to Sally. Jill, on the other hand, bragged about enough intimate encounters to fill a football stadium. Prone to embellish, Jill's lurid stories nagged at Sally. Books weighed down her arms. Written accounts of Greek gods, Jewish wisdom, and hatchet-made interlocking logs didn't stay in her brain as long as Jill's fictive dreams. Of course, even in *'Lilith'* God was described as male and female entwined to ensure an all-knowing being. Gods from India displayed four arms, too. And in Tahiti, under the encouraging cheers of female priests, the holy-of-holies included the pure act of creation between altar-prone teenagers.

Sally shook her head. In her birth religion, the consecration of the flat Host at Mass certainly held less excitement. All these sterile descriptions of intercourse, even Jill's tales, failed to mention the intensity of her body's reaction to touch -- Art's touch. Could she ever return to her serene world of books?

* * *

First Wednesday in January

In John's home the bedside telephone rang, waking first John and then Sally from their naps. "Sheriff Woods." John handed the phone to Sally.

"Tim's been telling me some interesting stories," Sheriff Woods said.

"About Matilda?" Sally guessed.

"No. Is there something more I should ask Tim about Mrs. Armstrong? Tim's told me who Bret was having an affair with."

"This, I need to hear in person." Sally looked at her watch. Eight o'clock.

"Wait until morning." John advised.

"How about if I bring Tim out to your house?" Sheriff Woods asked. He must have heard John's opinion on the urgency issue. Art Woods understood her too well.

She couldn't wait through the night for crucial news about the arson. "Bring Kentucky Fried Chicken for all of us and come right over."

"You just think you can boss me around because you used to love me." Sheriff Woods laughed as he hung up his end. Sally looked at John. Had he overheard Art's flippant remark?

"You used to date Sheriff Woods?".

Sally fled into the dining room keeping busy with setting the table for four. "Oh, back in high-school, John."

"But did you love him?" John stuffed linen napkins into napkin rings.

"He was the first boy I loved."

"The first you kissed?"

"No. No he wasn't." Sally stopped John's domestic activities and kissed him soundly. "And you, Sirrah, are the last man I am ever going to kiss."

"You've got that straight." John held her, returning the kiss. When he let go, he was still entranced with the idea. "Who was the first boy you kissed?"

"Samuel Immanuel Tucker. On board a moonlit cruise on the Potomac River on our junior class trip. The boy was from South Carolina. He wrote to me for about a month. He owned a white stallion, he said."

"You've got a story for everything."

"Mark Twain said some of his best stories about himself were probably not even the truth."

"But you're telling me the truth?"

Sally turned the oven up to 450 degrees, found a jar of honey and a large rectangular glass-baking dish. Skylights let the moonlight dance on the black slate kitchen counters. Cobalt blue walls caused the stainless steel appliances to reflect a cerulean glow to the white Amish cabinetry. Sally found no reason to redecorate the well-designed room in which she planned to spend less than any time.

When Tim and Sheriff Woods arrived with the Kentucky Fried Chicken, Sally directed them to bring the food into the kitchen. "Set those down." She pointed to the island sink. "Just let me jazz this chicken up a bit."

She started to shoo them back into the dining room, but John blocked the doorway. "You don't want to miss anything they tell me, do you?"

Sally agreed, thankful John understood her priorities. She

placed the chicken pieces into the glass pan and drenched them entirely with honey before popping the heaping pan into the preheated oven.

"Give me your coats, gents. And we'll observe a national phenomenon, Sally Bianco…Nelson actually cooking."

"Gabby loves to cook." Art said.

Tim rubbed a non-existent stomach. "I can attest to that."

"Don't you usually cook for your husband?" Sheriff Woods asked Sally.

John returned. "All the time I've known Sally, we've been chasing criminals or sitting in court rooms."

"Surely, not all the time." Sheriff Woods winked at Sally.

"You're an animal." Sally swatted at him with a handy dishtowel. She deposited a package of frozen corn into a bowl, sprinkled salt and a tablespoon of sugar over the square lump, topped it with a healthy dab of butter and jammed the bowl into the microwave, pushing the buttons for five minutes. She dumped the mashed potatoes and gravy from the Kentucky Colonel into separate oven-safe bake ware and slid them into the hot oven. "John, set those biscuits in the toaster oven, on warm."

"Hey," Woods said. "I thought you said we would see her cook."

"This is as close as you're going to get." Sally laughed. "Tim, take a few minutes and tell me about your affair with Matilda."

Tim checked the face of the sheriff to see if the news shocked him. "Since you already know we're in love, what can I tell you?"

Sally stepped closer to Tim so as not to miss any flickering reaction in his eyes. "Don't tell us you're involved because you know Matilda's husband is fooling around. Anyone who has spent a minute with Bret knows he doesn't own an ounce of philandering blood in him. Besides you knew Matilda, in the Biblical sense, before she married."

Sheriff Woods elbowed John. "No wonder she doesn't cook."

"Sally," John said. "Why don't you three sit down at the table and I'll bring in the food."

"I could use a drink," Tim said.

"Not in this house." John informed him.

"There was liquor yesterday," Sheriff Woods argued.

"My new sister-in-law, Betty Nelson's party." Sally explained. "Booze yesterday, booze tomorrow, but no alcohol today. I need to thank her for inviting you both."

Tim rubbed his handsome chin. "Bret only loves Matilda's money."

Sheriff Woods looked at Sally. "We always think our love is of the highest order. Nevertheless, Bret comes from a rich family."

John brought in the hot dishes from the kitchen. "Bret told me Matilda's father paid for the castle renovations."

"Wedding present." Woods said, and then sheepishly asked, "Could I have a bowl for the potatoes and another dish for the corn?" The three other people in the room stared at him. "I don't like my food to touch," Sheriff Woods said.

"It all …" John began.

"Never mind," Sally said. "I understand. My brother, Dick, has the same obsession."

"It's not an obsession." Sheriff Woods received the extra bowls from Sally.

Tim poked at his honey-baked chicken. "Do you glaze the chicken because you don't like the taste?"

"I love the Colonel's chicken," Sally said. "Did you know their secret is they pressure cook the raw chicken before they bread and fry it?"

"Dig in, boy," John said.

"Not really hungry." Tim broke off a piece of biscuit. "I feel you three have me under a pressure cooker."

"What part of the truth is difficult to spit out?" Sally asked.

Tim laughed. "Well," he sipped at his glass of water. "How about the fact I think I followed the dead woman. I lost her at the corner of Dunham and Territorial Road. When I reached route 31 on the way to Elgin, I turned around. I could have turned east when I got back to Territorial Road, but I turned towards Matilda's folk's house."

"Any reason?" Woods asked.

"Matilda, I guess."

"He meant why were you following the dead woman." Sally turned to Sheriff Woods. "I suspect you know her name by now."

"Not yet. Tim thinks Enid Krimm might be the woman."

"She's a member of the country club," Tim said. "Everyone in Wayne knows her." The table grew silent. Sally was hungry and did the feast justice. Sheriff Woods delicately forked food from the separate plates into his mouth. John was busy with his food, too.

"Why sugar on the corn?" Tim asked.

"They call it sweet corn, don't they?" Sally defended her attempt at cooking. "Tim, why were you following Enid? Is she married?"

"Divorced." Sheriff Woods provided between bites.

Tim studied his filled plate. "I followed her from her apartment. She's been blackmailing people for a long time."

Sheriff Woods laid his fork down. "For what?"

"Infidelity."

"Do you have any proof anyone was Enid's lover?" John asked.

Sally changed the subject. "Mrs. Masters hinted you harmed Bret."

Tim abruptly stood up, knocking over his chair. "Sorry." He righted the chair. "It was an accident."

"What happened?" the sheriff asked his junior officer.

"Bret came home unexpectedly." Tim rubbed the hint of a blond beard on his chin. "I was rushing out the servant entrance of the castle, thinking Bret would be coming in the front door from the garages. Instead, he took the garbage bins back behind the house and used the back entrance. I knocked him over when I bolted out the door."

"Did he ask why you were there?" John asked.

"I don't even remember what I told him," Tim unfolded his

napkin and placed it on his lap. "We took him to the hospital for stitches. The butler drove the three of us in Matilda's car. I kept saying how sorry I was. Bret just let it go. It was an accident."

"Why do you put up with Matilda?" Sally asked.

"Always loved her," Tim said. "I can't seem to tell her no."

"Did you actually see Matilda's husband with Enid?" John asked.

"Never. That's why I was following her. I didn't tell Matilda."

Sally asked, again. "Why did you think Enid was blackmailing people for infidelity? With her, I assume?"

"You thought it would make a difference to Matilda," John said.

Sally tried another tactic. "What time did the fire start?"

"Six o'clock."

"How do you know that?" John asked.

"I was driving up the lane of the Master's home, when I saw the flames in the back of the house shooting over the roof. The horses were racing around the front pasture in a panic. I found Enid's car parked on the lane. I suspect she walked to the house to surprise us." Tim raised a fork of mashed potatoes to his mouth, but then laid the fork back in his plate. "I might as well tell you. Matilda said both her parents were in Dallas and we could use their house to meet. But Matilda's car wasn't there."

"Where was Enid's car?" Sheriff Woods asked.

"About half-way down the lane. The fire trucks drove part-way in the ditch to get around it."

"So," John mulled over Tim's story. "You were following Enid from her apartment. But you were also hoping Matilda's car would be at her parents' house to signal she would be available for a rendezvous?"

"Didn't you consider Enid could already be blackmailing Matilda?" Sally asked. "Did you think she knew you and Matilda were having an affair?"

"No, because Enid told me Bret was involved with her."

John shook his head. "The only reason she came up with the lie was because she understood you were linked with Matilda."

"You could be right," Tim said. "Maybe Bret is innocent."

Sheriff Woods interjected. "Matilda and Bret may not know who the dead woman was."

"I would like to see their faces." Tim coughed with embarrassment at his obvious vindictiveness.

"How long have you known Enid?" Sally asked Sheriff Woods.

"Loose woman?" John asked.

"Loose tongue," Sheriff Woods said. "Do you want to see Enid's apartment or go out to the castle to harass those folks?"

"Mrs. Masters might be back from Dallas tomorrow," Sally said. "Let's go look at Enid's digs."

"Tomorrow morning." John proceeded to the front closet and brought back Sheriff Woods and Tim's coats.

"Hint, hint," Sheriff Woods winked at Sally.

"Will you be all right, Tim," Sally asked. The young man

seemed lost.

"Right," Sheriff Woods said. "Tim, you're going to be my house guest tonight."

"I'm okay." Tim said, almost as a question.

"That's an order." Sheriff Woods slapped the young man's back.

"Tim?" Sally recalled another question. "Did the butler know Matilda and you were lovers?"

Tim shook his head. "I could never figure it out. Matilda didn't seem to care. I know I never laid eyes on the butler, didn't even know his name, until Bret was injured."

"So he was in the house while you were with Matilda." Sally surmised.

"I guess so," Tim said, and then as if dawn had risen, "That's why Bret wasn't suspicious."

"And why I need to talk to the butler," Sheriff Woods said. "Thanks, Sally … and John, thanks."

* * *

"I'll clean up." John pushed Sally down the hall towards their bedroom. "Go start the fireplace in the bedroom and take a shower."

"I feel as if smoke and dirt seeped into every pore of my body." Sally gladly headed for the shower. Once under the warm water, Sally couldn't keep from traveling the memory lanes as a young girl in St. Charles.

* * *

Rohn Federbush

May, 1957

Sauntering down the grassy hill from school the day Art Woods first touched her hand, Sally wanted to throw her books to the ground and run all the way to Route 47. The rush of energy from Art's minute of attention tempted her to walk the forty miles instead of the four blocks to the house on Dean Street. Forty miles would take her straight out west on route 64, the main street of St. Charles; all the way to Route 47, the road her family took south to visit her grandmother Kerner in Bloomington.

Turning right onto Dean Street, Sally changed arms for her usual load of library and schoolbooks. Too bad, she couldn't stylishly use her little brother's red wagon to pull the tomes home. The family abandoned the wagon on the Rossmoor farm.

Her brother, Dick, owned a bike, too. But, Sally learned to ride on her sisters' bikes. Back then, Madelyn was temporarily at the convent in Indiana, and Loretta wasn't athletic. Not owning a bike mattered to Sally. Funny how things turned out. Sally lived with her folks all by herself for five years. Both sisters married their first year out of high school and Dick entered the seminary right out of grade school, at fourteen, for religious training to become a priest.

A warm breeze swirled dust up from the shoulder of the road as Art's car passed. She closed her eyes as the mini whirlwind crossed the sidewalk. She replayed her worst nightmare, which involved taking care of her dying parents. They weren't dying. They were hale and hearty; but the thought of being responsible for their care was frightening. She was, after all, the remaining inmate of the

Dean Street house. Neither of her parents loved her. Too ugly in comparison, their favorite, Madelyn, was blonde and blue eyed like Mother. Loretta's dark eyes and thick, black hair resembled Daddy's. Maybe longing to flee parents caused kids to link up with a mate. Art Woods was the only target, at the time.

* * *

First Wednesday night in January

Sally took a deep breath in the warm air from John's bedroom fireplace. She thought she could smell sweet alfalfa from the Rossmoor farm, her first real home. John came in and offered to rub her back. "Never mind. I'm dead on my feet. How about a promise for tomorrow morning?"

"Hey," John hadn't released her. "As long as you're in the house, I'm happy to make love with you anytime you want, or not."

Sally was asleep before John was out of the shower. She was looking forward to dreaming about the pasture on the Rossmoor farm, where she'd roamed as much as possible. From the age of ten to thirteen, she claimed the grass and trees as her own. She appreciated each bend of the creek, each patch of swampy low land in the grassy acre. The pasture along the creek's deep ravine shielded her from the farmhouse's view. Sally spent complete summers out there, warming herself like a frog on a comfortable flat boulder, summoning her future from the sparkling brook. Daddy often sent their Border collie, Bob, to herd her back to the house when she was finally missed. Would she always feel like a lonesome gypsy or some day in the distant future, could she make a home for a family?

In the continuing dream, Sally adjourned to her bedroom in the Dean Street house, where the tool-and-die factories provided a constant thudding. She could see herself in the full-length mirror, as a young teenager. Her hair floated around her head like a cloud of dark feathers with no constant color, no weight to hold a style. Her dark eyes peered back through thick, plastic-rimmed glasses, with the left eye slightly crossing from eyestrain. Nothing attractive there. Who would look at her long enough to care what she was thinking, let alone start a life with her?

A freight train blew its whistle for the Dean Street crossing. Her window shook slightly. She reached up to smooth down her flyaway hair. In the crook of her arm, the mirror framed the dresser top with her white statue of the Virgin Mary shuddering to the train's rumble, like an egg rocking in the nest before the chick pecks free. The reverberations from the train reminded her of Art's effect on her nerves. She'd been run over by him, and he hadn't even stopped to notice.

Tossing in her sleep, Sally forced herself to focus on the Rossmoor pastoral landscape, the water's sweet rushing, the warmth of the sun. Sally snuggled next to John in her peaceful slumber.

Chapter Three

First Thursday in January

To visit Enid Grimm's condo, Sheriff Woods arrived at the Nelson's at eight o'clock in the morning. John answered the door, not too happy to see the two policemen. Tim appeared rumpled and sleepy.

"We need to eat breakfast," John said.

Sheriff Woods handed him a bag of donuts. "There's a thermos of coffee in the cruiser. I thought you and Sally would be familiar with cop timetables."

"What time did you tell the Armstrongs we wanted to see them?" Sally struggled into her car coat. "I need to attend a meeting in Geneva at noon."

Tim answered. "Ten o'clock. But we need to drive out to the Montgomery's place. The Masters are guests of theirs until their house is rebuilt, I guess."

"Not staying at the castle?" John asked, opening the back door of the cruiser for Sally.

"Peter says they want to keep an eye on the reconstruction," Sheriff Woods said.

Between the Fox River and the lumberyard in St. Charles, Enid's condominium was set in the crook of an L-shaped arrangement of attached units. Common architecture for the late Sixties, the entire complex used barn siding on the exteriors. Evergreen trees were taller than the two-story units. Several of them sparkled with Christmas lights and the leavings of the ice storm.

"Tim, were you in here before?" Sally asked when they opened Enid's front door. A sickly, cloying odor hung in the air, as if the carpeting was sprayed with cheap perfume.

"Actually, no. I met her outside, before she drove off."

"So, she told you about Bret on the doorstep?" John asked.

"She was in a hurry to meet someone," Tim said. "She didn't tell me who. That's why I followed her."

"The lady needed money," John said.

"Or she was partially moved to another address," Sally said. "Sheriff, someone needs to canvass the neighbors and the country club."

On the second floor of the place, an unusual empty two-story well could be accessed only from a large side-hinged window in the bathroom. A clothesline stretched diagonally across the strange aperture. Sally couldn't imagine how the clothesline was originally rigged, unless it was planned during construction. Odd architecture. Why didn't Enid use a Laundromat or install a washer and dryer in the basement? Off the kitchen, a back door opened to a roof-covered and shuttered lawn. Weeds grew among broken patio stones.

"Strange place," John said.

"Unless you are a nudist," Sally said.

"Great come on." Sheriff Woods said. He led them back inside and pointed to the top cupboards in the small kitchen. "Looks like a moving company moved her belongings out."

The movers left the top shelves untouched. Potato chips were still in a large blue bowl, candies and nuts filled other crystal dishes. "Entertained, a lot," John said. "Didn't even cover the potato chips."

The cabinet above the empty refrigerator was filled with whiskey, gin, vodka and expensive brandy bottles. "Do you remember the term, blind pig," Sally asked Sheriff Woods.

"Yeah. But this looks more like a Madame's pad."

"There's blackmailing details enough for you," Tim said.

"We need to find the movers," Sally said. "What time is it?"

* * *

Montgomerys' House in Wayne

The Masters' temporary home with the Montgomerys was as lavish as Sally expected John's to be. Set on a hilltop among a glade of nude trees, the cedar siding of the three story house folded its diagonal room lines around an oak, and between the gnarled stands of apple trees. A small creek was encompassed into the house itself. A musical ripple could be heard in the glassed-in foyer. "How do you keep the water from freezing over?" Sally asked.

"Heated pipes along the sides." Carolyn Montgomery whispered. Sally wanted to pattern her manners after this elegant, older woman with auburn hair and either a flawless complexion or an artisan's cosmetics.

Peter Masters briefly appeared and then retired to a back study.

Carolyn showed Sally's team into the front room. A roaring fire and two orange cats greeted them. Sally sat near the fire in a plush green chair. One cat jumped in her lap. Carolyn put one foot behind the other and floated down on a nearby couch. "You must be new here."

"I knew your son, Tony," Sally said. "When I was much younger, Jill Wisniewski was a friend of mine."

Carolyn Montgomery abruptly rose, but then regained her composure. "Excuse me. I'll just go gather the men."

"Nice work," Sheriff Woods said, sarcastically. "Did you need to mention Tony?"

"Give it a break," John said, taking Carolyn's place on the couch.

Sally petted the cat. Her hometown was not feeling homey. She might as well be living in snooty Ann Arbor. She wanted to leave but didn't want to disturb the cat. Would the AA meeting members welcome her? Time enough for the noon meeting. However, a lot of questions needed answering. "I thought the Montgomerys were too poor to send Tony to an ivy-league college." Sally looked around the place.

"Insurance money," the sheriff muttered.

"From a suicide?" Sally asked.

"Just shut up!" Sheriff Woods shouted.

John stood. "Apologize, you idiot." He looked at Sally as if for approval and then resumed his seat.

"Sorry, Sally, John." Sheriff Woods ran his fingers through his hair. At least he had hair, not like the bald man Sally had just married. "They cheated, okay? What do you want me to do, prosecute them for fraud?" He slumped down on the couch so heavily John gave a little jump. Police discretion. Of course, he should have prosecuted the Montgomerys, but what good would have occurred. They already suffered enough. After Tony's lover Jill Wisniewski broke up with him, Tony dropped out of school. On Jill's wedding day to the tax assessor, Tony slaughtered himself in the room next to the honeymoon suite. "I need to erase the bloody details."

"Explains why Jill is still rather odd," John said.

Woods gave a bitter laugh. "The black hound Gabby told you about at the reception, Sally, the one who follows Jill everywhere, is named Tony."

"What did happen?" Tim asked.

Sheriff Woods heard Sally tell him, "Tony taped his mouth shut with duct tape. Then he tried to castorate himself. He bled to death in the hotel corridor outside his room. Tony's corpse was the first thing the newlyweds encountered the next morning."

Tim said, "He went crazy."

"With love." Woods was surprised at the force of free-floating anger rising in his body. He brushed his sleeve against his wet face and stood.

John stood next to him. "He was your friend."

"Was." Sheriff Woods said.

* * *

"God forgive him." Tim hugged the sheriff who shortly pushed him away.

Sally regained her admiration for Tim. She expected his affair with Matilda was ended, not only by the gruesome story about Tony but because of Enid's suspicious death. Nevertheless everywhere Sally turned, St. Charles offered evidence of the ungodly actions of the inhabitants. She pulled John down to whisper, "Ann Arbor looks pretty good from here."

The Montgomerys and Peter Masters returned to the living room. "Bret and Matilda will be here shortly," Peter said. "I phoned them when you arrived."

"And Mrs. Masters?" Sheriff Woods asked.

"She hasn't been able to get a flight." Peter said.

Sally innocently continued to stroke the Montgomery's cat. "What did you tell her to do when she called you yesterday?" Peter didn't reply. "At the police station. Your cell rang while you were in the briefing room."

"I didn't speak to her then."

"Who did you talk to?" Sheriff Woods asked.

"Her lawyer."

"But you said you hadn't talked to her lawyer, when I questioned you," Sheriff Woods said.

"Sorry. I guess I got mixed up."

"Mrs. Masters isn't coming back, is she?" Sally asked.

"Not unless you win an extradition case," Peter said, pleased with himself.

Bret and Matilda arrived and Carolyn ushered them into the

front room. Matilda stayed close to Bret, holding his hand after he helped her off with her coat. Bret gave the coat to her father, who transferred the garment to Carolyn Montgomery. As Sheriff Woods settled into the green armchair opposite Sally's, the matching orange cat asserted her right to his lap.

"We had a terrible fight." Peter began. The Montgomerys exchanged wary glances but then sat down on the couch opposite the one the Armstrong couple chose. Tim and John remained standing on each side of Peter Masters near the door to the hall.

"Geraldine accused me of having an affair," Peter continued. "With the receptionist at the country club. The crazy woman was harassing her, telling her when I would leave for a trip, implying she was my lover. I swear, Matilda, I never touched a woman since I married your mother. I look at women, you know how it is. Sorry, but I've never pursued anyone."

The cat on Sally's lap mewed as Sally stood to get a better view of the Armstrongs. She maneuvered herself to stand behind Sheriff Woods' chair on the other side of the fireplace.

Sheriff Woods took the hint. "The receptionist, Enid Grimm, died in the fire."

Matilda gripped Bret's hand harder but didn't look at his face. Bret reacted to his wife's obvious concern. "Did you know her?"

"Did you?" Matilda asked.

"Sure," Bret said, "from the club." He looked at Sheriff Woods. "Why did you wait for Matilda and me to arrive before you told her father who the victim was?"

"Because Enid was blackmailing your wife." Tim concentrated on Matilda's reaction to his words.

"She's the body." Peter started walking in circles but was stopped from leaving by Tim and John's presence in the entrance to the hallway.

Mr. Montgomery stood. "I think we all could use a drink."

Sheriff Woods motioned for him to sit down. "Matilda, when did you last see Enid Grimm?"

Matilda looked at her lap, afraid to confront either Bret or Tim. "At the country club, after the Nelsons' party."

"Did you make an appointment to meet her at your father's the next day?" Sally asked.

"I did," Matilda said to Sally. "I didn't realize Bret invited you and John over to see the castle. I tried to call Enid, but they said her phone was disconnected."

Tim said. "She planned to move away after she received money from you."

Matilda finally looked at her amazed husband. "Bret," she said. "You two were having an affair."

"Why would you pay her money?" Bret asked. "I could have told you I was as faithful as you are."

A steady blush settled on Matilda's face. Tim turned away.

Sally interrupted. "Peter, was your wife planning to meet Enid?"

"You need to speak to her lawyer."

Matilda rose from the couch. She put her arms around her

father's waist. "Daddy," was all she said.

"Why did you tell Matilda you found your house on fire after you returned from Dallas?" Sally asked. "You couldn't go to Dallas and return by ten o'clock in the morning, after staying at our house the night before, could you?"

"The ticket is in my coat. I knew Geraldine was with her mother. The fight I told you about was for New Year's Eve, when she threw her ring in the fireplace."

Sally believed only half of Peter's words. "Sheriff Woods, do you have Mrs. Masters' ring with you?"

"I'm afraid the ring is evidence." Woods was still seated in the Montgomery's fireside chair. The orange cat who appropriated his lap seemed inclined to stay put.

"Peter, you assume your wife was the last person to see Enid alive," John said.

Peter waved the question away. "Her lawyer …"

"Could I see your boarding passes to and from Dallas?" Sally asked.

"I, I threw them away."

"Right," Tim said. "We don't believe you traveled to Dallas."

Carolyn Montgomery asserted her hostess duties. "I'm sorry; I must ask you all to leave. I can hardly allow you to call a guest in my house a liar." Mr. Montgomery offered coats to Sally and John. Peter retired to a back study.

"Tell Peter it is advisable for him not to leave the state." Sheriff Woods stated for the record.

Tim delayed leaving, as if he expected Matilda to give him some sign. On the doorstep, he sighed. "She loves him, too?"

Sally answered him. "Legally she is bound to him. You gave her every opportunity to declare her affection for you."

"I guess I'm free, and I didn't even have to pay for a divorce."

The sheriff patted Tim's back. "We should get started canvassing Enid's neighbors."

John offered, "I can locate the movers for her furniture."

"Aren't you going to ask the state's attorney to extradite Mrs. Masters?" Sally asked.

Sheriff Woods nodded. "I'll speak to her lawyer, first. If she hasn't committed a crime, I can't understand why she won't come home. If she doesn't return voluntarily, I will start proceedings." He opened the cruiser's passenger door. "Tim, could you drive. I'm exhausted."

Sally followed Sheriff Woods to the car. "Your emotions about Tony are wearing you out."

Woods shook his head. "I hope I never enter the Montgomery home again."

After the police car left, John drove Sally back east to Dunham Road. A freezing rain began to fall. The Honda's windshield wipers and defrosters couldn't keep up with the ice.

"Let's pull off until the car warms up," Sally said. "The defrosters will work better."

John turned into the parking lot of the Wayne Riding Club at the corner of Dunham and Territorial Roads cattycorner across from the castle. "I'm more worried about the roads than the windshield." He got out and scraped on the back window, then chipped away at the ice above the windshield wipers reach. He ran his glove along the wiper blade showing Sally the caked ice.

When he returned to the car, Sally said, "A country club is a great place for a Madame to contact rich clients."

The defroster began to work, so John cautiously drove south on Dunham Road to Route 64, the main street of St. Charles. "How long did Enid live in her condo?"

"Probably since they were built. Remember the crazy clothesline from the bathroom window. The entire enclosure smelled like bleach."

"I hate that smell. Why didn't she use a laundry service."

"Nothing was hanging on the line," Sally said. "We need to find out if she did convert to an outside source for clean linens."

Back on the road, the pavement glistened as the weather continued turning rain to ice. In town, the Honda slipped, fishtailing down the eastern hill of St. Charles' main street. At the intersection of Routes 64 and 31, they both sighed when the car stopped in time at the light.

"Good job," Sally said.

"You just have to drive slowly."

"I remember getting into a crash right here with Art, Sheriff Woods," Sally said. "A northern bound car slammed on its brakes and spun into a pick-up truck in the oncoming lane. As if in slow motion, the pick-up slid sideways, slamming into my side of the car.

My glasses and the windshield were broken."

"Were you injured?"

"The other drivers weren't injured and one of them helped me out of the driver's side of the car. For some reason, I waited for the tow-truck in Burger Drugs with the driver of the pick-up. They had an ice-cream counter and booths back then. When I reached to push my hair away from my face, he asked me not to move. Then he picked a sliver of glass off my cheek."

John talked about the time required to get home with the roads the way they were. "The normal fifteen-minute ride might take an hour."

"What time is it now?" Sally pushed the sleeve of her winter coat up to find her watch. "Eleven thirty! I need to find an AA meeting at noon in Geneva. It's not an open meeting."

"I could wait in the bar. Just kidding. I'll get groceries. How long will you be."

"Usually not longer than an hour. It really depends on how many people are at a table and how long they need to share. St. Mark's is on Franklin Street."

After they arrived at the address, Sally asked John to wait. "I don't know which door is open." After trying two back doors and even the front door of the church, she returned to the car. "Grace is going to have my head."

"Probably canceled because of the weather. Let's go home and order pizza. I'm tired."

"You're a safe driver," Sally said, receding into a daydream of times past. Before she lost complete consciousness of the winter scene around her, she wondered, briefly, if it were true, one of the symptoms of Alzheimer's was a tendency to nap at every opportunity.

* * *

January, 1958

"I see more glass," the pick-up driver said. "Close your eyes."

Sally heard the driver, Terry Grove, call for help from the pharmacist. Terry gently laid a piece of scotch tape along her eyebrows. He showed Sally the miniature flakes of glass. Bobby Burger, the pharmacist's son, came over with a pair of tweezers and a magnifying glass. None of the glass penetrated her skin. Instead, the shower of shards peppered her hair and face. The tow truck carried off the wrecked cars, before Art and the helpful driver deemed Sally ready to travel to the hospital. The emergency room was thankfully empty. A young doctor gave her a careful eye exam before releasing her.

Sally and Art took a taxi to the house on Dean Street. Instead of going in the front door, Sally asked Art to lift the garage door. She opened the kitchen door a crack before calling Daddy out into the garage. "I broke my glasses. I can use the old pair, until I replace them."

"We were in an accident," Art explained.

Sally's father turned on the garage light. "Are you hurt?" he asked Sally and then Art. "Come on in, Marie, are there any of those

Christmas cookies we can sample? Someone smashed into the kids."

"Art, call your mother." Mother said, before raiding the cookie jar's holiday stash.

"I wrecked the car." They overheard Art tell his mother. "No we're fine. Sally's glasses broke. "Sally, will you me drive home?" When she agreed, Art relayed the news. "No. I was not upset. We were stopped at the intersection, but two other cars could not and a pick-up hit Sally's side of the car. Okay. Thanks, Mother." Art sat down next to Sally at the kitchen table. His legs spread out halfway across the room. "My father's upset. Sally told on me." Art grinned. "I'm taking catechism lessons."

"A lot of wars were fought over religion," Daddy said.

"Even in this house." Mother laughed as she refilled the glasses of cold milk.

"Terry Grove was the guy who was knocked into us. He acted like a guardian angel afterwards," Sally said.

"He drove us to the hospital in his wreck." Art agreed.

"And he saved my eyes," Sally said.

Her mother stood and tipped Sally's head back.

Art tried to reassure them. "My windshield broke. Terry Grove and Bob Burger picked all kinds of glass off her face before Terry drove us to the emergency room."

Mother sat back down. "Sally only has one eye with enough vision to read."

"She's okay." Daddy repeated, as if to himself.

They did love her. Sally munched on another cookie. When

did it happen? Then she understood, this was a performance piece for a prospective suitor.

"What was the angel's name," Mother asked.

"Terry, Terry Grove," Art said.

* * *

First Thursday in January

When their Honda stopped in the driveway, Sally woke up to hear John ask. "I don't understand why Tony Montgomery committed suicide. Tim's been as rebuffed and none of us expect him to do away with himself."

"Tony was high-strung. Tim's a lot older than Tony was at the time of his death, too. I think younger people suffer more than adults. They have fewer interests, less work to do, fewer responsibilities, certainly less experience in dealing with life. Everything passes and the Lord is a real help."

"I suppose Tony wasn't religious."

"You're right. But he was a lovable scamp. Part of the motivation behind his suicide was vengeance against Jill. He probably hated her by the time he died. I remember her at the time."

As they entered the house, Sally's new husband struggled to hang up her coat while Ginger danced around him. The cleaning people had done their best to restore the house to a clean and orderly home after the reception. Her sister-in-law's caterers had retrieved their serving utensils.

Sally settled down on the couch in front of the fireplace,

reached forward to flick on the gas flame, and tried to feel at home. She could hear John's cheerful scolding of Ginger. Who were his parents? How did they compare to hers? She admitted marrying a man in her late sixties left her ignorant about important details throughout fifty years in his life. John said he didn't marry because he loved her since high school; but what or who filled his days? When he returned rosy-cheeked from the cold she asked him, sort of. "I've reminisced a lot about my parents since I returned. Do you miss yours?"

He sat down and pulled his long legs up on the couch. Facing her, he scanned the open area behind the couch. Ginger leaned into the couch. John stopped petting her and pointed. "Both their hospital beds sat right there. They held hands most of the time. My bedroom television was situated against the wall of windows. They were bedridden with liver and ovarian cancer, died within a week of each other. Dad called it their private falling satellite. He meant they were lucky to die together."

"You nursed them."

"No. We hired a male nurse to help. Dad died first. Mother said she was glad he didn't need to live without her. She only lasted six more days. The doctor said they both gave up living."

Sally stroked his toes in his heavy winter socks. "What furniture did you remove from the room when their hospital beds arrived?"

John rubbed his baldness. "A red rug, with designs. You know, from India."

"Persian?"

"That's it. James and Betty have the carpeting in their front room, now." John surveyed the empty space behind the couch. "With the chairs that match this couch."

Case closed. The news certainly explained the failed decorating scheme. "Did James and Betty relieve your vigil?"

"Sometimes." Ginger laid her head in John's lap, as if anticipating his sorrow. "Ginger saved my sanity."

"I'm sure she did." Sally examined the fire. His lonely death watch made her cry.

"Oh, don't." John scooped her unto his lap. "I'm happy. You're here. We have work to do, a career in righting wrongs. I couldn't ask for more."

As the fire and his secure embrace comforted her, Sally's mind returned to the days she spent as a teenager in St. Charles.

* * *

July, 1957

In the summer between Sally's junior and senior year, Jill Wisnewski called early one Saturday morning. "Would you like to go horseback riding again?"

"Wear a sweater," Sally's mother said, as if she really cared.

Jill's head start on riding techniques was due to a year's riding lessons at the country club in Wayne. At the rental stables on Route 47, Jill rode a four-reined, roan horse. Sally's white mare, Flicka, sported wide haunches. Not a pretty thing. When Sally first placed her hand on the mare's neck, Flicka steadied her stance listening to Sally's quiet introduction and request for permission to ride. Her father claimed genetic retention allowed Sally to copy Jill's posting. Sally preferred the skimpy English saddle to the western saddles, which distanced her from the animal's movements. Flicka easily accommodated herself to Sally's gentle commands.

There was one problem. Flicka didn't like to be passed and Jill's lean, high-stepping horse wasn't happy until he was out in front of the riding group.

"Just get her attention." Mr. Spradlin, the stable owner, cautioned Sally. "Talk to her until her ears come up. If they're down, someone's gaining on her and she's planning to kick."

The cool summer morning promised to keep the mosquitoes manageable. They let the horses walk comfortably through the first stand of trees to get to the riding path. Sally prompted Jill to describe her latest date with Tony. The non-stop chatter might include news of Tony Montgomery's friend, Art Woods.

Jill mentioned the movie, the hamburger, the romantic parking spot. At the most interesting point, when Tony tipped Jill's head back for a kiss, Jill's horse chose to speed up to be first on the trail. Adjusting her posting to the rapid trot, Sally failed to perceive the change in Flicka's ears.

Bang! Flicka kicked at Jill's horse.

They both pulled up their horses. Jill's wooden stirrup was shattered by Flicka's rude kick, but Jill was not injured.

Sally never heard about the rest of Tony's kiss. In fact, Jill quit riding at the rental stable, with a polite excuse about her trainer arranging for her to ride free at the Wayne club. So, Sally borrowed her father's Buick when she wanted to ride Flicka. She relished returning to the country, even for an hour among other rented horses. She felt one with the peaceful, flat open spaces of yellow grasses bordered with straight rows of pioneers' fencing, where patches of willows pointed patiently to the refreshing brooks. Claiming ownership of earth, sun and sky, Sally found a place to call home her last summer on Dean Street to replace the quiet Rossmoor farm.

* * *

September, 1956

During Sally's junior high-school year, the family visited her brother at the Sacred Heart Seminary on Sunday afternoons, once a month. Just fourteen, Dick was the shortest boy in his class. Sally's married sisters and their husbands also attended. The first grandbaby, beautiful and blonde, provided the entertainment. Bare banquet tables filled the seminary's gym. Her mother's apple pie, paper plates and napkins adorned their table. After her father swallowed his share of pie, he deserted the group. Cigarettes demanded his constant attention. Her sisters' husbands didn't last much longer.

Dick seemed okay; not needing the female attention, trying to act grown up or bored with their non-stop questions. "Some of the guys wake me up at night crying."

A rush of hated at Mother's shortcut for getting into heaven by handing over her children to God overwhelmed Sally. At least,

Madelyn escaped her mother's plan for a life spent in a convent praying for their salvation. "Remember when you made us get in the basement, the summer when the sky turned green?"

"I do," Loretta said.

Madelyn contributed, too. "You dragged Sally out of the bathtub."

Sally's father came back in to claim the last piece of pie. "I pulled them up out of the basement into the garage," he told the husbands. "Mother made them quake in their boots. I showed them the storm sweeping right by the open garage door."

"You made us promise to be nuns and priests." Sally grumbled at the direction of Mother's cold, blue eyes.

"Never happened." Her blonde mother gathered up the plastic silverware and paper plates.

Sally folded her paper napkin into an origami swan. Trying to remember the exact story about Mark Twain, she listened to Mother's voice as she chatted with blonde Madelyn about a modeling job for a Junior League benefit. The loving warmth in Mother's tone dissolved when her attention was drawn back to the rest of the family -- except for Dick, who was also blond. That was when, Sally witnessed real joy. She could almost hear Mother's increased heart rate. Sally wondered if she would ever love a son too much.

In the story about Mark Twain, Mrs. Clemens stood at the bottom of the main staircase listening to her husband's string of riverboat curses, after his single-edged razor took a nick out of his ornery hide. Mrs. Clemens repeated every one of her husband's swear words. He leaned over the banister and critiqued her performance. "You've got the words right but the tune's all wrong."

Mother said all the correct, charitable things to the brunettes in the family; to Sally, Loretta and Daddy, but the song was out of key. The dulcet tones of love shied away from her tongue when speaking to them. Would she recognize love, if ever she was loved? How did it feel to be truly loved by a mother?" Sally tried to draw Dick's attention into the conversation but he was off chasing his little blonde niece, lost in Mother's dream of sainthood.

* * *

May 1958

For the last day of high school, Sally wore black silk bell-bottoms with a wide cummerbund waist. Her yellow blouse with buttoned sleeves above the elbow caused the sleeve to puff up at the top of her shoulders. Her hair, for once, behaved into a pageboy curl, resting symmetrically near her neck. In front of the mirror, she thought she looked as perfect as possible. Smiling at herself, she felt oddly confident. But the day turned harsh. Jill asked what she was all dressed up for, instead of returning a goodbye hug. Two of her classmates, Alan and Greg, acted as if she were a stranger instead of a member of their small study-hall group. As she left school for the last time by the side exit, Art Woods and his buddy, Tony Montgomery, stood outside on the steps. They were home from college for Jill's graduation. Sally stopped short, her hand on the door.

"There she is," Art said to Tony. "Watch this." Art held the door open, smiling into her eyes. "How's Sally?"

"Fine," she managed to whisper. Her heart seemed stuck on one of her ribs, swelling to a warning beat.

Six-feet-two inches of Art brushed against her as she stood transfixed by his stare. Her face was red with embarrassment, but Art's eyes stayed locked on hers as he passed. Then his gaze burned a path down her upturned throat, over her rising chest, into her stomach, heating the blood all the way to her knees. At the open door, a breeze from the school's ancient oak tree blew away the hall's stale odors. Breathing in the shadow's coolness, Sally restored herself to some semblance of order.

In the corridor behind her, Tony expressed his awe to Art. "I thought she was going to faint."

Before the door closed, she also heard Art's boastful reply. "I told you!"

Sally walked dejectedly away. She would miss school, not the kids and their idiotic games. Instead, the smell of new books and the opening of new ways of thinking would be missed. She yearned for those continuing pathways, new avenues for her brain to embrace. The prejudices taught at home, by Daddy, who hadn't graduated from eighth grade but provided an answer for everything, and Mother, who lived within narrow religious confines, were proven wrong. They were not mean-spirited, just ignorant of a wider world's perspective.

She counted the schools she attended as she numbered her steps down Dean Street. First grade in Huntley, second grade in Algonquin, third grade in Crystal Lake, fourth grade in Wayne, fifth, sixth and seventh in Plato Center on the Rossmoor farm, and eighth grade was spent at St. Patrick's. The family moved nearly every year until Daddy stopped managing farms for other people to start house painting. His hot temper wasn't fit for steady employment. If he left a customer as a house painter, the family could at least stay put in the same community. As a consequence, Sally endured a friendless existence. She was most comfortable talking to strangers. The entire world was filled with interesting people.

Her middle name was Alice, and as Lewis Carroll said of his brave Alice in the journey through the Looking Glass, she found in her world, "Everything happened so oddly she didn't feel a bit surprised." She certainly couldn't control much. The family's extras went to support her brother in the seminary. No one encouraged her to apply to college.

As she was growing up, her older sisters and Dick, four years younger than Sally, were spirited away to school or worse. In Algonquin when her mother fell down a haymow in a suspicious accident, they were at school, her father in town. The farm's crop failed to turn a profit. Their unpaid wages were deemed a further investment in their share of the land. Her father contacted a lawyer, which only added fuel to the dispute. The family was asked to vacate the premises in the middle of the school year, so her mother's convenient accident solved their lodging problem. An aunt opened her home for Mother while her broken pelvis healed. Madelyn and Dick accompanied her. Loretta and Sally were shipped off to grandmothers; first Daddy's and then Grandma Kerner gave them a home.

Nearing the end of Dean Street, Sally thought she could taste an apple pie. The factories behind the house smelled of rust and oil. Maybe there would be no pie tonight. No siblings either. One sister lived five blocks east; the eldest across Main Street, six blocks away. Dick was still tucked away in the Seminary.

Art Woods was playing games with her to entertain his buddy. What was it with guys? Jill probably presented her fantastic stories for the same reason. Sally stopped before opening the front door. They were more immature than she was.

Sure she dived into books at the first hint of trouble, but at least she knew who she was. They were all pretending, while she was content to what, read scripts? Almost the same thing! Understanding their need for escape helped Sally draw her next, more mature, breath as she called hello to Mother.

Nevertheless, Sally longed to return to a simpler time on the farm when copulation was only fit for farm animals.

* * *

September 1958

On the first Monday in September after Art and Tony returned to college for their second year, Jill called asking Sally to spend the weekend with her down in Lincoln, Illinois, where the boys attended

Lincoln College. "Art Woods asked Tony if you could come down with me. Are you dating Art?"

"I know him from school." Sally couldn't understand why she was defending herself.

"So you have been dating."

"No. We just ran into each other." Sally didn't want to share the details of the last time she'd seen Art Woods in June.

Sixty miles west of Chicago the mighty Fox River cuts a north-south meandering path through the farming plains of Illinois. In St. Charles, 'streets' were laid out parallel to the river on the west side balancing the 'avenues' which terraced the riverbed's rising slope to the east. As a teenager, she hoped to escape the valley.

The first week out of school, she accepted a job at DuKane, a privately owned electronics firm. Each day she drove her father's Buick east to her secretarial job. Each night she returned west. She often thought if the sun would stop blinding her, she might find a way out of the river valley. Typing dull business letters left her hungry for more exciting worlds—and words.

Watching Sally grumble through their scant bookshelves one Friday night, Mother reminded her the public library was only eighteen blocks away on the other side of town. Daddy needed the car in the morning but she could walk the short distance.

Bright and early Saturday morning Sally headed for the library. The four blocks of Dean Street ended at the high-school hill, which was the highest point on the west side of town. Descending east toward the Fox River, she passed St. Patrick's school, the priest house and the church where they attended seven o'clock Mass each Sunday. Regulars, her mother was pious, Daddy off-handed. Sally's beliefs claimed the one constant and sanctioned toehold on life.

Past the gas station and hardware store, she slowed her pace, gawking into the windows of Carson's, the most expensive women's clothing store in town. Across the street the shoe store beckoned. Daddy said she owned enough shoes to put soles on a caterpillar. The Hotel Baker's Nelson's jewelry-shop window held a few trinkets of interest, but the sound of the wide Fox River spilling over the north dam drew her down the hill to the bridge.

She would check out the south dam on her return trip. Maybe all farmers' daughters love to watch water flowing toward promised destinations. The past made sense standing next to the talking stream. But she was a house painter's daughter now, making her weekend more pleasurable with a gallery of books. The steepest hill, thankfully on the way to the library, passed between twin peaks of the modest Methodist and the fancy Presbyterian churches. Planning to carry as many books as possible back from the library, she calculated each slight incline. She scheduled her trek early enough to arrive cool and un-rumpled as the main doors opened.

The domed, modest brick structure boasted Ionic columns outside and mahogany paneling inside. If souls needed buildings, Sally's spirit chose a library over a church, anytime. She breathed better among books. The promise of friends remaining constant on the shelves, their words of wisdom unchanged, their homes secure in idyllic sites, compelled her to appreciate each book's binding, each category's rightness, each hushed word appropriate to the hallowed air. The smells of leather, glue, and mildew rose as a heady incense in the diffuse light from the rim of high windows in the oval room.

The librarian recognized her as a frequent patron; but never presumed on her privacy by asking about her family. Besides, Sally underwent the creation of a new personality each time she entered, transformed by the content of the latest, borrowed books written by Kafka, Maugham, Stevenson, and Emily Dickinson. It was a miracle her feet still reached the pavement because her mind rose another inch above reality. She brought a pillowcase to lug new books home. After two hours careful selection, Sally picked eight red books by Anatole France, a slim blue volume by Voltaire, a yellow one by Christopher Fry, Shakespeare's <u>Romeo and Juliet</u> and <u>Othello</u>, and three volumes of the <u>History of the Jews</u>. Trying to ignore the frowning librarian, Sally filled her cloth bag with the treasures.

The summer heat of late June made the burden heavier than expected. Tempted to drag the bag, Sally rested at the bridge before hitching the load up onto the other shoulder.

"Santa Claus." Art Woods taunted as he slowly drove up in his father's MG. "Need a lift?"

Sally stopped to put down her load. "Is there room in that little thing for these and me?"

He double-parked and came over, lifted the bag of books into the trunk. "Way too many. I thought you were too smart for summer school?"

"Don't you read?" She asked, trying not to sound snobbish as she stretched out her grateful legs in the little car.

"Not in summer. College will come fast enough."

Sally wished she'd brought more Kleenex as she dabbed at her forehead and nose.

In the car, Art chatted about not getting accepted at Princeton the year before, and his father's disappointment. Lincoln College would do for a second year, if he could maintain a passing grade. "Dad says one more semester of bad grades and I'm out."

Sally couldn't seriously consider going away to college. Mother insisted she take shorthand and typing the last two years of high school. Her little brother needed the family's extra funds for the Seminary. "If I can afford it, I guess I'll take evening courses at Elgin Community this fall."

"We should trade parents. My dad would love to have a kid with your brains."

"You've read Robinson Crusoe, right?"

"Everybody had to."

"No they didn't." Sally pulled the visor down and checked her hair in the mirror. "You own a brain."

"When I told my father I was reading Crusoe, he told me I was still reading kids' books."

Sally didn't want to discuss the merits of parents. "Remember how Crusoe read a bible passage to sustain him every day? "I can't remember where now; but I read a book where a businessman picked up Robinson Crusoe each morning the same way—to hear what the universe was saying to him."

"I'll try it in Lincoln." Art went on to describe dinners with his parents. Not fun. The night before he stared at his emptied plate listening to his father demean Tony Montgomery. "My dad says I might amount to something if Tony would leave me alone. But Tony's grades are better than mine."

"Folks always want us to be better than themselves."

'But never as bad." Art laughed.

As Art slowed, before downshifting for the turn from Main to the Dean Street turn-off, Sally's imagination went into high gear. She envisioned them escaping their parents, riding off to catch the sunset, starting a life together, talking forever into the night, even laying embraced in each other's arms on some uninhabited island. She sighed as Art made the turn.

"What?' he asked.

"I've missed you." She gathered her wits.

In the driveway Art sat quietly with the car's engine purring. As Sally started to open the door, he reached across her and closed it. "It's nice to have a fan club at home." The he kissed her cheek.

"I'm it." She smiled at him. Her appreciation for every line of his body, every tone of his being, made her forget for a moment all the doubts about her own attractiveness. As she got out of the car, she glanced back. Art's arm was outstretched toward her empty seat. She smiled good-bye again, content. She would hear from him.

Still on the telephone with Jill, Sally contemplated falsely claiming to have dated Art. There was no sense lying. "A ride home, just a ride home from the library."

"Sure, sure," Jill said. "Will your mother let you come down with me?"

"I'm nineteen. What shall I pack?"

"It's homecoming. You could take your prom dress."

When Sally hung up, the dreadful high-school prom night replayed itself. Her sister, Loretta, had arranged a date with a friend of her husband. Bill, the date's name was, didn't say three words the entire evening. In her nervousness, Sally talked non-stop from the moment she got in the boy's car until they stood in the dark, smelly gym maneuvering around the dippy decorations she helped put up. Bill's zombie appearance remained intact while he danced. At times, she experienced an overwhelming pity for the guy. He probably thought she was the worst date in the place. Jill and Tony stopped by their table. Tony complimented Sally's dress; but when Bill remained silent, Jill had rolled her eyes and pulled Tony away. It was stupid to go out with the idiot. Fifteen library books on Sally's bookshelf stood ready to provide more heartbeats. She couldn't bring herself to ask, if Bill was paid to accompany her.

So, Art Woods had asked to see her, to visit him at college, not directly, but by way of Jill. Why hadn't he called her? She would take the dumb dress, which needed at least a second night out before her mother gave it away to the church's auction.

* * *

June 1958

On the day of the Lincoln trip, Sally wore blue-and-white checked, thigh-gripping shorts which showed off her fitness. Thank God for Flicka, the rental horse she road every rainless Saturday. The posting exercise firmed up the last of her baby fat. The blouse with a matching collar could be turned up so her hair wouldn't cling to her neck in the heat. Her prescription sunglasses might even impress Jill.

The drive down to Lincoln was tiresome, with monotonous flat landscape creeping by. They stopped for gas once. After handing Jill a ten spot for the gas, Sally hurried into the dirty bathroom. The walls were gray from fumes, the sink untouchable. When she tried unlocking the door to leave, it wouldn't open. She pulled and pounded until Jill came over and yelled directions. The sticky lock finally gave way and the door opened. "Locked in a dirty, gas station washroom for eternity," Sally said, as she got in the car. "There's a description of Dante's Inferno."

"We wasted ten minutes." Jill's short red hair never dared slip out of place. Her khaki shorts kept their pleat and her dark green blouse remained free of any perspiration stains. Easy to become acquainted with on the surface, Jill kept her inner self hidden. Jill didn't delve into the workings of her own mind. A block of some kind rose to shield her from self-scrutiny. Outside she exuded perfection, while her soul stayed crouched in a morass of fear. Fear of what? Probably rejection. Jill continued to harp on two subjects. One was how much her father hated Tony and the other was how long did Sally know Art.

Sally devised a defense. Whenever Art was the subject of inquiry, she would ask a question about Tony. Jill said she didn't know why she was so attracted to Tony.

"The lack of moral severity could make Tony a delight."

"Moral severity?" Jill hooted. "Half the time people don't know what you're talking about. What is Dante's Inferno? All I know is my father wants Tony to leave me alone!"

When they finally reached the Lincoln campus, Sally escaped the confining car. Tall elms provided slim shade on the leaf-strewn paths to the dormitory. A hint of wintry breeze cooled her lungs, heightened her spirits. Awkward around Tony and Jill, Sally thought Art's cold hello meant he was as uncomfortable. Tony's mocking remarks about Sally's appearance sounded too familiar, insincere. Art suggested lunch. Sally was too excited to eat in the diner.

Tony told an off-color joke. Sally couldn't laugh, it was so gross. Art groaned, but Jill laughed on cue. Sally ordered coffee, but when the black sludge arrived it proved too tepid to drink.

Jill scolded her. "We're all waiting for you to finish your coffee."

"I don't want it." She was embarrassed by Jill's vehemence.

"Then why did you order it?" Tony demanded.

"Never mind." Art defended her.

"It's too cold." Sally looked into Art's eyes.

He squeezed her hand. "It's okay." Then turning to Jill and Tony, he offered, "Let's go for a ride."

"Good idea." Tony winked. He drove Jill's car with Art and Sally in the back seat.

Art slid over next to Sally and put his arm around her shoulder with his other hand on her knee. "Why do you smell like fresh cut grass?"

Sally laughed. "I was born on a farm?" She gave herself up to the delicious pleasure of being held by Art. Every few miles, she pushed his hand back down to her knee, twice. Finally, Art put his head in her lap pulling her down for a kiss. Sally returned his sweet kisses. How had she existed, survived so long without them. Her hair swept his face whenever she straightened up. She loved his face. His great dark eyes were offset with long black lashes. She wanted to bite them they seemed so tantalizing. His nose was straight and not too thin. Changing expressions caused his forehead to seem prominent when his thick brows lowered giving his eyes a predatory hood. His square jawline kept his full lips in balance. "It's a wonder," she said, "women don't lay down in front of you in the street so you can walk on them."

"Wow! Tony, did you hear what she said?"

Tony turned around in the driver's seat causing Jill to cry out as she rescued the abandoned wheel. "The kid likes you." Tony laughed, but Sally turned away from his lecherous grin.

Art kissed her a full minute, then whispered in her ear. "I like you, too."

Tony found a bumpy, country path behind a field of standing corn. Jill and Tony slipped out of the car leaving Art and Sally alone.

"Have fun." Tony called as Jill pulled him into the rows of corn.

Art held Sally close, wrapping his arms around her, burying his sweet head in her shoulder. "I'm so glad you came. You feel like home to me."

"We're safe now." They clung together for an hour. Art fell asleep in her arms. She roused him with a kiss when she spied Tony and a rumpled Jill returning.

"Hey let the guy come up for air." Tony slammed into the car.

Art stretched into a yawn. "Boy am I thirsty."

"Sally sucked him dry," Tony rescued a corn shuck out of Jill's hair, then explained to Sally with a leer, "We rolled around a bit in the hay."

"He's just kidding."

"Oh no I'm not, Miss Priss." No one commented as they drove to the motel where Jill and Sally needed to change clothes for the dance.

"We'll be right back." Tony slapped Jill on the bottom. "Keep it warm for me."

After they left Sally said, "I can see why your father hates Tony."

"And why I have to have him." Jill stripped for her shower.

The boys came back with a six-pack. Tony joined Jill in the shower. Art tried to make polite conversation. He finally turned on the television. They sat on the edge of the bed, feet on the floor, watching some football heroes smash into each other for half an hour.

"Who's winning?" Tony asked, zipping up his pants as further evidence when he joined them.

Jill finally came out decently wrapped in a robe, with her red hair up in one of the motel towels. "Your turn," she said to Sally. "You guys get out of here so we can get ready. And don't forget the corsages."

"Geez!" Tony grabbed the six-pack.

"Leave it here," Art said. "Just take a swig. We don't need to get arrested for drunk driving." He waved at Sally and they were gone.

Jill got under the covers, "That guy wears me out! Don't let me sleep past six. They'll be back at seven." She rolled over and was out like a light.

Sally turned off the television set and undressed in the bathroom. The couple left one towel untouched.

At the dance, Art continued to compliment Sally's dress. "Blue is really your color and you have the sweetest body."

"Now if I could just stop blushing."

"It suits you." Art moved his hand up and down the back of the gown. "Your blush let me know you were a passionate girl. Remember in the library when we first spoke?"

"I didn't think you would remember."

"I do. And then I was so stupid showing off in front of Tony."

Sally smiled as Art led her out onto the floor. Their steps weren't intricate. She loved being held in his arms with the sweet music and pushing crowd around them. "I wish this could go on forever."

When they rejoined Tony and Jill at their table, Sally could tell something was amiss. Tony pounded the table. "Guess why she came down here?" He pointed to a tearful Jill with his thumb. "Her daddy wants her to date Chuck Reddinger, that rich wimp." Tony slumped in his chair for a moment before hissing, "Slut!" He stomped out of the college dance hall.

Jill combed her hair with her fingers. "Daddy never liked him."

Sally shuddered. Art draped his arm around Sally's shoulders as if to protect her. The three of them sat in silence until a small, almost fat girl came up and asked Art in a halting voice to dance with her. Art turned a questioning look to Sally, who nodded politely. Encouraged by his willingness to dance, four other girls lined up for Sally's permission.

After the sixth beauty whisked Art away, Jill couldn't resist. "Art seems to be having a good time away at school." Sally admitted Art made a lot of friends, but then how could a handsome man not be flattered by all the attention. When Art sat down again, Jill said, "We have to get back. I want to start out early for home."

Art kissed Sally in a long embrace before he let her get into the car. "I haven't had a chance to talk to you. I'm reading Robinson Crusoe every day. Can you get a car of your own?"

"I will." Sally planned to come down every weekend.

Even though Sally bought her own car, events surrounding Jill and Tony stopped the planned trips to Lincoln

Chapter Four

First Thursday in January

Sheriff Woods was glad to let Tim drive the police car from Wayne to Geneva's countywide police station. The visit to Tony Montgomery parents' home flooded him with memories of Sally, Mrs. John Nelson now, and the fate of his friend, Tony. When he was only twenty years old, Art wanted Tony to see the light, stop being such a stud and develop a few feelings. But Tony jumped off an emotional cliff. After Jill dumped him, his friend wouldn't attend classes at Lincoln College, wouldn't eat, couldn't seem to sleep.

* * *

October 1958

"There are other girls," Art said to Tony, once.

Tony met his eyes, let him see the agony. "You should take me out somewhere, behind a deserted barn and put me out of my misery, the way you would a dying dog. I'm not good for anything now."

Art started staying with Tony, offering him water, soup, to call his folks, anything. Two weeks after homecoming, Tony's father came down south to Lincoln College to pick up his failing son. "He's high-strung like his mother." Mr. Montgomery had said, before he took Tony's last suitcase out to the car. "Hard work will snap him right out of this."

Art wasn't sure of a cure for Tony's fixation with Jill. He'd had no experience with people suffering to the degree Tony allowed.

Alone now in the dorm room he had shared with Tony, Art reached for Robinson Crusoe. The page he opened read. "When I came down the hill to the shore, I was perfectly confounded and amazed; nor is it possible for me to express the horror of my mind, at seeing the shore spread with skulls, hands, feet, and other bones, where the savage wretches had sat down to their inhumane feastings upon the bodies of their fellow creatures."

Art summoned up a vision of the strutting braggart Tony was the last time he drove him home from high school. Jill had spit Tony out like a prune pit. Now, Tony was shriveled up in the back seat of his father's car.

Art went back to Crusoe. "Recovering myself, I looked up with the utmost affection of my soul, and with a flood of tears in my eyes, gave God thanks that had cast my first lot in a part of the world where I was distinguished from such dreadful creatures."

Surely, Sally would never have thrown him away for someone with more money, as easily as Jill discarded Tony.

Sheriff Woods tried to remember why he broke up with Sally. They'd separated after Jill's wedding, after Tony suicide. He couldn't remember the cause. He doubted he'd ever allow himself to love again. Love became a dangerous word, an emotion to be avoided. He often told Gabby he cared for her because *she* loved him.

His contentment was real, but not the passionate love Tony claimed for Jill. Sheriff Woods kept himself sane by staying free of deep emotional entanglements. He didn't want to experience the fearful degree of rejection Tony suffered. It was sadly simple, he wanted to survive, so he limited his emotional range.

* * *

First Thursday in January

Recovering from her memories of Tony and her teenage crush on Art, Sally surveyed the masculine frontroom of her new husband's house, their home. The black leather couch was huge and comfortable. The ceiling-high stone fireplace dominated the room. Jarring modern art canvases on the opposite wall provided the only color. She should think about making some changes if she wanted to feel at home here. "Coffee," she begged and John responded in a short time with a full cup.

"Did you microwave it?" Sally asked.

"No, I set up the coffee maker earlier. You seem to inhale coffee. I just needed to plug it in."

"Thank you. Microwave coffee lacks the aroma of newly brewed coffee."

John got cozy on the couch with her again. "So tell me again about Sheriff Woods and the Montgomerys."

Sally groaned. "I rather talk to you about redecorating."

"Another touchy subject." John described where he bought the modern art, who the painters were, how much the artwork cost, into an entire soliloquy of his love of art. Poor Sally could not concentrate. Her mind roved teenage recesses, dragging out old memories of Jill and Tony and the promise to buy a car to visit Art.

* * *

November 1958

Sally thought her peach linen suit ought to do the trick. Taking a deep breath, she straightened the shoulder strap of her purse. After standing in line to make deposits each week, she knew where to find the loan desk. Mr. Westland, the loan officer, was acquainted with her father and Jack Stone, her boss at DuKane. "Good morning, Sally. What can we do for you?"

"I don't want you to call my father to co-sign for a car loan." Sally eased into the arm-less chair next to his desk, one foot behind the other for balance, back straight. "Mr. Stone's private secretary should be able to afford car payments on a used car. How long will it take before the bank will approve my loan?" She had practiced the speech in front of her mirror at home five times.

Without letting his good-natured smile falter, Mr. Westland tapped his pen on a small note pad. "Have you picked out the car?"

"The Naylor's Chevy is two years old." She couldn't remember the price of the car.

"Sally, you've done your homework." Mr. Westland said. "Before you sign the papers out at Naylor's, they'll call me. We need the vehicle registration number. Give me your social security number for the loan."

Trying not to seem too childishly elated, she thanked him and walked out of the bank. Loretta waited to drive her to the dealership, where an older salesman made the call to Mr. Westland. Sally had nervously smiled as he nodded at her, still talking on the phone to Westland. After a lot of paperwork and a promise to return with the bank's check, the salesman handed Sally the keys to her first car.

Sally called Art as soon as she rushed into the house after parking the white and blue Chevy next to her father's paint truck behind the house. "I bought a car, Art!"

"So your mother won't worry," he said, not sounding nearly as giddy as she felt. "Tell them you're bringing me home from school."

"Oh, Art!"

"Tony couldn't survive school without Jill. I'm coming home, too."

"How's your dad taking it?"

"I only talked to Mother." Sally thought she heard Art's voice break as he hung up.

* * *

Down in Lincoln, Sally stopped her car at the same spot Jill parked two weeks earlier. A freak snowfall iced the green campus. Barren elms stood along the empty sidewalk. Art hugged Sally before she stepped into his room. Tony's side of the room was empty, the mattress bare. "His father came for him." Art said, before she could ask.

"He loved her, then."

"If that's love, I never want to fall in love." He held Sally by the shoulders. "That wasn't love, Sally. It was a thing without affection. It consumed his mind and body, leaving no place for his soul to rest."

"You're right." Sally tried to calm his fierceness. Nevertheless, as she got into her second-hand car to drive home, she judged Tony to be a romantic because he grieved so much for his lost mate. Without thinking of her words effect on Art's nerves, she said, "Black swans die within twenty-four hours of the other swan's death. Their hearts stop."

"He wants to die."

"I never understood Jill. Once when I was talking to the boys in my study hall, she took me aside. She told me not to waste my time on them. They couldn't afford cars." Art didn't respond. "And another time after Mrs. Forbes invited the Latin Club over for Christmas, Jill estimated the cost of every lamp in the place."

"Her first love," Art said.

"Money?"

"My dad called," Art said, once they turned north on to Route 66 heading for St. Charles. "He's arranged for me to work at DuKane, in Customer Relations."

"Wow." Sally kept her eyes on the scant rural traffic.

"He's not happy."

Rich people seldom are, Sally's head replayed Daddy's saying. Then she offered Art an invitation, one guaranteed to please Mother. "Could we stop off in Bloomington and say hello to my grandmother?"

"It's your car."

"She'll love you."

Grandmother Kerner could be counted on to hug the poor guy and fill him full of soup, certainly enough cookies to raise his sugar level out of any depression. "Do you like oatmeal-raison or pecan ice-box cookies?"

"Both." Art smiled slightly.

When they stopped for gas, Sally called her grandmother to say she was bringing a friend to taste-test cookies. "I've got'ta plenty in the freezer," Grandma Kerner said. "Bring more milk if you want any."

Grandma's German accent struck a chord of homesickness in Sally. She wanted to be eight years old again without a care in the world to fully enjoy her share of Grandma's hugs and cookies. For an entire summer she stayed in Bloomington, when her mother broke her pelvis in a fall from a barn's hayloft in Algonquin, Illinois. Loretta came too, but Loretta was put to work helping with Aunt Rosie's brood of nine. Loretta could bake bread and iron by the age of eleven. Sally only dusted the steps up to the bedrooms every day with a damp cloth for Grandma with a pat on the behind if she missed a speck. Somehow, her grandmother convinced Sally in those four summer months that she was a lovable and wanted person, not like at home.

Rejudging the brown, tar-shingled house of her grandmother, Sally tried to see the house from Art's viewpoint. The grape arbor in the side yard stood ugly with its cap of dripping snow. The window boxes on the front porch were empty of flowers. Art Woods started up the front steps. "No, no," Sally called. "Come this way."

As Sally opened the side door, the familiar odors of a tomato and cabbage soup reached her. The dark stairway up to the kitchen needed guidance. She held Art's hand until they stepped into the bright kitchen. "Hello," she called and heard a muffled reply. She went around the refrigerator to open the door to the bedrooms' stairwell.

"I'm on the throne," Grandma called.

"She'll be right down." Before Sally found a place in the packed refrigerator for the milk, Grandma appeared...even shorter than she recalled.

Grandma peered up at Art, after the introduction. At four-foot eleven and shrinking, Sally thought her grandma would be impressed with Art's six feet two inches. "I've got three grandchildren taller than you." Grandma cut Art down to size. "Are you a good Catholic boy, hanging around our Sally?"

"No, Ma'am." Art sat down to get eye to eye. "I'm Protestant."

"Go to church?"

"No, Ma'am."

"Sally, you take this boy in hand now."

Sally intended to. "About those cookies, Grandma." She retrieved the milk carton and placed it on the oilcloth covering of the table.

"Get that off of there." Grandma spanked her behind. "Pour the young man a glass of milk and put the rest away."

Sally poured three glasses as Grandma briskly went down the narrow hall between the parlor and the front room out to the giant freezer housed on the front porch. Returning with plastic containers balanced up to her chin, Grandma went to the cupboard corner next to the sink and set out an array of cookies on a green glass platter. "You drink coffee?" she asked, pouring Sally and herself each a full cup.

"Not yet," Art said.

Grandma put her hand on Sally's arm, a warm gesture making Sally feel a part of Grandma's life.

Art devoured the plate of cookies with appropriate "oohs" and "ahs" of appreciation. "They're the best." Art turned in his chair to ask Sally, "Can you bake these?"

Grandma laughed. "She's a third daughter. Marie, her mother, got tired of teaching by the time Sally was old enough to learn. All this child does is stick her nose in books. But we love her."

For an hour they traded gossip about the four generations in the family. Who married, gave birth, died. Art moved around restlessly. "We better head home," Sally finally said.

"Well, use the bathroom at the head of the steps before you leave, while I pack up a few cookies to take back with you."

"Could I have a few for my mother?" Art asked. "She doesn't bake."

"He's a sweet boy," Grandma said as Art headed upstairs. "You make sure he takes those catechism lessons, like your daddy, before you agree to marry him."

"He hasn't asked."

"He will." Grandma gave her an extra good-bye hug. "I'll call Marie; tell her you're on your way. No sense worrying her beads."

As they got on the road with Art driving, he said, "That's the kind of mother I want my kids to have!"

Sally caught a sob in her throat. "Me too. I miss her already."

Art didn't notice. "My grandmother lives in Florida. Grandpa has Parkinson's, but she's fine. She plays tennis and bridge every day. She says I'm the cat's pajamas."

"Grandmothers love us best."

"Yeah, we don't have to prove our worth to them," Art said, somewhat restored from his college trauma. "They're just happy we're alive."

* * *

First Thursday in January

Tuning back into her husband's one-way conversation about the merits of the various modern art pieces hanging in their front room, Sally asked him, "What do you think caused you to fixate on me, fifty years ago?"

"You didn't even know I existed, did you?"

"I remember you as part of a pair of identical twins. You were both on the football team. The truth is, unless one of you told me your name, I couldn't keep you apart."

"But you can now," John said with a hopeful tone in his voice.

Sally laughed. "I don't really know. I've not seen James

without that horrid hairpiece."

"I told him. But he won't listen to me. Betty likes the thing, I guess."

"Her wig is a bit odd." Sally noted John's surprise, so she added, "for her age."

"Nevertheless, it is a good question. I mean about fixating on another human being when we're teenagers."

"Almost like a duckling out of an egg."

John characteristically rubbed his bald head to stimulate his thinking. "Must be all those hormones let loose in a rush. I remember feeling as if I might crack."

"Tony certainly did."

"He didn't believe in the power of tomorrow. Mother always said when I was down, "just wait until tomorrow." When I looked at the problem again the next day, somehow something would be altered, not always diminished, but I could find another angle to the problem."

"If Tony waited for the day after the wedding, he might have survived."

"Being here, in St. Charles …" John drew Sally closer to him on the couch. "Has brought back a lot of vivid memories for you."

"I feel overwhelmed. I'm sure Sheriff Woods suffered from being in such close contact with the Montgomerys."

"I think Tim will be free of Matilda, at least. She doesn't seem like a bad person."

"I'm sure she's not. It's hard to let go of affection for

someone, even when we know it is wrong."

"Have you let go of Sheriff Woods?" John seemed compelled to ask.

Sally put her arms around his neck. "I'd like to bury the fifty-year-old memories somewhere."

"Memories are not infidelities."

Sally wasn't sure. First loves seemed to hang on. She did not want anything to do emotionally with Sheriff Woods, but her energy seemed sapped by the constant thoughts of herself as a teenager. Probably trying to recapture your youth, she chastised herself. Attempting to return to the subject of redecorating, she asked, "Would Betty like to store this artwork for you, or buy them?"

"I can't see the room without them."

"Would they find a home in one of the bedrooms, after I redecorate it for your study?"

"Why don't we wait until we finish this arson case, before you start on the house?"

"Good idea. I can restrain myself until we figure out why Enid Krimm died in the Masters' home."

John stood up and swung his arms around, addressing the art hanging on the walls of his comfortable home. "You're safe for now, guys."

The front room might never seem anything but a bachelor's pad to Sally. Her home in Ann Arbor kept calling. Her books were still on the shelves in every room. The kitchen cupboards stood at the ready for any future attempt at cooking. At least, she complied with

John's dictate about cleaning out the refrigerator and leaving a forwarding address. Nevertheless without her cache of books, she suspected she was only vacationing, not living, in St. Charles.

* * *

First Friday in January

John and James were working at the Hotel Baker, going over the books, ordering supplies, and doing whatever hotel owners do, when Sally planned to visit the police station in Geneva. For the five years she lived in St. Charles, neither Sally nor her family members provoked any circumstances requiring law enforcement officials.

Daddy said anyone carrying a gun was crazy. He was never a hunter and the slaughter of farm animals wasn't carried out on the farms he managed, except for the chickens Mother axed. He included police officers in the people he considered dangerous because they carried guns, cautioning her to always follow their orders. She wished she questioned him further. Had he ever come up against the law? With his temper, he must have set limits for himself. Arguing with government officials was out of bounds.

Sally wrinkled her nose at her reflection in the mirror above the telephone table in John's front hall as she dialed Sheriff Woods. Curiosity demanded she proceed. "How is the extradition order coming?"

"Well," Sheriff Woods drawled, "I talked to Geraldine and convinced her to come home. She should be at the Montgomerys later tonight." Sally heard him sigh. "I'm getting depressed already."

"Why don't you let John and me question her? She might respond more readily to an arson detective than a police officer."

"Do I need to speak to John?"

"We'll be glad to help," Sally replied. "But do you mind asking Tim to join us."

"Won't he put a crimp in Geraldine's ruffles?"

"Oh, I hope so."

* * *

Montgomery Home in Wayne

Tim picked up Sally at seven o'clock in the evening for their appointment at the Montgomerys. John still pleaded urgent hotel business. At Carolyn Montgomery's, her frosty welcome prompted Sally to keep her coat on.

Tim retained his fur-collared overcoat as well. "We shouldn't take very much time," he said as if to explain his decision.

Geraldine Masters was, indeed, six feet tall. Her white hair was perfectly styled and her clothes showed the cut and taste only three generations of moneyed families guarantee. "I understand I was the last person to speak to Enid."

"Could you describe your meeting?" Sally positioned herself in the green armchair by the fireplace, even though she was not invited to sit. The familiar orange cat thought her action acceptable and jumped onto her lap. Sally took out her note pad and pencil, then motioned for Tim to take the matching chair on the other side of the fireplace. "You know Tim."

"Unfortunately," Geraldine said.

Sally ignored the insult. "Were you expecting Enid?"

"No, I was not.".

"Take your time," Sally urged. "We're in no rush."

"Well!" Carolyn Montgomery flounced out of the room.

Geraldine and her husband, Peter, both sat down on one of the couches, perpendicular to the fireplace. Sally stayed where she was. As far as she was concerned they could crane their stuck-up necks.

"Enid has been calling me, whenever Peter …" Peter patted his wife's knee. "Whenever," Geraldine continued, "Peter left for a business trip."

"What is your business, Mr. Masters," Tim asked.

"None of your…" Peter stopped, thinking better of his tone of voice. "I manage a software company with offices in several states."

"Did you find your boarding passes?" Sally asked, knowing full well Peter never traveled to Dallas on New Year's Eve.

"No," he said, hanging his head.

Geraldine came to his rescue. "You wanted to hear about Enid's visit."

"Yes," Sally said. "Please, go on."

"Enid showed up, uninvited, on New Year's Day. I was afraid I would miss my flight out of O'Hare."

"What time did she arrive?" Tim asked.

"In the morning, about 9:30, maybe 9:15." Tim said the house was on fire at ten o'clock. Turning away from Sally and Tim, Geraldine ran her finger along her husband's shoulder and arm, as if checking for dust. "I fell into the rescuer's trap with Enid. Victims provide such a wellspring of need. You are getting busier and busier. Matilda doesn't need daily interference." She looked back at Sally, "The woman's shelter soaked up all of my attention. I guess it made me feel valuable. Enid called every day with some new calamity or cause for outrage."

Sally speculated on why a Madame would try to pass herself off as an abused woman. "Did you first meet Enid at the country club?"

"Yes, of course," Peter answered.

The other orange cat leaned into Tim's ankle. Tim wrapped his arms around the cat, after it jumped on his lap. "We would like to hear your wife's version of the disaster. Do we need to invite her to the station?"

Peter grumbled but didn't interrupt again.

"Enid said she dropped by for a cup of coffee. I told her I was sorry but my taxi was coming within minutes to take me to the airport. She wanted to know if Peter confessed, confessed he was with her whenever he traveled." Geraldine stood up, as if to divest herself of her husband's influence on her story. "With her...intimately."

Peter squirmed on the couch.

The cat abandoned Tim's lap and the room. Its twin on Sally's lap followed suit, as if deserting the troubled married couple and their secrets.

"...the first time in the riding stable..." Geraldine choked out.

Tim interrupted. "She tried to grab me there."

Geraldine shook her head. "Enid expanded on her tale to include exploits..." she turned to her husband, grinning slightly. "Gymnastics even, at meetings. I must have supplied her with the dates and cities in earlier casual conversations."

Tim said, "I remember Enid leaning in my car window, talking about Matilda's father's trips. She was fishing for information."

"When I defended Peter's integrity, Enid insisted my son-in-law, Bret, was her lover since he turned sixteen. I asked her to leave my house." Geraldine strolled back and forth in front of the fireplace, as she finished the story. "Enid went crazy. She grabbed a candlestick and shook it at me, screaming Peter's house was her house. I ran out. The cab was there. That's all."

"Was the candle lit?" Sally asked.

Geraldine sat down again next to her husband. She shook her head. "I do have candles in them for the Holiday's, but I never light them. Pewter is hard to clean, and they're very old."

"Your colonial grandmother's," Sally said. "Your daughter said you rarely touched the heirlooms."

"She's right," Peter said.

"Thank you for coming home. We will need to question you further, once the arson report is filed."

"There will be an inquest." Tim stood to leave. "Into the cause of Enid's death."

Chapter Five

First Friday in January

On the return drive to Geneva's police station, Sally and Tim discussed the case in light of Geraldine Masters' answers. Tim thumped the steering wheel. "I think Mrs. Masters was telling the truth."

"Did Sheriff Woods interrogate Enid's neighbors?"

Tim tilted his cap, as he scratched his blond curls. "He said he was familiar with what she did."

"But, the neighbors …" Then she remembered John would look into who Enid's movers were. In downtown St. Charles about to turn onto Route 31 toward Geneva, Sally checked her watch. Noon. "Do you mind if we drive out to check with John, before we report into Sheriff Woods?"

"No that's fine. Does John cook?"

"Are you hungry?"

"I am." Tim laughed.

As Tim parked in front of the unattached garage, a strange premonition caused a chill to run up Sally's back. "Is there another cold wave coming through?"

"These plains states let northern winds howl across five states before they slam into us." Tim pulled up the fur collar on his uniform as they walked to the front door, shielding Sally from the worst of the northwestern wind. An impending storm front darkened the winter sky. The house was lit up, except for the bedrooms. They could hear Ginger barking.

"John's home," Sally said, as she opened the front door.

Bret Armstrong stood just inside. He held a small gun in his hand. Standing at the fireplace with one hand on Ginger's collar, John waved at Sally, as if to tell her to leave. Bret pointed the gun at Sally. "You've ruined my marriage."

Tim stepped in front of her as John lunged for Bret.

Bret fired in John's direction.

Tim tackled the fool to the floor, quickly disarming him. He rolled Bret on his stomach and attached handcuffs behind his back. John was still standing, holding onto the couch and his throat. Ginger was whining.

"No," Sally screamed. "Tim, call 911." She wadded her winter scarf into a bandage, as John slipped down onto the leather couch. "Don't talk," she said, scared, too scared.

With the hand not clutching her scarf against his wound, John reached for her face, but his arm dropped before she felt his touch.

"John, John," Sally called louder and louder into his eyes, as they faded into unconsciousness, or worse. "Tim," she screamed. "Are they coming?"

Tim knelt next to John, took his pulse. "Mrs. Nelson."

"No." Sally tried to stand. Instead, she slipped down unto the carpeted floor, where the blood from John pooled. "No," was all she could say.

Ginger was growling at Bret.

"I didn't mean to kill him." Bret said from the floor behind the couch.

Sally's anger recharged her energy. She jumped up, lifting the lamp from the end table and smashing John's killer on his head, twice.

Tim rescued her from her frenzy. He slipped her coat down to her elbows and pushed her onto the couch where John lay. "Did I kill him?"

"No," Tim said. "But he's out …"

"Like a light." Sally suffered no remorse. Her busy mind went blank. Where were the questions she should be asking? What next? "Better get me a drink of water." Her heart was making those flipping motions warning this was way too much excitement for a sixty-seven year old woman. "Widow," Sally said out loud before Tim returned with a glass of water. "I'm a widow, again."

* * *

First Monday in January
Hotel Baker, St. Charles, Illinois

For the next seventy-two hours, Sally feared for her sanity. Surreal memories of her teen years in St. Charles attempted to crowd the horrible reality of John's death out of her conscious mind. Violent daydreams meshed with the awful truths in reality during sleepless nights of utter confusion.

Several days were filled with Tim, James Nelson and his wife, Betty, as well as Sheriff Woods and Gabby keeping constant vigils. Nevertheless, Sally searched the assembled crowd for the man's face filled with love who would never meet her smile again in her lifetime. Her friends kept reminding her, John was dead.

On Monday, the funeral baskets of white roses from St. Patrick's altar arrived at Hotel Baker, where they lined the foyer walls. Unlit candles in giant brass holders were stationed along the main hall to the ballroom. Sally reminisced about being here before, among white roses and unlit candles. "Where is Jill?" Sally asked an usher.

Dressed in somber black, Tim shook his head.

An older man pushed Tim aside. "Jill?" Sheriff Woods asked.

A woman dressed oddly in black for a wedding seemed to have half the answer. "Sally," Gabby said. "We didn't think to invite her."

"For her own wedding?" Sally tried to laugh but the frowns of the people surrounding her delayed the effort.

An old person, Sally longed to hug stepped forward. "You're exhausted, Sally," James said. "Come and sit down for a minute."

"What happened to your head?" Sally judged the top of the man's head was too hairy to be real.

James touched his wig. He fished in his pockets for something. The woman next to him also in the day's fashion of black handed him a handkerchief. He freely applied the white lace to his wet face. Sally looked down at her hands. She touched a wedding ring on her left hand. Who did it belong to, and why did she hurt all over? "I don't think I'm well," she said to the youngest person in the group.

Tim helped her to a cushioned chair in the hotel's lobby. "You've had a shock. Give yourself time to absorb the blow."

Sally rested her head against the chair's soft back cushion. Tim sat down in a chair beside her. "I know you, don't I?" Sally put both hands to her head. Someone she knew did the same thing whenever he tried to think. John. No. She did not want to think of John. She closed her eyes and searched for Jill in her past.

* * *

December 1958

Jill had called Sally at work. "I never catch you at home."

"Night school," Sally answered. She hadn't heard from Jill since the homecoming debacle in Lincoln, nearly four months earlier.

"I'd like you to be my maid-of-honor," Jill said.

"Good Heavens! Who are you marrying, and when?"

"Next Saturday to Charlie. I picked out your dress for you. I'm paying for it."

"Thank you," Sally managed. "Should I try it on before the wedding?"

"I'll bring the dress by tonight." Jill sounded matter of fact, in control. "Tony won't leave me alone. My father finally let me invite him to the wedding. Could you ask Art Woods to talk to him? Art and his folks are invited too." After a pause, Jill added, "Yours are too."

Jill was stiff and apologetic when she brought over the dress, keeping her coat and hat on and declining a piece of Sally's mother's pie. Sally tried on the flowing, emerald satin gown.

"Wow," Daddy said.

"How should I wear my hair?" Sally asked.

Jill jumped up hitting her knee on the table. "Ouch. I forgot the hat." She ran out to the car, retrieving a mammoth hatbox and a wedding invitation. Sally's mother said they would enjoy coming, as Sally tried to figure out the wide-brimmed hat. "Can you make it down the aisle without your glasses?" Jill asked.

"I will. I just won't be able to see who you're marrying."

Jill managed a small smile. "Maybe I could take just a taste of your pie. It smells so good." Sally's mother obliged. When Jill took off her coat and hat to sit down at the table, she revealed coal black dyed hair.

Sally and her mother chorused, "Your hair!"

"It was red." Sally explained to her father. Jill concentrated on devouring the pie. "After Lincoln, I dyed it black. When I first met Charlie, he really liked it."

"Does he know you are a strawberry blonde?" Sally asked.

"Sure," Jill said, "but he says the contrast with my complexion is striking."

"It certainly is," Sally's mother said, without too much sarcasm.

Jill excused herself. "I've got to run. So much to do."

Rubbing his five-o'clock shadow after Jill left, Daddy said, "She doesn't look happy."

Mother stood at the window, watching Jill barrel out of the driveway. "You know, I read somewhere black hair dye can seep into the brain."

* * *

First Monday in January

Sheriff Woods asked Tim to let him try to talk to Sally. "Sally, we need you to wake up. People are arriving for John's service." Sally opened her eyes wide. Sheriff Woods could read Sally's frightened bewilderment in her darting eyes. He turned to his wife. "Gabby, perhaps we should let Sally rest upstairs."

"No," Sally said. "I need to be here."

"For the memorial service." Gabby stated, to make sure Sally was completely present.

"For the wedding." Sally looked down at her long black dress. "What happened to the emerald green?"

"The one you wore New Year's Day?" Gabby asked.

"No." Sally plucked at the black linen. "For Jill's wedding. Did Art get to talk to Tony?"

Then Sheriff Woods remembered. Jill's reception was held in the Hotel Baker. He also recalled searching frantically for Tony Montgomery.

* * *

December 1958

Art couldn't find Tony in his usual haunts. He finally called him at the farm and set up a lunch at Casey's Bar. Asking Sally along to cushion any emotional scenes, Art couldn't imagine what he might say to Tony to help.

Hiding in a corner booth Tony looked thinner, pale even. "Oh sure, you two are still together and you haven't even made love." Tony drained his glass of beer. "Sorry, bonded." He shook his finger at Art. "I never believed the lies you tried to sell me. Look at her; Sally, the saintly virgin, raises her eyebrows at the mere mention of intercourse." Sally slid in next to Tony.

Art seemed to forget how to bend his frame into a sitting position. "You look terrible."

"Oh, thanks. No chance Jill sent you to say she changed her mind?"

"No." Avoiding his direct glance, Sally said to her hands. "We will all be at the wedding." A low moan broke from Tony.

"You shouldn't go." Art waved away the waitress after she sat down three water glasses.

"I will though, if I can stand up long enough."

Sally tried to reason. "You'll find someone else." She ventured a look at him.

Tony's harrowed glance showed all his pain. "Jill is all I can think about."

"What about going back to college?" Art asked.

"Books?" Tony spread his hands palm up on the table flipping them back and forth, as if they were pages of a book. "Nothing there, when I can't touch her."

Sally put her hand on Tony's arm. "Don't."

"Don't?" Tony yelled. He grabbed the back of her hair. Sally's head had time to bounce off the back of the booth before Art's fist slammed into the bridge of Tony's nose.

"Never touch her!" Art sat back down on his side of the booth, before offering Tony his handkerchief for Tony's bleeding nose.

"Sorry." Tony's tears mixed with the dripping blood. "I'm insane." He nodded to Sally. "Sorry."

"Lean your head back." Sally gathered ice from the water glasses into a napkin and then held it to his nose.

"Shall we order?" Tony made them laugh.

***

December 1958

At Jill's reception at the Hotel Baker, Tony showed up with an older woman whose close fitting, gold-lamè dress shimmered seductively. Art told Sally her name was Kathleen, Kathy, Krimm. Everyone seemed to know the small blonde. Sally's parents, Mrs. Woods, Jill's parents, even the Reddinger clan welcomed her. Sally didn't remember if Kathy attended the wedding, but the reception seemed filled with twice the number of people St. Patrick's could hold.

Tony urged Kathy to dance with him. She held onto the back of her chair, resisting. Tony got louder and louder. Sitting next to

Sally at the bride's table, Jill studied her empty glass. Finally, Kathy gave in, dancing the first dance, the bride's dance, with Tony. The couple danced all the way to the front table, even after Charles Reddinger stood and motioned for the band to stop playing.

Tony yelled at a cowering Jill, "First in and first to dance!"

Kathy fled back to their table. Art apologized to the bride, rescuing a wilted Tony and guiding him off the floor. Charles Reddinger's best man unfolded his fists.

When Charles and Jill began to dance, the best man moved over to sit next to Sally. "I don't dance." Sally nodded, thankful. He looked as if he recently gave up dragging his knuckles on the ground. She smiled at the thought. The brute misjudged her grin, thinking it an invitation to talk. "Chuck and I are Navy buddies."

Sally continued to nod at the details of their service experience. Drinking to excess, walking through screen doors, and urinating into their officers' beer seemed to comprise the gist of their endeavors. One strange story about a broken transformer on a small island in the Philippines drew her attention. The natives fixed the equipment by encircling the area with miniature tomatoes to keep the midget spirits from playing games. Manna-who-knees, he called the south-sea leprechauns.

Sally caught a glimpse of her father standing at the Woods' table. Mr. Woods didn't look friendly. However, Mrs. Woods stood up and offered Sally's father her chair. Mr. Woods reached up to detain her, but she ignored him, joining Sally's mother at her table. Wishing she could read lips, Sally turned back to the best man's deep grumble.

* * *

Art Woods stayed close to Tony and Kathy. Kathy seemed more interested in Art than Tony. Art kept shaking her advances off, while trying to slow down Tony's drinking. Tony's conversation increased in coarseness as the evening progressed. The lug at the main table was talking Sally's ear off. She turned toward Art, sensing his gaze. She smiled and gestured with her chin for him to come over. Without looking back at Tony to gauge his condition, Art rushed to the front table rescuing Sally from the hulking ghoul at her side. Sally stood, before Art reached out his hand for the dance. Then they were in each other's arms on the crowded dance floor.

"I met your mother," Sally said as they danced.

"What did she ask you?" Art stiffened under her hands.

"If we were friends."

Art moved closer, as if relieved. "We are. And you are more beautiful than the bride."

* * *

Sally hoped the comment was half-way true. Maybe being in Art's arms made her shine. They hadn't danced since homecoming. She stayed close to his body, matching his movements. The world certainly forced them to consider mature subjects. Sally reacted to Art's guilty glance at Tony's table. "How's he taking it?"

Art missed a step. "He's drowning his sorrows." He tightened his grip on her waist. Sally clasped their hands to her chest. They were with each other for now. They seemed to be thinking the same thought, holding eye contact until the end of the dance.

Kathy tried to cut in. "I get him for the next dance."

Sally held on. "No. I'm not giving him up."

* * *

Back in the safety of the dancing crowd, Art whispered, "Thank you for saving me."

"You're welcome. And remember, I'm never going to stop loving you."

Art grinned. "Never?" He accepted her love without thinking of the need to return the affection. His mother loved him, he generally beat off women, like Kathy. And, he appreciated Sally loving him. A qualm hit his stomach. Now all he needed was a career to support her. Maybe DuKane would keep them gainfully employed. Or, maybe they could travel around the world, get married by a sea captain. Sally questioned his change of mood with a look. "You cheer me up, Sally." He moved her hand to his lips. "Expound on my good points. Why will you love me forever?"

Sally laughed, catching Mrs. Woods' attention. "You're modest, trustworthy, loyal friend. And, you're ugly."

"Ugly?" Art frowned.

"Beautiful. You were paying attention," Sally said, as they stepped in time to the quickening music. "We're getting pretty good at this. What did you think of the ceremony?" Sally planned a simpler wedding in her head.

"A bit overdone. I looked back down the aisle for the string of circus elephants needed to properly cement the union."

"Jill was terrified."

"Rightly so. I doubted the universe would keep silent during such a match."

"See, why I love you to distraction." Art kissed her then, right in front of his father's table. Sally spotted Father Fitzgerald and introduced Art to him with. "This is a priest concerned for each person's soul."

"Have you read Crusoe?" Art asked the clergyman out of the blue.

"Priest craft? Yes, he mentioned my profession," Father Fitzgerald said. "You two have a lot in common."

"Books and crazy friends." Sally agreed.

Father Fitzgerald said, "I'm reading Stendhal's book 'On Love.' I find my main enjoyment in literature. Stendhal promises, if I keep reading, in ten years my intelligence will be doubled."

"Marcus Aurelius would tell you to give up your love of books or you will die murmuring." Sally blushed, embarrassed to be showing off in front of the priest. "Could it be a sin to act as the witness to a wedding, when the bride doesn't love the groom?"

"Scruples can be troublesome," Father Fitzgerald said. "I can tell you are Marie's daughter. Did you confront Jill?"

"No," Art and Sally both said, as they reached for each other's hands.

"Well, it's too late now. God will handle their problems," the priest said.

When the band took a break, Sally went off to help Jill mend a rip in her hem.

Art escorted Tony outside to sober up. They walked to the middle of the Main Street bridge. The lights of the hotel ballroom sparkled on the gathering ice jam at the dam. A north wind blowing off the river caused both young men to pull up their collars. The triangular roof skylight of the Art-Deco bus terminal on the other side of the bridge turned from blue, to green, to yellow, orange, and red, and then purple. Tony spoke quietly, "Let's go back inside."

"Tony, I don't know what to say; except she's wrong." Art tucked his hands deep into his coat pockets away from the cold. "Especially in feigning affection. Have you read Desiderata?"

"White." Tony held onto the cold stone railing for support. "White, like Jill's dress." He turned away for a moment watching the black water pooling beneath them. Against the sound of the falls and crashing ice, Art strained to listen to Tony. "The void I can't broach is not being allowed to love." Then he pounded Art's back. His voice regained its authority. "White holds all the colors."

Art nodded. "And black is the absence of all colors. No, Tony, that's the opposite of the truth."

"It's okay, Pal." Tony stumbled as they headed back across the icy bridge. "It's over, really."

"I'm glad." Art wanted to believe his friend.

"I better let Kathy drive me out to the farm." Tony forced a smile. As they stamped their feet inside the hotel doors, Tony's icy hand gripped Art's. "Make sure, Jill is okay."

* * *

First Monday in January

In the Hotel Baker's ballroom memorial service, where friends of John Nelson were extolling the virtues and naming the values he held dear, Sally tried to hold herself together. Sheriff Woods heard her tell Tim, who seemed permanently tied to her hip, "Harper Lee has Atticus say, '…before I can live with other folks, I've got to live with myself.'"

After the eulogies and before the crowd of mourners surrounded Sally and Tim, Sheriff Woods observed Sally and Tim bow their heads in agreement, or prayer.

Chapter Six

Second Tuesday in January

Sheriff Woods and Gabby seemed to realize the full extent of Sally's pain. Gabby carried a box of stationary and addresses into Sally's suite of rooms at the Hotel Baker. "I thought I would spend the afternoon with you, if you'll let me."

Sally sat in front of her hotel bedroom's Victorian vanity, brushing her white hair. "Thank you, Gabby. But you surely have more interesting places to spend your time than in a drippy widow's rooms."

"Sally, I would love to help you send out your condolence thank-you notes."

"I'll have to include the wedding present thank-you notes, too." Sally laid down her brush and moved her aching body into the sitting room to examine the boxes Gabby brought. Stepping through the doorway out of the bedroom seemed to relieve a heaviness from Sally's shoulders. "I can't remember too much of the memorial service. She sat on the sofa facing the tea table loaded down with Gabby's box. "Did I behave badly?"

"You were very gracious." Gabby lied. "We all understood being widowed five days after your wedding, at your age, was a terrible shock. Reverend Warner said it was a miracle you survived."

A spark of anger ignited Sally's stomach. She laughed, then explained for Gabby. "It is a miracle to feel any life at all in these old bones. Thank God for sparing me for whatever purpose He has in mind."

The unspeakable truth was the first real feeling Sally experienced of primal anger at poor Gabby, who was only trying to be of service. A miracle at her age, indeed! Sally thanked the Lord she was conscious enough not to react negatively during the service.

Sally's conversation with Grace, her AA sponsor in Ann Arbor, helped her accept her widowhood. Now she could thank God. At least she recognized where home was. Neither St. Charles nor Ann Arbor counted as final destinations. The good Lord always showed His abundant love to her restoring her peace, more than any mortal could.

She went to the hotel's desk phone and ordered room service to provide high tea for the two of them. Her mind catalogued her recent contacts with death. She already came to terms with Danny's death. And Danny Bianco was her life's grand passion. She loved him as much as Tony Montgomery ever loved Jill. Nevertheless, Sally owned the good sense to survive. Robert Koelz's death was painful to bear. There was nothing else to do but continue, in spite of her real loss of his steadying friendship.

In a way, John Nelson was still a stranger. Naturally, he was a very dear stranger; but she'd only known him for a year. Poor John loved her since high school. Even so, Sally wasn't privy to the information until her search for Mary Jo Cardoniè, the missing abused wife, brought her back to St. Charles. John's help with the Leonard university drug scandal mystery was invaluable and the reason for their marriage, really. If John had failed to stay in Ann Arbor to help solve the Leonard case, she would hardly have considered him a friend, more less a partner in the detective agency, finally a husband, and an endearing lover.

"I suppose your husband is working on Bret's case as well as Enid's?" She asked Gabby, as she began to sort through the addresses, which included notes describing the various gifts.

"Yes, but Art specifically told me to wait until he arrives to discuss either of the cases. Is that okay with you?"

"Of course. Will Tim be coming along, too?"

"I think so." Gabby busied herself with arranging the condolence card addresses alphabetically.

Sally redialed the hotel's service desk and doubled the order of guests for tea, before attacking her social obligations. The thirteen wedding gift cards now seemed a paltry amount of work compared to the 150 or more sympathy cards needing acknowledgement. "I'll write the notes and sign them, if you could help me address the cards."

"We'll make short work of it." Gabby promised. In fact, they completed the wedding thank-you notes and were half-way through the sympathy cards, when James arrived with a waiter and the tea service.

"Could you move your stationary to the desk?" He asked.

Gabby jumped up to comply, but Sally raised her hand.

"Nonsense, James, your man can set up the tea on the desk." She touched Gabby's arm. "Gabby, spent two hours getting me organized."

James sat down on the couch with Sally. He craned his neck to watch the waiter arrange the tea things. "Sally, did you ask for tea for four?"

"I did," Sally confessed, feeling annoyed again at James' interference. The stages of grief she'd been counseled during her grieving process for Danny: here was free-floating anger for being deserted by her lover landing on everyone and everything within a country mile. "Is my controlling nature over-asserting itself? My world seems extremely uncontrollable, so I snap at everyone."

"No explanation needed." James started to rub his head the way his twin brother often did. He stopped the action, when he noticed Sally's shocked expression. "I know John always buffed that bald head of his. I'm probably as touchy as you are. I feel as if half of me disappeared."

Sally touched James' face. "I know you'll be lost without him." She continued to stare at James, wondering if she could ask him to take off his wig. But she didn't want to see the closer resemblance to her John, quite yet. Nevertheless, the wig always bothered her. "James?" She touched his knee. "Have you thought about not wearing your wig?" Sally rushed on, hoping he wouldn't contradict her. "Nobody will mistake you for John. And, John was so much more attractive. I mean. He didn't need to cover his gorgeous head."

James laughed and whisked off the horrid wig. Sally drew in a quick breath, then relaxed. James wasn't John. There was no love light in James' eyes, no warmth for her.

Just then, James' wife knocked on the open hotel door and entered. Betty dropped her purse, but quickly picked it up. Her own black wig slipped half-an inch to one side. She flopped down on the other couch where Gabby sat, knocking askew a pile of carefully stacked thank-you notes. The cards tumbled to the floor. "Oh, no," Betty shouted, and then apologized. She was sobbing.

Sally understood too well. Betty missed John, too. "Never mind." Sally ushered Betty into the bedroom and shut the door. "Betty, I know you miss him, too. Don't you?"

"Oh, I didn't realize." Betty continued to sob. "Until I saw James without, without his hair." She sat down at the vanity and straightened her long black wig.

Not fully understanding her motivation, Sally tried to comfort the rival. "John loved you, too. He said you always arranged everything."

"Did he?" Betty stopped crying. "I didn't think he even noticed me."

"You were an important person in his life." Maybe it was true, Sally didn't even know John well enough to judge how great a part his sister-in-law played in his prolonged single life. Sally grasped one thing; this woman loved John Nelson as much as she had. Of course, Sally didn't imply they were lovers, but Betty owned a real affection for her brother-in-law.

"Do you think it's all right, if James doesn't wear his wig?" Betty asked, with all her defenses down. "Won't people laugh at him for mimicking his brother's looks?"

To Sally the whole subject was suddenly comical. She tried not to laugh and managed to keep her smile in check. "James is an identical twin, after all."

"Right." Betty turned away from her reflection in the vanity's mirror.

"What color is your real hair, Betty?"

"White." Betty turned back to the mirror. "I look one hundred years old. James disagrees. He's always pulling at my wig."

"Is your own hair long?"

"Do you want to see it?" Betty slid off her wig.

Sally was astounded to see a spiky, modern cut of thick, beautiful white hair. "It's glorious!"

"Really?" Betty smiled at herself in the mirror. "I do like it and I hate this wig, but I want to stay stylish for James."

"Let Gabby see you. She'll tell you how great and up-to-date you look." Betty dropped her rat-colored wig into the wastepaper basket. "Betty," Sally hoped she didn't seem cold-hearted to ask, "Could you pack up my clothes from John's house. I don't think I can bear going out there again."

"I'd be glad to." Betty stopped, realizing she seemed all too eager to shed John's house of his wife's belongings. "Is there anything of John's you would like to have?"

"Could you bring Ginger to me? Is she okay?"

"Thank you. She's fine. I'm not really a dog lover." Betty preceded Sally into the living room.

"Betty," Gabby said. "Never wear that wig again. You look fifty."

"Really," Betty said, all smiles.

James hugged his wife. "She wouldn't listen to me."

Gabby rescued the cards from the carpet and stacked them by zip code. "Most of these people live on the same two roads in Wayne." She pointed to the largest pile.

Sally placed the stack on her lap. "All these people recognized Enid."

James, with his bald head shining and his arm around his snazzy wife, said his goodbye. Betty, with her happy mission to clean Sally's belongings out of John's home and shed herself of dog-walking duties, left without partaking of the tea.

Sally was in the process of pouring a cup of tea for Gabby when the sheriff and Tim Hanson arrived. "Hello, boys," Sally said, maybe too cheerfully.

Sheriff Woods looked at his wife, as if asking her assessment. "Sally's doing fine. We got some work done, too. James and Betty just left, without their wigs. Sally's going to stay at the hotel, instead of going back out to John's place."

"Good idea." Tim took the cup of tea Sally offered after filling a small plate with sweets from the tea tray.

"Did you talk to Enid's neighbors, yet?" Sally asked Sheriff Woods.

"Why is it so important?"

Sally shook her head, glad the brain cells were finally starting to make connections. "We don't know the full extent of Enid's shenanigans. Gabby was just showing me how many people came to John's memorial service. The majority of them probably were acquainted with Enid."

"Why?" Woods asked his wife, who shrugged her shoulders.

"They all live in Wayne. They, no doubt, belonged to the riding club where Enid worked, where she honed in on potential customers or her victims for blackmail."

"She's back." Tim crowed, then sheepishly filled his mouth with more sweets when Sheriff Woods scowled at him.

"I'll bite. I'll question every one of these." The sheriff reached for the envelopes with Wayne addresses. "You and Tim scour Enid's neighbors and see what you can find."

Sally's mind approached a painful subject. "Do we know what set Bret Armstrong off? I was under the impression Matilda was not going to reveal her lover."

Gabby's attention zeroed in on Sally. "Who was Matilda's lover?"

"We'd rather not say," Woods said.

When the tea tray was depleted of everything edible, Tim and the sheriff left with Gabby. Sally picked up the phone to call Grace in Ann Arbor.

"Thank God you called," she said. "I've been praying for you. Are you able to attend a meeting?"

"God knows I need one." Sally laughed. "I'm feeling like my old crazy self. Do you think I'm going to be okay?"

"Self-pity is a cruel hook. Alcohol just loves grieving widows."

"I'll go tonight. Grace, thanks for being there."

"You're welcome. Don't forget to thank our Maker. His mercy endures forever."

Sally called the hotel's front desk to find out if the Honda was parked nearby or if she would need to call a cab. When she slid behind the wheel of John's car, she thought about driving all the way to Ann Arbor. Instead, the numerous loose ends concerning Enid Krimm's death convinced her to search out the Bethlehem Lutheran's AA meeting place. The modern flagstone façade was adequately labeled with a low AA symbol near the street; however, none of the doors were open.

Consulting her pocket calendar, Sally recalled the Lutheran Church held a Monday night meeting, not a Tuesday night. She repeated her third step prayer as a substitute for the meeting. "Lord, I offer myself to you to do with me and to build with me what you will. Save me from the bondage of self. Free me from my present difficulties so that I may bear witness to those I'm trying to help of Thy power, Thy love, and Thy way of life. Help me to do Your will always." She also promised herself to attend a Thursday noon meeting at St. Mark's in Geneva.

Sally slept well Tuesday night. The two cases needed solving in the morning and she needed her rest. The ghosts surrounding her could wait their turn for her attention.

* * *

Second Wednesday in January

When she woke, a list of questions filled her mind. Did they find Geraldine's ring in the Masters' blackened fireplace? Who set the fire? How long was Enid in the house alone after Geraldine left? Where was Peter Masters at the time? Who laundered Enid's linens? Did John find out who the movers of her furniture were? What was her destination? Most importantly, who triggered Bret's ire enough to want to kill her? She tried not to dwell on John's death. How many people had been blackmailed?

Tim phoned early to find out when Sally would be ready to interrogate Enid's neighbors. "I thought we could bring them into the station. Then, they would understand how serious we are." When Sally didn't respond quickly enough, he added, "You know, about any information they might give us."

"Wait a minute," Sally said. "We can always threaten to question them at the police station, if they won't help us."

"What time will you be ready?"

"Nine. What time is it now?"

"Eight. Do you really need an hour for breakfast?"

"You haven't eaten?"

"No," he said.

Sally laughed. "Why don't you eat. You're always hungry."

"I forget about it. I still live in my folks' house in Geneva, the one you cleaned for us. Jeff is out of the house by five for his job in Chicago. Molly teaches in Elgin, so nobody's here when I wake up."

"Poor bachelor. Come on over. The hotel's breakfast has a long menu. Wait half-an-hour before you start." Sally glimpsed her smile reflected in the hotel room's mirror. Young people were such a joy to be around.

* * *

Enid Krimm's Neighborhood

Tim parked the police cruiser in Enid's driveway. "Which side of the condo do you want to interrogate?"

"Better stick together," Sally said, "to act as each other's witness for any facts we might uncover."

Only one housing unit was attached to the left of Enid's. In the small dooryard, a wooden wheelbarrow held a peck of snow. Sally imagined flowers were expected to bloom in its interior in the spring. She knocked on the door, checking her watch -- ten o'clock.

Taking her own sweet time to answer the door, or perhaps jumping out of a bed in the upstairs, a skimpy-haired woman appeared in a long fleece bathrobe. "Yes?" she asked, quickly adding, as she began to shut the door. "I'm not interested." Tim stopped the door with his arm. He poked his police badge through the opening. "You're not allowed to come in," the woman said. "I know my rights."

"We want to inquire about your neighbor." Sally positioned herself in front of Tim.

A faint odor of something like alfalfa, Sally remembered from her years on the farm, issued from the house.

"The Krimms?" the woman asked, opening the door an inch more.

"Yes." Sally moderated her tone to friendly. "Have you known them long? Mrs.?"

"Sederbush," the older woman said. "Don't know them at all. Minded the traffic, though."

"Traffic?" Sally pushed lightly on the door.

"Well, come in if you're about to. You'll have to sit yourself down. I need to get presentable. Or, go ask the other neighbors and come back."

"We will," Sally said. "I don't suppose you kept notes."

"I certainly did. License numbers and all."

Sally thought about protesting against the closing door, but decided the information was too valuable to irritate the source. "Thank you." Sally managed as she followed Tim down the front stoop.

The neighbor on the Krimm's right was more welcoming, but less helpful. "Enid Krimm?" Another older woman answered their question. "Was that the daughter's name? I met her mother, Kathleen, for exactly two seconds. Come in, come in, I love company."

Sally and Tim followed the fragile woman into her dining room, where she folded up her walker before easing into a soft chair. "Young man, there's coffee on the kitchen counter. Why don't you pour your mother and me a cup? Donuts in the fridge. I like cream, too."

Sally took out her notebook. "You are Mrs.?"

"Pierce, Miss Pierce, thank you very much. You can write down ninety years old, if you've a mind to."

Tim busied himself in the kitchen and then served them coffee and donuts. Sally asked, "Have you thought there was anything odd about your neighbor?"

"Always been odd. But then, who isn't. Did notice the movers." Miss Pierce broke a piece off one of the un-iced donuts and dunked it into her coffee, without apology. "Those guys had a heck of a job. They packed up everything into huge wooden crates. The truck's crane mechanism pulled the crates up a ramp to its flatbed. Took them all day. I went to sleep before they finished."

"Did you happen to see the name on the truck?" Tim asked between mouthfuls of donuts.

"International Seaways, something like that I'm sure."

"We thought Enid lived alone," Sally said.

"She did for the last fifteen years. Her mother died from AIDs. One of the first cases I heard about. I don't suppose anyone will be wanting to buy the place for a long time."

Mrs. Walker and her son, Gary, the neighbors to the right of Miss Pierce's unit, were not as welcoming. Tim and Sally stood in the hall during for the entire interview. Mrs. Walker summoned her son from the basement, where a television was blaring drug commercials. "Gar-ryee, get up here. Police officers want to know if you knew the Krimms?" Mrs. Walker winked at Tim. "In the biblical sense, I assume."

Tim stepped away from the woman. So, Sally questioned the two, who resembled each other enough to play Tweedle Dum and Tweedle Dee. Both sported thick long yellow hair. Their height, stomach, blue eyes, and lack of eyebrows also matched. Even their blue jeans, fleece-lined slippers and sweatshirts were identical. Each shirt was emblazoned with reindeers, sporting Christmas bells in their noses. Trying not to reveal her astonishment, Sally asked. "When was the last time you met with the Krimms?"

"Christmas Eve," they answered in unison. They smiled at each other and then added in perfect harmony, "She moved out."

The son stepped forward, which caused the bell on his shirt's reindeer to tinkle. His mother also moved toward Sally and Tim with the same tinkling of bells. "Laundry," they said, together.

The son deferred to his mother with a courteous sweep of his hand. Mrs. Walker said, "We thought it odd, after we moved in. A linen service made deliveries once a week."

"What name was on the delivery truck?" Sally asked.

Simultaneously they answered. "Stuart's."

"They lived here, how long?" Tim asked.

Mother and son smiled at each other, and answered in concert. "Ten years."

Tim pulled at Sally's sleeve. "Thank you, both."

Once outside, Sally and Tim hurried to the cruiser. Tim drove the car a block away, out of sight of the Walker's windows. He parked as quickly as he could. "Good Lord," was all he said.

"See what can happen." Sally couldn't stop laughing. "When, when a mother and son live together."

"Gave me the shudders."

"I haven't laughed, since seeing Bret in John's house." Sally wiped her forehead free of irrelevant cobwebs.

"We better get back and see Mrs. Sederbush." Tim suggested.

"Did you see Matilda, after?"

"With Sheriff Woods. We drove her to the Montgomerys, where her mother and father are staying. We didn't think we should leave her alone."

"I don't wish to get into your personal business." Sally equivocated. "What did she say for herself?"

"She said she did not mention me to Bret. She was shocked by his violence. He never said a word about me to her."

"Where was the butler?"

"He is never around, when I show up to see Matilda."

"Yes, but," Sally began and then changed the direction of her question. "Do you know his name?"

"J. K. Reeves."

Back at Mrs. Sederbush's condominium, Sally was astonished at the woman's transformation. She no longer looked over sixty. In fact, if you ignored the out-of-style wig and the condition of the skin on her neck, she might pass for the heavy side of fifty.

Tim seemed oblivious to how nicely Mrs. Sederbush cleaned up. He was busy writing down license plate numbers from the list she provided.

"Oh, don't waste time." Mrs. Sederbush scolded. "Just take the list with you."

"When did you start recording Enid's visitors?" Sally asked.

"They're dated." Mrs. Sederbush pointed to the list. "When I first retired from DuKane, I marveled at the different cars. First, I thought I wasn't acquainted with how busy people could be at home. You know, if they didn't work for a living."

"How long have you been retired?" Tim paged through four pages of numbers.

"Six months." Then Mrs. Sederbush laughed. "I should tell you. One night, about 1:00 in the morning, mind you; I crept outside and used a flashlight to read the plate on a Cadillac." She pointed to the final entry on the last sheet of paper Tim spread out on the dining room table. "For about three days, there were no visitors. Then the movers showed up. How's that for a successful neighborhood action committee of one."

"Very brave." Sally decided to put the fear of God where it belonged. "Enid Krimm died in a suspicious fire."

Mrs. Sederbush shuddered and reached for her list.

Tim kept the evidence safely away from her. However, he saw fit to add to the proud vigilante. "And a man who drove a Cadillac shot and killed Sally's husband last week."

"Please," Mrs. Sederbush said, completely chagrined, "Will I need to testify against anyone?"

"You might," Sally said. "In the future, you would be safer to call the police when there is a problem."

* * *

Kane County Sheriff's Office

At the Geneva police station, Sally entered the sheriff's empty office. The large squad room could be viewed through the office's glass walls. Tim was explaining, to a female officer, how the license number list should be checked against the stack of addressed cards Sally provided.

Woods' wooden desk held a minimum of personal belongings. A picture of Gabby stood behind a silver paperweight with a Chinese inscription. Sally studied the bookcases around the window behind the desk. A credenza with three, model sailing ships added a nice touch. The room was his safe haunt, since his father retired from the hardware store.

Sheriff Woods returned with a pot of coffee.

"Fifty years? Is that how long you've been here?" Sally asked.

"About." He handed her a filled cup of coffee. "Can't complain. Jill Wisnewski-Reddinger did not fare as well."

"Gabby said she's okay."

"After a long stay in Elgin's mental ward. Didn't your mother write you about her?"

"Mother?" Sally easily summoned up her mother's reaction to Tony Montgomery's suicide.

* * *

December 1958

The night Tony slaughtered himself in the Hotel Baker's fourteenth-floor hallway, Art had telephoned Sally. In shaking sobs, he described the details of Tony's last moments. That morning when Jill, the new Mrs. Charles Reddinger, opened the bridal suite's door, she found Tony sprawled on his back. He'd bled to death. At the funeral, Jill's new husband supported her as they walked down a side aisle at St. Patrick's, leaving Art to sit with Tony's parents. Sally sat next to Jill. Jill held out her hand for Sally. Sally grasped Jill's cold hand with both of hers, unable to speak.

Jill pulled her hand away and then thrust it close to Sally's face, whispering, "Can you see it? The devil is trying to get out of my hand?"

Sally stood up and pulled Charles Reddinger to his feet. "We've got to get her out of here."

Jill began to cry, then wail.

By the time Charlie, with Art Woods coming at last to help, and the three of them shoved Jill into the back seat of the Reddinger's car, even closing all the doors didn't cut down the noise of Jill's hysterics.

"What should I do?" Charles wrung his hands as he stood at the driver's door.

"Art, go back inside," Sally said. "Explain to my folks." Then deciding for them all she added. "We'll take her to the hospital. They'll know what to do."

In the back seat of the car with Jill's cries in her ears, Sally turned to see Art still standing on the steps of St. Patrick's. His shoulders slumped, his hands hung at his side. Finally, he lumbered back inside. Sally's heart went out to him. If only she could mend all the grief and hurt he suffered since she'd met him.

At the hospital, Charlie signed forms and nurses stuck sedative needles into Jill. Jill's screams diminished and the staff wheeled her away.

"They said to wait here," Charlie said, as if glad to be told what to do next.

Sally tried to get him to talk, but he only shrugged his shoulders, shaking his head in despair at every question. After two hours of inhaling disinfectants, a doctor as young as Charlie explained Jill would need to stay. Waiting for Charlie to bring the car around, Sally questioned the doctor about how long Jill would be hospitalized.

"Oh, she may never recover," the doctor said, cheerfully. "There's a chemical imbalance, indicating she may be institutionalized for the rest of her life." He left Sally standing in the lobby. Charlie coaxed her into the car, and then wheedled her into giving directions to her Dean Street home.

Two days later, Sally was finally able to tell her mother about the doctor's diagnosis.

If patience had been a ticket to heaven, Mother would not have needed a priest for a son. She waited for Sally to bring up the wedding disaster. She did prime the pump by expounding on the unvirtuous acts of Kathy Krimm, Tony's date for Jill's wedding.

Kathy, it seems, came early to church auctions, picking through the donated jewelry. Kathy pocketed the best pieces and then bought a bag of costume jewelry for a quarter. "She's a money grubber; I don't care how fancy she dresses. She's old enough to be Tony's mother."

Sally opened a line of inquiry as mildly as she could. "Do you think craziness is hereditary?"

"Well, Tony's mother is -- different."

"He wasn't buried in hallowed ground?" Sally realized what the answer would be.

"We can't be sure he didn't repent." Her mother was being unusually charitable. "He died alone."

"You were right about the hair dye," Sally said. "Jill won't be getting out of the mental hospital. Charlie will probably divorce her."

Sally's mother pulled a kitchen chair out to sit down next to Sally. "Jill reminds me of a girl I knew when I was little older than you, before I married."

Sally looked into her coffee cup. Nothing tasted right anymore. She realized she was losing weight.

Mother had continued, when Sally looked up again. "She married a concert violinist. They were Jewish, the family of the guy. I couldn't very well accept his proposal, so Tyke married him. I visited them once in Bloomington. Their back door entrance was through a wood-latticed porch, covered in morning glories." Her mother rose and fussed around the sink. "I've never been able to grow morning glories either."

"Mother?" Sally asked, missing the morale of the story.

"Oh." Mother returned to her chair at the table. "She, Tyke, kept house non-stop. If she offered you a cup of coffee, she'd pick it up and wipe imaginary spills away from under the saucer. They gave birth to one child. Tyke nicknamed him Chicken. The kid was a scrawny, an un-cuddly thing."

"I don't get the connection." Sally realized she spoke the same way her mother did. Books were not the cause of Sally's miscommunication with her fellows. The problem occurred because she copied the stream-of-consciousness manner of speaking her mother indulged in. "Why are you telling me about Tyke's baby? Because I was so ugly you couldn't love me either?"

"I always loved you. When you were little and so sick all the time, you needed more attention than I could give. Now we're off the farm and I'm freer, you don't need all my attention." Jumping back to her story, she said, "Marvin was killed." As if that explained everything.

Sally sighed ready to give up trying to make any sense of the story.

Stroking her throat, her mother went on with the pointless tale. "Marvin was offered first chair in the New York Symphony. He killed a boy in a car accident."

Nodding, Sally tried to encourage the end of the story.

"Marvin opened the door and the father of the boy he'd run over, shot him, dead."

Sally realized her mother's tragedy. "He'd asked you to marry him."

"I worked for his parents, cleaning house like you did while you were in high school."

"Why are you telling me now?"

"Because Tyke reminds me of Jill. They didn't put Tyke away but she was crazy. It wasn't hair dye. Without love growing between people, they shouldn't live under the same roof."

"Like Jill and Charlie?"

Her mother nodded. "When love is denied, negative elements are pulled toward the void." She stared quietly at Sally, waiting for her to talk.

"Somehow I think Jill believed she was unlovable, not able to accept Tony's affection." On their first ride to Lincoln, Sally recognized Jill kept herself sealed away from any incrimination from her conscience. "Maybe Art was right. Jill found it easier to lust for money than to search for love."

The monsters in the dark, unexplored territory of Jill's mind grew stronger from the lust and greed she fed on. Love's light from Tony could have weakened her fears. Instead, they overwhelmed and destroyed her.

Sally wanted a safe world. "You wouldn't let me marry someone I didn't love?"

Her mother put her arms around her shoulders, pressing Sally's head to her amble breast. "No," she said, adding in a lighter tone. "Art loves to dance."

Even though Sally loved Art Woods, could he sustain the level of lifetime devotion a commitment of marriage required? They had eaten at the Log Cabin restaurant across from the Hotel Baker. The waitress knew them well enough to make sure Sally's coffee remained hot. Sally consistently left a two-dollar bill under the saucer each time she ate there with Art. The couple sat silently throughout their meal.

The waitress tried to cheer them up. "Hey. Did somebody die, or are you two love birds fighting?"

"Somebody died," Art growled.

The waitress' voice dropped an octave. "I'm so sorry. Forgive my big mouth." With her coffee pot still in her hand, she sat down next to Sally. "One of your parents, and now you're putting off the wedding. Just elope."

"Art's best friend," Sally swallowed, "killed himself."

"Over a girl, I bet." The waitress patted Art's hand.

Art clenched his jaw muscles. "Well, while we're telling all. The girl, who married someone else, is now in a mental institution!"

His angry voice blew the waitress out of the booth; but not before she leaned over and whispered to Sally, "Be careful."

Sally thought she might need to be cautious. Out loud, she repeated Hawthorne's passage in the 'Scarlet Letter', "The sufferer's conscience...corrupted his spiritual being."

Art held his head with his hands. "I hate all women. Maybe only Jill. Most of the girls at school chased money, too."

"Tony was comfortable. Jill's father didn't like his course

language." Sally argued. "And you know they made love."

"She wanted it! She used him the morning of her wedding"

"Oh, Art! My sister, Loretta, was right." Art eyes snapped, asking what her sister could possibly reveal. Sally quoted her. "Once you make love you can't stop."

"No," Art said with patient sarcasm. "The fortune of the Montgomery family is a tenth that of the Reddinger family."

Properly chastised, Sally said, "Jill didn't talk about their money."

Art pounded the table with both fists. "Because your family doesn't have any!"

Sally commenced to cry. Didn't Art understand he was trying to get even, to prove Tony right? Sally looked at him again. His actions were tainted with the angry burden of grief. He resembled a wounded, cornered animal fighting for its life, unwilling to look at the heart she held out to him. If she waited long enough, would he come back to her? Choose love, Sally telepathed to him, choose me.

"I want to go to bed with you," Art said, as if astonished at his candor.

"I do too." Sally took off her glasses to wipe away the tears. While she focused with her large myopic eyes, her lashes still wet from crying, she witnessed Art's heart soften.

He reached for her hand. "It's okay. I'm sorry I upset you. I think the world of you. I never leave you without feeling better about myself." He stopped talking, and his head seemed cleared of a degree of agony. "...a better person, Sally."

She smiled. He didn't know he loved her. She crooned to him. "All night I could not sleep, because of the moonlight on my bed."

Art released her hand. "Don't bring it up." He ran his hands through his hair as if hoping evil thoughts wouldn't land on his brain, so soon."

"It's only from 'Chinese Translations'." She tried again to soothe him.

"Books can't answer everything. Your head lets words leak out without logical antecedents. I often want to scream at you." Staring as if hoping to find an answer in the depth of her eyes, he asked, "How long will Tony torment me?" Sally didn't respond. The waitress re-entered their space, smiling at what she perceived was their happiness. She silently poured Sally a congratulatory cup of hot coffee. Then squeezing Sally's hand, Art said, "It is as if you were given a sacred mission to defend me against a hostile world, even against myself."

Sally recognized the quote. "Somewhere in 'Evocations of Love'."

"Yes, I'm not all the way through the book." Art smiled sheepishly.

"Wasn't it said between brothers?'

"Maybe Tony was my brother. I sure failed to defend him from Jill."

"We all failed. Mostly, Tony chose to fail himself."

* * *

Second Wednesday in January

Kane County Sheriff Office

"Did you two find out anything at Enid's?" Sheriff Woods asked Tim, when they joined him in his office.

"Probably an international move was planned, or carried out. We should go through Enid's belongings, once we locate them." Tim rubbed his forehead.

"The Stuart Linen Service records could add evidence to our theory," Sally said. "Enid was running a house of ill-repute."

"Evidence for the opportunity for blackmail," Tim said.

"I'd like to question the butler, too." Sally ran her finger over the book bindings on Sheriff Woods' shelves.

"Oh, come on," Woods kidded with her. "You don't think the butler did it."

"He knew Tim was no longer Matilda's lover." Sally pulled out the sheriff's copy of Robinson Crusoe. "Do you still refer to this book, each day?"

"I do." Woods smiled. "Try it."

Sally opened the worn copy to the face page to check the publication date. Chicago was the place, but no date survived the printing. so she scanned a page at random. From page 149, she read aloud. "But it is never too late to be wise. ...they are proof of the converse of spirits, and a secret commination between those embodied and those unembodied...."

"You think the butler told Bret, you mean?" Tim asked.

"We'll pick him up," Woods said. "Is John still helping us?"

"I don't think you will be able to find the butler at the

Armstrongs' castle," Sally said. "I suspect he's long gone. If John Nelson could send us a clue, he would."

Sheriff Woods set a file folder on the desk for Sally to review. "The fire inspector sent me the arson report for the Masters' home. I'll go file a missing person report on the butler." He left the office.

Sally read parts of the report to Tim, "Mrs. Masters didn't close the door, when she fled Enid."

"What about the candle?"

"They found wax droppings. Enid used the candle to set fire, first to the couple's bedding in the master bedroom, then the tablecloth in the dining room, and finally the couch skirt in front of the fireplace."

"Did she set fire to herself then?"

Sally read. "At some point the heat in the low rooms and the fires Enid set flashed into the front room."

"She could have escaped through the open front door."

Sally shook her head. "The open door added oxygen for the fire."

"No one else was in the house." Woods said, as he walked back in. "Peter Masters is off the hook."

"Then why did he keep lying to us about going to Dallas?" Sally asked.

"They did find the ring Geraldine threw in the fireplace." The sheriff placed a blackened object on his desk. One diamond on the soot encrusted ring winked at them.

Just then, the policewoman Tim gave the task of identifying

license plates numbers knocked on the door. "Officer Hanson, Bret Armstrong is the owner of the Cadillac on the list."

"About Bret," Sheriff Woods said. "His lawyer has asked for a psych evaluation."

Sally shied away from the news. She purposefully avoided speaking by finishing her cup of coffee. The hot liquid helped to unclench her throat. "I know John's death is connected to Enid's. Whoever harmed Enid, aimed Bret's gun at my husband."

* * *

Later that evening, Sally ate supper in the Hotel Baker's dining room. A table next to the two-story windows provided a wondrous view. White Christmas lights trimmed the small trees lining the bank of the Fox River. The ice jam near the dam sparkled from the reflections. Changing tints in the city-hall tower across the river added their colors to the winter scene. She didn't recognize any of the hotel's other patrons. She left half the food on her plate, when memories of John bringing her a second cup of hot coffee when she was working on her first case overwhelmed her and negated her appetite.

Safely back in her suite of rooms, Sally reminded herself room service was a better option. Three of her suitcases and several storage boxes were dumped in the dining alcove of the hotel room. She recognized Betty's handiwork. Too tired to unpack her clothes, Sally dragged one of the storage boxes over to the couch.

Ginger raced out of the bedroom nearly knocking her down with his greeting. Then she ran around the room with her nose to the floor. She was searching for John. "Ginger," Sally called only once.

With her tail between her legs as if she was to blame for losing John, Ginger approached the couch. Sally patted the hotel's couch. "Never mind, Ginger. We still have each other."

The dog jumped on the couch and laid her head in Sally's lap. Sally turned on the television for company and opened the lid of a storage box. A file folder marked with a black felt pen in John's handwriting, read, "Movers."

Ginger sniffed the file, apparently not relieved to only smell her master's presence. Sally held the folder to her face. She could smell John's cologne, too. His presence surrounded them for a moment. She kept her emotions in check. There was work to be done to find out why her sweet husband was annihilated.

John's copious notes from telephone conversations were numbered and rated by possibilities. Sally read through the twenty legal-pad pages, before she came to one signified with a number 10. 'French Flyways' held Sally's attention. A signed contract was faxed by the company to John. The signature at the bottom of the contract read, "J. K. Reeves."

Sally checked her watch. Too late to accomplish anything. Ten o'clock. Nevertheless, she dialed the Woods' home number. "Gabby, I apologize. Could I speak to your husband for a moment?"

"Absolutely. We were watching 'Law and Order,' of course."

"Yeah," Woods said. "Who is this?"

"Sally. Who else owns the balls to call you this late?"

"What do you have?"

"The butler signed Enid's moving contract." Sally tried to keep a triumphant tone out of her voice. "We need a search warrant of the Armstrong castle."

"Boy, this will crimp their breeches."

Sally laughed. "And you, Sirrah, have been reading way too many Elizabeth George mysteries."

"Could be; but I'll call Judge Schonemann tonight. Will you be ready to roll with Tim in the morning?"

"Yes, but," Sally re-considered the ramifications, "With Tim so, shall we say, intimately involved, perhaps you and I should tackle this one."

"Tim's nose would be permanently out of joint. I'll come along with you two, just to protect you."

"Great," Sally said, thinking she didn't need protection. She needed more answers and quickly, if justice was going to be served in her lifetime.

Chapter Seven

⁕

Second Thursday in January
Hotel Baker, St. Charles

Sally's mind drifted among the pillows. 'Safe, Lord,' she thanked her Maker. 'Where?' was her next thought. She fought against the answer: 'Lost.'

Her pride in the intelligence still granted at her age demanded she sort things out. She straightened her body in the warm sheets and folded her hands over her solar plexus, right hand on top of the sinister left. The Hotel Baker's walls acknowledged she was still in St. Charles, where she attended high school. The loss of John pressed her down into the hotel's mattress. Grief was heavier than the thermal blankets. Her mind sought sleep, her spirit denied the oblivion. The rigor of memorized prayers struggled to focus her mind away from the terrors of a future without the steadying influence of her new, but late, husband. "Our Father, who art in heaven, hallowed be Thy Name."

She relaxed in the safe routine of chasing the goal of sanity against a backdrop of jumbled thoughts. Would Tim marry the young policewoman in Sheriff Woods' squad room?

"Thy kingdom come, Thy will be done on earth." Sally's toes stroked the soft sheets, when she repeated the word 'earth,' as if checking to see if she was still tethered to the mortal realm. "As it is in heaven."

John surely waited for her in God's safest place, away from thoughtless criminals ready to snuff out life in a second. "Give us this day our daily bread and forgive us our trespasses, as we forgive those who trespass against us."

Of course, she would need to forgive Bret for killing her husband. Maybe not today. Resentments would lead her to drink, if not resolved. "And lead us not into temptation, but deliver us from evil." Perhaps vengeance was the only evil in the world. All wars were fought to get even. "For Thine is the kingdom and the power and the glory, now and forever, Amen."

Without waiting for troublesome realities to present themselves, Sally followed the prayer with St. Francis' favorite. "God make me a channel of Thy Peace. Where there is hatred, let me sow seeds of love." Perhaps the Lord could forgive Bret for her.

Did the Montgomerys and Peter Masters hate her for delving into their personal lives? Someone needed to solve the reason for Enid's mysterious death. Of course, John wasn't killed by Bret alone. Someone knew Bret well enough to break his heart and cause him to seek a violent remedy.

There was a joke with St. Francis and St. Anthony arguing about who could concentrate better when praying. St. Francis asked St. Anthony to bet his horse. St. Francis claimed he could pray without interrupting the prayer with divergent thoughts. St. Anthony agreed to the bet. So, St. Francis began, "Hail Mary full of grace, the

Lord is with Thee. Can I have the saddle, too?"

Sally continued his prayer. "Where there is wrong, let me bring the spirit of forgiveness." Sally agreed to surround Bret with a cloud of forgiveness, not specifically for any deed, not outright forgiveness, but at least she owned sufficient motivation to find out who triggered Bret's mad attack.

Forgetting was never an option for cruelty. Sally mulled over her upbringing for a brief moment, which had left her self-image in the pits. Without tapping the source of all love and realizing the Lord found her beautiful in His eyes, her fate and addictions would have predicted a shorter life. "Thank you, Lord, for today," she prayed. She was alive still. Supposedly the Lord wasn't through with her journey on earth.

She scooted to the edge of the bed, sat up and as her feet touched the floor, she asked earnestly, "Help me trust you more, Lord."

Now where to find more black clothing. For six days she'd worn the traditional grieving color. Her wardrobe did not anticipate widowhood when she packed for the move to St. Charles. She yearned for home, where a closet in her condo's basement held the clothes she'd worn after Danny Bianco died. Robert Koelz's death required tapping the source, too. She longed for her books lining the walls in her condo. Ann Arbor awaited her return. Nevertheless, unfinished business loomed in St. Charles.

The emerald green jacket from the Nelson's New Year's Day party would serve. If she wore the dark jacket with black slacks and a black turtle neck sweater, the world might recognize her grief. "Where there is discord, let me bring harmony." Sally concentrated on her unfinished prayers. "Where there is despair, let me bring hope. Where there is doubt, let me bring faith."

Sheriff Woods and his life with Gabby came to mind. Gabby was a blessing. Sally assumed Gabby demanded little attention from her husband. Perhaps she was content with his presence. And Art, did he find peace? Losing Tony Montgomery left a mark on him. A key part of the young Art Woods was snuffed out when Tony took his own life.

"Where there is darkness, let me bring light." A tall order, but she was willing to try. "Where there is sadness, let me bring joy." She thanked the Lord again for being alive and able to think. "Grant that I may seek to comfort, rather than be comforted; to understand, rather than be understood; to love, rather than to be loved."

She enjoyed the end of the prayer. The relinquishment of the need to feel loved by others was liberating, sane and grounding. Of course, loving others was all she could do to fulfill God's will. "For it is by forgiving that we are forgiven, by self-forgetting that we find, and by dying that we awaken to eternal life." What would life after death resemble. Would she see her loved ones?

"The Lord is my shepherd, I shall not want." Sally uttered the 23rd Psalm as she headed for the shower. "He maketh me to lie down in green pastures." The Hotel Baker's plush carpeting was a dark green. "He leadeth me beside the still waters." A hot shower would relieve some of her morning stiffness. "He restoreth my soul." As always happened, her ribs seemed to melt away as her soul stretched out to the ends of the earth.

"He leadeth me in paths of righteousness for His Name's sake. Yea, though I walk through the valley of the shadow of death, I shall fear no evil. For Thou art with me. Thy rod and Thy staff they comfort me. Thou preparest a table in the presence of mine enemies. Thou annointest my head with oil. My cup runneth over. Surely goodness and mercy will follow me all the days of my life, and I shall dwell in the house of the Lord forever."

She stopped before closing the bathroom door to confront the daylight in the windows facing the Fox River.

Ginger stuck her nose around the door. "You need a walk, right?" Ginger waged her tail. There was a lot to do. "God grant me the serenity to accept the things I cannot change." John was gone from earth, but she still sensed his love and the pride he showed in winning her as his wife and friend. "The courage to change the things I can." Whoever masterminded the deaths of John and Enid needed to be caught and charged, before she returned to Ann Arbor. "And the wisdom to know the difference." Sally sniggered to herself. Wisdom was the rub. Old age did not guarantee any such accouterment.

"God," Sally prayed a second AA prayer as she ducked her head under the shower. "I offer myself to You to do with me or build with me what Thou wilt. Save me from the bondage to self. Grant me victory over my present difficulties so I may be a witness to those I seek to help of Thy power, Thy love and Thy way of life.

Help me to do Thy will always."

Stepping out of the shower, she pulled down the large hotel towel from the rack and faced the morning's mirror.

* * *

Sally reached Hotel Baker's dining room at eight o'clock. Sheriff Woods and Tim were already waiting for her. "My, I'm impressed by you two early birds."

Tim said the breakfast menu was worth the trip.

Sheriff Woods stood. "We waited to order."

Tim pushed in her chair as she sat down, blushing slightly.

"I love company for breakfast." She reminded herself not to tease Tim about his appetite. A young man needed calories. Her chair faced the doorway to the restaurant. She drew in a sharp breath. For a split second, she thought John stood at the entrance.

Of course, James was the person. When Betty stepped next to him, James placed an arm around her shoulder and then played with Betty's short hair with his other hand.

'Lovers' Sally thought, feeling a sharp pang below her left breast. "Oh," she tried to muffle a cry from real pain.

"What is it?" Sheriff Woods followed her gaze. "Betty, right?"

Sally nodded. The pain ceased. She fished in her purse for a handkerchief and whisked away a tear, before John's relatives arrived at the table. The waitress came by and Sheriff Woods, Tim and Sally ordered their breakfasts.

"We ate earlier," James explained.

The waitress pulled up two more chairs at the small table.

"Coffee?"

James waved her away politely. "No, thank you."

"Sally," Betty said. "Please come with us to John's lawyer. He wants to read us the will."

Sally managed not to break down by concentrating on the snow starting to fall outside the hotel restaurant windows. "I doubt John had time to even consider including me in his will. My finances don't need any help from his estate." She smiled at Betty. "Let me know, if you need me for anything."

James stood up first. Betty was quick to follow; however, she leaned down and whispered in Sally's ear. "Bless you for getting me out from under my horrid wig."

Sally took Betty's hand and held it to her cheek. "Very welcome."

After they left, Sheriff Woods and Tim minded their coffee. Their posture telegraphed how uneasy they were around a grieving widow. Sally placed her notebook on the table next to her plate which contained a dry and cold ham and cheese omelet. The waitress started to pour coffee into her cold cup. "Could you bring me a fresh cup with a cheese Danish? Thank you. You can take away my plate, too."

"Still can't abide lukewarm coffee," Sheriff Woods said.

Tim tilted his head, indicating he needed enlightenment.

Sally explained, "We dated in high school, before I moved to Michigan."

Sheriff Woods said, "I can't stop thinking about Tony

Montgomery."

"I keep playing those bad tapes, too."

"Relevant to the case?" Tim tried to keep up with references in their shared history.

"I don't know," Sheriff Woods said. "Sally, remember Kathy Krimm."

"Enid's mother?" Tim asked.

"There's your connection," Sally said. "Tony brought a prostitute to Jill's wedding reception."

"Was that the only date he could get?" Tim was foolish enough to ask.

Both Sheriff Woods and Sally glared at him. Sally said quietly. "Tony was a beautiful young man, just tortured beyond belief."

"Would Tony's father try to get even for his suicide with Kathy's daughter, at this late date?" Tim asked.

Sally dismissed the idea. "Kathy wasn't the problem. Jill Wisnewski-Reddinger was the villain. And she paid the price."

"How?" Tim asked.

"A lifetime of suffering," Sheriff Woods said.

Sally understood he included himself in that sentence of pain. She turned the pages in her notebook to change the subject away from Tony. She penciled in Tim's red herring about Tony's parents' motivation. Sheriff Woods sat on her right and leaned over to try to read her notations. "Should I read my notes aloud?" Both men nodded, so Sally listed her clues: "Number one, January 1st, John says Tim Hanson knows something that needs investigating.

Solved."

"I was suspicious of Enid. She was always asking questions about Peter Masters, Matilda's father. Of course, you probably noticed how guilty I am about Matilda, too."

Sheriff Woods said, "Remember Geraldine Masters said Enid Krimm recited a list of dates her husband was out of town as the basis for her claim of an affair."

"Peter denied it," Tim said.

"In front of his daughter, Matilda." Sally recalled for them. "But who called his cell phone when he was in the interrogation room. I don't believe it was his wife's lawyer. Geraldine never hired a lawyer. Matilda and I spoke to her. Supposedly, Geraldine went to Matilda's grand-mother's home in Dallas to get away from her husband."

"Nevertheless," Tim said. "They're both at the Montgomerys'."

"With their daughter," Sally added. "People do strange things for their children."

"What else do you have listed in there?" Sheriff Woods asked.

"Number two," Sally read. "January 2nd, Where is Peter Master's boarding passes to Dallas?" She looked up from the notebook. "Why is he still lying to us? Where was he during the fire? Unsolved."

Sheriff Woods said, "When we are through searching Dunham Castle, we'll get an answer from him or take him into custody for withholding evidence."

Sally nodded in agreement. "Number three and four of January 2nd, we already solved. The candlestick was used by Enid, and she was the dead woman, not Geraldine. I should include clue number five and six as solved, also. Geraldine's ring was where Peter said she threw it on New Year's Eve. And Tim explained how he injured Bret accidentally."

Tim asked Sheriff Woods, "When you questioned Peter Masters did you come across anything suspicious?"

Sally answered for him. "Clue number eight, Enid told Tim, Matilda, and Geraldine that Bret was having an affair with her."

"You said you didn't believe it, at the time," Tim said.

Sally throat and mouth went suddenly dry. She sipped her tepid coffee again and frowned. Sheriff Woods motioned for the waitress to bring another hot cup of coffee. "Even though, he killed John," Sally managed. "I don't believe Bret could cheat on his wife."

"Ouch," Tim said.

"Matilda's a very manipulative woman," Sally said. "But you admitted, you were in error."

The waitress arrived. "I microwaved the cup, before I poured in fresh coffee."

Sally tucked on the girl's apron. "Wait a minute." She dug in her purse and slipped the girl a folded twenty dollar bill. "Thank you for your thoughtfulness."

Tim said. "Why did Enid insist Bret was having an affair with her?"

"Good question," the sheriff said. "A very effective

blackmailing ploy? Probably worked on most of the citizens of Wayne."

Sally nodded. "The addresses on the thank-you notes and Mrs. Sederbush's list of license plates establishes the facts." The waitress waved a thank-you, after she unfolded the money.

"How many unsolved clues are left?" Tim asked.

"Number two is not solved," Sheriff Woods said. "Peter Masters needs to clear up a few things."

"Number ten, January 3rd, Bret shoots John. But why." Sally finished her coffee for once. "I'm not even sure Bret would have aimed the gun at John, if John hadn't lunged for him."

"Do you think Bret meant I ruined his marriage?" Tim asked. "Or you?"

"Initially, I thought Bret meant you, but my snooping around probably prompted someone to tell Bret about Matilda. I thought about letting you two handle the case. If stopping my involvement in the case was the reason for upsetting Bret; it almost worked."

"We have established some of the circumstances surrounding Bret before he committed murder," Woods said.

Tim nodded his head. "He visited Enid, three days before the movers shipped most of her belongings to France."

"Who was threatening whom?" Sally asked.

"Bret lawyered up," Sheriff Woods said. "I assume we'll find out at Bret's trial Enid pushed him into a corner, or at least his family's reputation was about to suffer."

"But Bret said," Sally said looking at her notes. "Number

eleven, January 3rd, Bret said, 'You ruined my marriage,' before the gun went off."

"Matilda claimed Bret only loved their castle," Tim said. "She even kidded if the castle hadn't been part of the marriage deal, she'd probably still be single."

"We know what evil the love of money can produce between people," Sally said to Sheriff Woods, who agreed by pounding the table. Sally read the last clue to them, "Number eleven, January ninth, the butler. J K. Reeves signed the moving contract. Why? Unsolved."

* * *

By nine in the morning the snow was four inches thick, but the salt trucks were efficiently ridding the roads of the hazardous conditions. Sheriff Woods, Tim and Sally drove north on Dunham Road, rehearsing the possible evidence they might find at the Armstrongs' Castle.

"Will Matilda be there?" Tim worried.

"You handle yourself all right around her." Sheriff Woods complimented him. "But I think she'll be with her folks at the Montgomery's."

"If she is there," Sally said, "I can question her about why she asked Enid to meet her at her mother's house. Was she trying to cover up for her mother?"

"The list of people who dropped in on Enid and lived in Wayne is pretty long," Tim said. "It's not a crime to pay blackmail, is it?"

"Perpetrating a felonious act?" Sheriff Woods said aloud.

"But blackmailing is a punishable crime," Sally said, from the backseat of the cruiser, "as is murdering the blackmailer."

"I'll search Bret's room," Woods said. "Tim, go through the butler's things. We sent out an international search for him."

"Did you contact French Seaways?" Sally asked.

Tim answered. "Officer Caldwell said the crates were off-loaded in France. They were transferred to a mover based in Rome. She's following up to find the crates' final destination."

"Interpol might need to be included in the search for J. K. Reeves," Sally said.

"You keep insisting the butler did it." Sheriff Woods laughed.

"I suspect he's sitting somewhere in France or Italy, counting out the money Enid earned by blackmailing half the village of Wayne." Sally hoped they were getting close to answering all her questions.

"He didn't seem evil to me," Tim said.

"You were just happy he disappeared during your affair with Matilda," Sally reminded him. Tim nodded his head. "Sorry," Sally said. "That was an unnecessary comment."

"Nevertheless," Tim said. "Facts are facts.

* * *

Dunham Castle, Wayne

Four inches of snow covered the circular drive in front of the Dunham Castle. Hundred-year-old oaks and evergreens bordered the extensive grounds. Fresh snow caressed their fronds and lined their limbs, accentuating the beauty of the trees. Yellowed rough stones of the gothic walls reached toward the glistening snow on the spired roofs of the top windows, on the round caps of the three towers, and on the slopes of the mansard roof. Long icicles hung at the edges, picking up light from the brightening cloud cover. Larger than usual flakes of snow, proclaiming white innocence, drifted down on the haunting, lonely scene.

One set of tracks plowed through two of the four inches of snow before the squad car crunched up the drive. When Sheriff Woods got out of the cruiser, he examined the trampled snow up the steps to the front door. "A woman drove away about an hour ago."

"Heap big Indian guide," Sally surprised herself by teasing.

Woods grinned. "I'm glad you're back to your old ornery self."

"Aren't you going to miss us?" Tim blushed furiously and added, "if you return to Ann Arbor."

Sally adjusted her purse. "First things first. Who is going to get us past the front door?"

Tim knocked uselessly and then opened the door with his key.

"Convenient, right?" Woods winked at Sally.

"Will the search hold up in court?"

"Tim was given the key by the owner."

"Not for this," Sally said. "Be a shame to lose any evidence on a technicality." Nevertheless, Sally crossed the threshold. "Time's a wasting."

"Check every room." Sheriff Woods opened one of the two evidence toolboxes he carried into the house. After he put on plastic gloves, he pointed to the other box. "Yours is over there, Sally."

Tim went up the main staircase, after donning gloves from his case.

"I'll take the downstairs," Sally said.

The sheriff followed Tim upstairs. "We'll help you, when we get done up here." His voice bounced around the circular entryway.

Sally headed for the library. The evidence case was too heavy to lug around, so she set the metal box on the couch, which faced a long desk. On the right-hand corner of the desk, an open dictionary was propped open on a sandalwood stand. She read the page headings, just in case they were relevant. 'lacriminal sac,' something to do with tears, nothing about criminals. If AA allowed belief in psychic phenomena, Sally would assume John was near her. 'lady, lady apple and lagena,' were the other headings. 'Lagena,' meant some part of a fish's body mammals shared. Sally wasn't interested enough to search further.

The red leather bindings of the books with titles embossed in gold did tempt her curiosity. She excused her lack of concentration on the case by imagining a letter might fall out of any of the books she chose to open. The entire wall behind the desk was dedicated to war. Wars throughout history were captured in a plethora of printed matter. Famous battles, generals and spies with more than one book named for them lined the shelves. Behind the couch, a freestanding, bookcase with glass pull-up doors held over a hundred books about

Lincoln and the Civil War.

The narrower shelves on either side of the entrance were filled with first editions of novels. Trying to focus like a detective on a case, Sally lifted out Anatole Frances' 'Under the Rose.' No letter or stray notes were tucked inside its covers even though the title promised secrets were kept there.

Nonfiction books on architecture and decorating subjects faced the entrance. Their covers were not leather. A colorful array of paper book jackets brightened an otherwise dull gathering of books. Were the books purchased as they stood on the shelves when the castle changed hands, or had Matilda or Bret collected them.

She went back to the library desk to examine its drawers. Matilda used the desk to write invitations, greeting cards and thank you notes. An expensive array of stationery filled the drawers. One drawer held a card index with addresses and phone numbers. Sally checked, but no cards listed the names of Kathy, Enid Krimm or J. K. Reeves, for that matter.

Thinking she soaked up enough literary vibes, she headed for the dining room. She ran her hand under the edge of the mahogany table, not expecting to find anything, but checking nonetheless. She pulled the floral portraits off the wall and looked at the back of the canvases for clues. She couldn't summon the energy necessary to replace them or up-end the chairs, but she thought about it. Instead of tackling the kitchen, she chose to look around the visitor's parlor where Reeves ushered John and Sally on their first visit.

John's fur hat lay abandoned on the green-and-white silk

couch. She clutched it to her. "Help me," she prayed to the Lord, or to any remaining force of soul which might allow her husband to guide her.

A drop leaf desk, with two filled bookshelves occupying its lower section, was the only piece of furniture in the room except for the upholstered chairs and marble end tables. Before opening the lid of the desk, Sally looked out the side window of the room. An unobstructed view of the front stoop could let anyone in the room see who was entering the house. A butler could easily choose not to appear in the entranceway. Reeves could avoid meeting Tim on his illicit visits.

So the desk might contain the butler's belongings. She returned to the library to retrieve the evidence case. After tearing one plastic glove on her diamond wedding ring, she opened the desk's only drawer.

Travel brochures and train schedules were jammed to overflowing. She let down the lid of the desk onto the open drawer. A small, gold framed picture of Bret confused her for a moment. She thought perhaps the desk was Matilda's. Bret would not keep a picture of himself on his own desk. Would the butler keep a picture of his boss?

Each vertical section of the desk held paid receipts addressed to Reeves. "Bingo." Sally filled cloth evidence bags with the material.

After all the dividers were emptied, she reached up inside the desk. A shelf between the top and the first lengthwise panel held yellow vaccination cards for Reeves and Enid Krimm. Enid's useless passport was also on the hidden shelf. Sally put the cards into a plastic evidence bag and ran out of the room. "I found it," she cried up the staircase. "The butler did it!"

* * *

Before Woods heard Sally's cry, he was congratulating himself on his own success. The central suite of rooms at the top of the stairs contained a large sitting room. A fireplace flanked by filled bookcases vied for attention with the back wall, where a two-story high window invited a view of slumbering gardens and a fountain layered with snow.

Bret's bedroom to the right of the suite was decorated with reds and deep browns. The fireplace was copper. The sheriff was tempted to test the winged back leather chair and its footstool, but headed for the mirrored wall of closets. He rummaged through each pocket of Bret's suits, throwing the clothes onto the four-poster bed to facilitate his search. He found no reason to waste time by re-hanging the garments of a murderer.

Bret was a fastidious man. No scraps of paper, receipts or coins were left in his pockets. Maybe the butler did do it. Reeves cleaned up after his boss. Sheriff Woods caught a reflection in the closet mirror of his own smile. Sally, she could turn a stone to butter. He secretly hoped she would stay in town. But if another interesting case didn't appeal to her, he was pretty sure she would be off to Ann Arbor again. Tim was right. They would miss her.

Bret's dresser drawers yielded nothing of interest. Was the gun

Bret used to kill John even his? Something else to check on. Maybe Sally was right. Maybe someone instigated John's death by revealing Matilda's infidelity.

He wanted to be thorough, so he knelt down and poked his head under the leather dust ruffle of Bret's bed. He pulled out a long white box. Expecting to find a spare blanket, he opened the box. Instead, letters filled the box. A pink diary, strange knick-knacks and pieces of rocks, leaves and twigs were also stuffed in the box. He recognized the paraphernalia as a lover's stash. Tim's name was written on the bottom of a birthday card. Bret found, or was shown, Matilda's personal keepsakes. Fingerprint experts needed to go over the evidence.

When he opened Matilda's door on the left side of the main room, he was taken aback by the contrast to Bret's room. Here all was light and fluff. No other color than white was used on the furniture, bed draping's, rug or chairs. Even the fireplace was white marble. The two-timing lady was surrounded with white profusions of virtuousness.

He didn't bother with Matilda's closet or dressers. Bret's room divulged all he needed in the way of evidence. He wondered if Reeves' fingerprints were on file in some national data bank for a traffic infraction, or worse.

* * *

On the third floor of the castle, Tim found storage rooms filled with extra furnishings, trunks, and boxes labeled with their contents. Reeves' bedroom and bath were the only habitable areas. He was surprised at the starkness of the furnishings in the butler's room. They consisted of a low cot, a caned chair, and one beat up dresser. No pictures, not even curtains on the pointed windows. 'A monk,' Tim thought. Or a man on the move, with a better future or pickings planned.

In the bathroom, he used a plastic bag for the water tumbler on the sink, hoping for fingerprints. He found a few hairs in the shower's drain for DNA evidence. Reeves cleared out every personal possession, wherever he was. Tim bet Reeves was the person who made sure Bret found out about his visits to Matilda. If he was going to reveal her indiscretion, why had he waited so long?

* * *

Back on the main floor Tim called out for the rest of the team, "Where are you guys?"

"In here." Sally called from the dining room. The room's pictures were stacked in one corner. Sheriff Woods was upending the chairs. Sally held up a plastic evidence bag with yellow cards inside and another with a passport. "Reeves knew Enid Krimm."

Sheriff Woods patted a long white box on the table. "Your love letters were under Bret's bed."

Tim sat down. The weight of the consequences of his affair with Matilda pushed his head to the table.

"You didn't harm John." Sally rubbed Tim's shoulders. "Remember you stepped in front of me, when Bret pointed the gun at us."

"Reeves was an evil man." Sheriff Woods coughed to hide his

emotion.

Tim recovered himself enough to ask. "Could I look through the box?"

Sally tugged on Woods's uniform. "Give the kid a break."

"We'll wait for you in the car."

* * *

"Don't start the car," Tim said, when he got in the back seat. "How does Reeves' link to Enid clear up why Matilda's father lied about his whereabouts during the fire?"

"And who called him on his cell?" Sally asked.

Sheriff Woods said, "He acted as if he suspected his wife was involved."

"Why don't we drive over to the Montgomery place and ask a few questions?" Tim asked.

Sally knew the answer. Woods hated any contact with the parents of Tony Montgomery. The sheriff started the car; but at the corner of Territorial Road and Dunham, he went straight through the intersection. "I want to take this evidence directly to the station."

Sally met Tim's astonished look. She slightly shook her head. The Montgomery household of guests, Peter and Geraldine Masters, as well as Matilda Armstrong could wait long enough for Sheriff Woods to recover his bearings. "I wonder why Reeves kept a picture of Bret on his desk?"

"His room was cleaned out," Tim said. "But, I bagged a water tumbler from his sink."

"Good," Woods said. "I'm hoping we can match the

fingerprints on Matilda's box to Reeves to prove he's the one who ratted you out."

"Maybe Reeves was gay," Sally said.

"Hatred of women might cover his motivations," Sheriff Woods said. "But how would hurting Bret make sense if he loved him?"

"Revenge," Tim said. "He made a pass at Bret and was rebuffed. Reeves' cot looked uncomfortable enough for a suffering sinner's penance."

"Bret's bed was big enough for two," the sheriff said. "I remember there was a chain lock on the door between his room and the sitting room. I thought it strange for a married couple. But if Bret was hiding an affair with Reeves, it might explain why Matilda thought Bret loved the castle more than he cared for her."

"Might explain the delay in revealing Matilda's indiscretions," Sally tried to believe. "But don't forget, Reeves held Enid's passport. Maybe he knew she wouldn't need it." Sally recalled Bret's words and said them aloud. "You ruined my marriage."

"Bret's marriage included enough secrets, why couldn't he bear hearing about Tim and Matilda?" Woods asked.

"Maybe it was Reeves who jilted Bret," Tim said.

Sally said, "After Reeves showed Bret the evidence against Matilda, Bret might have refused to divorce her; so Reeves left him."

In St. Charles, Sheriff Woods pulled up in front of the Hotel Baker. "Sally, there are tons of paperwork Tim and I need to do to get this evidence properly catalogued."

"Don't forget to feed the kid," Sally said as she got out. "Pick me up by two o'clock?"

"Deal. I'll let Tim ring up Matilda and have the group prepare their lies for us."

"You might be surprised," Sally said. "Truth wills its way out."

* * *

In her quiet hotel room, Sally blessed the sheriff for allowing her a break. She was surprised how debilitating investigating her husband's murder was. She reminded herself she'd become involved initially because of John. The arson at the Masters' house was thrust upon her because of the Armstrongs' invitation to visit the castle during their wedding reception. As she laid down to rest for a minute, a dream or the parallel universe where John had resided for such a short time claimed her reassessment.

It was in the early afternoon of New Year's Day when John had carried her over the threshold of his childhood home. His small border collie, Ginger, ran between his legs. Nearly stumbling over the dog, John said he fancied his youth when he could depend on his strength. He said he wanted to raise Sally above his head as a show of victory to the universe. Instead, he clasped her closer to his chest.

Sally had whispered into his shoulder. "You better set me down before you permanently ruin your back."

John carefully placed her on her feet before sweeping his arms out to include the large front room. "How do you like the joint?"

"Not bad." Sally unbuttoned her coat. "Not bad for a

bachelor's pad."

Ceiling to floor windows faced each other on the east and west sides of the room. Winter snow drifts crisscrossed by the tree limbs' long shadows provided a stunning contrast to the modern paintings claiming the south wall. Slashes of primary colors randomly streaked three unframed canvases. The north wall sported a mammoth stone fireplace flanked by separate hallways. Facing the fireplace, the furniture consisted of a leather couch flanked by two glass-topped end tables.

"Make any changes you want."

Sally had heard no enthusiasm for alterations in his tone. 'Stark' described the room. Her condominium's colorful, book-stuffed hominess called to her from Michigan. Thank the Lord, no buyers had presented themselves to purchase her sanctuary. John's carpet was grey or well used? Liberal donations from Ginger's fur rolled about. The paintings resembled her father's house painting skills. "You spent a lot of your time running your family's hotel, didn't you?"

"True; but my folks lived here until they passed away."

One high-school trophy claimed the stone shelf above the fireplace. Sally pointed. "Is that your trophy?"

"No." John swiped at a cobweb attaching the metal statue to the stonewall. "Mother thought James' tennis stardom deserved a place of honor."

"I wouldn't touch a thing." Sally returned her arms to John's neck. "You're perfect."

"I'm glad you approve." John's warm kiss had been interrupted by the telephone. He let go and threw his black overcoat on the couch before answering. "We're home," he announced, triumphant. Then he turned to Sally. "James wants to know if he should bring Betty over. You didn't meet his wife when you were here solving your Ann Arbor friend's case."

Sally felt obliged to meet his twin brother's wife. "Of course," she said, as convincingly as she could. The six-hour drive from Ann Arbor to St. Charles had been too long for her old joints. She had wanted to take the more leisurely ferry from Ludington to make the shorter drive down from Milwaukee. John had argued against the plan. The construction delays on the I94 loop around the southern shore of Lake Michigan proved she'd been correct. They sat in stalled traffic for two hours after they'd passed Gary, Indiana. How long would she accommodate her new husband?

"I usually invite people over for New Year's Day." John helped Sally off with her blue alpaca coat. "Our parents served up to three hundred when they were the hosts."

"How many people are coming today?"

"Not to worry." John laid her coat next to his. "Betty has her favorite caterer in gear."

Sally put her hands on her hips. "John?"

"You're tired." He picked up the phone.

"Never mind." Sally reminded herself how much she loved him. "Just tell me how many you expect."

"I don't know." John busied himself with hanging their coats in the entryway closet. "You look great. I am sorry. I did not expect Betty to plan a New Year's Day party this year; although, she usually handles the affair for me."

Sally needed help to face all the strangers. She might recognize a few classmates from when she was in high school nearly fifty years earlier. She wondered if her Michigan AA sponsor would mind an emergency call on New Year's Day. "Could I ask for a cup of coffee before the shivaree?"

"Oh, heavens!" John put both hands up to his bald head. "They wouldn't?"

"I hope not! My daddy told me a story about people coming over in the country in southern Illinois keeping everybody up 'til dawn with their shenanigans and then getting right into bed with the newlyweds."

"Well, that's not going to happen. But they may turn this into a wedding reception. I better take Ginger for a walk while I can."

Happy to have his owner home, the border collie was romping about the place, down the halls, out into the kitchen. Ginger leapt at John when he opened the door for their walk. John's laughter rang through the empty rooms as he closed the door behind him.

* * *

Sally had focused on the source of a heightened sense of fear. She admitted her natural shyness was a problem, one she was now unwilling to alleviate with alcohol. She called Grace, her AA sponsor in Michigan. "I think I can add new directions to my spending addiction, redecorating John's house."

"Set a budget for each room and stick to it," Grace said, "then you won't need to add to your fourth step list."

"I will. Of course, that's the answer. The program is simple."

"Complications arrive when we let them. Next time you call, I expect you to tell me about two different meeting locations and the speakers."

"I'll be awfully busy."

"No excuses, First things first."

"You're right. I'll see to it. Thanks for being there."

Sally was also thankful for enough time to change her clothes before the party, even if she couldn't unpack. Which dresser drawers would be designated as hers and which side of the mirrored closet could she claim?

In the master bedroom decorated in masculine black and gray colors, Sally tried on three outfits. The black dress didn't seem festive enough or the colors in the room negated its elegance. Red was too Christmassy, so the emerald green velvet won. Her white hair retained a modicum of style which she fortified with additional hairspray. Anticipating a long evening, she chose black-strapped slippers. She congratulated herself for keeping slim at sixty-seven and with a prayer for strength from the heavens, she pronounced herself ready.

* * *

Betty Nelson, Sally's new sister-in-law, accompanied an entire tribe of caterers, who scattered around the couple. "Hello, hello." She nodded to Sally after John's brief introduction.

"What time is it?" James asked as he hugged Sally. "We invited everyone for six o'clock."

Sally stared at her new brother-in-law. "Without making sure we arrived?"

"James has a key," John explained.

Betty took a moment out of her busy schedule of directing caterers to inform the bride and groom. "Wedding reception."

Betty proceeded to order her team to dress the dining room table, find the best china and glassware, stock the bar, and lay out a spread to vie with the most lavish wedding reception.

The dark shadows from Betty's black tresses emphasized the lines around her eyes and mouth. Her shoulder-length hair brought attention to the downward pull of the extra skin beneath her chin -- all and all not a youthful choice of hairstyles. Unable to ignore the bad hairpiece sitting on James' head, in direct contrast to his identical twin brother's baldness, Sally surmised Betty's hair was stuck-on, too.

"Might as well go with the flow." John advised a dubious Sally.

When the doorbell rang again, a florist arrived with a decorated tree and an entire truckload of poinsettias.

Sally tried to place her coffee cup on a dresser near the front closet, to escape into the powder room, but Betty re-instructed her, "Not there, dear. The presents are going there."

"I would like to gossip with you about the wife of a friend of mine. I know you don't have time now," Sally said. "She stayed in your Safe-House, before I met her."

"Is she all right?" Betty directed five catering staff members at the same time.

"Couldn't be better." Sally kept the details to a minimum. "Married a policeman in Ann Arbor." She wished some etiquette book covered how to celebrate marriages for older couples.

Sheriff Art Woods, Sally's high-school friend, as well as the Sheriff's wife, Gabby, were the first to arrive. Gabby stuck close to Sally, giving her gossipy details about the lives of the guests and making sure everyone knew Sally and John ran a successful detective agency in Michigan. Sally listened at least six times to stories about the destruction of their unfinished home.

During the wedding reception, Sally tried to attach names to the faces after the thirteenth pair of feet arrived. The presents piled up and she dreaded trying to send personal thank-you notes to the horde. Every new bride faced the same dilemma; but at her age, Sally was a bit guilty for accepting presents they didn't need or already possessed. Sally and John were not able to move any furnishings into their dream home before the arsonist involved in her latest case in Ann Arbor burnt the barely started home to the ground.

Another high-school mate of John and Sally's, Reverend Rosemary Warner's conversation held sway during the shank of the evening. The tall, mammoth-hipped, single woman traveled around the globe, preaching to native-born pagans she could hog-tie long enough to listen. From her conversation, Sally discovered the remaining holdouts from Christianity were literate and argumentative. Opinions of the indigenous citizens, Rosemary quoted word for word, were logical and hard to dispute, unless you considered faith a blessed gift from God. The religious clerics, known previously to the natives, were themselves cruel, bigoted, and without shame.

Sally stopped Reverend Warner's monologue. "Every missionary should be given a copy of 'The Poisonwood Bible' before being allowed out of the country."

Rev. Warner nodded. "We need to force the Commander in Chief of our armed forces to do the same. Democracy makes half the people in any nation unhappy."

"Agreed," the listeners chorused.

Gabby had tugged at the emerald lace on Sally's sleeve. "Don Jenny just told me he dated your older sisters."

"Where is the scamp?" Sally looked around for the jolly boy her family knew.

Instead, a frail, melancholy oldster approached. "Sally." He took her hand.

"My sisters, Madelyn and Loretta, both live in Florida." Sally swallowed hard. She coughed but failed to hide her shock.

"Been a little under the weather since the Korean prisoner camp." Don held up his shaky hands.

Embarrassed at her rudeness, Sally sought to bring out the boy she admired. "Are you still able to mimic Jerry Lewis?"

The glimmer of a smile creased his face. "At least I'm not a porker like he's turned into."

"Did you marry?" Sally attempted a more positive subject.

"She's over there." Don pointed to a round-faced woman speaking to Betty. "Gossiping about us. Name's Tina. She loves bread."

"Not much to say about my family." Sally poured a glass of punch for her family's old friend. "Madelyn's husband is gone. Loretta divorced her children's father and married a man as young as our little brother. Do you remember Dick?"

"Yeah." Don sipped the cranberry juice. "Priest, right?"

"No, no." Sally motioned for John to join them. "Dick left the seminary before his final vows. He has a son, and a daughter-in-law from India no less, as well as a beautiful granddaughter and grandson."

"We didn't have children," Don said.

"Me either," Sally said.

"I asked her," John teased and placed his arm possessively around Sally's shoulder.

"I told him, no."

"Can you imagine a ten-year-old with a seventy-year-old Dad?" Sally snuggled against John's shoulder.

Tim, Jeff, and Molly Hanson had turned up at the party, too. As a teenager, Sally cleaned house for their family to help with high school expenses. She also babysat for the brothers before their sister was born. Tim Hanson stayed next to Sally when his brother and sister went off to freshen their drinks. "Remember when you used to yell at me?"

The Appropriate Way

"I do." She included John and Gabby in the conversation. "Tim always talked to me when the vacuum was running. I would shout, 'What?' over and over and louder and louder, until I finally turned off the machine."

"We looked forward to the day you cleaned. You rearranged our toys into stories."

"She's still telling stories." John patted Sally's back. "She picks up a few clues and points the police in the right direction."

"I read all about the Tedler brothers helping you in Michigan. I'd like to apply for a similar position on your next case."

"The Tedlers were both police officers." Sally accepted a cup of cranberry punch from John.

"Sheriff Woods encouraged me to come to the party to speak to you." Tim straightened his shoulders and stretched his neck to reveal his entire height. "I've been on the force for two years."

Sally had always been fond of the boy, now a young man. "God forbid, we're needed in peaceful old St. Charles; but I certainly wouldn't mind working with you. You're used to my yelling!"

"Thank you." Tim shook both Sally and John's hands good-bye. "I'll let Sheriff Woods know."

John had watched the attractive young man saunter away. "He acts like he knows something he's not telling us."

Another young couple, the Armstrongs, and a man called Masters were also guests. Mr. Masters couldn't place who Sally was, until Sheriff Woods nailed her identity down for him. "She's the house painter's daughter."

"I remember." Mr. Masters turned to Sheriff Woods. "Tony always …"

The room turned quiet for a moment. They all dredged up their memories of Sheriff Wood's best friend, Tony Montgomery -- and his horrible suicide.

"Too bad the idiot can't celebrate the New Year." Sheriff Woods raised his glass for a toast.

But the pall was cast. Very shortly, guests began to set their drinks down and mosey toward the door. Sally was sorry the party ended on such a sad note, but she was not unhappy to see the crowd disperse.

Evidently, Betty and James didn't plan to clean up after the caterers. "They'll come by tomorrow morning for their serving trays." Betty instructed when they started to leave.

John appeared next to Sally. "The cleaning ladies come tomorrow. We'll leave the mess for them to deal with."

Sally drew John's arm closer to her. A flicker in Betty's eyes alerted her. This party was a get-even shindig for John's new wife. As far as Sally was concerned Betty had counted on twin escorts long enough, but Sally produced a gracious good-bye. "Thank you for going to all the trouble of rounding up people who knew me. Anytime you want to bring over a party," Sally lied, "just let us know."

James was quick to understand. "I'm sure this is the last time we'll make use of Mother's dishes."

"Oh." John pointed to the mess. "You're welcome to them

right now."

Sally wrinkled her nose as she surveyed the stacks of dirty dishes littering the dining room table. She imagined the kitchen counters were filled with glassware and dishes waiting to be cleaned. She agreed with John, they could pack up everything right now. The two couples laughed at each other before parting, but the turf was well marked, John and Sally's new home wouldn't be so easily available to Betty in the future.

Later that night a winter storm glazed everything with an inch of ice.

Sally awoke to the loud crack of a tree's demise. Without waking her new husband, she peered out the back bedroom window. The weight of un-pruned branches split the trunk of a fruit tree down the middle. She'd chosen not to accept the event as a bad omen. She planned to hold up her half of the marriage commitment, with the Lord's help. John's gentle lovemaking endeared him more to her each time they slept together.

In bed the very next morning, John urged Sally to accept an invitation from Bret Armstrong to tour his castle in nearby Wayne. "He asked us to come. Bret probably wants us to see the place all decked out for the Holidays."

"Shouldn't we call?" Sally reluctantly climbed out of bed. "They're so young. What if he was just in his cups?"

"I don't want to lose the opportunity." John pouted. "I've never been inside the castle. Bret was quite open about Matilda's father providing all the renovation funds. Peter Masters, he's the guy who didn't recognize you."

Sally argued with herself. She needed to find an AA meeting location, before she called her sponsor. "First things first, John. Let me locate the addresses of a couple AA meetings while you start the coffee and then we'll go."

"Dress warm," John called as he headed for the kitchen. "The weather looks treacherous."

The information operator found an Alcoholics Anonymous number. Sally spoke briefly to the woman answering the phone and wrote down two meeting sites, one in Geneva and one in Batavia. Then she called Grace. "There's no meeting today; but I'll attend a noon meeting on Thursday in Geneva and a morning meeting on Monday in Batavia."

"How was your first day in your new home?"

"My sister-in-law arranged a wedding reception." Sally sat back down on the bed, looking at the broken tree outside.

"With alcohol?" Grace sounded concerned.

"Yep. I'm okay."

"Good. It wasn't easy, was it?"

"No." Sally ran her hand through her hair, hoping she could coax it into some suitable style for a castle visit. "But John hung onto me, or me him, most of the evening."

"Ask John to pack up all the alcohol."

"He could take it to the hotel." Sally stood to begin getting ready.

"Good idea. Relocations aren't easy for alcoholics."

The Appropriate Way

"All those new faces." Sally stared at her reflection in the dresser's mirror. "Actually, old faces. I mean familiar faces, aged."

"You better call me daily, until you nail down a new sponsor."

"Thanks." Sally felt ashamed of a catch in her throat. "Hanging on to you, means a lot to me."

"It's the program you're holding onto." Grace sighed. "Don't forget you're helping me stay sober, too. God loves us, doesn't he?"

* * *

St. Mark's AA Meeting

Sally awoke from her reverie of John as she reached down to acknowledge Ginger's cheerful tongue anointing of her fingertips. Her watch claimed the hour was eleven. Time to make a noon AA meeting at St. Mark's in Geneva. She would be welcomed without knowing anyone at the meeting. When she walked into the large room, a greeter stuck out his hand. "Welcome."

"Is this a step meeting?" she asked, after shaking his hand.

"We just share at the tables. Is this your first meeting?"

"No, I'm new in town." Sally realized the awful truth. She wouldn't be staying in her hometown for long. "Just visiting really."

"We're glad you could make a meeting," the white-haired guy said.

A round table with six chairs filled with comfortable looking women, sported one empty seat. Sally claimed it. Most of the women seemed to know each other. After the Serenity Prayer, the man who opened the meeting asked several people in the room to read sections out of the Big Book. Sally read a list of the twelve steps out loud with the rest of the group, when one of the members read "How It Works." She tuned back into the goings-on when the "Promises" were repeated.

She raised her hand when newcomers were asked to. "Sally," she said, "a gratefully recovering alcoholic." She was the only new person in the room where five tables were filled with Fox River Valley alcoholics.

After the room dividers were pulled around the tables, a white-haired stunning woman began their tables' meeting. "Any special topics?"

"Widowhood," was out of Sally's mouth before she could think.

"Loss," another woman nodded.

The leader asked, "Who would like to start?"

Sally kept her mouth shut wondering what in the world she was going to say to these strangers.

"My boyfriend of ten years moved out," a woman with a destroyed hair style offered. "And my dog died."

After immediate murmurings of consolation for the loss of her dog, they listened to her tell them how badly she felt, how tempted she was to drink, and how grateful she was for a place to come for solace.

The woman who first nodded said her mother died two months earlier and she couldn't seem to move on. She was praying for strength to let the grief dispel; but her mother was her best friend and her loneliness was eating her up. She prayed for God's will every day. She enrolled in an evening class in watercolors, because she didn't want to throw out her mother's wealth of painting supplies.

Another older woman said her name, but wouldn't admit to being an alcoholic. "The judge and my husband insist I come here."

The leader asked if she could sign her checklist. After signing, which meant the woman attended the meeting, she asked, "Would you like to leave now or would you like to talk?"

"Could I just listen?" she asked.

"Absolutely," the leader said. "If you change your mind, let me know."

"My name is Sally, and I'm still a recovering alcoholic. Last week my husband was shot to death. The killer might have wanted me dead, but my husband saved me. I'm still sober."

"Thank God," the leader said. "Are you going to counseling?"

"No," Sally said, feeling too weepy. "John was my second husband, and I lost my best friend, a bookman, earlier last year."

"My Lord," the new person said. "How do you do it?"

"No cross talk," the leader said in a kindly tone. "We just listen to each other."

"Well you told her to see a psychiatrist. I want to know how she survives…without drinking."

Sally answered, "I pray like a crazy person. Every time I see a white van with ladders on the top, I say the Our Father. Daddy was a house painter, but I figure the universe is reminding me prayers are needed regularly…"

"Would you both explain the first step to our newcomer," the leader asked.

"We admitted we were powerless over alcohol and our lives had become unmanageable," one of the remaining women said. "I always drank differently than other people. They mixed soda with the alcohol, or would leave a glass half-finished. Not me. I could never get enough of the stuff. Then when I decided I wouldn't drink, I kept on going to bars, partying, speculating on why I couldn't stop. The program taught me to find a Higher Power, something or someone I could count on, outside of myself. First, I just kept coming to meetings trying to figure out how you all kept sober. This is my second time in the program, but I have a sponsor and three sponsees now."

"When I first came to the tables. I thought I figured out the deal. It was a God thing. I knew all about that. So I didn't attend and didn't get a sponsor. I just stopped drinking. I was a dry drunk for ten years. Then I joined Overeater's Anonymous and even did a fourth step. But after about five years, I started drinking, not much. But it just increased and increased, until one day before a party, I was 'testing' the wine at three o'clock in the afternoon. So I started coming back. I have a sponsor and I've been sober for nearly five years."

It was Sally's turn to say something. "I'm glad you're here for me. I'm going to go home to Ann Arbor, Michigan, where my sponsor lives."

"Good idea," the leader said.

They closed the meeting with the Lord's Prayer.

* * *

Kane County Sheriff Office

Back at the police station in Geneva, Officer Caldwell helped Tim and Sheriff Woods separate the contents of Matilda's box. Tim warned her, "Don't be surprised to find my name on all the letters. Matilda and I were lovers before she married." He coughed out the truth, "and after."

Officer Caldwell's eyes widened, but she kept her thoughts to herself.

Woods detected what was going on between them. "Why don't you two take this evidence down to the lab boys in Chicago. Tim, take along Reeves' water glass, too."

Officer Caldwell stood and almost snapped to attention. "I won't need Officer Hanson's help. I'll run this batch down by myself. I'm sure you two have other work to do on the case."

After her abrupt departure, Tim shook his head. "She likes me, but she won't be able to get over this. How would she explain to her friends or her family? She's in love with a rounder? Besides, it would be wrong to encourage her. Is it fair to marry someone because they love you? After this case is closed, I plan to leave the force. Leave town."

Sheriff Woods wanted to say, yes. You can marry someone who loves you. He hoped Gabby was happy with him. He was content. He liked his life and his wife. But he didn't know how to console his young officer or surmount his problems. "Ask Sally if she needs a partner in Ann Arbor. You could keep me informed, if she gets into anything she can't handle."

Tim seemed to see Sheriff Woods in a new light. "You loved her, once."

"If this old heart ever gave a beat for anyone but myself," Sheriff Woods said, "Sally was the cause."

"Why did you two break up?"

"I've been racking my brains," Sheriff Woods said. "Can't remember, or don't want to. Don't think I don't care for Gabby, by the way."

"She's a good wife."

"She's mine," Sheriff Woods said, keeping some of his personal business to himself.

Chapter Eight

Hotel Baker

Sally's bedside phone rang. She struggled to stay in her nap' daydream. Ginger and she were in the beautiful kitchen in John's house. She was explaining to the dog why she wasn't convinced she could make John happy. "I didn't buy him any presents, yet." Ginger cocked her head and raised her ears. "I wish we talked more about God. I wanted to tell him Mathew's Biblical comment about whoever provides a drink of water to a believer, is also saved."

In the dream Ginger barked and waged her tail. So Sally turned around to face the doorway. John was just leaving. She called his name, but he didn't turn. She thought she heard him say, "I'm okay, don't worry."

Her dreamscape shifted to the bookshop in Ann Arbor. Her first husband, Danny Bianco, with his shock of white hair and John with his bald head were arguing with Robert Koelz about which sweater to wear.

Sally answered into the receiver, cupped to her ear, "It doesn't matter."

"Well," Sheriff Woods said, "I'll probably agree, but tell me anyway."

"Tell you what?" Sally asked, coming fully to her senses.

"I can't remember and it is slowly driving me crazy. You know I'm happily married. As happy as I assume I should be. This is not a ploy."

She could hear him take a deep breath. "You want to know why we broke up."

"Exactly. Do you know the chapter and verse?"

"I do. You were in a funk about Tony. Angry at all women for his suicide." Sally stopped. "Are you sure you want to go over this?"

"It is gnawing at me. I probably acted like a dim-witted fool. Please, just tell me what I did."

"Nothing horrible. I was shy and couldn't tell you about a physical complication."

"What?"

"You demanded intercourse with me. We were not even engaged. I told you no. So, you said not to call you until I was ready. I think your exact words were, 'to give it up.' I thought I would never see you again. I'd enrolled in an English night course at Elgin's Community College. One of the teachers hit a nerve when he said most of the people attending were not interested in learning, they were looking for mates because they didn't connect to anyone in high school. I'd already spent six lonely months and I remember thinking the virginity stuff wasn't all it was cracked up to be. So, I called you." Sally brushed her white hair away from her eyes.

"What did I do?"

"Well after I called you to make the date, my period arrived. Thank the Lord. I thought we would date for a while before you demanded more again. And I missed you. I think I really did love you at the time. Anyway, we went to a movie, or something, before you made your move, as we used to call it. I told you no. But I couldn't tell you why I needed to delay. I was too embarrassed. We weren't as open back then as teenagers are now. You called me a tease and took me home in silence. I never called you again."

Sheriff Woods said, "I was so stupid. Will you accept an apology, at this late date?"

"We were very young. I forgave you years ago. Do you remember any of the scenes, now?"

"The truth is I don't. The last thing I remember is sitting with you in the Log Cabin restaurant and getting incredibly angry at a waitress."

Someone was knocking on the hotel's door. "Art, I mean Sheriff Woods, someone is at the door."

"Good-bye, Sally. And, thanks. Tim and I will be over about four."

Betty and James Nelson invited themselves in. "We have good news for you," bald James said.

Ginger stayed glued to Sally's heels, following her around the room. The dog didn't notice James' physical resemblance to his former master.

"True." Betty sat down in the small dining room, placing her purse on her lap. Her white hair sparkled from the light over the table.

"John did change his will," James explained. "The house,

stock holdings, share of the hotel and savings accounts are all yours."

"Oh, he complicated everything, didn't he? Betty, should I ring for room service? Would you like a cup of coffee, or tea?"

Betty shook her head. "I'm happy for you."

"What is the name of the lawyer?"

"Silas Pike," James said.

"I'll call him to arrange a Quit Claim Deed to turn over the house and the hotel to you," Sally looked directly at Betty. "I'm sure John would understand."

James said. "John wanted you to live in the house."

Sally tried to explain. "If I grew old with John, as we planned to, this would make sense. However, after this case is solved, I intend to return home to my condominium in Ann Arbor. You understand, don't you, Betty?"

"James is right," Betty placed her purse on the floor and cozied up to the table. "You are being very generous."

"You're welcome. It's fun to play lady bountiful. But really, I'm sure John would approve. Now how about tea? Sheriff Woods and Tim should be here directly. We're going out to the Montgomerys' to ask a slew of questions."

"I could use a drink," Betty said.

"Not in this room," James said, sounding exactly like John for a second.

Sally called room service for tea. "Five people, three of whom are men. In other words, bring enough for eight. And a carafe of coffee, too. You don't keep dog biscuits, do you."

Ginger wagged her tail at the word biscuit.

* * *

After Tim and the sheriff consumed every morsel of food Sally provided at the hotel, they drove her to Wayne. Sally appropriated the back seat, hoping to prime the two police officers with enough unanswered questions to make the trip a decisive, perhaps final, visit. "We need to know why Peter is lying."

"Tim is quitting the force," Sheriff Woods said.

"Why is that?" Sally hoped to turn the conversation back to the case as quickly as possible.

"My reputation," Tim said, in a tone implying Sally already knew the answer.

"A little humility will patch up your honor in no time." Sally prayed she sounded encouraging, not just impatient. "Would you like a dog to keep you company? Ginger seemed to switch loyalties as soon as you entered the hotel room."

"He's interested in returning to Ann Arbor with you." Woods kept his eyes on the winter road ahead of them.

"To work for you." Tim turned around to face Sally. "I like Ginger. I guess a dog would give me someone to take care of."

"I'd be glad for you to join the Tedler detective agency. I miss Ann Arbor. I made a few friends I hope don't forget me. I'm not really a dog person though. Walking Ginger at five degrees below zero in the early morning doesn't sound appealing to me.

"I could write you a recommendation for the police

department," Sheriff Woods said.

"But Tim," Sally said. "I think you should spend some time evaluating your future," She tried not to lecture. "Will you succumb to …"

"Temptation?" Tim finished for her.

"I don't mean just women." Sally wanted to state the job's requirements for integrity clearly. "Tim, I met you when you were two years old, but I don't know what your priorities are."

"Not money." Tim turned in the front seat to smile at Sally.

"Okay, good. But spiritually, Tim? What is your relationship with the Lord, as you understand Him?"

"I'm thankful to own the will power to stop seeing Matilda."

"I believe I'm powerless." Sally waited for the shift in attitude to sink in, before she added, "I'm only speaking for myself, but I turned my will over to my Higher Power. I don't know how I could exist as a sober, ethical person without my conscious contact with God."

"You mean, He talks to you?" the sheriff slowed the car to a crawl.

"No. I mean I ask His help to do His will."

"How do you know what it is?" Tim asked.

"I'm never sure, but I ask, daily, for help to trust Him more."

"I could." Tim faced the road ahead. "I'm looking forward to claiming Ginger."

"Can't ask more of the boy," Sheriff Woods said.

Sally laughed. "I'm sure I'll be asking a great deal of Detective

Tim Hanson."

As they turned west on Territorial Road, Sally was startled to see the sun so low in the sky. She struggled to uncover her watch from the sleeve of her alpaca coat. "What time is it?"

"Nearly four," Tim said.

"Shouldn't the days be getting longer?"

"Not yet, Sally," Woods said. "It is only the tenth of January."

"A lot has happened, since the first." Tim's tone was sympathetic.

Sally admitted her world completely changed in those five days. John was killed on the fifth. She vaguely recalled the memorial service in the Hotel Baker. "Was I given any sedatives?"

"Why do you ask?" Woods slowed the car again.

"The grieving process jumbled memories of Jill's wedding reception with the going's on at John's affair. I complained about the dress I was wearing, didn't I?"

"We understood." Tim and the sheriff commented in unison.

Sally felt a warm touch on her cheek bone, where John usually gave her a peck when he was leaving. "I'm okay," she said to John and the police officers in the front seat.

*　*　*

They drove by the Masters' home, where a bevy of new two-by-fours rose above the ruins of the arsoned home. "I thought they would wait for spring," Woods said.

"Money," Tim said, "With enough money, the earth would spin counter-clockwise."

"No," Sally said. "It wouldn't. But money can pay enough wages for workers to get frostbite."

"She doesn't approve," Woods kidded.

"I used to get beat up in grade school," Sally said. "I was always the do-gooder. The kids would pound me right to the ground for not keeping my mouth shut."

Tim struggled with his seat belt to face Sally. "I'm glad you talked to me."

Sally smiled at him. "Before we pull into the Montgomerys' drive, let's go over the case."

"Peter's lying," Tim said.

"Why did Peter think his wife needed a lawyer?" Woods asked.

"And who rang Peter's cell phone, when he was at the police station?" Sally asked.

* * *

Montgomery Home in Wayne

Sally counted six people in the Montgomery living room. Peter and Geraldine Masters were seated across from the couch where their daughter, Matilda, and Reverend Rosemary Warner sat. After hanging the officers' and Sally's coats in the entranceway, Carolyn and Anthony Montgomery brought extra chairs into the living room. Sally wondered why no one arranged for a lawyer to be present.

"Is your wife's lawyer coming?" Sheriff Woods asked, as he stood with his back to the fireplace. He motioned for Tim and Sally to sit in the green wingback chairs on either side of the fire. The twin orange cats assumed their positions on Tim and Sally's laps.

"We intend to cooperate," Peter Masters answered.

Matilda turned toward Tim. "I want to apologize, publicly."

Sally concluded Reverend Warner had enacted a miracle. "How long have you known the Montgomerys?" she asked the minister.

"Since they lost their son," Rev. Warner said.

Sally reminded herself she was sitting in a house purchased with funds obtained by fraud. "You know Tony committed suicide?"

"Yes," Rev. Warner said. "A real loss."

Sally looked at Woods who glared at her. 'Police discretion,' Sally's mind repeated a phrase from a justice system course she took in college. The sheriff would not prosecute the Montgomerys for using Tony's insurance, even if he believed a crime was committed. Nothing would bring Tony back from the grave, or John Nelson for that matter.

Rev. Warner asked Sally, "How are you holding up?"

"With the Lord's help." Sally hoped she didn't answer too quickly. She didn't mean to imply she took God's grace and her renewal of strength lightly. So she repeated. "His real support."

Rev. Warner nodded her head in understanding.

Woods asked again. "Mr. Masters, why did you think your wife was involved in Enid Krimm's death?"

Matilda answered. "We're going to tell you everything."

Carolyn Montgomery placed an extra chair next to Peter's side of the couch. Carolyn nodded and then smiled at Peter.

Matilda continued, "I had been asking Mother repeatedly for a picture of my grandfather. But because the house burned down, I told her at breakfast I wouldn't be bugging her for the picture anymore."

Geraldine Masters looked at her husband. "Peter thought Matilda asked me for his picture."

"Then they called me," Reverend Warner interrupted to explain. "This morning."

Peter acted as if he was going to stand, but changed his mind and sank even lower in the upholstered couch. "I gave the picture I thought they meant to Carolyn."

Officer Tim Hanson leaned forward as if he needed to be closer to hear correctly.

So, Peter repeated the information, "I gave a picture of myself I thought my daughter wanted to Carolyn."

"Because?" the sheriff asked. Sally thought he should have guessed the answer.

"Carolyn and my husband are involved in an affair," Geraldine said. "Whenever he decided to pound on me enough to make me escape to my mother's in Colorado, sweet Carolyn here would come over and commensurate with him, physically."

Carolyn's husband coughed, trying to conceal his misery.

"Did you wait for Reverend Warner's arrival?" Sally asked. "Before you revealed your infidelities?"

"Yes," Carolyn and Peter said.

"I advised them to forgive each other." Rev Warner clutched her hands in her lap, as if she realized the extent of her religious help.

Sally thought forgiveness would be a tall order for Geraldine Masters and Anthony Montgomery, at least for the immediate future.

"I'm not leaving my husband," Carolyn said, in a plea for the assembled to condone her actions.

Mr. Montgomery stood. "Sheriff Woods, are there any questions you need to ask of me?"

"No. You're free to go."

Mr. Montgomery walked toward the hall leading to the bedrooms. He returned shortly. "Carolyn, I hated every moment we lived here." He started to cough again, trying not to weep in public. "The house was built on Tony's tortured bones. I'm leaving you to your own crazy devices."

Carolyn refused to turn in her husband's direction. Perhaps, she hoped her guests would assign less credence to the damaging words. She focused her attention on Rev. Warner, hoping for some miraculous wisdom to negate her husband's insults, a reprieve from the consequences of her actions.

The minister rose and followed Mr. Montgomery out of the room. They retired in the direction of the bedrooms. Everyone in the living room could hear Mr. Montgomery's mumbled but continuing distress.

Sally brought them back to another distressing topic. "Peter, you thought you recognized your wife leaving your house, before the flames started." Peter nodded his head.

Carolyn reached for his hand, but he pulled away from her.

"I love my wife," he said directly to Geraldine.

"Not enough," Geraldine said. She crossed over to Matilda's side of the room, sitting in Rev. Warner's vacated position.

Carolyn said, "Peter, that was me returning from the house."

"Did you talk to Enid Krimm?" Tim asked her.

"I didn't know anyone was in the house," Carolyn said. "The taxi left, so I walked over to wait for Peter."

"What changed your mind?" Sally asked.

"When I left by my back door, I noticed a car parked down the Montgomery's lane. I couldn't see the car from inside the house because Peter's blocks my view of part of his drive. Anyway, I walked across the field trying to identify the car, but I didn't even knock on the door." She smiled nervously at Peter. "Peter might have seen me walking back across the field to my home."

Peter turned away.

Carolyn sighed. "When I got home, I looked back when I heard a car coming down Territorial Road. Then I became aware of Peter's house. The flames were shooting higher than the roof!" She gestured to show the extent of the blaze, but no one reacted. "It couldn't have taken me ten minutes to cross the field. The horses were acting weird. Running in circles. I didn't know at first that they were panicking from the fire."

"Peter?" Sally asked. "Why did you tell us you returned from Dallas?"

"When I first told Matilda and the rest of you about the fire at the castle, I thought Geraldine was dead. I tried to cover up my meeting with Carolyn New Year's Eve by saying I returned from Dallas." Peter looked at his wife. "On New Year's Eve, Geraldine told me she was divorcing me for abuse."

Rev. Warner walked with Mr. Montgomery past the living room to the front door. He carried two suitcases. Rev. Warner returned to the group without Carolyn's husband. Then, she sat down next to Peter Masters. "I'm afraid he's left you, Carolyn."

"He'll be back," Carolyn said.

"I don't think so. He said he'll arrange for movers to pick up the rest of his belongings."

Sally thought Mr. Montgomery was well out of the place which fraud built and deceit entered. "How long have each of you known J. K. Reeves and Enid Krimm?"

Matilda looked at her mother. "Mother recommended Reeves to Bret."

"Peter wasn't home enough to need a butler," Geraldine said. "I thought Bret was such a nice boy." She turned to face Sally. "Sorry for your loss."

Sally lost focus. Mentioning John's murder caused her to evaluate her clothing. The dark green jacket over her black turtleneck sweater and black slacks could pass for mourning clothes. 'No one would notice on a galloping Palomino,' was Danny Bianco's favorite saying, whenever she asked him how she looked.

Carolyn was dressed in festive white wool slacks and matching sweater. Geraldine wore a dark maroon dress. Sally couldn't shake her mind's retreat from her task. Instead her concentration seemed fixated on clothing, a safer subject. Matilda wore a short blue skirt of what looked like a suede material. She constantly tugged at the hem to draw attention to her fabulous legs. Tim seemed immune to the ploy. Matilda's blouse was silk and lacey, but too tight for Sally's taste.

"Do you remember who recommended Reeves to you, Mrs. Masters?" Sheriff Woods rescued the inquiry, while Sally gathered her wits.

"Enid's mother," Geraldine said. "What was her name?"

"Kathy," Peter said.

"Were you involved with her, too," Matilda asked.

"I was," Peter said. "When she contracted AIDs, I stopped seeing her."

"Nice of you," his wife said.

"You people," Tim Hanson said in a condescending tone.

Sally shook her finger at him, but she didn't quote the verse about throwing the first stone. Tim could certainly not defend his own behavior.

"What was Bret's relationship with Reeves," Sheriff Woods asked.

"Normal," Matilda lied.

Geraldine, her mother, caught the lie and turned in Matilda's direction. Was it an unfamiliar tone or her daughter's slightly elongated spacing of the pronunciation? "What was going on?"

Geraldine asked.

Matilda shook her head.

Woods said, "I was speculating, too. Why did Bret have a chain slip lock on the inside of his door?"

"He didn't like to be disturbed," Matilda said.

"Or interrupted?" her mother asked.

Matilda broke down. She pointed at Tim. "I tried to tell him. Bret loved the castle more than me."

"Or a resident of the castle?" Tim asked. "You haven't been straight with me since the day I met you. I need to apologize to your family for letting you use me."

"What a marvelous family," Geraldine said. "What else?"

"What do you mean, Mother."

"What else have you done?" Geraldine asked, standing in frustration. "You're just like your father. I always know when you're lying to me." She turned to her husband. "That's why you beat me, you idiot. I could see right through you."

Matilda said very quietly, "I put my keepsake box under Bret's bed."

Woods heard. "Why would you do that?"

"I hoped if you thought Bret went crazy because of me," Matilda pulled on her skirt for the fourteenth time. "You might be more lenient with him."

"Tim," Sheriff Woods said, "Grab a phone and call Chicago. We won't be needing lab reports on the contents of that box."

"Who did you think I put the box under Bret's bed?" Matilda

asked.

"His lover," Tim told her. "J. K. Reeves." Matilda's hands strayed to her hair. Tim shook his head. He wasn't buying anymore of her tricks.

"Back to Enid," Sally's mind rejoined the case.

"Enid was the dining room manager at the club." Geraldine sat next to her daughter again.

"You told us Enid claimed to be Peter's lover," Tim said.

"My husband only goes for older women," Geraldine said to Carolyn.

"But did you know it at the time?" Sally asked.

"I did not," Geraldine said. "All I wanted was a divorce."

"Why didn't you tell me?" Her daughter asked.

"I was going to, but I didn't want to wreck your Holidays. I thought you were happy with the castle, the Christmas decorations, and Bret seemed content. It would ruin the season."

"It has," Peter said.

"And whose fault is that?" Geraldine yelled.

Rev. Warner held up her hand for peace.

"Matilda." Sally stroked the cat in her lap. "When John and I came by to see the decorations and the castle, you were supposed to be meeting Tim at your mother's house?"

"Enid. I told Tim my folks were out of town. Mother was visiting my grandmother. Actually, I thought she planned to leave earlier in the morning. I wanted Enid to meet with Tim and me so she would shut up about our affair."

Woods said, "Enid and Reeves were blackmailing most of the citizens in Wayne."

"Really," Peter said. "By the way, where is Reeves?"

"In Europe with Enid's earnings," Sally said.

Matilda got up and went over to Sally. She knelt down next to her and placed her hands on the orange cat. The cat made an evil swipe at Matilda's face, slashing a keen wound across her nose. "Ouch" Matilda yelled.

Tim jumped up and deposited the cat which was on his lap onto the floor. Sally reached for her purse to find a handkerchief to stop the profusion of blood on Matilda's face, which was rapidly dripping onto Matilda's exquisite white blouse. Carolyn swooned onto the couch, effectively obstructing Peter from coming to his daughter's aid.

Geraldine reached Matilda first, halting the flow of blood with the hem of her maroon dress. "Lie down, dear. It's not fatal."

Woods looked at the wound. "Needs a few stitches. We don't want your pretty face scarred."

Peter disengaged himself from Carolyn's fake faint and knelt down next to his wife and daughter. "I'll drive."

Geraldine brushed him aside. "We won't be needing your help. Rev. Warner, will you take us to the hospital?"

"The usual suspects are dwindling in number," Sally said, as the three women left.

The sheriff shook his head at her. "Your daughter is out of the house, now. Mr. Masters, did you want to tell us about your affair with Reeves?"

"Why not. He ruined my daughter's happiness. I nailed down my own unhappiness." Carolyn reached for him. "No. I'll not add to my guilt."

"Does Reeves vacation in Paris or Rome?" Sally asked.

"Rome. The priests with all their vows of celibacy are great targets."

"For blackmail?" Sally tried to maintain her sense of decorum.

"We might need to question you further," Woods said to Peter and then to Carolyn. "after we extradite Reeves. So stay in town."

Peter walked out with them. "I won't be staying here any longer. You can find me at the Pheasant Run Motel."

Sally thanked the Lord that Peter had not chosen Hotel Baker for accommodations. "Who called you? At the police station?" Sally pulled her collar up against the cold.

"On your cell phone?" Woods blocked Peter's access to his car.

"Reeves," Peter said. "He said whoever killed Enid would pay."

"Why didn't you tell us?" Woods asked. "He sent Bret to kill Sally and murdered her husband instead."

Peter shook his head. "I thought he was threatening Geraldine."

"This doesn't make sense." Sally was pretty sure the mention of John was letting her mind go fuzzy again.

Peter took a step toward Sally, but Sheriff Woods intervened.

"Time to go." Woods waved for Tim to come closer. "Sally wants to keep warm in the cruiser."

Tim guided Sally away, but they heard Peter curse. "A housepainter's daughter defeated all of us." He slammed the door of his car and drove away.

Carolyn waved after him from the open door of her empty house. The silvery house lights spread over the snow, but the blackness of the winter night snuffed out any cheerful effect.

"Do you envy the house, now?" Woods asked Sally as he got behind the wheel of the police car.

"I never envied her. I don't think a house should be built on fraud."

Chapter Nine

Hotel Baker

Sally stretched out under the covers. Every bone in her body let her know the cold weather and the stress of interrogating all those people at the Montgomerys' had caught up with her. She repeated the Lord's Prayer and then recited the tenth step from AA's Big Book to review her actions of the day.

Was she angry? Yes. John was snuffed out by the consequences of three married couples' infidelities.

Was she resentful? No, but she recognized Tim's ire stemmed from his strong resentment from being used by Matilda. Sally reminded herself she was taking Tim's inventory instead of her own.

Was she dishonest? No.

Had she been fearful? Yes. Peter Masters' anger had been frightening. She was in the Lord's hands, under his protection and let her fear and anger dissipate as she meditated.

Without changing her normal breathing, she counted from one to four, concentrating on the sound of the words in her mind. When her brain rebelled, she gently guided her thoughts back to the tedious repetitions until the technique let her drift off to sleep.

Sally dreamt a road construction crew busily replaced a section of broken pavement. At least twenty men removed orange road barriers, swept debris from the curbs, and concerned themselves with making the road smooth and drivable.

* * *

Second Friday in January

Sally planned to take a day of rest. She ordered room service at ten o'clock and was involved in making a list of loose ends to wrap up before she moved to Ann Arbor, when there was a knock on her door. Thinking room service wanted their dishes, she opened the door still in her bathrobe. Ginger gave a happy bark. Tim Hanson and his brother, Jeff, and his sister, Molly, stood in the hall. Ginger joined them in the hall.

"Sorry." Tim reached down to pet the dog. "I should have called ahead."

"Come in, come in. Ginger, behave. Retain a little dignity. I know you love the guy. I'll call room service for you. Did you eat, Tim?"

"He hasn't even slept." His sister pushed him into the room.

"Just open the door for the staff, when they get here. I'll be presentable in a minute." Before she dressed, Sally made a quick call for the mountain of food necessary to feed three young people. No more black, she told herself. Life needed to go on. She chose a light blue sweater set with a pair of matching wool slacks.

Black was assigned to her shoes. 'God bless John's soul,' she prayed.

Tim was finishing a last bite of bacon from his plate, when

Sally returned "He won't eat at home," his big brother Jeff said. "We're both worried about him."

"Tim, what's going on?"

"I'm sick." Tim touched his own forehead for a temperature. "Maybe. I can't think."

"What's your predominant thought?" She poured herself a cup of coffee and joined the siblings in the small dining room.

"Hurting Bret when I knocked him down at the castle." Tim shook his head. "Do you think I might have caused a tumor to grow, or...?"

"You haven't rid yourself of the resentment you feel against Matilda." Sally diagnosed.

"Who wouldn't be angry with her?" Tim shouted. Ginger barked at him.

"Ginger, hush," Sally ears hurt from all the noise.

"Someone who admitted he was a party to the sin," Molly said.

Jeff's gesture included his sister. "Molly and I accepted Jesus as our Savior. Tim refuses to believe his problems would be over if he did the same."

"In AA we're taught to only talk about ourselves." Prompted by her knowledge of AA's spiritual steps, Sally relaxed "Jeff, explain to Tim why you thought it was necessary to personally search for the Lord's way of life."

"Work was driving me crazy," Jeff began. "If my co-workers and supervisors weren't stealing my ideas outright, they found ways to undercut my decisions. They even sabotaged my test results."

"Jeff works in a safety laboratory for Federal Express," Molly explained.

"One night, I thought about stopping everything. Quitting. Finding another job in this economy seemed hopeless. I considered ending my life. I even thought about joining the army to die in combat. I was a wreck." Jeff took his sister's hand. "I complained to Molly and she told me about a new boyfriend of hers who challenged her to accept Jesus."

"My decision made all the difference in the world to me," Molly said. "I treated my fiancée with new respect. My temper tantrums disappeared. I feel as if I'm stepping on new ground, every day."

"Safe ground," Sally said. "What do you think, Tim?"

"I don't know." Tim scratched his head. "Isn't it just an easy way out of your troubles? Religion is called a crutch."

"Exactly," Jeff, Molly, and Sally agreed.

"Lord," Tim said, as if he meant the call. "At this point I'll try anything. What do I need to do?"

"Is there a Gideon Bible here?" Jeff asked.

"I'll get it." Sally returned to the bedroom. She found the bible in her bedside table, right where the Gideons placed it for just such an emergency. She handed the book to Molly. As Molly searched for the verse she wanted, Sally talked about her beliefs. "I first comprehended the peace, the oceanic swelling of the soul people write about, when I was in my twenties. At some point in my long life, I lost sight of my active trust in Jesus. Alcohol is a cunning adversary. Remember how Jesus was chastised for spending time with the winebibbers. I think he tried to understand how someone who is addicted wants to avoid the drug or drink but cannot control themselves, without divine intervention. After I was sober, I returned to the Lord."

"Here's one," Molly smiled at Tim. "They are legion in the bible."

"Okay," Tim said. "Read it."

"Tim," Sally advised. "Why don't you read the verse and let your soul find its Maker?"

"Shouldn't I kneel down?" Tim asked.

Jeff explained. "God loves you just the way you are, Tim. You present yourself to him the way that feels most comfortable."

Tim knelt down and placed the Bible on the seat of his chair. To accommodate his preference, his sister, brother, and Sally joined him in kneeling. "I am the door; by me if any man enter in, he shall be saved, and shall go in and out, and find pasture." Tim read John 10:9 and then 10:11. "I am the good shepherd: the good shepherd giveth his life for the sheep."

"He is our Passover." Sally evoked a part of the Episcopal communion prayer.

Tim's head was bent in prayer. Ginger was curled up at his knees. Molly and Jeff kept their silent vigil, as the Lord swept Tim's sins away. "Amen." Tim stood, then immediately sat down. "Thank you."

Jeff and Molly rose easily and resumed their chairs. Sally's creaking knees complained. So, she used the chair to help her stand. "It's best to take the Lord for your Savior, while you can still kneel down."

"I'm not being silly," Tim said. "Or maybe I am. I feel lighter. I think the Lord took away a burden I could feel actually weighing me down. Now what?"

"One day at a time." Sally said and laughed.

"I'm late for work. And I need to call Matilda at the castle." Tim immediately headed for the phone.

Sally was wondering if she should advise Tim not to encourage Matilda, when a knock was heard on her hotel door.

With a nod from Sally, Jeff got up and answered the door. "Yes?"

Sally could see the back of a girl in a grey sweatshirt and baggy jogging pants standing in the hall. When she heard Jeff's voice, the girl started to walk away; but then stopped. As the disheveled woman turned around, Sally realized it was Matilda. Her face wore no makeup. Her hair looked like she just jumped out of bed.

"Mother said to ask for Sally Nelson." Without waiting for a reply, she wailed. "I'm pregnant!"

Tim gently pushed past his brother and Sally and enclosed Matilda in his arms. "Matilda, everything is going to be fine, now."

Ginger looked once at Sally, whined and joined Tim and Matilda in the hall.

"She's Tim's dog now," Sally said.

Jeff shut the door, leaving the dog and the young couple to their privacy in the hall.

"The Lord giveth, too." Molly handed the Gideon Bible back to Sally.

* * *

Jeff and Molly Hanson were only gone a minute, when the phone rang. Sally's first thought was that the Lord did not agreed to her day of rest. Sheriff Woods asked if Tim was with her.

"How did you know?"

"Gabby says you're a safe harbor for a lot of people. I thought you should know, James Reeves was found."

"Are they sending him back?"

"No, no need for that." Before Sally could protest, he added, "He's dead. He slit his wrists while he was in his bathtub."

"Just like a dishonored Roman citizen. Now we will never learn why Bret shot my husband, unless you offer Bret a deal."

"For murdering John?"

"I don't think he meant to harm John. Tim or I were the intended targets. Would his lawyer let him tell us why he arrived with the gun, if the prosecutor settles for manslaughter?"

"What would his brother think?"

"I'll ask him, before I come over. Could you ask the prosecutor, hypothetically?"

* * *

James and Betty were at the front desk when Sally asked their approval for her plan. James nodded, but Betty was not buying any of it. "Never! I hope he gets the chair."

"Illinois no longer allows the death penalty," Sally reminded her.

"Then he can rot in jail."

"Vengeance won't bring John back." James held his weeping wife and nodded again. "Sally needs to find out the truth.

* * *

Bret was brought into Sheriff Woods' office in handcuffs. When he spotted Sally, he stepped back against his handler. "Why is she here?"

"Why don't you remove the handcuffs," Sally said. "Bret, we're offering you manslaughter instead of being tried for the first degree murder of my husband."

"Why?" Bret sat down rubbing his wrists from the impress of cold steel.

Sheriff Woods answered. "We want to know what happened. I'm sorry to tell you, we found James Reeves." Bret's posture changed. He showed his interest. Bret's female lawyer reached for his hand. Sheriff Woods did not give Bret good news. "Reeves took his own life."

Bret's body sunk into his prison garb, as if a balloon had deflated. "Gone, too."

"Please, Bret," Sally pleaded. "I want to understand."

"You don't care anything about me." Bret face was red with anger. "You just want the bloody details."

"Take him back," Sheriff Woods said, infuriated with the process.

Sally held up her hand. "Ask your lawyer, Bret?"

After a whispered, frenzied conversation, Bret sunk down further in his chair. "Okay. I'll try to explain."

Sheriff Woods signaled for the stenographer to turn on her court-recording machine.

Bret began, "I'm not a trusting person. I suppose people in my position find it difficult to put faith in anyone. All the lies I told, keeping them all straight wore me out. Of course, the lying made me suspicious of everyone else. I knew before I married Matilda that she and Tim were lovers. Actually, their affair helped sanction my own. The Masters were so nice to me. I know Geraldine didn't realize I was gay, but I appreciated her sending James to me – probably to get him away from Peter."

"James Reeves," Sheriff Woods added for the recorder.

"I was happy at the castle. When Tim knocked me down with the backdoor, the whole family came to see how I was doing. My own parents didn't even call back to see if I was all right. I'm sure they're happy now."

"Bret, if you could." Sally wanted more details about John's murder. She honestly wasn't interested in the details of how he lived his life.

Bret acknowledged he was expounding about himself more than was necessary for the case. "I thought James was bisexual when I followed him to Enid's condo one night. I threw a fit and

The Appropriate Way

threatened to fire him. Of course, I was bluffing. I just didn't want him to frequent a prostitute, or any woman, or man. James promised never to see Enid again." Bret's face showed his satisfaction for a moment, and then his frown returned. "When Peter told Matilda the police were sure the dead woman was Enid, I went to James." Sally focused on his words. "I thought James would be pleased Enid wouldn't be blackmailing Matilda or Geraldine for indiscretions any longer." Bret relaxed, as he replayed the scene. "I told him, our world was safe."

"Your intimate world?" Sheriff Woods wanted on the record.

"Yes," Bret stretched his neck and jutted his chin. "We were lovers." Then he shivered and a frown dominated his face again.

"James was frantic. He went all to pieces, actually grinding his teeth." Bret looked up, as if he expected their sympathy. "He wouldn't let me touch him. He dashed out of my bedroom and I followed him outside to his car. He wouldn't tell me where he was going. By then I was weeping, but James wouldn't relent." He wiped his eyes. "I laid down in the snow, in front of his car. Then he told me."

Bret looked directly at Sally. "Enid was his illegitimate daughter, not his lover. He said you and Tim would find out everything. He said we were through. I told him you didn't know we were lovers. He said you would figure out his connections to me. Enid's blackmailing racket would implicate him. I was sitting next to the wheel of his car, hugging his ankle. James shook me off. He acted disgusted when he finally told me Matilda was going to divorce me. She was pregnant."

Bret smiled, "Funny. My butler knew before I did. James shoved his passport in my face. He was leaving me, for good. After he left, I went into the house to kill myself. I own several guns. While I searched for the bullets and loaded the gun, I kept getting angrier and angrier. Why should everyone else be off the hook after Enid died? I was the only one suffering, because James would leave."

"It was all your fault!" He pointed at Sally as he had aimed the gun at her the night John died. His volume increased with each word. "I didn't care if I killed you and Tim. I wanted everyone to suffer."

Bret stopped speaking for a moment, then said in almost a whisper, "but when John jumped at me, I shot in his direction."

Sally relived the nightmare.

"I liked John," Bret said. "He listened to me. He seemed thrilled to be able to visit the castle."

"But you killed him," Sally said.

Chapter Ten

Tim and Matilda asked if they could lunch with Sally at the hotel before she left for Ann Arbor. She couldn't deny the couple who appeared to be deeply in love. Matilda was intent on canceling out any fears Sally might hold about Tim's future. "I think Tim should stay in law enforcement."

"She wants to redecorate the castle," Tim said.

"Upstairs, I'm buying a queen size bed for the central room. Mother is going to stay with us, too. I'll turn the bedrooms on each side of the master bedroom into nurseries."

"I'm sure you two were meant to be together," Sally said. "Make room for the Lord in your lives, too."

"We will," Tim promised. "We know who to thank."

"Me, too," Sally said, thinking of her many blessings and the safe harbor she still owned in Ann Arbor.

PART III

The Recorder's Way

Prologue

"And while the meat was yet between their teeth, ere it was chewed, the wrath of the Almighty was kindled against the people, and God emaciated their souls." Numbers 11:33

1990, Ann Arbor
Schneider Residence

The victim, seven-year-old Larry Schneider came home early from Little League. His mother, Amy, invited his coach in, even though the house was a wreck, and she was still wearing her bathrobe. The coach instructed her to check Larry's temperature. He needed to get back to the game to tell the other parents about Larry's rash. After he left, Amy found the digital thermometer in the bathroom's catch-all drawer. When she read how high her son's temperature was, she immediately called his father at the computer company office.

"104 degrees?" Tom asked.

Amy was accustomed to hearing censure in her husband's voice. "The coach brought him home. I guess he played too hard. I thought his cold was better this morning. Dr. Handler's advice did keep the fever down with all that aspirin. Larry's lying down on the sofa, watching the news."

"Larry's too young to watch the news."

When Tom wasn't making her feel guilty, he settled for treating her like an idiot. She tried to ameliorate the situation. "He seems happy enough. He did complain about too many cobwebs. I don't see any."

"Force some fluids down him." Tom was shouting. "I'll be right home."

Amy rinsed a glass and made a chocolate shake for her son. Larry took one sip and set his glass down on the littered coffee table. She didn't press him. She dressed and busied herself clearing some of the debris out of the room. Actually, Tom was a stickler for tidiness. Some might even call him compulsive. She could *not* care less. Life was too important to chase dust around. Books needed to be read, thoughts followed. One room would get cleaned just long enough for the rest of the house to appear messy in comparison. Amy would no sooner succeed in removing all the grime from Larry's train set, which ran around a high ledge in the front room, before Tom would complain the plants around the front windows had sprouted spider webs, again. The dog, her puppies, and three cats seemed to choose the neatest room to shed their ceaseless balls of fur. Amy actually loved rainy days, because her husband could spy less of the prevailing dust.

"Can't you reach those cobwebs?" Larry waved his thin arms above his head, frowning as if fresh pain from his headache stabbed him.

Amy twisted ice water from the washcloth before tenderly replacing it on her son's searing brow. "Daddy will be here soon."

"Good," the child said. "He'll be able to reach the spiders for you."

There were no cobwebs, no spiders either. To entertain him while they waited for his father, Amy switched on the Lionel train set. As the cars circled the eight-inch wide shelf, accumulated dust particles from the tracks danced down slants of the late afternoon sun. Amy shoved last night's supper dishes into the dishwasher just as her husband slammed the front door.

* * *

Tom Schneider centered his briefcase on the marble entrance table. He hung his raincoat by its inside label onto the antique coat rack before entering the cluttered front room. He picked up his son's chocolate shake, tasted it and glared at his wife.

"What's wrong, now?" Amy's voice never lost its tinge of whine to his ears.

"You're hopeless. The chocolate milk is sour. How is he supposed to drink this? Give him a glass of water. With ice!" He sat down next to his son and felt his brow. "Not feeling chipper?"

Larry grinned. "You came home."

Tom examined the glass of water Amy offered before handing it to his son. His wife, whose nose was constantly in a book, was not a stringent housekeeper, but she was a loving mother. Larry only sipped the water and leaned back against the pillows. "Rough game?" Tom asked.

"No. I dressed, but when it was my turn to bat, the coach felt my head. Mom can't reach those cobwebs." Larry's arm jerked toward the clean ceiling.

"So you haven't been running around all day?" Tom unbuttoned the throat of his son's sweaty baseball jersey. A purple rash ran down his neck, covering his chest.

"I fell asleep in class. Mrs. Dobson sent home a note for you. She thinks I stay up too late at night."

"Get his coat," Tom directed Amy. "Call that quack, Dr. Handler, and tell him to meet us at the hospital."

After he'd wrapped his lethargic son in a blanket, Tom noticed Larry didn't want to keep his head upright. The boy leaned back on his father's arm. He whispered his throat hurt. In the car, Tom kept the boy cradled in his arms.

In an unbuttoned trench coat hastily thrown over a dingy housedress, his wife sped through red lights, frantically laying on the horn to race to St. Anthony's emergency room. Tom wasn't happy with her explanation about Dr. Handler's answering service taking her message about Larry's bumps.

The hospital entrance area was filled with frantic parents and children dressed in Little League outfits. The other kids looked tired and hungry, but healthy. The general bedlam was punctuated by worried admonishments to, "Sit still," by more than a dozen anxious parents.

"Larry's coach must have warned the parents about Larry's hives," Tom told Amy. When Larry moaned and tried to push away from Tom's arms, saying there was a fire in front of his eyes, Tom screamed at the nurses, "Do something!"

Amy pulled the collar of her trench coat over her ears. She rocked back and forth, singing a biblical dirge to herself, "Why has the wrath of the Almighty been kindled against the people? Why has God emaciated our souls?"

The other occupants of the waiting room grew silent and moved away, as if Tom Schneider might become violent, or Amy might go berserk.

When Larry was finally wheeled into an isolation room, Nurse Sharon Daley knew immediately what was wrong. The child was delirious and hallucinating from the high fever. Without waiting for permission, Sharon started an IV needle in the boy's arm and prepared an antibiotic drip.

Her supervisor, Marilyn Helms asked the parents to wait outside, telling them their doctor would be sending the boy down for an MRI.

Sharon and Marilyn took turns staying with the dying child waiting for Dr. Benjamin Hnndler. They traded off making trips to monitor two other patients of the University's consultant staff. Jean Bacon, an end-stage diabetic, was in a coma and slipping rapidly. Dr. Cornell was notified they were making her comfortable. Charlie Klondike, a seriously ill alcoholic, was resting comfortably after a tiring bout of D.T.'s. His doctor was also his younger sister, Dr. Dorothy Whidbey, who told Sharon to keep her informed if his condition changed.

Half an hour later, Marilyn closed the door in the isolation room and shook her head at Sharon. "Dr. Handler called. Said to tell the doctor on-call to authorize the antibiotic drip. All the University's consultant services were terminated by St. Anthony's for budget reasons. He told *me* to find the kid another doctor. It's seven o'clock at night. Where am I going to come up with another pediatrician?"

"Dr. Cornell never mentioned being let go." Sharon placed a pillow under Larry's shoulders to allow his swelling head to loll back even farther.

"Neither did Dr. Whidbey," Marilyn said. "I doubt Charlie's sister wants anyone else to be called in to witness their family's problem child."

When St. Anthony's staff doctor came in, Sharon showed him how the boy's knee wouldn't relax after she bent it towards his stomach. His body was covered with a darkening inflammation.

"You're right," The small Indian doctor said on his way out. "It's spinal meningitis, advanced. Make him comfortable. There's nothing to be done at this late stage. I've got more than I can handle reassuring the mob outside their offspring haven't been infected."

After he left, Marilyn twisted the buttons on her tight uniform. "I'm not going to tell his parents Dr. Handler is not coming."

"I'll do it." Sharon knew the parents would be hysterical, but it was already too late. Even when the kid was given a spinal tap, his brain would be far beyond damaged.

"Wait a half-hour," Marilyn ordered.

"He'll be dead by then. I'll take his parents to the chapel to pray. Maybe they'll be better prepared."

Marilyn agreed. "At least they'll be spared the anguish of scurrying around hopelessly trying to find help."

Sharon returned to Larry Schneider's bedside after she had seen to settling the parents as best she could. "I prayed for his early release to death."

The two nurses waited together then, keeping the boy clean from the vomit and diarrhea. When Larry's suffering seemed unbearable, Marilyn asked Sharon to check on Charlie Klondike for her.

Before she left, Sharon saw Marilyn preparing to give the writhing child a large dose of morphine. She knew Marilyn would lose her nursing position at St. Anthony's Hospital for the infraction. Dr. Handler might create a position for her at the University hospital to cover up his part in the disaster. Nurses were always needed. Sharon planned to suggest Marilyn join the National Guard. She seemed tough enough. Sharon didn't know who to blame more, Dr. Handler or Marilyn Helms, but murder had been committed.

Later, a doctor drained Larry's spine. Only then did the hospital release the child's body to the funeral parlor. If they hadn't resorted to the cosmetic drains, the boy's swollen skin under his scalp, the fluids around his neck and tragic bloated face would *not* have permitted the parents to recognize their own child.

Sharon never discussed the fact those exact procedures might have saved the abandoned lad earlier. Marilyn agreed, Dr. Handler failed his Hippocratic Oaths, "to keep the good of the patient as the highest priority."

* * *

First Week of March, 2008
Interstate 94, Michigan

Eighteen years later after her stint in Iraq, Marilyn Helms reluctantly rolled down the window of her Ford Taurus. "My dog jumped on me."

"License." The short state trooper was all business.

Marilyn fished around her candy-bar stuffed purse to find the identification card. "Is it all right if I get out of the car to dump out my purse?"

The officer stepped back from the driver's door.

Marilyn deposited the contents of her bag onto the car's hood. "It's in here somewhere." She had purposefully left the door open and Rufus took advantage of the situation, hopping onto the roadway. "Oh, catch my dog!" she yelled.

The officer stood still, watchful of her movements. "Call him."

Marilyn did call him. She snickered inside, from the effect of the prescription diet pills or the knowledge her Irish setter appeared to be no threat. She'd rescued him from the Army's attack unit. Actually, they rescued each other, when she'd been dishonorably discharged and the dog was listed to be put down. Rufus sat at her side as she handed her license to the cop.

"I've been following you for two miles." The trooper scrutinized her reaction. "You're weaving all over the road. I need you to take a breath test."

"No problem." Marilyn had the misfortune of giggling. Rufus wagged his tail.

The officer frowned. "And that's funny because ...?"

"Nothing. Sorry." The irony of being able to pass the test for alcohol while still being high on diet pills amused Marilyn. She repacked her purse trying to suppress her laughter.

The officer moved closer and Rufus growled a warning. "Drugs?"

"Yep!" Marilyn laughed openly. "You can't touch me. They're prescribed."

"Hands on the car!" the officer cried, moving in to push her shoulders down.

But Marilyn possessed a concealed weapon. "Rufus, attack!"

Within a matter of seconds, the cop, gun drawn, was on his back on the pavement with Rufus' fangs at the ready on his neck. "Get this dog off me before I shoot him!"

"Rufus, sit."

The cop kept his gun on the dog. "Now put your hound in your car and climb into the back seat of the cruiser."

* * *

First Sunday in May, 2008
Adrian, Michigan

Marilyn Helms moved the sautéed chicken parts to the far corner of the salad buffet hoping the ravenous horde would fill their plates with raw vegetables before homing in on the good stuff. The next entrée table was heaped with roast beef and salmon roll-ups. The addicts attending the convent's recovery retreat would not starve to death. They treated Marilyn as if she were a part of their group. A tall woman commented that she, too, was a member of OA, Overeaters Anonymous.

Marilyn's knowledge of the various twelve-step programs was purely hearsay. She did, however, understand the need for a fix. Prescription diet pills alleviated her eating binges. She knew the first step of the twelve was a statement about believing in God. That would be a problem. Marilyn surmised from her nursing experience if there was a mastermind, He or She failed to protect the innocent from suffering. No sense believing in a cruel or uninterested God.

The smells from sliced onions and bacon in the heaps of German potato salad caused Marilyn's mammoth stomach to growl in protest.

Sister James Marine had instructed her to wait until everyone else had eaten before choosing her own food. It hardly seemed fair. Of course, since she was a kitchen helper serving out a community-service sentence, Marilyn couldn't complain. "Sister," Marilyn asked instead, "what does it mean to be free from the bondage of self?"

"We are free from the old self when we have a new sense of being in Christ." The good woman seemed to think Marilyn understood her mumbo jumbo.

Marilyn found it difficult to tell her honestly not a word in the answer penetrated her brain, nor did her soul embrace any meaning.

Rufus bumped into her leg. At least the Dominican nuns at St.

Anthony's allowed her Irish setter to accompany her. Dogs were sweeter to her than any man had been. Dr. Cornell had been the most considerate of the three doctors in her life. Now he was gone. Death was so inconvenient. At the start, Dr. Cornell was sixty, so she told him she was only twenty to secure his sympathy, guilt really. Self-reproach was an easy sell. Marilyn could teach telemarketers a thing or two about the lucrative benefits of guilt. Her own remorse lasted until she got angry enough to find a monetary solution for her job loss. She'd done all she knew how to do for the patients eightteen years earlier. All three of the doctors agreed with her, but now there were only two medical benefactors.

Marilyn scratched behind her dog's ears. She immediately checked to see if one of the sisters might ask her to change the bothersome plastic gloves, again. Rufus was her only friend. Of course, one had to look at a dog in the light of reality. Dogs, pets were all really parasites. If you didn't feed them, like if a person died and the pets were locked in the room, they would probably eat their owners, if need be. She didn't like the idea of anything gnawing on her bones. She stifled a laugh at herself, as if anyone could dig through her fat to find bones.

Rufus slept in the corridor outside Marilyn's room at the convent precisely for that reason. Her room was filled with a stash of food stolen from the sisters. Once, when she'd swiped a full box of chocolates off the reception desk, she was forced to consume the whole box sitting in one of the main floor bathroom stalls. The sisters washed their hands and speculated on what had happened to the candy. Marilyn left the empty box in the waste bin stuffed under a handy supply of used paper towels.

If boredom could kill a person, Marilyn knew she must be close to dying. Her knees ached. She knew without looking her ankles were swollen after standing around for an hour, waiting for the skinny old biddies to peck around the cafeteria's spread. Not one of them had an ounce of extra meat on their bones. Marilyn knew she could be as slim as any of them, some day. Some day soon if she could get out of the convent long enough to hit up the doctors for a few more prescription diet pills. Dr. Handler would require a visit, but Dr. Whidbey would phone in a prescription to Adrian. Mother Superior wouldn't need to know what the pills were for, confidentiality and all that.

As if evoked by her thoughts, Sister James Marine quietly reappeared next to the empty cash register. Marilyn had learned, unhappily, the guests paid for their rooms and food when they registered.

"Has Sally Bianco eaten?" Mother Superior asked.

"Which one is she?" All the short old women looked alike to Marilyn.

"White haired, sprightly. She's a detective from Ann Arbor. You might want to tell her your story about the St. Anthony's Hospital slip-up."

Marilyn tried to understand how Mother Superior pulled off looking so elegant, regal even. Her light blue blouse hung loosely over an ankle-length white linen skirt. Her short ash-blonde hair was tucked neatly behind her ears. Her bangs were not luxurious. No jewelry was in evidence, except for the cross, not even earrings. Her shoes were sensible sandals. Yet the gracefulness of her stance, walk and gestures made you wonder if a diamond-studded mother had raised her on a palatial estate. Marilyn nursed a comforting antithesis. Maybe Sister James Marine was the poised but estranged daughter of a mobster. "Mrs. Bianco won't be interested in something from way back in 1990."

"She might be. Didn't you say three patients died? Justice will be served."

As if summoned, Sally Bianco squinted at the food layout after acknowledging their presence with a nod. She placed a few cherry tomatoes, a boiled egg, and three pieces of Marilyn's coveted chicken on her plate before adding a salmon roll-up.

Marilyn compared her to Sister James Marine as the two women chatted. Mrs. Bianco was much older, but her frumpiness had nothing to do with age. She wore a navy-blue, shapeless sweatshirt over a pair of black jeans. Her sparse white hair sort of flew around her head. She walked in a fog. As if to recall herself to the real world, she would peer jerkily at objects like the table before setting her tray down with a bang, or her chair previous to moving it closer to the table. If you didn't know better, you would think she was either blind, or drunk.

Marilyn's own white kitchen outfit covered up quite a few temporary lumps of fat. The apron was a godsend. She didn't bother to tie the strings, so the wide bib and skirt hung straight down from her neck. She looked more like a nun than the sisters did in their modern clothes. She even folded her hands under the apron, resting them comfortably on her hungry stomach.

Mother Superior nudged her, affectionately. "Fill up your tray now and go join Mrs. Bianco."

* * *

Earlier on the First Sunday in May
Adrian Convent

The retreat began well enough for Sally Bianco. A lanky valet in a blinding white shirt and a green tie asked for her Honda's keys. Stiff blond spikes of hair enhanced his cherub face.

The convent's double oak doors encased etched and beveled glass panels. The entranceway's terrazzo floor welcomed Sally to St. Anthony's Convent. According to the convent's smiling guide, a defrocked Dominican sister, the large room to the left of the lobby served as a funeral parlor. The opposite room furnished with a mammoth table and high-backed chairs was the priests' dining room. Only the prettiest and youngest nuns served food to the priests. All that sort of thing changed in the Sixties, when reason allowed women a few rights even if they weren't deemed equal enough to join the priesthood.

The sleeping rooms in the new wing were as modern as the media station in the middle of the ancient conference room. The newly built church had the pews arranged in a semi-circle around a central altar. A library transformed the older edifice. Three sides of

The Recorder's Way

the old house of worship's balcony were tiered with bookshelves. Each wall on the main floor between the stained-glass windows held religious books. Attached ladders reached the uppermost shelves.

Sally's weekend retreat had promised peace and guidance. Five of the AA group of twenty admitted to receiving no particular message from their Higher Power during the careful stepping of the flagstones of the labyrinth's garden walk. The tour book said the path, patterned after one in Notre Dame Cathedral, represented a pilgrimage to Jerusalem.

Sally was more interested in the placement of purses and water bottles on the lawn and benches surrounding the labyrinth than any inspired chatter in her conscious mind. Each turn in the path required letting her purse become temporarily out of sight. Her years as a practicing detective resulted in a quandary, whether to trust in the honesty of her fellow travelers or to be discreetly aware of her belongings. The tyranny of her training negated the possibility of making any friendships among the attendees. Sally lost her struggle with the AA slogan, 'Trust to be trusted.'

After spending too much time and money in the gift shop, Sally hurried to her room to drop off her purchases of encouraging religious books. The digital clock above the dresser read '12:48.' She grabbed her keys and sprinted through the basement passages. The nuns might already be clearing away the retreat's luncheon.

"Just in time," Sister James Marine said, as Sally picked out a clean food tray.

"Time is the only terror in the world." She smiled at Mother

Superior. "I need to write a longer amends list before my time runs out."

The only waitress on duty smiled. A yellow hound sitting near the young woman's feet eyed Sally's progress down the food line. The server helpfully pulled the coffee urn toward Sally's cup. Black, bitter-smelling liquid bubbled out.

Sally was determined to make at least one acquaintance on her last day in the peaceful Adrian countryside. Getting older included friends dying off faster than she could replace them. In the seating area of the cafeteria, one luncheon straggler shared a table littered with dirty dishes on green and gray food trays. Sally waffled against her best intentions and chose a germ-free table near the window facing the labyrinth. As Sally set her luncheon tray down on the isolated table, the waitress from the buffet joined her with a tray positively overflowing with food.

"I'm Marilyn." She pulled a chair up and commanded her dog to sit behind her.

Sally refrained from gathering up her things and moving to another table. Here, obviously, was a member of Overeaters' Anonymous, forty pounds overweight, who needed a friendly chat. "What are your plans for the day?"

"Another drag." Marilyn shoved food into her mouth and began to chew.

"If Mother Superior agrees, would you like a drive in the country? Waterloo is a lovely stretch of woodlands north of I-94. The farmers gave the land to Roosevelt during the Depression to pay their taxes. They thought the lakes and hills un-farmable."

Marilyn's manners included waiting until her mouth was almost empty to ask, "Can Rufus come, too?"

"If you keep him on a leash. I think there are rules." Sally noticed Marilyn's formidable frown. "Waterloo stretches twenty miles long and eight miles wide. We might never find poor Rufus again if he takes after a rabbit or a deer."

Rufus heard his name and slunk from behind Marilyn's chair to nudge Sally's hand with his wet nose. Marilyn finished off the last of her roll-up sandwich in one chomp followed by the rest of her coffee. "Could we leave right after lunch? I could get out of cleaning up for once."

"Absolutely." Why shouldn't the poor girl get a break from her chores?

"Mother Superior told me you were a detective?" Sally nodded as Marilyn continued. "When I worked at the University Hospital in Ann Arbor, one of the doctors, who was a worse addict than me, told me a story about St. Anthony's Hospital. In 1990, there were three questionable deaths. Why do rich doctors get away with murder and I can't cross the street without getting arrested?"

"There is no statute of limitations on murder. Were the doctors from St. Anthony's or the university?"

"The university. They were consulting. St. Anthony's was trying to save money and stopped using them. After the patients died, the dippy guys were reinstated."

* * *

When Sally knocked on Mother Superior's office door, she hoped the nun wouldn't notice her mouth was watering from her zeal to question Marilyn about the suspected St. Anthony's Hospital murders. "The countryside is soothing. Waterloo is lovely this time of year. We'll be back by four o'clock."

"Weekends are hard on the live-in staff." Sister James Marine offered. "Could you pick up a few videos in town? I'll have someone return them on Monday."

Back in her room, Sally zipped up her hooded rain jacket before she dialed The Firm, the detective agency she still moonlighted for, hoping to reach Max or Helen. The phone rang too long. Sure enough, The Firm's answering machine pleaded for her message. Sally stalled coming up with the correct wording, hung up and dialed again. "I've found a case. St. Anthony's Hospital allowed three patients to die in 1990. See you tomorrow afternoon, about two. We need to find records of the deaths."

Chapter One

"A river of blood..." The Egyptian Plagues
Ann Arbor, 2008

First Monday in May

On the corner of Huron and Division, the smell of gasoline greeted Helen Costello each morning when she opened the front door of the detective agency because petrol fumes permeated the concrete walls of the converted service station. Helen's father, Andrew, greeted her at The Firm's reception desk. "Did your mother pick out your suit?"

Helen brushed her hip, letting her fingers linger on the red silk. "She thought I should wear something for spring."

They both noticed a silver Mercedes stop out front to deliver Helen's partner, Max Hunt. Helen caught a glimpse of the driver's shoulder-length blonde hair. Once inside, Max found it necessary to comment on Helen's clothing selection, too. "Isn't red for fall?"

"Pinks spring from a core of red." Andrew leafed through the appointment calendar.

"Mother said we should feel our blood thinning with the warmer weather."

Max scuffed his shoe on the carpeting. "Is that why the carpets are red, for all the blood-letting work we do?"

Andrew roared. "Egad! Not murder. Murder most foul!"

Helen pretended to strangle Max. The rims of his ears reddened. She let go of him, backing up to see if the stained-glass lamps had shed the rosy glow. No. Max's ears were definitely blushing. Helen changed the subject. "Two different groups of mothers in Burns Park were airing out their children."

"Like pillows." Andrew said.

"Beat them soundly, did they?" Max poured himself a cup of coffee.

"Never." Andrew said, seriously. "Never teach hitting."

Helen wished she could hide her reactions to Max's teasing under her hair. Instead, she touched her flaming cheeks. Yep, they were telling more than she intended. Max obviously wasn't interested in hearing about the darling babies she'd seen toddling down the sidewalk. The mothers were saints of patience as the children repeatedly examined some treasure on the sidewalk or in the neighbors' yards. Helen attempted to change the direction of the conversation, again. "Mother has an entire album of Ann Arbor's spring gardens."

"I was with her when she accosted the gardeners," Andrew said.

"What did they do to stop her?" Max asked. "Throw petals?"

"They concluded she was odd." Andrew smoothed down a message pad. "I tried to encourage her to join a garden club."

"Too much work?" Max asked.

Helen watched her father shake his head. "Let's get to work."

Her father's off-hand comments made Helen wonder for the hundredth time why she still lived at home. Truthfully, she couldn't imagine what would fill her mother's day if she didn't cook, clean, and fold laundry for her only child. Unlike Helen's gregarious father, her mother lived the friendless life of a shy hermit.

Nevertheless, Helen prayed each morning for the strength and courage to leave their home in Burns Park. When she drove her father's antique Oldsmobile to work, the pink-blossomed trees along the way triggered the thought. She was like a fledgling bird, not ready to be kicked out of the nest into some man's marital bed. She'd seen first-hand how unwise the leap could be. Four of her college acquaintances were already divorced.

Andrew grumbled into his coffee. "That persistent Sally Bianco left a cryptic message on Sunday. She acts like she owns the place."

"Don't start, Dad. She's promised to be on the look-out for new cases."

"Then why does she sputter about when I find work for you and Max?"

"Mrs. Bianco thinks our goal of serving justice with the truth is intrusive." Helen sounded like a schoolmarm to herself. "--except when there's a violent crime involved."

Max checked his grin in the mirror near the front door. "Is the voice of the turtle heard?"

Helen didn't comment on her partner's metaphor for truth.

They initiated the concept of an ideal detective agency in the throes of a coffee jag, while sitting in the basement of the espresso shop across the street from the University's School of Social Science. The agency would pursue the whole truth and nothing but the truth for their clients.

Max came up with the name "The Firm" to stand for the permanence and integrity clients would rely on.

Helen was fifteen years younger than Max, but they had graduated together. Max had returned to college after the first Iraq war. Neither of them wanted to assume the roles for which they'd trained. Eventually, as social workers, they were convinced they would be labeled as failed do-gooders. According to their shared value system, court-ordered social controls artificially manipulated marriages and intruded into the lives of innocent children.

Helen remembered the previous June's coffee-klatch at the agency's inception.

Max had pulled at the back of her tight curls. "Do you remember the cartoon with Tom Terrific?"

She had swatted his hand away. "I think my grandfather talked about his sidekick, Froggy, and his magic twanger."

Max drained caffeine from the biodegradable cup. "Wasn't Froggy with Buster Brown in a shoe commercial? Were you even walking when I was in high school?" He pulled her chair closer and whispered in her ear, "Didn't Tom Terrific save the day with his partner, Crusader Rabbit?"

Helen had scooted her chair back to its original position. "A rabbit is better than a cold-blooded frog."

She reminded herself Max liked her and claimed she was a smart cookie. They never dated, because his manners with women bordered on the obscene. She wondered what sort of woman his mother had been. He'd lost both parents before enlisting in the army.

The glamour of working as a snoop intrigued Helen. She understood Max entertained dreams of sexual conquests along with the thrill of the hunt for truth. Helen refused to delve into Max's bottomless pit of revenge resulting from his military service.

Helen's dad, an injured retired cop, sold them the abandoned gas station. The city had removed the tanks because of leakage problems; but didn't reimburse Mr. Costello for the cost of clean landfill and re-pavement. Helen believed she was repaying her dad for her expensive education by renting the place as The Firm's office. Andrew intended to spend his retirement providing The Firm with information from the authorities. And,because Max was a veteran, her father trusted him.

They couldn't get a better deal, Max agreed with Helen, an interest-free mortgage and an in-house expert. Within a month of start-up, five computers along the windowless back wall were running searches. Helen ordered the ferns and philodendrons for the side windows. Initially, she watered the plants with consummate care. When business picked up, her father took over the chore.

Helen once looked forward to hiring a secretary for female companionship. However, The Firm relied on a sophisticated answering machine, which triggered an overhead camera and a document scanner. Few of the first thirty people in the door refused to ink their fingers to provide basic information. Walk-in clients placed their social security and driver's license identification on the computer's copier. The process of intake also required disclosure of gun permits.

Both Helen's dad and Max agreed they would not handle a client if guns were involved. Helen's mother, Julia, did insist Andrew accompany Helen to a handgun range to wield the firepower she carried. For Helen, the time lost in the noisy practice was worth the security of the gun's weight in her briefcase.

Money rolled in faster than Helen and Max had ever dreamed. The Firm, with Andrew's help, connected a wealth of website data to reveal unreported income, outstanding warrants, and pending litigations in the lives of the subjects of investigations, as well as the agency's customers. Clients needed the wherewithal to afford $400-an-hour for The Firm's truth-finding services.

Helen replayed Sally Bianco's Sunday phone message for Max. "I've found a case. St. Anthony's Hospital allowed three patients to die in 1990. See you tomorrow afternoon, about two. We need to find records of the deaths."

Max shook his mop of dark curls at the machine. A wife would have reminded him a haircut was overdue.

Andrew pointed at Max's peace symbol, which hung on a string of rawhide over his red-and-black striped shirt. "Hey, did you two kids call each other to wear matching colors?"

"You don't own a change of uniform?" Max tugged at the

collar of Andrew's black suit.

"I do own a red tie."

Unlike the boys Helen had dated in college, Max's build reminded her of a dance-club's bouncer. But Max was not all brawn. His mind was razor keen when not dreaming about one of his consorts. Helen was surprised at the level of her interest. She trusted him about as far as she could throw him in his dealings with women. Max's moods swung from black depressions to teenage gushing, usually over his newest female conquests. Hardly steady husband material. Helen did realize women found his muscular body attractive.

Max met her eyes, then studied his watch. "Mrs. Bianco won't be here until after lunch?"

Andrew checked the appointment book. "I set up an appointment for you at ten, Max. A suit with a diamond stud in his red tie paid us a $10,000 retainer. Owns the Honda dealership. Name's Brent."

Max looked back at Helen. "Andrew, Helen and I prefer to be a team. We'll both take on Mr. Brent, won't we?"

Helen nodded. "Two for the price of one."

* * *

When the whiney-voiced Mr. Brent arrived, they didn't invite him up to Max's comfortable second-floor office of leather, mahogany and greenery. Instead, the stocky man stomped around the reception area. They did not offer him a drink to calm his obviously ragged nerves.

"Aren't you going to take notes?" Mr. Brent offered his pen to Max.

Max tapped his temple. "Your wife, I assume?"

"You're good." Mr. Brent opened his coat and sat down in one of the wingback chairs. He took out his handkerchief, looked at its snowy whiteness and replaced it unused in his inside pocket. "Anita isn't speaking to me these days. May I smoke?"

"I think Dad would fry us." Helen sat down in the chair perpendicular to Mr. Brent's, crossing her slim legs.

Smokeless, Mr. Brent continued, "She wants children and I … We haven't been having much luck. Now she wants to adopt brats." The man spread his palms face up on his knees. "Some other man's child?" He glanced briefly at Helen. "I talk to her. Ask her where she's been. If we can't just get along. She still allows me my marital rights, in bed. Even then, not a word. Nothing." He sighed. "You two are my only hope. I should ask her for a divorce, but the pre-nuptial agreement was very generous. I'm the only Honda dealer in Washtenaw County." He stood and buttoned his suit coat. "The marriage contract does have a clause negating the agreement in instances of infidelity."

Something about the tone of Mr. Brent's wheedling voice probably offended his wife, as it did Max. No one would want to prolong a conversation with the man. "Could you describe her?"

"I should have brought a picture." Mr. Brent furrowed his brow. "Her teeth are not opaque white." He pulled out his clean handkerchief, again. "Whiter than this. Bluer. Can teeth be blue?

Anyway, they're so white they shine. Anita never had them touched, you know - painted or bleached." Mr. Brent rubbed his finger over his closed upper lip. "Mine are permanently stained from tobacco."

"Besides her teeth?" Helen asked.

"Green eyes, orbs. Big irises in large eyes. She stares without blinking. Lots of tears. Nearly washes her face in tears." Mr. Brent smiled to himself. "Faucets really. I once asked her if she could cry on command. Anita denied it. I can't cry like that."

"How tall is she? Hair color?" Max stroked the rawhide string and then his peace symbol.

"A goddess. Taller than me." Mr. Brent shook his head. "I wish I could brainwash her. Take children out of the equation. At our dinner parties, she talks - even brags I give her anything she wants. I love being around her. A stylish woman. I've always been an elitist. What else is money for?"

Max wanted the creep out of the office. "Shall we call you when we find out anything?"

Helen escaped to the computer room.

"Sure, sure." Mr. Brent offered his hand to Max.

Max coughed into his own. "Have you been vaccinated for this latest fungus thing?"

"I'll wait to hear from you, before I contact a divorce lawyer."

When the door shut behind the unctuous man, Max wanted to open the windows, install an exhaust fan, spray room deodorizer around, something.

Max never imagined, after getting out of the army, life would be sweet again. While he was getting his degree, he ran around with his army buddies. Max had stopped drinking after a saloon waitress asked him if he thought he might end up like his friends. One of them died in a car crash and another was in a state-ordered recovery program. Max didn't need the stuff, and his newest girlfriend, Maybell, didn't drink.

Max had managed to instill enough respect in the street people in town to insure they wouldn't approach him for a handout when he accompanied a date. He stared them down if they came too close, or were stupid enough to speak. When he was alone, he paid them their due the way all affluent pedestrians ought to those who dwell in the street.

His present flame's skin was as milky as a lily-of-the-valley. Maybell's delicacy entranced him. He was content to let women paw him, but Maybell only looked at him. Her intelligent eyes dominated her features. They scoured the pit of his stomach. She was someone who made a man with his social skills feel humbled. He knew he would be willing to spend his whole life with her, but he couldn't touch her hand. He first ran across her at the City Club while he was chasing down another older woman in an investigation.

One cold Friday night when he refused to take comfort in wine or easily accessible women, Max decided to make his intentions known to Maybell. The pursuit of happiness was his due. After all, he put up with the indignities of the armed services to afford life and liberty. He needed a wife to crown his success at the detective agency. Everything else had been too easy. He relished the challenge of courting her, on her terms. He felt akin to mountain climbers making resolutions about the peaks they would reach. His highest aspiration was to show Maybell how much love he could bestow.

The watercolor classes Maybell attended every Thursday morning at the City Club had allowed Max easy access. He'd opened the door for her one morning and carried her things from the car the next week. He admired the leaning lighthouse picture she shared with him. He praised her astounding freedom of colors, the yellow skies, the pink lakes. After one class, Max asked her to go to lunch.

Maybell's table manners put him to shame. He endeavored to keep his feet under his side of the table, but the temptation to touch or bump her leg caused his feet to creep. Her perfume diverted his best intentions. His witticisms failed to elicit more than brief smiles. After he escaped the Club, he felt ridiculous. He pounded the steering wheel, trying to stop an insane urge to open his mouth and pant. He wanted Maybell's lingering scent to reach his innermost recesses.

The next week, Max asked Maybell why she didn't wear rings. The remark came out without forethought. The sight of her ringless hands made him deliriously happy. He doubted if he could have stopped the question from blurting out.

Maybell examined her manicured nails. "My hands swell in the night, and in the morning I can't remove my rings."

Her hands were as perfect as a model's, as far as Max was concerned. He wondered if the painting caused them to swell from overwork.

She lifted the heavy lids of her magnificent eyes. "I wear bracelets instead."

Max planned to immediately purchase her every available round piece of jewelry in the world. "Is one of those made of ivory?"

Maybell blushed. "I know ivory is illegal, but I think this is an antique."

Max wanted to stop her embarrassment. Who was he to cause her any discomfort? In the next breath, it was out. "Will you marry me?"

She laughed, heartily. Tears came to her eyes. She used her napkin to hush her hysterics, but she never stopped looking into his eyes.

As Max watched the mirthful tears roll down Maybell's cheeks, he thought all was lost.

She patted his hand. "Would you like any of my watercolors?"

"Could I have all of them?"

In the parking lot, to say good-bye, Maybell stretched up on the toes of her classy shoes to plant a warm kiss on his hot lips. She pulled the back of his hair, and Max lost all semblance of order. He engulfed her slenderness against him, kissed her with his mouth shut. He held her beautiful face in his hands until she opened her eyes. "When will you marry me?"

"Some day," she said without the laughter, but with the tears. "Some day, soon."

Max was so besotted with Maybell he thought he could, even now, smell her essence in the reception area of The Firm. "Helen?"

he yelled.

The clock behind him chimed one o'clock.

Helen emerged from the computer room. "Dad wants us to visit Mother. Big case in the works. Twenty thousand to find out the background of a young man, who just happens to want to marry into the rich Clapton family."

Andrew followed Helen into the reception area. "Your mother knows Mrs. Clapton." Max didn't enjoy Andrew's lurid wink. "So did I, before I met my wife, Julia."

***

In the Costello's immaculate living room, Helen Costello's mother pumped Mrs. Clapton for information about the future groom.

Mrs. Clapton smiled endlessly at Max, as if modeling for a toothpaste commercial.

In the dining room, Helen paged through stacks of bridal magazines with the daughter of her mother's high-school acquaintance. The younger women faced the living room, where their mothers were talking with Max.

The matrons in matching chairs on each side of the fireplace faced Max whose largeness was distributed across most of the love seat's cushions. He resembled an over-sized teddy bear come to tea with delicate china dolls. Helen searched her mother's face. Julia Costello's hands were steady as she handed the delicate china cup-and-saucer to Max and the toothy Mrs. Clapton.

No speck of dust, no newspapers, shoes or sweaters were

allowed to rest in her mother's house, especially not in the white-carpeted dining room and visitors' parlor. Even the family room's shiny wood floors brooked no mess for long. The fireplace tiles sparkled a day after a cozy fire as they had the day before. Every stray item was returned to its proper place, and every inappropriate emotion hidden. The only time Helen heard her father complain about her mother's compulsive cleaning was when she threw away notices for plays and concerts as she opened the mail.

Julia Costello *did* allow storage of important items. All of Helen's prom dresses were cleaned and kept in individual hanging fabric bags. However, after each style season, Helen was required to justify why each piece of clothing in her closet and dresser drawers should be kept for the following year. If her mother couldn't remember seeing her wear a particular outfit, the entire ensemble was sent to Purple Heart, as were books which would not be read a second time.

The work of constant upkeep occurred whenever Helen and her father were out of the house. Nevertheless, Helen recognized the sustained effort housekeeping, or homemaking required. The paraphernalia necessary to embark on a single life even in an apartment boggled her mind. Raising children couldn't be contemplated because of the sheer enormity of the work involved. Supposedly, children just happened to most people as if caught unaware as a hurricane or tornado approached their lives.

If Helen moved out of her parents' home, where would she store her collection of dollhouses? The twenty-five diminutive homes decorated in furniture spanning decades from the 15th through the 21st centuries, lined her bedroom walls and the upstairs hallways. She would need an extra bedroom for the multitude of miniature abodes. Helen spent an inordinate amount of time justifying her present status as an unmarried daughter satisfactorily living at home.

Her mother entertained not at all. Except for church functions, Julia Costello didn't keep up with people in town. No grandparents on either side of the family, no aunts or uncles added to their small family. For a detective, Helen realized she knew nothing about the cause of her mother's social isolation. Maybe she'd been raised to be a recluse, too.

Helen asked Mrs. Clapton's daughter, Millicent, "A June wedding?"

Millicent rubbed her reddening nose. "A year from now. Mother insists you will take that long to secure a man's background."

"Is his family questionable?"

"I don't know." Millicent sniffed. "He's so beautiful!" She lowered her eyes to whisper, "I'd like to lick the sweat off his back." She straightened in her chair, rubbing her palms down the thighs of her slacks. "He plays tennis at the club. Swims there too."

"Millicent," pink-haired Mrs. Clapton called. "Come join us."

Before Helen replenished the tea service with more cucumber sandwiches, she wondered who she should inform the girl was in lust, not love.

Instead, she heard Max tell Mrs. Clapton, "We provide a

wealth of information for our clients. I assume there is one subject you are concerned about?"

"The usual. Business dealings, family connections, habits." Mrs. Clapton ate another sandwich, before adding, "That sort of thing."

"Is he non-communicative?" Helen's mother asked.

"Oh, it isn't that!" Millicent interrupted.

"I've informed Millicent." Mrs. Clapton looked adoringly at her somewhat ugly daughter. "It's best not to encourage a man one knows so little about. For instance, Helen, did you know I dated your father, before he caught sight of your mother?"

Millicent dropped her eyes and spoke softly. "George Clemmons doesn't yet know I'm interested."

Julia Costello spilled her tea onto the immaculate white carpeting.

***

Later the same afternoon, Helen explained to her father, "Mother says we should return the check."

Andrew shook his head. "George Clemmons? His son, no doubt."

Max moodily flicked paperclips into a wastebasket across the room. "Didn't we say there would be cases we didn't need? Andrew, is it three o'clock? Should I call Sally Bianco at home?"

"You dated that mean Mrs. Clapton." Helen could see why her father had ended any contact with the vindictive woman. "Give her another hour, Max. Sally doesn't move that fast anymore."

Andrew nodded sheepishly, waving his hands as if his opinions were of no consequence.

Max changed the subject by plowing his own field. "Why can't I stand that creep? What's his name? Brent? Do I feel sorry for his wife?" He tossed another paper clip. It bounced off the wall into the plastic basket. "Why does Brent act like he purchased his wife at a dime store?"

"Dime stores don't exist, never did as far as I know." Andrew shook his head. "You said you wouldn't take cases involving gun-packing clients. I never agreed to judge who else could or could not be investigated. You kids aren't going to stay in business long with this attitude. What are we going to do? Hand back $30,000?"

Helen felt she should take off her shoes or wash her hands. A shower would help. "I know we owe you money, Dad."

"Andrew," he said.

"Why worry your dad about a guy we don't even know?"

"It's not like you know Mrs. Brent." Guilty about sparring with Max, Helen asked, "What's her Christian name?"

"Anita Brent, isn't it?" Max shook his head at the distasteful tasks they'd undertaken.

For the first time, Helen experienced a profound sympathy for her partner. They had not agreed to start The Firm to get rich. "The Truth." Helen was surprised to hear herself say the two words aloud. Max turned in her direction and shrugged. Helen walked toward the computer chair he was sitting in. She hadn't repeated their motto to nag him. "We never knew recording the truth would be this sticky."

"Gruesome? Were we idealists?" Max reached out his hand as she passed behind him.

When she touched his huge hand, he gripped hers. The warmth of his hand, or the meaning of the gesture, softened her heart, even more. Helen quickly withdrew her hand.

Max swung his chair towards her. "Did you know cats pull away when they want to be petted?"

"George Clemmons." Andrew interrupted their interplay. "I remember now. Your mother dated him big-time, before I got in the picture."

"I wondered why she was upset." Actually, Helen's mother refused to discuss the Claptons' visit or George Clemmons, the younger.

"Mrs. Clapton knows they dated." Andrew positioned his chair to start searching the Web. "I always thought I broke your mother's engagement with George." He spoke over his shoulder to Helen. "Don't bother your mother anymore about the guy."

"Okay." Helen felt unaccountably worried. "Mrs. Clapton gave me a creepy feeling." Her father wasn't listening so she addressed Max. "Didn't she act gleeful?"

Andrew turned in the swivel chair to face them. "Promise."

"We'll find out all we need to know," Max said, "with your expert help."

"Here's his address and phone. Good luck." Andrew pushed in his chair. "I'm going to talk to your mother about the check … and George."

When they were alone in the huge computer room, Helen remembered Sally Bianco's comment about their naive reason for starting The Firm. "We're both recorders of the truth; but Sally said the third recorder's way of handling the truth was superior to ours. She meant God's way of life."

Max stood up to leave. "Well if we take the Clapton case which you don't relish, I guess we need to drive over to Anita's house, too?"

"Drive?" As long as Helen had known Max, she had never seen him drive his yellow Mustang convertible. Some gorgeous woman was always at his disposal. Not the same woman. Lots of them. All about Helen's age or younger. Andrew had commented the stupid ones seemed younger than they actually were. Helen agreed. Some of the women's faces were unlined because they never entertained a serious thought.

After one of Max's women started stalking him, he suggested wooden shutters on the front windows to keep down the utility bills. Helen thought the shutters helped him stay out of trouble with his entourage. Max installed fake greenery in the plant hangers and lined the reception area walls with law books. He added a bar enclosed in a roll-top desk. Dark green wingback chairs, an antique pendulum clock, and standing brass light fixtures changed the reception area from a technological nightmare into a set ready for Sherlock Holmes's entrance.

Max shoved his hands into his pockets. "Did you think I couldn't drive? Having a woman chauffer me around wasn't good cover?"

"More of a way to entice them under the covers."

Max sat back down. "Wasn't there some bed-hopping in your own family?"

Helen tsk'd. "Dad says most people were promiscuous in the Sixties because of the birth-control pill. When AIDS came onto the scene, everything went back to the romantic Fifties."

"You don't believe that, do you?" Max scratched his head. Max's voice dropped an octave. He seemed to be speaking to himself. Helen needed to lean forward to hear each word. "Aren't times more romantic now? Isn't that why Maybell and I spend most of our time together talking about the future?" Max turned his attention back to Helen. "Are we following our hearts right over a cliff?"

Chapter Two

"...raining frogs and the dust turned to lice..."
The Egyptian Plagues

First Monday in May
Ann Arbor

George Clemmons was not going to be a problem. Max and Helen followed him from his home into a coffee shop on West Stadium and Packard. The different blends of coffee filled the small shop with a rich variety of coffee aromas. Max asked, "Could we get a caffeine high by breathing too deeply?"

When George noticed Helen standing behind him, he fell all over her. "You're Helen Costello, aren't you?"

"How did you know?" Max asked.

A warm wind from the brewing coffee machines or George's inappropriate enthusiasm made Helen's cheeks flush. She needed to get out more; stop copying her mother's isolating behavior.

"Mrs. Clapton pointed you out to me last week at St. Andrew's church." George paid for the three coffees. "We need to talk."

Helen was lost for words. Max guided them to a corner table. Helen seated herself with as much dignity as she could and waited for George to continue. Something about him seemed familiar. Ann

Arbor faces meshed together after seeing people again and again. He said he was a churchgoer. George was good looking, so she smiled as he patted her hand.

"You're my half-sister," he said.

"Am not." Helen sounded like a six-year-old in an argument she couldn't win.

"Mrs. Clapton assures me your mother was pregnant when she married Mr. Costello."

"She was not."

"Your mother was engaged to my father before she met your stepdad."

"Her father," Max insisted.

George leaned back as if to get a better picture of Helen. Helen touched her hair. It did match George's sandy color. "Mother would have said something, when we took the case."

"What case?"

"Never mind, I'm Max Hunt."

George shook Max's hand. "How tall are you?"

Max grunted. "Tall enough for all practical purposes."

Helen finished her coffee, wondering if the caffeine would help her swimming thoughts come to any conclusion. "How old are you?"

"Twenty." George smiled at her, again. "You?"

"Twenty-two." Helen felt the doors of her lonely world open a crack. "Is your dad still alive?"

"No. But my mother is."

The Recorder's Way

"Do you live at home?" Max asked.

"No." George said the word as if that would be unseemly for a young man of twenty.

"I do." Helen wondered if she would ever say those two words in an environment a little more pompous than a coffee house ... like in a flower-filled church, when she wouldn't ever return to her mother's house, where she could start to really plan on how many children she wanted in her own home, where the world would open up to an infinity of possibilities.

"I haven't told my mother that I was going to seek you out," George said. "Only Mrs. Clapton knows."

"And my mother." Helen felt like weeping for her mother. That evil, grinning Mrs. Clapton's need for revenge might open a fissure of shame between Helen and her mother. All this high-minded talk about letting everyone live with the truth didn't take into account the injuries encountered. The truth could descend on a peaceful family like a swarm of flies or ants at a picnic. There was no telling what might be ruined.

"How would your mother know we would meet?" George asked. "Don't cry."

Max offered Helen his handkerchief. He glared at George. "See the havoc you've wreaked?"

Their combined sympathy released more of Helen's tears. "Mrs. Clapton mentioned your name in front of my mother." Helen felt she was being too cagey to what might be a family member. "Have you met Millicent?"

"Her scrawny daughter?"

"Did you know Millicent is quite interested in you?" Max asked.

"She plans to marry you a year from now." Helen dried her eyes. "I helped pick out a bridal dress for her."

"I've never said a word to the child. Mrs. Clapton sought me out at my father's investment firm."

Max pulled out their business card. "The Firm," didn't enlighten George. Helen turned the card over so George could read the words. George shook his head. "He that knows least commonly presumes most." Too much cream in his coffee, Helen could see the caffeine had been neutralized in George's brain. Max spelled the truth out for him. "Mrs. Clapton hired us to find out if you were a suitable groom for Millicent."

Helen added, "I think her motives were more vindictive. My father dated her in high school. Now, after all these years, she's found a way to get even with my mother by shaming her. Max and I are partners in a detective agency."

* * *

The Day Before, which was the First Sunday in May
Waterloo Recreation Area

Rufus, the yellow Irish setter, was making a sloppy mess of the back seat in Sally Bianco's Honda. Marilyn spread her bulk over the parking brake, as she handed her dog crumbling potato chips from the giant bag resting on her stomach's bulge.

Overeaters, Sally reminded herself, were as privy to the Twelve Step Program as alcoholics. "What step are you on in your program?"

Marilyn struggled with her seatbelt. "I have thirty more hours of community service at the convent. I'm on the first step. God's knows a drug addict's life is unmanageable."

"I've been sober five years, but I needed the retreat to keep me focused."

"Don't you ever graduate?" Marilyn grunted as she leaned forward to replace a gargantuan cup of diet-pop in the car's holder.

"I'll be an alcoholic the rest of my life, so I'll be a member of AA for that long, too." The outing up route M50 to Waterloo, just north of I-94, seemed longer than Sally anticipated. "Do you enjoy hiking in the woods?"

Marilyn remained intent on cramming food in her mouth. "I wish I had a fix right now. It's the only thing that keeps my weight down. How bad of a drunk were you?"

"Bad enough." Sally berated herself for inviting the girl for a ride in the country. Marilyn didn't seem the type of person to keep confidences. Sally had wanted to take home at least one acquaintance from the recovery retreat. Being magnanimous probably was not a humble enough stance to fit into God's plan. "Do you have a sponsor?"

"Sister James Marine said she would sponsor me."

"Was Mother Superior an addict?"

"Of course not. Didn't you experience her aura of peace?"

"Your sponsor should be someone familiar with the nature of addictive diseases as well as its spiritual program. How long have you been sober?"

"Three weeks. No one is more spiritual than Mother Superior. I think she floats instead of walking." Marilyn laughed and Rufus barked.

In Chelsea, Sally exited M50 taking I-94 to Pierce Road. At the road's dead-end, she turned west on the gravel road winding through the state-owned forest. She slowed the car to a crawl past a hunter's blind on the passenger side of the car, but the field of winter wheat was nude of deer.

Rufus' ears pricked up. Sally hoped he wouldn't bark if they spotted any wildlife. The tree trunks were black from recent rains. Every so often Sally would spot the white petals of cottonwood seeming to float against the ungreen landscape. Marilyn remained unmoved by the obvious approach of spring. The rutted road skirted the gravel pit presenting a bird's-eye view of an extensive swamp lined with spring's offering of pussy-willow hedges.

Sally stopped the car and pointed across Marilyn's bulk. "Those sand-hill cranes nest here."

"They're the color of deer." Marilyn said. "Why aren't they afraid of cars?"

"No one is allowed to hunt them." Sally had plied the dirt roads to Seymour Road since 1969, the year she had deserted her tyrant of a first husband. Oaks, maples, dying elms and pines fought for turf in the deep ravines and rolling hills surrounding the numerous small lakes. The trees soothed her soul with century shadows of unconcern. She drew Marilyn's attention to the beauty. "God's glory."

"Wasted space." Marilyn dismissed the scenic drive between mouthfuls of potato chips.

Easing her Honda into the small picnic site near Mud Lake, Sally pushed down all the automatic window buttons down to listen to the birds singing their hearts out. A flock of Canadian geese flew over to splash, still squabbling, into the lake's blue expanse. "This place probably hasn't changed since before Native Americans camped here."

"Boring," Marilyn said.

Rufus was more appreciative. He licked the window frames as if trying to taste the birds or the beauty. Sally was disappointed this young stranger couldn't bring herself to enjoy the pleasures offered by nature. As they left the turnabout, they faced freshly planted fields revealing the earth's gentle slopes. Sally pointed to the village graveyard outside the line of trees. "My friend, Robert Koelz, is buried here. He ran a used bookshop in Jackson before alcohol killed him."

"Were any of your friends not alcoholics?"

Sally laughed. "Most of my new friends don't have drinking problems." She continued to drive toward the small town of Waterloo, a collection of houses around a gristmill's pond.

"Dr. Whidbey lives out here," Marilyn said. "Somewhere. I don't remember her exact address."

Sally heard the change of tone in Marilyn's lie. "I tried to buy a parcel of land, years ago." Sally hoped she didn't appear too cagey. "Is Dr. Whidbey one of the doctors involved?"

"No. No." Marilyn grabbed her drink. "She's my addiction shrink."

Probably not. Sally decided not to directly pursue the subject. "I couldn't afford the forty grand they wanted for a lot the size of half a football field. Can you imagine?"

"Too far from civilization for me." Marilyn replaced her empty cup. "They probably can't even get cable out here, or a pizza delivered. I thought you said Rufus could walk around some lake?"

"Portage Lake." Sally thanked God in her heart. "We're almost there."

After they arrived, Sally watched Rufus trot down the Portage Lake path to his tall, sturdy owner. Marilyn scratched his ears.

Sally was tired of waltzing around the woods with Rufus interfering with every step. She repeated one of AA's 'Just for Today' slogans to herself to keep calm. "I will adjust myself to what is, and not try to adjust everything to my own desires. I will take my luck as it comes, and fit myself to it." At least, Sally smiled to herself, memorizing all the advice in the AA program kept her mind sharp.

Marilyn did not re-attach the leash on her dog. "I've kept in contact with two of the doctors."

"Why?" Sally had not lost interest in the case.

"The Bible. I memorized two verses in Ezekiel, Chapter 38,

'Thus saith the Lord God: It shall come to pass that at the same time shall things come into thy mind, and thou shalt think an evil thought. And thou shall say, I will go to them that are at rest, that dwell safely: to take a spoil, and to take a prey; to turn thine hand upon the desolate places and upon the people.'"

Sally wiped her eyes. Marilyn was standing with her back to the sun. Sally's cataract made her eyes water and caused Marilyn's face to appear black. Sally tilted her head to see better.

A flash in the woods, up the hill from where she stood, caught her attention. A large buck moved in the sunlight. Shimmering foliage draped his shoulders in a mirage of cottonwood flowers as he strutted away into brighter sun. Sally tried to point him out to Marilyn, who had finished quoting scripture to justify her immoral actions.

"My drug habit requires the doctors' prescriptions and financing." Marilyn placed one fat finger on her top lip. "Hush money, you know."

Sally took her car keys out of her pocket. She started back down the trail to her car. This trip was ended as far as she was concerned. Blackmailers were not endearing companions.

* * *

First Tuesday in May
The Firm

Helen opened her drenched umbrella once she was safely within the reception area of the office.

"Bad luck," her dad said, "to open an umbrella inside."

"It will get moldy, if I don't let it air out." Helen clapped her dad's shoulder as she passed behind the automated reception counter. "Any word from Sally Bianco?"

"None. Max is already here this morning."

Why Max was changing his habits? Arriving before noon, driving his own car. She knocked on his office door. Opened it to say good morning. "What's up?"

Max turned toward her. His handsome face seemed aged.

Emotions clamped Helen's throat shut. She quietly amended her question. "What's wrong?"

* * *

"What's going to be right, ever again?" Max struggled to get control of his face. His emotions were bouncing off the ceiling, caving in his chest. God help me? He hadn't prayed in earnest since he left the desert in Iraq.

The day before when they found Anita Brent wasn't home, Max had dropped Helen off at her home in Burns Park before he headed for his studio apartment. Next to the north-facing windows, Maybell was painting a yellow barn on a huge canvass. He couldn't help smiling at the silly lopsided thing.

She returned his grin. Max wondered why Anita's husband fixated on his wife's teeth. Maybell's couldn't be any whiter than the wife of the strange bloke. "How lucky was I to convince you to take a key to the place last month? Would you believe I think it's nice to have a woman around?"

Maybell wiped off a spot of yellow paint from her palm. Her bracelets jangled enticingly. "I thought we might hit the sheets again."

"Do you mean hit the deck?" Max was in no hurry. "Don't sailors say 'hit the deck?'" Maybe she'd fix a potpie for supper again. Not only was she a blonde doll, she cooked.

"I thought you were in the army." Maybell had a way of sidling up to him leaving Max without any defenses.

After Maybell had worn him out and served him a cup of soup in bed, she let him know her big news. "I passed the pregnancy test this morning."

Max sat up too quickly. Tomato soup spilled on the sheets. Maybe the news made his hand shake. He placed the offending cup on the bedside table, then pulled her down next to him. But, Maybell sat up and swung her knees over the edge of the bed. She wiggled her green painted toenails. Max wrapped his arms around her small waist to steady himself. He nudged his head into her lap. She ran her fingers through his curls and looked down at his upturned face. So, he asked, "Now we have to move up our wedding date?"

"I thought you knew." When she cradled his ears, her bracelets clanked.

"Knew what?" Max asked, wanting to nuzzle her breasts again.

"I'm already married."

Max moved his head to the pillow at the head of the bed. No rings, repeated over and over in his awe-struck brain. Maybell snuggled beside him. Max tried to calm down, rationalize the effects of this new reality. She was temporarily married. "Divorces don't take long, do they?" Something was terribly wrong here. Evil, disloyal thoughts tempted him. "Why don't you wear rings? Didn't you say your hands swelled?"

"A lie." She nodded, as the truth swept over him.

"The baby?" Max didn't recognize his voice. He felt as if he'd been punched out. The feeling was similar to shocks of noise and blasts from shells falling too close. He rubbed his stinging eyes from Iraq's thrown sand.

"The baby," Maybell was saying, "needs a good home. My husband can provide everything." She smiled again, licking her glistening teeth. "He'll think it's his. You don't want to make trouble."

Max placed his hands over his head, pushing them hard against the wall. He had never struck a woman in his life. Not like his father. "Didn't you know I loved you?" He heard the pitiful whine in his voice. Max remembered the client, Mr. Brent, with the diamond stud in his red tie. Mr. Brent's voice pleaded in that same sickening, unmanly pitch.

"That's what makes it so nice." Maybell knelt astride him. "I'll be raising our love child."

Max's mind couldn't take it all in. His crowning glory, the beautiful lover he intended to make a permanent joy in his life, tricked him into fathering a child for another man. She used him the way he used women. She didn't care if the rest of his life was ruined.

She got what she wanted: a child and all the money she needed from her husband. Max couldn't recall what color Mr. Brent said his wife's hair was. "Anita?" he asked.

"Yes," she responded from somewhere near his hip.

* * *

At the firm, Helen moved quietly to stand behind Max's desk chair. She stroked his hair. "Maybell?" She watched the six-foot-five, iron man who only yesterday adhered to romantic principles, dissolve into a broken-hearted boy.

"Gone?" Max asked, with despair in his tone. A surge of anger or pride straightened his spine. "Gone, with my child in her belly?"

Helen felt her knees give way. Max swung the chair around in time to catch her from falling. He embraced her, drew her to his lap. Helen kissed the side of his cheek. "I'm so sorry."

Max briskly pushed her to a standing position. "What did *you* do? Can't you see, I'm the idiot?"

"She's wrong to use you."

"Sound like any jerk you knew in the past?"

"But you've changed." Helen wanted to keep alive the sweet, openhearted man who only yesterday made her sound cynical in comparison to his dreams.

"Can people really change?" Max pounded the arms of his chair with his fists.

Helen retreated to the business side of his desk. She dropped into the nearest client chair. "Emotions are so exhausting."

Max nodded agreement. They sat together quietly, not

speaking, somehow in tune with each other. "Will you tell me I'll get over her?" He didn't sound convinced. "Should I have known when I thought I smelled her perfume in the office, that first day? Do we need to return Mr. Brent's money?" Helen tilted her head to question the connection. "You think I'm much of a detective? Didn't her husband describe her teeth, eyes, tears, that she wanted a baby? Did I want to remain blind to everything? Can't you see Maybell's first name is Anita, the last is Brent?"

"Maybell drove a Mercedes." Too much information lacked time to process in Helen's brain. "Isn't Brent the Honda dealer?"

"I guess a Honda wasn't good enough for the likes of her?"

"Oh, Max." An explosion of contradictions rocked Helen's brain. "If you return the money, won't he suspect something's wrong?"

"Should I wait until Brent calls off the investigation?" Max ran his fingers through his dark curls. "Would I be telling the whole truth by waiting?"

"What about your child?"

"How can I interfere when she asked me not to cause trouble?"

Helen wanted to hold his giant head against her, make the whole problem disappear. "You love her enough to give up your parental rights?"

"Didn't God ask as much of Abraham?" Max lowered his head into his hands.

Helen moved around the desk again to rub Max's hunched shoulders. "God stayed Abraham's hand, Max. Pray about it. You could ask for a blood test after the child is born." She wanted to fix everything for Max, but Helen knew asking for God's will was a better idea. She did not want Max to waste time focusing on resentments against Maybell -- Anita. Helen stopped touching Max. Her inexperience and confusion about her own feelings and plans for him made her ill equipped to discuss Anita's wickedness. She returned to the client chair on the safe side of Max's desk. "We should get started on Sally's case."

Max sighed. "Do you think I'm acting like a wimp?"

Helen embraced him with her words. "Any woman would be proud to own that much emotion from a man."

"Love?" Max pronounced the word stoically, as if the question was carved on a moldy gravestone.

All Helen could offer him was Sally's new case. "Mrs. Bianco will wonder why we haven't pinned down any information by now. She should be popping in the door any minute."

Chapter Three

"A darkness that was felt…ashes turned to boils…"
The Egyptian Plagues

First Wednesday in May
The Firm

As Helen approached the front door of The Firm, she was surprised at her eagerness to talk about her half-brother. Max had been too upset about Anita for her to mention her concerns. Once inside however, she sought out her father instead of climbing the stairs to her partner's office. Andrew was busily scrolling through computer screens when Helen arrived. His back was to the entrance. Helen thought he'd heard her open the door; but when she touched his shoulder, she startled him.

He hit the minimize button for the screen. "Helen. Are you early?"

"What are you researching?" She kissed the side of her father's cheek.

Except for the act of producing a half-brother, George Clemmons Senior barely affected Helen's life. Andrew had shared each of her hours. He was there for each childish trauma and triumphant. Andrew fathered her. Helen thanked the Lord for

Andrew, her mother's champion, her dear father.

"Sally Bianco's past." Andrew answered his daughter. "Thought I might find something to explain where she is. Her fourth husband was shot dead in front of her during an arson investigation in St. Charles, Illinois."

"That's her hometown. Captain Tedler gave Max and me details on three of Mrs. Bianco's cases when we asked for an employment reference. Two were arsons." After tucking her briefcase next to her computer desk, Helen poured herself a cup of coffee. "I met with George Clemmons. We're both blondes."

"Not surprising." Andrew limped over to the coffee pot for a refill. "Could any of the perpetrators in Sally's cases be released, to do her harm?"

"I remember one woman died in the fire she'd set. The man who shot her husband wasn't the arsonist, just crazy." Helen sipped the hot liquid. No odor accompanied the stale coffee. "A professor was killed by his common-law wife, who then died of a pill overdose. Their henchman is still in jail. A wife-beater killed his first wife. He's still in jail in Missouri." Helen carefully watched Andrew's reaction when she asked, "What did you and Mother agree I should do about George?"

"We think we should invite him to dinner." Andrew gave her a rare smile. "Maybe with Max? Now that Julia is convinced everyone knows about George, she seems relieved. Did she tell you she ordered a second-hand player piano? Needs it to entertain people when they come over. Been shopping for clothes. You're not going to believe it, she asked me to put the dishes in the dishwasher after you'd gone to bed."

"Mother?"

"She filled two boxes with her old clothes for Purple Heart. Bought two weeks worth of nightgowns. Says she's tired of doing laundry every week. The truth about George did her no harm. Far from it. She's acting like a new bride, learning to spread her wings."

"Not to fly away?"

Andrew shook his head. "To claim her own beauty."

Helen hugged his shoulders. "You love her."

"More every day. But I think you should pick-up after yourself now, make your own bed -- that sort of thing."

Thinking about the prospect of two strangers descending on her previously shy mother, Helen automatically made a fresh pot of coffee without firing one synapse for the process. "I'll go up and ask Max, then call George." After pouring two cups of coffee, she addressed her father's back. "Maybe Mother is looking forward to associating more with people. The truth didn't kill her, or us?"

Andrew swung his chair away from the computer before sitting down with his fresh cup of coffee. "If I'd known your mother was carrying you, I *still* would have asked her to marry me. George's grandmother refused to allow his father's marriage to Julia. It doesn't matter now. We're all civilized adults, Helen. Don't worry so much. Your mother has always owned a gracious heart."

"I'm glad she found you." Helen thought she might cry at the thought of never having had Andrew in her life. "No girl could ask for a more loving father."

"You're my best girl. Nothing's changed, except the Lord has seen fit to hand you a grown brother. You might need one to help you handle Max."

"I think you'll like George."

"Hey, he's part of you and your mother, isn't he?"

* * *

Upstairs, Max bestowed his best smile on the gift of coffee from Helen and accepted the invitation to dinner. "Do you think George will let me share him? I never enjoyed being an only child, did you?"

Helen felt rooted to the spot after she handed Max his coffee cup. If anything, she wanted to move closer. She realized for the first time Max never uttered a complete sentence. All his words were coached in tentative questions. "You want to share my brother?"

"Weren't you taught to go halves with the neighbor kids?" He punched her shoulder.

Helen could smell the soap he used from where she was standing. As easily as she had kissed her father she bent closer to kiss his cheek. But Max slipped his hand around her neck and drew her head down for a real kiss. She felt unwilling to move away from his lips, but blinked and took a step back.

"You don't kiss like a sister."

Helen slapped at his shoulder. "I believe I have just heard the first unqualified statement you ever made."

"Do you think it will be my last?"

She laughed at the ornery twinkle in his eyes.

* * *

Max studied Helen's changing behavor. She wore a soft blue sweater which complemented her coloring better than her red suit. Her slim body seemed tense, her hands clenched and unclenched. "What else is going on?" He rose and walked over to her. He stretched out his arms for a brotherly embrace. "We took on more than we could chew, asking for the whole truth from the universe, didn't we?"

Helen melted into his chest. "Sally Bianco was right. We should only invade people's privacy when a crime has been committed."

He touched her soft hair and patted her back, as if to burp any hurt away. She lifted her head and looked into his eyes. She seemed frightened, trembling. It seemed so natural. Max kissed her teary face.

Helen pushed him away. "Sally Bianco could be dead?"

"No. Sorry. I mean, kisses just happen, don't they?" Helen stood there wiping her mouth, brown eyes dilating. Neither of them noticed Andrew Costello turn away from the open office door. Max searched for a safe subject. "Should we listen to Sally's message again? Could we have missed anything?"

Max heard Helen sigh as she followed him down the stairs to the computer room. Max did not want to analyze what had just happened. They needed to find Sally Bianco before delving into their feelings about each other…whatever they might be. "Andrew?" Max called too urgently. "Do you want to listen to Sally's message again?"

"Sure," Andrew didn't look directly at either partner as he restarted the messages. "Helen, write down the phone number on the ID screen."

Max listened to the excitement in Sally's voice, as Helen wrote down the number. "I've found a case. St. Anthony's Hospital allowed three patients to die in 1990. See you tomorrow afternoon, about two. We need to find records of the deaths."

* * *

Sure enough, when they started to play back Mrs. Bianco's message, a phone number appeared on the small identity screen. After hitting the speakerphone button, Helen dialed the number. "St. Anthony's Retreat Center. Please dial one for the main reception desk."

Helen hung up. "She could have been at an AA retreat."

Max ran his fingers through his thick hair. "Don't AA people like to stay anonymous? They won't be able to tell us if she attended, will they?"

"Monday and this is already Wednesday." Helen pulled at her sweater's hem. "The convent in Adrian is run by Dominican nuns. The nuns will take our inquiry more seriously, if a male descends on them."

Max smiled halfheartedly. "Well, I proved I'm a man, haven't I?"

Helen's father gave her a questioning look. Helen had no

intention of commenting on the subject of fathering children. "Dad, while we are gone find someone at the police department to issue a warrant for St. Anthony's Hospital records."

As Helen put on her coat to leave, Max called, "Helen?"

She stopped, then turned around with her prepared let's-go-get-'em smile firmly in place.

"Is the convent connected to the hospital?" Max was pulling on his curls.

"We'll find out, won't we?" She realized she was mimicking Max's mode of communication. He certainly filled a room. She couldn't help wondering how tall his children might be.

* * *

Trip Ann Arbor to Adrian

Max barely remembered which roads led to the Adrian convent. He briefly considered finding a new apartment on the way and drove to the east side of town before heading south. Helen asked him where he was going. "Without Maybell, my studio on First Street doesn't seem habitable." He could engage a mover to pack up his belongings. In the meantime, he'd live in a motel and shop for changes of clothing at Briarwood Mall.

"Your lifestyle doesn't match the families in the enclaves of condominiums and gated communities on the outskirts of Ann Arbor."

Max nodded in agreement. He noticed Helen emphasized the word *families*. If they became a family, married, and had maybe five children, then they would fit into the newer affluent housing settlements. But for now thoughts of downtown Ann Arbor's busy pedestrian nightlife, with the sidewalk restaurant trade and street musicians swiftly negated thoughts of relocating. Home meant living near main campus with young people, summer festivals with street fairs, antique car shows, concerts, live theatre, movies. The non-stop cultural life of Ann Arbor was only blocks away from his apartment.

Helen asked, "Are you going to allow Maybell, Anita, to ruin your bachelor pad?"

Max grunted. "Of course, if I'd demanded to be married before being with her, nothing would have happened. No baby harvest while she was married to another man."

He remembered an aunt, his mother's sister, who helped him retain his sanity after his parents' violent deaths. "Aunt Rose Emery," Max said. He had lost touch with her after he joined the army to serve in Iraq.

"Where is your aunt?" Helen asked.

"When I was thirteen, my father committed suicide after killing my mother in a jealous rage. My aunt comforted me. I remember smelling her freshness, a baby-powder odor clung to her mourning dress. She said she could help."

Helen didn't comment.

"At that promise, I broke down, sobbed like a three-year-old." Max kept his eyes on the road. "Aunt Rose let me weep. Finally, she patted my back and told me, 'If you want to accept Jesus Christ as your Savior, he will take away all your pain.'"

"I didn't believe anyone could stop the raging feelings clenching my guts." Max looked over at Helen. "I remember hanging my head. It was hopeless."

'What do you have to lose?' She asked me and handed me her open Bible, saying, 'Read aloud Verse 16 of John's Third Chapter.'"

I blinked through tears to read the words of Jesus, which were printed in red ink. "For God so loved the world that he gave his only begotten son that whosoever believeth in him should not perish, but have everlasting life."

"You memorized the verse," Helen said.

"Aunt Rose asked me if I wanted to believe." Max kept his eyes on the traffic. "I remember asking her how. She tugged on my curls and told me she knew I trusted her. 'I'm not going to put bad food in front of you when you come to live with me and belief in our Savior will do you no harm. Try to accept the Lord into your heart.'"

"Words sprang from my grief, 'Lord, help me accept you as my Savior.'" Helen touched his arm. Max continued, "I remember Aunt Rose wept, while a feeling without end, as far as the ocean's reach, filled me with a warmth and unexplainable peace. 'Wow,' I said as I reached for Aunt Rose's hand out of thankfulness."

Suddenly to Max, the reality of a child in his future, his child, didn't feel like a disaster. "Now part of me is going to walk on the same earth I'm treading." He tried to shoot down his growing elation as he viewed freshly tilled earth on past both sides of the Mustang's windows. "The weather isn't warm enough to put the convertible top down."

The Recorder's Way

"Without catching pneumonia," Helen said as if in harmony to his mood change.

Keeping his eyes on Carpenter Road's two-lane traffic, Max touched the subject of his unborn child again, as if sucking on a sore tooth. "Helen, you could be right. After the baby is born, I could ask for a blood test … and parental rights of visitation. I'll never sign over adoption rights. My son, or maybe a beautiful daughter might live in Ann Arbor, go to school at the university."

Max stopped the car at a four-way stop, put on his emergency flashers, leaned over the wheel and wept for his lost dream of marriage. He hated women, all of them. He would never touch another woman for as long as he lived. That scared him. He looked over at Helen, who seemed confused by his changing emotions. He was not a homosexual, was he – all those army buddies? Helen recited the Lord's Prayer out loud.

Max allowed God's will to regain preeminence in his life. He asked for forgiveness for his transgressions as he forgave Anita-Maybell. He turned off the flashers and put the car in gear. He was not a homosexual, bless them all, and would eventually, no doubt, mate with a woman. 'Please God,' he prayed, silently. 'Don't let me be such a fool again. When I fall in love, I'll propose marriage and wait until after the wedding to consummate the marriage. I never want to be used by another woman."

"The Lord's rules make life more manageable," Helen said.

Max agreed. God's verdant landscape, a patchwork of color, stretched out before him, restoring hope into the recesses of his soul.

"I'm not going to move."

The rolling hills around Adrian welcomed their progress toward their destination. Max voiced a prayer of "Thank you, God, for the peace residing again in my soul."

"Amen," Helen chorused.

* * *

Helen wondered if she should confide in Max as freely as he had with her, before they reached Adrian. "I should tell you the dream I had last night."

"Was I in it?" Max seemed relaxed, comfortable with her.

"I don't think so. I was at a church service for children. Little boys in suits and girls in white flowered caps received, I think, their first communion. It was a little confusing, the way dreams always are. The children walked down the aisle in pairs, boy-and-girl couples. I think someone told me, or I was supposed to know, they were promising to marry each other when they grew up."

Max seemed to have trouble keeping his attention on the road. "They do that in India, don't they?"

"Ahh, but these children were American."

"Were you one of the children, Helen?"

"No." Helen remembered one of the little dream girls had let her wear her white flowered hat. Helen turned her head towards the passenger window so Max couldn't see her reddening face. "I'm not very mature for a woman of twenty-five."

"You're fine, Helen." Max patted her shoulder. "Maybe the dream was about missing your childhood with your new brother."

Helen forced a bright smile for Max. She knew better. The dream was her wish for a husband, someone like Dad, Andrew. Someone guaranteed to marry her. She regarded Max, the giant next to her. Would he ever think of her as the mother of his children; especially now that another woman was going to give birth to his first child. Helen intended to fight for all of Max's rights in regard to the child, who she might some day share in mothering. Max's child. Of course, she would want her own children, too. Maybe with Max. Hopefully, she wouldn't need to scour the land to find a husband. Surely the Lord would provide a man close at hand, like Max.

* * *

At the convent, Helen rang an old-fashioned library bell on the desk blocking access to the convents' central stairwell.

"Anybody here?" Max hadn't meant to raise his voice, but the marble corridors down each side hall from the stairs echoed with his deep tones. He turned back to ring the bell but his elbow knocked a vase of white lilacs to the floor, smashing the vase, spreading water and crushed flowers for yards.

Helen apologized to a lady who peeked her head around an office door. "Do you know where we might find Sally Bianco?"

"She hasn't returned." The woman moved toward them, calling back over her shoulder. "I'll take care of these people, Sister Alice. Could you clean up out here?" She extended her hand to Max and then Helen. "I'm Mother Superior, or you can call me: Sister James Marine."

Max settled on "Sister." He didn't feel comfortable calling

anyone Mother. Not because of the death of his own parents, but because the word was more of a swear word in the army. "Could I examine Mrs. Bianco's room?"

"Do you have a warrant?"

"Do we look like a policemen?" Helen asked.

Max smiled his best attempt at Cary Grant's famous grin. "Mrs. Bianco didn't tell you she uses our detective agency?"

"Uses?"

Max wiped the dead actor's grin off his face.

Helen opened her purse to present her detective license. "Sally Bianco left a message about a case and said we would see her in Ann Arbor on Monday."

"We haven't;" Max said. "When did you last speak to her?"

"I expected her at four on Sunday." Sister J. M. crossed her arms. "What day did she leave her message?"

Max reached for his notepad and pen. "Sunday, a little after one o'clock, why?"

"Right before they drove to Waterloo."

Max looked up from his note taking. "They? Waterloo?"

Sister J. M. seemed upset by his questions. She directed them back to her sparsely decorated office. "Sister Antoinette, you may leave the filing for later."

"Yes, Mother Superior." The ancient nun quietly closed the door behind her.

Sister J. M. noticed and got up to re-open the door.

"Could I do that for you, Sister?" Max supposed there must be a rule about being in a room with a man. The square room's ceiling was twice as high above them as the width of the room. He would need a ladder to touch the copper tiles.

"Mrs. Bianco offered to give Marilyn Helms and her dog an outing in Waterloo." Sister J. M. touched her throat above the securely buttoned blouse. "I should call the police."

"Don't you think so?" Helen said.

"Could you describe Marilyn?" Max was on point. "Was she attending the recovery retreat, too?"

"AA, means anonymous, you know." Sister reached for the phone. "However, Marilyn was working out a community service penance ... sentence, I mean."

"From what charge?" Helen asked.

"I'm not sure." Sister J. M. seemed to be weighing her options to tell the whole truth, or only part. "Marilyn is addicted to prescription drugs."

"How did she hook-up with Sally Bianco?" Max flipped a page in his notebook.

"My fault, I'm afraid. Marilyn is very resentful. One of her sources for the drugs died last year. Apparently, the doctor was involved in the death of patients at St. Anthony's Hospital. No connection with our convent. I told Marilyn that Sally Bianco was a detective and might be interested in her story."

"The doctor was writing her prescriptions?" Helen exchanged a glance with Max.

"Marilyn said he was an addict too, but yes, I think either that or he paid for the drugs."

Max felt his temper rise under his open collar. "You let an old woman take a drug addict for a drive to the woods?"

"You make it sound unconscionable." Sister J. M. started to twist the end of a lacy handkerchief. "They were all recovering addicts of some kind. Mrs. Bianco was going to bring a video back for the staff to enjoy on Sunday tonight."

Helen was letting her sympathy for the nun's predicament show by nodding.

Max held out his hand. "If you give me Sally Bianco's key, Sister Alice could show us the way?"

"Of course." Sister J. M. sniffed as she opened a small cabinet hanging on the wall behind her desk.

Helen saw fit to glare at him while the nun's back was turned.

Sister James Marine handed him the key and called in Sister Alice, who must have been waiting in the hall. "Show Mr. Hunt and Miss Costello to Sally Bianco's and Marilyn Helm's rooms."

Max and Helen stepped into the hall.

"Miss Costello," Sister J. M. called. "I remember there were three doctors involved with the three dead patients." She came around her desk and touched Max's arm. "Promise me you will keep me informed."

Max looked at her hand on his arm. He covered her small hand with his free hand. "When we find either of them, we'll let you know."

"Bless you," she said. "Bless you both and those you love."

The Recorder's Way

Max felt touched to the quick. Who did he love now Maybell, Anita, had tricked him? Only himself?

* * *

Mrs. Bianco's room at the convent was devoid of decoration. The modern ceiling nearly touched Max's head, which was quite a contrast from the Mother Superior's ancient office. Helen supposed all the rooms for visitors to the convent were identical: a telephone, but no television, computer or radio.

"Do you have a box to pack up Sally's and Marilyn's belongings?" Max asked. Sister Alice nodded and scooted off. "I hope she comes up with boxes without consulting Mother Superior. I'm glad you're here to deal with the fussy business." Max pulled out each drawer in the dresser and dumped the contents onto the bed.

Helen found Sally's journal in the bedside table. Helen worried about all the women at the convent, who had made decisions never to give birth, none. Nuns would never caress their own babies; never see them grow into the parents' image, never love a person who belonged, while growing up, entirely under their care. Helen prayed the Lord would see fit to grant her children of her own…all she could provide for. The responsibility for their souls seemed light compared to the wealth of comfort and love her children and husband would endow. "Please God," she prayed aloud.

"For what?" Max asked.

"Not to be a nun." Helen laughed.

"Never fear," Max said in a sexy voice that unnerved Helen.

Without commenting on the mess he'd made, Sister Alice

precisely folded Mrs. Bianco's belongings and packed them neatly into Sally's suitcase. Max filled a small box with the books, while Helen turned her attention back to Sally's journal.

The last entry, first Sunday in May, read, "List more amends." With an exclamation point, twice as large as the lettering, were the words, "Write down each of the sixty!"

"I liked her dog." Sister Alice interrupted Helen's speculations.

"Marilyn's dog?" Max asked. "What breed was he?"

"Beautiful and friendly, an Irish setter. Yellow." Sister Alice coughed. "Maybe he knew I'm Irish."

"The dog knew?" Max failed to hide his disdain.

Sister Alice lifted her prideful chin. "Rufus. That was his name." She left the room in a huff.

"I understand these sexless schmoos are all a little off kilter." Without sufficient reason, Max seemed to congratulate himself for being sexually active. Helen watched Max's shoulders slump when his memory of Maybell shot him down. Sister Alice returned with another box. With renewed respect in his tone, Max said. "I like dogs better than people, don't you?"

Sister Alice clapped her hands. "Oh yes! Don't repeat that to Mother Superior."

"Our little secret?" Helen said.

Max picked up the suitcase and knocked a framed tile sitting on the bedside table to the tiled floor. He tried to place the broken pieces back together like a jigsaw puzzle. The motto on the broken tile, *"Grant that I may seek to comfort, rather than to be comforted; to understand rather than to be understood; to love rather than to be loved."* "Can anyone keep that advice?" Max asked Sister Alice, who swept the pieces into a wastepaper basket.

"Just for today is even more difficult." Sister Alice smiled up at him.

Max acted like a chagrined bear in a very delicate glass house. Helen and Sister Alice followed Max as he toted the suitcase and boxes down to the reception desk. Then, Sister Alice guided them through a series of connecting poorly-lit tunnels under the convent and church to the back windowless, basement bedrooms of the hired help.

The room smelled of mildew and chocolate. The only light was a goose necked lamp on the bed. Marilyn's clothing gave away her size. "Big woman?" Max stated. "Under thirty?"

"You are good at this." Sister Alice actually cooed.

Among Marilyn's few belongings was a diet journal with scribbling in all the margins. Helen sat down on the squeaking bed to examine the book. A flea jumped onto Helen's arm. Helen leapt up. "Fleas," she cried.

Sister Alice screamed. "The dog must have slept in here sometimes. Marilyn said he laid down in the hall each night. Mother Superior will have a fit. Marilyn complained the food was giving her boils but I bet they were flea bites."

As the three of them stood in the hall, Max craned his neck to look over Helen's shoulder at the diet journal. "What are those, drawing in the margins?"

"That's Gregg shorthand," Sister Alice said. "My mother wanted me to be a secretary. I bet Marilyn's mother wanted her to be a stenographer, too." Max cocked his head to indicate he didn't understand her ramblings about mothers. "…So Marilyn became a nurse. You know," Sister Alice said. "Like I became a nun."

"Daughters often go against their mothers' wishes," Helen said.

"Is that right?" Max winked at her.

They had found no other reading material. Every available corner of the dresser and bookshelves had been stuffed with food. Tupperware packaged cookies and potato chips, tin cans filled with licorice and chocolates crammed the room.

Helen asked, "How long was Marilyn supposed to work here?"

"One month, 150 hours. For a five-hour day. She loved the grounds. Marilyn was always off somewhere with Rufus. We have a labyrinth, you know." Sister Alice chatted away as if talking didn't need an audience. "They were originally made to substitute for pilgrimages to Jerusalem. You know." Max nodded. "You know about the Holy City and the Crusaders?" Sister Alice duly regarded Max. "You're terrific."

Playing Tom Terrific to the hilt, Max winked at his crusader rabbit, Helen.

Helen understood why Marilyn took her first opportunity to escape the convent's boredom. She probably car-jacked Sally Bianco as soon as they were far enough away from the convent.

"Sally Bianco probably didn't have a chance against a very large drug-addict," Max said. "One, who obviously needed a fix."

Helen called her father on her cell phone. "Better give the police Sally's license number. I think she's in trouble."

Chapter Four

"...plagues upon thy heart, a pestilence..."
The Egyptian Plagues

First Wednesday in May
St. Anthony's Hospital

The basement of the St. Anthony Hospital was a maze of identical corridors to Helen. Was Max ready to give up?

"Let's call the records room from The Firm," he said. "We can ask for the files to be delivered."

Helen shook her head. "You're more effective in person."

She watched as Max let his vanity assess the compliment. "You should know."

The truth was she wanted to keep Max interested in the agency long enough to convince him she was the only woman necessary in his life. She stopped every second person in the sterile halls to ask directions to the file room. Eventually, they found the small reception area for seekers of patient files.

The basement room's walls were covered with cheerful prints by Gauguin. A horizontally placed mirror over the sliding window of the receptionist's desk let Max adjust his smile. Helen squinted to read the file clerk's name as she showed The Firm's credentials.

"Sharon, could we wait until you find the medical records for Larry Schneider?"

* * *

"Did you pack a lunch?" Sharon Daley crowed. Sharon thought her filing job was demeaning compared to her nursing career. If the doctors weren't lording it over you, some patient with a beef was willing to let you work all night to find a relevant file. Everyone wanted you to believe you would share in the financial rewards from damage settlements. Of course, Sharon was required to first produce enough facts to prosecute incompetent fools, like those with framed degrees littering their office walls. At least as a file clerk, there were no unpleasant bedpans to empty unlike her loftier years as a registered nurse.

Sharon re-read the request form. "The names of all patients who died between the time the University of Michigan consultants were terminated in 1990 and then reinstated." She knew the names too well.

Larry Schneider, the little boy, was the hardest death to witness. Her friend, Marilyn, went crazy because of it. Stupid drug addict. Sharon hadn't heard from her since her latest arrest. If the doctors hadn't been so ready to pay up to keep her quiet, Marilyn wouldn't have been able to afford her prescription drug habit.

Sharon scrutinized the couple in the waiting room. Helen Costello wore a pretty blue sweater. The big guy had flashed some sort of detective badge before they made themselves comfortable in the waiting room.

"Who started the investigation?" Sharon handed over the boy's file.

"I'm not at liberty to say." The curly-headed chick grabbed onto one end of the folder.

"If you tell me," Sharon promised, "I'll give you the name of a nurse I worked with on all three cases."

"Sally Bianco came up with the case," Max said, "during a retreat in Adrian with the same name as this hospital, St. Anthony."

Sharon caught her breath. "St. Anthony is the patron saint of lost people and things." Was she speaking to a friend or foe of Marilyn's. "My friend. Well we're not friends anymore, according to her. Anyway Marilyn Helms was doing community service in Adrian. She was arrested with too many prescription drugs in her car. They thought she was a drug pusher, which wasn't true. She needed every pill for herself. I told her lawyer, but he wouldn't let me take the stand. I'm sure Marilyn thought I didn't try hard enough to get her off. She did need help. I was hoping she would be put in a recovery center. She had worked off and on in Ann Arbor with the doctors involved in the cases. They supplied the prescriptions for her elephant of a drug habit." Sharon thought she might cry. "Looked pretty much like one, too."

Helen offered her a tissue from the desk. "Maybe Marilyn told Sally Bianco about the deaths in 1990."

"No." Sharon didn't think Marilyn would be that stupid. "I don't think so."

* * *

First Wednesday in May
The Firm

Max opened the door for Helen who ran into the back room. "We found one file at St. Anthony's Hospital."

Andrew held out his hand for the file as he smiled. "Now that's a good day's work, isn't it, Max?"

"What did the police say when you reported Sally as missing?" Max put his hand on Helen's shoulder.

Andrew reached for the phone, rested his hand on the handset. "I gave them her license number, RDS WAY." He shook his head. "They were more interested in decoding the plate's meaning than the fact that she could be missing."

"The Recorder's Way," Max said. Sally Bianco wasn't one of Max's favorite people, kind of preachy and cold at the same time; but he didn't want any harm to come to her on his watch. "Do they know she was investigating a case for us?"

Andrew rolled his eyes. "Not much of a case, so far. I told them we all thought she'd been the victim of a car-jacking."

"Captain Tedler was surely upset." Helen put her arm around her dad.

Max apologized. "Sorry, Andrew. I know you and Mrs. Costello are friends of Sally Bianco."

Andrew nodded unable to speak for a moment. "Let's look at the file."

"The file clerk, Sharon Daley, says a Marilyn Helms worked with her on the cases." Helen pointed to Marilyn's name in the file.

"Larry Schneider was only a boy when he died in the emergency room."

Max tugged on his curls. "I think the same Marilyn was doing community service at the convent. Sally invited her for a drive in Waterloo, according to the Mother Superior. They're both missing, now."

Helen said. "The nurses were both fired after the three deaths."

"Nurses don't hurt people, Andrew." Max wasn't as sure of his statement as he wanted to be but he wanted to relieve Andrew from any unnecessary worry."

"I've got to see Tedler," Andrew said.

Helen took a step toward Max as her father left. She slipped her arm around his waist. He knew she needed something or someone to hold onto. as if they were playing tag and Max was home base.

"We shouldn't get involved, with each other?" Max disengaged himself and sorted through the file Andrew had abandoned. "We shouldn't jump to conclusions about Sally either. Larry Schneider," he read. "Spinal meningitis was the cause of death?"

"Sharon said University of Michigan consultants were let go during a budget crisis at St. Anthony's Hospital."

"A Dr. Benjamin Handler signed the death certificate?"

"After the patients died, the doctors were reinstated." Helen's professionalism returned.

"In time to ward off any damage suits to the hospital?" Max

asked.

* * *

In the car, Andrew Costello rubbed his bum thigh. Whenever he needed to think, his leg acted up almost demanding his attention to painful subjects. He didn't want to talk to Tedler or Julia. He wanted to think. Helen and Max were no longer just friends. They were falling in love. He liked Max. The self-doubt Max exhibited reassured Andrew. The man owned a reflective soul. But was Helen, his daughter, his baby mature enough for marriage and children? Those dollhouses of hers, no one would want to marry a child. Raising one of your own was fine, but marriage required a mature mate.

Julia was such a treasure now. He felt his wife was showing him new aspects of her personality, more to love. The secret of Helen's birth father must have dogged every one of her steps, censured every thought. The deception had been a plaque on her heart. The truth had set her free of the pestilence. She no longer needed to place every fork directly on top of the next. She finally agreed after twenty-one years his tee shirts did not need to be ironed. The living room could appear lived in and they could afford to eat at restaurants as often as she liked. Their lovemaking was becoming a little more exploratory, healthy. Andrew smiled. He wondered if he should talk to Julia about Max and their daughter. So much was happening; maybe he'd wait until Julia came to him about their romance from her point of view. He'd try to act surprised.

* * *

The Day of the Crime, First Sunday in May
Portage Lake

Marilyn Helms walked her dog down to the boat ramp. His muzzle and fur were drenched in red. Finding several sticks, Marilyn threw them one at a time into Portage Lake until Rufus was immaculate. "Good dog," she said. "Time to go."

The Honda waited for them. The weather was beautiful. Rufus needed a long walk to calm him down from his little adventure. Marilyn re-attached the leash but let it run all the way out. She didn't feel like patting his ears. She would drive to Brighton for lunch, and keep going east. Easterners were easy to con. Once she was settled with her grandmother in Cape May, she could always phone Dr. Handler and Dr. Whidbey. They'd probably congratulate her for moving away.

She could start clean…free of her drug habit. Three weeks wasn't much sobriety, but maybe she wouldn't call the doctors. Penance enough for what? Maybe *not* for letting Rufus attack the old woman. What did the program say? First things first. First, Marilyn needed to survive.

That old hag would have seen her in prison quicker than jack snap for blackmailing the doctors. If she stayed clean, she wouldn't need to call the doctors for drug money. In addition, the long drive out east might slim her down enough not to need her perfect diet pills.

Rufus would be a problem. Marilyn called him and undid the leash. To let him know he could leave, she threw another stick into a fern covered ravine. Rufus bounded off. Marilyn wished she could feel as happy about her freedom.

As she started Sally's car, her mouth tasted bitter. The Mayapple leaves were making her feel sick. She reached for the half-empty bag of potato chips. As she sped up, Marilyn noticed Rufus in the rear-view mirror. He was standing in the middle of Seymour Road, with the stick she had thrown in his mouth. She didn't slow down, but it was comforting to think maybe the dog hadn't been a parasite after all. Maybe he had liked her, a little.

If Rufus was in the passenger seat, she would have told him whenever her collections exceeded her drug habit, she bought gold necklaces. They, the necklaces, were never around her neck for longer than two months. Something always set off a binge with its requirement to increase her stash of pills by hocking the gold.

The stupid policeman Rufus had jumped thought she sold pills. Idiot. She needed each one of the blamed things or would before she reached her ideal weight. She couldn't remember anymore what it used to be. Once 130, 150. At the rate she was going, 160 seemed her next reachable goal. The only reason she wasn't in jail was because Dr. Handler could out talk any buzzard of a cop or judge. He should have been a lawyer instead of a doctor. Wasn't much of a doctor anyway…and that was the truth!

When she first met Dr. Handler, he was always trying to impress her with some outlandish extravagance. Oh, they were never gifts for her. A cap from Scotland for himself, a sweater from Ireland, shoes from Italy. She kept track of the doctor's excesses in her diet book. Who gave a rat's ass? She didn't, as long as she got her share of his string of rich wives' money. The whole scam was a hoot, until she got stopped. Now she needed her grandmother's out-of-state pad to crash in.

* * *

First Thursday in May
The Firm

When Max first heard the knock on his office door, he thought Helen might want to persuade him to have Dr. Handler arrested. Max was still of the opinion they should wait until all three doctors' whereabouts were known. He didn't want any of the medical men to circumvent justice by fleeing the country. Instead, Andrew was at the door with Helen standing behind him. "What now?" Max asked. Andrew's face was all wrong. Max tried to lighten the mood. "Who died?"

"Sally." Helen spoke behind her father.

Max stood up. "Sorry. How do you know?"

Andrew collapsed into one of the client chairs. "A Waterloo ranger found her body."

"Should we go out there?" Max offered his arm to Helen, to help her into the other chair. Civilians were not accustomed to sudden death. As a veteran, Max's stoicism was won at a terrible cost. The sight of friends dropping dead in their tracks – right next to him, gained him a measure of detachment. His bout of post-traumatic stress disorder was not as severe as other veterans' cases because of the violent history of his parents' death.

Helen seemed to be moving into the chair in slow motion. Max's natural tendency to assist the weaker sex triggered his sexual response to her lithe body. His next thought was for his lost dream. Maybell's presence made a room glow with an unnatural brilliance. He grumbled to his soul. Fool, the whole set-up was a trap. You were the only one under any delusions of love. But, Max congratulated himself for his new self-honesty. He was not in love with Helen. He liked her, but she was not the girl he wanted as a life-mate.

Helen looked up at him and he stepped away. Women and their eyes. Helen's were dark for such a towhead. Dark and mysterious. Max returned to the commanding position of his tall-backed desk chair.

"You're right." Helen rose. "We need to view the scene."

Andrew was still seated. "You two go ahead. I've known Sally for too long. I need to call her friends. I'll wait for the funeral."

'Max followed Helen out of the office. "Should you wait a day before scheduling the funeral?" He spoke to Andrew over his shoulder, not wanting to lose sight of Helen. "Doesn't an autopsy take a couple days?"

Chapter Five

"...rain a grievous hail and fire ran along the ground...barley and flax destroyed. Wheat and rye were not smitten because they were not grown up." - The Egyptian Plagues

First Thursday in May
Waterloo

Helen eased herself out of Max's yellow Mustang. He had parked next to the ambulance at Portage Lake. A black and white State vehicle, a ranger's green car, and the county sheriff's police car were lined up along the boat launch. A perfect Michigan sky with a fresh breeze off the placid lake denied the quiet wooded area could be the scene of a vicious crime. Helen held onto Max's shirtsleeve. Learning that someone she knew personally was the victim of a crime was devastating. She wanted to keep her wits sharp to catch the perpetrator. Helen released her partner's sleeve. Max rubbed his arm and looked down at her sympathetically, as if ready to excuse her from their appointed task. "I can do this." She meant to reassure Max, but found the words helped her, too. She silently prayed, with God's help.

The attendant opened the back door of the ambulance. Helen prayed again for strength and climbed in, next to the body bag.

When she turned towards Max, she was surprised to see he was dealing with deep emotions, too.

* * *

Day of the Crime First <u>Sunday</u> in May
Waterloo

"Never enough time." With the smell of spring in the air, Sally's last words flew out of her shattered brain as her skull crashed against the rocks at the bottom of Portage Lake's thirty-foot cliff. Her eyes beheld the blue sky's portal to her afterlife.

* * *

First Thursday in May
Waterloo

Max was knocked for a loop when Helen stepped into the ambulance van. Her black skirt hiked up dangerously close to her bottom, high enough for him to receive a jolt of raw lust. God, deliver us from evil. He was not ashamed of praying. He could see Helen was wondering what kept him from climbing in behind her. Max commanded himself to pull his act together. He donned his inspection gloves.

Helen unzipped the body bag and leaned back from the shock and fishy odor. The victim's face, Sally Bianco's face, was chalk white and bloated. Sally's throat was torn out from her neck.

"Do we need to check her hands?" Max pulled the zipper down far enough to lift out Sally's right hand. The fingers were locked in a fist.

The attendant leaned forward. "Rigor mortis."

"I've seen this before, in the war?" Max kept his voice steady, as he pried Sally's fingers open. In the ball of her hand was a clump of wet hair. He removed the hair and bagged the evidence. "Could you give this to the state trooper in charge of the scene?"

The attendant nodded, as he watched Helen examine Sally's left hand. "She hung onto somebody." The kid sighed, accepting an identical offering of evidence from Helen.

"Could a dog do this?" Helen climbed out of the ambulance, with Max's help.

"You wouldn't believe how my army unit's attack dogs could make a mess of a man."

"Maybe rabies?"

"Wouldn't Mother Superior have noticed if anything was wrong with Marilyn's dog? Can you remind me to call the Sister about Mrs. Bianco?" Max walked over to the state trooper to ask about Sally's Honda.

As he stepped back after receiving an unenlightened answer, he almost knocked Helen to the ground. "Sorry." He caught her and let go of her as soon as she seemed steady. At least he managed to control his reactions to her closeness.

"I heard the trooper say there was an all points bulletin out for the car since Tuesday." Helen walked beside Max back to his car. "No witnesses. The dog would have been a mess."

"They think Mrs. Bianco was attacked up there." Max pointed

through a stand of oaks to a hill of trees surrounding that section of the lake.

"And pushed over the cliff? Did the dog fall with her, or let go?"

"They haven't found the dog, yet." Max noticed Helen was asking more questions than he was. "We may never know what really happened."

Max drove his convertible slowly back to Ann Arbor on Seymour Road to Pierce Road. He chose I-94 to drive into town. He couldn't control the workings of his mind. The questions about the death of his own parents would always remain unanswered.

Maybe that was why every word out of his mouth seemed to end in a question. If he could be sure of how they died. Did his mother suffer long when his father was strangling her? Did she weep for their lost love as he was killing her? Is that why he shot and killed himself? Was it remorse? Did God accept both their souls? Would he see them in eternity? Could he trust God enough to let go of his questioning nature? He wondered how his state of insecurity, his unsureness affected those around him. He promised to try to state only declarative statements.

Helen was sitting next to him quietly lost in her own thoughts, probably of the recent horror of seeing Mrs. Bianco's body.

Max wanted to comfort her, reassure her of his devotion to duty as her partner in the detective agency. "We need to work on Mrs. Bianco's case." He sounded like a repetitive parrot. "The evidence will tell us where Marilyn Helms can be found."

Helen rubbed her temples with her fingertips. "We didn't say we wouldn't take cases with deadly dogs."

Max stifled a laugh. "No, we didn't."

"It's a good thing people pay us outrageous retainers. No one will fund our work to find Sally's murderer."

"But it will be our priority."

"It will." Helen patted his shoulder.

Max was sure she wasn't aware of the effect her touch produced in his unprincipled body.

* * *

First Thursday in May
Costello Home

Max wasn't hungry, but he accepted Helen's invitation to share an evening meal with her family. He told himself they needed to review the case, but he was more interested in staying close to Helen until he could talk himself out of his attraction to her. Good business ethics demanded he *not* get involved with his partner, didn't they?

The garage door was open. Max followed Helen. She opened the door from the attached garage into the house. The kitchen aroma of cabbages and onions cooking in tomatoes sent him back to memories of his Aunt Rose's home. Max didn't want to think of his mother's family, or his father. He blamed most of his foolishness and stupidity on his dad's side of the family. After the drunken tragedy, his mother's sister provided refuge from the age of thirteen until he was sixteen.

She had signed the agreement that allowed him to join the Army. That's how he escaped the mess in Bloomington, Illinois. Half the people in town were afraid of him because of his violent father. The other half couldn't treat him like a normal kid because of their pity over the loss of his mother. He had been embarrassed, even felt guilty when he was lucky enough to find something to laugh about. Orphans were not supposed to laugh.

"Smells great." Max touched Mrs. Costello's shoulder.

She jumped a bit and blushed at her foolishness. "Max, Max. We never see you anymore. Now that you finished your degrees, you're both so busy at The Firm."

Max hugged her plump figure, thankful for her welcome.

Andrew came into the kitchen from the dining room. "Grab some plates from the cupboard. And, let go of my wife. We're about to sit down."

Helen had shed her suit jacket. Her silk blouse enhanced her full figure. Max's throat tightened, but he managed to say, "I don't think I'm hungry after our Portage Lake trip."

Helen nodded. When they were seated, Andrew said grace.

The dining-room windows faced the back garden of the house. Lilacs, apple blossoms, and redbud trees surrounded the lawn. Max relaxed. He thanked his Maker for the abounding beauty set before him. The soup was great. The bread seemed homemade. The carrots, potatoes, turnips and parsnips from the pot roast were spread out in separate serving dishes. Max noticed his hunger returned with each bite. He smiled at Helen. "Was I lying about not being hungry?"

"Julia's cooking always does that to me." Andrew lifted his water glass. "A toast, to the best cook in Ann Arbor."

"Andrew, stop that." Mrs. Costello blushed, but Max could see she was pleased. "Max might not enjoy my strawberry-rhubarb pie."

Max groaned. "Isn't that an unfair advantage? Shouldn't I know the menu, before I overindulge?"

"You'll find room." Helen nudged his shoulder as she took away his plate.

In response, Max almost reached out to grab Helen's leg, but stopped himself in time. That was all Andrew needed at his family's table, a letch for a guest. Max changed the subject to give his out-of-control body a break. "If we give the police our evidence for one doctor, the other might escape."

"I thought Sally Bianco said three doctors were involved." Andrew stirred his coffee.

"Mother Superior said Marilyn was upset because one of the doctors had died. Helen, you promised to call her when we found out what happened to Sally."

"No," Helen smiled at him. "You promised her."

Max's brain took a break to savor the flavors of the scrumptious pie. "Can she bake a cherry pie, Billy boy, Billy boy?"

"She can bake a cherry pie, quick as a cat can wink its eye," Julia Costello sang a phrase from the old song.

Helen ended the song. "She's a young thing and cannot leave her mother." Max noticed Helen's cheeks flame. Was she interested in him?

* * *

Helen sipped her coffee, hoping Max would think the caffeine affected her complexion. "We should tail Dr. Handler. You could interview him at his office while I check out his home. His mismanagement of the Schneider's case leaves few excuses."

The phone rang and her dad excused himself to answer it in the kitchen. When he returned, his company smile had vanished. "Hey, Max, Mr. Brent wants to call off the investigation of his wife. He said to keep the retainer." Andrew returned to his pie. "Seems they're expecting a baby."

Max lurched from the table. Helen pointed to the guest bathroom, near the front door. They could all hear him retching. "Weak stomach," Helen told her mother. "He loved your food."

Max re-appeared, and couldn't stop apologizing to her mother. "The army or Iraq? If I eat a bite too much, this can happen? I guess your food was too good?"

"Never mind." Helen's mother brought him a glass of ginger ale. "Drink this. You boys are never thanked enough for your service to keep us all safe."

Helen avoided meeting Max's eyes. Unexpectedly hearing about Max's child caused his stomach's revolt. "We need to go over the case, Mother."

"Of course." Her mother nodded in her father's direction. "We think you should invite George Clemmons to supper. We'd both like to meet him."

"Sure." Helen gulped. "If you think you want to. Could Max come too? He'll keep things light, you know."

"Max, you're always welcome." Helen's mother patted Max's shoulder. As she walked into the kitchen, they heard her say, "We need clowns in the house."

The phone rang again and Julia Costello answered. They heard her asking a few questions. Julia reappeared in the dining room. She read from her note pad, "A Sharon Daley from St. Anthony's Hospital found two more files for you. One is a Jean Bacon and the other is a Charlie Klondike. I told her you would pick up the files within the hour. She's about to leave work for the day."

"I'll help Mother with the dishes," her dad offered. "You two better get started."

Helen directed Max out to the garage to her father's antique Oldsmobile. "Sorry, Max." She backed the car out of the drive. "I wonder which doctor is dead. Didn't the Mother Superior mention which of Marilyn Helm's doctors died?"

"What? I'm sorry. I wasn't listening. I guess my nerves are shot." Max occupied more than his side of the front seat.

He was so big. Helen could smell his scent of clean soap; Irish Spring, she'd bet. She had never noticed before how small her parent's home was. Max was too tall to stand up straight as he passed through the doorway out to the garage. She glanced at him as she drove to St. Anthony's hospital in Ann Arbor. She felt she was a plotting, laying traps to catch him, while acting uninterested -- just the way Maybell, Anita, had done.

Max took her hand from the steering wheel. "Why didn't you rat me out?"

Warmth traveled through Helen's body at Max's touch. She wanted more of him. Perhaps her mother was right about the thinning blood stream running its spring course through her tensing body. Where was she headed with all this pent-up heat? Helen shook her head. "What are you going to do about your child?"

Max let go of her fingertips. "Can't handle it yet, I guess." Then he laughed. "Shall I wait until I'm over the morning sickness?"

Helen didn't laugh. The poor guy. She'd misjudged him. He really loved Maybell, Anita. What a mess he was in. "I was surprised Mother wants you to meet George."

"I wonder if my child is a girl or boy?" Max rubbed his dark curls. "I really enjoy living close to downtown."

"I wouldn't like to eat on the street the way I see other people." Helen wondered what his apartment was like. "I collect doll houses." She could feel a childish blush rise. "I mean, I'm curious about how a man decorates a place."

"It's two stories tall. I put some rods up, you know, those thin pieces of wood? Anyway, I strung several bolts of blue silk cloth up there, to look like the sky?"

"Sounds neat."

"How many doll houses have you collected?"

"Twenty-five."

"Geez! Where do you keep them all?"

"Upstairs, at home. Dad built shelves in my room and along

the hall. Double shelves."

Max dusted his curls again. "I build model ships. How do you keep control of the dust?"

"Plastic wrap on the open side. How do you?" Helen thought he was more interesting than she'd imagined.

"Computer keyboards are sprayed with a can of compressed air. Do you want to come up sometime?"

"You sound like Mae West."

Max squirmed. "Nothing like that. When I take my girlfriends for a walk down Main Street for my buddies at the Earle, the waiters at Gratzi, and the cooks at Mongolian Barbecue, I get to smell all the different foods."

"Do your girlfriends know they're being shown off?" Helen laughed, feeling like a teasing sister rather than the interested woman she was.

* * *

Max frowned. "Did your father know your mother was pregnant? They seem reconciled now, don't they?" He felt ashamed for putting Helen on the spot. Why was he being so defensive, attacking her? The answer was he wanted to push her away before he injured her by using her, too. He liked her too much to disrespect. "I should tell you what my drinking buddies say about me." Max stared at his huge hands. "They told me I reach for women the way they see drunks reach for a bottle, drain them, and toss them into the garbage."

When Max heard Helen's shocked intake of breath, he

instantly repented for showing her his bad side. He dug his hands into his suit coat pockets. Summoning up his courage, he asked, "Did I tell you I was orphaned at thirteen by my drunken parents?"

"Did you want to tell me what happened?"

"Aunt Rose said they were both addicted to rage. People can drink too much. My father strangled my mother and then shot himself."

Helen stopped the car in St. Anthony's Hospital parking lot. She knelt beside him on the front seat put her arms around his head, her cheek next to his. "I'm sorry."

"They were traveling in Europe." Helen's comfort was genuine. He might need her in his life. Max's voice was close to a whisper. "To me, they just disappeared. But from my viewpoint everyone treated me as if I'd killed them. I'm sure they were trying to be sympathetic. I carried a cement block of resentment on my shoulder for years. The army kicked the self-pity out of me." Max rubbed the back of his hand against Helen's cheek. She sat down beside him, her warm hip next to his hip.

Max escaped tasting her mouth by opening the passenger door and sliding out. He offered her his hand. "Let's hang these doctors out to dry."

* * *

When the children left even before the dishes were in the dishwasher, Julia Costello decided to ask her husband to take a walk around the block. Andrew never blinked an eye. Julia knew all her behavioral changes must be driving him crazy, but she didn't want to talk about them. "I'm worried about Helen," she said to start the conversation.

"Max is a good person."

"I know. It's Helen I think might have a problem, because of me. I've been so isolated; I think I allowed her to be a hermit, too."

"She's a smart cookie, good detective."

Julia slipped her arm through her husband's arm. She wondered if the neighbors might be inclined to call the cops. Strangers were cruising their street. How she could have denied herself all this beauty? "For years …."

"Never mind," Andrew said, as if he understood. "We're here now."

"We are," she said. "And happier?"

"Much," Andrew said and tugged her arm closer to his side. "Much happier."

"Would it be cruel to suggest Helen find her own apartment?"

"I wouldn't call it cruel. She needs to expand her life past our home and the office, hopefully before she marries Max." Andrew stopped. He turned back to stare at their home. "She needs to live somewhere other than Burns Park, but I hope she stays in Ann Arbor. God, I would miss her, if they left town."

"She's not going to leave town." Julia hoped. "We need the grandchildren close. She'll be a working mother. I don't want to baby-sit while she works, but I do want to be available when she needs me."

"We sound like we have her entire life planned." Andrew

The Recorder's Way

shook his head. "I know we should wait until Helen decides to move out, but I can't wait." He pinched Julia arm. "I'll be able to chase you around the house."

"Likely story," Julia said, but she laughed…and she didn't try to silence her merriment. God was good and she felt she had finally forgiven herself for the deceitful way she caught Andrew. "You never thought I trapped you?"

"You're kidding! Remember me; I'm the one who wouldn't go home. Sat on your doorstep until George would bring you home from a date. Me. I was there waiting for my girl." Andrew kissed her, standing right there on the sidewalk in front of their home.

"The neighbors?" Julia said.

"Are either missing a good show, or are happy for us." Andrew opened the front door and swept his arm towards the inside, as if he were inviting the Queen. "Did I tell you I don't think Max thinks he's good enough for Helen?"

"He might be right."

"I see them together more than you do, even caught them kissing."

"In a full body embrace?"

"My aren't we getting technical." Andrew laughed as he headed for the kitchen. "Any coffee left?"

Julia was serious. "I want to know how far this has gone."

"I think they both surprised themselves," Andrew said as he embraced his wife. "Love is a gift from God, surely. Aren't you surprised our love keeps growing?"

"You are the man. I mean you stayed the course, when I offered only half of myself."

Andrew drew away from a kiss he seemed to want to prolong. "You offered every ounce of yourself that was free to be loved. Now you've forgiven yourself and I can love you even more, more of your entire self."

"I feel more of God's love, too."

"The good Lord has blessed us with a wonderful daughter." Andrew led the way up the stairs for an afternoon of lovemaking. "I think that's why God made man a helpmate, so they could nourish each other to grow toward his love."

"I love you, Andrew Costello." Julia invited her husband down on the sheets beside her. "When are the dishes going to get done?"

"They'll wait for us," he said.

* * *

First Friday in May
St. Anthony's Convent

Sharon Daley occupied the back seat of the Oldsmobile. Helen had invited her to accompany them to meet with Sister James Marine. After Sharon handed over the files for two more victims, Charley Klondike and Jean Bacon, she insisted they tell her everything they knew about Sally Bianco's death.

"Sister James Marine insisted we come right down." Max was trying to explain.

"Mother Superior?" Helen clarified for Sharon as they tooled down Carpenter Road, headed for Route 12.

"She sounded so upset when I told her we found Sally Bianco's body, I couldn't tell her no." Max's hands were in his hair.

Helen thought Max would surely be bald by the time he was fifty. Sally Bianco told her bald men were sexy. She said she'd only been married a short time to a bald husband who had loved her since she was a teenager. 'They try harder.' Helen swore she could still hear Sally's clipped way of speaking, as if you could understand every nuance of meaning in the sparse words she deigned to throw in your direction. Nevertheless, Helen did like the way Max, balding or not, bothered to consider Mother Superior's worry about Marilyn's connection to Sally's death.

Sharon said she understood the need to drive to Adrian. "I'm sure Marilyn would never injure another human being. That's why she was sent to the convent for her community service."

Max asked, "Did you know her dog?"

"Rufus. Sure. He's harmless, devoted to Marilyn." Sharon coughed. "Oh. Did you know Marilyn served in the National Guard? She didn't live with me after they discharged her. She said she would be too much of a burden, with the dog and all."

"Did you like dogs?" Max asked.

"Rufus was okay." After two miles of silence, Sharon continued. "Actually, I was glad Marilyn didn't ask to move back in with me. She'd changed. I mean, she was more angry than before she went into the service. I was so hopeful, when she first told me about the job they offered her. Part of the problem, I think, was she never stopped her contact with those three doctors. They kept the memory of our patients fresh in her mind."

"Then why did she keep in touch with them?" Helen was glad to be able to pump Sharon for information on the way down to Adrian. But she knew in her heart she would have enjoyed not sharing Max's company even more.

Sharon grumbled. "They always gave her new prescriptions for diet pills. Crazy business. Marilyn tried to stuff down her anger with food. She took the pills and continued to eat. Did you know Rufus was an attack dog? The National Guard was going to him put down. Marilyn told me one of the soldiers Rufus attacked came close to dying. The dog was very devoted to her."

Max tapped Helen's shoulder. "Remind your dad to look up Marilyn's record. We need the name of the arresting officer."

* * *

Sister James Marine seemed to gauge their shock and sadness. "What can I do? Have they found Marilyn yet, or her dog?"

Max introduced Sharon as a friend of Marilyn's. "The police have been searching for Sally's car since Tuesday. Helen called them from here. Marilyn probably has the car now."

"It's my fault." Sister James Marine twisted a fresh handkerchief.

"Marilyn was sober, I mean not on drugs when she was with you, right?" Sharon still stood in the open doorway.

"Her room was filled with food." The sister motioned for Sharon to come into the room. "We didn't find any diet pills."

"Or prescriptions?" Sharon asked.

"None." Sister J. M. spread her hands palm down on her desk. "When you find her, I want to help. Please call me. I'm sure Marilyn will do the right thing."

Sharon nodded. "Her dog could have gone off on Sally Bianco. Marilyn might just be frightened. She wouldn't want to return here if Rufus hurt Sally." Max could tell Sharon was offering some relief for the sister.

"I want to explain." Sister James Marine walked to Sharon, took her arm, and moved her over the threshold into the room and shut the door behind her. "When I met Sally Bianco, I thought her job was the most interesting and useful thing I had ever heard of. God forgive me, I'm bored to death here. I want to work for your agency, find the truth for people, serve God's justice."

Max looked at Helen to help dissuade the woman. "Often times, Sister, we find the truth hurts more than it's worth."

"Please," Sister J. M. said. "I want to be of more use to God than doling out kitchen assignments."

"I understand." Helen stood up, slightly brushing against Max. "You're such a giant," she complained.

Max backed up against the wall. That girl! Was she trying to cause him problems?

Helen looked innocent enough as she went around the desk to look at the sister's computer. "How up-to-date is your computer?"

"State of the art." Sister J. M. seemed excited.

"Google CSI. There is an investigator's license course you can apply for." Helen smiled at the sister's enthusiasm.

"The course is fairly complicated." Max opened the door ready to escape the close quarters. "We'll keep in touch."

"Anything I can do, before I'm licensed, to help. I could talk to Marilyn, maybe." Sister James Marine was back to wringing her handkerchief.

Back in the car, Sharon said, "Mother Superior might be able to interrogate or maneuver Marilyn, if you ever find her."

Max patted Helen's knee, just to reassure her. "We'll find her." Who was he kidding? He had no idea where Marilyn was. What seemed more important at the moment was, did Helen know how much she affected him? Should she? Max couldn't bring up the subject of his passion for his best friend. He felt his spirits plunge into his boots. "Please God."

He hadn't realized he'd prayed aloud for strength to follow God's will, until both Sharon and Helen chimed in with an, "Amen."

Chapter Six

"floods, caterpillars, and sycamore trees' frost, locusts...and the firstborn shall die." - The Egyptian Plagues

Second Sunday in May
University Art Museum

Standing near the atrium of the art gallery's central, circular hall, Helen asked her father to explain to George Clemmons why Sally Bianco's memorial service was so crowded with people they had never met.

"Half are policemen or plain-clothes detectives," Andrew said.

"Helen thought I could meet you all casually," George said, "before I come to dinner."

Andrew shook George's hand. "Your father was our hero in high school."

Max said, "With all these out-of-state crime experts available, Helen is convinced Sally's murder will be solved in record time."

Captain Tedler touched Helen's shoulder before introducing himself to Sister James Marine. "Helen tells me you're interested in filling in for Sally with The Firm."

"As soon as I complete my training," Sister said. Ten of her fellow nuns were scattered about the room. Helen spotted several of them on the second-floor balcony, which circled the main hall. Helen tuned back into the nun's conversation with Captain Tedler. "In the meantime," Sister replaced her handkerchief in her jacket's side pocket. "I might possess some sway with Marilyn. She trusts me to keep her best interests at heart."

Captain Tedler agreed. "Trust is a valuable tool."

Helen's father asked the Mother Superior to lead the mourners in the short serenity prayer from AA. As a footnote, Sister said, "St. Anthony is the patron saint of lost items and people. I would like to ask for all believers to pray that we find Marilyn Helms, who we think knows more about the circumstances surrounding Sally Bianco's passing than we presently do."

Sally's AA sponsor, Phyllis Reed, mentioned specifics about Sally's generous nature. "During one retreat, we nicknamed her 'Lady Bountiful'."

Captain Tedler closed the memorial service. "Sally Bianco once described a cartoon she'd seen of a hunter and his dog. Underneath the two, a rabbit hole hides a rabbit larger than the hunter. 'Go get him,' the hunter says to the dog, who doesn't appear very eager to ferret out the monster. Sally was always ready to pursue wrong doers no matter how huge their reputation in society."

Julia Costello spoke, too, inviting the crowd to a brunch at their home. Helen was amazed to see her recluse mother hand out maps to the crowd of complete strangers.

The mourners included three couples from St. Charles, Illinois. A police captain and his wife explained their association with Sally spanned two of her cases. Apparently, Sally reclaimed her previous husband's name after she was widowed during the investigation of an arson death in St. Charles. She was married only a week to the twin brother of a bald, handsome man. The younger couple from Illinois wept openly.

Four children and a babe in arms accompanied Captain Tedler's brother and his wife from Missouri for the memorial service; Helen heard them apologize to Julia for not attending the brunch. Their ride home would take six hours due to weekend traffic.

Two older men in wheelchairs, an enormous man and his grim-faced wife, a slim fellow with a pronounced limp, another fuzzyheaded elderly man with two grown sons, and a white-haired man from India and his blonde wife added to the gathering, which nearly filled the University's art gallery.

Helen checked the guest register after a group of ten, black-suited men signed the book. Gilbert Commonwealth was written after their names. Apparently, they were fellow workers from Sally's past. Helen realized to her, most of Sally Bianco's life was a blank slate compared to the stories the assembled mourners could reveal. Arizona, Florida, Louisiana, Missouri, Montana, Washington and Wisconsin sent more than a hundred grieving guests to Mrs. Bianco's funeral service.

Andrew leaned over Helen's shoulder to read the book. "Sally kept in contact with people involved in the various cases she worked on."

"I hadn't realized the full extent of her friendships," Max said.

Costello Home

At home after checking on the caterer, Helen found Max leaning against the wall in a corner of the living room, taking notes. Because of his height, his head practically touched the ceiling. They would need a bigger house, higher ceilings, at least. What was she thinking? Helen shook her head to stop her speculations. "What are you doing? This is a funeral, Max, not part of our investigation."

Max put away his notebook. "I was counting. Sally's journal said she needed to make amends to sixty people."

"Mrs. Bianco's friends, these people, are not attending the funeral of someone who injured them. Most of them are probably from AA."

"True." Max's hand strayed to his curls. "I thought maybe sixty were old lovers."

Helen pulled him by the hand into the backyard. The birds were singing away. She needed to tug on his arm to get his attention away from the birds' romantic melodies. "Sally Bianco was a moral person."

"Maybe not while she was drinking." Max loosened his tie. "Remember your dad's theory about the sixties when the birth control pill was available – before the AIDS epidemic arrived?"

"Sally Bianco possessed too much self-esteem to be promiscuous."

Max shook his head, like a dog with a bone. "I've been

calculating various breakdowns of the number. Sixty. If she was thirty when she was first divorced and has only been sober for five years, sixty breaks down to a minimum of two lovers a year. And, wasn't she married a few times, too?"

"I think a couple of her husbands attended the service. Just drop the subject, Max. It's not appropriate at a funeral," Helen said. "Besides I'm sure her Higher Power has forgiven her for using people to salve her ego."

* * *

"Is that what you think I did?" Max's mouth watered. Helen's perfume, Chanel No. 5, caused him to anticipate his next breath of scented air.

"You tried to fill the empty space left by your parents," Helen said. "I'm proud of you loving and trusting Maybell. You changed before my eyes. I think she was wrong to use you."

"I have forgiven her." Max opened a folding chair, sat down and rubbed the arms of the chair.

"You're a very loving person, Max."

The hemline of Helen's black dress was inches away from Max's fingertips. He stood, tapped the top of Helen's head, then wound his arm around her midriff. "We should *not* get involved, sexually. While we're partners."

Helen pushed him away. "What makes you think …?"

George Clemmons called to her from the back door. "Helen, is your ornery partner bothering you?" Helen laughed, perhaps too hysterically for the occasion. George was slimmer and shorter than

Max. "Unless my sister invites your attentions, I suggest you keep your hands to yourself."

Max attempted to shove the guy who was standing way too close to him. "Your *newly* recognized half-sister knows how to handle herself."

"While I'm around, Helen can count on me." George didn't give an inch of turf. "What are you going to do, stomp me into the ground?"

"Easier than stepping on a bug." Max spat out the words.

"Max, stop it." Helen tried to wave him off. "Go in and see if Mother needs any help with the caterer."

Max let go of George's shoulders and stormed off.

* * *

George dusted himself off. "Did you need to hire a goniff for your agency?"

"He's a sweet guy, with lots of problems."

"No doubt." George looked around their beautiful yard. Her brother inhaled the scents from the flowering trees deeply, as if to calm down. "Nevertheless, I would avoid being alone with him."

"Really?" Helen felt she'd been given the best compliment she'd received in years.

* * *

Second Monday in May
Ann Arbor Police Station

Captain Tedler was pacing around his desk when Helen and Max arrived.

"Andrew said you have something for us." Max folded his sunglasses and sat down at one of the two chairs facing the Captain's desk.

"I have." Seemingly relieved, Captain Tedler collapsed into his chair. "Beautiful day?"

Helen continued standing, as if preparing herself for worse news. Max wondered if he touched the shoulder of her white blouse if he would feel the warmth from her body.

Captain Tedler waved for Helen to sit and didn't speak until she did. Helen placed her hand on Max's arm.

"We found Sally's Honda." Captain Tedler consulted the notes on his desk. "It was abandoned in the surf in Cape May, New Jersey."

Max stood up. "I'll go." Mostly, Max needed to move away from Helen's hand on his arm. His body's early warning system let him know his interest in this slip of a girl was not abating.

Helen shook her head in disagreement.

"Sorry I couldn't come to the house after Sally Bianco's service." Captain Tedler seemed to think Helen's gesture was in censure. "We've been busy around here."

Helen asked, "Did you find out anything more about what transpired at Portage Lake?"

"We found a yellow dog whose fur matches the fur in Mrs. Bianco's hands." Captain Tedler swiped at what might have been angry tears on his face.

"Did he have rabies?" Max asked.

"No, we checked. The Humane Shelter put him down, after he tried to attack one of the Waterloo rangers."

"I'll fly to Cape May," Helen said.

"I should go with you." Max knew she should go, but he didn't want to be without her. Captain Tedler shook his head no. Max felt confused.

First Helen's half-brother took an instant dislike to him, and now Captain Tedler appeared distrustful. Max hadn't demanded to go with Helen because of the likelihood something untoward would happen between them. He worried about how to continue a working relationship with a woman he obviously intended to know better. With the hope of a reprieve, he admitted to God his fixation was not entirely honorable.

Max suggested an alternate agenda to the Captain, "The file clerk from St. Anthony's Hospital should be brought in for formal questioning. She gave us two more files connected to Sally's investigation."

"What investigation?" Captain Tedler pounded the desk with his fist. "What investigation?"

"Mrs. Bianco told us three doctors were involved in deaths at St. Anthony's Hospital, in 1990." Helen's voice was apologetic. "I thought you knew. My father obtained a warrant to search …."

"Not through this office! And you didn't bother to inform us when we found Sally's body?" Captain Tedler's face resembled bright hamburger before fire darkened it. He tapped the holster of his gun.

"Have you found a Marilyn Helms? She's the owner of a dog called Rufus."

Captain Tedler tore pages out of his notebook. "The shelter said the dog's tag had his name on it. Here it is. Rufus!" Tedler lifted his telephone. "We need an extradition order for a Marilyn Helms now visiting in Cape May, New Jersey. And bring in … "He held the phone away from his ear. "What's the file clerk's name?"

"Sharon Daley," Max said.

"Sharon Daley, St. Anthony's Hospital." Captain Tedler hung up the phone. His face was not yet its normal color. "Do you realize you jeopardized Sally's life by not coming forward with this information?"

Helen tried to calm him down. "You're upset about losing your friend, but Sally was probably killed Sunday afternoon. We didn't know she was involved in a case until Monday morning. By Wednesday, Andrew had called you to look for her car, because she was missing." Helen stood. "Max, it could take days before the extradition process succeeds in bringing Marilyn Helms here. I knew Sally Bianco longer than you. Let me do this for her."

Max wanted to hug her out of relief. She could handle herself like a pro. She backed Captain Tedler down without insulting him. At least there would be no question of sharing a motel with her. He'd be in Michigan and she'd be safe in New Jersey. He would decide how to handle his attraction while she was gone. "Don't tell her about her dog's death until you need to."

"Before you go," Captain Tedler said, "Who are the other two doctors?"

"Show him the files, Max," Helen said. "I'm going to call Sister James Marine. She wants to help with Marilyn. Dad will drive us to the airport."

Captain Tedler was rummaging in his desk. Max told Helen to wait a moment. He watched as Captain Tedler presented her with a deputy's badge.

"You're right. I personally miss Sally." Captain Tedler shook her hand. "This badge will help you get clearance to question Marilyn. I know your father's taught you enough about police procedures not to mess up any case against the girl."

Max felt his chest expand with pride. This was his partner. Nice to know someone else appreciated her as a first-rate detective. But, he wasn't going to kiss her goodbye in front of Captain Tedler. Too risky, even in private, now.

"Helen, interview Sharon with me," Max said. "Then we'll make a threesome attack on Marilyn Helms in Cape May after we nail down a few more facts about the deaths."

Helen held out her hand to Captain Tedler. "Max needs a badge too."

* * *

Second Monday in May
Ann Arbor Police Station

Captain Tedler ordered lunch, which arrived simultaneously with Sharon Daley from St. Anthony's Hospital. Max offered to talk to the young woman. Captain Tedler sized him up. "Yep, girls go for you big guys."

Helen played with her salad, not meeting Max's glance.

"You just want your lunch." Max slapped a bit of hot mustard on his roast beef on rye and took a bite, before walking into the interrogation room. Sharon was one of those hefty women who didn't attract many men. Her perfume was innocent enough, lilac. Max got right to the point, so she wouldn't miss too many work hours. "Do you know where Marilyn Helms might be staying in Cape May?"

"Yes. I visited her grandmother with her in Cape May." Sharon scratched the back of her head. "She lives in a purple Victorian bed-and-breakfast facing the ocean."

"Address?"

"No. Sorry."

Max nodded at the two-way mirror. He knew Captain Tedler or Helen would be relaying Marilyn's position to the Cape May police. "Were you aware that Marilyn was blackmailing three doctors?"

Sharon clicked her tongue. "Will I get in trouble for not going to the police?"

"Not if you tell us everything you know." Max wasn't sure she couldn't be prosecuted, but he needed information.

"Not directly through Marilyn, but a waitress at the City Club knows a woman who doesn't like one of the doctors involved."

"Which doctor is that?"

"Dr. Dorothy Whidbey."

"Charley Klondike's doctor." Max remembered the file. "What is the woman's name who's not keen on Dr. Whidbey?"

"Mary Livingston. She knows about Charley's death, too. Hepatic coma. Marilyn and I thought he was sleeping after the D.T.'s. He looked exhausted; his hands slumped down to his sides. I learned too late the hands were the clue. He was very near death. I doubt that Dr. Whidbey would have bothered to visit him anyway."

"And the other doctors?"

"Larry Schneider's." Sharon clutched her purse to her chest. "That would be Dr. Handler. He's a tricky one. I doubt you'll be able to pin anything on him."

"And one died?"

"Dr. Cornell. Jean Bacon's doctor. I don't know why he paid Marilyn. Diabetes is a tricky business. I wonder if her file still includes the notes I made about how the disease was slowly eating away her fat. She deflated while we watched. Jean probably couldn't have been saved if Dr. Cornell had lived at her bedside." Sharon brushed dandruff from her sweater.

"Three died in one night?" Max asked to make sure he had gleaned all the details from the nurse.

"Marilyn went a little mad, I think." Sharon choked up. "Can I go home now?"

"Let me check." Max stood. "You have been very helpful."

"I can see why Helen Costello chose you for her partner."

Max placed his hand on the doorknob, grinned at the mirror, where he hoped Helen was smiling back.

"She's a lucky girl." Sharon said.

"Thanks." Max flashed his rehearsed smile before leaving. As Max walked down the hall from the witness room, he wondered if he should explain his relationship with Helen Costello to Captain Tedler. What could the Captain say in response? Max barely understood his feelings for his partner, didn't know if he could find the right words to express them to Captain Tedler. He wasn't in love, was he?

Chapter Seven

︽

"He rained flesh upon them as dust, and feathered fowls like the sand of the sea: And he let it fall in the midst of their camp, round about their habitation. So they did eat, and were well filled. For he gave them their own desire: They were not estranged from their lust..." Psalm 78:27-30

Second Tuesday in May
Cape May

Chatting with Sister James Marine and Max made Helen's trip from the Newark airport to Cape May almost enjoyable, even in the rain. She relaxed in the passenger's seat as Max drove down the long, forested peninsula. The proud trees had watched more than one President of the United States pass by their shadows. Cape May was the Camp David for presidents for over a century. Towards the east were glimpses of the ocean's whitecaps while the calm bay on the west side of the car could be seen through breaks in the tree line, where brave homeowners settled to enjoy and to weather the elements. Helen was seduced into a momentary state of denial.

In the back seat, Sister read Helen's mind. "Hard to believe we're in this beautiful landscape to find out why someone killed Sally Bianco."

As they reached the beach highway, Helen said she preferred the Victorian, bed-and-breakfast houses to the more modern establishments. "The decorating colors probably help travelers find their accommodations." Transported to an earlier time, Helen hit her automatic window button. May birds she couldn't name were singing along with the seagulls. When Max opened the driver's window, she could hear the waves on the black outcroppings of rock between the long stretches of beach.

Max slowed the car. "Try imagining riding in a horse-drawn carriage."

"I know an old story about the father of a sick woman," Sister said. "He carpeted the cobblestone street outside their home with bales of hay. The hay softened the sounds of buggy wheels."

"My father would have been such a man," Helen said. "I still live at home."

"They will understand your need to prove yourself," Max said, "when you move out."

"Do you think we can trap Marilyn Helms into confessing the murder?" Helen asked.

"I think …," Sister said. "We can convince Marilyn she would be doing herself more harm by *not* cooperating."

Helen returned to the previous subject. "I do want to live alone, for a while."

"Before you marry?" Sister asked.

Max coughed.

Helen had been tempted to add, 'even if Max is in love with me.' Instead, she chose a less emotional subject. "These Victorian houses remind me of my favorite doll houses."

"How many do you own? The sisters, who went upstairs at your mother's after the funeral, mentioned seeing quite a few."

"Twenty-five," Max said.

Helen didn't hear any disapproval in Max's voice. "I don't know what I'm going to do with all of them, when I finally move into my own place."

Sister tapped Helen's shoulder. "I'd love to see them. We, the sisters, I mean are all a little childish."

"I have enough to give each of them two." Helen laughed.

"One a piece would be great. Good therapy for their homesickness. Actually just to decorate their rooms."

"You do live rather like Spartans." Max laughed. "I can't think of a better home for the collection."

"Maybe some of the abuse shelters would like a few," Sister said. "The doll houses might relieve the sisters' thwarted nesting instincts."

"I'll keep my favorite Victorian one. It has those long windows and high ceilings. Modern homes have two-story ceilings in the entrance way."

Max said, "I need head room in every room."

Sister laughed. "You will require higher ceilings like the ones in these old-fashioned houses."

"My studio ceilings are two-stories high." Max smiled at Helen.

She recognized she was making premature statements. "I need to focus on the goals of our trip to the ocean."

"Grim business, murder," Max said.

On the beach highway near a curve in the highway, Helen pointed to a low sign, "Police." Max turned the rental car at the street, leading them away from God's beauty. As if in the thrall of their trip back in time, the station-house doorway sported twin antique glass globes lighting the black letters of the word, 'Police' atop each column.

Max parked behind the building. The gray day and the old walls of the station finally worked their depressing enchantment on Helen's spirits. "I half expect one of the shuttered windows to be opened with the bonneted old witch yelling, 'Peter Grimes, Peter Grimes.'"

Max stepped out of the car. "In the opera, wasn't the murderer hounded into killing an innocent boy?" Max held his umbrella over the two women.

Helen loved being close enough to smell his Irish Spring soap. "I wonder," she said, "if Mrs. Bianco inadvertently forced a dangerous person, a drug addict like Marilyn, to kill her."

Sister nodded. "... if only to gain her freedom."

"I left the lights on." Max announced handing the umbrella to Helen and racing back to the car.

Watching him run back to the car, another chilling thought crossed Helen's mind: Huge Max Hunt and his impenetrable hide would never belong to her. She whispered to Sister, "Max will never be mine. I'm too immature."

"He does seem too wily to be caught easily."

Helen wanted to be loved above anyone else by him, to be admired by him, even to be esteemed. "It's hopeless. What do I have to offer a man of his experience?

"Innocence," Sister whispered back and Helen believed her.

The back door of the station opened and a woman officer called to them, "Helen Costello?" Helen didn't respond quickly enough and the policewoman repeated, "Helen Costello?"

A little shocked at the similarity to her previous thoughts about the Peter Grimes opera, Helen raised an arm in reply. "I'm here."

"Come in before you drown. I'm Orange Creeper. Officer Creeper to you all."

"Officer," Max said.

Helen dared not ask the origin of her name, as they were ushered into the station's back door. She introduced her companions as the Mother Superior of the convent where Marilyn Helms was last seen and her partner and fellow deputy, Max Hunt.

However, as Helen climbed the ancient steps to the officer's second floor room, she prayed silently to herself about an entirely different matter. She asked God to find her a good man if Max was wrong for her. 'Lord. One I can love with all my heart, with confidence and trust in your will.'

Officer Creeper wore a white military-looking uniform. Helen hoped her own black suit and turtleneck appeared professional enough. Sister wrinkled her nose as if she noticed the smell of tobacco, too. Did it come from the entrance hall, or was Officer Creeper addicted to smoking?

***

Max, Helen and Sister searched for Marilyn's grandmother's house among the line of houses facing the Atlantic Ocean.

Max pointed. "There is only one house painted purple."

Helen called Officer Creeper on her cell phone. They waited patiently for the police to arrive and take Marilyn Helms into custody. Then, they followed the squad car back to the police station. After speaking to Captain Tedler in Ann Arbor, Officer Creeper allowed the newly sworn deputies to question Marilyn with some reservations. "I don't know enough about the case to ask pertinent questions."

Sister patted Helen's shoulder. "If you need me, pull your left ear lobe and I'll knock on the door."

In the small interrogation room, Marilyn Helm's belligerence surprised Max. The woman was a head taller and maybe three times Helen's girth. Helen set her briefcase next to her chair and opened the clasp in case she needed swift access to her weapon. Max didn't carry a gun.

"I don't understand why you upset my poor grandmother." Marilyn tapped her chubby fingers on the steel tabletop. "Has my lawyer arrived?"

Max unbuttoned his suit jacket in the warm Cape May questioning room. "Should we wait for your lawyer?" He tried to appear relaxed, able to wait until doomsday.

Marilyn squirmed. Her stomach growled in the silent room. "Could I answer something and go home?"

Helen switched on the tape machine. "Why are your fingerprints on Sally Bianco's car?"

"They're not." Marilyn seemed too sure of that.

"Did you remember to wipe off the gear shift when you ditched Sally's Honda in the ocean?" Max noted Marilyn's eyes flicked from the incriminating oversight.

Marilyn rubbed her wrists as if the handcuffs were just removed or awaiting her. "Could I have something to drink? I was in the middle of lunch when the police *arrested* me. Are you at least going to tell me the charges?"

"Murder," Helen said and waited for the word to sink into the woman's massive bulk.

"I haven't killed anyone. I only blackmailed three criminals. I'm a nurse. We help people, not kill them. We're not doctors. Sally Bianco said they were culpable. Sharon Daley will tell you; we did everything we could for those patients." Marilyn started to cry.

Max wondered if he misjudged the tears. Were they contrite? The water jettisoned out of Marilyn's besieged brain could be caused by anger and frustration at being discovered. "We found your dog," Max said, asking God's forgiveness for being cruel.

"What makes you think he's my dog?"

"He was with you at the convent." Helen said. "Mother Superior is waiting outside, if you want to talk to her about Rufus."

Suddenly, Marilyn stood, knocking her chair to the floor as she lunged across the table at Helen. Helen felt Marilyn's fist graze her curls as she ducked to retrieve her gun. She stuck the gun between

Marilyn's eyes. "Sit back down or I'll blow your head off." Marilyn's right fist slammed into Helen's left ear. Helen fell sideways off her chair. She fired her gun away from Marilyn and Max's general direction. "Stop!"

"Shoot me!" Marilyn shouted, looming over Helen's sprawled body. "You chicken-shit!"

Blows rained down on Helen, who tucked her arms and her loaded gun over her face. Max grabbed Marilyn from behind, lifting her off the floor.

Marilyn kicked a chair over on top of Helen. "Shoot me. Put me out of my misery!"

Through increasing consciousness of pain and real fear, Helen heard the room's door open. Officer Creeper struck Marilyn's head with her nightstick. Max let go of the woman and Marilyn fell like a giant tree.

Sister James Marine assisted Helen to the chair she had righted. "Are you seriously hurt? Bleeding?"

"My ribs." Helen couldn't help but moan.

"Call an ambulance!" Max shouted. Then he whispered as he stroked Helen's forehead. "We'll check you out at the hospital."

"Let me put my gun away," Helen said, but fainted as she dropped the gun back into her briefcase.

* * *

Second Wednesday in May
Ann Arbor Police Station

Max turned toward Captain Tedler's open office door a moment before Helen entered. He wondered if he had smelled her perfume, that had alerted him to her presence. She stood at the threshold, hands on her hips.

"Say hello to Captain Tedler." Max couldn't help teasing.

His mood lightened with the sight of her. Helen's navy-blue suit was trimmed with light blue piping along the lapels. Fluorescent rainbows danced off her blonde curls. She could have been wearing sackcloth as far as Max was concerned. He thanked God his partner, his friend, had *not* been seriously injured in Cape May.

Captain Tedler offered Helen a paper cup of coffee. "We searched Dr. Cornell's house. I read his diary. Dr. Cornell's son is here to tell us what he knows of Marilyn's blackmailing scheme."

"Hi, Max." Helen's genuine smile warmed Max's heart, more than it should have. Max had noticed for the first time that Helen wrinkled her nose before smiling, as if she might sneeze.

"Could we talk to him?" Her face turned serious. "Sister stayed in Cape May, in case we need more answers from Marilyn."

"Did Marilyn confess?" Captain Tedler asked.

Helen shook her head. "She lawyered up, but she's open to a deal."

"For murder?" Max didn't want to hear about any such arrangement.

"She says nurses never hurt other human beings." Helen turned to set her coffee cup down. Max caught sight of the large bruise on Helen's left cheek. "But she admitted," Helen continued, "Rufus was her dog, before she blew her top."

"She obviously took Sally's car to Cape May." Captain Tedler shifted papers on his desk. "But the DA thinks we need more evidence for a trial for murder."

"I am coming with you to talk to Jason Cornell?" Max rose to accompany Helen.

Captain Tedler waved for them to go. "I'll be listening."

When they entered the interrogation room, Jason Cornell clicked his cowboy boots like a German officer. He wore a denim shirt with a leather string tie. After introductions, he went to the heart of the matter. "I know Marilyn Helms was blackmailing my dad, but I never knew why."

Max took his time arranging himself at the table. "Your father thought he was negligent when a patient of his died at St. Anthony's Hospital, after they stopped using his services as a consultant."

"Someone died?"

"Jean Bacon." Helen remained standing. She walked from the table to the door and back again. Her shoulders were tense as if her ribs still pained her. Her heels made sharp jabbing sounds on the tiled floor. "Miss Bacon was diabetic. The nurse in charge swears Dr. Cornell would not have been able to reverse what was clearly a gradual decline."

"Then why did he pay the money?" Jason asked.

"He might not have wanted a scandal." Max couldn't keep his hands from his hair. He really wanted to touch Helen. "Or, Doctors Whidbey and Handler colluded to keep him ignorant of the facts.

They might have wanted to give Marilyn Helms a third blackmail victim to share the financial burden."

Jason shined the knees of his jeans. "We always thought he was a skinflint, not helping with our college expenses. Mother went without things she might have enjoyed. My father spent money on himself: bagpipes, trips for out-of-state lessons. Our home was huge to keep up appearances. Colleagues can harass you into doing things their way. I wish he had owned more courage."

"Captain Tedler tried not to rummage about too much in our search of his belongings." Helen said. "Did you read his diary?"

"No. Should I?"

"I think you would find out how much he thought of his children." Max said. "According to Captain Tedler, your father thought you were the happiest. You raise horses?"

"I do. Thank you for your kindness in this matter."

"We won't be needing you further." Max said.

"Even if Dr. Whidbey and Dr. Handler claim my father was part of the mess?"

"We can guarantee we intend to keep your father's name out of the newspapers." Helen sat down finally as Dr. Cornell's son left the room.

Max stayed behind, too. "I should have prevented Marilyn from injuring you."

"Marilyn might decide to plead insanity for Sally's murder." Helen held her side.

Max felt the sand from Iraq descend from some inner cache.

His eyes smarted and his nose itched. "I let you down."

Helen stood up and moved behind him, pressed his head against her breasts. "You are my truest friend. You could never disappoint me."

Max let himself be comforted by her closeness. He knew he didn't deserve her tenderness. He took her hand and kissed it, not noticing his tears also anointed her ring finger.

* * *

Helen withdrew her hand, stared at the teardrops. "Max," she said, moved at his concern.

Abruptly, Max's mood changed. The lines of his face soured his expression. He stood and faced her. "I need to speak to your dad."

"Come to supper." Helen wanted to cheer him up. His seriousness unnerved her. "George will be there. You know how much George loves you."

"He hates me."

She thought he might actually be ready to weep again. "No. No. He doesn't, Max. He's just flexing his new half-brother muscles."

Max didn't say anything. He acted as if he'd just realized she owned a face, staring as if he needed to attach a name. He seemed confused as conflicting emotions held him sway. She straightened her jacket in the interrogation room's two-way mirror. There wasn't a fly sitting on her nose. She cocked her head, preparing to ask him what had just happened. She could tell he wouldn't answer.

He turned his back to her, missed a beat and then produced his well-rehearsed smile. "I'm starving. What is your mother cooking tonight?"

"She doesn't issue menus for the day."

Max laughed, so Helen tucked her worries away.

* * *

Second Wednesday in May
Costello Residence

George Clemmons was sitting on the front steps of Helen's home. Max stuck out his hand to show he harbored no hard feelings. "Hello, George." George didn't shake his hand. Max felt his temper rising. He'd kick this interfering baggage into the next county if he wasn't careful.

Helen sat down next to the lump and put her arm around George's shoulder.

George looked up at Max as if he should explain. "Helen's mother is weeping and her dad asked me to wait out here."

"What did you say to her? She's the nicest woman on the planet, besides her daughter." Max wanted to hit something, anything. He picked up a pot of geraniums to pitch at George, but Helen gently took the weapon away from him.

"Dad will come back out." She patted the stone step next to her as if Max should make nice.

"George must have said something awful." Max tried not to shout.

"I didn't say a word." George shook his head. "She took one look at me and burst into tears."

"You idiot," Max said. "Your probably look like your father."

"I guess that's the trouble." George appealed to Helen. "Should I go home?"

Max was all for that, but Helen insisted George stay. She left them sitting there like two mismatched bookends while she went into the house to find out how matters stood.

George seemed to need conversation. "Mr. Costello said you two have solved Sally Bianco's murder case."

Max looked at the kid. Was this jerk going to stay in his life? As soon as Mr. Costello had time to listen to him, Max was sure he wouldn't be invited back to Helen's home. Finally, Helen opened the front door and ushered the two of them into the living room.

Julia Costello held out her hand for George. "I don't know why I was so shocked today. When you were here for Mrs. Bianco's funeral, I didn't react at all. You see, your father always wore a red baseball cap when we dated. I think that's what triggered my outburst. You're very welcome here and I do apologize.

George threw the red hat he was holding behind him, as if to toss it out the door. Instead, the bill of the cap hit Max right in the eye.

"Oh, Max." Helen recognized Max was trying not to swear a blue streak. "Dad, check Max's eye."

"Sit down, you giant." Mr. Costello pushed him into a chair and took a good look into Max's watering eye. "You're all right.

Nothing a good helping of orange duck won't fix."

Helen could see Max's mouth water with the thought of food. He wiped his tearing eyes and smiled. "No injury, no foul."

* * *

Helen's mother motioned for George to sit next to Helen. Max was seated across from them. Usually Helen could peg Max's moods, at least to the positive or negative side of a chart, but today she regarded him warily. Under stress, his PTSD loomed into his awareness. She disagreed with his private assessment of the ailment. Even if his parents died a violent death, Max must have been affected deeply by the war. She should try harder to make him open up to vent the horrid tales; but dinner with her newly found half-brother hardly seemed the time to assure Max a comfortable enough environment to render his war experiences.

But, George broached the subject just as Max finished his first bite of roast duck. "Max, a fair number of my company's investors are veterans."

"Which war?" Max asked, intent on his plate.

Andrew coughed. "Hey, we were recently given a graphic example of Max's capacity to handle stress. Why don't we wait to discuss his war experiences after the table is cleared?"

Max waved his free hand. "I'm okay. I served in the first Iraq war."

George seemed to try to back out of the discussion, after Andrew's warning. "Most of these guys are younger than you."

"Any signs of PTSD?" Max asked. George nodded. He filled

his mouth and tried to avoid answering. But Max was like a cat waiting for a mouse to spring away from his gaze. Julia tried to pass Max more orange sauce, but he waved her away without breaking eye contact with George.

"A few." George admitted. "They attend a group session at the VA."

"I heard it helps to talk about events – with other veterans." Max began to attack his plate again. "Details are not conducive to good digestion."

"Of course," George said.

Helen thanked God the subject was closed. George blushed with as much color as she did. A shared family trait, no doubt. "Max, we haven't told George about the trial we're going to be involved with."

"The murder trial," Andrew offered.

Max shook his head. "I doubt Handler will serve any time for endangering Larry Schneider's life."

"What about Sally's murderer?" Julia asked.

Helen touched her left ear gingerly. "Marilyn Helms may not admit to blackmailing Handler unless she can get off with manslaughter."

George reached for the sauce ladle. "You and Max live more exciting lives than my girlfriend, Mitzi, and I do."

Helen wondered if Max caught the fact George thought Max was her boyfriend, as well as partner in the detective agency.

"Tell us about your friend," Julia said as she started clearing the table. She tugged on Max's plate. He seemed unwilling to let her take his. "Now, Max. Drink some water and sit awhile. We'll have cake and coffee later in the evening."

"I met Mitzi at the Back Door," George said. "I volunteer once a month to hand out groceries at St. Clare's. People only sign their names and tell us how many are in their families. A family of four receives two bags a week."

"Hardly enough," Max said.

"I agree," George said. "Mitzi gets in trouble because she walks them to the car and hands out twenty-dollar bills."

Max asked, "Is she rich?"

"Uh, no." George blushed. "She asks me for the money."

Max laughed. "You remind me of your sister, I mean half-sister. You both have good hearts."

* * *

After dinner, Max asked Mr. Costello if he could speak to him, "Privately." Andrew led him down to the basement room he used as his den. "It's me." Max ducked his head as he walked into the small room. After waiting for Andrew to claim his desk chair, Max plopped down into an enormous beanbag. "I'll never get out of here."

"We'll rent a crane. What did you want to talk about?"

"Your daughter." Max felt he shouldn't need to explain further, but Andrew didn't react to the news.

Andrew only stared at him. "What about my daughter?" Andrew seemed to find it necessary to add a negative edge to his voice.

"No. Nothing to complain about." Max noticed again how gigantic his frame was compared to Andrew's. "See, I think I'm in love with her…and you shouldn't let me near her. I mean, you know…I'm no good for a decent woman."

Andrew held up his hand to stop his babbling. "You want to marry Helen?"

"No that's just it." Max pulled on his curls. "Why would you want me to marry Helen?"

"You said you loved her."

"I know, but it's me you're talking to. You don't want me to marry your daughter, do you?"

"What's wrong with her?"

"Not her! Me."

Andrew's hands tugged at the remains of his hairline. "Okay. Start over. Why don't I want you to marry my daughter?"

"I'm no good for her." Max felt that should do it. He'd said it all. Andrew would understand the matter now.

"Have you asked Helen to marry you?"

"Of course not!" Max was shocked. "That's why I'm talking to you. To explain I shouldn't."

"Because you're no good for her?"

"Exactly." Max struggled out of the beanbag, resulting in actually getting down on his hands and knees in order to stand up. "So that's settled." Andrew didn't say anything. Max cocked his head. Obviously, Andrew had missed something.

Helen's father stood up and opened the door. "I suppose we both need to see what Helen has to say about all this."

Max grabbed the door to close it, pushing Andrew back into the room. "Don't say a word. I just wanted you to understand my position."

Andrew stood his ground. "Oh, I understand." He actually laughed. "You don't have a chance, Max. Give it up." With that Andrew opened the door and left the basement.

Max thought his brain might have dried up, suffered a lingering injury from when he was in Iraq. He couldn't make heads nor tails out of what had just happened. He dusted off his shoulders as if from falling bomb debris in the war zone. He'd explained, Andrew understood, but what? Andrew wanted Helen to decide her own fate? Max thought Andrew was being imprudent. Very cautiously, Max climbed the basement stairs to the kitchen where he could hear Helen and her mother laughing with George.

Chapter Eight

⁂

"...But while their meat was yet in their mouths, the wrath of God came upon them, and slew the fattest of them, and smote down the chosen... For all this they sinned still, and believed not for his wondrous ways."
- Psalm 78: 30-34

Second Thursday in May
Ann Arbor City Club

"Mary Livingston is in the library." The City Club's sharp-eyed receptionist realized Max and Helen had no idea where the library was. "I'll be glad to show you." She directed them through a set of glass doors into a long room crowded with bridge players huddled in silence around a dozen or more tables. Max winked at one of the elderly ladies. She disgustedly waved him away.

The receptionist pointed to a flight of stairs situated between the next group of parlors. She whispered. "To your left at the top of the landing."

"Big place," Max said, but was shushed by more than one bridge player.

The library was stuffed into the smallest room in the building. The place would have served as a walk-in closet. Besides the bookshelves, there was room for a black leather chair and a decent lamp and table. The only other furnishing was a miniature gate-leg table with an occupied chair. Max made himself comfortable in the leather reading chair.

"Mrs. Livingston?" Helen asked

For a lady past her prime, Mrs. Livingston was stylishly dressed. "Are you picking up a book for a member?"

Max held out The Firm's business card. "We would appreciate any information about a doctor our agency is investigating for the police."

"I don't think I can help you about any of our members."

"I understand." Max put his card back in his wallet and started to rise. "We did hear you might be able to help …"

"Who is it? Is she in any trouble?"

"We don't know, yet," Helen said. "Dr. Dorothy Whidbey was identified as a friend of yours."

Mrs. Livingston motioned for them to follow her. "Give me your card. We need more privacy." Max and Helen followed her to a slightly bigger room decorated with white wicker furniture, pink pillows and a full-length mirror. "This is the bride's room." Mrs. Livingston held the door open for them "No one will walk in on us here."

Max held onto the arms of the delicate looking wicker chair and eased down gingerly into the pillows. Helen half expected the chair to disintegrate under his weight. A swift thought of a scene from the old black and white movie, *The Bishop's Wife*, came to mind. In the movie, several servants were needed to pry off a chair glued to the preacher. Max pulled the folding card table toward himself and spread out Charley Klondike's file.

'Please God,' Helen prayed, 'Pry every bit of truthful information from this lead.' She wondered if God's will included such trifles when the world needed major overhauling.

Mrs. Livingston closed the door and sat down opposite Max. "Mr. Hunt?"

"Yes." Max remembered to smile. "I hope you can help my partner, Helen Costello, and me."

Mrs. Livingston acknowledged Helen's presence and turned over The Firm's business card. "He that knows least commonly presumes most." She looked up, as if startled. "I should have gone to the police before. One seldom wishes to interfere in a couple's problems. Of course, wife-abuse wasn't always a crime against the state."

Helen nodded, keeping her astonishment to herself.

"Were you a witness to her husband's violence?" Max asked.

"Of course not!" Mrs. Livingston straightened her purple vest. She checked the heart-shaped watch pinned to its collar. "We share a gardener …." Max cocked his head to indicate he didn't understand. "…the Whidbeys and I. He's a sturdy fellow. Old but, you know," Mrs. Livingston included Helen with a look, "able."

Max slipped his notebook out of his jacket pocket. "The gardener's name?"

"Willets. John, I believe. We call him Willets."

"Did Willets witness the abuse?" Helen asked.

Mrs. Livingston squirmed. "It's so distasteful to discuss."

"We could go down to the police station." Max's tone was hard-edged. "I'm sure a policewoman would be happy to take down your statement." He slowly began to rise.

Helen hoped Mrs. Livingston would stop him. Waving twice for Max to remain seated, Mrs. Livingston allowed the gruesome facts to tumble out, as if she were spitting bad tasting soup onto the rug. "He's untied her more than once. Mr. Whidbey just leaves her stranded in the bed for hours. Willets helped her change the sheets after more than one urinary accident."

Max and Helen got the picture quickly enough. "Bondage?" Max prompted.

Mrs. Livingston secured a flowered handkerchief from her purse and dried her sweaty palms. "I suspect Willets did more than untie Doctor Whidbey, at times."

"Is there anything else?" Helen had heard all she wanted to know about the personal life of Dr. Dorothy Whidbey.

Shaking her head, no, Mrs. Livingston added. "Her wrists are usually bruised. I asked about them. She told me she used too many blood thinners."

"She never mentioned a patient of hers?" Max leaned forward. "Charles Klondike?"

"Oh yes she did! My late husband was an alcoholic too. Charley gave her quite a run for her money before he died. Her brother, you know. Lived out of state for years. But when his wife left him in Alaska, he tried to move in with Dorothy. Couldn't hold a job. He was a salesman. Heavy equipment, you know, for factories.

The Recorder's Way

Wrote bad checks to cover the cost of the alcohol."

Max made a note after he asked, "Did you know Mr. Klondike personally?"

"I met him after my husband talked him into attending an open AA meeting." Mrs. Livingston pursed her lips on the sour truth. "I think Charley only went once. Decided it was a God thing he didn't need. Honestly," Mrs. Livingston turned from Max to address Helen, as if a woman might empathize. "I could never understand why my husband attended the group. If he could stop with their help, he should have been able to stop drinking on his own." Mrs. Livingston inhaled.

Max held up his hand to ask a question, but she ignored him.

"His cat was a drunk too. What was his name? You wouldn't remember. I know, Stalin. See Charley used the cat to move in once with the Whidbeys after they had set him up in an apartment in Ashley Terrace. Seems the cat drank whatever Charley spilled, which must have been precious little. But the cat, Stalin, went crazy from the alcohol, I guess. He attacked Charley at every opportunity. Tore up everything in the apartment he couldn't break and had to be tranquilized just to be taken to the vet to be put down. Poor cat. Anyway the cat's destruction of Charley's apartment was why Dorothy took her brother in for a month."

Helen tried to inject a question, but Mrs. Livingston was too fast for her, too.

"Charley never stopped." Mrs. Livingston She rattled on, "Well near the end, he was hospitalized. DTs Dorothy said. She sent him to St. Anthony's Hospital to cut down on the talk. He died there."

"She was her brother's doctor?" Max shook his head.

"Yes." Mrs. Livingston dusted off her skirt as if her words left a residue she could see. "The Whidbeys were very close with their fortunes. Dorothy said her grandchildren were her priority. Never gave to charities. I asked more than once. She gave a pat answer, 'Families-first.' I know it's wrong to judge but animals take care of their families. People are supposed to rise above that type of selfishness to embrace a wider world, don't you agree?" Mrs. Livingston's hands swept in their opposing directions as if gathering applause to herself.

Max nodded. "Thank you for your help."

"You'll be hearing more from us," Helen offered.

"Oh, I hope not." Mrs. Livingston said, sincerely shocked.

***

Second Thursday in May
Whidbey Residence in Waterloo

Waterloo's millponds formed a figure eight with the smaller of the two filled with a several brightly-feathered, migrating waterfowl. Helen nudged Max. "The Whidbey couple has an intriguing view through their sitting room windows.

Captain Tedler tapped his holster when he stepped out of the police car. "I do not envy the Whidbeys' vista."

"Are you being honest with yourself?" Max asked himself the

same question. Should he acknowledge Helen's reference to coupling or let it pass. Was she thinking of him as more than a partner in the agency? Was he avoiding his feelings for Helen?

Once in the house after they listened to Dr. Whidbey's tirade for twenty minutes, Captain Tedler shook his head. "Madame, I don't care who you know. Your husband can tell your lawyer to meet us at the station. You are under arrest for murdering your brother, Charles Klondike."

Doctor Whidbey fell forward and screamed. "My ankle. You've broken my ankle."

Captain Tedler sat down on the hall's bench. He waved for Helen. "Call an ambulance. We need to transport Doctor Whidbey to emergency."

Max noted that Mr. Whidbey stood in the living room, staring at the view of the duck pond with his back to the fracas.

Doctor Whidbey screamed at him. "Call someone, you idiot."

Max wanted to flee the scene. But, they needed to get on with the business of wrapping up the loose ends of Sally Bianco's final caseload. "Call for back-up, Captain Tedler, Helen and I will run by John Willet's home."

Mr. Whidbey finally spoke up. "Does this concern St. Anthony's Hospital?"

"Yes, sir, it does." Captain Tedler stood with his feet placed firmly apart as if anticipating an attack.

"We were all fired from St. Anthony's Hospital." Doctor Whidbey's ankle didn't seem to require much attention from her.

"Reinstated," Helen contributed, "after three patients died?"

"Yes."

"That's the problem." Captain Tedler opened the door for the ambulance staff.

"That we were re-hired?"

"No, just the three murders."

Max and Helen were barred from leaving by the crush of ambulance workers at the door.

"You won't be able to prosecute any of us." Doctor Whidbey sounded confident. "Handler's a fixer, and Cornell is dead."

"I'd start worrying about your own case," her husband said without turning around, about as coldly as one would speak to a telephone solicitor. "You were told your brother was experiencing DT's at four in the afternoon. You never visited his room until you were sure he was dead."

* * *

Second Friday in May
Dr. Handler's Office

Helen considered telling Dr. Handler's patients why she needed to see their pediatrician. Four young women with their children were seated around the most luxurious waiting room Helen had ever frequented. Four domed teardrop chandeliers provided light. Max busied himself examining the swarms of colorful exotic fish in narrow tanks, which lined the walls all the way to the ceiling. The chairs were upholstered, the carpeting was a deep maroon pile, and the paintings were original oils. Flowering hedges topped by blooming tulip trees graced each windowed view. Pots of forced daffodils bulbs decorated the magazine tables.

Helen speculated about what the cold-faced, elegantly dressed mother, eyeing Max, would do with the red-cheeked urchin who sat between her designer boots happily chewing on her bootlaces. Would the sweet mother of twin two-year-olds rush them out of the office as if a fire alarm had gone off? The over-weight mother might take longer to convince her three-year-old to give up the visiting room's TV cartoons. The mom who was concentrating on a Nora Roberts' romance might not pay any attention to the fate of her sleeping infant.

Being sued for defamation of Dr. Handler's character might actually be enjoyable. Helen checked her watch before heading for the reception desk for the third time. "We've been waiting for forty-five minutes. I may not have explained the exact nature of my visit to Dr. Handler." Helen turned slightly so the reception area could hear and raised her voice to a strident tone. "Dr. Handler's mismanagement of a spinal meningitis case resulted in the death of a seven-year-old boy. I would like to hear his side of the case."

The receptionist immediately ushered them into the inner sanctum. Helen wasn't able to see if the waiting room emptied out with the news.

"Come this way." The nurse encouraged them to enter an office clearly marked, 'Private.'

During their long wait, Helen appreciated the ambiance of the doctor's consultation room. Dark green walls held old-fashioned English foxhunt scenes. The desk was as long as a coffin. The massive dark oak was carved with baby angels flapping wooden wings up the sides of the desk. Rows of matching leather-bound medical volumes attested to the doctor's qualifications.

Max chose to wait standing next to arched doors framing a view of the garden. Prepared flowerbeds awaited their blooms.

Dr. Handler finally arrived. "And you are?"

"Detectives Helen Costello and I'm Max Hunt from The Firm here in Ann Arbor." He handed the doctor their card.

Dr. Handler motioned for them to sit as he turned the card over to read Thomas Fuller's words aloud. "He that knows least commonly presumes most." Before Max sat down, he restated the reason for their visit. Dr. Handler nodded. "Yes, yes, that's what my receptionist said. She also said you emptied out the reception room."

Helen tried not to smile, but she knew she'd failed in hiding her delight. "Could you explain what happened the evening Larry Schneider died?"

Still unseated, Dr. Handler walked to his office door and opened it. The invitation to leave was obvious. "I can fully explain, but not to you two and not here."

"When can we expect you to drop by Captain Tedler's office?" Max asked.

"When he produces an arrest warrant and my lawyer accompanies me."

Helen straightened her briefcase strap on her shoulder in the middle of the doorway. She remembered it was a good place to stand during earthquakes, too. "Marilyn Helms has been very forthcoming. She's facing a murder charge."

Dr. Handler shoved her back into his office. "I think you better explain yourself, young lady."

Helen felt intimidated. She was glad Max insisted they should both approach the good doctor. She remembered the gun in her briefcase and backed away from the man to keep her balance. If he intended to attack her like Marilyn had, she could deal with him.

"I expect you owe Helen an apology for manhandling her?" Max demanded.

Helen cocked her head, letting Dr. Handler know her unguarded moment had passed.

"Yes, yes, of course." Helen half-expected to see oil drip from his mouth. "You surprised me." Dr. Handler motioned for both of them to sit back down. "Please tell me what has happened to Marilyn Helms?"

"Besides blackmailing you, Dr. Whidbey, and Dr. Cornell, she pushed an elderly detective off a cliff in Waterloo."

Dr. Handler looked ill. He pushed a button on the wall next to the door and a fully assembled bar swung into view. "Excuse me," he said, as he poured and drank a quick shot of bourbon. "Would you like a drink?"

"Do you admit to paying blackmail?" Max asked.

Dr. Handler slung back another shot of whiskey before taking his time to walk around his desk and sit down in his leather chair. He leaned his head against the back. "Marilyn Helms is a young woman I tried to help out financially. After her involvement in the deaths at St. Anthony's, no one would hire her. Did you know she is a drug addict?"

"Yes." Helen decided to sit down, too.

Max took out his notebook. "The victim, Sally Bianco, met Marilyn in Adrian at a recovery retreat at St. Anthony's convent."

"Ironic, isn't it?" Dr. Handler said.

"I don't think so." Helen consulted Max.

"I mean the hospital and the convent both being named for St. Anthony." Neither Max nor Helen responded. Helen could see Dr. Handler's mind was racing around inside that handsome old skull, looking for believable excuses. "Marilyn Helms was my lover," Dr. Handler proffered.

"We've met Marilyn," Max said.

"Oh, I'm not saying she was attractive," Dr. Handler stroked his chin. "Just convenient."

Helen felt as if a sewer had opened at her feet. Her nose twitched and she needed to bathe, to change her clothes as soon as possible. Max stood and Helen followed him to the door. The fresh air from the hall helped revive her.

"Captain Tedler will be contacting you," Max said with his back still turned away from the doctor. Helen didn't want to see the man alive on earth, either. 'God forgive me,' she prayed for her violent thought.

* * *

Seven wives married that guy?" Max opened the passenger door of his Mustang for Helen.

"Will Captain Tedler ask the wives to testify against Handler?"

Max banged the steering wheel. "I wonder how long number seven will last."

"Does money make women blind?"

Max knew Maybell used money to justify her actions. "I'd like to meet the present Mrs. Handler."

Helen seemed to read his mind. "Alone?"

"I might find a different angle on the case."

"I agree, Max. She'll be inhibited with me tagging along."

"I think I should go now, before Handler gets a chance to prepare her.

"Just drop me at home, Max." Helen fastened her seat belt. "It's on the way."

* * *

Second Friday in May
Dr. Handler's home

Dr. Handler's wife inserted her key into the front door, as Max Hunt strolled up behind her. "Mrs. Handler?"

"Yes. You're not allowed to solicit in this neighborhood, young man."

Max flashed his detective badge. "The police are interested in Dr. Handler's association with Marilyn Helms. She's a nurse who works for him. We have her in custody for the murder of a colleague of mine, Sally Bianco."

"You'll need to wait for him." Mrs. Handler opened the unusual front door. The doorway wasn't double, but it was wider than most. The home was white-painted brick. A '1909' historical plaque was displayed prominently near the recessed entrance.

Max stepped over the threshold. "This is wide enough for a coffin and pallbearers."

"The house has been owned by doctors since it was built." Mrs. Handler led the way to the right of the entrance past a chiming clock. "My husband should be home in ten minutes."

The entrance rug was a zebra skin. The floors were tiled white, the stairway facing the doorway was carpeted in white, the walls, the latticework on the windows, the piano, the couch, the lampshades, and all the knick-knacks were white. In the main room, the mounted heads of a white buffalo, an African elephant, a horned rhinoceros, and a tall long-horned sheep marred the innocence-claiming, immaculately white decorating scheme.

In Dr. Handler's den at the back of the house where Mrs. Handler deposited Max, the walls were a deep maroon. Max was tempted to touch the textured material on the walls, which looked like tanned hides, dyed to match each other. Fifteen more animal heads of antelope, moose, and deer were hung two and three high around the stuffy room. "Could you open a window?" Max felt he might pass out from the lack of oxygen or the surrounding horrors.

Mrs. Handler swung open the French doors. A breeze wafting over a wall of red roses entered the room, but its sweetness reminded

Max of the smell of fresh blood in Iraq. Instead of taking the chair Mrs. Handler pointed to, Max stepped out into the small garden. A stone bench served him well. Max wished he smoked. He could cover his queasiness better by lighting up. "Could I ask for a drink of water?"

"You look quite ill, young man. I'll be right back."

When Mrs. Handler returned, Dr. Handler accompanied her. "We have already spoken at my office," Dr. Handler explained to his wife. He pointed the way out for Max. "I'll have to ask you to leave." Max stood up, held onto the frame of the French doors and wobbled past the doctor and his wife. "Have you been drinking?" Dr. Handler shouted after him. Max managed to find the front door, but his knees failed him. He fell head first across the threshold.

"Call 911, Margaret!" Dr. Handler knelt beside Max. "What's wrong with you?"

Max thought he might have broken his nose on the pavement. Blood gushed everywhere. He tried to sit up, but the blood threatened to ruin his clothes. Still on all fours, Max gained access to his handkerchief to stop the nosebleed. "Post Traumatic Stress Disorder," he managed to say before passing out from the sight of his own blood.

* * *

Second Friday in May
Costello Residence

"But, Mother." Helen shook her head at the plethora of empty boxes in her bedroom. "I like my clothes. You *have* been busy today. I know you like me in emerald green now but I don't want to give any more of my things to Purple Heart."

"Of course you don't." Mother sat down on Helen's single bed. "I'm sorry. You know I've managed this household with an iron fist for so long, I don't know how to stop."

"You were never a tyrant." Helen joined her mother on the bed. "You know Dad and I love you."

"But you are getting too old for me to manipulate." Mother smiled, but then handed Helen the housing section of the newspaper. Three advertisements were circled in red.

"Oh, Mother." Helen thought she might break down in childish tears. "You want me to move out?"

Mother hugged her. "I want you to be happy, as happy as your father and I are." They could hear the phone ringing downstairs. Julia's new social life included an unusual increase in calls. Helen's extension rang only when customers called The Firm. Dad would answer the house phone.

"With whom will I be as happy as you and Dad?"

"Why Max, of course."

"I don't want to move in with Max."

Mother stood and dusted off her hands. "I should hope not! I moved from my parents' home into Andrew's apartment after we married. But I think you should learn how to live on your own. Decorate your own house, buy groceries, get a cat."

"Like a spinster?"

"Like someone who needs a pet to warm up a place." Mother lined the boxes up under the windows. "Something to come home to."

"I guess I could use the boxes to pack. Sister James Marine is taking ten of my dollhouses for the convent. She thinks an abuse shelter will take the rest." Helen tapped the roof of her blue Victorian dollhouse. "I'm keeping this one."

"I bet you and Max will end up in an old house like this." Mother bent over to move one of the tiny chairs away from the miniature dining room table. She set it on the floor outside the house.

Helen saw the action as a metaphor for moving her chair away from the Costello table. Did her presence remind her mother too much of the first George Clemmons? Her injury of rejection by the Clemmons family and by the man she had loved must be fresh in her mind.

Mother asked, "Did I ever tell you Sally Bianco and I tried to volunteer at the Safe House?" Dad came up the stairs and stood in the doorway. Mother saw him, too; but continued her story. "The shelter fired us because Sally told the women to wait until their husbands fell asleep, then to take an iron skillet and beat them around the head and privates."

"No wonder they asked you to leave." Helen rescued the discarded dollhouse chair, repositioning it under the table in the miniature dining room.

Dad tried to interrupt. "That phone call was from…"

Helen did not want to concede her point. "You were supposed

to let women gain back their inner strength before they moved out on their own."

"While they were penniless and so beaten up no one would hire them?" Mother clicked her tongue. "Didn't make sense to Sally and it didn't make sense to me."

"The hospital!" Dad finished his bit of news.

Helen hugged her mother. "Okay, we can look at the places you picked out for me."

Dad coughed as he stood at the door. Mother laughed and pointed at him. "Your dad circled those apartments."

Helen's mouth dropped open. "*Et tu Bruté?*"

Her dad took the offending paper. "This condo is just two blocks from Max's, walking distance. You could cook for him, invite him over."

"Max?"

"He's at the hospital?" Dad limped over to her, shook her shoulders. "Max loves you but doesn't think he's good enough for you."

"Max?"

"Anyone else been sniffing around you?"

"Dad!"

Mother asked him to repeat himself. "Max is in the hospital? That's what you said?"

"Yes. We have to go." Dad herded the two women down the stairs.

Once in the car, he said, "Max collapsed at Dr. Handler's

home. The ambulance took him to the university hospital." He turned slightly to speak to Helen who sat as if stunned in the back seat of the car. "Helen, your mother and I are not blind. We know you care for Max." The three of them drove in silence until Dad added, "By the way, your condo has three trees and flowering hedges. The window boxes are filled, now, with daffodils."

"Each unit has its own laundry room." Mother said.

Dad slowed the car to ask, "Did Max's PTSD cause his vomiting the other day?"

Helen discovered she could speak. "Max had previously told me his shell shock was hardly noticeable because of his parents' deaths."

"His dad strangled his mother," Dad explained to Mother. "then shot himself."

"I'm sure the war could trump that," Julia said. "Is he under a doctor's care?"

"He will be from now on," Helen promised them. She tried to explain why Max was not seeing a therapist currently. "We both studied the symptoms for shell shock at school. PTSD is just the new name for war injuries to the soul. The smallest thing can trigger a bout of debilitating fear." Helen remembered Max's shock and shame at hearing Dad mention Mrs. Brent's pregnancy.

She had Google'd his symptoms of Post Traumatic Stress Disorder to find if a cure existed. EMDR, Eye Movement Desensitization and Reprocessing, sessions might allow Max to distance himself from his memories and set up defense mechanisms to cope with reoccurrences. "I wonder what happened at the Handlers." Helen asked.

"Something must have triggered the episode?" Dad said, rubbing his bum leg.

Chapter Nine

"Therefore their days did he consume in vanity and their years in trouble. When he slew them, then they sought him: and they returned and enquired early after God." Psalm 78: 30-34

Third Monday in May
Ann Arbor Police Station

Dr. Handler wore designer jeans with a black silk shirt for his visit to the police station. Max priced out the sneakers on the doctor's feet. Three hundred dollars was a lot to pay for a pair of shoes. Dr. Handler's attire telegraphed he was not destitute. When the newspapers reported Dr. Whidbey had been arrested in connection with a blackmailing scheme, Dr. Handler decided to make himself available to the police. "I'll be glad to authorize handing over all my bank records." Handler spoke to Captain Tedler, who stayed in the hall closing the interrogation room door without commenting. Max spread the doctor's file contents onto the metal table. Dr. Handler refused to take a seat. "Isn't Tedler joining us?"

Max pointed to the stack of accounting records. "He's recording our session with a visitor on the other side of the mirror. We received a warrant yesterday for the information. Why did you find it necessary to pay Marilyn Helms $30,000?"

Handler hid his curiosity about the mystery visitor by becoming overly chatty. "I'm glad you've recovered so quickly from your bout of PTSD." Dr. Handler refused to examine the file Max thrust to his side of the table. "I know Dr. Whidbey and Dr. Cornell didn't match my outlay. They paid Marilyn blackmail for keeping their slip-ups secret. I, however, was not included in the debacle. I paid Marilyn for sexual favors."

Max raised one eyebrow. "You think a jury is going to believe you paid over $30,000 for sex?"

Dr. Handler tapped his delicate fingers on the metal table. "I admit when Marilyn first started, her prescriptions were easier to finance. I've kept detailed financial records and a few videos before Marilyn became so enormous. My journals are very explicit."

Max realized the doctor might slip away from them. He remembered Sharon Daley and Helen cautioning him. "Your wives … ?"

Dr. Handler rubbed his hands together. "Were seven. Every time Marilyn needed a raise, she would threaten to expose us. I always told her to go ahead, no one would believe her. However, six of my very wealthy wives did take her side in the affair. Apparently, their sensibilities were outraged I would pay for serves rendered." Handler stared unflinchingly at his reflection in the two-way mirror. "I merely countered with the fact each of them paid my bills to enjoy being with me."

Max nodded in a state of shock. "Of course, the whole truth and nothing but the truth always ended the relationships."

"However," Dr. Handler raised one ringed hand for Max and the secret visitor to examine. "My seventh wife and I are no longer interested. So the issue is moot. We like to travel. We've been married for three months."

Max remembered why he didn't enjoy the detective business and why Helen declined to interview Handler. He opened Larry Schneider's file folder. "Your patient, who died at St. Anthony's Hospital …?"

Dr. Handler condescended to sit down. "Larry's parents were very negligent. They never told me about the boy's rash. I personally had not examined the boy when he was taken to St. Anthony's emergency room. I was no longer employed with the hospital. The attending doctor was apparently quite busy with a flurry of panicky mothers bringing in their children to be tested for spinal meningitis. If Larry's mother had bathed him the night before, she would have seen red skin eruptions. It's a wonder he lived as long as he did, before Marilyn gave him an overdose of morphine."

"Is your lawyer expected soon?" With those words, Max scooped up the files and fled the room as if to search for Dr. Handler's lawyer. He wasn't sure Dr. Handler even considered needing an attorney. Mostly, Max needed an excuse for leaving the room without admitting to Dr. Handler that there might *not* be enough evidence to extract any punishment for his neglect in Larry Schneider's death. Captain Tedler and the fictitious visitor could show Dr. Handler the door.

Driving down I-94, Max clamped his right arm down on the file of Dr. Handler's bank statements. When the wind had flipped open the folder, pages had taken flight behind the convertible. Max tucked the bank records under the passenger seat, without a thought about retrieving the lost documents. Max wished his thoughts of Helen could fly away as easily. He wanted the woman, needed her close, missed her whenever they were separated. He berated himself for his deception to her father. Andrew needed to know all the facts about his affair with Maybell (Anita Brent) and the impending birth of his child. "My child," he said aloud and acknowledged for the first time all the pride he felt.

"Also …," Max felt the weight of his next idea. "Helen and I need to talk to Larry Schneider's parents."

* * *

Tom Schneider's Apartment

Tom Schneider's stark penthouse was unrelieved by the ambiance of books or fabrics. No rugs were scattered about the slate flooring. Leather pillows perched on the black leather couch and chairs. Vertical blinds with mirrored slats blocked out the fading light of the spring day. Black brass sculptures of men and prancing horses were tastefully placed about the living room.

Helen wondered if Max's studio apartment would feel like this negative block of space, too. After Tom asked them to remove their shoes, a mangy, longhaired black mutt sniffed Max's gigantic loafers and Helen's high heels. Max let the dog lick his hand. "What is your dog's name?"

"I fixed her after her last litter, but I failed to name her." Tom stretched out his arms to offer Helen and Max glasses of iced tea wrapped in paper towels.

Helen wanted to spoon feed the discouraging information about Dr. Handler's case with a compliment about Tom's apartment. Her mind drew a blank. Instead, she heard Max say. "You haven't lived here long."

"I'm not in town very often. Sit, sit. My son deserved better."

Max plopped down on the couch. Helen sat on the arm of one of the leather chairs. She found it difficult to ask for painful details. Max asked for her, "Dr. Handler reassured you Larry would be all right?"

"He spoke to my wife." Tom ground his teeth. The dog growled.

* * *

Amy Schneider's Home

Max and Helen found Amy Schneider's nest glorified in pink and mauve peony designs, which spread over chintz-covered, matching love seats and hassocks. Three Siamese cats reclined in various poses of disinterest. Lamp tables strained under the weight of books. Tomes were left opened. Others were cracking their spines under precarious stacks. Every bookshelf was stuffed with horizontal and vertical disorderly piles of books. Verdant philodendrons grew on top of the bookshelves as if sustained by the volumes of deep, captured thoughts. Light rose carpeting clashed with the coffee table lilacs, which splayed out their luxuriant hypnotic odors.

"What a lovely home you've made for yourself." Helen accepted tea in a china cup.

"Tell me the names of your cats," Max said.

Amy stroked the cats as she passed them. "Hamlet is white, of course. Rosencrantz is the calico and Guildenstern is all black."

"Was Larry your only son?" Max sank into one of the loveseats.

"He was our only child. Tom has never forgiven me."

Max sipped the tea as he stalled, hoping for Divine aid to give this bereft mother an offering of comfort. He placed his empty cup and saucer on the stack of books next to him, before his answer arrived from Helen. "You forgave your husband?" Hamlet positioned himself on Helen's lap.

"Tom never does anything wrong," Amy said.

"He left you," Max said.

Amy brushed her fingers over her dry forehead. "Because of Larry's death."

Max bent forward with his elbows resting on his knees. "Dr. Handler is the person to blame, not you." He wanted to fix the chasm between this husband and wife. "Would you accept your husband's return?"

Amy shook her head. "He won't want to come back. I remind him of Larry's death."

"All your husband's memories of your son include you." Max

stood up to leave.

"Has Tom seen your lovely home?" Helen asked.

Amy smiled; a hint of happiness moistened her eyes. "You're right, I should invite him."

* * *

Third Wednesday in May
The Firm

Max greeted Andrew with less hesitation than he felt. "Helen phoned. You expect the district attorney this morning?"

"First thing." Andrew carried a watering can into the back computer room. He stopped with his foot holding open the door to the reception area. "Could you carry a couple chairs up to your office? It's the most impressive room."

"No problem." Max easily slung one computer chair under each arm and mounted the steps to his office. Andrew quickly followed on his heels with a pot of coffee and warmer. Max piled up some of the papers on his desk. "Should I let Mr. Warner sit behind my desk?"

"I don't think we have to go that far." Andrew surveyed the room. "We look like we know what we're doing."

"Hello?" They heard Helen's voice sing out downstairs.

"Come on up," Andrew called. "I'll wait for Roger downstairs. We don't need to call him 'Mister,' do we?"

When Helen arrived in his office, Max felt his heart rate change. He sat down behind the desk to calm down. She was dressed professionally, suit and blouse. She was so endearing, small and capable all at the same time. He felt a little dizzy with the realization he might one day ask this beauty to marry him, if he ever found the nerve to be rejected. 'Please, God,' he prayed for he knew not what. 'Your will be done.'

Six-foot-eight District Attorney Roger Warner was all business as soon as he thanked Andrew for the delicious coffee blend. "We will need every bit of hard evidence you can find on Handler if we're going to prosecute him for negligence in Larry Schneider's death. What do you have besides claiming he paid a nurse to keep quiet?"

After looking up for once to shake a man's hand, six-foot-five Max knew if anyone could nail Handler, Warner would have the best shot. "Seven wives can be called to testify that he was involved with Marilyn Helms."

Helen spoke up. "He claims he was paying her for sex. The woman is enormous."

Roger Warner shook his head. "Anything else?"

"Both the boy's parents will testify." Max said. "Do we need to make a deal with the nurse to testify?"

"She's accused of murdering Sally Bianco to keep the racket intact?" Warner asked.

Max could see the case against Handler contained more problems than solutions. "Are you going to offer her a deal to testify against Handler?"

"Sally gave her life to bring these doctors to justice." Helen's voice held the same note of despair Max felt.

Roger Warner stood up. "I'd like to crucify the guy, too. Andrew, give me affidavits from each of the wives. I understand Marilyn Helms is friends with another nurse and a nun? I'd like both of them to be at the trial with Marilyn. Is there anything else I should know?"

"Yes." Max pulled out his middle drawer to delay breaking the bad news. "Handler said he has tapes of Marilyn."

"Videos?" the D.A. asked.

Helen nodded. "Should we ask for them before the trial?"

"No," Roger said. "Let's hope the matter won't come up."

After he left, Max was sure Handler would be freed. "The tapes are his only defense."

"Maybe he possesses a thread of decency," Helen said.

"No." Max was sorry he could not reassure her. "There's no question of any integrity on his part."

"I'll ask Sister James Marine to talk to Marilyn." Helen walked around the desk, hugged his shoulder, and kissed the side of his face.

Max was afraid to move. Andrew appeared with his watering can and began to water Max's silk plant hangings.

Helen and Max shouted at him together, "They're silk!"

Then they laughed at Andrew's surprised face and dripping watering can. "Sorry." Andrew said. "I've been watering them since you went to Cape May." Andrew laughed. "I wondered why Max's office floor kept getting wet. Listen, Max, I printed out the list of Handler's wives. Take a tape recorder. Let's hope their resentments will help dig a hole for Handler to fall into."

* * *

"We need to talk, again." Max's tone was too serious when he spoke to Andrew. On the way down the steps from Max's office, Helen wondered if it was possible Max might quit The Firm. She nervously turned on the message machine.

Sister James Marine sounded urgent. "It's Marilyn," she said. "I told her Dr. Handler might get off by claiming she was a prostitute. If you can settle on manslaughter for Sally Bianco, Marilyn says she left evidence at the convent which will prove she only blackmailed Dr. Handler. She said to ask Sharon Daley about the point. Marilyn says she and Sharon were lovers. Neither one of them have been with a man. I think you told me Sharon was a long-time friend of hers. Call me. I'm back at the convent. Marilyn should be arriving with Officer Creeper at the Ann Arbor jail today or tomorrow. Sister Alice says there are notes in shorthand in the margins of her diet book. Apparently Marilyn's mother wanted her to be a secretary instead of a nurse, so of course she became a nurse."

"The diary is there," Max had followed her down the stairs. "Sister Alice said there were Gregg shorthand notes in the margins."

"Great," Helen said. "Do you want to go down with me to retrieve it?"

"No." Max seemed to lose his excitement about the new evidence. "I need to talk to your dad."

* * *

Third Wednesday in May
Adrian Convent

In Adrian, Sister Alice was paging through the diet book while she waited at the entranceway of St. Anthony's Convent. Helen was a little disappointed not to be invited in.

"The place is filled with guests," Sister Alice explained. "We only charge $55 a night, which includes three meals."

"No wonder you're mobbed," Helen said. "Sister James Marine said the sisters might enjoy my collection of dollhouses. I brought ten with me."

Sister Alice started to follow her down the steps, then changed her mind. "Oh, wait right here. I'll get help."

Helen didn't count, but she was soon surrounded by a bevy of nuns oohing over her dollhouses. "Please," she said. "Pick whichever ones you want." Within minutes, the Honda was devoid of Helen's childhood memories.

Sister Alice cradled her choice, a twin-gabled bungalow. "Mother Superior said to tell you she will be at Dr. Handler's trial."

Helen would have been happier seeing where each of her dollhouses were positioned in the sisters' rooms. Letting go of all the hours spent with each of the homes seemed to tug at her heart. 'Indian giver' she told herself. She tried to take comfort in the knowledge each of the nuns might be replaying their childhood reminiscences. The world was a better place by giving away her precious clutter. God awarded riches in order to share with others. But the silly grief of loss was real.

Helen raced her father's new gas-saving Honda back to Ann Arbor. She did obey the speed limit, not like when she was younger and sped down the roads in Waterloo at a hundred miles an hour. As she placed her briefcase under the desk of the accounting data computer, she wondered why it never occurred to her to make one end of the long back room into an office for herself. She could bring her best dollhouse in to decorate.

A coldness in the pit of her stomach alerted her to the ridiculous immaturity of the idea. She needed to grow up and stop acting like a dim-witted Barbie doll. She would call the contractor to start work on the new office. Helen didn't want a second floor place to work like Max's, even though there was room on the roof. She could afford the outlay. What she wanted was to be close to her dad, close to the front door. She laughed at herself. Helen wanted to be in control of the choice of cases. Her new clients should have a place to meet with her privately.

The reception area was out, as was her home, where her mother's weekly mah-jongg group packed every available inch. The game resembled gin rummy using plastic tiles instead of cards. At Helen's last count, three tables were also crammed into the kitchen. Her mother ought to join the City Club before the ladies wore out the flooring and eventually her mother's new gift of hospitality.

Helen tried to make sense of her father's accounting spreadsheets on the computer as he pulled up a chair next to her.

"Dad, didn't you return Mr. Brent's and Mrs. Clapton's fees?"

"I tried. They both said they were happy with our services." Her dad patted her arm to get her attention away from the computer screen. "Max is insisting on another chat with me."

"Has he decided what he's going to do about the baby?"

"What baby?"

"His baby. Anita Brent tricked him into fathering a child for her."

"I think you let the cat out of the bag. But the child is something you two should decide."

Helen felt confused. "What do I have to do with Max's decision?"

"Probably everything." Dad scratched his head. "For smart people, you two are emotional midgets."

"Have you asked Max to leave The Firm?"

Andrew shook his head. "Of course not. Why would you even think that?"

Relief spread through Helen. She had worried after her father learned about Max's child he might not trust him to stay at the Firm. "I'd miss his voice."

"His voice? Child when are you going to wake up and realize you're in love with the hulk?" Helen stared at her father.

Max interrupted them. He came into the back room, chose a chair with its back to the computer next to Helen's and spread out his long legs. "Did you get the diary?"

"Yes." After handing Max the diary, Helen put her hand on

Max's knee. Max brushed her hand away, rose and stalked around the room.

Helen acknowledged the rejection to her father. What good was loving Max, if he wouldn't accept her touch?

Max coughed. "Helen, who do you know that reads shorthand?"

Dad answered, "Julia does. I'll take it home with me."

"Helen," Max coughed again. "There's a movie at the Michigan Theatre you might enjoy. Jane Austen?"

Helen turned back to the computer. "George and his friend Mitzi are going. Do you want to meet us there?"

Dad threw up his hands. "Youth! I'll take the diet book over to the DA after Julia types up the notes."

Chapter Ten

"Then the congregation shall Judge between the slayer and revenger of blood accordingly." Numbers 35:24

Second Friday in June
Washtenaw County Court House

At the end of the courthouse's second-floor corridor, Helen opened the heavy door into the courtroom's old-fashioned, glassed-in entranceway. Sister James Marine waltzed in and settled into a front row seat in the spectators' gallery behind the D.A.'s table. Helen assumed the nun had attended more than one court case. Along the opposite wall, on the left side of the room, Marilyn Helms and a burly police matron were seated in uncomfortable looking chairs. Marilyn was gnawing at her fingernails.

Sharon Daley waved at Marilyn, who nodded. Then Sharon scooted into the bench row to sit next to Helen. "I'm still betting Dr. Handler will con his way out of trouble."

A low wooden fence separated them from Roger Warner and Captain Tedler, who dwarfed the prosecutor's table.

At the defense table, Verne Chapski, Dr. Handler's attorney, was of slight build but his carrot-red ring of hair drew further attention to his green plaid suit. At perhaps four-foot-eleven, the man resembled a Trappist monk with a shaved bald spot to acknowledge God's austerity.

Dr. Handler wore an expensive blue suit the same color as his suede shoes. His crop-haired wife leaned forward to touch him, once. He dismissed her presence with a perfunctory shrug.

Several well-dressed women sat a few rows behind Helen. She drew Captain Tedler's attention to the group and he nodded. The group of various ages was undoubtedly the collection of Dr. Handler's ex-wives.

Andrew and Julia Costello had slipped into the courtroom without Helen noticing. Her mother whispered to her, "We rented a truck for you for Saturday."

Helen appreciated her parents' assistance. However, their eagerness triggered a certain nervousness. "Max and George will help carry out my bed and dresser."

"Take the furniture in your sitting room, too," her father said. "We ordered tread mills and a digital TV screen for the wall. We plan to exercise in rainy weather."

Helen wanted to ask how long her parents had planned for her to leave home, but she knew enough about courtroom tactics not to ask a question to which she might not like the answer. She had scheduled to arrange her things in the condo while Dr. Handler's trial progressed. Her mother had shown her a catalog with pans, silverware, dishes – linens. Helen dutifully pointed out the ones she liked but didn't order anything. Apparently, she was going to be living alone a lot sooner than she had anticipated.

The entire courtroom noticed when Max Hunt arrived. He banged his shoulder into the entranceway door and the glass panels rattled in response. Nothing broke. Max rubbed his arm.

After her mother and father made room for him, Max sat behind Helen. "The ox has landed," he whispered.

Helen only had time to pat Max's hand as it rested on her shoulder before the bailiff requested everyone to stand for Judge Joe Wilcox's entrance.

* * *

When Helen touched Max's hand, his senses came alive. His awareness telescoped to the back of her fragile neck where her curls attempted to create ringlets. Max glared at Marilyn Helms who was trying to read Sandra Daley's lip-sync. He wished he could throw Marilyn out of the wooden chair she was sprawled on and pummel her with it the way she had beaten his Helen. Marilyn was lucky Helen didn't let her get her wish for 'suicide by cop.'

The jury members seated themselves in tiered rows along the right side of the room, which was as far away from Dr. Handler's persuasive tricks as possible.

Helen, Max, and Andrew had participated behind the scenes. Their careful background profiles contributed to the selection process of the six women and six men. Four of the men were churchgoers. Two were divorced more than once. Five of the women were married to their original husbands. One older woman was unmarried and an atheist. The moral persuasions of each sounded conservative. However, their leanings for or against Dr. Handler's mismanagement of Larry Schneider's case were unknown.

Then Max recognized Maybell's long blonde hair in the crowd behind Dr. Handler's present wife. He touched his nose with his left hand to stop a sneeze. Had he suddenly developed an allergic reaction to his old lover? When he included Mr. Brent in his survey, Max grabbed his onyx belt buckle. He relaxed recalling his Iraq PTSD mantra 'Stay at peace in a safe place.' Here was the mother of his embryonic child…in the same room with him…and Helen. Max's temptation to touch Helen's neck was quelled by the bailiff's call for attention.

* * *

Marilyn Helms was the prosecutor's first witness. Prison food seemed to agree with her. Helen was not surprised when Sister J. M. whispered, "She's lost weight."

Sharon agreed. "Maybe her five-year sentence will break her drug habit."

Helen knew enforced abstinence would not alter Marilyn's addictive personality. Once people were free to follow their own wills, only God could intervene. "Is she in a twelve-step program in prison?" Neither Sister J. M. nor Sharon seemed to know.

Roger Warner asked Marilyn his first question. "Dr. Handler says he possesses video tapes of you when you first became involved with him. Is that true?"

"Have you seen them?"

"Do they exist?"

"Of course not. He's going to say anything to get off."

The Recorder's Way

Roger Warner walked to where Dr. Handler was seated. "So, Dr. Handler is not going to produce tapes to prove his association and payments to you were for sexual favors?"

"In his dreams," Marilyn shouted.

"Keep a civil tongue in your head, young lady." Judge Wilcox chided Marilyn.

"Explain your relationship to Dr. Handler, in your own words." Roger Warner hinted that Marilyn had not been well-rehearsed.

"He was one of three doctors who paid me to keep quiet about their three patients." Marilyn sat up straighter. "The patients died in St. Anthony's Hospital in 1990."

Roger Warner faced the jury. "How much money have the doctors paid you in the last eighteen years?"

"I only kept track of Dr. Handler's." Marilyn started eating her fingernails.

"Why was that?"

"Because the other two, one I'm not supposed to name, and Dr. Whidbey were easier to handle. I always suspected Handler would cover his tracks. But I never thought he would claim to have had sex with me, paid me for sex. Geez! Sometimes when he wasn't flush, I accepted a stack of prescriptions from him. But usually he just paid cash. That's why I kept records. You typed up my notes."

"Yes, we did, your Honor." Roger placed Marilyn's journal and a stack of blue sheets of paper on the clerk's desk. "The defense attorney was given copies. I would like Marilyn to read a few excerpts to the jury."

Judge Wilcox motioned for the clerk to hand him the pile of papers. He read quietly for a minute or two. "Any objections, Mr. Chapski?"

Chapski shook his head. "No, Sir." Dr. Handler whispered urgently to him, but Chapski ignored his protest.

Marilyn was given the file. "Begin anywhere?"

"Yes," the D. A. said, "and mention the date."

Marilyn cleared her throat and started reading. "September 8, 1991: Handler showed me his winter cap from Scotland. He wrote me prescriptions for a year's supply of diet pills. March 15, 1992: Handler says he's not going to write any more prescriptions for me. He was wearing a white sweater fresh from his trip to Ireland. I called Mrs. Mary Alice Handler and said we needed to talk. Handler called back and said my prescriptions would be at the pharmacy. He also said his wife was divorcing him."

"Judge," Roger Warner held up his hand. "Could I excuse this witness temporarily to corroborate her evidence with Mrs. Mary Alice Handler's testimony?"

"Any objections, Mr. Chapski?"

"No, your Honor." More arm tugging and angry whispers occurred at the defense table.

The clerk called the first Mrs. Handler to the stand. A dignified gray-haired lady disengaged herself from the gaggle of Handler's ex-wives. She opened the gate between the audience and the court proper with a white-gloved hand. When the gate had the audacity to creak, the first Mrs. Handler allowed the D.A. to hold it open so that she could pass through.

"You were married how long to Dr. Handler?" Roger Warner backed away from the stand so the jury could witness the interchange between ex-wife and ex-husband.

"Thirteen terrible years." Mrs. Handler glared for a second at her ex-husband and then turned to the jury. "When Marilyn Helms called me, Benjamin claimed she was a prostitute. The marriage was essentially over years before I learned of Marilyn."

"Do you believe they were lovers?" Roger Warner motioned for her to answer in the jury's general direction.

"If I were you ...," Mrs. Handler touched her perfectly arranged white hair. "I would believe her. My analyst told me Benjamin was probably gay."

"Your honor?" Verne Chapski found a reason to object.

"The jury is to disregard the hearsay evidence presented by Mrs. Handler's therapist." Judge Wilcox glared at the jury. "Is that understood?"

Each member of the jury nodded. The unmarried lady even smiled.

"Could you tell us why your therapist would conclude such a thing?" The D.A. asked.

The first Mrs. Handler shook her head no. "I told him how excited Benjamin became before his hunting trips south of Adrian. The deer are fed there. Ben hunted from ground blinds or raised platforms. They were heated, too, the enclosures. He killed them and brought home a mounted head as a trophy every year we were married. The heads range from eight to thirty points – that's the number of antler points. I insisted he take the horrific things with him when I asked him to move out."

"You're excused," the D.A. stated.

"That's my job," Judge Wilcox said. "Any questions, Mr. Chapski?"

"No, your Honor."

The rest of Marilyn's evidence followed the same pattern. Notes were read and the relevant wife gave confirmation. Dr. Handler consistently claimed he was paying a prostitute, Marilyn, for sexual favors. Each wife handled the news slightly differently.

A jolly woman who had only been married a year to the doctor laughed. "Actually, Marilyn did me a favor. I was looking for a good excuse to back out of the sexless marriage."

A delicate looking woman with a German accent said after four years in their unhappy, expensive relationship, she, too, was delighted to end the marriage. She said, "Ben kept dragging home those horrible heads."

"Heads?" The D.A. asked.

"I went along on all four trips. First to Alaska. Healey was the town's name. I did enjoy seeing the Aurora Borealis. He went on a horseback hunt on the Central Alaskan Range. The next day he brought back a dead sheep, the one of those long-horned ones with the inward curved horns." The lady gestured to make sure the jury understood the type of mountain goat she was referring to. "He had it mounted and sent home. He always let the tour guides send the trophies to him here in Ann Arbor. Quite expensive: fleshed, salted, mounted and packaged for shipment. I can tell you!" The D. A. was not required to prompt her lengthy testimony. "He didn't kill anything at Seal Bay. However, in Manitoba he killed a black bear at Dorothy Lake. I love bears and wouldn't let him bring the mounted head into my house. I think he kept it in the storage unit I paid rent on."

"We went to Africa on a safari the next year, Southern Africa, Botswana, Zimbabwe. We stayed sixteen days so he could bring home an elephant head. He also bagged, that's what they call the dead beasts, a Cape Buffalo, a horned Rhino, and a zebra skin. I don't think he killed the zebra." The third Mrs. Handler dapped at her forehead with a wad of tissue. "I stayed in the hotels and shopped while he went off with the male guides. What makes a man commit violence against innocent animals?" Her lawyer made sure the divorce decree included a statement, "Benjamin Handler considers the act of sexual contact too packed with the chance of infection to participate."

"Your Honor?" Mr. Chapski objected.

Judge Wilcox banged his gavel several times when the audience decided to enjoy themselves over the third Mrs. Handler's remarks. "The statement is in the public record; therefore, the jury is allowed to consider it as evidence."

Helen noticed even Sister James Marine giggled slightly.

Judge Wilcox called the lawyers into his chambers. When

Roger Warner came out, Helen overheard him tell Captain Tedler, "Dr. Handler is unable to find the video tapes of Marilyn, but he insists they exist."

Sharon Daley reached for the D.A.'s arm. "You should let me testify."

Roger Warner nodded. "Shortly."

The jury heard again from Marilyn and thereafter from a slip of a girl under twenty, Kathy Handler, who described a sailing trip with Dr. Handler. After an uneventful vacation, she found women's underwear in her husband's suitcase. He claimed they were Marilyn's. Kathy's divorce lawyer claimed in the decree Dr. Handler was a cross-dresser.

Next a bug-eyed woman and an intense, sharp-jawed woman, both ex-wives, testified to Marilyn's timely interruptions of platonic but expensive alliances with Dr. Handler, who continued to bring home the mounted heads of deer.

Marilyn Helms was recalled to the stand by Verne Chapski. "Where did you meet your doctors for the prescriptions?"

Marilyn looked at the district attorney, before she answered. "What do you mean?"

Mr. Chapski moved to block Marilyn's view of Roger Warner. "In a bookstore, a laundry, your apartment, where?"

"It varied." Marilyn crossed her arms. "Dr. Whidbey only needed a phone call. The unnamed doctor was nice. He was a widower, and I usually took donuts to his house."

"How nice was he?" Mr. Chapski voice implied an

assignation.

Marilyn came to attention in the witness stand. "He once touched my face and told me God thought I was a beautiful woman."

"Was that the only touching?" Marilyn refused to answer. Mr. Chapski appealed to the judge.

"Young lady, answer the question."

"That was the only time he touched me. And no other man ever laid a hand on me!"

Judge Wilcox warned Marilyn again. "There is no reason to shout. Do you want to be held in contempt of court?"

"No, your Honor. He's making me mad."

"Sorry." Mr. Chapski walked back to his table. Marilyn stood as if dismissed, but Judge Wilcox waved for her to sit back down. Mr. Chapski picked up the stack of blue notes. He turned slowly to Marilyn as he paged through the notes. "You mentioned quite a few dates in your testimony: September 8, 1991." Chapski turned a page. "March 15, 1992. Should I go on?"

"What's your point?" Judge Wilcox asked.

Mr. Chapski handed his list to the judge. "Dr. Handler has attached his motel receipts for all of the dates mentioned, your Honor."

The audience hushed a common gasp.

Judge Wilcox returned the evidence. "The clerk will accept these."

Mr. Chapski motioned to Marilyn and then swung his arm to include the jury. "You're angry because you've been caught in a lie.

Isn't that the truth?"

"He never touched me."

Mr. Chapski walked over to Marilyn, standing dangerously close.

Helen Costello sucked in her breath. Her sore ribs reminded her to relax into the pain.

Chapski stuck his face within an inch of Marilyn's chubby cheeks. "So you touched him?"

Bam! Marilyn punched his face.

Mr. Chapski screamed like a woman.

Judge Wilcox stood and pounded the gavel. The court came to its feet when the judge stood, only they were shouting and laughing. Finally, the policewoman, who had accompanied Marilyn into the courtroom and the officer of the court handcuffed a resistant Marilyn to the witness stand. "He had it coming." Marilyn said, once she calmed down.

"And your sentence gained six months for contempt of court." Judge Wilcox sat back down. "This seems like a good time for a lunch break. The jury is cautioned not to talk about the case. We will resume at 1:30 for a more peaceful session. Will you be all right by then, Mr. Chapski?"

Chapski held a reddening handkerchief to his nose. He nodded.

* * *

Max had taken Helen's hand, drawing her into a conference ᵈrew, Captain Tedler and the district attorney. "Do the gate all the other testimony?"

Roger Warner shook his head. "The jury will have a lot to consider. I'll call Sharon to the stand if Chapski thinks he's finished with Marilyn." He couldn't suppress a laugh.

"Well, let's go over to Angelo's and grab a bite." Andrew held out his hand for Julia.

"That will take forever, Dad." Helen still held Max's hand.

Max didn't want to let go either. "You go ahead. Helen and I need to talk about Saturday's move."

When they were alone in the hall, Helen looked up at him. "We could get a sandwich downstairs."

They still held hands in the elevator. Max thought the crowd, which included the Brents, would not appreciate their embracing. However, once they were in the hall leading to the cafeteria, Max couldn't wait any longer. He stopped and drew her to him. Placed a hand under her chin and kissed her. He felt as if he'd never kissed a woman before. This innocent friend was so trusting, so open to his advances. Max stopped, releasing her mouth, letting her step away, but keeping Helen's hand. "You move me," was all he could say.

"You know I love you, Max."

"And I love you ... more than I should." Max rubbed his curls with his free hand. He still hadn't explained about his child to her father.

"Living alone for a year will put me on a better footing. I'll appreciate another person more, don't you think?" Helen tugged her hand away to secure a lunchroom tray.

Max's predominant thought was his child would be born

before Helen's year of innocence was completed.

* * *

The afternoon sun poured into the paneled courtroom. Helen smiled at Sister James Marine. Tiny translucent hairs on the nun's upper lip were highlighted by the brightness. Helen tried to concentrate on the court proceedings once they were underway again. Nothing seemed important anymore because Max said he loved her! More than he should? Nevertheless, she found herself looking forward to living alone. Max now sat next to Helen, a mountain of steadiness in her changing world.

Mr. Chapski continued his cross-examination of Marilyn. "You received a manslaughter sentence for killing Mrs. Sally Bianco?"

"I didn't kill her." Marilyn looked at her handcuffs.

"Your attack dog ripped her throat out before knocking her over a cliff?"

The jury drew in shocked breaths, shifting positions on their rigid pews.

Marilyn whispered her answer, "He was trained by the National Guard."

"The jury didn't hear the witness, your Honor."

"Speak up."

Marilyn glared at him and shouted. "Make up your mind."

Judge Wilcox refused to take offense.

~ever, Mr. Chapski stepped back as if expecting another

ıy did you let your dog attack Mrs. Bianco?"

Marilyn pointed at Sister James Marine. "It's her fault!" All eyes turned toward the Mother Superior.

Sister James Marine smiled ruefully. "It's true." She nudged Helen. Tears were running down the nun's usually placid face.

Helen took her hand. "You know you're not to blame."

Judge Wilcox sighed. "Explain yourself."

"She wanted me to tell that old hag …."

The room became ominously silent. Captain Tedler, Andrew and Julie had risen from their seats. Their anguish was palpable. Helen, Max, and Sister J. M. joined the tribute to a lady's passing. Judge Wilcox maintained the silence for five minutes. Captain Tedler was the first to take his chair, the others followed.

"If I were allowed to strike you," Judge Wilcox said to Marilyn in a stage whisper loud enough for everyone to hear, "I would."

Properly chastised, Marilyn continued, "Mother Superior told me Sally Bianco was a detective who might be interested in my story about the three deaths at St. Anthony's Hospital in 1990."

Mr. Chapski stayed out of reach, standing close to the defendant's table. "Were you surprised at Sally Bianco's reaction to your claim?"

"She said they could go to jail." Marilyn looked directly at the jury as if to ask for understanding. "I told her patients die all the time. Doctors get away with murder."

"Your honor?" Chapski took a step toward the bench, but changed his mind.

"You asked her what happened." Judge Wilcox gave a nod to Marilyn. "Continue."

"Sally said they were culpable. I had to ask her what that meant. She said they would go to jail. Well," Marilyn made a gesture to the jury as if her reasoning was obvious. "How were they going to provide me with diet pills if they were in jail?"

"Paying you for sexual services rendered with diet pills?" Chapski asked, keeping his distance.

"No." Marilyn acted as if the lawyer had turned stupid. "Paying me to keep my mouth shut."

The D.A. asked for permission to re-examine Marilyn. "Weren't you suspicious when Dr. Handler invited you to a motel – to receive your payments?"

"I knew I could handle the good Doctor Handler." Marilyn glared at Roger Warner.

"Did you tell his wives you provided sex?"

"No." Marilyn again petitioned the jury. "All I said was I wanted to talk to them privately about Dr. Handler. I can't help it if they all assumed I meant I was his lover. I was prepared to tell them about the death of Larry Schneider, if they had the nerve to ask."

"But you knew they would assume you were involved sexually?" Roger Warner rubbed his palms together.

"I never denied it," Marilyn said, "because they never asked me."

"Did Sally Bianco know you were blackmailing the doctors?"

Marilyn became very quiet. She looked up at the judge, then

the jury, then back at the district attorney. "I told you in the deposition to receive the manslaughter sentence."

"Repeat your words," Roger Warner motioned, "to the jury."

"I told Sally, if the doctors went to jail they wouldn't be able to pay me."

"Blackmail?"

"I'm sure she knew what I meant. Sally took out her keys and started back down the path. When I first saw her keys, I only intended to take her car and run. But, she had way too much information. She would have stopped them." Marilyn pounded her stomach. "I never would have gotten rid of this. No diet pills." She hung her head, as if she knew there was no sympathy forthcoming from anyone in the room. "I wanted Rufus to scare her, but Sally struck him on the nose with her keys. Then he attacked her. She dropped her keys before she went over the cliff. I cleaned up Rufus and set him free. Then I drove to my grandmother's in Cape May."

Verne Chapski got to his feet. "You expect this jury to believe, after you killed another human being, that your allegations about Dr. Handler paying you blackmail are true."

"Have you heard of the twelve-step program?" Marilyn asked.

Verne Chapski nodded.

"I'm addicted to diet pills. Diet-pill addicts are insane. Their only friends are pills. I had friends, real ones like everyone else, before the deaths at St. Anthony's. Sharon Daley is here. She'll tell you. I was a good nurse. Actually I think I would have remained sane if only Charley Klondike and Jean Bacon died that weekend, but the poor kid …" Marilyn motioned in the direction of the Schneiders. "Handler could have helped, should have known earlier what was wrong. I killed him you know. I gave the boy his last dose of morphine. We chouldn't let the parents see his horrible condition." Tears streamed down her face. Judge Wilcox handed her a box of tissues. Marilyn coughed. "I lost my job at the hospital. No one would hire me. Then one morning I was reading the Bible." Marilyn looked up at the judge. "I recited the passage to Sally Bianco. Do you want to hear it?" Judge Wilcox's sympathy was showing for the dishonored nurse. He nodded.

So, Marilyn delivered her biblical motivation. "I memorized two verses in Ezekiel, Chapter 38, 'Thus saith the Lord God; It shall come to pass that at the same time shall things come into thy mind, and thou shalt think an evil thought: And thou shall say, I will go up to them that are at rest, that dwell safely, to take a spoil, and to take a prey; to turn thine hand upon the desolate places and upon the people.'"

Marilyn hung her head. "I did blackmail Dr. Handler, for pills. But I'm gay. I've never been interested in men. I'm sorry Sally Bianco got involved. She seemed to want to help, but I couldn't let her." Marilyn didn't look up. "My life was unmanageable as an addict. Look where I am. I hope a Higher Power can restore me to sanity, someday. But you can believe me about him." Marilyn pointed to Dr. Handler. "Dr. Handler paid me blackmail to keep quiet about the Schneider's son. They should have taken his license and sent *him* to jail!"

Marilyn was excused from the witness box.

The Schneiders, Larry's parents, were the next to testify about the details of their son's death. They wrapped their arms together when they returned to their seats. Helen thanked God she had prompted Amy Schneider to ask her husband over to her new home so Tom Schneider would know he was forgiven for leaving her. Helen was pleased they were no longer living alone, not like she would be shortly.

Helen asked God to forgive her anger towards Marilyn. Sally Bianco had taught her the daily tenth step prayer 'to stay free of self-pity, anger, resentment and fear.' Fear was evil. It crept up on her like a hungry cat. If she trusted God, how could she insult Him by living in fear?

Larry Schneider's Little League coach and Larry's teacher, a Mrs. Dobson, also gave evidence about Larry's symptoms.

Sharon Daley testified about her memories of Larry Schneider's death. When she mentioned her lesbian relationship with Marilyn, she battled tears of frustration over Marilyn's increasing reliance on prescription drugs. "Those doctors did her no favors."

Mr. Chapski sought to change the jury's view of her statements. "Aren't many overweight people helped with diet pills?"

"Don't you understand?" Sharon turned to the judge to make her point. "Marilyn was addicted to them."

"But the doctors were only trying to help," Mr. Chapski insisted.

"All three of those doctors were paying Marilyn to keep her

mouth shut about their dead patients!"

Mr. Chapski rubbed his nude chin. "Why didn't you bring charges against the doctors if you thought they were in error?"

Sharon laughed. "I'd worked too long in the profession to try anything stupid. Look how long it took to even bring one of them to trial. I was lucky enough to find a job filing in the hospital. No one would hire Marilyn because the medical community knew she injected the boy with enough morphine to put him out of his misery. If the detective, Sally Bianco, hadn't lost her life, the police would never have taken the murder case this far."

"Neglect allegations have been made." Mr. Chapski addressed the jury. "This is not a murder trial.

"Larry's just as dead," Sharon said, before she was excused.

Judge Wilcox closed the hearing for the day, cautioning the jury not to read papers, speak to each other, or to anyone outside the courtroom about the case, which would resume on Monday.

* * *

The district attorney invited Max and Helen to join him at the Earle restaurant for dinner. Captain Tedler and Max seemed particularly optimistic about the outcome. Helen didn't feel confident about the jury's persuasions.

"You did a good job." Roger Warner cuffed Max's back. "You found Marilyn's diary."

"But Chapski used the dates against her." Helen had watched the jurors closely. "The women weren't happy Marilyn met the doctor in a motel."

"Sally's murder could be a reason for the jurors not to believe Marilyn blackmailed Dr. Handler." Captain Tedler ordered a Manhattan. "A double."

Roger Warner waved the drink waitress away. "I've had my share."

"When did you quit?" Captain Tedler asked, as if interested in the process.

"Last summer. I visited my four brothers in Missouri. We're a hotheaded lot, tease each other mercilessly. I'm the tallest. We were out in my dad's barn, drinking, scuffling around. My brother…he's three inches shorter than me. But he's built like a Mac truck. Anyway, he started kidding me about my poetry. Called me a wimp!" Roger glared at them as if they would comment. "I grabbed the first thing I could and threw it at him." They waited for the end of the story, as the district attorney drained his water glass. "The pitchfork went right through my brother's shoe, missing his toes." Roger wiped his brow with his napkin. "That was enough liquor-inspired craziness for me."

***

Second Saturday in June
Helen's New Condo

Helen opened the kitchen cupboard next to the back window. It was filled with glassware.

Her mother stood behind her. "I sent for the ones you picked out. Do you like them?"

"I do. Mother, you didn't need to do that." Julia started opening the other cabinet doors. Dad came in and exposed the contents of the refrigerator, which was fully stocked with Helen's favorite foods. All the houseware items she chose previously from her mother's catalogues were in place.

"Your dining room table and chairs will arrive tomorrow." Dad included Max, George and Mitzi in his invitation. "We're having pizza delivered at our house tonight."

"You've thought of everything," Helen said. What she didn't say was how shocked she felt at their speedy dismissal of her living arrangements with them. Max might misunderstand if she mentioned any hint of complaint against their generosity. She did want to live alone. Was it really necessary to throw her out entirely in one fell swoop?

Max put his hand on her shoulder and squeezed gently. He handed her a fairly large package wrapped in blue with a gigantic white bow. She smiled at him before opening it, trying not to cry. He guided her into the front room.

"I'll just make a pot of coffee." Mother called from the kitchen. "Is that all right, dear?"

"Fine," Helen called. "Everything's fine."

Max handed her his handkerchief. "I know what you're going through."

"Do you?" He couldn't know what she was feeling. But tears tumbled down her face. Helen didn't know herself. Was she crying because she was angry, would she miss her parents? What?

"It's the letting go," Max said.

George had introduced them to Mitzi. She was an African-American of significant beauty and enough spunk for four people. Helen adored her immediately. Mitzi said she was living with George to see if she ought to marry him.

George and Mitzi were sitting on the floor, cross-legged, knee-to-knee. They both nodded at Max's sage judgment call about letting go of her parents.

Max pulled Helen down on the loveseat next to him.

"Open it," Mitzi demanded.

Inside the box was a blue and white china coffee pot with creamer and sugar bowl. "I asked your mother what pattern to choose," Max said.

"They're beautiful!" She kissed his cheek.

"Oh, George. You left ours in the car!" Mitzi kicked him.

"Be right back," George promised. When he returned, Max held the door open for him. George balanced five heavy-appearing cardboard boxes in his arms. He set them on the floor, and they all proceeded to rip them open. Five Tiffany lamp reproductions were quickly assembled.

Helen clapped her hands. "Perfect. They're perfect. Thank you."

* * *

Over pizza back at her mother's, Helen felt like a stranger in her parents' home. Though all of her personal possessions had been moved out, nothing had changed except herself.

Max seemed a little nervous; as if he knew she was planning to trap him. All he could talk about was how Dr. Handler was not going to go to jail for his lapse in care for Larry Schneider, corrupting Marilyn, colluding with Dr. Whidbey to involve Dr. Cornell in the financing scheme, and how terrible and devious the world was becoming.

George, on the other hand, was quite cheerful about Dr. Handler's chances of becoming a jailbird. "Mitzi," George put his arm around his girlfriend's shoulder. "says doctors need to pay for their mistakes by going to jail instead of paying civil suit penalties."

"That's what the D.A. is hoping for." Dad sliced the third pizza for the big eaters at the party.

"Helen," Mitzi said. "George says you're trying to sell your father's Oldsmobile. I know a collector of antique cars."

"See how old we are, Julia." Helen's father embraced his wife. "It's too late for us to begin romping around the world like we owned it."

"After I'm buried," Mother laughed. "You can give my suitcases to Purple Heart. But for now we're going to see the world."

"You are?" Helen asked.

"Count on it," Dad said. "By the way you kids need to check the message machine at the office. Some woman claims she's a friend of the wife of an FBI agent. Delores Gant is her name. Knows a secret that will ruin the agency's reputation and save the lives of twelve innocent children."

"A nut case?" Max asked.

"Let's check her out anyway, Max." Helen wanted something to work on with Max at her side, even if it was only to get a crazy person off the streets of Ann Arbor.

"That will keep you busy until we get back." Dad touched the back of Mother's neck. "When is that, Julia?"

"August 1st," Julia said.

* * *

On Sunday afternoon, Mitzi drove Helen out to the animal shelter in Dixboro to choose two Siamese kittens. Mitzi explained to the staff Helen didn't want the cats to be lonely when she wasn't home.

Mitzi was also kind enough to accompany Helen to a car dealership. Helen bought a Honda from Mr. Brent, who gave her a good deal on a used hybrid. Anita's husband didn't recognize her from The Firm or the courthouse. Helen couldn't help feeling nervous, because she knew Max and she would be seeing more of Mr. Brent and his wife after Max's child was born, something she couldn't yet share with her new friend, Mitzi.

Living alone was not as traumatic as Helen thought it might be. Rather, she felt she was playing house in her own life-size dollhouse. On Monday, she made breakfast for herself and the cats, chose her own clothes, and popped the few dishes in the dishwasher. She left the television on the Turner channel in case the cats got lonesome for a human voice.

* * *

Third Monday in June

Washtenaw County Courthouse

The district attorney, Roger Warner, began the second day of Dr. Handler's trial by calling Dr. Dorothy Whidbey to the stand. The eighty-year-old woman limped to the stand and raised a bruised arm to take the oath. Helen's parents had begged off coming to court. "Dr. Whidbey, you plead guilty to a misdemeanor charge concerning your late brother?" Roger Warner consulted his notes. "Charles Klondike. Could you explain your relationship with Marilyn Helms, the head nurse on duty the night Mr. Klondike died?"

Dr. Whidbey wrinkled her nose and tipped her chin even higher. "When I could pour Charley out of his shoes long enough, he praised Marilyn's care."

The D.A. moved closer to Dr. Whidbey. "Did you pay Marilyn to keep quiet about the details of your brother's death?"

Dr. Whidbey moved her body to the side of the chair so she could see around huge Roger Warner. "My husband thought it was a good idea." Mr. Whidbey, Dorothy's husband, stood and left the courtroom.

Verne Chapski, Dr. Handler's attorney asked for permission to question the witness. "Your husband has left the room, do you want to change your testimony?"

"I paid her." Dr. Whidbey black eyes snapped. "Don't you dare say a word against my husband."

Roger Warner pointed to John Willets and Mary Livingston, who were seated where Dr. Handler's wives previously sat the first day of the trial. "Would you like to make formal charges against your husband for wife-abuse?"

"No," Dr. Whidbey began to shake. "I would not."

Judge Wilcox said, "The witness is excused. Bailiff, help Dr. Whidbey out of the courtroom."

The D.A. called Sister James Marine to the stand to explain how Marilyn was accepted at the convent to serve out her community service sentence. "She was deeply upset about the recent death of a doctor, whose name we're not mentioning. Marilyn literally stuffs her emotions down by overeating. I want to believe Sally Bianco's death was a horrible accident."

Marilyn Helms interrupted the proceedings by weeping, loudly and hysterically. Judge Wilcox banged his gavel and then motioned for the police to accompany Marilyn out of the courtroom and back to her holding cell. Sharon Daley followed but was stopped at the exit and returned to her seat.

Helen Costello was called to the stand. She let go of Max's hand and walked the long distance under the jury's surveillance to the witness box. Roger Warner smiled before asking her to replay the investigation of Sally Bianco's lead into the suspicious St. Anthony Hospital deaths. Helen used her notes to summarize the case. When Mr. Chapski questioned her, Helen flipped the pages of her account, sometimes to stall for time to reach for the appropriate word.

"Even after Marilyn Helms beat you," Mr. Chapski asked. "You believe she is telling the truth about her relationship with Dr.

Handler?"

Helen cocked her head and then responded facing the jury. "No one has given any evidence of any sexual relationship with Dr. Handler, not even his seven distinguished wives."

"Your honor!" Mr. Chapski waved in the Judge's direction, but Judge Joe Wilcox was smiling.

Roger Warner chose to call Max Hunt to the stand to verify Helen's testimony about the investigation of Mrs. Bianco's death and the motivation behind it.

* * *

Max was not happy with Verne Chapski. After reading from his notes, Max could feel a wall of anger rising toward the defense attorney. "Dr. Handler has failed to produce any incriminating tapes he claimed to have in his possession. Clearly Marilyn Helms met him to pick up prescriptions for her drug habit or money to buy the drugs as blackmail payments to keep silent about Dr. Handler's mismanagement of Larry Schneider's case."

"You were never present when Dr. Handler 'paid' Marilyn, were you?" Verne Chapski let his tone imply the worst possible meaning.

"Of course not."

Mr. Chapski took refuge behind the defense table. He motioned in the direction of Mr. and Mrs. Brent. "The Brents were clients of yours, too?"

"For a short time." Max could feel a rolling cloud of terror building on the deserts of Iraq. He shifted in his chair so he could hold onto his belt buckle under his suit jacket.

"The Brents are expecting their first child, aren't they?"

"How is this relevant?" The D.A. objected.

"I'm showing the jury the kind of people The Firm hires to investigate decent citizens of Ann Arbor." Mr. Chapski's words seemed to give him more courage. He moved closer to Max.

"You visited Mrs. Handler?"

"I did." Max answered. He could feel the sand pulling at his boots, knew he was in trouble, wouldn't escape.

"Dr. Handler arrived unexpectedly and claims you were drunk."

"I was not drunk." Max found his throat already felt like dust.

'You were weaving around," Mr. Chapski insisted. "You bloodied your nose when you fell on your face leaving the house."

"I did." Max said.

"If you weren't drunk, explain yourself."

"PTSD"

"Really? And how do you explain a request for a blood sample of Mrs. Brent's child?"

Max stood. Rather he held onto both sides of the witness box and let his rubbery legs fall down the step. He followed a back-peddling Chapski out through the squeaking gate into the aisle between the audiences' pews, past the row the Brents were sitting in. Max was on his knees eye to eye with the short, flame-haired leprechaun when he heard his own whisper. "She tricked me." Max couldn't believe his own words, but he believed the wave of unconsciousness greeting his declaration.

* * *

Helen knelt next to Max. She waved off the Bailiff. "He'll be all right."

Captain Tedler helped Max out of the courtroom. Pushed him to a seated position on the bench outside. "Should I call Andrew?"

"No." Max wiped his wet brow with his handkerchief. "It's passing. I'm glad your parents didn't hear about the Brents – in public."

"No one is going to throw stones at you, Max." Helen shook Captain Tedler's hand. "Go back inside. Let us know what happens." Max tried to stand. Helen placed her hand on his shoulder. "Wait a minute or two, then we'll leave."

"I don't want to see the Brents, right now."

"I know." Helen patted his knee.

"I could have ruined the case."

"Dr. Handler's errors are not yours. You had the misfortune of being injured in the service of your country and …."

"Being used by one woman the way I had used every one I touch." Max took both of Helen's hands in his. "Until now, Helen. I won't make love to you until we're married, even though I love you."

"I know," she said. "We just need to get you home to rest."

* * *

Third Tuesday in July
Washtenaw County Courthouse

Max watched the jury over the top of Helen's blonde curls. If they, the jury, could feel half the affection he held for this courageous friend of his, they would surely acquit a confessed mass-murderer. He hoped his terrible collapse in the witness stand wouldn't sway any of them. He prayed the jury had carefully weighed the evidence against Dr. Handler. The closing arguments had been fairly brief.

Sister James Marine was recalled to the stand to reiterate her testimony as a character witness for Marilyn Helms. "The Dominican nuns at St. Anthony's Convent in Adrian elected me as their Mother Superior. We accepted Marilyn Helms as a community service worker to fulfill her sentence for a DUI, driving under the influence, conviction. Her pet, Rufus, was very well mannered while she was with us. He slept outside her door at night. Am I taking too long?" Sister asked the judge who waved his hand to relieve her of any worry. "I think you all should know the reason I became a nun. I was inspired by a woman, a Dominican nun who visited prisons. Actually, she only visited death-row inmates. She said she found every person is more similar to us than we first think. It was true the people she met had gigantic sins on the surface of their souls, but the rest was as pure as if you'd noticed a dot of dust on a fresh white handkerchief. More good is present in all persons than bad." Sister James Marine folded her hands in her lap. "I do want to add from Matthew, Chapter Seven, Verse One, my belief of how you should see Marilyn's plight and her truthful statements about Dr. Handler's mishandling of Larry Schneider's life."

"That won't be necessary." Verne Chapski, Dr. Handler's defense attorney tried to usher the nun from the witness box.

"Yes," Judge Wilcox said, "It is necessary."

Sister received a nod to proceed from the judge. "I want you to remember the words of Jesus when you are together in the jury room. 'Judge not, that ye be not judged. For with what judgment ye judge, ye shall be judged: and with what measure ye mete, it shall be measured to you, again.'"

"Your Honor!" Verne Chapski stormed around the area in front of the jury box. He waved in their direction. "Direct the jury to disregard that sentimental drivel."

"I beg your pardon." Judge Wilcox's stare was not friendly.

"I give up!" Verne Chapski slapped his sides in exasperation and sat down.

"I take that as your closing statement." Judge Wilcox dared the attorney to argue. "Mr. Warner are you prepared to give your closing arguments?"

Roger Warner turned slowly and faced the jury. "I'll let the Lord's words burden the jury."

The jury responded by removing Handler's license and charging 255 million dollars for a wrongful death payment to the Schneides.

Chapter Eleven

⁓⁓

"And if any man hear my words, and believe not, I judge him not: for I came not to judge the world, but to save the world."
John 12:47

First Monday in July
The Firm

Max shut his second-floor office door behind Andrew. He considered locking it to avoid letting Helen walk into the middle of an embarrassing conversation. "Maybe you should sit down, Andrew? I don't think you understand the complications involved."

"What are you so serious about?"

"Can you hear me out?" Max slumped into his desk chair. "I'll talk and you listen. I'll ask you what you think afterwards, okay?"

"Sure, Max."

"As I tried to tell you when Helen was still living at home, I like your daughter." His brain provided a bridge detour for the flow of truthful words he had intended to convey. The silence between the men grew. Frustrated, Max finally said, "I need to start at the beginning, don't I?" Andrew encouraged him with a nod. Max looked around his office. Would he need to call the movers to store his mahogany desk, file cabinets, the clock downstairs, the wingback chairs, the ruined fake greenery, until he found a new job? "Mr. Brent's case threw me a curve ball. I think I needed the sucker punch. You can believe I didn't know I was dating his wife. Now she's pregnant with my child." Andrew didn't comment. His eyes widened slightly, but his face remained friendly, concerned. "She called herself Maybell and lied about not wearing rings, but that doesn't excuse my actions. Anita was the mirror of my sins, like Don Quixote's when he recanted his lofty goals. I asked her to marry me, before we had sex; but it doesn't relieve me of the responsibility, does it? What I'm trying to explain to you is…." Max felt his throat clog. "… even though I think your daughter is getting too involved with me," each word caused real pain as he pushed it past his lips, past his deceit-encrusted soul, "I'm not fit husband material."

Andrew sighed. The truth was laid bare.

Max added, "The Iraq buddies I partied with, before Maybell, said I reach for women the way drunks grab their next bottle, drain them and toss them in the garbage. I already told Helen about Anita and the baby."

Andrew sat very still, too still.

"Say something, please?"

"I think women can break or make a man. My daughter is one of those who creates the man she loves. You've changed since meeting Maybell. I didn't know she was Anita, but part of you changed. The human soul you've kept buried since Iraq or your parents' deaths, it's still here, caring. Your feelings for my daughter are not my concern. I can see you are suffering. I know what she thinks of you. Do you? I would strongly advise you to leave the future of your involvement, or not, with Helen. If you love her, you will confidently leave your fate in her hands. She's not going to rush you into anything you're not ready to undertake."

Max stared. "But, Andrew…."

"No buts. I think the world of you, Max. That's not going to change, even if you and Helen never marry."

"I promise…"

Andrew held up his hand. "Please. Let's pretend we never had this talk."

"Okay?"

"Okay." Andrew left, but didn't close the door.

Max felt fine, better. If Andrew knew the score and didn't throw him out of The Firm, he must be okay. Max patted his desktop as if to reassure the thing they were not packing up. He wondered how soon Helen would make her move on him.

Max hooked his seat belt before driving home to his apartment. Helen had never seen his place. If Mrs. Schneider could invite her estranged husband over, he could certainly ask the woman he loved, Helen Costello, to visit him. Maybe he could include George and Mitzi in the invitation, just to keep the atmosphere safe for Helen.

* * *

George laughed when Helen drove up in her new Honda. He stepped aside after opening the elevator door to Max's apartment so Mitzi and Helen could precede him. "Why did you drive the gas-guzzling Oldsmobile anyway?"

"I miss Dad's car." Helen cocked an ornery eye at George and Mitzi. "Have you ever flown down a country dirt road at 100 miles an hour in a heavy car?"

"That tank couldn't go that fast." George scoffed. "It didn't even own seat belts."

Helen tugged at the neckline of her white cotton dress. "I drove through Waterloo on moonlit nights with the lights off, too."

"You are one crazy child." Mitzi laughed.

"I'm older than George. I am glad I finally moved out of my parents' house." Helen sighed. "Mitzi, you might want one of my dollhouses. I gave ten of them to the nuns at St. Anthony's convent."

"Oh," Mitzi clapped her hands. "I never owned a doll house when I was a kid."

"You're still a kid." George whacked Mitzi's bottom.

Mitzi punched him hard on the arm for the infraction.

On the ride up the elevator to Max's apartment, Helen checked off her recent advancements toward maturity. She'd received a dollhouse from her father for each birthday. With the gift for Mitzi and the convent's presents of ten that might mean that she had shed eleven years of her childhood. Fourteen more to go, before she could claim womanhood at twenty-five. She planned to be a first-time mother before the age of thirty. She wondered if she should let Max in on her plans for his added fatherhood.

"Mother is giving the final thirteen abodes to a shelter for abused women. They usually aren't allowed time to pack their children's toys. Did you see the Victorian one I brought with me? It's in my condo's bedroom. I was thinking, Max is so tall, if we ever do get together, like you two, we'll need a house with high ceilings." Helen knew she was chattering away. Why was she so nervous? She knew Mitzi and George were with her. It wasn't as if she was going to Max's apartment by herself.

Helen laughed. "I like buying groceries, cleaning up after myself, living alone, taking care of my cats…before I think about marrying. Too many of my friends left their parents' domination only to succumb to some idiot's idea of a happy home…usually answering to them, too much."

"Good for you." George patted her shoulder.

"What about you, George?" Mitzi asked. "Are you a confirmed bachelor?"

"Not me." George laughed. "Helen, have you seen Max's apartment before?"

Helen stayed in the elevator after George and Mitzi got off. "I have been curious. He says the ceilings are two stories high. He's arranged some sort of temporary ceiling with bolts of silk cloth hung on wires or rods."

"Sounds innovative." Mitzi tugged on Helen's arm to pull her out of the elevator.

"You like him, George, don't you?" Helen didn't really care if George hated him. She knew she was in love.

George rolled his eyes at Mitzi. "If you like the guy, he's fine with me. Just remember you have a brother to lean on, now."

"Yeah." Helen said. "I like that. I feel braver, you know, to venture out into the real world, because of you."

"Thank you. Now let's give Max a good time."

"He deserves one, George. A married client of ours is carrying his child."

George stroked his chin. "Does he need a lawyer?"

"Exactly," Helen said glad again for the attributes of her sibling. "I knew you would take his side."

* * *

Max wasn't sure George would be a pleasant guest. He was surprised at how well they all got along. He couldn't keep his mouth shut. Max filled an entire half-hour describing the glories of his apartment complex. "They did a good job converting the old factory." Helen chose his favorite chair.

George seemed to imply he was more interested in Helen's business than Max. "Do you like pets?"

"Mitzi and I just picked out two Siamese cats." Helen stroked the leather arm of Max's chair.

Her smile melted Max's reserve not to say another bragging word. "I'm buying a sailboat with a slip on Lake St. Claire."

Helen's brown eyes widened. "As soon as you help me pick one out."

The End

Printed in the USA
CPSIA information can be obtained
at www.ICGtesting.com
JSHW010310210424
61452JS00001B/16